ACCLAIM

PREST

BRIMSTONE

"An outrageously entertaining thriller from these accomplished coauthors...a gripping climax...a smashing epilogue...[an] exhilarating series. As good as the genre gets. Don't miss it."

—*Kirkus Reviews* (starred review)

"Red-hot action...a wild ride...one hell of a book...No one mixes science and the supernatural better than Preston and Child, and BRIMSTONE just may be their ultimate collaboration...the supreme beach read."

—*Flint Journal* (MI)

"The perfect thriller."

—*Publishers Weekly* (starred review)

"Too scary, too much fun, to put this one down."

—*Freelance Star* (VA)

"[A] page-turner...a plot that is as complex as it is entertaining, leaving the reader most assuredly wanting more."

—*Times Record News* (TX)

"The authors have outdone themselves with marvelous set pieces and an intriguing mystery. Fans will be excited to see old friends, yet the story will still captivate newcomers."

—*Library Journal* (starred review)

"Explosive."

—*New Mexican*

"Delivers the action and the twists...a good, old-fashioned thriller mystery with a great hook."

—*Edge Boston*

WHITE FIRE

ONE OF THE BEST BOOKS OF THE YEAR BY *LIBRARY JOURNAL*

"Excellent...Small-town politics, murder, a century-old conspiracy, arson, and a detective who embodies a modern-day Holmes add up to an amazing journey...Preston and Child's best novel to date."

—Associated Press

"Sherlock Holmes fans will relish [this novel]...one of their best in this popular series...easily stands on its own with only passing references to Pendergast's complex backstory."

—*Publishers Weekly* (starred review)

"A mile-a-minute thriller with a deeply entertaining plot and marvelous characters."

—Diana Gabaldon

"Through myriad shocks, surprises, twists, and turns, the suspense never lets up...Great fun to the last page."

—Anne Rice

"The best Pendergast book yet—a collision between past and present that will leave you breathless."

—Lee Child

"A terrific mix of mystery and the unexpected...They promise a great read and they have delivered."

—Clive Cussler

"As a fan of both Oscar Wilde and Arthur Conan Doyle, I began this book with great expectations...Get ready for the ride of your life."

—David Baldacci

"[Preston and Child] are a bestselling team for a reason...You can't flip the pages fast enough to discover who survives."

—*Newark Star-Ledger*

"These dynamic authors' best thriller to date."

—*Library Journal*

"Pendergast isn't the only offbeat detective in the latest thriller by Preston and Child. With a deft hand, the pair create a new mystery for Sherlock Holmes."

—*Oklahoman*

"Fans of Sherlock Holmes will devour Preston and Child's latest thriller, not only because of its connection to Conan Doyle, but because Pendergast bears a striking resemblance to the iconic detective, and has powers as eerily uncanny as Sherlock's. Readers will race toward the final page, and once there, will thirst for more."

—BookReporter.com

"It has everything that has made this reader eagerly await the next book in this series: a great story, solid supporting characters, an element of the macabre (or two), and an original touch."

—TheMysterySite.com

"A remarkable plot that ties together multiple killings...a secret Sherlock Holmes story and a meeting between Oscar Wilde and Arthur Conan Doyle keep readers glued to the page."

—*RT Book Reviews*

TWO GRAVES

"A good thriller forces the reader to finish the book in one sitting. An exceptional thriller does that plus forces the reader to slow down to savor every word. With *Two Graves,* Preston and Child have delivered another exceptional book...The gothic atmosphere that oozes from the pages will envelop the reader...Pendergast is a modern-day Sherlock Holmes, quirks and all...The mystery tantalizes, and the shocks throughout the narrative are like bolts of lightning. Fans will love the conclusion to the trilogy, and newcomers will seek out the authors' earlier titles."

—Associated Press

"A unique reading experience...*Two Graves* delivers the high thrills one expects from the two masters."

—*Washington Post*

"Pendergast—an always-black-clad pale blond polymath, gaunt yet physically deadly, an FBI agent operating without supervision or reprimand—lurks at the dark, sharp edge of crime fiction protagonists."

—*Kirkus Reviews*

"A lavish story and one that takes the time for some skillful vignettes and characterizations."

—*Charlotte Observer*

"Preston and Child's high-adrenaline thriller wraps up the trilogy...with a bang...[An] intelligent suspense novel."

—*Publishers Weekly*

"*Two Graves* provides readers exactly what they would expect from a Preston and Child novel—thrills, high adventure, treacherous plot twists, and well-researched scientific intrigue. The story is never predictable, and Pendergast is a multi-layered personality who keeps you guessing throughout."

—BookReporter.com

"The action is constant and starts with a bang.

—*RT Book Reviews*

"Another fast-paced murder mystery that crosses the country, dips into Mexico and then wallops Manhattan hotels. It's the perfect holiday gift for that thriller-genre lover in your life."

—*Asbury Park Press*

COLD VENGEANCE

"Before you even open the cover of a Preston and Child book, you know you're in for a good, if chilling, even thrilling time."

—*Asbury Park Press*

"[Preston and Child are] still going strong...Such is the talent of our authors that we happily follow their characters...all over the globe, from the moors of Scotland to the loony bins of New York City; the recipe is mixed well with a dash of assassins here and a soupcon of Nazis there, a couple of traitors and some really fascinating secondary characters...*Cold Vengeance* is a hot hell of a fun read."

—Examiner.com

"4½ stars! Top Pick! Preston and Child continue their dominance of the thriller genre with stellar writing and twists that come at a furious pace. Others may try to write like them, but no one can come close. The best in the business deliver another winner."

—*RT Book Reviews*

"Douglas Preston and Lincoln Child have outdone themselves once again, and with *Cold Vengeance* at the #1 spot on the *New York Times* bestseller list, it's proof this is without a doubt the best in the entire series."

—GoodReads.com

"5 stars! This fast-paced series continues to provide the reader with many twists. What you thought you knew from prior Pendergast novels may not necessarily be true."

—TheMysteryReader.com

FEVER DREAM

"This is no dream; it's the authors' best book in years."

—*Library Journal* (starred review)

"A thrill a minute."

—*San Jose Mercury News*

"[One of the] summer's best beach books."

—*Newark Star-Ledger*

"Preston and Child up the emotional ante considerably in this thriller featuring brilliant and eccentric Pendergast...Once again, the bestselling authors show they have few peers at creating taut scenes of suspense."

—*Publishers Weekly* (starred review)

"Together [Preston and Child] reach an entirely different level, achieving a stylistic grace and thematic resonance neither has so far matched alone. This may be the best of the Pendergast novels…a definite must-read."

—*Booklist* (starred review)

"Pendergast has never been more brilliant, eccentric, and intriguing."

—TucsonCitizen.com

BY DOUGLAS PRESTON AND LINCOLN CHILD

Pendergast novels

White Fire
*Two Graves**
*Cold Vengeance**
*Fever Dream**
Cemetery Dance
The Wheel of Darkness
*The Book of the Dead***
*Dance of Death***
*Brimstone***
Still Life with Crows
The Cabinet of Curiosities
Reliquary†
Relic†

Gideon Crew novels

Gideon's Corpse
Gideon's Sword

Other Novels

The Ice Limit
Thunderhead
Riptide
Mount Dragon

*The Helen Trilogy
**The Diogenes Trilogy
†*Relic* and *Reliquary* are ideally read in sequence

BY DOUGLAS PRESTON

The Kraken Mission
Impact
The Monster of Florence
(with Mario Spezi)
Blasphemy
Tyrannosaur Canyon
The Codex
Ribbons of Time
The Royal Road
Talking to the Ground
Jennie
Cities of Gold
Dinosaurs in the Attic

BY LINCOLN CHILD

The Third Gate
Terminal Freeze
Deep Storm
Death Match
Utopia
Tales of the Dark 1-3
Dark Banquet
Dark Company

DOUGLAS PRESTON
AND LINCOLN CHILD

BRIMSTONE

GRAND CENTRAL
PUBLISHING

NEW YORK BOSTON

This book is a work of fiction. Names, characters, places, and incidents are the product of the author's imagination or are used fictitiously. Any resemblance to actual events, locales, or persons, living or dead, is coincidental.

Grand Central Publishing
Hachette Book Group
237 Park Avenue
New York, NY 10017
www.HachetteBookGroup.com

Grand Central Publishing is a division of Hachette Book Group, Inc.
The Grand Central Publishing name and logo is a trademark of Hachette Book Group, Inc.

Printed in the United States of America

Originally published in hardcover by Hachette Book Group
First mass market edition: May 2005
First one-time only mass market edition: April 2010
First oversize mass market edition: May 2014

10 9 8 7 6 5 4 3 2 1
OPM

Douglas Preston
dedicates this book to
Barry and Jody Turkus.

Lincoln Child
dedicates this book to
his daughter, Veronica.

{ 1 }

Agnes Torres parked her white Ford Escort in the little parking area outside the hedge and stepped into the cool dawn air. The hedges were twelve feet high and as impenetrable as a brick wall; only the shingled peak of the big house could be seen from the street. But she could hear the surf thundering and smell the salt air of the invisible ocean beyond.

Agnes carefully locked the car—it paid to be careful, even in this neighborhood—and, fumbling with the massive set of keys, found the right one and stuck it into the lock. The heavy sheet-metal gate swung inward, exposing a broad expanse of green lawn that swept three hundred yards down to the beach, flanked by two dunes. A red light on a keypad just inside the gate began blinking, and she entered the code with nervous fingers. She had thirty seconds before the sirens went off. Once, she had dropped her keys and couldn't punch in the code in time, and the thing had awakened practically the whole town and brought three police cars. Mr. Jeremy had been so angry she thought he would breathe fire. It had been awful.

Agnes punched the last button and the light turned green. She breathed a sigh of relief, locked the gate, and paused to cross herself. Then she drew out her rosary, held the first bead reverently between her fingers. Fully armed now, she turned and began waddling across the lawn on short, thick legs, walking slowly to allow herself time to intone the Our Fathers, the Hail Marys, and the Glory Bes in quiet Spanish. She always said a decade on her rosary when entering the Grove Estate.

The vast gray house loomed in front of her, a single eyebrow window in the roof peak frowning like the eye of a Cyclops, yellow against the steel gray of the house and sky. Seagulls circled above, crying restlessly.

Agnes was surprised. She never remembered that light on before. What was Mr. Jeremy doing in the attic at seven o'clock in the morning? Normally he didn't get out of bed until noon.

Finishing her prayers, she replaced the rosary and crossed herself again: a swift, automatic gesture, made with a rough hand that had seen decades of domestic work. She hoped Mr. Jeremy wasn't still awake. She liked to work in an empty house, and when he was up, everything was so unpleasant: the cigarette ashes he dropped just behind her mop, the dishes he heaped in the sink just after she had washed, the comments and the endless swearing to himself, into the phone or at the newspaper, always followed by a harsh laugh. His voice was like a rusty knife—it cut and slashed the air. He was thin and mean and stank of cigarettes and drank brandy at lunch and entertained sodomites at all hours of the day and night. Once he had tried to speak Spanish with her but she had quickly put an end to that.

Nobody spoke Spanish to her except family and friends, and Agnes Torres spoke English perfectly well enough.

On the other hand, Agnes had worked for many people in her life, and Mr. Jeremy was very correct with her employment. He paid her well, always on time, he never asked her to stay late, never changed her schedule, and never accused her of stealing. Once, early on, he had blasphemed against the Lord in her presence, and she had spoken to him about it, and he had apologized quite civilly and had never done it again.

She came up the curving flagstone path to the back door, inserted a second key, and once again fumbled nervously with the keypad, turning off the internal alarm.

The house was gloomy and gray, the mullioned windows in front looking out on a long seaweed-strewn beach to an angry ocean. The sound of the surf was muffled here and the house was hot. Unusually hot.

She sniffed. There was a strange smell in the air, like a greasy roast left too long in the oven. She waddled into the kitchen but it was empty. The dishes were heaped up, and the place was a mess as usual, stale food everywhere, and yet the smell wasn't coming from here. It looked like Mr. Jeremy had cooked fish the night before. She didn't usually clean his house on Tuesdays, but he'd had one of his countless dinner parties the prior evening. Labor Day had come and gone a month before, but Mr. Jeremy's weekend parties wouldn't end until November.

She went into the living room and sniffed the air again. Something was definitely cooking somewhere. And there was another smell on top of it, as if somebody had been playing with matches.

Agnes Torres felt a vague sense of alarm. Everything was more or less as she had left it when she went away yesterday, at two in the afternoon, except that the ashtrays were overflowing with butts and the usual empty wine bottles stood on the sideboard, dirty dishes were piled in the sink, and someone had dropped soft cheese on the rug and stepped in it.

She raised her plump face and sniffed again. The smell came from above.

She mounted the sweep of stairs, treading softly, and paused to sniff at the landing. She tiptoed past Grove's study, past his bedroom door, continued down the hall, turned the dogleg, and came to the door to the third floor. The smell was stronger here and the air was heavier, warmer. She tried to open the door but found it locked.

She took out her bunch of keys, clinked through them, and unlocked the door. *Madre de Dios*—the smell was much worse. She mounted the steep unfinished stairs, one, two, three, resting her arthritic legs for a moment on each tread. She rested again at the top, breathing heavily.

The attic was vast, with one long hall off which were half a dozen unused children's bedrooms, a playroom, several bathrooms, and an unfinished attic space jammed with furniture and boxes and horrible modern paintings.

At the far end of the hall, she saw a bar of yellow light under the door to the last bedroom.

She took a few tentative steps forward, paused, crossed herself again. Her heart was hammering, but with her hand clutching the rosary she knew she was safe. As she approached the door, the smell grew steadily worse.

She tapped lightly on it, just in case some guest of Mr. Jeremy was sleeping in there, hungover or sick. But there was no response. She grasped the doorknob and was surprised to find it slightly warm to the touch. Was there a fire? Had somebody fallen asleep, cigarette in hand? There was definitely a faint smell of smoke, but it wasn't just smoke somehow: it was something stronger. Something foul.

She tried the doorknob, found it locked. It reminded her of the time, when she was a little girl at the convent school, when crazy old Sister Ana had died and they had to force open her door.

Somebody on the other side might need her assistance; might be sick or incapacitated. Once again she fumbled with the keys. She had no idea which one went to the door, so it wasn't until perhaps the tenth try that the key turned. Holding her breath, she opened the door, but it moved only an inch before stopping, blocked by something. She pushed, pushed harder, heard a crash on the other side.

Santa María, it was going to wake up Mr. Jeremy. She waited, but there was no sound of his tread, no slamming bathroom door or flushing toilet, none of the sounds that signaled his irascible rising.

She pushed at the door and was able to get her head inside, holding her breath against the smell. A thin screen of haze drifted in the room, and it was as hot as an oven. The room had been shut up for years—Mr. Jeremy despised children—and dirty spiderwebs hung from the peeling beadboard walls. The crash had been caused by the toppling of an old armoire that had been pushed up against the door. In fact, all the furniture in the room seemed to have been piled against the door, except for the bed. The bed, she could see, was on the far side of the room. Mr. Jeremy lay on it, fully clothed.

"Mr. Jeremy?"

But Agnes Torres knew there would be no answer. Mr. Jeremy wasn't sleeping, not with his charred eyes burned permanently open, the ashy cone of his mouth frozen in a scream and his blackened tongue—swelled to the size of a chorizo sausage—sticking straight up from it like a flagpole. A sleeping man wouldn't be lying with his elbows raised above the bed, fists clenched so hard that blood had leaked between the fingers. A sleeping man wouldn't have his torso scorched and caved in upon itself like a burned log. She had seen many dead people during her childhood in Colombia, and Mr. Jeremy looked deader than any of them. He was as dead as they come.

She heard someone speaking and realized it was herself, murmuring *En el nombre del Padre, y del Hijo, y del Espíritu Santo*... She crossed herself yet again, fumbling out her rosary, unable to move her feet or take her eyes from the scene in the room. There was a scorched mark on the floor, right at the foot of the bed: a mark which Agnes recognized.

In that moment, she understood exactly what had happened to Mr. Jeremy Grove.

A muffled cry escaped her throat and she suddenly had the energy to back out of the room and shut the door. She fumbled with the keys and relocked it, all the while murmuring *Creo en Dios, Padre todopoderoso, cre-*

ador del cielo y de la tierra. She crossed herself again and again and again, clutching the rosary and holding it up to her chest as she backed down the hall, step by step, sobs mingling with her mumbled prayers.

The cloven hoofprint burned into the floor told her everything she needed to know. The devil had finally come for Jeremy Grove.

{ 2 }

The sergeant paused from stretching the yellow police tape to take in the scene with a jaundiced eye. It was a mess that was about to become a fucking mess. The barricades had been set up too late, and rubberneckers had overrun the beach and dunes, ruining any clues the sand might have held. Then the barricades had been set up in the wrong places and had to be moved, trapping a matched set of his-and-hers Range Rovers, and the two people were now out of their cars, yelling about important appointments (hairdresser, tennis) and brandishing their cell phones, threatening to call their lawyers.

That wet sound over his shoulder was the shit already hitting the fan. It was the sixteenth of October in Southampton, Long Island, and the town's most notorious resident had just been found murdered in bed.

He heard Lieutenant Braskie's voice. "Sergeant, you haven't done these hedges! Didn't I tell you I wanted the *whole* crime scene taped?"

Without bothering to respond, the sergeant began hanging the yellow tape along the hedge surrounding the Grove Estate. As if the twelve-foot hedge with the concertina wire hidden within wasn't enough to stop a reporter, but the plastic tape was. He could see the TV trucks already arriving, vans with satellite uplinks, and could hear the distant dull thud of a chopper. The local press were piling up against the Dune Road barricade, arguing with the cops. Meanwhile, backup squad cars were arriving from Sag Harbor and East Hampton along with the South Fork homicide squad. The lieutenant was deploying these newcomers along the beaches and dunes in a failing attempt to keep the public at bay. The SOC boys were arriving, and the sergeant watched them entering the house, carrying their metal crime lab suitcases. There was a time when he would have been with them, even directing them—but that was a long time ago, in another place.

He continued hanging tape on the hedges until he reached the dunes along the beach. A few cops were already there, keeping back the curious. They were pretty much a docile crowd, staring like dumb animals toward the shingled mansion with its peaks and turrets and funny-looking windows. It was already turning into a party. Someone had fired up a boom box and some buffed-up guys were cracking beers. It was an unusually hot Indian summer day and they were all in shorts or swimming trunks, as if in denial over the end of summer. The sergeant scoffed, imagined what those cut bodies would look like after twenty years of beer and chips. Probably a lot like his.

He glanced back at the house and saw the SOC boys crawling across the lawn on hands and knees, the lieutenant striding alongside. The guy didn't have a clue. He felt another pang. Here he was, pulling crowd control, his training and talent wasted while the real police work went on somewhere else.

No use thinking about that now.

Now the TV trucks had unpacked, and their cameras were set up in a cluster, with a good angle on the mansion, while the glamour-boy correspondents yammered into their microphones. And wouldn't you know it: Lieutenant Braskie had left the SOC boys and was heading over to the cameras like a fly to a fresh pile.

The sergeant shook his head. Unbelievable.

He saw a man running low through the dunes, zigzagging this way and that, and he took off after him, cutting him off at the edge of the lawn. It was a photographer. By the time the sergeant reached him, he'd already dropped to his knee and was shooting with a telephoto as long as an elephant's dick toward one of the homicide detectives from East Hampton, who was interviewing a maid on the veranda.

The sergeant laid a hand on the lens, gently turning it aside.

"Out."

"Officer, come on, please—"

"You don't want me to confiscate your film, do you?" He spoke kindly. He'd always had a soft spot for people who were just trying to do their job, even if they were press.

The man got up, walked a few paces, turned for one final quick shot, and then scurried off. The sergeant walked back up toward the house. He was downwind of the rambling old place, and there was a funny smell in the air, like fireworks or something. He noticed the lieutenant was now standing in the middle of the semicircle of TV cameras, having the time of his life. Braskie was planning to run for chief in the next election, and with the current chief on vacation, he couldn't have gotten a better break than if he'd committed the murder himself.

The sergeant took a detour around the lawn and cut behind a small duck pond and fountain, keeping out of the way of the SOC team. As he came around some hedges he saw a man in the distance, standing by the duck pond, throwing pieces of bread to the ducks. He was dressed in the gaudiest day-tripper style imaginable, complete with Hawaiian shirt, Oakley Eye Jacket shades, and giant baggy shorts. Even though summer had ended over a month ago, it looked like this was the man's first day in the sun after a long, cold winter. Maybe a dozen winters. While the sergeant had some sympathy for a photographer or reporter trying to do his job, he had absolutely no tolerance for tourists. They were the scum of the earth.

"Hey. You."

The man looked up.

"What do you think you're doing? Don't you know this is a crime scene?"

"Yes, Officer, and I do apologize—"

"Get the hell out."

"But, Sergeant, it's important the ducks be fed. They're hungry. I imagine that someone feeds them every morning, but this morning, as you know—" He smiled and shrugged.

The sergeant could hardly believe it. A guy gets murdered, and this idiot is worried about ducks?

"Let's see some ID."

"Of course, of course." The man started fishing in his pocket, fished in another, then looked up sheepishly. "Sorry about that, Officer. I threw on these shorts as soon as I heard the terrible news, but it appears my wallet is still in the pocket of the jacket I was wearing last night." His New York accent grated on the sergeant's nerves.

The sergeant looked at the guy. Normally he would just chase him back behind the barriers. But there was something about him that didn't quite wash. For one thing, the clothes he was wearing were so new they still smelled of a menswear shop. For another thing, they were such a hideous mixture of colors and patterns that it looked like he'd plucked them randomly from a rack in the village boutique. This was more than just bad taste—this was a disguise.

"I'll be going—"

"No, you won't." The sergeant took out his notebook, flipped back a wad of pages, licked his pencil. "You live around here?"

"I've taken a house in Amagansett for a week."

"Address?"

"The Brickman House, Windmill Lane."

Another rich asshole. "And your permanent address?"

"That would be the Dakota, Central Park West."

The sergeant paused. *Now, that's a coincidence.* Aloud, he said, "Name?"

"Look, Sergeant, honestly, if it's a problem, I'll just go on back—"

"Your first name, *sir*?" he said more sharply.

"Is that really necessary? It's difficult to spell, even more difficult to pronounce. I often wonder what my mother was thinking—"

The sergeant gave him a look that shut him up quick. One more quip from this asshole, and it would be the cuffs.

"Let's try again. First name?"

"Aloysius."

"Spell it."

The man spelled it.

"Last?"

"Pendergast."

The pencil in the sergeant's hand began writing this down, too. Then it paused. Slowly the sergeant looked up. The Oakleys had come off, and he found himself staring into that face he knew so well, with the blond-white hair, gray eyes, finely chiseled features, skin as pale and translucent as Carrara marble.

"Pendergast?"

"In the very flesh, my dear Vincent." The New York accent was gone, replaced by the cultured southern drawl he remembered vividly.

"What are you doing here?"

"The same might be asked of you."

Vincent D'Agosta felt himself coloring. The last time he had seen Pendergast he had been a proud New York City police lieutenant. And now here he was in Shithampton, a lowly sergeant decorating hedges with police tape.

"I was in Amagansett when the news arrived that Jeremy Grove had met an untimely end. How could I resist? I apologize for the outfit, but I was hard-pressed to get here as soon as possible."

"You're on the case?"

"Until I'm officially *assigned* to the case, I can do

nothing but feed the ducks. I worked on my last case without full authorization, and it, shall we say, strained some high-level nerves. I must say, Vincent, running into you is a most welcome surprise."

"For me, too," said D'Agosta, coloring again. "Sorry, I'm really not at my best here—"

Pendergast laid a hand on his arm. "We shall have plenty of time to talk later. For now, I see a large individual approaching who appears to be suffering from emphraxis."

A low-pitched, menacing voice intruded from behind. "I hate to break up this little conversation." D'Agosta turned to see Lieutenant Braskie.

Braskie stopped, stared at Pendergast, then turned back to D'Agosta. "Perhaps I'm a little confused here, Sergeant, but isn't this individual *trespassing at the scene of a crime?*"

"Well, uh, Lieutenant, we were—" D'Agosta looked at Pendergast.

"This man isn't a *friend* of yours, now, is he?"

"As a matter of fact—"

"The sergeant was just telling me to leave," interjected Pendergast smoothly.

"Oh, he was, was he? And if I may be so bold as to inquire what you were doing here in the first place, sir?"

"Feeding the ducks."

"Feeding the ducks." D'Agosta could see Braskie's face flushing. He wished Pendergast would hurry up and pull out his shield.

"Well, sir," Braskie went on, "that's a beautiful thing to do. Let's see some ID."

D'Agosta waited smugly. This was going to be good.

"As I was just explaining to the officer here, I left my wallet back at the house—"

Braskie turned on D'Agosta, saw the notebook in his hand. "You got this man's information?"

"Yes." D'Agosta looked at Pendergast almost pleadingly, but the FBI agent's face had shut down completely.

"Did you ask him how he got through the police cordon?"

"No—"

"Don't you think maybe you should?"

"I came through the side gate in Little Dune Road," Pendergast said.

"Not possible. It's locked. I checked it myself."

"Perhaps the lock is defective. At least, it seemed to fall open in my hands."

Braskie turned to D'Agosta. "Now, at last, there's something useful you can do. Go plug that hole, Sergeant. And report back to me at eleven o'clock *sharp.* We need to talk. And as for you, sir, I will escort you off the premises."

"Thank you, Lieutenant."

D'Agosta looked with dismay at the retreating form of Lieutenant Braskie, with Pendergast strolling along behind him, hands in the pockets of his baggy surfer shorts, head tilted back as if taking the air.

{ 3 }

Lieutenant L. P. Braskie Jr. of the Southampton Police Department stood beneath the trellis of the mansion's grape arbor, watching the SOC team comb the endless acreage of lawn for clues. His face wore a stolid mask of professionalism as he thought of Chief MacCready playing golf in the Highlands of Scotland. He pictured in his mind the links of St. Andrews in autumn: the narrow doglegs of greensward, the grim castle, the barren moors beyond. He'd wait until tomorrow to give the chief a call, let him know what was going on. MacCready had been chief for twenty years, and this golf trip was one more reason why Southampton needed fresh blood. Braskie was a local boy with roots in the town and friends in City Hall, and he'd also managed to build up some powerful relationships among the summer people. A favor here and a favor there worked wonders. A foot in both worlds. He'd played his cards well.

And now this. They'd have the perp in the bag in a week or two, and come November and the elections, he'd be a shoo-in. Maybe he'd call MacCready the day *after* tomorrow: *Gee, Chief, I really hesitated to interrupt your hard-earned vacation...*

Braskie knew, from long experience in South Fork homicide, that the first twenty-four hours of a murder investigation were often the most crucial. Fact was, if you didn't get on the trail and follow it right away, you might as well hang up your hat. Find ingress and egress, and everything that followed—forensic evidence, murder weapon, witnesses, motive—would form a chain leading to the perp. Braskie's job wasn't to do the work himself but to make sure everyone else did theirs. And there was little question in his mind that the weak link in this chain was Sergeant Vincent D'Agosta. He didn't do what he was told. He knew better. Story was, D'Agosta had once been a homicide lieutenant himself in the NYPD, and a good one. Quit to write mystery novels, moved to Canada, went broke, and had to come back with his tail tucked firmly between his butt cheeks. Couldn't get a job in the city and ended up out here. If Braskie were chief, he'd never have hired someone like that in the first place—the guy might know his stuff, but he was guaranteed trouble. Not a team player. Had a chip on his shoulder the size of Manhattan.

Braskie checked his watch. Eleven o'clock, and speak of the devil. He watched D'Agosta approach the trellis—a real type, fringe of black hair hanging over his collar, growing gut, attitude oozing from his pores like B.O. Here in Southampton, he stuck out like a bunion. No great surprise the man's wife had decided to stay behind in Canada with their only kid.

"Sir," said D'Agosta, able to make even that single word a trifle insolent.

Braskie shifted his gaze back to the SOC team combing the lawn. "We've got an important case here, Sergeant."

The man nodded.

Braskie narrowed his eyes, looked toward the mansion, toward the sea. "We don't have the luxury of screwing it up."

"No, sir."

"I'm glad to hear you say that. I have to tell you, D'Agosta, that ever since you came on the force, you've made it pretty clear that Southampton isn't where you want to be."

D'Agosta said nothing.

He sighed and looked straight at D'Agosta, only to find the pugnacious face staring back at him. His "go ahead, make my day" face. "Sergeant D'Agosta, do I really need to spell it out? You're *here*. You're a sergeant in the Southampton Police Department. Get over it."

"I don't understand what you mean, sir."

This was getting irritating. "D'Agosta, I can read your mind like a book. I don't give a shit what happened before in your life. What I need is for you to get with the program."

D'Agosta didn't answer.

"Take this morning. I saw you talking to that intruder for a good five minutes, which is why I had to intervene. I don't *want* to be riding your ass, but I can't have one of my sergeants eating up his time explaining to some shitcake why he has to leave. That man should've been ejected immediately, no discussion. You think you can do things your way. I can't have that."

He paused, scrutinizing Sergeant D'Agosta carefully, thinking he might have detected a smirk. This guy really had a problem.

The lieutenant caught the glimpse of a loudly dressed presence to his right. It was that same scumbag in the Hawaiian shirt, baggy shorts, and expensive sculpted shades, approaching the grape arbor as cool as could be, once again *inside* the police cordon.

Braskie turned to D'Agosta, speaking calmly. "Sergeant, arrest that man and read him his rights."

"Wait, Lieutenant—"

He couldn't believe it: D'Agosta was going to argue with him. After everything he'd just told him. His voice became even quieter. "Sergeant, I believe I just gave you an order." He turned to the man. "I hope you brought your wallet with you this time."

"As a matter of fact, I did." The man reached into his pocket.

"No, I don't want to see it, for chrissakes. Save it for the booking sergeant down at the station."

But the man had already extracted the wallet in one smooth movement, and as it fell open, Braskie caught the flash of gold.

"What the—?" The lieutenant stared.

"Special Agent Pendergast, Federal Bureau of Investigation."

The lieutenant felt the blood rush to his face. The man had set him up. And there was no reason, none, for the FBI to justify their involvement. Or was there? He swallowed. This needed to be dealt with carefully. "I see."

The wallet shut with a slap and disappeared.

"Any particular reason for the federal interest?"

asked Braskie, trying to control his voice. "We've been treating it as a simple murder."

"There's a possibility that the killer or killers might have come and left by boat from across the sound. Perhaps Connecticut."

"And?"

"Interstate flight."

"That's a bit of a stretch, isn't it?"

"It's a reason."

Yeah, right. Grove had probably been laundering money or dealing drugs. Or maybe he was even involved in terrorism. These days, with all the shit going down in the world, you couldn't break wind without a phalanx of feds dropping down on you like a ton of manure. Whatever the case, this put a whole new spin on things, and he had to make the best of it.

The lieutenant swallowed, held out his hand. "Welcome to Southampton, Agent Pendergast. If there's anything I or the Southampton P.D. can do for you, just let me know. While the chief is on vacation, I'm acting chief, so you just come to me for anything. We're here to serve."

The man's handshake was cool and dry. Just like the man himself. Braskie hadn't seen a fed quite like him before. He looked even paler than that artist who used to come out here—what was his name?—the weird blond guy who did the Marilyn Monroes. Autumn or not, by the end of the day, this guy was going to need a quart of Solarcaine and a pitcher of martinis before he could even sit down.

"And now that we've straightened things out," the man named Pendergast said pleasantly, "may I ask you for the courtesy of a tour? I trust the immediate workups have been completed, clearing the way for us." He looked at D'Agosta. "You will accompany us, Sergeant?"

"Yes, sir."

Braskie sighed. When the FBI arrived, it was like getting the flu: nothing you could do about it but wait for the headache, fever, and diarrhea to go away.

{ 4 }

Vincent D'Agosta followed Pendergast and Braskie across the lawn. Over in the shade of a vast patio, the South Fork homicide squad had set up an impromptu interrogation center with a video camera. There weren't too many people to interview beyond the domestic who'd found the body, but it was toward this shady spot that Pendergast directed his footsteps, walking so swiftly that D'Agosta and Braskie almost had to jog to keep up.

The chief detective from East Hampton rose. He was a guy D'Agosta had never seen before, small and dark, with large black eyes and long lashes.

"Detective Tony Innocente," said Braskie. "Special Agent Pendergast, FBI."

Innocente rose, held out his hand.

The domestic sat at the table, a short, stolid-looking woman. For someone who had just discovered a stiff, she looked pretty composed, except for a certain unsettled gleam in the eyes.

Pendergast bowed to her, held out his hand. "Agent Pendergast."

"Agnes Torres," she said.

"May I?" Pendergast looked inquisitively at Innocente.

"Be my guest. Videotape's rolling, FYI."

"Mrs. Torres—"

"Miss."

"Thank you. Miss Torres, do you believe in God?"

Innocente exchanged a glance with the other detectives. There was an awkward silence.

"Yes," she said.

"You are a devout Catholic?"

"Yes, I am."

"Do you believe in the devil?"

Another long pause.

"Yes, I do."

"And you have drawn your own conclusions from what you saw upstairs in the house, have you not?"

"Yes, I have," said the woman, so matter-of-factly it sent an odd shudder through D'Agosta.

"Do you really think the lady's beliefs are relevant?" Braskie interjected.

Pendergast turned his pale eyes on the man. "What we believe, Lieutenant, shapes what we see." He turned back to her. "Thank you, Miss Torres."

They continued to the side door of the house. A policeman opened it for them, nodding at the lieutenant. They gathered in the foyer, where Braskie paused.

"We're still trying to get a handle on ingress and egress," he said. "The gate was locked and the grounds were alarmed. Circuit breakers and motion sensors, activated by keypad. We're checking out who had the codes. The doors and windows to the house were also locked and alarmed. There are motion detectors throughout the house as well as infrared sensors and lasers. We've tested the alarm system and it's working perfectly. As you can see, Mr. Grove had a rather valuable collection of art, but nothing seems to be missing."

Pendergast cast an admiring glance toward one of the nearby paintings. To D'Agosta, it looked like a cross between a pig, a pair of dice, and a naked woman.

"Mr. Grove had a party last night. It was a small party, five in all."

"Do you have the guest list?"

Braskie turned to D'Agosta. "Get the list from Innocente."

Pendergast stayed D'Agosta with a hand. "I should prefer that the sergeant stay here and listen, Lieutenant, if you could spare another officer."

Braskie paused long enough to cast a suspicious glance at D'Agosta, then gestured to another cop in the room.

"Pray continue."

"By all accounts, the last guest was gone by 12:30. They all pretty much left together. From that point until 7:30 this morning, Grove was alone."

"Do you have a time of death?"

"Not yet. The M.E. is still upstairs. We know he was alive at 3:10 A.M. because that's when he called a Father Cappi."

"Grove called a priest?" Pendergast seemed surprised.

"It seems Cappi had been an old friend, but he hadn't seen Grove in thirty, forty years. They had some kind of falling-out. Anyway, it didn't matter: all Grove got was the answering machine."

"I'll need a copy of the message."

"Certainly. Grove was hysterical. He wanted Father Cappi to come over right away."

"With a Bible, cross, and holy water, by chance?" Pendergast asked.

"I see you've already heard about the call."

"No, it was just a guess."

"Father Cappi arrived at eight this morning. He came straight after getting the message. But, of course, by then it was too late, and all he could do was give the body the last rites."

"Have the guests been questioned?"

"Preliminary statements. That's how we know when the party broke up. It seems Grove was not in good form last night. He was excited, garrulous, some say frightened."

"Could anyone have stayed behind, or perhaps slipped back inside after the guests had left?"

"That's a theory we're working on. Mr. Grove had, ah, perverse sexual tastes."

Pendergast raised his eyebrows. "How so?"

"He liked men and women."

"And the perverse sexual tastes?"

"Just what I said. Men and women."

"You mean he was bisexual? As I understand it, thirty percent of all men have such tendencies."

"Not in Southampton they don't."

D'Agosta stifled a laugh with a burst of coughing.

"Excellent work so far, Lieutenant. Shall we move on to the scene of the crime?"

Braskie turned, and they followed him through the house. The peculiar smell that D'Agosta had caught a whiff of out on the lawn was much stronger here.

Matches, fireworks, gunpowder—what exactly was that? It mingled with a smell of burned wood and a gamy roast of some kind. It reminded D'Agosta of the bear meat he had once tried roasting at his house outside Invermere, British Columbia, brought to him by a friend. His wife had walked out in disgust. They'd ended up ordering pizza.

They mounted one set of stairs, threaded a winding hallway, came to a second staircase.

"This door was locked," said Braskie. "The housekeeper opened it."

They climbed the narrow, creaking staircase to the attic floor. At the top was a long hall with doors left and right. At the far end, one door was open and a bright light shone out. D'Agosta breathed through his mouth.

"The door to that far room and its window were also locked," Braskie continued. "The deceased, it appears, piled furniture up against it from the inside." He stepped across the threshold, Pendergast and D'Agosta following. The stench was now overpowering.

It was a small bedroom tucked beneath the eaves of the house, with a single dormer window looking out toward Dune Road. Jeremy Grove lay on the bed at the far side of the room. He was fully dressed, although the clothes had been slit in places to accommodate the M.E.'s investigations. The M.E. was standing beside the bed, back turned, writing on a clipboard.

D'Agosta dabbed his brow. Maybe it was the sun on the roof, maybe the bright lights in the room, but it was stifling. The smell of badly baked meat clung to him like greasy perspiration. He waited near the door while Pendergast circled the corpse, his body tensed like an eagle, examining it from every angle, the look on his face so eager it was unsettling.

The dead man lay on the bed, eyes goggled with blood, his hands clenched. The flesh was a strange tallow color, and its texture seemed off somehow. But it was the expression on the man's face, the rictus of horror and pain, that forced D'Agosta to look away. In his long years as a New York cop, D'Agosta had accumulated a small, unwelcome library of images stored in his mind that he'd never forget as long as he lived. This added one more.

The M.E. was putting away his tools, and two newly arrived assistants were getting ready to bag the body and load it onto a stretcher. Another cop was kneeling on the floor, cutting out a piece of floorboard that had a mark burned into it.

"Doctor?" Pendergast said. The M.E. turned and D'Agosta was surprised to see it was a woman, hair hidden under her cap, a young and very attractive blonde. "Yes?"

Pendergast swept open his shield. "FBI. May I trouble you with a few questions?"

The woman nodded.

"Have you established the time of death?"

"No, and I can tell you that's going to be a problem."

Pendergast raised his eyebrows. "How so?"

"We knew we were in trouble when the anal probe came back at one hundred eight degrees."

"That's what I was going to tell you," said Braskie. "The body's been heated somehow."

"Correct," said the doctor. "The heating took place most strongly on the inside."

"The inside?" Pendergast asked.

D'Agosta could have sworn he'd heard a note of disbelief in the voice.

"Yes. It was as if—as if the body was cooked from the inside out."

Pendergast looked closely at the doctor. "Was there any evidence of burning, surface lesions, on the skin?"

"No. Externally, the body is virtually unmarked. Fully dressed. Aside from a single, rather unusual burn on the chest, the skin appears unbroken and unbruised."

Pendergast paused a moment. "How could that be? A fever spike?"

"No. The body had already cooled from a temperature greater than one hundred twenty degrees—far too high to be biological. At that temperature, the flesh partially cooks. All the usual things you use to establish time of death were completely disrupted by this heating process. The blood's cooked solid in the veins. Solid. At those temperatures, the muscle proteins begin to denature, so there's no rigor—and the temperature killed most bacteria, so there's been no decomposition to speak of. And without the usual spontaneous enzymatic digestion, there's no autolysis, either. All I can say now is he died between 3:10 A.M., when he apparently made a telephone call, and 7:30, when he was discovered dead. But, of course, that's a nonmedical judgment."

"That, I assume, is the burn you referred to earlier?" Pendergast pointed at the man's chest. There, burned and charred into the sallow skin like a brand, was the unmistakable imprint of a cross.

"He was found wearing a cross around his neck,

very expensive by all appearances. But the metal had partially melted and the wood burned away. It seemed to have been set with diamonds and rubies; they were found among the ashes."

Pendergast nodded slowly. After a moment, he thanked the doctor and turned his attention to the man working on the floor. "May I?"

The officer stepped back and Pendergast knelt beside him.

"Sergeant?"

D'Agosta came over and Braskie hastened to follow.

"What do you make of that?"

D'Agosta looked at the image burned into the floor. The finish around it was blistered and cracked, but there was no mistaking the mark of a huge cloven hoof, deeply branded into the wood.

"Looks like the murderer had a sense of humor," D'Agosta muttered.

"My dear Vincent, do you really think it's a joke?"

"*You* don't?"

"No."

D'Agosta found Braskie staring at him. The "my dear Vincent" hadn't gone down well at all. Meanwhile, Pendergast had gotten down on his hands and knees and was sniffing around the floor almost like a dog. Suddenly a test tube and tweezers appeared out of his baggy shorts. The FBI agent picked up a brownish particle, held it to his nose a moment; then, sniffing, stretched it out toward the lieutenant.

Braskie frowned. "What's that?"

"Brimstone, Lieutenant," said Pendergast. "Good Old Testament brimstone."

{ 5 }

The Chaunticleer was a tiny six-table restaurant, tucked into an Amagansett side street between Bluff Road and Main. From his narrow wooden seat, D'Agosta looked around, blinking. Everything seemed to be yellow: the yellow daffodils in the window boxes; the yellow taffeta curtains on the yellow-painted windows; the yellow linen tablecloths. And what wasn't yellow was an accent of green or red. The whole place looked like one of those octagonal French dinner plates everybody paid so much money for. D'Agosta closed his eyes for a moment. After the musty dark of Jeremy Grove's attic, this place seemed almost unbearably cheerful.

The proprietress, a short, red-faced, middle-aged woman, bustled up. "Ah, Monsieur Pendergast," she said. *"Comment ça va?"*

"Bien, madame."

"The usual, *monsieur*?"

"Oui, merci."

The woman turned her gaze on D'Agosta. "And you, Officer?"

D'Agosta glanced at the menu—scrawled in white

chalk on a slate near the door—but half the dishes he didn't recognize, and the other half held no interest for him. The reek of Jeremy Grove's flesh was still strong in his nostrils. "Nothing for me, thanks."

"Anything to drink?"

"A Bud. Frosty."

"So sorry, *monsieur*, but we have no liquor license."

D'Agosta licked his lips. "Then bring me an iced tea, please."

He watched the woman depart, then glanced across the table at Pendergast, now dressed in his usual black suit. He still couldn't get over the shock of running into him like this. The man looked no different than the last time he'd seen him, years before. D'Agosta, embarrassed, knew the same couldn't be said for himself. He was five years older, ten years heavier, and two stripes lighter. What a life.

"How'd you find this place?" he asked.

"Quite by accident. It's just a few blocks from where I'm staying. It may well be the only decent restaurant in the Hamptons undiscovered by the beautiful people. Sure you won't change your mind about lunch? I really do recommend the eggs Benedict. Madame Merle makes the best hollandaise sauce I've tasted outside Paris: light yet silky, with the merest hint of tarragon."

D'Agosta shook his head quickly. "You still haven't told me why you're out here."

"As I mentioned, I've taken a house here for the week. I'm—what is that phrase?—location scouting."

"Location scouting? For what?"

"For the, shall we say, *convalescence* of a friend. You'll meet her in due course. And now I'd like to hear your story. The last I knew, you were in British Columbia, writing novels. I have to say, I found *Angels of Purgatory* to be readable."

"Readable?"

Pendergast waved his hand. "I'm not much of a judge when it comes to police procedurals. My taste for sensational fiction ends with M. R. James."

D'Agosta thought he probably meant P. D. James but let it pass. The last thing he wanted to do was have a "literary conversation." He'd had more than enough of those the last few years.

The drinks arrived. D'Agosta took a big gulp of iced tea, found it was unsweetened, tore open a packet of sugar. "My story's soon told, Pendergast. I couldn't make a living at writing, so I came home. Couldn't get my old place back on the NYPD. The new mayor's downsizing the force, and besides, I'd made more than my share of enemies on the job. I was getting desperate. Heard about the opening in Southampton and took it."

"I imagine there are worse places to work."

"Yeah, you'd think so. But after spending a summer chasing people whose dogs have just left a steaming load on the beach, you'd think different. And the people out here—you give a guy a speeding ticket, and the next thing you know, some high-priced lawyer's down at the station with writs and subpoenas, raising hell. You should see our legal bills."

Pendergast took a sip of what appeared to be tea. "And how is working with Lieutenant Braskie?"

"He's an asshole. Totally political. Gonna run for chief."

"He seemed competent enough."

"A competent asshole, then."

He found Pendergast's cool gaze on him, and he fidgeted. He'd forgotten about those eyes. They made you feel like you had just been stripped of your secrets.

"There's a part of your story you left out. Back when we last worked together, you had a wife and son. Vincent Junior, I believe."

D'Agosta nodded. "Still got a son. He's back in Canada, living with my wife. Well, my wife on paper, anyway."

Pendergast said nothing. After a moment, D'Agosta fetched a sigh.

"Lydia and I weren't that close anymore. You know how it is: being on the force, working long hours. She didn't want to move to Canada to begin with, especially a place as remote as Invermere. When we got there, having me in the house all day long, trying to write... well, we got on each other's nerves. And that's putting it mildly." He shrugged, shook his head. "Funny thing was, she grew to like it up there. Seems my moving back here was just about the final straw."

Madame Merle returned with Pendergast's order, and D'Agosta decided it was time to change the subject. "What about you?" he asked almost aggressively. "What have you been up to? New York keeping you busy?"

"Actually, I've recently returned from the Midwest. Kansas, to be precise, where I was handling a case—a small case, but not without its, ah, interesting features."

"And Grove?"

"As you know, Vincent, I have an interest—some might call it an unhealthy interest—in unusual homicides. I've traveled to places far more distant than Long

Island in pursuit of them. A bad habit, but very hard to break." Pendergast pierced an egg with his knife, and yolk flooded out over the plate. More yellow.

"So, are you official?"

"My freelancing days are over. The FBI is a different place. Yes, I'm official." And he patted the cell phone in his pocket.

"What's the hook? I mean, for the feds. Drugs? Terrorism?"

"Just what I told Lieutenant Braskie—possibility of interstate flight. It's weak, but it will have to serve." Pendergast leaned forward, lowering his voice slightly. "I need your help, Vincent."

D'Agosta looked over. Was he kidding?

"We made a good team once."

"But I'm..." He hesitated. "You don't need my help." He said it more angrily than he meant. He found those damn eyes on him again.

"Not as much as you need my help, perhaps."

"What do you mean? I don't need anybody's help. I'm doing fine."

"Forgive the liberty, but you are not doing fine."

"What the hell are you talking about?"

"You're working far below your capacity. Not only is that a waste of your talents, but it's all too clear in your attitude. Lieutenant Braskie seems to be basically decent, and he may be somewhat intelligent, but you do not belong under his supervision. Once he's chief, your relationship will only grow worse."

"You think that asshole is intelligent and decent? Christ, if you could spend a day working for him, you'd change your tune."

"It's you, Vincent, who needs to change your tune. There are far worse policemen than Lieutenant Braskie, and we've worked with them."

"So you're going to save me, is that it?"

"No, Vincent. It's the case that will save you. From yourself."

D'Agosta stood up. "I don't have to take this shit from you or anyone." He pulled out his wallet, dropped a crumpled five on the table, and stalked out.

Ten minutes later D'Agosta found Pendergast in the same place he'd left him, the crumpled bill still sitting there. He pulled out the chair, sat down, and ordered another iced tea, his face burning. Pendergast merely nodded as he finished the last bite of his lunch. Then he removed a piece of paper from his jacket pocket and laid it gently on the table.

"This is a list of the four people who attended Jeremy Grove's last party, and the name and number of the priest who received his final phone call. It's as good a place to start as any. Considering how short the list is, there are some rather interesting names on it." He pushed the paper across the table.

D'Agosta nodded. The burning sensation began to ebb as he looked at the names and addresses. Something began to stir in him: the old excitement of working a case. A good case.

"How's this going to work, with me being on the Southampton P.D. and all?"

"I will arrange with Lieutenant Braskie to get you assigned as the local FBI liaison officer."

"He'll never go for it."

"On the contrary, he will be only too happy to get rid of you. And in any case, it won't be presented as a request. Braskie, as you pointed out, is a political animal, and he will do as he is told."

D'Agosta nodded.

Pendergast checked his watch. "Almost two. Come on, Vincent, we've got a long drive ahead of us. Priests dine early, but we might just catch Father Cappi if we hurry."

{ 6 }

D'Agosta felt like he'd been swallowed by Ahab's white whale, cushioned as he was in the white leather interior of a '59 Rolls-Royce Silver Wraith. Chauffeured, no less. Pendergast had certainly come up in the world since the bad old days of the museum murders, when he drove a late-model Buick from the Bureau pool. Maybe a relative died and left him a few billion. He glanced over. Or maybe the time for dissembling had simply passed.

The car was cruising up Route 9, along a beautiful stretch of the middle Hudson Valley north of Poughkeepsie. After months spent among low sand dunes and beach scrub, D'Agosta found the lush greenery and rolling hills a relief to the eyes. Here and there, old mansions could be seen: set far back from the road, overlooking the river or tucked in among copses of trees. Some had signs identifying them as monasteries or retreats; others still seemed to be in private ownership. Despite the warmth of the day, there were already strong traces of fall coloring in the trees that marched up the gentle slopes.

The car slowed, then slid into a long cobbled driveway, coming at last to a noiseless stop beneath a red-brick porte-cochère. As he stepped out of the car, D'Agosta found himself before a rambling, Flemish-style mansion. A narrow bell tower at the flank of the building appeared to be a later addition. Beyond, well-tended greensward swept down toward the Hudson. A plaque screwed into the facade announced that the structure was built in 1874 and was now designated a historic site on the National Register of Historic Places.

Their knock was answered by a cowled monk in brown robes, a silken rope tied around his waist. Without a word, he ushered them into an elegant interior smelling of time and wax polish. Pendergast bowed and presented the monk with a card; in turn, the monk nodded and beckoned. They followed him through several turnings and twistings of corridors to a spartan room, whitewashed and bare save for a single crucifix and two rows of hard wooden chairs along opposite walls. A single window near the exposed rafters let in a bar of light.

The monk bowed and withdrew. Moments later, another figure appeared in the door. He, too, was dressed in a monk's habit, but when he drew back the collar, D'Agosta was surprised to find a man well over six feet, broad-shouldered, square-jawed, with black eyes that sparkled with vigor. In the background, he could hear the faint peal of bells as the changes began to ring in the tower. Somehow it gave him the shivers.

"I'm Father Bernard Cappi," the man said. "Welcome to the Hyde Park Carthaginian Monastery. Here we're under a vow of silence, but we meet in this particular room once a week to talk. We call it the Disputation Chamber, because this is where we piss and moan. You build up a lot of resentments in a week of silence." He swept his robes back, taking a seat.

"This is my associate, Sergeant D'Agosta," Pendergast said, following the monk's lead. "He may want to ask questions as well."

"Pleased to make your acquaintance." The priest crushed his hand in greeting. *This is no gentle lamb of God,* thought D'Agosta. He eased down in the chair, shifting, trying hard to get comfortable. He failed. The room, despite the sunny day outside, felt cold and damp. God, he would never make a good monk.

"I sincerely apologize for this intrusion," said Pendergast.

"Quite all right. I just hope I can be of help. This is a tragic business."

"We'll take as little of your time as possible. Perhaps we should begin with the telephone call."

"As I told the police, the call came to my home at 3:10 in the morning—the answering machine registered the time—but every year I take a two-week retreat here, and so I wasn't home to receive it. I check my messages upon rising—it's a violation of the rules, but I've got an elderly mother. I immediately headed out to Long Island, but, of course, it was too late."

"Why did he call you?"

"That's a complicated question requiring a long answer."

Pendergast nodded at him to proceed.

"Jeremy Grove and I go way back. We met at Columbia as students many years ago. I went on to the priesthood, and he went to Florence to study art. In those days, we were both—well, I wouldn't call us religious in the usual sense of the word. We were both spiritually *intrigued.* We used to argue to all hours of the morning about questions of faith, epistemology, the nature of good and evil, and so forth. I went on to study theology at Mount St. Mary's. We continued our friendship, and a few years later I officiated over Grove's marriage."

"I see," murmured Pendergast.

"Grove stayed in Florence and I visited him several times. He was living in a beautiful villa in the hills south of the city."

D'Agosta cleared his throat. "Where'd he get his money?"

"An interesting story, Sergeant. He bought a painting at an auction at Sotheby's that was billed as being by a late follower of Raphael. Grove was able to prove it as the hand of the master himself, turned around and sold it for thirty million dollars to the Met."

"Nice."

"Indeed. Anyway, while living in Florence, Grove had become quite devout. In an intellectual kind of way, as some people do. He loved to engage me in discussion. There is, Mr. Pendergast, such a thing as a Catholic intellectual, and that was Grove."

Pendergast nodded.

"He was very happily married. He adored his wife. And then, quite abruptly, she left him, ran off with another man. To say that Grove was devastated is not saying enough. He was destroyed. And he focused his anger on God."

"I see," Pendergast replied.

"Grove felt betrayed by God. He became... well, you certainly couldn't call him an atheist or an agnostic. Rather, he picked a fight with God. He deliberately embarked on a life of sin and violence against God, which in reality was a life of violence against his own higher self. He became an art critic. Criticism is a profession which allows one a certain license to be vicious outside the bounds of normal civilized behavior. One would never tell another person in private that his painting was a revolting piece of trash, but the critic thinks nothing of making the same pronouncement to the world as if he were performing a high moral duty. There is no profession more ignoble than that of the critic—except perhaps that of the physician presiding at an execution."

"You're right there," said D'Agosta with feeling. "Those who can't do, teach, and those who can't teach, critique."

Father Cappi laughed. "Very true, Sergeant D'Agosta."

"Sergeant D'Agosta is a writer of mysteries," explained Pendergast.

"Is that so! I love detective stories. Give me a title."

"*Angels of Purgatory* is his latest."

"I'll buy it immediately."

D'Agosta mumbled his thanks. For the second time that day, he found himself feeling embarrassed. He would have to talk to Pendergast about sounding off about his abortive writing career.

"Suffice to say," the priest continued, "Grove made a splendid critic. He surrounded himself with the most degraded, selfish, and cruel people he could find. Everything he did was excessive—drinking, eating, sex, money, gossip. He gave dinner parties like a Roman emperor, and he was often on television, savaging this person or that—in the most charming way, of course. His articles in the *New York Review of Books* were avidly read. Naturally he was a huge hit in New York City society."

"And your relationship to him?"

"He couldn't forgive me for what I represented. Our relationship simply couldn't continue."

"When was this?" D'Agosta asked.

"Grove's wife ran off in 1974, and we had our falling-out shortly thereafter. I haven't heard from him since. Not until this morning, that is."

"The message?"

The priest removed a microcassette recorder from his pocket. "I made a copy before turning it over to the police."

Holding it up in one hand, he pressed the play button. There was a beep. Then:

Bernard? Bernard! It's Jeremy Grove. Are you there? Pick up the phone, for God's sake!

The voice was high, strained, tinny.

Listen, Bernard, I need you here, now. You've got to come. Southampton, 3001 Dune Road. Come immediately. It's... it's horrible. Bring a cross, Bible, holy water. My God, Bernard, he's coming for me. Do you hear? He's coming for me! I need to confess, I need forgiveness, absolution... For the love of God, Bernard, pick up the phone—

His voice was cut off by the message machine using up its allotted time. The harsh voice echoed into silence in the bare, whitewashed room. D'Agosta felt a shiver of horror.

"Well," said Pendergast after a moment. "I'd be curious to hear your thoughts on that, Father."

Father Cappi's face was grim. "I believe he felt damnation was upon him."

"Damnation? Or the devil?"

Cappi shifted uncomfortably. "For whatever reason, Jeremy Grove knew his death was imminent. He wanted to obtain forgiveness before the end. That was even more important to him than calling the police. Grove, you see, never stopped believing."

"Are you familiar with the physical evidence at the scene of the crime: the burned hoofprint, the traces of sulfur and brimstone, the peculiar heating of the body?"

"I was told, yes."

"How do you explain it?"

"The work of a mortal man. Grove's killer wished to make a statement about what kind of man Grove was. Hence the hoofprint, brimstone, and all the rest." Father Cappi slid the tape recorder back into his cassock. "There's nothing mysterious about evil, Mr. Pendergast. It's here all around us, I see it every day. And I somehow doubt the real devil, whatever form he might take, would wish to draw such unwelcome attention to his way of doing business."

{ 7 }

In the first darkness following sunset, the man known only as Wren walked up the broad, trash-strewn thoroughfare of upper Riverside Drive. To his left lay the black outlines of Riverside Park and the Hudson River beyond; to his right, the vast hulks of once-great mansions, now empty and decaying. Wren's shadow flitted from streetlamp to streetlamp as the last touch of red left the incarnadine sky. Despite the gentrification creeping up from southern Manhattan, this remained a dangerous neighborhood, one in which few would wish to be caught after dark. But there was something about Wren—the cadaverousness of his features, perhaps; or his quick, stealthy scuttle of a walk; or the wild shock of white hair, unnaturally thick for a man of his years—that kept predators at bay.

Now Wren stopped before a large Beaux Arts mansion that fronted Riverside Drive from 137th to 138th Streets. The four-story pile was surrounded by a tall spiked-iron fence, furred in rust. Beyond the fence, the lawn was overgrown with weeds and ancient ailanthus bushes. The mansion itself seemed in decrepitude:

windows securely boarded up with tin, slate roof tiles chipped, widow's walk missing half its metal posts.

The iron gate blocking the entrance was ajar. Without pausing, Wren slipped through the opening and down the cobbled drive to the porte-cochère. Here, trash had accumulated in the corners, blown by the wind into fantastic shapes. In the blackness beneath the carriageway entrance was set a lone oaken door, festooned with graffiti but solid-looking nonetheless. Wren raised his bony hand, rapped once, then again.

The echo of his knock was lost in the vast spaces within. For a minute, perhaps two, all remained still. Then there was the rasp of a heavy lock being turned, and the door slowly creaked open. Yellow light filtered out. Pendergast stood in the doorway, one hand on the knob, the paleness of his features enhanced by the incandescent glow of the hallway. Without a word, he ushered Wren in, then closed and locked the door behind them.

Wren followed the FBI agent through the marbled entranceway and into a long, wood-paneled gallery. Then he stopped abruptly. The last time he had seen this house was during the summer, when he'd spent several weeks cataloging the mansion's vast collections while Pendergast was taking his vacation in Kansas. At the time, the inside of the house had been as much a ruin as the outside: paneling torn away, floorboards ripped up, plaster and lath exposed, the by-products of an intense search. Along with Pendergast, Wren was one of only four—no, that would be five—living beings who knew the results of that search, and what those results meant.

But now the chestnut wainscoting shone with fresh polish; the walls had been replastered and covered in muted Victorian wallpaper; and everywhere, brass and copper fittings glowed in the dim light. In dozens of inlaid nooks and on marble plinths sat specimens from a magnificent collection: meteorites, gemstones, rare butterflies, fossils of long-extinct species. Within this house, a cabinet of curiosities unmatched by any other had been restored to a magnificence it had not enjoyed in a hundred years. Yet it was a cabinet destined to remain hidden from the world.

"I love what you've done with the place," Wren said, waving his hand around the room.

Pendergast inclined his head.

"I'm amazed you accomplished it so quickly. Just two months ago the house was a shambles."

Pendergast began leading the way down the gallery. "Cajun craftsmen and carpenters from south of the Bayou Têche served my family well in earlier years. They proved themselves invaluable once again. Though they did not approve of the—shall we say—environs?"

Wren chuckled faintly, tunelessly. "I have to agree with them. It seems odd, you taking up residence here, when you have such a delightful place down at the Dakota that's—" He stopped in midsentence, eyes widening in understanding. "Unless...?"

Pendergast nodded. "Yes, Wren. That is the reason. One of them, anyway."

They were now passing into a vast reception hall, its domed ceiling repainted a Wedgwood blue. Rippled glass cabinets lined the walls, full of more artifacts, beautifully displayed. Small mounted dinosaur skeletons and taxidermied animals were arrayed around the parquet floor. Wren plucked at Pendergast's sleeve. "How is she?"

Pendergast stopped. "She is well. Physically. Emotionally, as well as could be expected. We're making slow progress. It's been so long, you see."

Wren nodded his understanding. Then he reached into his pocket and withdrew a DVD.

"Here it is," he said, passing it to Pendergast. "A complete inventory of the collections within this house, cataloged and indexed to the best of my ability."

Pendergast nodded.

"It still amazes me that the world's preeminent cabinet of curiosities is housed under this roof."

"Indeed. And I trust you found the pieces I gave you from it payment enough for your services?"

"Oh, yes," Wren whispered. "Yes, yes, they were definitely payment enough."

"As I recall, you were so long on restoring a certain Indian ledger book I was afraid the rightful owner would get restive."

"One can't hurry art," Wren sniffed. "And it was such a *beautiful* ledger book. It's just that...it's just *time*, you know. Time bears away all things, as Virgil said. It's bearing away my books right now, my lovely books, faster than I can restore them." Wren's domicile was the seventh and deepest sub-basement of the New York Public Library, where he held court over uncataloged legions of decaying books, their endless stacks navigable by no one but himself.

"Indeed. Then it must be a relief to know that your work here is done."

"I'd have inventoried the library as well, but *she* seems to retain everything about it in her head." And Wren allowed himself a bitter laugh.

"Her knowledge of this house is remarkable, and I've found uses for it already."

Wren glanced at him inquiringly.

"I'm planning to ask her to examine the library's holdings on Satan."

"Satan? That's a broad topic, *hypocrite lecteur.*"

"As it happens, I'm interested in just one aspect. The death of human beings at the hand of the devil."

"You mean, as in selling one's soul? Payment for services rendered, that kind of thing?"

Pendergast nodded.

"It's *still* a broad topic."

"I'm not interested in literature, Wren. I'm interested solely in nonfiction sources. Primary sources. Preferably first-person and eyewitness accounts."

"You've been in this house too long."

"I find it's beneficial to keep her occupied. And, as you said yourself, she knows the library's holdings so well."

"I see." And Wren let his gaze stray toward a set of doors in the far wall.

Pendergast followed his gaze. "You wish to see her?"

"Are you surprised? I'm practically her godfather, after what happened here this summer. You forget my role."

"I forget nothing, and will always be in your debt for that, if nothing else." And without another word, Pendergast stepped forward and noiselessly opened the doors.

Wren peered through them. His yellow eyes grew bright. On the far side lay a large and sumptuously appointed library. Case after case of richly bound books rose to the ceiling, firelight warming their leather spines. A dozen small sofas and wing chairs were arranged across a thick Persian carpet. In one of the chairs, sitting before the fire, was a young woman, paging through an oversize book of lithographs. She was wearing a pinafore over a white dress and black stockings, and as she turned another page, the firelight shone on her slender limbs, her dark hair and eyes. On a low table nearby sat a tea service, laid out for two.

Pendergast cleared his throat gently and the girl looked up. Her eyes went from the FBI agent to Wren, and for a moment, fear flashed through them. But then recognition spread across her features. She put the book aside, stood up, smoothed her pinafore, and waited for the two men to approach.

"How are you, Constance?" Wren asked in as soothing a croak as he could manage.

"Very well, Mr. Wren, thank you." Constance gave a small curtsy. "And yourself?"

"Busy, very busy. My books take up all my time."

"I shouldn't think one would speak grudgingly of such a noble occupation." Constance's tone was grave, but the faintest of smiles touched her lips—in amusement? condescension?—and was gone again before Wren could be sure.

"No, no, of course not." Wren tried not to stare. How, in such a short time, could he have forgotten that studied voice with its quaint constructions? How could he forget those eyes, so very ancient, yet set in such a young and beautiful face? He cleared his throat. "So tell me, Constance, how you pass your days."

"Rather tranquilly. In the mornings, I read Latin and Greek, under the direction of Aloysius. My afternoons are my own, and I generally spend them browsing the collections, correcting the occasional inaccurate label I happen to come across."

Wren darted a quick look at Pendergast.

"We have a late tea, during which Aloysius generally reads to me from the newspapers. After dinner, I practice the violin. Wretchedly. Aloysius suffers me to believe he finds my playing bearable."

"Dr. Pendergast is the most honest of people."

"Let us say Dr. Pendergast is the most tactful of people."

"Be that as it may, I'd love to hear you play sometime."

"I would be delighted." And Constance curtsied again.

Wren nodded, turned to leave.

"Mr. Wren?" Constance called after him.

Wren turned, beetled eyebrows raised in query.

She looked back at him. "Thank you again. For everything."

Pendergast quietly shut the doors to the library and accompanied Wren back down the echoing galleries.

"You read her the *newspapers*?" Wren asked.

"Just selected articles, of course. It seemed the easiest form of—how best to put it?—social decompression. We're now up to the 1960s."

"And her nocturnal, ah, rambles?"

"Now that she's under my care, there's no need

for foraging. And I've decided on the site of her recuperation: my great-aunt's estate on the Hudson. It's deserted these days. It should be a good reintroduction to sunlight, if handled gently enough."

"Sunlight." Wren repeated the word slowly, as if tasting it. "It still seems impossible she was there all that time, after what happened, in those tunnels down by the river access. I keep wondering why she revealed herself to me."

"Perhaps she'd grown to trust you. She'd watched you at work long enough, over the summer. You clearly loved the collections, which are precious to her as well. Or perhaps she had just reached the point where human contact was necessary, no matter what the risk."

Wren shook his head. "Are you sure, really sure, she's only nineteen years old?"

"That question is more difficult than it sounds. Physically, her body is that of a nineteen-year-old."

They had reached the front door, and Wren waited for Pendergast to unlock it. "Thank you, Wren," the FBI agent said, opening the door. Night air rushed in, carrying with it the faint sounds of traffic.

Wren stepped through the door, paused, turned back. "Have you decided what you're going to do about her?"

For a moment, Pendergast did not reply. Then he nodded silently.

{ 8 }

The Renaissance Salon of the Metropolitan Museum of Art was one of the museum's most remarkable spaces. Taken piece by piece, stone by stone, from the ancient Palazzo Dati of Florence and reassembled in Manhattan, it re-created in perfect detail a late Renaissance *salone.* It was the most imposing and austere of all the grand galleries in the museum, and for this reason, it was chosen for the memorial service of Jeremy Grove.

D'Agosta felt like an idiot in his cop's uniform, with its Southampton P.D. patch in gold and blue and its lowly sergeant's stripes. People turned toward him quickly, stared as if he was some kind of freak, and then just as quickly dismissed him as hired help and turned away.

As he followed Pendergast into the hall, D'Agosta was surprised to see a long table groaning with food, and another sporting enough bottles of wine and liquor to lay low a herd of rhinos. Some memorial service. More like an Irish wake. D'Agosta had been to a few of those during his NYPD days and felt lucky to have survived them. They'd obviously set this whole thing up with remarkable speed—Grove had been dead only two days.

The room was crowded. There were no chairs: people were meant to mingle, not sit reverentially. Several television crews had set up their gear near a carpet-covered stage, which was bare save for a small podium. A harpsichord stood in a far corner of the salon, but it was barely audible over the noise of the crowd. If there was anybody shedding tears over Grove, they were hiding it pretty well.

Pendergast leaned over. "Vincent, if you are interested in any comestibles, now is the time to act. With a crowd like this, they won't last long."

"Comestibles? You mean that food on the table? No, thanks." His dalliance with the literary world had taught him that events like these served things like fish eggs and cheese that smelled so bad it encouraged you to check the bottom of your shoes.

"Then shall we circulate?" Pendergast began moving sylphlike through the crowd. Now a lone man mounted the stage: impeccably dressed, tall, hair carefully groomed back, face glistening with a professional makeup job. The crowd hushed even before he reached the microphone.

Pendergast took D'Agosta's elbow. "Sir Gervase de Vache, director of the museum."

The man plucked the microphone from the podium, his elegant figure straight and dignified.

"I welcome you all," he said, apparently feeling it unnecessary to introduce himself. "We are here to memorialize our friend and colleague Jeremy Grove—but as he would have wanted it: with food, drink, music, and good cheer, not long faces and lugubrious speeches." He spoke with a trace of a French accent.

Although Pendergast had stopped the moment the director gained the stage, D'Agosta noticed that the FBI agent was still scouring the room with his restless eyes.

"I first met Jeremy Grove some twenty years ago, when he reviewed our Monet exhibition for *Downtown*. It was—how shall I say it?—a classic Grove review."

There was a ripple of knowing laughter.

"Jeremy Grove was, above all else, a man who told the truth as he saw it, unflinchingly and with style. His rapier wit and irreverent sallies enlivened many a dinner party..."

D'Agosta tuned out. Pendergast was still ceaselessly scanning the room, and now he began moving again, slowly, like a shark that has just scented blood in the water. D'Agosta followed. He liked to watch Pendergast in action. There, at the liquor table, pouring himself a stiff drink, was a striking young man dressed entirely in black, with a neat goatee. He had exceptionally large, deep, liquid eyes, and fingers that were even more spidery than Pendergast's.

"Maurice Vilnius, the abstract expressionist painter," Pendergast murmured. "One of many beneficiaries of Grove's ministrations."

"What's that supposed to mean?"

"I recall a review Grove wrote of Vilnius's paintings some years back. The phrase that best sticks in my mind is: *These paintings are so bad they inspire respect, even awe. It takes a special kind of talent to produce mediocrity at this level. Vilnius has such talent in abundance.*"

D'Agosta swallowed a laugh. "That's worth killing over." He hastily put his face in order; Vilnius had turned to see them approach.

"Ah, Maurice, how are you?" Pendergast asked.

The painter raised two very black eyebrows. As a fellow sufferer of bad reviews, D'Agosta had expected to see anger, or at least resentment, on the flushed face. Instead, it wore a broad smile.

"Have we met?"

"My name's Pendergast. We met briefly at your opening at Galerie Dellitte last year. Beautiful work. I've been considering acquiring a piece for my apartment in the Dakota."

Vilnius's smile grew broader. "Delighted." He spoke with a Russian accent. "Come by anytime. Come by today. It would make my fifth sale this week."

"Indeed?" D'Agosta noticed Pendergast was careful to keep surprise from his voice. In the background, the director's voice droned on: *"...a man of courage and determination, who did not go gently into that good night..."*

"Maurice," Pendergast continued, "I'd like to speak with you about Grove's last—"

Suddenly, a middle-aged woman came up to Vilnius, her cadaverous figure draped in a sequined dress. In tow was a tall man in a black tuxedo, his bald head polished to gemstone brilliance.

The woman tugged at Vilnius's sleeve. "Maurice, darling, I just *had* to congratulate you in person. That new review is simply wonderful. And *so* long overdue."

"You've seen it already?" Vilnius replied, turning toward these new arrivals.

"Just this afternoon," the tall man replied. "A proof copy was faxed to my gallery."

"...and now, one of Jeremy's beloved sonatas by Haydn..."

People continued talking, ignoring the man at the podium. Vilnius glanced back toward Pendergast for a moment. "Nice to have met you again, Mr. Pendergast," he said, drawing a card from his pocket and handing it to the FBI agent. "Please drop by the studio anytime." Then he turned back to the woman and her escort. As they walked away, D'Agosta could hear Vilnius saying, "It's remarkable to me how quickly news spreads. The review isn't even due to be published for another day."

D'Agosta looked at Pendergast. He, too, was watching Vilnius walk away. "Interesting," he murmured under his breath.

They drifted back into the crowd. De Vache had concluded his speech, and the noise level had risen once again. The harpischord had resumed but was now completely inaudible over the drinking, eating, and gossiping.

Suddenly, Pendergast took off at high speed, arrowing through the crowd. D'Agosta realized his aim was the director of the Met, stepping down from the stage.

De Vache paused at their approach. "Ah, Pendergast. Don't tell me *you're* on the case."

Pendergast nodded.

The Frenchman pursed his lips. "Is this official? Or were you perhaps a friend of his?"

"Did Grove *have* any friends?"

De Vache chuckled. "True, very true. Friendship was a stranger to Jeremy, something he kept at arm's length.

The last time I met him was—let me see—at a dinner party. I recall he asked the man across from him—a perfectly harmless old gentleman with dentures—to stop clacking his front incisors while he ate; that he was a man, not a rat. Someone later dripped sauce on his tie, and Jeremy inquired if perchance he was related to Jackson Pollock." Sir Gervase chuckled. "And that was just one dinner party. Can a man who routinely talks this way have friends?"

Sir Gervase was called away by a group of jewelry-laden matrons. He apologized to Pendergast, nodded at D'Agosta, then turned away. Pendergast's eyes went back to roaming the room, finally locking on a group of people near the harpsichord. "*Voilà,*" he said. "The mother lode."

"Who?"

"Those three talking together. Along with Vilnius, whom you just met, they were the guests at Grove's last dinner party. And our reason for being here."

D'Agosta's eye landed first on an unexceptional-looking man in a gray suit. Beside him stood a wraith-like elderly woman, covered with powder and rouge, dressed to the nines, manicured, coiffed, and no doubt Botoxed in an ultimately failed attempt to look less than sixty. She wore a necklace of emeralds so big D'Agosta feared her scrawny shoulders would tire carrying their weight. But the standout among the group was the figure at her other elbow: an enormously fat man in a gorgeous, dove-gray suit, replete with silk waistcoat, white gloves, and gold chain.

"The woman," murmured Pendergast, "is Lady Milbanke, widow of the seventh Baron Milbanke. She is said to be a poisonous gossip, a drinker of absinthe, and an indefatigable séance organizer and raiser of the dead."

"She looks like she needs a little raising from the dead herself."

"Vincent, I have missed your trenchant sense of humor. The heavyset gentleman is undoubtedly Count Fosco. I have long heard of him, but this is the first time I've seen him."

"He must weigh three hundred pounds if he weighs an ounce."

"And yet observe how lightly he carries himself. And the tall gentleman in the gray suit is Jonathan Frederick, the art critic for *Art & Antiques.*"

D'Agosta nodded.

"Shall we venture into the lion's den?"

"You're the boss."

Immediately, Pendergast strode over, smoothly and shamelessly insinuated himself into the group, and, seizing Lady Milbanke's hand, raised it toward his lips.

The old woman blushed beneath her makeup. "Have we had the pleasure—?"

"No," said Pendergast. "More's the pity. My name is Pendergast."

"Pendergast. And who is your friend? A bodyguard?" This elicited a round of titters from the group.

Pendergast chuckled along with them. "In a manner of speaking."

"If he's moonlighting," the tall man named Frederick said, "he should do so out of uniform. This is, after all, a memorial service."

D'Agosta noted that Pendergast did not bother to

correct the man about the moonlighting. Instead, he shook his head sadly, ignoring the comment. "Terribly sad about Grove, don't you think?"

Nods all around.

"I heard a rumor he gave a dinner party the night of his death."

There was a sudden silence.

"Well now, Mr. Pendergast," said Lady Milbanke. "What an extraordinary comment. You see, we were all at that dinner party."

"Indeed. They say the murderer might have been a guest at the party."

"How exciting!" cried Lady Milbanke. "It's just like an Agatha Christie novel. As a matter of fact, we each had our own motives to do away with Grove. At least, we *used* to." She exchanged brief glances with the others. "But then, we weren't the only ones. Isn't that so, Jason?" And, raising her voice, she beckoned a young man who was passing by, champagne flute in one hand. An orchid drooped from the buttonhole of his fawn jacket, and his hair was the color of marmalade.

The youth stopped, frowned. "What are you talking about?"

"This is Jason Prince." She laughed teasingly. "Jason, I was just telling Mr. Pendergast here how many people in this room had cause to murder Jeremy Grove. And you're known to be a jealous lad."

"She's full of crap, as usual," said Prince, his face flushing. Turning on his heels, he strode away.

Lady Milbanke issued another tinkle of laughter. "And Jonathan here had been skewered by Grove more than once in his time. Right, Jonathan?"

The gray-haired man smiled ironically. "I joined a rather large club."

"He called you the inflatable love doll of art critics, didn't he?"

The man didn't bat an eye. "Grove did have a turn of phrase. But I thought we agreed this was all behind us, Evelyn. That was more than five years ago."

"And then there's the count. A prime suspect. Look at him! Obviously a man of dark secrets. He's Italian, and you know *them*."

The count smiled. "We Italians are devious creatures."

D'Agosta looked at the count with curiosity. He was struck by the man's eyes, which were a dark gray color, with the unique clearness of deep water. The man had long gray hair, swept back, and skin as pink as a baby's, despite his age, which had to approach sixty.

"And then there's *me*," Lady Milbanke continued. "You might think I had the best motive of all to murder him. We were once lovers. *Cherchez la dame*."

D'Agosta shuddered and wondered if such a thing was physically possible.

The critic, Frederick, seemed to be equally put off by this image, because he began backing off. "Excuse me, there's someone I need to speak with."

Lady Milbanke smiled. "About your new appointment, I suppose?"

"As a matter of fact, yes. Mr. Pendergast, a pleasure to have met you."

There was a brief pause in the conversation. D'Agosta found that the count's gray eyes had settled on Pendergast and that a small smile was playing about his lips.

"Pray tell, Mr. Pendergast," said the count. "What *is* your official interest in this case?"

Pendergast didn't react. By way of response, he slipped a hand into his jacket and removed his wallet, opening it slowly and reverently, as if it was a case of jewels. The gold badge flashed in the lights of the great hall.

"Ecce signum!" the count cried delightedly.

The old lady took a step back. "You? Police?"

"Special Agent Pendergast, Federal Bureau of Investigation."

Lady Milbanke rounded on the count. "You knew and didn't *tell* me? And here I've made all of us into suspects!" Her voice had lost its undertone of amusement.

The count smiled. "I knew the minute he approached that he was of the constabulary."

"He doesn't look like an FBI agent to *me*."

The count turned to Pendergast. "I hope Evelyn's information will be useful to you, sir?"

"Very," said Pendergast. "I have heard much about you, Count Fosco."

The count smiled.

"I believe you and Grove have been friends a long time?"

"We shared a love of music and art, and that highest marriage of the two: opera. Are you by chance a lover of opera?"

"I am not."

"No?" The count arched his eyebrows. "And why not?"

"Opera has always struck me as vulgar and infantile. I prefer the symphonic form: pure music, without such props as sets, costumes, melodrama, sex, and violence."

It seemed to D'Agosta the count had gone stock-still. But then he realized Fosco was laughing silently, visible only from an internal convulsion. The laugh went on for quite a long time. Then he wiped the corners of his eyes with a handkerchief and patted his plump hands together lightly, in appreciation. "Well, well. I see you are a gentleman with firm opinions." He paused, leaned toward Pendergast, and began to sing in a low tone, his deep bass voice barely keeping above the noise of the room.

Braveggia, urla! T'affretta
a palesarmi il fondo dell'alma ria!

He paused, leaned back, beaming around. "*Tosca*, one of my favorites."

D'Agosta saw Pendergast's lips tighten a little. "Shout, braggart," he translated. "What a rush you're in to show me the last dregs of your vile soul!"

The group became still at what appeared to be an insult directed at the count. But the count only broke into a smile himself. "Bravo. You speak Italian."

"Ci provo," said Pendergast.

"My dear fellow, if you can translate Puccini that well, I should say you do much better than merely trying. So you dislike opera. I can only hope you are less of a philistine when it comes to art. Have you had a chance to admire that Ghirlandaio over there? Sublime."

"Getting to the case," said Pendergast, "I wonder, Count, if you could answer a few questions?"

The count nodded.

"What was Grove's mood on the night of his death? Was he upset? Frightened?"

"Yes, he was. But come, shall we take a closer look?" The count moved toward the painting. The others followed.

"Count Fosco, you were one of the last people to see Jeremy Grove alive. I would appreciate your help."

The count patted his hands together again. "Forgive me if I seem flippant. I want to help. As it happens, your line of work has always fascinated me. I'm an ardent reader of English mysteries; they are perhaps the only thing the English are good for. But I must confess myself unused to being the *subject* of detection. Not an altogether agreeable feeling."

"It is never agreeable. What makes you think Grove was upset that night?"

"Over the course of the evening, he couldn't sit still for more than a few minutes. He hardly drank at all, a striking departure from his usual habits. At times, he spoke loudly, almost giddily. Other times he wept."

"Do you know why he was upset?"

"Yes. He was in fear of the devil."

Lady Milbanke clapped her hands in an excess of excitement.

Pendergast peered at Fosco intently. "And what makes you think that?"

"As I was leaving, he asked me a most peculiar question. Knowing I was Catholic, he begged to borrow my cross."

"And?"

"I loaned it to him. And I must admit to being a trifle alarmed about its safety since reading the morning papers. How may I retrieve it?"

"You can't."

"And why not?"

"It's been entered into evidence."

"Ah!" the count said, relieved. "But in time I may retrieve it, yes?"

"I don't see why you'd want to, save perhaps the jewels it held."

"And why is that?"

"It's been burned and melted beyond all recognition."

"No!" the count cried. "A priceless family relic, passed down for a dozen generations. And it was a present to me from my nonno, on my confirmation!" He mastered himself quickly. "Fate is a capricious thing, Mr. Pendergast. Not only did Grove die a day too soon to do me an important service, but he took my prized heirloom as partner to his destruction. So goes life." He dusted his hands. "And now an exchange of information, perhaps? I have satisfied your curiosity, you satisfy mine."

"I regret I can't talk about the case."

"My dear sir, I don't speak of the case. I speak of this painting! I would value your opinion."

Pendergast turned to the painting and said, in an offhand way, "I detect the influence of the Portinari Triptych in those peasants' faces."

Count Fosco smiled. "What genius! What foresight!"

Pendergast inclined his head slightly.

"I speak not of you, my friend, but of the artist. You see, that must have been quite a feat, since Ghirlandaio painted this little panel *three years before* the Portinari Triptych arrived in Florence from Flanders." He beamed, looking around at his audience.

Pendergast coolly returned the gaze. "Ghirlandaio

saw the studies for the painting which were sent to the Portinari family five years before the altarpiece arrived. I'm surprised, Count, to find you not in possession of that fact."

The count lost his smile for only a moment. Then he clapped with genuine admiration. "Well done, well done! It seems you have bested me on my home turf. I really must get to know you better, Mr. Pendergast: for a member of the carabinieri, you are exceptionally cultivated."

{ 9 }

D'Agosta listened to the distant ringing from the earpiece, so faint the other phone could have been ringing on the moon. If only his son, Vincent, would answer. He really didn't want to talk to his wife.

There was a click and that familiar voice came on. "Yes?" She never said *hello*, she always said *yes*, as if his call was already an imposition.

"It's me."

"Yes?" she repeated.

Jesus Christ. "Me, Vinnie."

"I know who it is."

"I'd like to talk to my son, please."

There was a pause. "You can't."

D'Agosta felt a flare of anger. "Why not?"

"Here in Canada we have something called *school.*"

D'Agosta felt stupefied. Of course. It was Friday, close to noon. "I forgot."

"I know you forgot. Just like you forgot to call on his birthday."

"You left the phone off the hook."

"The dog must've knocked it off the hook. But you could have sent a card, a present."

"I *did* send a card and a present."

"It arrived the day after."

"I sent it ten days before his birthday, for chrissakes. You can't blame me for slow mail." This was insane. Once again he was letting himself get dragged into a senseless argument. Why did they feel this desperate need to fight? The best thing to do was just not respond.

"Look, Lydia, I'll call later tonight, okay?"

"Vincent's going out with friends."

"I'll call tomorrow morning."

"You'll probably miss him. He's got baseball practice all day—"

"Have him call *me*, then."

"You think we can afford to make long-distance calls on what you're paying?"

"You know I'm doing the best I can. No one's stopping you from moving back here, you know."

"Vinnie, you dragged us kicking and screaming up here. We didn't want to go. It was tough at first. But then something amazing happened. I made a life here. I *like* it here. And so does Vincent. We have *friends*, Vinnie. We've got a *life*. And now, just when we're on our feet again, you want us to go back to Queens. Let me tell you, I'm *never* going back to Queens."

D'Agosta said nothing. It was just the kind of declaration he hadn't wanted to provoke. Jesus, he had really blown it with this phone call. And all he wanted to do was talk to his son.

"Lydia, nothing's engraved in stone. We can work something out."

"Work something *out*? It's time we faced—"

"Don't say it, Lydia."

"I *am* going to say it. It's time we faced the facts. It's time—"

"Don't."

"—time we got divorced."

D'Agosta slowly hung up the phone. Twenty-five years, just like that. He felt short of breath; almost sick. He wouldn't think about it. He had work to do.

The Southampton police headquarters was located in a charming, if dilapidated, old wooden building that had once been the clubhouse of the Slate Rock Country Club. The police force must have labored hard, D'Agosta reflected bleakly, to turn its insides into a typical charmless linoleum, cinder-block, and puke-colored police station. It even had that universal headquarters smell: that combination of sweat, overheated photocopy machines, dirty metal, and chlorine cleaning agents.

D'Agosta felt a knot in his gut. He'd been out of the place for three days now, running around with Pendergast, reporting to the lieutenant by phone. Now he had to face the lieutenant in person. The phone call to his wife had left him a wreck. He really should have waited and called her later.

He walked through the outer offices, nodding this way and that. Nobody looked particularly glad to see him; he wasn't popular with the regular guys. He hadn't joined the bowling club or hung out with them at Tiny's, tossing darts. He'd always figured he was just passing through on his way back to NYC, hadn't thought it worth the time to make friends. Perhaps that had been a mistake.

Shaking such thoughts away, he rapped on the frosted-glass door that led to the lieutenant's small office. Faded gold letters, edged in black, spelled out *BRASKIE.*

"Yeah?" came the voice.

Inside, Braskie sat behind an old metal desk. To one side was a stack of newspapers, from the *Post* and the *Times* to the *East Hampton Record*, all with front-page stories about the case. The lieutenant looked terrible: dark circles under the eyes, face lined. D'Agosta almost felt sorry for him.

Braskie nodded him into a seat. "News?"

D'Agosta ran through everything while Braskie listened. When he was done, Braskie wiped his hand over his prematurely thinning scalp and sighed. "The chief gets back tomorrow, and basically all we've got so far is jack. No entry or egress, no latents, no hair or fiber, no eyewitnesses, no nothing. When's Pendergast coming?"

He sounded almost hopeful, he was that desperate.

"Half an hour. He wanted me to make sure it was all ready."

"It's ready." The lieutenant rose with a sigh. "Follow me."

The evidence room was housed in a series of portable, container-type structures, fitted end-to-end behind the police station, at the edge of one of Southampton's last remaining potato fields. The lieutenant swiped his card through the door scanner and entered. Within, D'Agosta saw that Joe Lillian, a fellow sergeant, was laying out the last of the evidence on a table in the middle of the long, narrow space. On both sides, shelves and lockers stretched back into the gloom, crammed with evidence going back God knew how many years.

D'Agosta eyed the table. Sergeant Lillian had done a nice job. Papers, glassine envelopes, sample tubes—everything was tagged and laid out neat as a pin.

"Think this'll meet with your special agent's approval?" Braskie asked.

D'Agosta wasn't sure if it was sarcasm or desperation he detected in Braskie's voice. But before he could contemplate a reply, he heard a familiar honeyed voice behind them.

"Indeed it does, Lieutenant Braskie; indeed it does."

Braskie fairly jumped. Pendergast stood inside the doorway, hands behind his back; he must've somehow slipped in behind them.

Pendergast strolled up to the table, hands still clasped behind his back, lips pursed, examining the evidence as keenly as a connoisseur admiring a table laden with precious art.

"Help yourself to anything," said Braskie. "I've no doubt your forensics lab is better than ours."

"And I doubt the killer left any forensic evidence beyond that which he *wanted* to leave. No, for the moment I'm merely browsing. But what's this? The melted cross. May I?"

Sergeant Lillian picked up the envelope holding the cross and handed it to Pendergast. The agent held it gingerly, turning it slowly this way and that. "I'd like to send this to a lab in New York."

"No problem." Lillian took it back and laid it in a plastic evidence container.

"And this charred material." Pendergast next picked up a test tube with some burned chunks of sulfur. He unstoppered it, waved it under his nose, restoppered it.

"Done."

Pendergast glanced at D'Agosta. "Anything that interests you, Sergeant?"

D'Agosta stepped forward. "Maybe." He swept an eye over the table, nodded toward a packet of letters.

"Everything's been gone over by forensics," said Lillian. "Go ahead and handle it."

D'Agosta picked up the letters and slipped one out. It was from the boy, Jason Prince, to Grove. Out of the corner of his eye, he saw a smirk growing on Lillian's face. What the hell did he think was so funny? D'Agosta began to read.

Jesus. Oh, Jesus. Reddening, D'Agosta put the letters down.

"Learn something new every day, huh, D'Agosta?" Lillian asked, grinning.

D'Agosta turned back to the table. There was a small stack of books: *Dr. Faustus* by Christopher Marlowe; *The New Book of Christian Prayers*; *Malleus Maleficarum.*

"The Witches Hammer," Pendergast said, nodding at the last title. "The professional witch-hunting manual of the Inquisition. A font of information on the black arts."

Beside the books was a stack of Web printouts.

D'Agosta picked up the top sheet. The site was called Maledicat Dominus; this particular page appeared to be devoted to charms or prayers for warding off the devil.

"He visited a bunch of sites like that in the last twenty-four hours of his life," said Braskie. "Those were the pages he printed out."

Pendergast was now examining a wine cork with a magnifying glass. "What was the menu?" he asked.

Braskie turned to a notebook, flipped open some pages, and passed it to Pendergast.

Pendergast read aloud. "Dover sole, grilled medallions of beef in a burgundy and mushroom reduction, julienned carrots, salad, lemon sherbet. Served with a '90 Petrus. Excellent taste in wine."

Handing back the notebook, Pendergast continued his prowl. He bent forward, picked up a wrinkled piece of paper.

"We found that balled up in the wastebasket. Appears to be a proof sheet of some kind."

"It's an advance print of an article for the next issue of *Art Review*. Due on the newsstands tomorrow, if I'm not mistaken." Pendergast smoothed the paper, once again began to read out loud. " 'Art history, like any other great discipline, has its own sacred temples: places and moments any self-respecting critic would give his eyeteeth to have attended. The first impressionist exhibition on the Boulevard des Capucines in 1874 was one; the day Braque first saw Picasso's *Les Demoiselles d'Avignon* is another. I am here now to tell you that the Golgotha series of Maurice Vilnius—now on display in his East Village studio—will be another such watershed moment in the history of art.' "

"At the memorial service yesterday, I thought you said Grove hated Vilnius's stuff," D'Agosta said.

"And so he did—in years past. But he seems to have suffered a change of heart." Pendergast replaced the paper on the desk with a thoughtful expression. "It certainly explains why Vilnius was in such a good mood last night."

"We found another, similar article sitting beside his computer," Braskie said, pointing to another sheet on the table. "Printed out but not signed. Appears to be by Grove, however."

Pendergast picked up the indicated sheet. "It's an article to *Burlington Magazine*, titled 'A Reappraisal of Georges de la Tour's *The Education of the Virgin.*'" He glanced over it quickly. "It's a short article by Grove retracting his own earlier review, where he labeled the de la Tour painting a forgery." He replaced the sheet. "He appears to have changed his mind about a lot of things in his final hours."

Pendergast glided along the table, then stopped once again, this time before a sheaf of telephone records. "Now, these will be helpful, don't you think, Vincent?" he said, handing them to D'Agosta.

"Just got the warrant for their release this morning," said Braskie. "Clipped to the back are names and addresses and a short identification of each person he called."

"Looks like he made a lot of calls on his last day," said D'Agosta, flipping through.

"He did," said Braskie. "To a lot of strange people."

D'Agosta turned over the records and looked at the list. It *was* strange: An international call to Professor

Iain Montcalm, New College, Oxford, Medieval Studies Department. Other, local calls to Evelyn Milbanke; Jonathan Frederick. A variety of calls to directory information. After midnight, calls to Locke Bullard, the industrialist; one Nigel Cutforth; and then—even later—the call to Father Cappi.

"We plan to interview them all. Montcalm, by the way, is one of the world's experts on medieval satanic practices."

Pendergast nodded.

"Milbanke and Frederick were at the last dinner party, and the calls were probably about organizing it. We have no idea why he called Bullard. We don't have any evidence that he ever met the guy. Cutforth is also a cipher. He's some kind of record producer, again no indication that he and Grove ever crossed paths. Yet in both cases, Grove had their private numbers."

"What about all these calls to directory information?" D'Agosta asked. "He must have called at least a dozen different cities."

"As far as we can tell, he was trying to track down somebody by the name of Beckmann. Ranier Beckmann. His Internet search activity bears this out, too."

Pendergast laid down a dirty napkin he had been examining. "Excellent work, Lieutenant. Do you mind if we interview some of these people as well?"

"Be my guest."

D'Agosta and Pendergast climbed into the agent's Rolls, idling ostentatiously in front of the police station, the driver in full livery. As the powerful vehicle accelerated away from the station, Pendergast slipped a leather notebook from his pocket, opened it to a fresh page, and began making notations with a gold pen. "We seem to have an embarrassment of suspects."

"Yeah. Like about everyone Grove ever knew."

"With the possible exception of Maurice Vilnius. Even so, I suspect the list will shorten itself rather quickly. Meanwhile, we have our work cut out for us tomorrow." He handed the list to D'Agosta. "You speak with Milbanke, Bullard, and Cutforth. I'll take Vilnius, Fosco, and Montcalm. And here are some identification cards from the FBI Southern District of Manhattan Field Office. If anybody objects to the questions, give them one of these."

"Anything in particular I should be looking for?"

"Strictly routine police work. We've reached the point in the case where we must regrettably put on those old-fashioned gumshoes. Isn't that how they say it in those detective novels you used to write?"

D'Agosta managed a wry smile. "Not exactly."

{ 10 }

Nigel Cutforth, sitting in his Bauhaus-style breakfast nook 1,052 feet above Fifth Avenue, lowered the latest issue of *Billboard* and sniffed the air. What was it with the ventilation in his apartment these past few days? This was the third time that sulfurous stink had come up into his apartment. Twice those yahoos from building maintenance had come up, and twice they'd found nothing.

Cutforth slapped down the paper. "Eliza!"

Eliza was Cutforth's second wife—he'd finally dumped the old bag who had worn herself out bearing him children and found something fresher—and there she stood in the doorway, in her exercise tights, brushing her long blonde hair with her head tilted to one side. Cutforth could hear the crackle of static.

"There's that smell again," he said.

"I've got a nose, too," she said, swinging one mass of hair back and pulling another forward.

There was a time not so long before when Cutforth liked watching her mess with her hair. Now it was beginning to get on his nerves. She wasted half an hour a day on it, at least.

As she continued brushing, Cutforth felt his irritation rise. "I paid five and a half mil for this apartment, and it smells like a goddamn science experiment. Why don't you call maintenance?"

"The phone's right there, next to your elbow."

Cutforth didn't care for the tone she was taking with him.

She swung the last part of her hair back, shook it out, straightened. "I've got my spin workout in fifteen minutes. I'm already late."

With that, she vanished from the doorway. Cutforth could hear her banging the hall closet, getting on her tennis shoes. A moment later there was the hum of the elevator in the hall beyond, and she was gone.

He stared at the closed door, trying to remind himself that he'd wanted something fresher; that he'd gotten something fresher. Too fucking fresh, in fact.

He sniffed again. If anything, the smell was worse. It would be a bitch getting maintenance up here a third time. Building management was useless; they did something only if you yelled loud enough. But there were only two apartments on this floor—the other had been purchased but not yet occupied—and nobody on the other floors had seemed to smell anything. So Cutforth was the only one yelling.

He stood up, feeling a prickle of disquiet. Grove had complained of a bad smell in that bizarre call of his—that, and about a hundred other strange things. He shook his head, trying to clear the clouds of apprehension that were slowly gathering. He was letting that old pillow-biter and his crazy worries get to him.

Was it coming from the vents? He moved around,

testing the air. It was stronger in the living room, even stronger in the library. He followed it to the door of the control room, sniffing like a dog. Stronger, ever stronger. He unlocked the door, entered the room, flicked on the light, and looked around. There was his beautiful 64-channel Studer, his RAID-striped hard disk recording system, and his racks of audio processing gear. On the far wall were several glass cases containing his treasured collections. The guitar Mick Jagger had smashed at Altamont: Keith Richards's prized 1950 Telecaster, dating from the first year of mass production, still sporting its original pickups. The scribbled music sheets to "Imagine," with the coffee stains and obscene doodles in the margins. His wife said the control room looked like Planet Hollywood. That really pissed him off. This space was one of the greatest collections of rock memorabilia anywhere. The place where he'd discovered the Suburban Lawnmowers from an over-the-transom four-track demo mailed from Cincinnati. This is where he'd first heard the sounds of Rappah Jowly and felt that special creeping sensation go up his spine. Cutforth had an ear. He had a knack of recognizing a big-money sound. He didn't know where the ear came from, and he didn't care. It worked, and that's all that mattered.

Planet Hollywood, my ass. Where the hell is that smell coming from?

Cutforth followed his nose toward the plate-glass window looking into the studio. It was definitely in there. Some piece of equipment frying, perhaps.

He opened the heavy soundproofed door. As he did so, the smell washed over him like an oily fog.

He hadn't noticed through the glass, but there was a light haze in the air here. And it wasn't just that sulfurous smell; there was something a lot worse now. It reminded him of a pig wallow on a hot summer day.

He glanced around the studio quickly, at the Bösendorfer piano and his beloved Neumann microphones, at the isolation chambers, the acoustically tiled walls.

Had some motherfucker been messing with his studio?

Cutforth searched the room with his eyes, anger vying with fear. It was impossible anyone had gotten into his apartment. It had state-of-the-art security. When you dealt with gangstas and others who settled business differences with lead instead of lawyers, you had to have good security.

He glanced around. Everything seemed to be in its place. The recording equipment was off. He laid his hand on the row of mic preamps: cool, the rows of LEDs all dark. But what was this? Over in the far corner there was something lying on the floor.

He stepped over, bent close to the blond wood, picked it up. It was a tooth. Or more like a tusk. Like a boar's tusk. With blood on it, still wet. And a knot of bloody gristle at one end.

He dropped it in violent disgust.

Some fucker has been in here.

Cutforth swallowed, backed away. It was impossible. No one could get in. Hadn't he just unlocked the door himself? Maybe it had happened yesterday, when he'd shown that promoter around, a guy he really didn't know. You dealt with a lot of weird people in this business. He quickly got a cloth, picked up the tooth with it, practically ran to the kitchen, dropped it down the garbage disposal, and turned it on, listening to the raw grinding noise. The thing exhaled a bad smell and he averted his face.

A shrill buzzer sounded, and he just about jumped through the wall. Taking deep breaths, he went to the intercom, pressed the buzzer.

"Mr. Cutforth? There's a police officer to see you."

Cutforth peered into the tiny video screen beside the intercom and saw a forty-something cop standing in the lobby, shifting from foot to foot.

"On a Saturday? What does he want?"

"He won't say, sir."

Cutforth finally got his breathing under control. The thought of a cop in his apartment right now was almost inviting. "Send him up."

On closer inspection, the officer looked just like any Italian-American cop, with the working-class Queens accent to boot. Cutforth settled the cop on the living room sofa and took a chair opposite. The guy had Southampton on his patch, which confirmed what Cutforth already suspected. This was about Grove. He had caller ID; he should never have answered that crazy son of a bitch's phone call.

The cop took out a notebook and pen, displayed a microcassette recorder.

"No taping," said Cutforth.

The cop shrugged, returned it to his pocket. "Funny smell in here."

"Ventilation problems."

The cop turned the pages of his notebook, got himself all positioned and ready to go. Cutforth settled back in the chair, crossing his arms. "Okay, Officer Dee-Agusta, what can I do for you?"

"Did you know Jeremy Grove?"

"No."

"He called you very early on the morning of October 16."

"Did he?"

"That's what I'm asking you."

Cutforth uncrossed his arms, crossed and recrossed his legs, already regretting having let the cop up. The only redeeming thing was, the cop didn't look too bright.

"The answer's yes, he did call me."

"What did you talk about?"

"Do I have to answer these questions?"

"No—at least not at this moment. If you wish, we could arrange something more formal."

Cutforth didn't like the sound of that. He thought quickly. "There's nothing to hide. I have a collection of musical instruments, rock memorabilia, that sort of thing. He was interested in buying something."

"What?"

"Just a letter."

"Show it to me."

Cutforth managed to suppress any look of surprise. He stood up. "Follow me."

They went back into the control room. Cutforth cast his eyes around. "That."

The cop went over, looked, frowning.

"A letter Janis Joplin wrote to Jim Morrison, but

never mailed. Just two lines. Called him the worst lay of her life." Cutforth mustered a chuckle.

The cop took out his notebook and began copying the letter. Cutforth rolled his eyes.

"And the price?"

"I told him it wasn't for sale."

"Did he give a reason why he was interested?"

"He just said he collected Doors paraphernalia. That's all."

"And you didn't mind getting a call in the wee hours of the morning?"

"In the music business, we keep late hours." Cutforth walked toward the control room door, held it open, giving the cop a big hint about leaving. But the man didn't budge. Instead, he seemed to be sniffing the air again.

"That smell, it's really peculiar."

"I'm about to call maintenance."

"There was exactly this smell at the site of Jeremy Grove's homicide."

Cutforth swallowed. What was it Grove had said? *The smell is the worst part of it. I can hardly think straight.* In his call, Grove said he'd found something—a lump of fur-covered meat the size of a golf ball. It had seemed to be alive...at least until Grove stomped on it and flushed it down the toilet. Cutforth felt his heart pounding in his rib cage, and he took a couple of breaths, let them out slowly, the way he'd been taught in those anxiety management classes. This was ridiculous. This was the twenty-first fucking century. *Cool it, Nigel.*

"Do you know a Locke Bullard, Mr. Cutforth? Or one Ranier Beckmann?"

These questions, coming on the heels of each other, almost physically staggered Cutforth. He shook his head, hoping his expression wasn't betraying him.

"You been in touch with Beckmann?" he pressed.

"No." Hell, he never should have let the cop in here.

"What about Bullard? You been in touch with him? You know, just a friendly chat about old times?"

"No. I don't know the man. I don't know either one of them."

The cop made a long notation in his notebook. Cutforth wondered what it was that took so long to write down. He felt the sweat trickling down his sides. He swallowed, but there was nothing to swallow. His mouth was dry.

"Sure you don't want to tell me more about that telephone call? Because everybody else who spoke to him that night said Grove was upset. Terribly upset. Not exactly in the mood to buy rock memorabilia."

"I already told you everything."

Now at last they returned to the living room. Cutforth didn't sit down or offer a seat to the cop. He just wanted him out.

"Do you always keep the apartment this hot, Mr. Cutforth?"

It *was* hot, Cutforth noticed; hot even for him. He didn't answer.

"It was also excessively warm at the site of the Grove homicide, despite the fact that the heat was off in the house." The cop looked at him inquiringly, but still Cutforth said nothing.

The cop grunted, slapped shut his notebook, returned the pen to its leather loop. "If I were you, Mr.

Cutforth, next time I'd decline to answer a police officer's questions without a lawyer present."

"Why?"

"Because a lawyer would advise you that keeping your mouth shut is better than lying."

Cutforth stared at the cop. "What makes you think I'm lying?"

"Grove hated rock music."

Cutforth stifled his response. This cop wasn't as dumb as he looked. In fact, he was about as dumb as a fox.

"I'll be back, Mr. Cutforth. And next time it will be on tape and under oath. Keep in mind that perjury is a serious crime. One way or the other, we *will* find out what you discussed with Grove. Thank you for your time."

As soon as the elevator had hummed its way down, Cutforth picked up the phone with a shaking hand and dialed. What he needed was a humping vacation on the beach. A beach on the other side of the earth. He knew a girl in Phuket who did amazing things. He couldn't leave tomorrow—Jowly, his biggest client, was coming in for an overdub session—but after that he'd be clean gone, fuck the rest of the clients. He was going to get the hell out of town. Away from his wife. Away from this cop and his questions. And, most especially, away from this apartment and its stench...

"Doris? Nigel here. I want to book a flight to Bangkok. Tomorrow night if possible, otherwise first thing Monday. No, just me. With a limo and driver for Phuket. And find me a nice big house on the beach, something really secure, with a cook, maid, personal trainer, bodyguard, the works. Don't tell anyone where I've gone, okay, Doris darling? Yeah, *Thai*land...I know it's hot this time of year, you let me worry about the heat."

Do you always keep the apartment this hot, Mr. Cutforth?

He slammed the phone down and went into the bedroom, threw a suitcase on the bed, and began hauling things out of his closet: bathing suits, sharkskin jacket and slacks, shades, sandals, money, watch, passport, satellite phone.

They couldn't nail him for perjury if they couldn't frigging *find* him.

{ 11 }

By the time Sergeant Vincent D'Agosta entered the back door of the New York Athletic Club, he was a very pissed-off cop. The doorman had stopped him at the Central Park South entrance—even though he was wearing a tie as part of his full dress uniform—and upon hearing his inquiry sent him around to the back door because he wasn't a member. That meant walking all the way to Sixth Avenue, down the block, and coming back around on 58th Street—almost a quarter of a mile.

D'Agosta cursed under his breath as he walked. Cutforth was lying, that much he was sure of. He'd taken a gamble, with that wild guess about Grove hating rock music, and Cutforth's eyes had given him away. Still, for all his tough talk, D'Agosta knew there was an entire legal system between him and a rich bastard like Cutforth. Milbanke had been a total wash: all she'd wanted to do was babble about her new emerald necklace. The nutcase hadn't given him a single decent lead, not one. And now here he was, taking an unexpected constitutional around one of Manhattan's long crosstown blocks. *Shit.*

Finally arriving at the back door of the Athletic Club, D'Agosta punched the button for the service elevator—the only elevator there—and when it opened at last, creaking and groaning after a good three-minute wait, he punched 9. The elevator ascended slowly, pissing and moaning the whole way, at long last opening its doors again with a wheeze. D'Agosta stepped out into a dim corridor—for a fancy club, this one was pretty dark—and followed a little wooden sign with a gold hand pointing a finger toward *Billiards.* There was a faint smell of cigar smoke in the air that made him crave a good Cuban. His wife had nagged him into giving up the habit before they moved to Canada. But maybe he'd take it up again. Hell, no reason not to anymore.

As he walked down the corridor, the smell grew stronger.

He came through a door into a spacious room, its far wall studded with grand windows. As he entered, another guardian of the order sprang up from a little desk with a "Sir!" Ignoring the man, D'Agosta peered around the room. His eye finally discerned a lone, dark figure, wreathed in smoke, hunched over the farthest billiard table.

"If I may inquire your business, sir—?"

"You may not." D'Agosta brushed by the attendant and strode past the billiard tables, low-hanging lamps casting pools of light over their emerald surfaces. It was six o'clock in the evening, and through the windows, the rectangle of Central Park was a graveyard of darkness. New York was at that magical twilight moment, neither light nor dark, where the glow of the city matched the glow of the sky behind it.

D'Agosta paused about ten feet from the man and pulled out his notebook. He flipped it open and wrote, *Bullard. October 20.* Then he waited.

He expected Bullard to look up and acknowledge him, but he didn't. Instead, the man leaned farther over the green baize, his face in shadow, and tapped another ball. He chalked his cue with a swift twist of the wrist, came around the table, hit again. The table was like no pool table D'Agosta had ever seen: much larger, with smaller pockets and smaller balls in just two colors, red and white.

"Mr. Bullard?"

The man ignored him, moving to make yet another shot. His back was huge, his shoulders broad, and the silk fabric of his suit strained taut across them. All D'Agosta could clearly discern was the glowing stump of a huge cigar and two great knotted hands that were thrust into the circle of light, the veins on their backs as thick and rolled as blue earthworms. One of the hands sported two immense gold rings. The man tapped, moved around, tapped again.

Just as D'Agosta was about to say something, the man abruptly straightened, turned, pulled the cigar from his mouth, and said:

"What do you want?"

D'Agosta didn't answer right away. Instead, he took a minute to observe the man's face. Quite possibly there wasn't an uglier man on God's earth. His head was huge and swarthy, and though the body it was perched on seemed as massive and thick as a grizzly's, the head still appeared oversize. A lantern jaw, anchored by popping muscles, rose toward a pair of undulant earlobes.

Centered between them were dry fleshy lips white against the dark skin: a particularly unpleasant combination. Above stuck out a thick, pitted nose. Massive, beetling brows jutted far over a pair of sunken eyes. From the bushy eyebrows above, a squat forehead led upward to a bald dome, its skin covered with freckles and liver spots. The impression the man gave was of enormous brute strength and self-assurance in both mind and body. When he moved, the blue silk that clad his frame rustled, and his movements were as heavy and deliberate as those of a well-muscled draft horse.

D'Agosta licked his lips. "I have a few questions for you."

Bullard looked at him for a moment, then shifted the cigar back into his mouth, leaned over the table, and gave one of the balls a little tap.

"If it's too distracting in here, we can always do this downtown."

"Just a minute."

D'Agosta checked his watch. He glanced back, saw the mincing attendant watching them from the far side of the room, his hands clasped in front of him as if he was an usher in church, smirking faintly.

Bullard now put his back to D'Agosta, leaning far over the table, the silk stretching and hiking up, exposing a crisp expanse of white cotton shirt and a pair of red suspenders. Another faint tap, more rustling silk.

"Bullard, your minute's up."

Bullard jerked his cue up, whisked some chalk on the tip, bent back down. The motherfucker was actually going to take a few more shots.

"You're pissing me off, you know that?"

Bullard took the shot, rounded the table for another. "Then maybe what you need is a course in anger management." He eased the cue back and forth and then, with the softest little push, sent the ball all of three inches so that it kissed another.

That did it. "Bullard, one more shot and I'm cuffing you and leading you out the front door, past the porter and anyone else who happens to come by. I'm going to march you down along Central Park South to Columbus Circle where I parked my squad car. And then I'm going to radio for backup and keep you standing at the curb at Columbus Circle, hands cuffed behind your back, through the ass end of a Saturday afternoon, until that backup arrives."

Bullard's hand paused on the cue stick. Then he straightened up, jaw muscles tight. He slipped his hand into his suit coat and began punching a call on his cell. "I think I'll just tell the mayor how one of his finest has just threatened me with four-letter expletives."

"You do that. In case you hadn't noticed, I'm Southampton P.D. and could give a flying fuck about your mayor."

Bullard raised the phone to his ear and inserted the cigar in his mouth. "Then you're out of your jurisdiction, and threatening me with arrest is misrepresentation."

"I'm an assigned liaison with the Federal Bureau of Investigation, Southern District of Manhattan Field Office." D'Agosta opened his wallet, pulled out one of the cards Pendergast had given him, tossed it onto the pool table. "If you want to complain to the supervisor, he's Special Agent Carlton and his number's right there."

That finally penetrated. Bullard slowly and deliberately snapped the phone shut. Then he dropped the cigar into a sand-filled spittoon in the corner, where it continued to smoke. "All right. You've managed to attract my attention."

D'Agosta flipped out his notebook. He wasn't going to waste any more time.

"On October 16, at 2:02 A.M., Jeremy Grove placed a call to your unlisted private number. On your yacht, I believe. The call lasted forty-two minutes. Is this correct?"

"I have no recollection of such a call."

"Yeah?" D'Agosta slipped a photocopy of the phone record out of his notebook and held it out. "Telephone company records say different."

"I don't need to see that."

"Who else was there at that time who might have taken the call? I'd like the names. Girlfriend, cook, babysitter, whatever." He poised his pen.

A long silence. "I was alone on my yacht at the time."

"So who picked up the phone? The cat?"

"I won't answer any more questions without my lawyer present."

The guy had a voice to match the face, deep and scarred, and when he spoke it was as if he was scratching a match along D'Agosta's spinal cord. "Let me tell you something, Mr. Bullard: you just lied to me. You lied to a police officer. That's obstruction of justice. You can call your lawyer if you like, but it'll be from downtown and I'll be escorting you out of here now. Is that how you want it? Or should we try it again?"

"This is a gentlemen's club, and I'll thank you not to raise your voice."

"I'm a little hard of hearing, see, and anyway, I'm not a gentleman."

He waited.

Bullard's white lips curled in what might have been a smile. "Now that you mention it, I do remember that call from Grove. We hadn't talked in a long time."

"What did you talk about?"

"This and that."

"This and that." D'Agosta wrote it down. *This and that.* "For forty-two minutes?"

"Catching up, that sort of thing."

"How well did you know Grove?"

"We'd run into each other a few times. We weren't friends."

"When did you first meet him?"

"Years ago. I don't remember."

"I ask again, what did you talk about?"

"He told me what he'd been up to lately—"

"Which was?"

"I can't remember specifically. Writing articles, dinner parties, that sort of thing."

It was just like Cutforth: the motherfucker was lying, lying, lying. "And you? What did you talk about with him?"

"Much of the same. My work, my company."

"What was the reason for the phone call?"

"You'll have to ask him. We were just catching up."

"He called you after midnight just to catch up?"

"That's right."

"How did he happen to know your number? It's unlisted."

"I suppose I must've given it to him once."

"I thought he wasn't your friend."

Bullard shrugged. "Maybe he got it from someone else."

D'Agosta paused to look at Bullard. He was standing off to one side, half in shadow, half in light. He still couldn't see the man's eyes.

"Did Grove seem frightened or apprehensive to you?"

"Not that I could tell. I really can't remember."

"Do you know a Nigel Cutforth?"

There was a slight beat before Bullard's response. "No."

"What about a Ranier Beckmann?"

"No." No pause this time.

"A Count Isidor Fosco?"

"The name's familiar. I think I've seen it in the society pages once or twice."

"Lady Milbanke? Jonathan Frederick?"

"No and no."

This was hopeless. D'Agosta knew when he was beaten. He slapped the notebook shut. "We're not done with you, Mr. Bullard."

Bullard had already turned back to his pool table. "But I am most certainly done with you, Sergeant."

D'Agosta turned on his heel, and then paused. He turned back. "I hope you're not planning any trips out of the country, Mr. Bullard."

Silence. Encouraged, D'Agosta pursued the line. "I could get you declared a material witness, restrict your movements." D'Agosta knew he could do no such thing, but his sixth sense told him he had finally struck a vein. "How'd you like that?"

It seemed as if Bullard hadn't heard, but D'Agosta

knew he had. He turned and walked toward the exit, past the huge green tables with their tiny little pockets. At the door he paused, glaring at the attendant. The smirk vanished, and his face became suddenly and completely neutral.

"What's this game here? Billiards?"

"Snooker, sir."

"Snooker?" D'Agosta stared at the man. Was he making fun of him? It sounded like something a prostitute might charge extra for. But the man's face betrayed nothing.

D'Agosta left the room, located the front elevator, and took it down. To hell with the porter and his rules.

The last of the evening light was slowly dying in the great billiard room of the New York Athletic Club. Locke Bullard stood over the table, cue in hand, no longer seeing the table or the balls. Sixty seconds passed. And then he placed the cue on the table, walked toward the bar, and picked up the phone. Something had to be done, and right now. He had important business to attend to in Italy, and nobody—especially this upstart sergeant—was going to cause him to miss it.

{ 12 }

D'Agosta paused on the steps of the New York Athletic Club and checked his watch. Only 6:30. Pendergast had asked him to come to what he called his "uptown residence" at nine so they could compare notes on the day's interviews. He checked his pocket, found the key Pendergast had given him. Nine. He had time to kill. If memory served, there was a dim little Irish pub called Mullin's on Broadway and 61st that served a decent burger. He could catch dinner and a cold one.

He glanced back into the lobby, caught the eye of the snooty doorman who'd made him walk around back earlier, and made a point of lingering a little longer on the steps. The man was at his kiosk, hanging up the house phone and looking back at him, a pinched expression on his mummified face. Damn, sometimes it seemed that being a fossilized old turd was the main job qualification of a Manhattan doorman.

Now, as he sauntered down the steps and turned left on Central Park South, his thoughts returned to Pendergast. Why the hell did he need a house uptown? From what he'd heard, Pendergast's apartment in the Dakota was bigger than most houses, anyway. He pulled the card from his pocket: 891 Riverside Drive. What cross street was that? Probably one of those elegant old buildings along Riverside Park up around 96th. He'd been out of New York too long. In years past, he could take any avenue address and calculate the cross street in his head.

Mullin's Pub was still where he remembered it, little more than a dim storefront with a long bar and old wooden tables along the opposite wall. D'Agosta entered, his heart warmed by the thought of a real New York cheeseburger, cooked rare, not one of those fussy avocado-arugula-Camembert-and-pancetta things they sold in Southampton for fifteen dollars.

An hour later, well fed, D'Agosta emerged, then headed north to the subway station at 66th. Even at 7:30, there were a million cars rushing, vying, and honking, a fuming chaos of steel and chrome, including one shitbox eighties-era gold Impala with smoked windows that nearly clipped off his toes. Laying a suitable string of curses in the car's wake, D'Agosta ducked down into the subway. He fumbled with the magnetic card, swiped it through the machine, then headed down the stairs for the platform of the uptown IRT local. Even having killed an hour, he was going to be early. Maybe he should have stayed in Mullin's for another brew.

In less than a minute a growing roar, along with a balloon of stale air that forced its way out of the dark tunnel, signaled the arrival of a train. He boarded, managed to find a seat, settled onto the hard plastic, and closed his eyes. Almost instinctually he counted the stops: 72nd, 79th, 86th. When the train slowed for 96th, he opened his eyes again, rose, and exited at the southern end of the station.

He crossed Broadway and walked west down 94th Street, past West End Avenue to Riverside Drive. On the far side of the leafy drive, past the thin green sliver of Riverside Park, he could make out the West Side Highway and the river beyond. It was a pleasant enough evening, but the sky was darkening and there was a smell of moisture in the air. The sluggish waters of the Hudson roiled along like black ink, and the lights of New Jersey speckled the far shore. There was a faint flicker of lightning.

He turned and scanned the address of the building on the nearest corner. Number 214.

Two fourteen? D'Agosta swore. He really had lost it in those few years in Canada. Eight ninety-one was a lot farther uptown than he realized, maybe close to Harlem. What the hell was Pendergast doing living up there?

He could go back to the subway, but that meant a long uphill walk back to Broadway, and perhaps a long wait in the station, then the local crawl farther uptown. He could grab a cab, but that still meant walking back to Broadway, and uptown cabs were almost impossible to find at that time of night.

Or he could hoof it.

D'Agosta turned north and began walking up the drive. It was probably only ten or fifteen short blocks. He slapped his gut. It would do him good, work off some of that greasy burger. Besides, he still had more than an hour to kill.

He set a brisk pace for himself, his cuffs and keys jangling. The wind was sighing through the trees along the edge of Riverside Park, and the facades of the elegant apartment buildings that faced the river were brightly lit, most sporting doormen or security guards. Even though it was almost eight, a lot of people were still coming home from work: men and women in suits, a musician carrying a cello, a couple of college professor types in tweedy jackets arguing loudly about somebody named Hegel. Once in a while someone glanced at him, smiled, nodded, glad that he was there. September 11 had changed a lot of things in New York City, and one of them was the way people looked at cops. Another reason to get himself rehired at the first opportunity.

D'Agosta hummed as he walked along, filling his lungs with the heady fragrance, that West Side perfume of salt air, car fumes, garbage, and asphalt. He caught a brief whiff of roasting coffee from some all-night delicatessen. New York City. Once it got into your blood, you could never get it out again. When the economy turned around and the city began hiring again, D'Agosta would be first in line. Christ, he'd start off as a tire-kicker in Far Rockaway if it meant working again for the NYPD.

He crossed 110th Street. The numbers were still only in the 400s, rising but not fast enough. What the hell was the cross-street rule for Riverside? Something divided by something minus 59...He couldn't even guess anymore—all he knew was it was going to be farther uptown than he thought.

At least he had plenty of time. Maybe Pendergast lived in one of those professorial brownstones up by

Columbia. That must be it: Pendergast, slumming with the academics. He quickened his pace. Now the buildings were less elegant, plainer, but still neat and trim. He was getting into the Columbia University neighborhood, with its students and their baggy clothes, a kid shouting down from a window to some other kid on the sidewalk, tossing down a book. D'Agosta wondered what his life would have been like if he'd come from a family that had sent him to college. He might be a big-time writer by now. Maybe the critics would have liked his books more. You made a lot of contacts in the right college, and a hell of a lot of those *New York Times* critics seemed to come from Columbia. And they all reviewed each other's books. The damn *Times Book Review* was like a private club.

He shook his head. As his old Italian grandfather used to say, it was *acqua passata*.

He paused at 122nd Street to catch his breath. He had reached the northern fringe of Columbia. Ahead was International House, standing like the last outpost on the edge of the frontier. Beyond was no-man's-land.

And the numbers were only up to 550.

Shit. He checked his watch. Ten past eight. He'd hiked a mile. He'd done his duty for the day. He still had plenty of time, but he was no longer enjoying himself. And this far uptown, there was zero chance of getting a cab. There were still one or two students in view, but there were also crowds of kids loitering on stoops, watching him pass, sometimes giving a little hiss or muttering something. He now realized that 891 Riverside would be somewhere around 135th Street, if not a little farther. He could make it in another ten minutes—and he would still be early—but it meant walking into the heart of Harlem.

Once again he pulled the card from his pocket. There was the address, in Pendergast's elegant script. It seemed impossible. But there could be no mistake.

He left the bright oasis of International House behind, neither hurrying nor loitering. There was no reason for him to be nervous: not in uniform and packing his Glock 9mm.

As he walked on, the neighborhood changed abruptly. Gone now were the students, the bustle of activity. The streetlights were broken, the apartment facades dim. It became quiet, almost deserted. At 130th Street, D'Agosta passed an empty mansion, one of the really old ones: the tin ripped off the empty window frames, the very frame of the building exhaling a smell of mold and urine into the street. A junkie palace. The next block contained a single-room-occupancy "hotel," the inhabitants sitting on the stoop and drinking beer. They fell silent and watched him go by with bleary eyes. A dog barked incessantly.

Though plenty of antiquated cars lined the curb—battered, windowless, sometimes even wheelless—there were fewer cars on the road now. An ancient, microscopic Honda Accord CVCC passed by, so rusted its original color was impossible to discern. A minute or so later it was followed by a gold Impala with smoked windows. It seemed to D'Agosta that it slowed as it went past. He watched as it took the next right.

A gold Impala. There must be a million of them in the city. Hell, he was starting to get paranoid. All that soft living in Southampton...

He continued steadily on, passing rows of abandoned buildings, old mansions broken into apartments and SROs. Dogshit littered the sidewalk now, along with garbage and broken bottles. Most of the streetlights were out—shooting at them was a favorite gang pastime—and with the city's general neglect of this area, it took forever to get them repaired.

He was now approaching the hard-core center of western Harlem. It seemed incredible that Pendergast had a place here: the guy was eccentric, but not *that* eccentric. The next block, 132nd, was completely dark, every streetlight out, the two remaining buildings on the block abandoned and boarded up. Even the lights on the park side had been blown away. It was a perfect muggers' block—except no one in his right mind would ever walk there at night.

D'Agosta reminded himself he was packing, in full uniform, with a radio. He shook his head. What a wimp he'd become. He strode resolutely forward, down the dark block.

That was when he noticed a car behind him, moving slowly. Way *too* slowly. As it passed under the last streetlight, D'Agosta saw the gleam of gold—the same Chevy Impala that had nearly taken off his toes on West 61st Street.

D'Agosta may have forgotten the street address formula, but his NYPD cop radar remained in perfect working order, and now it went off loudly. The car was moving at precisely the speed that would bring it next to D'Agosta at the middle of the dark block.

It was an ambush.

D'Agosta made an instant decision. Breaking into a

sudden run, he cut left and sprinted across the street in front of the approaching car. He heard the screeching acceleration of the tires, but he had moved too quickly and was already heading into Riverside Park by the time the car squealed to a stop along the curb.

As he sprinted into the darkness of the trees, he saw both doors open simultaneously.

{ 13 }

The door to the tenth-floor suite at the Sherry Netherland Hotel was opened by an English butler so impeccably outfitted he seemed to have stepped from the pages of a Wodehouse novel. He bowed to Pendergast, standing to one side. The man's double-breasted Prince Albert frock coat was immaculately brushed, and when he moved, his starched white shirtfront rustled faintly. One white-gloved hand took Pendergast's coat; the other held out a silver tray. Without hesitation, Pendergast reached into his pocket, removed a slim gold card case, and placed his card on the tray.

"If the gentleman would kindly wait." The butler gave another slight bow and disappeared into a long hallway, carrying the tray before him. There was the soft opening of a door, the faint sound of clicking and hammering. Another, farther door was opened. Minutes later the butler returned.

"If the gentleman will follow me," he said.

Pendergast followed the butler into a wood-paneled sitting room, where he was greeted by a birch fire, flickering merrily within a large fireplace.

"The gentleman is welcome to seat himself where he pleases," the butler said.

Pendergast, always attracted to heat, chose the red leather chair nearest the fire.

"The count will be available momentarily. Would the gentleman care for amontillado?"

"Thank you."

The butler retreated noiselessly and reappeared less than thirty seconds later, bearing a tray on which reposed a single crystal glass half filled with a pale amber liquid. He set it on the nearby table and, just as noiselessly, was gone.

Pendergast sipped the dry, delicate liquid and gazed about the room with growing interest. It had been furnished in exquisite and yet understated taste, managing to be both comfortable and beautiful at the same time. The floor was covered with a rare Safavid carpet of Shah Abbassid design. The fireplace was old, carved from gray Florentine *pietra serena*, and it bore the crest of an ancient and noble family. The table that held his glass also bore an interesting array of items: several pieces of old silver, an antique gasogene, some lovely Roman glass perfume bottles, and a small Etruscan bronze.

It was the painting above the mantelpiece, however, that startled Pendergast. It appeared to be a Vermeer, depicting a lady at a leaded-glass window examining a piece of lace; the cool Flemish light from the window shone through the lace, which cast a faint shadow across the woman's dress. Pendergast was familiar with all thirty-five of Vermeer's known paintings. This was not one of them. And yet it could not be a forgery: no forger had been able to duplicate Vermeer's light.

His eye roamed farther. On the opposite wall was an

unfinished painting in the Caravaggesque style, showing the conversion of Paul on the road to Damascus. It was a smaller and even more intense version of Caravaggio's famous painting in Santa Maria del Popolo in Rome. The more Pendergast looked at it, the more he doubted it was a copy or a "school of" rendering. In fact, it looked like a study in the master's own hand.

Pendergast now turned his attention to the right-hand wall, where a third painting hung: a little girl in a dark room, reading a book by candlelight. Pendergast recognized it as very similar to—yet not a copy of—a series of paintings on the same subject, *The Education of the Virgin* by the mysterious French painter Georges de la Tour. Could it possibly be real?

They were the only three paintings in the room: three breathtaking gems. But they weren't displayed with pomp and pretense; instead, they seemed to be part of the environment of the room, placed for private enjoyment rather than public envy. None of the paintings even bore a label.

His curiosity about Fosco increased.

More faint sounds emanated from chambers beyond. Immediately, the agent's preternatural hearing focused on them. A distant door had opened, and Pendergast could hear the whistling of a bird, the light patter of footsteps, and a deep, gentle voice.

Pendergast listened intently.

"Come out and hop upstairs! One, two, three, and up! Three, two, one—and down!"

A burst of chirping and twittering, combined with another sound—clacking and whirring—floated into the room from beyond, mingled with cheerful exhortations.

Then, softly, a beautiful tenor voice sounded, singing the notes of a bel canto aria. The bird—if that's what it was—fell silent, as if under a spell. The voice rose in pitch and volume, then faded slowly away, and as it did, the butler returned.

"The count will see you now."

Pendergast rose and followed him down a long, broad corridor, lined with books, to a studio beyond.

The count stood in all his corpulent majesty in a capacious studio, one end with floor-to-ceiling glass, his back turned, looking out on a small balcony framed with rosebushes, sinking into twilight. He was wearing slacks and a crisp white shirt, open at the collar. Beside him was an immaculate worktable. At least a hundred tools were lined up on the table in geometric precision: tiny screwdrivers, pinpoint soldering irons, tiny jeweler's saws, watchmaker's vises and files. Laid out next to them was an array of exquisitely small gears, ratchets, springs, levers, and other finely machined metal parts, along with chips, small circuit boards, bundles of fiber-optic cabling, LEDs, bits of rubber and plastic, and other electronic objects of mysterious function.

In the center of the worktable stood a wooden T-bar stand, and on the stand stood a strange object that at first glance looked like a Triton cockatoo, brilliant white with a lemon-colored crest, but which on closer inspection proved to be a mechanical device: a robotic bird.

The butler indicated politely for Pendergast to seat himself on a nearby stool. As if by magic, his half-drunken glass of amontillado appeared; then the butler vanished like a ghost.

Pendergast watched the count. With his free hand,

he plucked a casuarina nut from a tray, placed it between his fat lips, then protruded it. With a whistle of excitement, the robot cockatoo climbed to Fosco's shoulder, then to his ear, and—leaning forward with a whirring of gears—plucked the seed from the projecting lips, cracked it with its mechanical bill, and made every appearance of eating it.

"Ah! My pretty, playtime is over!" cooed the count. "Back to your perch." He gave his gloved hand a little wave. The cockatoo gave a screech of displeasure and flared his mechanical crest, but made no further movement.

"Ah, stubborn today, I see." The count spoke louder, more firmly. "Back to your perch, my pretty, or you will be eating millet instead of nuts the rest of the day."

With another screech, the cockatoo hopped off his shoulder onto the table, waddled over to the stand, climbed it with metal claws, and resumed its place, casting its beady LED eyes on Pendergast.

And now at last, the count turned with a smile and bow, offering Pendergast his hand. "I am so sorry to keep you waiting. My friend—as you see—requires his exercise."

"Most interesting," said Pendergast dryly.

"No doubt it is! It is true, I cut a ridiculous figure with my pets."

"Pets?"

"Yes. And you see how they love me! My cockatoo and—" He inclined his suety head toward the other side of the room, where what looked like a pack of mice were disporting themselves within an elaborate wire pagoda with various clicks and whirs and digital squeaks. "And my dear little white mice! But, of course, of all my pretties, Bucephalus here is my pride and joy." And Fosco turned toward the cockatoo. "Are you not, my pretty?"

The bird's only response was to bury its massive black bill within a fluff of fake beak feathers, as if rendered timid by the compliment.

"You must forgive Bucephalus!" Fosco said, tut-tutting. "He is not partial to strangers. He is slow to make friends and screams when displeased—ah, my friend, such screams as you would not believe! I have been forced to take the two apartments adjoining this and keep them unoccupied, at great personal expense. Mere walls, you see, are no defense against the lungs of this magnificent creature!"

The robotic cockatoo gave no acknowledgment of this panegyric, continuing to eye Pendergast motionlessly.

"But they are all quite fond of opera. As Congreve said, music hath charms et cetera. Perhaps you heard my poor singing. Did you recognize the piece?"

Pendergast nodded. "Pollione's aria from *Norma*, 'Abbandonarmi così potresti.' "

"Ah! Then you liked it."

"I said I recognized it. Tell me, Count, did you build these robots yourself?"

"Yes. I am a lover of animals and gadgets. Would you like to see my canaries? The real ones, I mean: I rarely distinguish between my own children and those of nature."

"Thank you, no."

"I should have been born an American, a Thomas Edison, where my inventiveness would have been encouraged. But instead I was born into the stifling, decaying

Florentine aristocracy, where skills such as mine are useless. Where I come from, counts are supposed to keep both feet firmly in the eighteenth century, if not earlier."

Pendergast stirred. "May I trouble you with some questions, Count Fosco?"

The count waved his hand. "Let us do away with this 'Count' business. We are in America, and here I am Isidor. May I call you Aloysius?"

There was a short silence before Pendergast spoke again, voice cool. "If it's all the same to you, Count, I would prefer to keep this interview on a formal level."

"As you like. I see the good Pinketts supplied you with refreshment. He's a treasure, don't you think? The English lorded it over the Italians for so many centuries that it gives me pleasure to have at least one Englishman under my thumb. You're not English, are you?"

"No."

"Well then, we can speak freely of the English. Bah! Imagine, the only composer of note they ever produced was a man named Byrd." The count settled himself into a wing chair opposite, and as he did so, Pendergast noted again how lightly and easily the enormous man seemed to move, how delicately he seated himself.

"My first question, Count Fosco, involves the dinner party. When did you arrive?"

The count placed his white hands together reverently, as if about to pray, and sighed. "Grove wanted us at seven. And on a Monday night, too—very unlike him. We came straggling in, fashionably late, between seven-thirty and eight. I was the first to arrive."

"What was Grove's mental state?"

"Very poor, I should say. As I told you, he seemed

nervous, high-strung. Not so much that he couldn't entertain. He had a cook, but he prepared the main dishes himself. He was quite a good chef. He prepared an exquisite sole, lightly grilled over the fire, with lemon. Nothing more, nothing less. Perfection. Then he followed with—"

"I already have the menu, thank you. Did he give any indication why he was nervous?"

"No. In fact, he seemed to be at great pains to hide it. His eyes darted everywhere. He locked the door after each guest was let in. He hardly drank, which was quite out of character. He was a man who normally liked a good claret, and even on this occasion, he served some excellent wines, starting with Tocai from Friuli and then a '90 Petrus, truly magnificent."

Château Petrus 1990, considered the best since the fabled '61, was one of Pendergast's own most prized wines; he had a dozen bottles of the $2,000 Pomerol laid down in his cellar in the Dakota. He chose not to mention this fact.

The count continued his description with great good humor and volubility. "Grove also opened, quite spontaneously, a wine from the Castello di Verrazzano, their so-called *bottiglia particolare*, the one with the silk label. Exceptional."

"Did you know the other guests?"

The count smiled. "Lady Milbanke I know quite well. Vilnius I'd met a few times. Jonathan Frederick I knew only from his writings."

"What did you talk about at dinner?"

The smile widened. "It was most peculiar."

"Yes?"

"The first part of the dinner was taken up with a

conversation about the Georges de la Tour painting you saw in my sitting room. What do you think of it, Agent Pendergast?"

"Shall we stay on the subject, Count Fosco?"

"This *is* the subject. Bear with me. Do you think it's a de la Tour?"

"Yes."

"Why?"

"The brushwork on the lace is very characteristic, and the glow of the candle through the fingers is handled in pure de la Tour fashion."

The count looked at Pendergast curiously, a faint gleam of something indefinable in his eyes. After a long silence, he said very quietly and seriously, "You surprise me very much, Pendergast. I am truly impressed." The jocular, familiar note had vanished from his voice. He paused, then continued. "Twenty years ago I found myself in a little financial embarrassment. I put that very painting up for sale at Sotheby's. The day before the auction, Grove wrote a little piece in the *Times* calling it one of the Delobre fakes, done around the turn of the century. It was pulled from the auction, and despite my having the provenance in hand, I lost fifteen million dollars."

Pendergast considered this. "And that's what you talked about? His branding your de la Tour a forgery?"

"Yes, in the beginning. Then the conversation moved to Vilnius and his paintings. Grove reminded us of Vilnius's first big show, in SoHo in the early eighties. At the time, Grove wrote a legendarily scathing review. Suffice to say, Vilnius's career never recovered."

"An odd topic of conversation."

"Indeed. And then Grove brought up the subject of

Lady Milbanke and the affair he'd had with her some years back."

"I imagine this was quite a lively dinner party."

"I have rarely seen its equal."

"And how did Lady Milbanke react?"

"How would you expect a lady to react? The affair broke up her marriage. And then Grove treated her abominably, left her for a *boy*."

"It sounds as if each of you had reason to be mortal enemies of Grove."

Fosco sighed. "We were. We all hated him, including Frederick. I don't know the man at all, but I understand that some years ago, when he was editor of *Art and Style*, he had the temerity to write something nasty about Grove. Grove had friends in high places, and the next thing Frederick knew he'd been fired. The poor fellow couldn't find a job for *years*."

"When did the dinner party break up?"

"After midnight."

"Who left first?"

"I was the first to stand and announce my departure. I have always required a great deal of sleep. The others rose at the same time. Grove was most reluctant to see us go. He kept pressing after-dinner drinks on us, coffee. He was most anxious that we stay."

"Do you know why?"

"He seemed frightened of being alone."

"Do you recall his precise words?"

"To a certain extent." Fosco broke out into a high-pitched, upper-class drawl that was startling in its realism. "*My friends! You're not going already? Why, it's just midnight! Come, let's toast our reconciliation and bid good riddance to my years of misguided pride. I have an excellent port that you must try, Fosco*—and he plucked my sleeve—*a Graham's Tawny, 1972 vintage.*" Fosco gave a sniff. "I was almost tempted to stay when I heard that."

"Did you all leave together?"

"More or less. We said our good-byes and straggled out across the lawn."

"And that was when? I'd like to know as precisely as possible, if you please."

"Twelve twenty-five." He looked at Pendergast for a moment and then said, "Mr. Pendergast, forgive me if I observe that, among all these questions, you haven't asked the most important one of all."

"And what question would that be, Count Fosco?"

"Why did Jeremy Grove ask us, his four mortal enemies, to be with him on the final night of his life?"

For a long time, Pendergast did not answer. He was carefully considering both the question and the man who had just posed it. Finally he said simply, "A good question. Consider it posed."

"It was the very question Grove himself asked when he gathered us around his table at the beginning of the dinner party. He repeated what his invitation said: that he invited us to his house that night because we were the four people he had most wronged. He wished to make amends."

"Do you have a copy of the invitation?"

With a smile, Fosco removed it from his shirt pocket and handed it over—a short, handwritten note.

"And he'd already begun to make amends. As with his reappraisal of Vilnius's work."

"A splendid review, don't you think? I understand Vilnius has just landed Gallery 10 to show his work, and they've doubled his prices."

"And Lady Milbanke? Jonathan Frederick? How did he make amends to them?"

"While Grove couldn't put Lady Milbanke's marriage back together, he did give her something in compensation. He passed her an exquisite emerald necklace across the table, more than enough to replace that dried-up old husk of a baron she lost. Forty carats of flawless Sri Lankan emeralds, worth a million dollars if a penny. She practically swooned. And Frederick? He was a long shot for the position of president of the Edsel Foundation, but Grove arranged the job for him."

"Extraordinary. And what did he do for you?"

"Surely you already know the answer to that."

Pendergast nodded. "The article he was writing for *Burlington Magazine*. 'A Reappraisal of Georges de la Tour's *The Education of the Virgin*.'"

"Precisely. Proclaiming himself in error, making appropriately abject apologies, beating his breast and affirming the glorious authenticity of the painting. He read the article aloud to us over the dinner table."

"It remained beside his computer. Unsigned and unmailed."

"Only too true, Mr. Pendergast. Of the four of us, I was the only one cheated by his death." He spread his hands. "If the murderer had waited a day, I would be forty million richer."

"Forty million? I thought it had been put up for sale at fifteen."

"That was Sotheby's estimate twenty years ago.

That painting would go for at least forty million today. But with Grove on record that it's one of the Delobre fakes..." Fosco shrugged. "An unsigned article beside a dead man's computer means nothing. There is one good thing: I'll have the lovely painting to look at for the rest of my life. *I* know it's real, and *you* know it's real, even if no one else does."

"Yes," Pendergast said. "Ultimately that's all that matters."

"Well put."

"And the Vermeer that hangs beside it?"

"Real."

"Indeed?"

"It has been dated to 1671, between the period of *Lady Writing a Letter with Her Maid* and *The Allegory of Faith.*"

"Where did it come from?"

"It's been in my family for several hundred years. The counts of Fosco never felt the need to trumpet their possessions."

"I'm truly astonished."

The count smiled, bowed. "Do you have time to see the rest of my collection?"

Pendergast hesitated for only a second. "As a matter of fact, I do."

The count rose and went to the door. Just before they exited, he turned to the mechanical cockatoo, still on his perch.

"Keep an eye on the place, Bucephalus, my pretty."

The bird gave a digitized squawk in reply.

{ 14 }

D'Agosta moved fast through the trees, seeking the darkest area of the park—a dense growth of trees and shrubs along an embankment leading down to the West Side Highway. He paused just long enough to glance back. Two figures were running after him, guns gleaming in their fists.

Staying low, weaving between the trees, D'Agosta unsnapped the holster of his Glock. He withdrew the weapon, racked the slide. It was the chosen weapon of most modern police departments, and D'Agosta hadn't been given a choice about carrying it, on duty or off. It didn't have the punch of his personal .45, but it was light and reliable, and best of all, it held fifteen rounds. He'd left his extra clip in his desk drawer that morning—who needed an extra clip for a day of interviews?

The men were already into the woods, moving fast. D'Agosta ran on, heedless of the noise he was making—the brush wasn't heavy enough to conceal him for more than a minute or two, at best. He headed south, twigs crackling underfoot. If he could lose them, even temporarily, maybe he could get back onto Riverside Drive and head toward Broadway. They wouldn't dare follow onto such a busy street. He quickly checked off his options. The nearest precinct house was located at 95th between Broadway and Amsterdam—that's where he'd head for.

He could hear the men running behind him. One shouted out to the other, and a fainter response came back. D'Agosta immediately understood what had happened: they had divided and were still pursuing, one on either side of the narrow strip of park.

Shit.

Keeping low, he ran through the woods, gun in hand. No time to stop and strategize; no time to use his radio; no time for anything but a flat-out run. The faint lights of Riverside Drive flickered through the trees on his left; to his right lay the long, brush-filled slope running steeply down toward the West Side Highway. He could hear the droning rush of cars far below him. He briefly considered running down the embankment and trying to get out on the highway, but it would be easy to get hung up in the nasty bracken that clogged the slope.

If that happened, he'd be a sitting duck, fired on from above.

The stretch of woods ended abruptly, and he burst out into a moonlit scene of parallel walkways overlooking the river, gardens and trees between them. It was exposed, but he had no choice but to keep moving.

Who the fuck's chasing me? Muggers? Cop haters? It didn't make sense. He was no longer just a target of opportunity. These killers were determined. They had followed him uptown. They were after him for a reason.

He ran past the first formal garden, behind rows of

iron benches, keeping low. Suddenly he saw something off to his left: a red spot of light chasing him, dancing around like an agitated firefly.

Laser sight.

He threw himself to the right as the shot came. It hit the metal bench with a sickening ricochet and hummed off into the darkness. D'Agosta fell into the flower bed, rolled clumsily, and rose on his knees in firing position. He saw a dark shape moving fast against the dimness of the open grass and fired—once, twice—rolled to the side, rose to his feet, and took off running again, cursing himself for not having kept up with his shooting practice. But even missed shots had a good effect—making them careful, slowing them down. At least that was the theory. He passed the far side of the garden and ducked in among the trees.

Another jiggling red dot. He threw himself to the asphalt as the shot came, rolled, tearing his knee open against the pavement, and was up again and running. The shooters were using some big-caliber sidearms and knew what they were doing. His own shots hadn't slowed them down at all.

These guys were professional assassins.

He ran through a playground, desperately leaping first the teeter-totter, then the sandbox, and across a small square with a fountain, gasping with the effort. Jeez, he was out of shape, gone to seed. Long gone were the days in the police gym, keeping trim and fit.

He cut across a small square with a fountain, jumped a stone parapet, and was back on the steep, woodsy embankment leading down to the highway. He crouched behind the stone wall, waiting. They would have to cross the open walkway. That's when he'd have a shot at them. He held the weapon tightly in a two-hand combat grip, steadied himself, tried to get control of his wild breathing. *Don't squeeze the trigger. When it goes off, it should almost be a surprise. Make every shot count.*

Now! The dark shapes emerged from the trees, moving fast. He fired: once, twice, thrice.

The red lights were dancing around the branches over his head, and he screamed an obscenity as he forgot his own careful advice and fired again and again at the dim shapes. He could hear nothing over the bark of his firearm, but he could feel the slap of bullets hitting the stone right before his face. These bastards didn't miss a beat.

He, on the other hand, had missed by a mile, and no wonder. He hadn't taken a turn at the range in three damn years, and his shooting was as old and stale as all those shooting awards that hung on his wall.

He scrambled back from the stone wall, running along it in a low crouch, praying his back wasn't exposed. As he ran, he popped the clip from the gun, peering at it in the dim light. Empty. That left him only two shots in the chamber... thirteen rounds wasted.

Suddenly he saw something come into view through the trees up ahead: the bridge over the 110th Street off-ramp. The whole thing was chain-linked like a cage. If he got caught in there, he'd be the proverbial fish in a barrel.

But turning back—jumping back over the stone wall and crossing the open walkway—meant running right into the arms of his pursuers. And that would be suicide.

He glanced down to his right. There was only one other choice. It was the highway or nothing. Get out on the West Side Highway, stop traffic, create a snarl, radio for help. They wouldn't pursue him or shoot at him out there.

Without waiting to reconsider, he charged down the steep embankment, clawing through the brambles and sumac and poison ivy, half falling, half rolling. The branches tore cruelly through the fabric of his uniform, and the sharp rocks of the embankment bruised his shoulders and knees.

Whang! sounded the shot.

Ahead, the embankment dropped away steeply. He fell, rolled as far as he could, forced himself back onto his feet, and began running again, casting one brief look back. He could hear them crashing through the brush not thirty feet above him. In desperation, he wheeled, squeezed off a shot at the closest figure. It ducked to the side, then charged forward again. D'Agosta turned and ran with all his might. His heart was racing dangerously. The rush of cars was suddenly louder, the lights flashing through the trees, flashing on him for a moment.

Whang! Whang!

He ducked, zigzagged. The highway was just fifty feet ahead. The headlights were now flashing across him, making a clear target.

Thirty more feet. The trees were thinning, giving way to garbage and weeds.

Whang!

The embankment leveled out. Twenty more feet to the edge of the trees and the highway. He ran flat out, making a beeline—

Boom. And he was thrown back.

D'Agosta lay there for a moment, stunned, thinking he'd been hit, that it was over. Then he realized he'd run full tilt into the chain-link fence that ran just above the highway. His eyes took it in within the space of a heartbeat: the concertina wire at the top, the crappy fence all mangled and twisted by junkies, the skeletons of cars lying on the verge below the far side. *Of course.* In the old days, he had driven that highway a million times, seen that fence leaning dangerously above him, stuffed with trash and decaying leaves. One more thing he'd forgotten in those years in British Columbia. He was trapped.

This was it. He rose on one knee and turned to make his stand. *One round, two men.*

The math wasn't good.

{ 15 }

A low fire burned in the grate, casting a ruddy light on the walls of books and chasing the damp chill from the air. Two wing chairs occupied the space on either side of the fire. In one sat Special Agent Pendergast, and in the other Constance Greene, pale and slender in a beautifully pressed and pleated dress. To one side sat the remains of an evening tea service: cups and saucers, strainer, creamer, digestive biscuits. The still air smelled of wood polish and buckram, and on all sides the bookshelves climbed, row after row, toward the high ceiling, the old leather-bound books that lined them gleaming with gold stamping in the firelight.

Pendergast's silvery eyes glanced toward a clock above the mantelpiece, then flickered back to the old newspaper he was reading. His murmured voice picked up where it had left off.

"'August 7, 1964. Washington—In an 88-4 vote today, the U.S. Senate authorized President Johnson the use of "all necessary measures" to repel armed attacks against U.S. forces in Vietnam. The vote was in response to the shelling of two U.S. Navy ships by North Vietnam in the Gulf of Tonkin'..."

Constance listened intently as he went on. There was a rustle as Pendergast gently turned the fragile, yellowed page.

The girl held up her hand, and Pendergast paused.

"I'm not sure I can bear another war. Will it be a bad one?"

"One of the worst. It will tear apart the country."

"Let us save this war for tomorrow, then."

Pendergast nodded, carefully folding up the newspaper and putting it aside.

"I can scarcely believe the cruelty of the last century. It staggers the soul."

Pendergast inclined his head in agreement.

She shook her head slowly, and the glow of the flames reflected in her dark eyes and straight black hair. "Do you think this new century will be as barbarous?"

"The twentieth century showed us the evil face of physics. This century will show us the evil face of biology. This will be humanity's last century, Constance."

"So cynical?"

"May God prove me wrong."

A bank of embers collapsed, opening a glowing wound in the fire. Pendergast stirred. "And now, perhaps, shall we move on to the results of your search?"

"Certainly." Constance rose and walked toward one wall of bookshelves, returning with several octavo volumes. "The abbot Trithemius, the *Liber de Angelis*, the McMaster text, *The Sworn Book of Honorius*, the *Secretum Philosophorum*, and, of course, *Ars Notorium*. Treatises on selling one's soul, raising the devil, and the like." She placed the volumes on a side table. "All alleged eyewitness accounts. Latin, Ancient Greek, Aramaic, Old French, Old Norse, and Middle English. Then there are the grimoires."

"Textbooks of magic," Pendergast said, nodding.

"*The Key of Solomon* is the best known. Many of these documents belonged to secret societies and orders, which were common among the nobility of the Middle Ages. Apparently, these societies were often active in satanic practices."

Pendergast nodded again. "I am particularly interested in accounts of the devil claiming his due."

"There are many. For example"—she indicated the wormy cover of the *Ars Notorium* with a faint look of distaste—"the Tale of Geoffrey, magister of Kent."

"Go on."

"The tales don't vary greatly from the Faustian theme, except in the details. A highly learned man, restless and dissatisfied; a manuscript; raising the devil; promises made, promises broken; a warm end. In this case, Magister Geoffrey was a doctor of philosophy at Oxford in the early 1400s, a chemist and mathematician. His great passion was the mystery of the prime numbers. He spent years in his studio, calculating the primes out to five digits. Some of the calculations involved more than a year of work, and they say he needed a little help to finish them. Hence, the pact with Lucifer. There was talk in Oriel College of chanting, ugly smells, unexplained noises, and strange lights burning in the scholar's chambers long after midnight. The magister continued to teach and do his alchemical experiments. His fame spread far and wide. He was said to have discovered the arcanum for transforming lead into gold, and he was admitted into the Order of the Golden Chalice by King Henry VI himself. He published his great work *The Nyne Numbers of God* and was known across Europe for his wisdom and learning.

"But then things began to change. At the height of his fame, he became nervous, suspicious, strange. He was often ill, confined to his chambers. He jumped at every noise. He seemed to grow thin, his eyes staring 'like the great hollow eyes of a calf in the slaughter.' He ordered brass locks and had his doors clad and banded in iron.

"And then one day his students missed him at breakfast. They went to his chambers. The door was locked, the iron hot to the touch. There was a smell of phosphorus and sulfur. Only with great effort could they break it down.

"They beheld a terrible sight. Geoffrey, magister of Kent, lay on his wooden pallet, fully dressed, as if laid out for burial. There were no cuts on his skin, no breaks, no bruising. And yet his heart lay next to the body, partially burned and still smoking. They said it wouldn't stop beating until it had been sprinkled with holy water. Then it burst. The details are rather . . . unpleasant."

Pendergast glanced at the girl. She leaned forward, took a sip of tea, replaced the cup, smiled.

"And do the texts describe just how the Prince of Darkness was conjured?"

"They drew circles around themselves. Generally, nine feet in diameter. They were usually drawn with an *arthame*, or ceremonial knife. Frequently, there were smaller circles or pentacles within the larger one.

Above all, it was critical that the circle not be broken during the ceremony—as long as he remained within the circle, the conjurer was safe from the demons he summoned."

"And once the demons were summoned?"

"A contract was made. The usual: wealth, power, knowledge, in return for one's immortal soul. Faust, of course, is the prototypical story—particularly in the way it ends."

Pendergast nodded encouragingly.

"After making his personal deal with the devil, Faust had all the power, earthly and unearthly, he had always craved. But he had other things as well. He complained of never being alone: of eyes in the walls watching him, of noises, strange noises like the clicking of teeth. Despite having everything mortal beings can possess, he grew restless. Eventually, as the days of his contract grew short, he took to reading the Bible, loudly proclaiming his repentance. He spent his last evening in the company of his drinking companions, weeping bitterly, bewailing his sins, begging heaven to slow the passage of hours."

"'O lente, lente, currite noctis equi,'" Pendergast intoned quietly.

"*Dr. Faustus*, Act 5, scene 2," Constance said immediately.

> *"The stars move still, time runs, the clock will strike,*
> *The devil will come, and Faustus must be damned."*

A small smile broke across Pendergast's features.

"According to legend, terrible screams were heard issuing from his rooms after midnight. None of his guests dared investigate. In the morning, they found his bedchamber turned into an abattoir. The walls were painted in blood. Somebody found a lone eyeball in a corner of the room. The crushed, limp remains of his skull clung to one wall. The rest of his body was found in the alley below, thrown over a pile of horse manure. They said—"

She was interrupted by a knock at the library door.

"That would be Sergeant D'Agosta," Pendergast said, glancing up at the clock. "Come in," he called in a louder voice.

The door opened slowly and Sergeant Vincent D'Agosta stepped into the library: dirty, clothes torn, scratched, bleeding.

Pendergast rose abruptly from his chair. "Vincent!"

{ 16 }

D'Agosta slumped in a chair, feeling dazed and in shock. It seemed one-half of his body was numb, and the half that wasn't was throbbing in pain. The old mansion gave him the creeps, so damp, cold, and dark. Was this really where Pendergast was now living? Here the guy had a beautiful place on Central Park West, but chose instead to live in deepest Harlem, in a spookhouse of a museum no less, all stuffed animals and skeletons and shelves covered with weird crap. At least this library was like an oasis: soft chairs, a roaring fire. Pendergast had a guest, it seemed, but for the moment D'Agosta felt too scratched, bruised, and wiped out to care.

"You look like you just escaped from the devil," Pendergast said.

"I did."

"Sherry?"

"You wouldn't happen to have a cold Bud?"

Pendergast looked pained. "Would a Pilsner Urquell do?"

"If it's beer, it'll do."

The other occupant of the library—a young woman

in a long salmon-colored dress—rose and left the room. Within a few minutes, she was back, bearing a glass of beer on a salver. D'Agosta took it and drank gratefully. "Thanks, uh..."

"Constance," came the soft reply.

"Constance Greene," said Pendergast. "My ward. This is Sergeant Vincent D'Agosta, a trusted associate of mine. He's assisting in this case."

D'Agosta glanced at Pendergast. His ward? What the hell did that mean? He looked back more curiously at the girl. She was beautiful, in a pale, delicate kind of way. Her dress was very proper and demure, but the breasts that swelled the lace-front brought a most *un*demure stirring to D'Agosta's loins. Despite the old-fashioned clothes, she looked no older than twenty. But those violet eyes of hers, so alert and intelligent, somehow didn't look like the eyes of a young girl at all. Not at all.

"Glad to meet you," said D'Agosta, straightening up in his chair and wincing.

"Are you hurt?" Pendergast asked.

"Just about everywhere." D'Agosta took another long pull.

"Tell us what happened."

D'Agosta set down the glass. "I'll start at the beginning. I visited Lady Milbanke first. She was a complete wash. All she wanted to do was talk about her new emerald necklace. Cutforth wasn't much better: lied about the reason Grove called him, answered questions evasively if at all. Last was Bullard, at the New York Athletic Club. Claims he hardly knew Grove, doesn't know why he called, can't really remember what they chatted about, doesn't know how Grove got his number. A liar through and through, and didn't even bother to hide it."

"Interesting."

"Yeah, a real piece of work. Big, ugly, arrogant motherf—" D'Agosta glanced at the girl. "Man. Basically, he blew me off. I left, ate dinner at Mullin's Pub over on Broadway. Caught sight of a gold Impala more than once. Took the subway to 96th and walked over to Riverside. Hoofed it from there. The Impala reappeared again around 130th."

"Heading north or south?"

D'Agosta wondered why that was important. "North."

Pendergast nodded.

"I saw something was about to come down, so I ran into Riverside Park. Two guys jumped out and chased me, shooting laser-sighted handguns: accurate, large-caliber. Chased me through the park. I ran down toward the West Side Highway and came up against a chain-link fence. I really thought it was over. Then I noticed a recent car wreck fifty yards on. Some shitbox had gone through the fence, making a gap. Just left the car rotting there. I dove through the gap, lost them on the highway, flagged down a car. It let me off at the next exit, but I couldn't get a cab and had to walk the thirty blocks back down. Sticking to the shadows the whole way, watching out for that Impala—it took quite some time."

Pendergast nodded again. "So one of the men followed you onto the subway, the other drove the car. They reconnected and tried to cut you off."

"That's how I figured it. An old trick."

"Did you return fire?"

"Lot of good it did me."

"Ah! And your vaunted shooting ability?"

D'Agosta looked down. "Little rusty."

"The question is, who sent them?"

"It seemed to happen awful damn fast after I got Bullard stirred up."

"Perhaps too fast."

"Bullard didn't look like the kind of guy who would wait. He's the decisive type."

Pendergast nodded.

Throughout this recitation, the young woman had listened politely. Now she rose from the couch. "With your permission, I'll leave you to discuss this matter amongst yourselves." She had a precise, mannered way of speaking, and a faint accent that for some reason reminded D'Agosta of old black-and-white movies. She came over and kissed Pendergast lightly on the cheek. "Good night, Aloysius." Then she turned toward D'Agosta and nodded. "A pleasure to make your acquaintance, Sergeant."

A moment later the door to the library closed, and silence fell.

"Ward, huh?" said D'Agosta.

Pendergast nodded.

"Where'd she come from?"

"I inherited her with the house."

"How the heck do you 'inherit' someone? She a relative?"

"Not a relative. It's rather complicated. This house and its collections were passed down to me from my great-uncle Antoine. She was discovered in the house by an acquaintance of mine who cataloged the mansion's collections during the summer. She'd been hiding here."

"For how long?"

There was a pause. "A good while."

"What is she, a runaway? Doesn't she have family?"

"She's an orphan. My great-uncle had taken her in, looked after her welfare, educated her."

"Yeah? He sounds like a saint."

"Hardly. As it happens, Constance was the only person he ever cared for. In fact, he continued caring for her long after he'd stopped caring even about himself. He was a misanthrope, but she was the exception that proved his rule. In any case, it seems I'm her only family now. But I must ask you not to mention any of this in her presence. The last six months have been exceptionally... trying for her."

"How so?"

"That is something better left in the past. Suffice it to say, Vincent, that Constance is the innocent beneficiary of a set of diabolical experiments conducted long ago. Seeing how her own family was victimized early on by those experiments, I feel bound to look after her well-being. It's a complication I certainly did not anticipate. However, her knowledge of this house and its library is proving invaluable. She will make an excellent research assistant and curator."

"At least she's not hard to look at." When he felt Pendergast's un-amused gaze on him D'Agosta cleared his throat and added hastily, "How did your own interviews go?"

"Montcalm could add little to what we already

know. He was away until yesterday, traveling. It seems that Grove left a frantic message with his assistant: *How does one break a contract with the devil?* The assistant threw the note away—apparently Montcalm is a magnet for cranks and gets many such messages. He could add nothing else. Fosco, on the other hand, proved to be most interesting."

"I hope you really sweated him."

"I'm not sure who sweated who."

D'Agosta could not imagine anyone sweating Pendergast. "Is he involved?"

"That depends on what you mean by involved. He is a remarkable man, and his recollections proved to be invaluable."

"Well, the jury's still out on both Cutforth and Bullard."

"You said Cutforth was a liar, as well as Bullard. How do you know?"

"He told me Grove had called him in the middle of the night, wishing to buy some piece of rock memorabilia. I bluffed him by saying Grove hated rock music. His look gave him away immediately."

"A crude lie."

"He's a crude man, and pretty stupid to boot. I imagine he's good at what he does, though, given all the dough he's made."

"Intelligence, culture, and education are not qualities generally associated with the popular music business."

"Well, Bullard's on another level. He's crude, too, but highly intelligent. I wouldn't underestimate him. The fact is they both know a lot more about Grove's death than they're telling. We can crack Cutforth, I'm pretty sure—he's a wuss—but Bullard's going to be a tough nut."

Pendergast nodded. "The forensic report on Grove's body should be ready tomorrow. That may give us badly needed information. The critical thing now is to find the connection between Bullard, Cutforth, and Grove. If we find that connection, Vincent, we'll have the key to this entire mystery."

{ 17 }

Dr. Jack Dienphong cast his eye about his laboratory: exam-ining the metal tables, the chemical hoods and glove boxes, microscopes, SEMs, microtomes, and titration setups. It wasn't pretty, but it was organized and functional. Dienphong was chief of the FBI's Forensic Science Division on Congress Street, and he was very curious to meet—at last—this Special Agent Pendergast he had heard so much about.

He glanced down at the scribbled index card in his hand, running through his notes one more time. Most of it was in his head: the index card was more for comfort than anything else. He felt a disquieting sense of apprehension. He didn't like what he was going to have to report, and he just hoped the famous—some said infamous—agent would understand. In Dienphong's opinion, the worst mistake one could make in forensic chemistry was to over-interpret results. Do that enough times, and eventually you'd send an innocent man to prison. It was Dienphong's greatest fear. He wouldn't stretch results for anyone, not even someone as formidable as Pendergast.

There was a stir at the door, and Dienphong glanced

at his watch. On time almost to the second, already confirming one thing he'd heard Pendergast was famous for. A moment later the door opened, and a slender man in a black suit entered, followed by Special Agent in Charge Carlton, chief of the Southern District Field Office, and a hushed group of junior agents and assistants. There was an almost palpable excitement in the air, the kind of excitement high-profile cases always generated. And only a high-profile case like this would bring somebody like Carlton in on a Sunday. All the pertinent evidence had been forwarded to the FBI by local police for in-depth analysis. And now it was up to Dienphong to piece everything together for them. His feeling of apprehension did not diminish.

Dienphong observed the stranger carefully. Pendergast was just as people had described him, moving with the efficiency and grace of a cat. His hair was so blond it was almost white, his face cool and patrician, his pale eyes restlessly taking in everything. Dienphong had met many FBI agents in his time, but this one was in another category altogether.

Those ice cool eyes alighted on Dienphong, and the agent came striding over. "Dr. Dienphong," the man said in the buttery tones of the Deep South.

"A pleasure." Dienphong took the dry hand.

"I thought your piece in the *Journal of Forensics* on the maturation rate of blowfly larvae in the human cadaver to be fine reading."

"Thank you." He hadn't quite thought of the article as "fine reading" himself, but then each to his own. Dienphong's idea of fine reading was Johnson's *Rambler* essays.

"The presentation is all ready," he said, gesturing toward a double row of metal chairs set up before a projection screen. "We're going to begin with a brief visual presentation."

"Excellent."

The agents seated themselves with murmurs, coughing, and scraping of chairs. Special Agent in Charge Carlton took up position in the front row center, his thick thighs spilling off the edges of the seat.

Dienphong nodded toward his assistant and the lights dimmed. He switched on the computer projector.

"Please feel free to interrupt with questions at any time." He called up the first image. "We'll go from simplest to most complex. This is a 50x sample of the sulfur recovered at the site. Our chemical analysis showed it to be natural, with trace elements that indicate a volcanic origin. It had been rapidly heated and burned by unknown means. When sulfur burns, it combines with oxygen to make sulfur dioxide gas, SO_2, which has a very strong odor—the smell of burned matches. If it then comes in contact with water, it creates H_2SO_4, also known as sulfuric acid.

"These fibers here"—the next image came up—"are from the victim's clothing. Note the pitting and curling: clear effects of sulfuric acid on the victim's clothes."

Three more images in quick succession. "As you can see, there was even microscopic pitting on the victim's plastic glasses, and in the varnish on the walls and floor, from the intense release of sulfur compounds."

"Any idea of the specific volcanic source?" It was Pendergast who spoke.

"That's almost impossible to answer. We'd have to analyze and compare this with thousands of known volcanic sources, an overwhelming job even if we could get the samples. What I can tell you is that the high proportion of silicon indicates a continental, as opposed to an oceanic, source. In other words, this sulfur didn't come from Hawaii or, say, the seafloor."

Pendergast settled back, his expression unreadable in the dark room.

"This next image shows some microsections of the burned wood of the floor from the so-called hoofprint." Several more images flashed across the screen. Dienphong cleared his throat. Here is where the difficulties began.

"You will note the very deep penetration of the burn into the wood. You can see it better at 200x."

Another slide. "This was not caused by a 'branding iron' effect." He paused, swallowed. "That is to say, this mark was not burned into the floor by a red-hot object being impressed into the wood. It was caused by an intense burst of nonionizing radiation, probably in the very short infrared wavelength range, which deeply penetrated the wood."

Carlton spoke up, as Dienphong knew he would. "You mean, the perp didn't heat something up and press it on the wood?"

"Exactly. Nothing actually *touched* the wood. The burn was made by a short blast of pure radiation."

Carlton shifted, the chair uttering a dangerous groan. "Wait a minute. How can that be?"

"My job is to describe, not interpret," said Dienphong, flicking up the next slide.

But the chief hadn't finished. "Are you saying the mark was made with some kind of *ray gun*?"

"I can't say what the source of the radiation was."

Carlton settled back with a dubious grunt.

"This brings us to the cross." The next slide came up. "Our art expert has identified this as a rare example of a seventeenth-century Tuscan cross, commonly worn by the noble classes. It is made of gold and silver, layered, fused, and hand-chased to produce a rather interesting effect known as *lamellés fines.* It was then set in wood, which has largely burned away."

"How much's it worth?" Carlton said, asking an intelligent question for a change.

"Given the precious stones, eighty, perhaps one hundred thousand dollars. Undamaged, that is."

Carlton whistled.

"The cross was found around the neck of the victim, touching his skin. Here is a photograph of it at the scene of the crime, still around the victim's neck."

The next slide came up, prompting noises of disgust and disbelief.

"As you can see, the cross heated to the point of melting, deeply burning the skin where it lay. But observe that the surrounding flesh is not scorched or even reddened. Something—and I really can't say what—selectively heated the cross *without heating the surrounding skin.* The cross then partially melted and burned itself into the victim's flesh in situ.

"And here"—he brought up the next image—"is an electron micrograph at 3,000x, showing this extraordinary pitting along the silver—but *not* the gold—surface of the cross. I can't account for this, either. I suspect it might have been caused by an intense and prolonged dose of radiation that seems to have stripped off the top layers of electrons and vaporized part of the metal. It acts much more strongly on silver than on gold. Again, I have no idea why."

Carlton was on his feet. "Can we have this in plain English?"

"Of course," Dienphong said dryly. "Something heated up and melted the cross without heating up anything around it. I guess it must have been some kind of radiation that was taken up by metal more strongly than flesh."

"Like maybe the same radiation that burned the hoofprint?"

Carlton, Dienphong had to admit, was not as stupid as he pretended to be.

"A good possibility."

Pendergast raised a finger.

"Agent Pendergast?"

"Were there any signs of radiation burns or heating in any other surfaces in the room?"

An even better question. "Yes, in fact, there were. The bedposts, which were varnished pine, showed signs of heat stress, as did the wall behind the bed, which was painted pine. In some areas, the paint had softened and bubbled."

He moused his way through the on-screen menu and pulled up another image. "Here's a cross section of the wall, showing four layers of paint. Now here's yet another small mystery: only the *lowest* layer of paint seems to have heated up and bubbled. The others were undisturbed and remained chemically unaltered."

"Did you analyze all four layers of paint?" Pendergast asked.

Dienphong nodded.

"Was the bottom layer a lead-based paint?"

Dienphong felt a sudden surprise. He quickly saw where the line of questioning would lead, and it was something that he had not thought of. "Let me check the book." He flipped through the lab reports, organized and categorized in a three-ring binder labeled *Brimstone.* All FBI investigations get a nickname, and this was the one he had given this case. Melodramatic, perhaps, but appropriate.

He looked up from the binder. "Yes, as a matter of fact it was lead-based."

"And the rest were not?"

"That's correct."

"Further proof that we are dealing with some kind of radiation."

"Very good, Agent Pendergast." It was the first time in his career that an FBI agent had beaten him to a conclusion. This Pendergast was living up to his reputation. Dienphong cleared his throat. "Any other questions or comments?"

Carlton sat down again, raised a weary hand.

"Yes?"

"I'm missing something. How could something affect the *bottom* layer of paint and not the upper ones?"

Pendergast turned. "It was the *lead* in the paint that reacted, like the metal in the cross. It absorbed the radiation more strongly. Was there any radioactivity present at the site, Doctor, during follow-up investigation?"

"None whatsoever."

Carlton nodded. "Check into that, Sam, will you?"

"Of course, sir," one of the junior agents replied.

Dienphong went to the next image. "Here's the final image: a close-up of a section of the cross. Note the very localized melting, completely inconsistent with a convective source of heat. Again an indication that radiation played a role."

"What type of radiation would selectively heat metal more than flesh?" Pendergast asked.

"X-rays, gamma rays, microwave, far infrared, certain wavelengths in the radio spectrum, not to mention alpha radiation and a flux of fast neutrons. This is not very unusual. What is unusual is the *intensity*."

Dienphong waited for the inevitable expostulation from Carlton, but this time the agent in charge said nothing.

"The pitting on the cross," Pendergast said, "might suggest to you something?"

"Not so far."

"Speculations?"

"I never speculate, Mr. Pendergast."

"An intense electron beam could cause it, don't you think?"

"Yes, but an electron beam would have to propagate through a vacuum. Air would disperse it in, say, a millimeter or two. As I said, it might have been in the infrared, microwave, or X-ray spectrum, except that it would take a transmitter of several tons to generate a beam that intense."

"Quite so. What do you think, Doctor, of the theory being pushed by the *New York Post*?"

Dienphong paused briefly at this sudden change of

tack. "I am not in the habit of taking my theories from the pages of the *Post.*"

"They've published speculation that the devil took his soul."

There was a brief silence, and then there was a smattering of nervous chuckles. Pendergast was evidently making a joke. Or was he? He didn't seem to be laughing.

"Mr. Pendergast, that's a theory I don't subscribe to."

"No?"

Dienphong smiled. "I am a Buddhist. The only devil we believe in is the one inside the human heart."

{ 18 }

Not much scanning of the crowd streaming into the Metro-politan Opera House was needed to locate Count Isidor Fosco: his huge presence, striking a dramatic pose beside the Lincoln Center fountain, was unmistakable. Pendergast drifted toward him with the crowd. All around, men in tuxedos and women in pearl necklaces were babbling excitedly. It was opening night at the Metropolitan Opera, and the program was Donizetti's *Lucrezia Borgia*. The count was wearing white tie and tails, beautifully tailored to his enormously fat figure. The cut was old-fashioned, and in place of the usual white waistcoat, Fosco was sporting one in gorgeous Hong Kong silk brocaded in white and dove gray. A gardenia was stuck in his buttonhole, his handsome face was patted and shaved and powdered to pink perfection, and his thick mane of gray hair was brushed back into leonine curls. His small, plump hands were perfectly fitted in gray kid gloves.

"My dear Pendergast, I was *hoping* you'd come in white tie!" Fosco said, rejoicing. "I cannot understand why people dress down so barbarously on a night such as this." He waved a dismissive hand at the tuxedoed patrons streaming past them into the hall. "There are only three occasions left to truly dress up in these dark days: at one's nuptials, at one's funeral, and at opening night at the opera. By far the happiest of these three is the last."

"That depends on your point of view," said Pendergast dryly.

"You are happily married, then?"

"I was referring to the other occasion."

"Ah!" Fosco laughed silently. "You are right, Pendergast. I've never seen a more contented smile on some people than at their own wake."

"I was referring to the deceased's heirs."

"You wicked fellow. Shall we go inside? I hope you don't mind sitting in the pit—I avoid the boxes because the acoustics are muddy. We have tickets for row N, center right, which I have found from experimentation to be the acoustical sweet spot in this hall, particularly seats twenty-three through thirty-one. But look, there go the houselights: we had better sit down." And with his giant head held erect, chin raised, Fosco moved swiftly through the milling crowd, which parted instinctively. For his part, Fosco looked neither to the right nor to the left as they moved through the central doors, brushing past several ushers offering programs and sweeping down the central aisle to row N. Fosco waited at the end of the row, gesturing a dozen people out of their seats and into the far aisle so he could make his way undisturbed. The count had purchased three seats for himself, and he seated himself in the center one, stretching his arms on the upturned seats on either side.

"Forgive me if we don't sit jowl-to-jowl, my dear Pendergast. My corpulence demands its space and will not be reined in." He slipped a small pair of bejeweled, pearl-inlaid opera glasses out of his waistcoat and placed them on the empty seat next to him. A more powerful brass spyglass also made an appearance and was arranged on the other seat.

The great house was filling up, and there was an air of excitement. From the orchestra pit came the murmur of instruments tuning, playing snatches of the opera to come.

Fosco leaned toward Pendergast, placing a neat gloved hand on his arm. "No one who loves music can fail to be moved by *Lucrezia Borgia*. But wait—what is this?" He peered more closely at Pendergast. "You are not wearing earplugs, are you, sir?"

"Not plugs, no. These merely attenuate the sound—my hearing is exceptionally acute, and any volume above a normal conversation is quite painful to me. Fear not, the music will get through all too well, I assure you."

"All too well, you say!"

"Count Fosco, I thank you for this invitation. But as I warned you once, I have yet to meet an opera I liked. Pure music and vulgar spectacle are fundamentally incompatible. Beethoven's string quartets are by far my preference—and even those, to be honest, I enjoy for their intellectual content more than their musical."

Fosco winced. "What, may I ask, is wrong with spectacle?" He spread his hands. "Isn't life itself a spectacle?"

"All the color, noise, flash, the embonpoint diva

prowling the stage, shrieking and howling and throwing herself from the ramparts of some castle—it distracts the mind from the music."

"But that is exactly what opera is! A feast of sight *and* sound. There is humor! There is tragedy! There are soaring heights of passion and depths of cruelty! There is love and betrayal!"

"You are making my points even better than I could, Count."

"Your mistake, Pendergast, is to think of opera as solely *music*. It is more than music. It is *life*! You must abandon yourself to it, throw yourself at its mercy."

Pendergast smiled. "I am afraid, Count, I never abandon myself to anything."

Fosco patted his arm. "You may have a French name, but you have an English heart. The English can never step outside themselves. Wherever they go they feel self-conscious. That is why the English make excellent anthropologists but dreadful composers." Fosco snorted. "Purcell. *Britten.*"

"You're forgetting Handel."

"A transplanted German." Fosco chuckled. "I am glad to have you here, Pendergast, and I *shall* show you the error of your ways."

"Speaking of that, how did you know where to deliver the invitation?"

The count turned a triumphant smile on Pendergast. "It was quite simple. I went to the Dakota and made inquiries there."

"They are under strict orders not to divulge my other addresses."

"But they were no match for Fosco! I've always been

interested in this profession of yours. I read all of Sir Arthur Conan Doyle in my youth. Dickens, Poe. And the sublime Wilkie Collins! Have you read *The Woman in White*?"

"Naturally."

"A tour de force! In my next life, perhaps, I'll choose to be a detective. Being a count from an ancient family is rather boring."

"The two are not mutually exclusive."

"Well put! We have all kinds of detectives these days, everyone from English lords to Navajo policemen. Why not a count from the lineage of Dante and Beatrice? I must confess, this case with Grove fascinates me, and not only because I was a guest at the—dare I say?—last supper. One week ago tonight, alas. I feel for the poor man, naturally, but it is a rather delicious mystery. I am at your assistance in the matter."

"I thank you, but I must confess it's unlikely I'll need your assistance."

"Quite right! I am speaking now—if I may—as a friend. I only wish to offer you my services as someone with a particular knowledge of art and music, and perhaps society. And in that last regard, I'd like to think I've already been helpful with the question of the dinner party."

"You were."

"Thank you." The count patted his gloved hands together, as excited as a small boy.

The lights darkened. A hush fell on the house. Fosco turned his attention to the stage, practically wriggling with excitement. The concertmaster appeared and sounded the A; the orchestra tuned to it; then all fell silent. The conductor came out to a thunderous burst of applause. Taking his position at the podium, he raised his baton, brought it sharply down, and the overture began.

Fosco listened with rapt attention, smiling and nodding his head from time to time, not a note of Donizetti's luxurious music lost on him. When the curtain rose on the first act, a murmur and scattered applause filled the hall; a look of annoyance darkened Fosco's face as he cast a disapproving glance at his neighbors.

There he sat, like a giant in the darkened hall, from time to time raising the opera glasses or spyglass to observe the scene. When the people near him applauded the close of an aria without any regard for the music to follow, Fosco raked them with a look of reproof and even held up his hands in forbearance, with a sad but compassionate shake of his head. After the more complex and difficult passages of music, which went unnoticed by his neighbors, he held up his gloved hands and patted them lightly together with relish, sometimes murmuring "Brava!" After a while, Fosco's enormous presence, his deep enthusiasm, and his evident connoisseurship began to communicate itself to the people seated around them. Many an eruption of applause in appreciation for some particular turn of the music originated in row N, right center, with the soft patting of Fosco's plump, kid-gloved hands.

The first act drew to a close with huge huzzahs, a storm of applause, and shouts of "Bravi!" led by Fosco, so vociferous that even the conductor's attention was drawn to him. When the uproar had at last died down, Fosco turned to Pendergast, wiping the sweat from his brow with an oversize handkerchief. He was breathing hard, blowing, damp with perspiration.

"You see, you see!" he cried, pointing with a cry of self-vindication. "You *are* enjoying yourself."

"And what gave rise to that deduction?"

"You cannot hide from Fosco! I saw you nodding in time just now to 'Vieni! La mia vendetta.'"

But Pendergast said nothing, merely inclining his head slightly as the houselights came up and the intermission began.

{ 19 }

Nigel Cutforth threw back the covers and sat up in an empty bed. Eliza had taken exception to his little trip to Thailand and had gone off to stay with a girlfriend in the Village. Good fucking riddance.

He looked around. The bedside clock glowed 10:34 in red letters. *Jesus, only 10:30?* His plane left at six in the morning, and around eight he'd knocked back two fingers of gin and crawled into bed, desperate for a little sleep. But sleep had been slow to come. And now here he was, suddenly wide awake, sitting up in bed, heart beating hard. Christ, it was hot. He flapped the covers, trying to stir up the dead air of the room, but it seemed only to draw the heat closer around him. With another curse, he flicked on the light, swung his legs over the bed, and put his feet on the floor. At the rate he was going, the jet lag to Bangkok would be so bad he might just have to extend his vacation another week. But that would be hard to pull off: the fall was a big time in the cutthroat music business, and you had to stay vigilant.

He stood up, padded across the floor, and checked the thermostat. It was off, as he knew it would be, but the thermometer itself registered eighty-five degrees. He put his hand over the forced-air grating, but it felt cool to the touch. No heat there.

Heat. It was just what Grove had complained about.

He reminded himself again that this was the twenty-first century and that Grove had been insane in the closing days of his sorry life. He walked over to the balcony, ran back the heavy curtains, unlocked and slid open the glass door. A welcome stream of cool October air washed over him, and the faint sounds of traffic rose from below. Cutforth breathed deeply and stepped out onto the balcony, feeling sanity return. There was New York: solid, modern, rational New York. The buildings of Midtown stood like glowing ramparts against the night sky, and Fifth Avenue was like a brilliant stripe of moving light, changing from white to red as it passed below his window. He breathed again and, feeling the sweat chill on his skin, stepped back inside. The heat within seemed worse than ever, and now he felt a prickling sensation beginning to creep over his scalp and face and move down his limbs. It was very odd, like nothing he'd ever felt before, this sensation of heat and cold at the same time.

He was getting sick. That's what was happening. An early case of the flu.

He put on his slippers and walked out the bedroom, across the living room, to the wet bar. He jerked open the cabinet doors, pulled out the bottle of Bombay Sapphire, some ice, and a jar of olives, and mixed himself another drink. A Xanax, three Tylenol capsules, five vitamin C tablets, two fish-liver-oil pills, a selenium tablet, and three tabs of coral calcium followed, each washed down with a generous gulp of gin. After finishing the glass, he mixed himself another and went to the floor-to-ceiling windows of the living room. These windows looked east, past Madison and Park to the 59th Street Bridge and Roosevelt Island. Beyond lay the dark wasteland of Queens.

Cutforth was finding it hard to think. His skin was crawling with unpleasant sensations, as if he was covered with spiders that were scuttling around and nipping at him. Or bees, maybe: he felt like he was wearing one of those human bee cloaks, and the bees were moving around, not exactly stinging him, but prickling him with their dry hairy legs.

Grove had been crazy, he had to remind himself. Grove lost it completely, he'd succumbed to his own fantasies. Not surprising, given the kind of life he'd led. And then there was that other thing: the thing Cutforth never, *ever* wanted to think about again...

He shook this thought away furiously and took another slug of gin, feeling the liquor and the sedative starting to kick in. Under any other circumstance, it would be delightful, relaxing, a sensation of slowly drifting down. But it didn't seem to be doing anything about that itchy, hot, crawling sensation on his skin. He rubbed a hand on his arm. Dry and hot: his skin felt like sandpaper.

Grove had complained about a strange sensation of heat, too. That and the smell.

He tossed back the drink with a shaking hand. *Don't get paranoid, Nigel dear.* He was getting sick, that was all. He hadn't had his flu shot, and it was hitting him early this year. Great timing, on the eve of his departure for Thailand.

"Fuck," he said out loud. The drink was gone. Should he mix himself yet another? Why the hell not? He reached for the bottle, grasped it, filled the glass, and set it back down on the bar.

I am coming.

Cutforth spun around. The apartment was empty.

Who the fuck had spoken? It was a low voice, lower than a whisper; more like a vibration, sensed rather than heard.

He swallowed, licked dry lips. "Who's there?" His tongue felt thick and foreign, and he could barely get out the words.

No answer.

He turned, his full drink slopping over the sides of the glass and running down his hand. He raised the glass and sucked at it greedily. It couldn't be. He'd never believed in anything and wasn't about to start now. God didn't exist, the devil didn't exist, life was just some random shitstorm, and when you were dead, you were dead.

Maledicat dominus.

He jerked his head up, drink sloshing wildly. What was that, Latin? Was this some kind of joke? Where was it coming from? One of his crazy rap clients, being an asshole? Or, more likely, former client? There was one Haitian rapper in particular who had threatened revenge. This was probably him or his boys, trying to goad him into a premature heart attack with some voodoo nonsense.

"All right!" he called out. "That's enough with the bullshit."

Silence.

His skin crawled, unnaturally hot and dry. Suddenly, it didn't feel like nonsense anymore. It felt real.

It was happening to him. It *was* happening, like Grove had said.

He raised the shaking glass to his lips, swallowing, tasting nothing.

But it couldn't really be happening, could it? This was the twenty-first century. Grove must have been crazy, he *must* have. But, oh dear Jesus, those things the newspapers had hinted at...The cops weren't really saying much about how Grove had died, but the tabloids had been full of gossip about the body, burned from the inside, the marks of Lucifer on the walls.

Was it really possible, after all this time?

He let the half-finished drink fall to the floor and began casting desperately about. His late mother had given him a crucifix, which he'd kept around more as a memento than anything else. He'd seen it just last month. Where? He rushed back into his bedroom, to the walk-in closet, drew out a drawer with savage tugs, felt in the back. Cuff links, buttons, tiepins, coins rained to the floor.

No crucifix. Where was it?

He jerked open another drawer, then another, pawing roughly through watches, jewelry, gold. A sob escaped him.

The crucifix! He grasped it tightly, sobbing with relief, held it to his breast, crossing himself.

The sensation of being covered with crawling bees began to grow worse. Now it felt as if the bees were really stinging him, billions of agonizing little pricks.

"Go away! Get away!" He sobbed. *"Our Father, who art in heaven—"* God, how did it go?

The crucifix felt hot in his hands. Now his ears were buzzing. His throat felt as if it was caked with ash, as if he was choking on the hot air.

I am coming now.

He held out the crucifix in his shaking arms, this way and that, as if warding off something invisible. "Get thee behind me, Satan!" he shrieked.

The crucifix felt very hot now. It was burning his fingers. Everything was hot: his nightclothes, even his eyebrows and the hairs on his arms, felt as if they were crisping.

"Get away!"

He dropped the crucifix with a cry. To his utter terror, smoke began curling from it, burning a mark into the rug. He gasped for breath, hands scrabbling at his throat, gagging in the sulfurous air.

He had to get out. He had to find sanctuary. If he could get to a chapel, a church, anything, maybe he'd be safe...

He rushed for the door, but just before he put his hand on the doorknob, there came a knocking.

Cutforth froze, suspended between relief and fear. Who was it?

Maybe there was a fire? Yes, of course, that was it: the building was on fire, and an evacuation was under way. Something must have gone wrong with the sprinkler system. "I'm in here!" He sobbed, half in pain and half in relief. "In here!"

He grasped the doorknob, felt the searing pain of red-hot metal, jerked his hand away. *"Fuck!"*

He looked at his hand in disbelief. His palm was burned, smoking, and it cracked as he opened it, blood and clear matter welling from the fissure and running down his wrist. Left on the doorknob was a large piece of his skin, curling and frying in the heat like pork cracklings.

The knock came again: slow, steady, like the tolling of a bell.

"Help me!" Cutforth cried at the door. "There's a fire! *Fire!*"

He felt a sudden wave of pain along his skin, as if it was being peeled away, and then a grotesque feeling deep in his belly, as if someone had just stirred his guts for him. He lurched back. *He* was at the door. The feeling came again, a strange internal pressure, a terrible writhing of the intestines. He screamed, gripping his stomach, doubling over. He managed to stagger back into the bedroom. As he moved, little darts of pain raced across his skin and his eyes clouded with red mist. He could feel the terrible pressure mounting within him, and then all went black and the pressure became unbearable, and there was a sound like frying eggs and suddenly the pressure was gone and a hot wetness was running down his face.

He screamed, writhing on the floor, his legs beating a frenzied tattoo on the rug, his hands tearing at his nightclothes, his hair, trying to claw the skin from his own body because it was searingly hot, so unbearably hot...

Here I am here I am here.

{ 20 }

Letitia Dallbridge lay awake, motionless, rigid in her bed. At last, she arose in cool fury, slipped into a satin robe, flicked open her glasses, and put them on. Then she checked the time: 11:15. She compressed her lips. This was intolerable. Intolerable.

She picked up the building telephone and buzzed the desk; instantly a voice was on the line.

"May I help you, Mrs. Dallbridge?"

"You certainly may, Jason. The gentleman in the apartment directly above me, number 17B, has been thumping incessantly on the floor. Shouting as well. It's been going on and on, and I don't mind telling you, this is the second time this month I've had to complain. I am an old woman, and I simply *cannot* tolerate this kind of noise in the middle of the night."

"Yes, Mrs. Dallbridge, we'll take care of it immediately."

"I shall speak to the condominium board about this at the next meeting."

"I don't blame you, Mrs. Dallbridge."

"Thank you, Jason."

She laid down the phone and listened. True, the

thumping was fainter now; more irregular. In fact, it seemed to have stopped, along with the shouting. But it would pick up again soon—it always did. That dreadfully coarse music producer was having another party, no doubt. With drinking, dancing, drugs, all kinds of carrying-on. And on a weeknight, no less. She pulled her robe tighter around her narrow frame. There was no point trying to go back to sleep now—at her age, it would be an exercise in futility.

She crossed the living room into the kitchen, put a kettle of water on to boil. She removed a silver teapot, put three bags of chamomile inside, and waited for the whistle. When it came, she removed the kettle from the heat, poured the water into the teapot, and slipped a tea cozy over the pot to keep it hot. A silver teaspoon and two slices of buttered toast completed her *petit déjeuner.* She lifted the tray and returned to the bedroom. She glanced up darkly at the ceiling. Then she propped up her satin pillows and poured her tea.

The flowery aroma and the warmth of the liquid soon calmed her. Life was too short to allow oneself to be disturbed longer than necessary. It was now quiet as a tomb in the apartment above. No matter: she would take strong measures to ensure she wasn't awakened like this again.

She heard a faint noise and listened. A faint pattering. Raining again, it seemed. She would have to remember the Burberry when she went out that morning to...

The pattering grew louder. And now there was a smell like frying bacon in the air, faint but distinct. Like the rain, it grew steadily stronger. It was not a pleasant smell, either: it was repellent, like burnt meat. She sniffed, looking around. Had she left the stove on? Impossible, she hadn't even—

Plop! A huge greasy drop landed in the middle of her tea, splashing her. Then another fat drop, and another, splattering tea all over her face, her dressing gown, her beautiful satin puff.

She looked up in horror to see a stain on her bedroom ceiling. It was spreading fast. It glistened, oleaginous, in the dim light of her reading lamp.

Letitia Dallbridge snatched the phone out of its cradle, buzzed downstairs again.

"Yes, Mrs. Dallbridge?"

"Now there's a leak from the apartment above! It's coming right through the ceiling of my bedroom!"

"We're sending someone up immediately. We'll turn the water off in that apartment now."

"This is an outrage! My beautiful English puff is ruined! *Ruined!*"

Now the liquid was pattering down from the ceiling in several places, accumulating in the corners of the crown molding, even streaming down the Venetian chandelier in the middle of the ceiling. It was raining on her Louis Quinze chairs, the Chippendale highboy. Against her better judgment, she leaned forward and touched one of the brown splatters on the china cup with her finger. It was warm and greasy, like tallow or candle wax. She shrank in horror.

"It's not water," she cried. "It's some kind of *grease*!"

"Grease?"

"Yes! Grease! From the apartment above!"

There was some confused talk in the background,

then the voice came back on, a little breathless. "We're getting some alarms down here. It seems there may be a fire in the apartment above you, Mrs. Dallbridge. Listen carefully. Don't leave your apartment. If smoke begins to come under your front door, place a damp towel against it. Wait for instructions—"

The voice was cut off by the unbearably shrill sound of the fire alarm in the hall, followed by the even louder blare of the siren within her apartment. She dropped the phone, covering her ears. A moment later there was a snapping noise as the sprinklers went off, and suddenly the room was full of water, streaming everywhere.

Mrs. Dallbridge was in such a state of shock that she remained frozen as a statue, uncomprehending, while the spray slowly darkened her gown and her lovely bedspread and refilled the teacup on her tray with gray, chill water.

{ 21 }

The stench hanging in the apartment entrance helped warn D'Agosta what was in store. It only grew worse as he walked through the dwelling on his way to the master bedroom. He'd been half asleep when he entered the building's lobby—filling out the incident report on the gunfire he'd exchanged in Riverside Park had taken longer than expected—but he sure as hell wasn't asleep now. It was amazing the way that stench just cut through everything: took away the 2 A.M. grogginess, took away the aches in his joints, the pain of the skinned knees, the itch of the poison ivy he'd managed to roll through while evading the thugs.

He had seen a lot of unpleasant homicides in his day, but nothing could have prepared him for what lay on the floor beside the bed. It was a corpse, that much at least was clear: it had ruptured in a way he'd never seen before, the corpse unzipping itself from pubis to sternum, vomiting a shrunken tangle of burned and blackened organs. In an almost unconscious gesture, he reached up and touched the cross underneath his shirt, feeling its reassuring presence. If there was a devil, this was how he'd do it. This was definitely how he'd do it.

He glanced over at Pendergast and felt faintly gratified to see that even the great detective was looking whiter than usual. Pendergast's normal impulses to poke, pry, and sniff seemed to have deserted him. He stood there, dressed in white tie and tails, something almost like shock on his face.

The last of the SOC boys—the fingernail picker—came back around the corpse on his hands and knees, bristling with test tubes and tweezers and swabs. He looked pretty green, too, and those guys were a tough bunch. They were the ones who had to find the fibers and hairs, swab stains, pick up all the bits and pieces. Close-in work, real close.

The M.E. ducked in. "Finished?"

"I sure hope so."

Pendergast held out his shield. "Mind if I ask a few questions, Doctor?"

"Shoot."

"Do you have a cause of death?"

"Not yet. Heating, *burning*, is clear. But as for the cause . . . I have no idea."

"Accelerants?"

"Negative, at least prelim," the SOC man answered. "There are other anomalies. Note the lack of the pugilistic effect—there's none of the contraction of the arm muscles one usually sees in such severe burn cases. Note also the heat fracturing in the bones of the extremities. Nearer the center of the body, the bones have actually been calcined. Do you have any idea how hot a fire would have to be to cause this kind of damage? Well over the combustion threshold. And yet there was no room flashover. In fact, from the look of things, the fire never even *approached* flashover. The heat was localized to the body, and the body only."

"What kind of heat was applied?"

The doctor shook his head. "No idea yet."

"Spontaneous combustion?"

The doctor looked up sharply. "You mean, like Mary Reeser?"

"You know of that case, Doctor?"

"It's kind of a legend in medical school. A joke, really. I seem to recall the FBI handled it."

"Yes. And if the case file can be believed, SHC—spontaneous human combustion, as it's referred to—is far from being a joke."

The doctor gave a low, cynical laugh. "You FBI fellows and your acronyms. I don't believe you'll find 'SHC' in the *Merck Manual*, Mr. Pendergast."

"There is more in the world than is dreamt of in your philosophy, Doctor—or in the *Merck Manual.* I will send over the case file for your perusal."

"As you wish." The doctor departed with the SOC man, leaving them alone with the body.

D'Agosta removed his notebook and pen. Nothing was coming into his head, but he needed a way to take his eyes off the scene, and this was it. He roused himself and wrote, *October 23, 2:20 a.m., 842 Fifth Avenue, Apt. 17B, Cutforth.* The pen faltered as he tried to breathe only through his mouth. From now on, he was going to carry a jar of Vicks VapoRub with him always. On dates. On vacation. Out for bowling. Always.

He heard murmured voices in the living room:

detectives from Homicide. They'd been interviewing a maintenance worker outside the hall—away from the stench—and D'Agosta had been thankful to duck past them on entering the apartment. He didn't want any of his old pals seeing him with the Southampton P.D. patch and sergeant stripes on his shoulder.

His gaze focused back on the page of his notebook. His mind wasn't working. He gave up and raised his eyes.

Pendergast seemed to have overcome his revulsion and was now on his hands and knees, examining the corpse. Like the SOC guy, he had a glass test tube and a pair of tweezers in his hands—where did he keep all that stuff in such a narrow-tailored suit?—and was putting something into it, moving around with great care. Then he moved toward a wall, where he stopped to examine a scorched area with a magnifying glass. He spent so much time staring at it that D'Agosta began to stare, too. The paint of the scorched patch was browned and bubbled. There was no hoofprint that he could see, but as he stared a creeping sensation began to tickle its way up his spine and dig into his scalp. It was blurry, indistinct, but—damn—was it just like those inkblot tests, all in his mind?

Pendergast suddenly turned and caught his eye. "You see it, too?"

"I think so."

"What exactly do you see?"

"A face."

"What kind?"

"Ugly as shit, thick lips, big eyes, with a mouth open as if to bite."

"Or swallow?"

"Yeah, more like swallow."

"It's uncannily reminiscent of Vasari's fresco of the devil swallowing sinners. The one inside of the cupola of the Duomo."

"Yeah? I mean, yeah."

Pendergast stepped back thoughtfully. "Are you familiar with the story of Dr. Faustus?"

"Faustus? You mean, Faust? The guy who sold his soul to the devil?"

Pendergast nodded. "There are any number of variants of the story. Most come down to us in manuscript accounts written in the Middle Ages. While each account has its unique characteristics, they all involve a death similar to that of Mrs. Mary Reeser."

"The case you mentioned to the M.E. just now."

"Exactly. Spontaneous human combustion. The medievals called it *the fire within*."

D'Agosta nodded. His brain felt like lead.

"Here, with Nigel Cutforth, we seem to have a classic example. Even more so than with Grove."

"Are you telling me you think the devil claimed this guy?"

"I offer the observation without attaching any hypothesis."

D'Agosta shook his head. The whole thing was creepy. Seriously creepy. He felt his hand stealing toward his cross again. It *couldn't* be the work of the devil... could it?

"Good evening, gentlemen." The voice came from behind: female, a rich contralto, calm, efficient.

D'Agosta turned to see a woman framed in the doorway, dressed in a gray pinstripe suit with captain's bars on the collar of her white shirt. Several detectives were visible behind her. He took in the features: petite, thin, large breasts, glossy black hair framing a pale, almost delicate face. Her eyes were a rich blue. She looked no more than thirty-five: amazingly young for a full captain in the Homicide Division. She looked familiar. He knew her. The sick feeling returned. Maybe he'd been a little premature in congratulating himself that he wouldn't run into any of his old buddies.

"I'm Captain Hayward," she said briskly, looking at D'Agosta a little too intently for comfort—recognizing him too, it seemed. "I know you already presented credentials at the door, but may I see them again?"

"Certainly, Captain." Pendergast had his badge out in one elegant movement.

Hayward took it, examined it, looked up. "Mr. Pendergast."

Pendergast bowed. "It's a pleasure to see you again, Captain Hayward. May I congratulate you on your return to the force, and most particularly on making captain?"

Hayward let that pass without comment and turned back to D'Agosta. He had removed his shield for her, but she wasn't looking at it. She was looking at him.

The name brought it all back: Laura Hayward, who'd been a transit cop back in his former life, going to school at the time, writing some book on the underground homeless in Manhattan, working toward a graduate degree or something. They had worked together briefly on the Pamela Wisher case. That was when she was the sergeant and he a lieutenant. He felt his gut sink.

"And you must be Lieutenant Vincent D'Agosta."

"Sergeant Vincent D'Agosta these days." He felt himself coloring. He really didn't feel like making more explanations. It was a frigging disgrace and there was no way around it.

"*Sergeant* D'Agosta? No longer NYPD?"

"Southampton P.D. You know, as in Long Island. I'm the FBI liaison on the Grove case."

He looked up to find her hand out. He took it, gave it a desultory shake. The hand was warm, a little damp. It gave D'Agosta a secret satisfaction to note she wasn't quite as cool as she seemed.

"Glad to be working with you again." The voice was crisp, devoid of morbid curiosity. D'Agosta felt relieved. There would be no chitchat, no prying questions. Totally professional.

"I, for one, am happy to see the case in such capable hands," Pendergast said.

"Thank you."

"You always struck me as an officer who could be relied on to conduct a vigorous investigation."

"Thanks again. And if I can be frank, you always struck me as somebody who never worried much about the chain of command or who let the formalities of standard police procedure get in your way."

If Pendergast was surprised by this, he gave no sign. "True."

"Well then, let's get this chain of command clear at the outset—shall we?"

"Excellent idea."

"This is *my* case. Bench warrants, subpoenas, whatever must be cleared through my office first, unless we're dealing with an emergency. Any communication with the press will be coordinated through my office. Perhaps that's not how you operate, but that's how *I* operate."

Pendergast nodded. "Understood."

"People talk about how the FBI sometimes has trouble getting along with local law enforcement. That's not going to happen here. For one thing, we're not 'local law enforcement.' We're the New York Police Department, Homicide Division. We will work with the Federal Bureau of Investigation as full equals and in no other way."

"Certainly, Captain."

"We will, naturally, return the courtesy."

"I should expect no less."

"I do things by the book, even when the book is stupid. You know why? That's how we get the conviction. Any funny business at all, and a New York jury will acquit."

"True, very true," Pendergast said.

"Tomorrow morning, 8 A.M. sharp, and every Tuesday thereafter for the duration of the case, we'll be meeting at One Police Plaza, seventeenth-floor situation room, you, me, and Lieutenant—I mean Sergeant—D'Agosta. All cards on the table."

"Eight A.M.," Pendergast repeated.

"Coffee and Danish on us."

A look of distaste settled on Pendergast's features. "I shall have already breakfasted, thank you."

Hayward looked at her watch. "How much more time do you gentlemen need?"

"I believe five more minutes should do it," said Pendergast. "Any information you can share with us now?"

"An elderly woman in the apartment below was the witness, or as close as we have to a witness. The murder occurred shortly after eleven. She seems to have heard the deceased having convulsions and screaming. She assumed he was having a party." A dry smile flickered across her face. "It grew quiet. And then, at 11:22, a substance began leaking through her ceiling: melted adipose tissue from the deceased."

Melted adipose tissue. D'Agosta began to write this down, then stopped. It didn't seem likely he'd forget it.

"About the same time, the smoke alarms and sprinklers went off—that would be at 11:24 and 11:25 respectively. Maintenance went up to check, found the door locked, no answer, and a foul smell emanating from the apartment. They opened the door with a master key at 11:29 and found the deceased as you see him now. The temperature in the apartment was almost one hundred degrees when we arrived, fifteen minutes later."

D'Agosta exchanged a glance with Pendergast. "Tell me about the adjacent neighbors."

"The man above heard nothing until the alarms went off but complained of a bad smell. There are only two apartments on this floor: the other one has been purchased but is still empty. The new owner is an Englishman, a Mr. Aspern." She pulled a pad from her breast pocket, scribbled something on it, and handed it to Pendergast. "Here are their names. Aspern is currently in England. Mr. Roland Beard is in the apartment above, and Letitia Dallbridge is in the apartment below. Do you wish to interview either of them now?"

"Not necessary." Pendergast glanced at her, then looked at the burn mark on the wall.

Hayward's lip curled, whether in amusement or something else D'Agosta wasn't sure. "You noticed it, I see."

"I did. Any thoughts?"

"Wasn't it you, Mr. Pendergast, who once cautioned me against forming premature hypotheses?"

Pendergast returned the smile. "You learned well."

"I learned from a master." She looked at D'Agosta as she spoke.

There was a brief silence.

"I'll leave you to it, gentlemen." She nodded to her men, who followed her out the door.

Pendergast turned to D'Agosta. "It seems our Laura Hayward has grown up, don't you think?"

D'Agosta simply nodded.

{ 22 }

Bryce Harriman stood on the corner of Fifth Avenue and 67th Street, staring up at one of those anonymous white-brick high-rises that infested the Upper East Side. It was a gray Tuesday afternoon, and Harriman had the dull ache of an old hangover pulsing somewhere behind his eyeballs. His editor, Ritts, had chewed him out for not covering the story the night before. Well, he wasn't on call, like a doctor, was he? He sure as hell wasn't being paid enough to go out sniffing up copy at three o'clock in the morning. And besides, he'd been in no condition to cover a murder. It was all he could do to find his way home on the subway.

He thought there might be some stragglers, but what he'd found instead was a crowd, generated by morning television news and the Internet. Here it was, past two in the afternoon, but at least a hundred people had converged on the block—rubberneckers, Goths, white witches, East Village weirdos, even a few Hare Krishnas, which he hadn't seen in New York in at least half a dozen years. Didn't any of these people have jobs? To his right, a bunch of satanists wearing what looked like medieval robes were drawing pentagrams on the sidewalk and chanting. To his left, a group of nuns were praying on their rosaries. A bunch of teenyboppers were holding a vigil, candles burning despite the time of day, singing to the accompaniment of a strummed guitar. It was unbelievable, something out of a Fellini film.

As he looked around, Harriman felt a swelling of excitement. He'd scored a mild success the week before with his piece about the Grove murder. Yet there had been little evidence to go on, and his story had been long on lurid speculation. But now he was here on the heels of a second murder—a murder that, from the whispered rumors that surged through the crowd like electricity, was even worse. Maybe his editor was right. Maybe he should have been here in the wee hours of the morning, despite all the single-malt Scotch he had unwisely imbibed at the Algonquin with his buddies the night before.

Another thought occurred to Harriman. This was his chance to stick it to his old nemesis Bill Smithback, busy dipping his wick on his honeymoon. Angkor Wat, of all places. Smithback, that bastard, who now had his old spot at the *Times*—not through brilliant journalism, or even just plain old pavement-pounding, but through sheer dumb luck. He'd happened to be at the right place at the right time, not once, but several times: during the subway murders a couple years back, and then again just last fall, with the Surgeon murders. That last was particularly bitter: Harriman owned the story—he'd already beaten Smithback to the punch—but then that stupid police captain, Custer, had stuffed him with false leads...

It wasn't fair. It was Harriman's connections that had gotten him the job at the *Times*, that and his distinguished last name. Harriman was the one—with his carefully pressed Brooks Brothers suits and his repp ties—who belonged in the rarefied and elevated atmosphere of the *Times*. Not rumpled, slovenly Smithback, who had been quite at home among the bottom-feeders at the *Post*...

Water under the bridge. Now this was hot and Smithback was ten thousand miles away. If the killings went on—and Harriman fervently hoped they would—the story would only get bigger. There might be television opportunities, magazine articles, a big book contract. Maybe even a Pulitzer. With any luck, the Times would be only too happy to get him back.

He was jostled by an old man in a wizard costume, gave a hard shove back. There was an almost hysterical frenzy to the crowd Harriman had never seen before, a potentially dangerous mixture if you stopped to think about it: volatile, like a tinderbox.

There was a sudden noise off to one side, and Harriman looked over. Some Elvis impersonator in gold lamé—a halfway-decent-looking one, for a change—was blaring "Burning Love" with the aid of a portable karaoke machine:

"I feel my temperature rising."

The crowd was growing noisier, more restless. Now and then Harriman could hear the distant shriek of a police siren.

"Lord Almighty, I'm burning a hole where I lay."

He had his tape recorder ready; he could pick up some color to add to what he already had on the murder itself. He looked around. There was a guy at his elbow, in leather boots and a Stetson, carrying a crystal wand in one hand and a live hamster in the other. Nah: too weird. Someone more representative. Like that kid with the Mohawk not far away, in black. A pimply middle-class suburban kid trying to be different.

"Excuse me!" He elbowed his way toward the youth. "Excuse me! *New York Post.* Can I ask a few questions?"

The kid looked toward him, eyes lighting up. They were all so eager for their fifteen nanoseconds of fame.

"Why are you here?"

"Haven't you heard? The devil has come!" The kid's face positively shone. "Some guy up there. He's just like the one out on Long Island. The devil took his soul, fried him to a crisp! Dragged him down to hell, kicking and screaming."

"How'd you hear about this?"

"It's all over the Web."

"By why are *you*, personally, here?"

The kid looked at him as if the question was idiotic. "Why do you think? To pay my respects to the Man in Red."

Now a group of aging hippies started to sing "Sympathy for the Devil" in cracked falsettos. The smell of pot wafted toward him. Harriman struggled to hear, to think, amidst the hubbub. "Where are you from?"

"Me and my buddies came over from Fort Lee." Some of his "buddies" were now crowding around, all dressed exactly like he was. "Who's this guy?" one asked.

"Reporter from the *Post.*"

"No kidding."

"Take my picture!"

To pay my respects to the Man in Red. There was his quote. Time to wrap it up. "Name? Spell it."

"Shawn O'Connor."

"Age?"

"Fourteen."

Unbelievable. "Okay, Shawn, one last question. Why the devil? What's so important about the devil?"

"He's the *man*!" he whooped, and his friends took up the cry, high-fiving each other. "The *man*!"

Harriman moved off. God, the world was full of morons; they were breeding like rabbits, especially in New Jersey. Now he needed a contrast, someone who took all this seriously. A priest—he needed a priest. Just his luck: there were two men with collars, quiet, standing not far away.

"Excuse me!" he called out, forcing his way toward them through the growing crowd. As the two turned to him, Harriman was taken aback by the expressions on their faces. Fear, real fear, mingled with the sorrow and pain.

"Harriman with the *Post*. May I ask what you're doing here?"

The older of the two men stepped forward. He had a lot of dignity; he really seemed out of place in this hysteria. "We're bearing witness."

"Witness to what?"

"The last earthly days." The way the man said it sent a flurry of goose bumps along Harriman's spine.

"You really think the world's coming to an end?"

The man quoted solemnly: "'Babylon the great is fallen, is fallen, and is become the habitation of devils, and the hold of every foul spirit.'"

The other, younger man nodded. "'She shall be utterly burned with fire: for strong is the Lord God who judgeth her. And the kings of the earth, who have committed fornication and lived deliciously with her, shall bewail her, and lament for her, when they shall see the smoke of her burning.'"

"'Alas, alas, that great city Babylon, that mighty city!'" the first priest went on. "'For in one hour is thy judgment come.'"

Harriman had drawn out his pad and was scribbling to get this down, but the first priest laid a gentle hand over his. "Revelation, chapter 18."

"Right, thanks. What church are you from?"

"Our Lady of Long Island City."

"Thanks." Harriman got their names and backed away hastily, tucking his notebook into his pocket. Their calmness, their certitude, spooked him more than all the hysteria around him.

There was a stirring along one edge of the crowd. A small convoy of police cars was approaching, lights flashing. There was a sudden eruption of flashes and television lights. He pushed forward, brutally shoving his way through a group of soundmen: he was Harriman of the *Post*, he wasn't going to sit at the back of the class. But the crowd itself was now surging forward, desperate for news.

A woman had stepped out of an unmarked cruiser at the rear of the convoy, dressed in a suit but with a shield riding shotgun on what looked like an amazing set of knockers: a really good-looking young woman, with a bunch of men now falling into place behind her. Young, but clearly in charge. It looked to Harriman like she didn't want to talk to the crowd at all, but needed to take charge before things grew any uglier.

She positioned herself behind a barricade of uniformed cops and held up her hand against the clamor of the press.

"Five minutes for questions. Then this crowd is going to have to disband."

More incoherent yelling as a thicket of boom microphones was thrust forward.

She waited, surveying the crowd, while the shouting continued. Finally she checked her watch and spoke again. "Four minutes."

That shut up the rows of press. The rest—the party people, the witches and satanists, the weirdos with crystals or perfumes—realized something interesting was about to happen and quieted down a little as well.

"I'm Captain Laura Hayward of NYPD Homicide." She spoke in a clear but soft voice, which forced the crowd to quiet further, straining to listen. "The deceased is Nigel Cutforth, who died at approximately 11:15 last night. Cause of death is unknown at this point, but homicide is suspected."

Tell me something new, Harriman said to himself.

"I'll take a few questions now," she said. There was an eruption of shouting, and she pointed at one frantically waving journalist.

The questions tumbled out. "Have the police noted connections between this and the death of Jeremy Grove? Are there similarities? Differences?"

A wry smile appeared on her lips. "We have. Yes and yes. Next?"

"Any suspects?"

"Not at this point."

"Was there a burned hoofprint or any other sign of the devil?"

"No hoofprint."

"We heard there was a face scorched into the wall?"

The smile left the woman's face briefly. "It was an irregular blotch that suggested a face to some."

"What kind of face?"

The wry smile. "Those who've claimed to see the face have labeled it ugly."

This caused a renewed clamor.

"Is it the face of the devil? Horns? Did it have horns?" These questions were shouted simultaneously by a dozen people. The mikes boomed in closer, knocking against each other.

"Not having seen the devil," Hayward answered, "I can't say. There were no horns I'm aware of."

Harriman scribbled frantically in his notebook. A bunch of reporters were now asking if she thought it was the devil, but she was ignoring this. Oh my God, was that Geraldo shouting over there? He definitely should've been here last night.

"Was it the devil? What's your opinion?" was cried from several quarters at once.

She held up a hand. "I'd like to answer that question."

That really shut them up.

"We have enough flesh-and-blood devils in this town, thank you, that we don't need to conjure up any supernatural ones."

"So how did he die?" a reporter shouted. "What were the injuries caused by? Was he cooked, like the other one?"

"An autopsy is currently under way. We'll be able to tell you more when it's completed." She was talking calmly and rationally, but Harriman wasn't fooled. The NYPD didn't even begin to have a handle on the case—and he'd be saying as much in his story.

"Thank you," she was saying, "and good afternoon. Now, let's break it up, people."

More clamor. More police were arriving and working to control the crowd at last, pushing them back, setting up barricades, directing traffic.

Harriman turned away, already writing the lead in his head. This was one hell of a story. At last—at long, long last—he was going to get a run for his money.

{ 23 }

As the vintage Rolls-Royce approached the gates of the East Cove Yacht Harbor, D'Agosta shifted in the backseat, staring out the window, trying to forget just how stiff and sore he felt. What with Cutforth's murder and all the attendant crime-scene business, he couldn't have gotten more than two hours' sleep.

For this particular errand, Pendergast had left his chauffeur, Proctor, behind, preferring to drive the big car himself. It was a beautiful fall day, and the morning sun shimmered on the bay like silver coins tossed on the waves. The Staten Island ferry was lumbering out of its berth, churning the water behind, flags snapping, trailed by a screaming flock of seagulls. The blue hump of Staten Island rose on the horizon, grading imperceptibly into the low outline of New Jersey. The smell of salt air flowed in the open windows.

D'Agosta turned his gaze toward the marina. A wall kept the gaze of the vulgar from the ranks of gleaming yachts, but from the top of Coenties Slip you could still see them lined up in their berths, splendid and sparkling in the bright sun.

"You're never going to get in without a warrant," said D'Agosta. "I talked to Bullard. I know what the guy's like."

"We shall see," said Pendergast. "I always prefer to start with a gentle approach."

"And if the gentle approach doesn't work?"

"Firmer measures might be in order."

D'Agosta wondered what Pendergast's idea of "firmer" was.

Pendergast slowed the Rolls and, turning to a custom-built cherrywood bay beside the driver's seat, tapped on the keys of the laptop set within it. They were approaching the chain-link gate leading into the marina's general parking area, but the man in the guardhouse had seen the Rolls approaching and was already opening the gate. Pendergast stopped the car just inside the lot, where they had a good view of the Upper Bay. On the screen of the laptop, the image of a magnificent yacht had appeared.

It didn't take long to locate the real thing among the forest of masts and spars riding at anchor just beyond the lot.

D'Agosta whistled. "That's some boat."

"Indeed. A 2003 Feadship motor yacht with a de Voogt custom-designed hull. Fifty-two meters in length, with a displacement of seven hundred and forty metric tons. Twin Caterpillar 2,500-horsepower diesels, cruising speed thirty knots. It's got enormous range and it's extremely comfortable."

"How much?"

"Bullard paid forty-eight million for it."

"Jesus. What does he need a boat like that for?"

"Perhaps he doesn't care for flying. Or perhaps he likes to operate away from prying ears and eyes. A boat like that makes keeping to international waters easy indeed."

"Funny, in the last interview with Bullard, I had the impression that he was anxious not to be detained in the country. That maybe he was planning an international trip."

Pendergast looked at him sharply. "Indeed?" He eased the car toward the second layer of security: the gate into VIP parking, manned by a pugnacious little redheaded security guard with a jutting chin. D'Agosta immediately knew the type. He was the kind who made it a point not to be impressed by anyone or anything: not even a '59 Rolls-Royce Silver Wraith.

"Yeah?"

Pendergast hung his shield out the window. "We're here to see Mr. Locke Bullard."

The man looked at the badge, looked back at Pendergast. His face was creased with suspicion. "And him?"

D'Agosta passed his own badge to the man.

"What's it about?"

"Police business."

"I gotta call."

The man took the shields back into his cubicle, got on the horn, spoke for a few minutes, came back with the badges and a cordless phone.

"He wants to talk to somebody named D'Agosta."

"That's me."

The man handed him the phone.

"D'Agosta here."

Bullard's deep voice filled the wire. "I figured you'd be back."

At the sound of the voice, D'Agosta immediately felt himself bristle. This was the man who had tried to humiliate him at the Athletic Club; who, just perhaps, had very nearly gotten him shot. Nevertheless, he tried hard to check his temper. "We can either do this nicely," he said as evenly as possible, "or it can get unpleasant. Up to you, Bullard."

A burst of laughter sounded at the other end. "You tried that same stale line on me back at the club. Let me tell you something. Since we had that pleasant little chat, I've had my people check into you. And now I know all about you. I got every sordid detail of your existence. For example, I know all about that wife of yours in Canada, the one who's been playing hide the salami behind your back these past six months. The guy's name is Chester Dominic, and he sells Winnebagos out of Edgewater—and hey, maybe she's doing him right now. Think about *that*, huh?"

D'Agosta's hand tightened around the phone.

"I also got the sales figures on your novels. Last one sold 6,215 copies. Hardcover *and* paperback. And that's counting all the copies your mother bought. Watch your back, Stephen King!" More harsh laughter. "Then I got your personnel files from your stint with the NYPD, including your disciplinary records. Interesting reading. And I got your medical and psychiatric records, too, even the ones from Canada. Too bad about those hard-on problems. Maybe that's why your wife's spreading her charms for old Chet. And depression, gee, that's tough. Did you take your Zoloft this morning? Amazing what you can find out when you own an HMO, isn't it? Reading all this over, a couple of phrases come to mind. Phrases like broken-down. Washed-up. Loser."

A thin curtain of red seemed to drop before D'Agosta's eyes. "You've just made the mistake of your life, Bullard."

More laughter and the line went dead.

D'Agosta handed the phone back to the attendant. His face was on fire. The son of a bitch. The son of a *bitch.* It was illegal—wasn't it? Digging up that kind of personal information. Bullard had been speaking loudly, and D'Agosta wondered if his voice had carried as far as Pendergast. He swallowed, fought hard to master his rising rage.

"You're blocking the gate," said the man in the booth. Then, as an afterthought, he added, "Sir."

"We'll drive around the block," Pendergast told the attendant, "and give Mr. Bullard time to change his mind."

"He's not going to change his mind."

Pendergast gave the attendant a long, sympathetic look. "You'll know when to step aside, I hope? For your own sake, of course."

"What do you mean?"

Without waiting for an answer, Pendergast put the Rolls in reverse and hit the gas, leaving a satisfying patch of rubber. He turned around in the parking lot, then nosed out onto State Street. He glanced over at D'Agosta. "Are you all right, Vincent?"

"I'm fine," D'Agosta said through gritted teeth.

Pendergast turned right and began circling the block. "Mr. Bullard, it seems, needs a firmer hand."

"Yeah."

Pendergast reached down with one hand and punched in a number on the in-dash cell phone.

A ring sounded over the speaker, then the phone was answered by a familiar voice. “Captain Hayward.”

“Captain? It’s Pendergast. We’re going to need that subpoena and warrant I called you about this morning.”

“On what grounds?”

“Refusal to cooperate. Imminent flight risk.”

“Come on. Bullard’s not some Colombian drug dealer or Middle Eastern terrorist. He’s a leading American industrialist.”

“Yes, with overseas accounts and overseas factories, who happens to be on his yacht, fueled to its maximum capacity and fully stocked for a transatlantic voyage. He can reach Canada, Mexico, South America, or Europe on one tank—take your pick.”

There was a sigh. “He’s an American. He’s got a passport. He’s free to leave.”

“He’s an uncooperative witness. He won’t answer questions.”

“A lot of people won’t answer questions.”

“Both Grove and Cutforth called him just before they were murdered. There’s a connection, and we need to find it.”

Another irritated sigh. “This is just the kind of irregular operation that looks bad in court.”

“He threatened Sergeant D’Agosta.”

“He did?” Her voice sounded a little sharper.

“An implied blackmail threat over personal information he collected through Northern HealthAtlantic Management, the HMO he owns.”

So he did hear, D'Agosta thought.

"That right?" There was a pause. "All right, then, go ahead. The papers are all ready and just need to be signed."

"Excellent." Pendergast gave a fax number.

"Agent Pendergast?"

"Yes?"

"Don't make a hash of this. I care about my career."

"I care about it, too."

The fax peeled out of the tiny impact printer just as they rounded Pearl Street and headed back toward the yacht harbor. Driving slowly through the outer lot, Pendergast tore it from the printer and handed it to the VIP attendant.

"You again?" the man said as he took the fax.

Pendergast smiled, put his fingers to his lips. "Not a word to Bullard."

The man read the fax, handed it back. There was something in his face that, perhaps, didn't look entirely displeased at the turn of events.

"Time to step aside," said Pendergast quietly.

"Yes, sir."

They parked in the VIP lot, and Pendergast opened the trunk. He gestured to D'Agosta. "For you."

D'Agosta peered in. A federal-issue battering ram lay inside, black and ugly and about three feet long, the kind DEA agents used in drug busts.

"You got to be kidding."

"Firmness, my dear Vincent," said Pendergast, smiling faintly.

D'Agosta grabbed the ram by its two handles and hefted it out. They headed down the walkway to the central dock. Ahead and to one side, tethered in its own private slip, the yacht loomed bigger than life: white with three enclosed decks, dozens of smoked windows, and a conning tower bristling with electronics. The name *Stormcloud* was stenciled on the stern.

"What about crew?" D'Agosta asked.

"My information is that Bullard's alone."

The private slip had its own dock behind a locked gate. Pendergast knelt before it, raising his hands to the lock. It looked to D'Agosta as if the FBI agent was just testing the lock to see if it might be ajar. Perhaps it was, because the gate swung open obediently in his hands.

"We need to be *brisk*," said Pendergast as he rose.

D'Agosta humped himself forward, lugging the ram. Despite renewed sessions in the gym since the gunfight in the park, he was still out of shape, the ram weighed at least forty pounds, and his bruised limbs protested with each thudding step. The gangplank of the *Stormcloud* was up, but in the rear, a locked boarding hatch lay just at dock level. Pendergast stopped, plucked his custom Les Baer .45 from his jacket, and stepped back, gesturing toward the hatch.

"After you, Vincent," he said.

D'Agosta reached deep down in his memory. What had they taught him at the Academy? *Don't run at the door, swing it into the door.* He took a deep breath, gripped the handles as tightly as he could, and heaved the ram forward. The door flew inward with a satisfying smack. Pendergast ducked inside, gun ready, and D'Agosta clambered in behind.

They were in a narrow corridor, with painted bulkheads along one side and smoked-glass windows along the other. Pendergast threw open a door set into the bulkheads, and suddenly they were in the grand salon of the boat, cocooned in plush cream carpeting with black lacquered tables piped in gold trim.

"FBI!" Pendergast barked. "Freeze!"

Bullard stood in the center of the room, wearing a pale blue warm-up suit, cigar in hand, with a look of complete astonishment and—it seemed to D'Agosta—momentary terror.

"Don't move!"

Bullard recovered immediately, his face reddening, the veins pulsing in his neck. Surprise gave way to ill-concealed rage. He raised the cigar to his thick lips, sucked in a lungful, exhaled. "So. The sorry fuck brought backup."

"Keep your hands in view," Pendergast warned as he advanced, gun aimed.

Bullard spread his hands. "Here's a scene for your next novel, D'Agosta. Bet you never saw anything like this boat in that slum you grew up in on Carmine Street, with a cheap, poolroom-hustling cop for a father and a mother who—"

D'Agosta rushed at the man but Pendergast was even quicker, interposing himself with lightning speed. "Sergeant, don't give him what he wants."

D'Agosta took a strangled breath. He could hardly breathe.

"Come on," Bullard sneered. "Let's see if there's anything at all hanging under that belly of yours. I'm sixty, and I could take your fat ass with one hand."

Pendergast held D'Agosta's gaze, shaking his head slowly. D'Agosta swallowed, stepped back.

Pendergast turned and fastened his silvery eyes on Bullard.

"And look at this, an undertaker playing FBI. White trash from the Deep South. *Very* white, it seems."

"At your service," Pendergast said quietly.

Bullard laughed and swelled like a black mamba, stretching the fabric of the warm-up suit. He still had his cigar tucked between two huge spatulate fingers, and now he stoppered the laugh by inserting it between his lips again and blowing a cloud of smoke in their direction.

Pendergast dropped the fax on an ebony table. Then he pointed to a large lacquered panel in the far wall. "Sergeant, open that panel, please."

"Just one goddamn minute, you need a warrant—"

Pendergast pointed a slender finger at the fax. "Read."

"I want my lawyer."

"First, we will secure the premises and obtain the evidence outlined in the warrant. One misstep will mean cuffs and an obstruction-of-justice charge. Is there anyone else on the boat with you?"

"Fuck you."

D'Agosta went to the panel that Pendergast pointed to, pressed the lone button. The panel slid back to reveal a wall of electronics, a monitor, and a keyboard.

"Seize the CPU."

D'Agosta pushed the monitor to one side, followed its cabling, and found the box tucked into a niche beneath.

"Don't you touch my computer."

Pendergast nodded toward the table. "It's listed in the warrant, Mr. Bullard."

D'Agosta yanked the cabling free with a satisfying jerk and hauled out the CPU. He dug into his pocket, pasted evidence labels over the drive bays and the plugs for the mouse and keyboard, set down the box, crossed his arms.

"Are you armed?" Pendergast asked Bullard.

"Of course not."

Pendergast tucked his Les Baer back into his suit. "All right," he said, voice low and suddenly pleasant, the southern accent rising like cream. "In addition to the warrant, there's a subpoena, Mr. Bullard, which I suggest you read."

"I want my lawyer."

"Naturally. We're going to take you to One Police Plaza and question you under oath. You may have a lawyer present at that time."

"I'm calling my lawyer now."

"You will *remain* in the center of the room with your hands in view at all times. You do not have a right to call a lawyer just because you feel like it. When appropriate, you will be *permitted* to call."

"My ass. You have no jurisdiction. I'll pull your badge and eat you for lunch, you albino prick. You have no idea who you're dealing with."

"I am sure your lawyer would advise you to dispense with the small talk."

"I'm not going to One Police Plaza."

Pendergast unclipped his police radio. "Manhattan South? To whom am I speaking, please? Shirley? This is Special Agent Pendergast of the Federal Bureau of Investigation. I'm at the East Cove Yacht Harbor, on the yacht of Mr. Locke Bullard—"

"You shut that radio off right now."

Pendergast's smooth voice continued. "That's right, Locke Bullard, on his yacht, the *Stormcloud*. We're taking him in for questioning in the Grove and Cutforth murder investigations."

D'Agosta watched Bullard go white. No doubt he knew that every news organization in New York monitored the police frequencies.

"No, he's not a suspect. I repeat: *not* a suspect."

The very emphasis Pendergast placed on the word had the curious effect of giving precisely the opposite impression.

Bullard glowered at them from beneath his beetled, Cro-Magnon brow, swallowed, made an effort to seem reasonable. "Look, Pendergast, there's no reason to play tough cop."

"Shirley, we're going to need backup, crowd control, and a squad car with escort to take Mr. Bullard downtown. That's right. Three should do it. On second thought, make it four. We're dealing with a well-known personality. It's likely to get busy."

Pendergast slipped the radio back into his suit, removed his cell phone, and tossed it to Bullard. "Now you may call your lawyer. One Police Plaza, interrogation section, basement floor, in forty minutes. We'll supply the coffee."

"You prick." Bullard dialed, spoke in low tones. When he was done, he handed the phone back to Pendergast.

"I imagine he just told you what I already advised: to keep your mouth firmly closed." Pendergast smiled.

Bullard said nothing.

Now Pendergast began poking around the grand salon, in a desultory kind of way, peeking here and there, admiring the sporting prints on the walls. It was almost as if he was killing time.

"Are we going?" Bullard finally burst out.

"He's talking again," said D'Agosta.

Pendergast nodded absently. "It seems our Mr. Bullard is a man who doesn't listen to his minders."

Bullard fell silent, his body shaking with malevolence.

"I think we need more time in here, Sergeant. Just to check things over, you understand."

"Right." Though he was still steaming, D'Agosta found he had to conceal a smile. Now he realized what Pendergast was up to.

Pendergast continued strolling about the room, adjusting a newspaper here, looking at a framed lithograph there. Ten more minutes passed as Bullard grew increasingly restive. Now D'Agosta began to hear faint sirens, the distant squawk of a bullhorn. Pendergast picked up a copy of *Fortune*, flipped through it, laid it back down. He checked his watch. "Do you see anything of interest I might have missed, Sergeant D'Agosta?"

"Have you checked the photo album?"

"An excellent idea." Pendergast opened the album, flipped through it. At a couple of pages, his hand paused and an intent look came into his face. He seemed to be memorizing faces; at least, it seemed so to D'Agosta.

He shut it with a sigh. "Shall we, Mr. Bullard?"

The man turned and shrugged into a windbreaker, his face dark. Pendergast led the way, followed by Bullard. D'Agosta brought up the rear, battering ram over his shoulder. As they stepped out of the hatch onto the dock, the crowd noise increased dramatically. There was shouting, the whoops of police sirens, the megaphoned voice of an official. Beyond the gates, photographers were jockeying for position. The police were struggling to clear a lane for their vehicles to pass.

Seeing this, Bullard stopped short. "You bastard." He almost spat the words at Pendergast. "You delayed deliberately, letting this build."

"Why hide your light under a bushel, Mr. Bullard?"

"Yeah," said D'Agosta. "And you're going to look great on the cover of the *Daily News* with your windbreaker draped over your head."

{ 24 }

Bryce Harriman headed back uptown behind the wheel of a *Post* press vehicle. The scene at the lower Manhattan marina had been a disaster. Except for a few rubber-neckers, it was New York City press at their finest—swearing, pushing, shoving. It reminded Harriman of the running of the bulls at Pamplona. What a waste of time. Nobody had answered questions, nobody knew anything, nothing but chaos and shouting. He should have gone straight back to his office to write up the scene of Cutforth's murder rather than wasting time chasing this radio call.

Ahead, the traffic coming in from West Street began to bunch up. He cursed, leaned on his horn. He should've taken the subway. At this rate, he wouldn't reach the office until after five, and he had to file by ten to make the morning edition.

He wrote and rewrote the lead, tearing it up again and again in his head. He thought back to the mob scene in front of Cutforth's apartment building earlier that afternoon. Those were the people he was writing for: people desperate for the story, hungry for it. And he had an open field, with Smithback gone and the *Times* treating the story as a kind of local embarrassment.

Cutforth's murder would be good for one headline, maybe two. But still, he was bound by the whim of the murderer, and there was no way of telling when—or if—the murderer would strike again. He *had* to have something new.

The traffic parted slightly and he switched lanes, flipping a bird at the blaring horn behind him, switched back, risking his life and those of half a dozen others to get one car length ahead. Flipped another bird. People were such assholes...

...And then it came to him. The fresh angle. What he needed was an expert to explain, to put it all in perspective. But who? Just as quickly the answer, the second stroke of genius, came as well.

He picked up his cell, dialed his office. "Iris, what's up?"

"What's up yourself?" his assistant retorted. "I've been as busy as a one-legged man at an ass-kicking contest answering the phones around here."

Harriman winced at the jokey, familiar tone she had taken with him. He was supposed to be the boss, not the secretary in the next cubicle.

"You want your messages?" she asked.

"No. Listen, I want you to get ahold of somebody for me, that researcher into the paranormal, what's his name, Monk, or Munch, something German. He had that Discovery Channel special on exorcism, remember? Yes, that's the one. No, I don't *care* how long it takes. Just get him for me."

He punched the call off and tossed the phone on the passenger seat, sat back, and smiled, letting the cacophony of honks, toots, and beeps that surrounded his car wash over him like a symphony.

{ 25 }

D'Agosta had to admire the genius that went into maintain-ing the interrogation section of One Police Plaza. It was perhaps the last place you could smoke in New York City without being arrested, and as a result, the painted cinder-block walls sported a tarry, brownish sheen. They made a point of keeping them grimy. The air was so dead and stale it felt like there must be a corpse hidden somewhere. And the linoleum floor was so old it could have been peeled up and put in a glass case in the Smithsonian.

D'Agosta felt a certain satisfaction in the surroundings. Locke Bullard, still dressed in blue warm-ups and deck shoes, sat in a chair at the greasy metal table, his eyes bloodshot with anger. Pendergast sat across from him, and D'Agosta stood behind, near the door. The civilian interrogations administrator—a mandatory presence these days—stood by the video camera, sucking in his belly and trying to look officious. They were all waiting on Bullard's lawyer, stuck somewhere in the traffic of their own making.

The door opened and Captain Hayward stepped

in. As she did so, D'Agosta felt the temperature in the room go down by about twenty degrees. She fastened cold eyes on Pendergast, then on D'Agosta, and motioned them to follow her into the hall.

She led the way to a disused office, ushered them in, closed the door. "Whose idea was the media circus?" she demanded.

"Unfortunately it was the only way," Pendergast answered.

"Don't give me that. This was staged, and you were both producer and director. There must be fifty press outside, every last one following you over from the marina. This is *exactly* what I didn't want to happen, the kind of hullabaloo I warned you against creating."

Pendergast spoke calmly. "Captain, I can assure you that Bullard left us no choice. For a moment, I thought I would have to handcuff him."

"You should've scheduled a meeting on the boat with his lawyer, so he wouldn't feel ambushed and defensive."

"There's a good chance that more advance warning would have caused him to flee the country."

Hayward expelled an irritated stream of air. "I'm a captain of detectives in the New York City police force. This is my case. Bullard's not a suspect and will *not* be treated as such." She swiveled to face D'Agosta. "You're going to manage the questioning, Sergeant. I want Special Agent Pendergast to remain well in the background with his mouth shut. He's caused enough trouble as it is."

"As you wish," Pendergast said politely to Hayward's turned back.

When they stepped back into the interrogation room, Bullard rose to his feet, pointing to Pendergast. "You're going to pay for this, both you and your fat fuck gofer here."

"Did you get that on videotape?" Hayward calmly asked the civilian administrator.

"Yes, ma'am. Tape's been rolling since he arrived."

She nodded. Bullard's pupils were pinpoints of hatred.

Silence fell, broken at last by a knock at the door.

"Come in," Hayward called.

The door opened, and a uniformed policeman admitted a man dressed in a charcoal suit. He had short-cropped gray hair, gray eyes, and a pleasant, friendly face. D'Agosta noticed the glint of a half-hidden cross beneath the officer's blue shirt as he turned and closed the door. *Hayward may not believe in the devil*, he thought, *but not all her minions have gotten the message.*

"Finally!" Bullard roared out, staring at the lawyer. "Jesus Christ, George, I called you forty minutes ago. Get me the hell out of here."

The lawyer, unruffled, greeted Bullard as if they were all at a cocktail party. Then he turned and shook Pendergast's hand. "George Marchand of Marchand & Quisling. I represent Mr. Bullard." His voice was almost musical in its pleasantness, but his eyes lingered first over Hayward's badge, then D'Agosta's.

"This is my colleague Sergeant D'Agosta."

"How do you do?"

There was a silence as Marchand turned his cool eyes around the room. "The subpoena?"

Pendergast slipped a copy from his black suit and handed it to the lawyer. The man scrutinized it.

"That's your copy," said Hayward. Her voice was deadpan, neutral.

"Thank you. May I ask why this questioning could not be done at Mr. Bullard's convenience in his offices or on his yacht?" He addressed the question in general, to all of them. Hayward nodded toward D'Agosta.

"On an earlier occasion at Mr. Bullard's club, he refused to answer questions. On this particular occasion, he threatened me with what I think a reasonable person might consider implied blackmail. He gave every sign of imminent departure from the country. His information is crucial in our investigation."

"Is he a suspect?"

"No. But he's an important witness."

"I see. And this implied threat of blackmail—what's that all about?"

"It's a goddamned—," Bullard began.

The lawyer cut Bullard off with a wave of his hand.

"The threat was made in my presence," Pendergast spoke up. "Mr. Bullard made a second threat, just before you arrived, for the benefit of the video recorder."

"You're a damned liar—"

"Not one more word, Mr. Bullard. I believe you've said more than enough as it is."

"For Christ's sake, George, these men are—"

"Quiet." The lawyer spoke pleasantly, but there was a curious emphasis in his tone.

Bullard fell silent.

"My client," the lawyer said, "is anxious to cooperate. Here's how it will work. First, you will ask the question. Then, if necessary, I will confer privately with my client in the hall. And then he will give his response. Agreed?"

"Agreed," said Hayward. "Swear him in."

They went through the process, the civilian administrator presiding, Bullard grunting his responses. At the conclusion, he turned again to his lawyer. "Damn it, George, you're supposed to be on my side!"

"My client and I need to confer privately."

Marchand took Bullard out into the hallway. A minute later they were back.

"First question," the lawyer said.

D'Agosta stepped forward, glanced down at his notes, and droned out, in his most stolid cop voice: "Mr. Bullard, on October 16, 2:02 A.M., Jeremy Grove called you. You spoke with him for forty-two minutes. What did you talk about? Start at the beginning and proceed through the call."

"I already—" He stopped when Marchand laid a firm hand on his shoulder. They went out into the hall again.

"You're not going to let him do this with every question, are you?" D'Agosta asked.

"Yes, I am," said Hayward. "He has a right to a lawyer."

The two men returned. "Grove called me to chat," Bullard said. "A social call."

"That late?"

Bullard looked at his lawyer and the lawyer nodded. "Yes."

"What did you chat about?"

"Just like I told you before. Pleasantries. How he was doing, how I was doing, how the family was doing, how the dog was doing, that sort of thing."

"What else?"

"I don't recall."

Silence. "Mr. Bullard. You talked for forty-two minutes about your dogs, then within hours Grove is murdered."

"That wasn't a question," said the lawyer crisply. "Next."

D'Agosta found Hayward's rather penetrating gaze on him. He turned the page.

"Where were you during this call?"

"On my yacht. Cruising the sound."

"How many crew were on board with you?"

"I went out without a crew. The yacht's computerized, I do it all the time."

There was a brief but significant silence.

"How did you meet Grove?"

"I don't recall."

"Was he a close friend?"

"No."

"Did you have any business dealings with him?"

"No."

"When was the last time you saw him?"

"I don't recall."

"So why would he call you then?"

"You'll have to ask him."

This was bullshit. It was the same runaround as before. D'Agosta moved on to the next call.

"On October 22, at 7:54 P.M., Nigel Cutforth placed a call to your home number. Did you take the call?"

Bullard glanced at the lawyer, who nodded.

"Yes."

"What did you talk about?"

"It was also a social call. We talked about mutual friends, family, news, that sort of thing."

"Dogs?" D'Agosta asked sarcastically.

"I don't remember if we talked about dogs."

Pendergast suddenly broke in. "Do you, in fact, have a dog, Mr. Bullard?"

There was a short silence. Hayward cast Pendergast a warning glance.

"I was speaking metaphorically. We talked about trivial social things, is what I meant."

D'Agosta resumed. "Cutforth was murdered just a few hours after you hung up the telephone. Did he seem nervous to you?"

"I don't recall."

"Did he express any sense to you that he was afraid?"

"Not that I recall."

"Did he ask for your help?"

"I don't recall."

"What was your relationship to Mr. Cutforth?"

"Superficial."

"When was the last time you saw him?"

A hesitation. "I don't recall."

"Did you ever have any business or other dealings with Mr. Cutforth?"

"No."

"How did you first meet?"

"I don't recall."

"*When* did you first meet?" Pendergast smoothly interjected.

"I don't remember."

This was *worse* than bullshit. The lawyer, George Marchand, was looking more and more satisfied. D'Agosta wasn't going to let it go at this.

"After Cutforth's call, you spent the rest of the night on your yacht?"

"Yes."

"Do you have a power launch?"

"Yes."

"Was it stowed?"

"No. It was docked next to the yacht."

"What kind of launch?"

"A Picnic Boat."

Pendergast broke in. "Are you referring to the Hinckley Picnic Boat, the kind with the jet drive?"

"That's right."

"With the 350-horsepower Yanmar or the 420?"

"The 420."

"With a top speed of over thirty knots, I believe?"

"That's about right."

"And a draft of eighteen inches."

"So they claim."

Pendergast settled back, ignoring Hayward's look. He'd clearly snuck in some research while Bullard was being processed.

D'Agosta picked up the line of questioning. "So after receiving the phone call, you could have gotten into your Picnic Boat and headed uptown. You could've landed the boat just about anywhere along the Manhattan shoreline with a draft like that. And the jet drive would give you maneuverability to go sideways, reverse, whatever. Am I right?"

"My client has already said he was on his yacht

that night," the lawyer said, equally pleasantly. "Next question?"

"Were you alone all night, Mr. Bullard?"

This prompted another trip to the hall.

"Yes, I was alone," Bullard said when they returned. "They keep track at the marina; they can verify I didn't leave the yacht all night or take the Picnic Boat out of its berth."

"We'll check that," said D'Agosta. "So you chitchatted with Cutforth about the weather for thirty minutes, just hours before he was murdered?"

"I don't believe we talked about the weather, Sergeant." There was a look of triumph in Bullard's eyes. He was winning again.

Pendergast asked, "Mr. Bullard, are you about to leave the country?"

Bullard looked at Marchand. "Do I have to answer that?"

Another trip to the hall. When Bullard came back, he said, "Yes."

"Where are you going?"

"That question falls outside the scope of the subpoena," said the lawyer. "My client wants to cooperate, but he also asks you to respect his privacy. You have already stated he is not a suspect."

Pendergast spoke to the lawyer. "Perhaps not a suspect. But your client may be a material witness, and it would not be beyond the bounds of probability he might be asked to surrender his passport—temporarily, of course."

D'Agosta had his eyes on Bullard's face and—even though he was expecting a change—he was startled by how dark it became. He seemed about to burst out again.

The lawyer smiled pleasantly. "An utterly absurd statement, Mr. Pendergast. Mr. Bullard will in no way be restrained in his movements. I am surprised and consider it most improper that you have even mentioned such a possibility, which might be construed as a threat."

Hayward cast a dark glance at Pendergast. "Mr. Pendergast—"

Pendergast held up his hand. "Mr. Bullard, do you believe in the existence of the devil?"

Something flickered across Bullard's face, some swift and powerful emotion, but it went by too fast for D'Agosta to get a sense of what it was. Bullard took his time leaning back in the chair, crossing his legs, smiling. "Of course not. Do you?"

The lawyer stood up. "It seems we've reached the end of our questions, gentlemen."

There was no contradiction. The lawyer handed around his card with smiles and handshakes. "The next time you need to communicate with Mr. Bullard," he said, "do so through me. Mr. Bullard is going abroad." He gave Pendergast a pointed smile.

"That," said Pendergast very quietly, "remains to be seen."

{ 26 }

Bullard and his lawyer had left, shoving their way through a second throng of shouting reporters. Pendergast had disappeared, too, leaving D'Agosta alone with Hayward. They were now lingering in the mud-colored lobby of Police Plaza. He had something he wanted to say; and so, it seemed, did she.

"Did Bullard really threaten you, Sergeant?" she asked.

D'Agosta hesitated.

"Just for my own information, off the record. I'm not asking you to tell tales out of school."

"In a way, yes." They began walking side by side toward the building's exit. Outside, the remaining news teams were grudgingly packing up. The sky in the west was smeared with red. As he walked, D'Agosta could almost feel waves of heat radiating from Hayward. She was clearly still pissed off.

"What kind of threat?"

"I'd rather not talk about it." *I know all about that wife of yours in Canada.* The image of Chester Dominic's smooth-shaven face came unbidden to his mind.

It couldn't be true. Well, on second thought, it *could* be true—they had been apart for a long time. The marriage was over—who was he fooling? But not Chester Dominic, with that cheesy shit-eating grin and the phony car-salesman cheer. And the polyester suits. Jesus. Anybody but him.

D'Agosta glanced over to see Hayward looking back at him. Her face showed concern mingled with skepticism. This wasn't easy for her, he thought. Pendergast was one hell of a good FBI agent, but he was no good at teamwork. It was his way or the highway—no compromise.

"You might have to talk about it if charges are brought."

"Fine. But not now." He took a deep breath. "Captain Hayward, Pendergast really did have to get tough with Bullard."

"I don't believe it. He could've gotten a subpoena, scheduled the interview on the boat, and probably gotten more information out of the guy in the process. As it is, we didn't get jack out of that interrogation."

"We went to the boat to ask questions. I was threatened. I don't see why you think scheduling it would have been more successful."

"Okay, you've got a point, but it turned into a pissing contest, and that's never successful."

They passed through the doors and paused on the broad marble steps. Hayward was still mad. More fence-mending was in order.

"You doing anything?" D'Agosta asked.

Hayward looked at him. "I was planning on going home."

"How about a drink? Strictly professional. I know—or at least I used to know—a place over on Church Street."

She gazed at him for a moment, her pale face framed by glossy black hair, her eyes still flashing with residual irritation. "All right."

D'Agosta descended the steps, Hayward by his side.

"Pendergast's got his own methods," said D'Agosta.

"That's exactly what I'm afraid of. Look, Sergeant—"

"How about calling me Vinnie?"

"Call me Laura, then. Here's what worries me: how many times has Pendergast had to testify against a perp in court?"

"I don't know."

"I'll tell you. Very few times. You know why?"

"Why?"

"Because most of his perps wind up dead. That's why."

"That's not his fault."

"I didn't say it was. It's just an observation. Let's say Bullard does become a suspect. This little shenanigan is going to look bad."

They made a left at Park Row, then a right at Vesey. Ahead, D'Agosta saw the little place still there, apparently unchanged. A couple of dying ferns hung from macramé in the basement window, just the right touch to keep out other cops. He liked it for that—and for the Guinness on tap.

"I never knew this place existed," said Hayward as they descended the steps and D'Agosta held open the door. He followed her into the cool, brew-fragrant interior. She took a table in the back and a man came up immediately.

"Guinness," she said.

"Two."

D'Agosta couldn't shake the image of Dominic with his wife. It was going to drive him crazy, he realized, until he did something about it. He got up. "Back in a moment."

He found the phone tucked into a nook in the back of the bar. It had been a long time since he used a pay phone, but this was one call he didn't want to make with his cell. He called information, got the Canadian operator, got the number, made the call. It took two trips to the bar and twenty quarters. Jesus.

"Kootenay RV," came a nasal voice.

"Chet Dominic there?"

"He's gone."

"Damn, I was supposed to meet him for an appointment, and I'm late. You got his cell?"

"Who's this?"

"Jack Torrance. I'm the one interested in the Itasca Sunflyer, you know, the one with the slide-out bedroom and Corian countertops? Chet's a friend from the club."

"Oh, yes, Mr. Torrance, of course," came the suddenly fake-friendly voice. "Just a moment." She gave him the number.

D'Agosta glanced at his watch, collected more quarters from the bar, dialed.

"Hello?"

It was Chester.

"This is Dr. Morgan at the hospital. There's been a terrible accident."

"What? Who?" The voice was instantly full of panic.

D'Agosta wondered if Dominic had a wife and kids. Probably did, the scumbag.

"I must speak to a Mrs. Lydia D'Agosta immediately."

"Well, ah, wait—yes, yes, of course." There was a fumbling sound, a muffled voice, and then his wife's voice came on. "Yes? What is it? What's happened?"

D'Agosta carefully depressed the hang-up bar, took a couple of deep breaths, and made his way back toward the table. Even before he got there, his cell phone was ringing. He answered.

"Vinnie? It's Lydia. Are you all right?"

"Sure. Why do you ask? You sound upset."

"No, no, I'm fine. I just heard…I don't know, something about the hospital. I was worried." She was all flustered and confused.

"Wasn't me."

"You know how it is, being out here like this, hearing everything secondhand…"

"You still at work?"

"I'm in the parking lot. Just pulling out now."

"Right. See you." D'Agosta snapped the phone shut and reseated himself. *You mean Chester Dominic was just pulling out, don't you?* He felt a horrible prickly heat crawling over his skin. The Guinness had arrived, in a real imperial pint, with two inches of cream on the top. He raised it and took a long pull, then another, feeling the cool liquid loosening the tightness in his throat. He put the pint down to find Laura Hayward looking at him intently.

"You were thirsty," she said.

"Yeah." To hide his face, he took another pull. Who was he kidding? They'd been separated half a year now.

He couldn't really blame her for that—not too much, anyway. And Vinnie Junior, his son, didn't want to move, either. Lydia wasn't a bad person at heart, but this was a low blow. A really low blow. He wondered if little Vinnie knew about it.

"Bad news?"

D'Agosta glanced at Hayward. "Sort of."

"Anything I can do?"

"No, thanks." He sat up. "I'm sorry. I'm lousy company tonight."

"Don't worry. It's not a date."

There was a silence, then Hayward said, "I read your two novels."

D'Agosta felt himself reddening. This was the last conversation he wanted to have.

"They were great. I just wanted to tell you that."

"Thanks."

"I loved the deadpan style. Gritty. Those books really captured what it's like to be on the job. Not like most of the phony police fiction around."

D'Agosta nodded. "So where'd you find them? On a remainder table?"

"I bought them when they were first published. As it happens, I've been sort of following your career."

"Really?" D'Agosta was surprised. When they'd worked together on the subway murders years ago, he hadn't thought he'd made much of an impression on her. Not a good impression, anyway. Then again, she'd always played her cards close.

"Really. I—" She hesitated. "I was still finishing up my master's at NYU when we worked together. That was my first big case. I was ambitious as hell, and to me, just starting, you looked like just the kind of cop I wanted to be. So I was really curious when you went off to Canada to write novels. I wondered why a cop as good as you would give it up."

"I had a lot I wanted to say—about crime, criminals, the justice system. And about people in general."

"You said it well."

"Not well enough."

Her pint was empty and so was his.

"Another round?" he asked.

"Sure. Vinnie, I've got to tell you, I couldn't believe it when I saw you in sergeant's stripes with a Southampton P.D. badge. I thought maybe I was dealing with a twin brother."

D'Agosta tried to muster a laugh. "Life."

"That was some case we worked on, those subway murders."

"Sure was. You remember the riot?"

She shook her head. "What a sight. Like something in a movie. I still have nightmares about it sometimes."

"I missed it. I was about half a mile underground, finishing what Captain Waxie started."

"Old Waxie. You know, he was sucked down so deep into those tunnels they never did find his body. Probably got eaten by an alligator."

"Or worse."

She paused. "The force is different now, really different. Thank God—what a cast of characters we had to deal with back then, when I was just a new jack."

"You remember McCarroll at the T.A.? They called him McCarrion because of his breath?" He chuckled.

"Do I. I had to work for that bastard for six months.

It was tough to be a woman on the T.A. force back then. I had two strikes against me: not only was I female, but I was in graduate school. Make that three strikes: I wouldn't sleep with McCarrion."

"He made a pass at you?"

"His idea of a pass was to get real close, breathe all over me, tell me I had a nice body, and pucker his lips."

D'Agosta made a face. "Oh, my God. You report him?"

"And kiss my career good-bye? He was just a harmless cretin, anyway, not worth reporting. Now the NYPD is like a different planet—totally professional. And anyway, nobody would dare pull a stunt like that on a captain."

The second round came, and D'Agosta buried his mug in it and listened to her reminisce, telling funny stories about McCarroll and another long-gone captain, Al "Crisco" DuPrisco. It brought back a lot of memories.

He shook his head. "Jesus, there's no better place to be a cop than in the Big Apple."

"You said it."

"I gotta get back on the job, Laura. I'm rotting out there in Southampton."

She said nothing. D'Agosta looked up, his eyes meeting hers and seeing what—pity? "Sorry." He looked away. Funny how life had reversed everything. Now here she was, probably the youngest captain on the force. And he... Well, if anyone deserved success, she did...

"Look," he said, suddenly professional again. "I really asked you for a drink because I wanted to make sure you were okay with Pendergast. I've worked with him on not just one big case, but two. Believe me, his methods may be unorthodox, but they work. You couldn't ask for a better fed on your side."

"I appreciate your loyalty. But the fact is, he's got a cooperation problem. I went out on a limb to have that subpoena and warrant ready to go, and he embarrassed me. I'm going to give him the benefit of the doubt this time, but please, Vinnie, keep the guy in line. He obviously respects you."

"He respects you, too."

There was a silence.

"So how come you gave up writing?" Hayward asked, shifting the subject back to him. "I thought you had a pretty good career going."

"Yeah, a career in bankruptcy court. I just couldn't make it. After two novels, I didn't have two nickels to rub together. Lydia—that's my wife—she couldn't take it anymore."

"You're married?" Her eyes rapidly glanced at his hand, but his wedding ring hadn't fit for years.

"Yeah."

"Why am I surprised? All the good guys are taken. Here's to Lydia."

She raised her pint. D'Agosta didn't raise his glass; instead, he said, "We're separated. She's still living in Canada."

"I'm sorry." She lowered her pint, but she did not look very sorry. Or was it just his imagination?

"You know that threat Bullard made against me?" D'Agosta swallowed. He wasn't sure why he was telling her this, but he suddenly felt he couldn't go another minute without getting it off his chest. "He somehow found out my wife was having an affair and told me about it. Along with a lot of other compromising personal information he dug up and threatened to make public."

"Bastard. In that case, I'm glad Pendergast stuck it to him." She hesitated. "You want to talk about it?"

"We are talking about it."

"I'm sorry, Vincent. That's tough. Is the marriage worth saving?"

"It was over half a year ago. We've just been in denial stage."

"Kids?"

"One. Lives with his mom. Going to college next year on scholarship. Great kid."

"How long were you married?"

"Twenty-five years. Married right out of high school."

"God. You sure there isn't something there worth holding on to?"

"Some good memories. But nothing now. It's over."

"Well then, Bullard just did you a favor." She extended her hand and laid it on his, comfortingly.

D'Agosta looked at her. She was right: in a way, Bullard had done him a favor. Maybe a really big favor.

{ 27 }

Midnight. The boat was still in its slip, the crew aboard, everything ready for a departure at first light. Bullard stood on deck, breathing the night air, looking across the bay toward Staten Island. There was one last thing he had to take care of before weighing anchor. He had made two serious mistakes, and they had to be corrected. The first was impulsively hiring those goons to cap D'Agosta. Damn stupid thing: he knew better than that. If you were going to kill a cop, you had to do it right. The bastard had mouthed off with a few empty threats, and in his nervous state he'd allowed himself to be spooked. Christ, he was jumpy these days. He wasn't thinking clearly. The fact was, that fat fuck was not his real enemy. He was just a gumshoe. The real enemy was the FBI agent, Pendergast. That man was dangerous as an adder: coiled up, cool, smooth, ready to strike. Pendergast played for keeps, and he was the brains in that team. Kill the brain and the body will die. Get Pendergast and the investigation would go away.

The same rule about cops was even truer for FBI agents. You didn't kill them unless there was no other way. It almost never made things better. But there were exceptions to every rule, and this was one of them. Bullard could allow nothing—*nothing*—to interfere with what he had to do.

He went belowdecks. All was quiet. He slipped into a soundproofed room, locked the door behind him, checked his watch. Still a few minutes. He pressed a few buttons, and a videoconferencing screen came to life. Pendergast had made off with one CPU and some of his files, but all his computers were networked, their business-related data folders encrypted. He used public encryption with 2,048-bit keys, unbreakable even by the most powerful computers in the world. He wasn't worried about what Pendergast might find. He was worried about the man himself.

He pressed a few more keys, and a dim face appeared on the screen. It was a face as smooth and tight as a drum, so thin it looked as if the wet skin had been stretched over the bones and allowed to dry. His head was shaved so smooth there wasn't even a five o'clock shadow on the scalp. It gave Bullard the creeps. But the man was good. More than good: he was the best there was. He called himself Vasquez.

The man said nothing, offered no greeting, just stared, hands folded, his face expressionless. Bullard eased back in his chair, smiled, although the smile made no difference. The image Vasquez was seeing on-screen was the computer-generated face of a nonexistent person.

Bullard spoke. "The target is Pendergast, first name unknown. Special Agent with the FBI. Lives at 891 Riverside Drive. I want two in the brainpan. I'll give you a million per bullet."

"I require full payment in advance," Vasquez said.

"What if you fail?"

"I don't."

"Bullshit. Everyone fails."

"The day I fail is the day I die. Now, do you agree?"

Bullard hesitated. Still, if you were going to do something, do it right.

"Very well," he said curtly. "But time is of the essence here." If Vasquez screwed him, there were other Vasquezes out there, willing to finish the job and reduce the competition; two killings wouldn't cost much more than one.

Vasquez held up a piece of paper with a number on it. He waited a moment, giving Bullard time to jot it down. "When the two million shows up in this account, I will undertake the assignment. We need never speak again."

The screen went black. Bullard realized Vasquez must have cut the transmission. He wasn't used to people hanging up on him. He felt a momentary irritation, then took a deep breath. He had worked with artists before, and they were all cut from the same cloth: egotistical, flamboyant, greedy.

And Vasquez was the best kind of artist: the kind that truly loved his work.

{ 28 }

D'Agosta pulled his Ford Taurus up to the iron gates, then stopped, wondering if he might have gotten the directions wrong. He was at least an hour late—the paperwork from the previous day's blowup with Bullard had taken all morning. Cops these days couldn't fire their gun, couldn't question a suspect, couldn't even break wind without having to fill out reports after the fact.

The rusty gates hung open, as if abandoned, mounted on two crumbling stone pillars. The graveled drive beyond was carpeted with sprouting ragweed well over a foot high, recently smashed down by the passage of a vehicle. But no, this had to be the place: a stone plaque mortared into one of the pillars bore the name, abraded by time and weather but still legible: *Ravenscry.*

D'Agosta got out of the car and shoved the groaning gate open a little farther, then got behind the wheel again and headed down the drive. He could see where the other car or cars had gone, flattening the weeds in two vague stripes. The drive wandered through an ancient beechwood forest, massive warped tree trunks rising on both sides, until at last it broke out into sunlight—a meadow dotted with wildflowers that had once evidently been a lawn. At the far end of the meadow rose a gaunt stone mansion: shaded by elms, shuttered tight, its roofs topped by at least twenty chimneys, a real haunted pile if ever there was one. D'Agosta shook his head slowly. Then, glancing at the directions Pendergast had given him, he followed the carriageway around the massive house and turned onto another road that led on through ancient gardens toward a stone millhouse on the banks of a stream. Pendergast's Rolls was parked here and he pulled in beside it. Pendergast's chauffeur, Proctor, was arranging something in the car's trunk; as D'Agosta got out of the car and approached, he bowed politely, then nodded in the direction of the stream.

D'Agosta began following a stone path that led down from the road. Farther ahead now, he could see two figures strolling along the path, dappled in shade, intent in conversation. One had to be Pendergast—the black suit and slim bearing gave him away. The other, who was wearing a sunbonnet and holding a parasol, could only be the girl staying in Pendergast's house. What was her name again? Constance.

As he approached the stream, he could hear the purling of water, hear the birds rustling in the beechwood. Pendergast turned and waved him over. "Vincent, you made it. Very good of you to come."

Constance turned, too, smiling gravely and holding out her hand. D'Agosta took it, mumbling a greeting. For some reason she made him eager to be on his best behavior, just the way his grandmother had done when he was a child. Her unusual eyes were concealed by a pair of very dark sunglasses.

He glanced down the shade-dappled path. The mill was no longer turning, but the shunt of water had been directed into a curious series of stone sluice tanks. "What is this place?"

"The estate belongs to my great-aunt Cornelia, who, alas, is not well and is confined to a home. I've begun bringing Constance up here to take the air."

"To complete my rehabilitation," said Constance with a faint smile. "Mr. Pendergast thinks I'm in delicate health."

"Quite a spread," D'Agosta said.

"The mill here was converted into a trout farm in the late nineteenth century," Pendergast replied. "Every year they stocked Dewing Brook with thousands of trout and kept the forest full of wild turkey, deer, pheasant, grouse, quail, and bear. Come Sunday there was quite a massacre around these parts, as my relations and their sporting friends took to the field."

"A hunting preserve. I'll bet the fishing was fantastic." D'Agosta looked at the brook purling over its cobbled bed, with deep pools and holes no doubt still thick with trout. Even as he watched, several fish, rising to a hatch, dimpled the surface.

"I never cared for fishing," Pendergast said. "I preferred blood sport."

"What's wrong with fishing?"

"I find it quotidian in the extreme."

"Quotidian. Right."

"After the sudden death of Aunt Cornelia's husband and children, most of the staff quit. Shortly thereafter, my aunt was obliged to leave. And now Ravenscry lies empty, decaying. In any case," Pendergast went on more briskly, "I asked you to come so we may take stock of the case in surroundings conducive to contemplation. Frankly, Vincent, the case is baffling. Normally by this stage I'd have found a piece of thread leading into the tangle. But this is different."

"It's a tough one," D'Agosta said. He glanced at the girl, wondering how much to say.

"We may speak freely in front of Constance."

The girl smiled with mock gravity. They strolled back through the dappled shade in the direction of the cars.

"Let us review what we know. We have two murders, each with inexplicable features, including the heating of the body and the various Mephistophelean appurtenances. We know that the two victims must have been connected with each other and to Bullard in some way. But I have not been able to find that connection."

"Hayward's been helping me with that end of things. We've pulled their telephone bills, credit card transactions, T&E records going back ten years. Nada. It doesn't look like they ever met. As for Bullard, most of the folders on that computer we seized are encrypted too strongly to break. I did get one nugget of interesting information from Hayward, though: they found a reference to the name Ranier Beckmann in a temporary Internet directory on the computer. Seems Bullard was trying to locate him, too."

"And yet you said Bullard denied knowing Beckmann when you questioned him at the Athletic Club. It's evident Bullard is concealing a great deal. He's angry, he's defensive. I might even say he's frightened. Of what?"

"Of arrest. As far as I'm concerned, Bullard is suspect number one. He doesn't have a good alibi for the Grove murder, either. He said he was on his yacht, cruising the sound that night. Without a crew. He could've been cruising the Atlantic side instead, slipped up on the beach at Southampton, done the job."

"Possible. But the fact that he has no alibi for either night, in my view, is actually a strike in his favor. Besides, what's Bullard's motivation? Why kill Grove and Cutforth? And why make it look like the devil?"

"He's got a macabre sense of humor."

"On the contrary, the man appears to have absolutely no sense of humor at all, apart from a kind of gangsterish schadenfreude. Somebody playing a mere joke would not take such a dangerous risk."

"He wants to send a message, then."

"Yes, but to whom? For what purpose?"

"I don't know. If it isn't Bullard, it might be some fundamentalist nutcase who wants to bring back the Inquisition. Somebody who thinks he's doing God's work."

"A second possibility."

There was a short silence. Then Pendergast added, "Vincent, you haven't mentioned the *other* possibility."

D'Agosta felt his gut tighten. Pendergast wasn't serious—was he? He found himself unconsciously fingering his cross.

"Where's Bullard now?" Pendergast asked.

"He left on his yacht this morning, heading to the open ocean."

"Any idea where?"

"Looks like Europe. At least he's heading east, at full speed. Better than full speed, in fact—the yacht must have a specially modified power plant. In any case, Hayward's got someone on it. We'll know where and when he lands—unless he evades customs and immigration, which seems improbable with a yacht like that."

"The admirable Hayward. Is she still upset?"

"You could say that."

Pendergast smiled thinly.

"So what's your theory?" D'Agosta asked.

"I am doing my best not to *have* a theory."

D'Agosta heard the crunching of tires on gravel, the slamming of doors, the distant chatter of voices. He glanced back across the meadows and spotted the new arrival: a long, old-fashioned limousine, its top down. A huge wicker basket was lashed across the rumble seat with leather straps.

"Who's this?" D'Agosta asked.

"Another guest," Pendergast said simply.

Now someone came around the side of the car: an enormous figure, grossly out of proportion to its surroundings but moving with a remarkable fluidity and ease. It was Fosco, who, it seemed, had somehow made the transition from witness to acquaintance.

D'Agosta looked over. "What's he doing here?"

"It seems he is in possession of some information of great value that he's most eager to pass on. And since he's expressed an interest in viewing what passes for antiquity here in America, I thought I'd invite him to Ravenscry. I owed him a return for an interesting night at the opera."

The figure came striding swiftly down the path, waving his arm in greeting long before he arrived.

"Marvelous place!" boomed the count, rubbing his white-gloved hands together. He bowed to Pendergast, then turned to D'Agosta. "The good sergeant. D'Agosta, is it not? Always pleased to make the acquaintance of a fellow Italian. How do you do?"

"Fine, thanks." D'Agosta hadn't liked the man and his flamboyant ways at the memorial service, and he liked him even less now.

"And this is my ward, Constance Greene," said Pendergast.

"Your ward, you say? I am delighted." Fosco bowed and brought her hand almost, but not quite, to his lips.

Constance inclined her head in acknowledgment. "I see you and Mr. Pendergast share an interest in exotic automobiles."

"Indeed we do; that and much more. Mr. Pendergast and I have become *friends*." He beamed. "We are very different in some ways. I am a lover of music and he is not. I am a lover of fine clothes, and he dresses like an undertaker. I am voluble and open, he is silent and closed. I am direct, he is diffident. But we do share a love of art, literature, fine food, wine, and culture—as well as a fascination with these dreadful and inexplicable crimes." He peered at Constance, smiled again.

"Crimes are interesting only when they are inexplicable. Unfortunately, few remain so."

"Unfortunately?"

"I was speaking from an aesthetic point of view."

The count turned to Pendergast. "This young lady is exceptional."

"And what is your interest in the case, Count, besides mere fascination?" Constance asked.

"I wish to help."

"Count Fosco has already been helpful," said Pendergast.

"And, as you shall see, I will be more helpful still! But first I must tell you how enchanted I am with this estate. Your great-aunt's, did you say? So picturesque! Falling into ruin and neglect, mysterious, haunted. It reminds me of Piranesi's engraving *Veduta degli Avanzi delle Terme di Tito*, the Ruins of the Baths of Titus. I much prefer a building in neglect and ruin—much of my own *castello* in Tuscany is in a delightful state of dilapidation."

D'Agosta wondered what the castle of a count looked like.

"As promised, I brought lunch," the count boomed. "Pinketts!" He clapped his hands and his driver, who was about as English as they come, unstrapped the huge wicker trunk and hefted it down the path, then proceeded to arrange a linen tablecloth, bottles of wine, cheeses, prosciutto, salami, silverware, and glasses on a stone table beneath the shade of an enormous copper beech.

"This is kind of you, Count," said Pendergast.

"Yes, I *am* kind, especially when you see the Villa Calcinaia '97 Chianti Classico Riserva I've brought, made by my neighbor, the good count Capponi. But I have something else for you. Something even better than wine, caviar, and fois gras. If such a thing is possible." The black eyes in his smooth, handsome face sparkled with pleasure.

"And that is?"

"In good time, in good time." The count began arranging, with fussy attention, the things on the table, uncorking and decanting a bottle of red wine, letting the anticipation build. At last, he turned with a conspiratorial grin. "By chance, I have made a discovery of the first importance." He turned to D'Agosta. "Does the name Ranier Beckmann mean anything to you, Sergeant?"

"We found that name on Bullard's computer. The guy he was trying to locate."

The count nodded as if he'd known it all along. "And?"

"Bullard had done an Internet search for a Ranier Beckmann, without success. Grove also seems to have been looking for Beckmann. But we don't know why."

"I was at a luncheon party yesterday and was seated beside Lady Milbanke. She told me—between frequent displays of her new necklace—that a few days before Jeremy Grove was murdered, he had asked if she could recommend a private detective. Turned out she could—scandalous people often can. I then went to this gentleman myself and soon pried from him the fact that Grove hired him . . . *to find a certain Ranier Beckmann.*"

He paused dramatically. "Grove was in a panic to find this man. When the detective asked him for details, he could provide none at all. None. The detective stopped his investigation when he heard of Grove's death."

"Interesting," D'Agosta said.

"It would be interesting to see if the name Beckmann turned up among Cutforth's effects, as well," Pendergast said.

D'Agosta removed his cell, dialed Hayward's direct line.

"Hayward here," came the cool voice.

"It's Sergeant D'Agosta. Vinnie. Have your people finished inventorying Cutforth's apartment?"

"Yes."

"The name Ranier Beckmann turn up, by any chance?"

"As a matter of fact, it did." D'Agosta heard a rustling of paper. "We found a notebook with his name written on the first page, in Cutforth's hand."

"The rest of the notebook?"

"Blank."

"Thanks." D'Agosta closed the phone and related what he'd heard.

Pendergast's face tensed with excitement. "This is precisely the thread we've been looking for. Grove, Cutforth, Bullard. Why were all three looking for Beckmann? Perhaps *we* should find this Beckmann and see what he has to tell us."

"You may find that a difficult proposition, my friend," said the count.

Pendergast glanced at him. "And why is that?"

"Because the private investigator told me something else. That he was unable to find any information *at all* on this Ranier Beckmann. No present or past address, no employment history, no family information. Nothing. But I leave that to you." The count, beaming with his success, extended his white hands. "And now, business concluded, let us be seated and enjoy our lunch." He turned and bowed to Constance. "May I be permitted to seat you here, on my right? I feel we have much to talk about."

{ 29 }

Even before entering, Harriman had formed a clear picture of Von Menck's sitting room in his mind. He figured he'd find it carpeted in Persian rugs, decked out with astrological charts, ancient pentacles, and perhaps Tibetan durgas made of human long bones. The room alone, he hoped, would make great copy. Thus he was crestfallen when the door drew back at his knock to reveal a simple, almost spartan study. There was a small fireplace, comfortable leather chairs, lithographs of Egyptian ruins on the walls. There were, in fact, only two clues that this room was not just another middle-class parlor: the wall of glass-fronted bookcases, bulging with books and manuscripts and papers, and the Emmy for Best Documentary that sat neglected on the desk beside the telephone and old-fashioned Rolodex.

Harriman took the proffered seat, hoping his hunch would prove correct: that Von Menck would give shape and voice to the devil-killings story. A typical scientist would merely debunk the business, while some crank satanist would have no credibility. What made Friedrich Von Menck perfect was that he straddled the gray area in between. While Von Menck's academic credentials were beyond reproach—doctor of philosophy from Heidelberg, doctor of medicine from Harvard, doctor of divinity from Canterbury—he had always made a specialty of mysticism, the paranormal, the unexplainable. His documentary on crop circles had aired on PBS to great acclaim, and it had been well done, salted with both skepticism and just the right frisson of the inexplicable. And, of course, his earlier documentary on the exorcisms in Cartagena, Spain, had won the Emmy. At the time, it had left even Harriman wondering—if only until the next commercial break—if there wasn't something to the idea of demonic possession.

Von Menck would provide more than just an opinion: he would provide a foundation, a launching pad, an engine. If Von Menck couldn't get this story into orbit, nobody could.

The doctor greeted him with courtesy, taking a seat in the leather chair opposite. Harriman liked him immediately. He was surprised to see that the compelling, almost magnetic personality projected on television was, in fact, real. It had a lot to do with the man's low, mellifluous voice and cool, ascetic features, with the prominent cheekbones and finely molded chin. Only one thing seemed to be missing. On television, Von Menck had frequently smiled—a raffish smile of wit and good humor, of a man who didn't take himself too seriously. It had the effect of keeping his rather technical investigations from getting too heavy. Now, however—though Von Menck was polite to a fault—the engaging smile was absent.

After a brief exchange of pleasantries, the doctor got

right to the point. "Your message stated you wished to speak with me about the recent killings."

"That's right." Harriman reached into his pocket for his digital voice recorder.

"What your paper has referred to as the devil killings."

"Right." Did he detect the slightest hint of disdain, or disapproval, in the doctor's polite inflections? "Dr. Von Menck, I've come to see if you've framed an opinion on these murders."

Dr. Von Menck leaned back in his chair, tented his fingers, and looked carefully at Harriman. When at last he spoke, it was in very slow and measured tones. It almost seemed to Harriman the man had been considering the question long before he asked it. "Yes. As it happens, I do have an opinion."

Harriman placed the recorder on the arm of his chair. "Do you mind if I record this?"

Von Menck gave a small wave of permission. "I've been debating the wisdom of making my opinions public."

Harriman felt himself go cold. *Oh, no,* he thought. *The guy's planning to do his own documentary on this. I'm about to get the royal shaft.*

Then Von Menck sighed. "In the end, I decided people had a right to know. In that way, your phone call was fortuitous."

The chill was replaced by relief. Harriman leaned forward, snapped the recorder on. "Then perhaps you can tell me your thoughts, sir. Why these two men, why in such a manner, and why at this time?"

Von Menck sighed again. "The two men, and the

manner, are of lesser importance. It's the *timing* that means everything."

"Explain."

Von Menck stood, walked toward one of the bookcases, opened it, and removed something. He placed it on the desk before Harriman. It was a cross section of a nautilus shell, its growth chambers spiraling outward from the center with beautiful regularity.

"Do you know, Mr. Harriman, what this shell has in common with the building of the Parthenon, the petals of a flower, and the paintings of Leonardo da Vinci?"

Harriman shook his head.

"It embodies that most perfect of nature's proportions, the golden ratio."

"I'm not sure I understand."

"It's the ratio obtained if you divide a line in such a way that the shorter segment is to the longer segment as the longer segment is to the entire line."

Harriman wrote this all down, hoping that he could figure it out later.

"The longer segment is 1.618054 times longer than the shorter segment. The shorter segment is 0.618054 percent of the longer. These two numbers, moreover, are exact reciprocals of each other, differing only in the first digit—the only two numbers to demonstrate that property."

"Right. Of course." Math had never been his strong suit.

"They have other remarkable properties. A rectangle constructed with sides of these two lengths is believed to be the most pleasing shape, called the golden rectangle. The Parthenon was built in this shape. Cathedrals and paintings were based on this shape. Such rectangles also have a remarkable property: if you cut a square off one side, you are left with a smaller golden rectangle of *exactly* the same proportions. You can keep cutting off squares and creating smaller golden rectangles ad infinitum."

"I see."

"Now, if you start with a large golden rectangle and reduce it, square by square, into an infinite series of smaller golden rectangles, and then connect the center of all these, you end up with a perfect natural logarithmic spiral. This is the spiral you see in the nautilus shell; in the packing of seeds into the head of the sunflower; in musical harmony; and indeed throughout all of nature. The golden ratio is a fundamental quality of the natural world."

"Yeah."

"This ratio is part of the basic structure of the universe. No one knows why."

Harriman watched as the doctor carefully put the shell back in the case and closed the glass front. Whatever he'd been expecting, this was not it. He was lost, and if he was lost, he knew that the *Post*'s readers would certainly be lost. What a waste of time. He'd have to escape at the earliest opportunity.

Von Menck stepped behind his desk and turned back to face the journalist. "Are you a religious man, Mr. Harriman?"

The question was so unexpected that, for a moment, Harriman did not know what to say.

"I don't necessarily mean in any organized sense: Catholic, Protestant, whatever. But do you believe there is a unifying force underlying our universe?"

"I'd never really thought about it," Harriman said. "I guess so." He had been raised Episcopalian, though he hadn't set foot inside a church—except for weddings and funerals—for almost twenty years.

"Then might you believe, as I do, that there is a purpose to our lives?"

Harriman shut off the tape recorder. Time to end this and get the hell out. If he wanted a lecture on religion, he could always call the Jehovah's Witnesses. "With all due respect, Doctor, I don't see what this has to do with the two recent deaths."

"Patience, Mr. Harriman. My proof is complex, but the conclusion will, to use a popular expression, blow your mind."

Harriman waited.

"Let me explain. All my life, I have been a student of the mysterious, the unexplained. Many of these mysteries I have solved to my own satisfaction. Others—oftentimes the greatest—remain dark to me." Von Menck took a piece of paper from his desk, wrote on it briefly, then placed it before Harriman:

3243
1239

"Those two numbers"—and he tapped the page—"have always represented the biggest mysteries of all to me. Do you recognize them?"

Harriman shook his head.

"They mark the single two greatest cataclysmic events ever to befall human civilization. In 3243 B.C., the island of Santorini explodes, generating tidal waves that wipe out the great Minoan civilization of Crete and devastate the entire Mediterranean world. This is the source of both the legend of Atlantis and the Great Flood. And 1239 B.C. is when the twin cities of Sodom and Gomorrah were reduced to ash by a rain of ruin from the sky."

"Atlantis? Sodom and Gomorrah?" This was getting worse.

Von Menck tapped the sheet again. "Plato described Atlantis in two of his dialogues, *Timaeus* and *Critias.* Some details he got wrong: for example, the date, which he put at around 9000 B.C. Recent extensive archaeological digs on Crete and Sardinia provide a more exact date. The story of the lost city of Atlantis has been sensationalized to the point where most people wrongly assume it's a myth. But legitimate archaeologists are convinced there is a foundation of truth: the volcanic explosion of the island of Santorini. Plato described Atlantis—that is, the Minoan civilization on Crete—as a powerful city-state, obsessed with commerce, money, self-improvement, and knowledge, but bereft of spiritual values. Archaeological excavations of the Minoan palaces at Knossos confirm this. The people of Atlantis, Plato said, had turned their backs on their god. They flaunted their vices, they openly questioned the existence of a divine, and they worshiped technology instead. Plato tells us they had canals and a so-called firestone that produced artificial power."

He paused. "Sounds like another city we know, doesn't it, Mr. Harriman?"

"New York."

Von Menck nodded. "Exactly. At the very height of

Atlantis's power, there were harbingers of some dread event. The weather was unnaturally cold, and skies were dark for days. There were strange rumblings in the ground. People died suddenly, unexpectedly, outrageously. One was said to have been hit 'by a bolt of lightning that came from the sky and from the bowels of the earth both together.' Another was abruptly torn apart, as if by an explosive device, 'his flesh and blood hanging in the air like a fine mist, while all around lay the most appalling stench.' Within a week came the explosion and flood that destroyed the city forever."

As Von Menck spoke, Harriman snapped on his recorder again. There might be something here, after all.

"Exactly two thousand and four years later, the area of the Dead Sea between what is now Israel and Jordan—the deepest naturally occurring spot on the surface of the earth—was breathtakingly lush and fertile. It was the home of the cities of Sodom and Gomorrah. Precisely how big these cities were remains unknown, although recent archaeological digs in the valley have uncovered massive cemeteries containing thousands of human remains. Clearly, they were the two most powerful cities in the Western world at that time. As with Atlantis, these cities had fallen into the last degree of sin, turning away from the natural order of things. Pride, sloth, the worship of earthly goods, decadence and debauchery, rejection of God and destruction of nature. As it says in Genesis, there were not fifty, not twenty, not even ten righteous men to be found in Sodom. And so the cities were destroyed from above, by 'brimstone and fire... the smoke of the country went up as the smoke of a furnace.' Again, archaeological excavations in the Dead Sea area confirm the biblical story to an amazing degree. In the days before this took place, there again were harbingers of the fate that was to come. One man burst into a pillar of yellow flame. Others were found calcified, not unlike Lot's wife, who was turned to a pillar of salt."

Von Menck came around the desk and sat on its edge, looking intently at the reporter. "Have you been to the Dead Sea, Mr. Harriman?"

"I can't say that I have."

"I've been there. Several times. The first time I went was right after I discovered a certain natural link in the timing of the disasters that befell Atlantis and Gomorrah. The Dead Sea is now a parched wasteland. Fish cannot live in it: the water is many times saltier than the ocean. Almost nothing grows on its edges, and what does is glazed and caked with salt. But if you walk across the dead plains near Tell es-Saidiyeh, where many scholars now place Sodom, you'll find a vast number of balls of pure, elemental sulfur riddling the salt surface. This sulfur is not rhombic, as found in naturally occurring geothermic areas. Rather, it is monoclinic: white, exceptionally pure, exposed to very high temperatures for long periods of time. Geologists have found no other pockets of such naturally occurring sulfur anywhere else on earth. Yet they are found in riotous abundance on the ruins of these two cities. What destroyed Sodom and Gomorrah was not some normal geological process. It remains a mystery to this day."

Von Menck reached for the scrap of paper, wrote another number beneath the first two:

3243
1239
2004

"2004 A.D., Mr. Harriman. It forms the end of the golden ratio. Do the math. The date 3243 B.C. is exactly 5,247 years ago: golden ratio. The date 1239 B.C. is exactly 3,243 years ago: golden ratio again. The next date in the series is 2004 A.D., which also happens to be the exact number of years separating the earlier disasters. Coincidence?"

Harriman stared at the paper. *Is he saying what I think he's saying?* It seemed unbelievable, crazy. And yet the quiet eyes that looked back at him with something like resignation did not look in the least bit crazy.

"I searched for years, Mr. Harriman, for proof that I was wrong. I thought perhaps the dates were incorrect, or that the evidence was flawed. But every discovery I made simply gave more credence to the theory." He walked to another cabinet and pulled out a sheet of white cardboard. On it, a large spiral—like that of the shell of a chambered nautilus—had been drawn. At its outermost point, it was labeled in red pencil: *3243* B.C.*—Santorini/Atlantis.* One-third of the way along its curve was another red marking: *1239* B.C.*—Sodom/Gomorrah.* At other spots along the spiral, smaller tick-marks in black listed dozens of other dates and places:

79 A.D.—Eruption of Vesuvius destroys Pompeii/Herculaneum
426 A.D.—Fall of Rome, sacked and destroyed by barbarians

1348 A.D.—Plague strikes Venice, two-thirds of the population die
1666 A.D.—The Great Fire of London

And at its very center, where the spiral closed in on itself and ended in a large spot of black, was a third red label:

2004 A.D.—???

He balanced the chart on his desk. "As you can see, I've charted many other disasters. They all fall *precisely* along the natural logarithmic spiral, all perfectly aligned in golden ratios. No matter how I cut the data, the last date in the sequence is always 2004 A.D. *Always.* And what do these natural disasters have in common? They have always struck an important world city, a city notable for its wealth, power, technology—and neglect of the spiritual."

He reached across his desk, picked a red pencil from a pewter cup. "I'd hoped I was wrong, hoped it was a mere coincidence. I waited for the arrival of the year 2004, expecting to be proved wrong. But I no longer think nature believes in coincidence. There is an order to all things, Mr. Harriman. We have a moral niche on this earth, just as we have an ecological niche. When species exhaust their ecological niche, there is a correction, a purification. Sometimes even an *extinction.* It's the way of nature. But what happens when a species exhausts its moral niche?"

He turned the pencil around, moved it to the center of the diagram, and erased the question marks:

2004 A.D.—

"In every instance there were harbingers. Small events, of seemingly limited significance. Many of these events have involved the death of morally dubious persons by the same means as the upcoming disaster. This happened in Pompeii before the eruption of Vesuvius, in London before the Great Fire, in Venice before the plague. So now perhaps you see, Mr. Harriman, why I say that Jeremy Grove and Nigel Cutforth are in themselves meaningless. Oh, to be sure, both men are remarkable for their hatred of religion and morals, their repudiation of decency, their outrageous excess. As such, they are role models for the greed, concupiscence, materialism, cruelty of our times—and particularly of this place, New York. But they are still merely harbingers—the first, I fear, of many."

Von Menck let the chart fall gently to the desk. "Are you a reader of poetry, Mr. Harriman?"

"No. Not since college, anyway."

"Perhaps you remember W. B. Yeats's poem 'The Second Coming'?

" Mere anarchy is loosed upon the world...
The best lack all conviction, while the worst
Are full of passionate intensity."

Von Menck leaned closer. "We live in a time of moral nihilism and a blind worship of technology, combined with a rejection of the spiritual dimension of life. Television, movies, computers, video games, the Internet, artificial intelligence. These are the gods of our times. Our leaders are morally bankrupt, shameless hypocrites, feigning piety but devoid of real spirituality. We live in a time in which university scholars belittle spirituality, scorn religion, and bow deeply to the altar of science. We live in a time when so many spurn the church and the synagogue, where radio commentators are shock jocks spewing hatred and vulgarity, where televised entertainment consists of *Real Sex* and *Celebrity Fear Factor*. We live in a time of suicide bombing, terrorism run amok, and nuclear blackmail."

The room fell silent, save for the faint beep of the recorder. At last, Von Menck stirred, spoke again.

"The ancients believed nature to be comprised of four elements: earth, air, fire, and water. Some talked of floods; others of earthquakes or mighty winds; others of the devil. When Atlantis had betrayed its niche in the moral order of nature, it was consumed by water. The destruction of Sodom and Gomorrah came by fire. The plague that struck Venice came by air. Like the golden ratio, it follows a cyclical pattern. I've charted it here."

He took out another diagram, very complex, covered with lines, charts, and numbers. All the lines seemed to converge on a central pentagram in which was written:

2004 A.D.—New York City—Fire

"So you think New York City will burn?"

"Not in any normal way. It will be consumed by a fire *within*, like Grove and Cutforth."

"You think this can be avoided if people turn back to God?"

Von Menck shook his head. "It's too late for that.

And please note, Mr. Harriman, I have not used the word *God*. What I'm talking about here is not necessarily God but a force of nature: a moral law of the universe as fixed as any physical law. We've created an imbalance that needs to be corrected. The year 2004." He tapped the pile of charts. "It's the big one. It's the one Nostradamus predicted, Edgar Cayce predicted, Revelation predicted."

Harriman nodded. He felt a crawling sensation along his spine. This was powerful stuff. But was it all claptrap? "Dr. Von Menck, you've devoted a great deal of time and research on this."

"It has been my overwhelming obsession. For over fifteen years, I've known the significance of the year 2004. I've been *waiting*."

"Are you really convinced, or is this just a theory?"

"I will answer by telling you this: I am leaving New York tomorrow."

"Leaving?"

"For the Galápagos Islands."

"Why the Galápagos?"

"As Darwin could tell you, they are *famous* for their isolation." Von Menck gestured at the recorder. "This time there will be no documentary. The story is all yours, Mr. Harriman."

"No documentary?" Harriman repeated, stupefied.

"If I'm the least bit right in my suspicions, Mr. Harriman, when this is over, there won't be much of an audience for a documentary—will there?" And, for the first time since Harriman had entered the room, Dr. Von Menck smiled—a small, sad smile utterly devoid of humor.

{ 30 }

D'Agosta gazed at the miserable-looking thing on his plate—long, thin, unidentifiable, swimming in a puddle of sauce. It smelled vaguely like fish. At least, he thought, it would help his diet. It had been ten days since Grove's death, and he'd lost five pounds already, what with the new weight routine and jogging regimens he'd instituted, not to mention the hours he'd put in at the shooting range, which were adding bulk and steadiness to his forearms and shoulders. Another two months, and he'd be back to his old NYPD condition.

Proctor flitted about in the background, presenting and whisking away plates with the least amount of warning gentility would allow. Pendergast sat at the head of the table, Constance to his left. She looked a little less pale than before: some sun, perhaps, from yesterday's outing. But the dining room of the ancient Riverside Drive mansion remained a dreary place, with its dark green wallpaper and equally dark oil paintings. The windows that once must have looked out over the Hudson had been boarded up a long time ago, and it appeared Pendergast was going to leave them that way.

No wonder the guy was so white, living in the dark like some cave creature. D'Agosta decided he'd trade the whole dinner, and its procession of mysterious dishes, for barbecued ribs and a cooler full of frosties in his sunny Suffolk County backyard. Even Fosco's exotic picnic basket of the day before had been preferable. He gave the dish an exploratory poke.

"Don't you like the cod roe?" Pendergast asked him. "It's an old Italian recipe."

"My grandmother was from Naples, and she never cooked anything like this in her life."

"I believe this dish comes from Liguria. But never mind: cod roe is not to everyone's taste." He signaled to Proctor, who whisked the plate away and, a few moments later, returned with a steak and a small silver beaker brimming with wonderful-smelling sauce. In his other hand was a can of Budweiser, still dripping chips of ice.

D'Agosta tucked in, then glanced up to see Pendergast smiling with amusement. "Constance cooks a sublime *tournedos bordelaise*. I had it waiting in the wings, just in case. Along with the, ah, iced beer."

"That was decent of you."

"Is the steak to your liking?" Constance asked from across the table. "I prepared it *saignant*, as the French prefer."

"I don't know about *saignant,* but it's rare, just the way I like it."

Constance smiled, pleased.

D'Agosta speared another forkful, washed it down with a swig. "So what's next?" he asked Pendergast.

"After dinner, Constance will indulge us by playing

a few of Bach's partitas. She is a rather accomplished violinist, though I fear I'm a poor judge of such things. And I think you'll find the violin she plays interesting. It was part of my great-uncle's collections, an old Amati, in fairly decent shape, though its tone has gone off somewhat."

"Sounds great." D'Agosta coughed delicately. "But what I meant was, what's next for the investigation?"

"Ah! I see. Our next move, actually, has two fronts. We track down this Ranier Beckmann, and we do more background research on the strange nature of our two deaths. I have somebody already at work on the former. And Constance is about to fill us in on the latter."

Constance dabbed primly at her mouth with a napkin. "Aloysius has asked me to look into historical precedents for SHC."

"Spontaneous human combustion," said D'Agosta. "As in the Mary Reeser case you mentioned to the M.E. at the Cutforth homicide?"

"Exactly."

"You don't really believe in that, do you?"

"The case of Mary Reeser is only the most famous of many, and it is well documented. Isn't that right, Constance?"

"Famous, impeccably documented, and very curious." She consulted some notes that lay at her elbow. "On July 1, 1951, Mrs. Reeser, a widow, went to sleep in an easy chair in her apartment in St. Petersburg, Florida. She was found the next morning by a friend who smelled smoke. When they broke down the door, they found that the chair Mary Reeser had sat in was now just a heap of charred coil springs. As for Mary Reeser herself, her one hundred and seventy pounds had been reduced to less than ten pounds of ash and bone. Only her left foot remained intact, still wearing a slipper, burned off at the ankle but otherwise undamaged. Also found were her liver and her skull, cracked and splintered by the intense heat. And yet the rest of the apartment was intact. The only burning occurred in the small circular area encompassing the remains of Mrs. Reeser, her chair, and a plastic electric wall outlet which had melted, stopping her clock at 4:20 A.M. When the clock was plugged into another outlet, it worked perfectly."

"You gotta be kidding."

"The Bureau was called in immediately, and their documentation was impeccable," said Pendergast. "Photographs, tests, analysis—it ran to more than a thousand pages. Our experts determined that a temperature of at least three thousand degrees would be necessary to cremate a body that thoroughly. A cigarette igniting her clothing would never have produced that temperature, and besides, Mary Reeser didn't smoke. There were no traces of gasoline or other accelerants. No short circuit. Even lightning was ruled out. The case was never officially closed."

D'Agosta shook his head in disbelief.

"And it's not just a recent phenomenon," Constance said. "Dickens wrote an account of spontaneous combustion into his novel *Bleak House.* He was roundly criticized by reviewers for it, so he later defended himself by recounting a real case of SHC in the preface to the 1853 edition."

D'Agosta, who had been about to take another bite of steak, put down his fork.

"On the evening of April 4, 1731, Dickens tells us, the countess Cornelia Zangari de' Bandi of Cesena, in Italy, complained of feeling 'dull and heavy.' A maid helped her to bed, and they spent several hours praying and talking together. The next morning, when the countess did not arise at her usual time, the maid called at the door. There was no answer—just a foul smell.

"The maid opened the door to a scene of horror. The air was full of bits of floating soot. The countess, or what remained of her, was lying on the stone floor about four feet from the bed. Her entire torso had burned to ashes, even the bones reduced to crumbled piles. Only her legs remained, from the knees down; a few fragments from her hands; and a piece of forehead with a lock of blonde hair attached. The rest of the body was merely an outline in ash and crumbled bone. It, and other early cases such as Madame Nicole of Rheims, were invariably ascribed to death by the 'visitation of God.'"

"Excellent research, Constance," Pendergast said.

She smiled. "There are several volumes devoted to spontaneous human combustion in the library here. Your great-uncle was fascinated by bizarre forms of death—but of course, you know that already. Unfortunately there are no books here more recent than 1954, but there are still many dozens of earlier accounts. SHC cases all have several elements in common. The torso is completely incinerated, but the extremities are frequently left intact. The blood is, quite literally, vaporized from the body: normal fires do not dehydrate body tissue to such a great degree. The inferno is extremely localized: nearby furniture or other items, even inflammable ones, remain untouched. Officials often speak of a 'circle of death': everything inside is consumed, while everything outside is spared."

Slowly, D'Agosta pushed away his half-eaten steak. This all sounded pretty similar to what happened to Grove and Cutforth, with one crucial difference: the branding of the cloven hoof and face, and the stench of brimstone.

Just then came a low, hollow knock at the distant front door.

"Neighborhood kids, I imagine," said Pendergast after a moment of silence.

The hollow knock came again—deliberate, insistent, echoing through the galleries and halls of the ancient mansion.

"That's not the knock of a delinquent," Constance murmured.

Proctor cast an inquiring glance at Pendergast. "Shall I?"

"With the usual precautions."

Within the space of a minute, the servant had ushered a man into the room: a tall man with thin lips and thinner brown hair. He wore a gray suit, and the knot of his tie had been pulled down from the collar of his white shirt. His features were regular, his face perhaps lined more than would be usual for a man his age, yet the lines spoke more of weariness than years. He was neither handsome nor ugly. In every way, the man was remarkable for his lack of expression and individuality. It seemed to D'Agosta an almost studied anonymity.

He paused in the doorway and his eyes roamed over the group, coming to rest on Pendergast.

"Yes?" Pendergast said.

"Come with me."

"May I ask who you are, and on what errand you come?"

"No."

A short silence greeted this.

"How did you know I lived here?"

The man continued gazing at Pendergast with that expressionless face. It wasn't natural. It gave D'Agosta the creeps.

"Come, please. I'd rather not ask again."

"Why should I go with you if you refuse to divulge your name or the nature of your business?"

"My name is not important. I have information for you. Information of a sensitive nature."

Pendergast looked at the man a moment longer. Then he casually removed his Les Baer .45 from his suit coat, made sure a round was in the chamber, replaced it in his suit. "Any objections?"

The expression never changed. "Won't make any difference either way."

"Wait a minute." D'Agosta rose. "I don't like this. I'm coming, too."

The man turned to him. "Not possible."

"Screw that."

The man's only response was to stare at D'Agosta. His features, if anything, grew even deader.

Pendergast laid an arm on D'Agosta's. "I think I'd better go alone."

"The hell with that. You don't know who this guy is, what he wants, anything. I don't like it."

The stranger turned and walked swiftly out of the room. A moment later, Pendergast followed. D'Agosta watched him go with a mounting feeling of dismay.

{ 31 }

The man drove north on the West Side Highway, saying nothing, and Pendergast was content to leave it that way. Rain began to fall, splattering the windshield. The car approached the on-ramp to the George Washington Bridge, its gleaming lights strung across the Hudson. Just before the ramp, the car veered off on a service road and bumped its way down the pitted, half-paved surface to a turnaround, hidden in a cluster of poison sumac at the foot of the bridge's enormous eastern tower.

Only now did the man speak. "Wired?"

"No."

"I ask only for your sake."

"CIA?"

The man nodded at the windshield. "I know you could ID me in a minute. I want your word that you won't."

"You have it."

The man tossed a blue folder into Pendergast's lap. Its label tab bore a single word: *BULLARD.* It was stamped *Classified: Top Secret.*

"Where did this come from?" Pendergast asked.

"I've been investigating Bullard for the past eighteen months."

"On what grounds?"

"It's all there. But I'll summarize it for you. Bullard's the founder, CEO, and majority shareholder of Bullard Aerospace Industries. BAI is a medium-sized, privately owned aerospace engineering firm. Mostly they design and test components for military aircraft, drones, and missiles. They're also one of the subcontractors for the space shuttle. Among other things, BAI was involved in developing the antiradar coating for the stealth bomber and fighter programs. It's a highly profitable company, and they're very good at what they do. Bullard has some of the best engineers money can buy. He is a very, very capable man, if hot-tempered and impulsive. But he's one of the really bad ones. Know what I mean? He doesn't hesitate to hurt, or eliminate, those who stand in his way. Civilian *or* official."

"Understood."

"Good. Now listen. BAI also does research work for foreign governments. Some aren't so friendly. That work is subject to strict export controls and transfer of technology prohibitions. It's watched very closely. So far, BAI has kept within the law—at least as far as its U.S. facilities go. The problem is with a small BAI plant in Italy, in an industrial suburb of Florence called Lastra a Signa. A few years ago, BAI bought a defunct factory there. It was once owned by Alfred Nobel." An ironic smile flickered across the man's face. "It's a sprawling, decaying place. They've turned its core into a highly sophisticated R&D facility."

Rain continued to drum on the roof. There was the flicker of lightning over the river, a faint roll of thunder.

"We don't really know what BAI does in this Italian plant, but we have some indirect evidence that they may be working on a project for the Chinese. Last year we monitored a string of ballistic missile tests over the Lop Nur desert testing grounds. It seems the missile in question is a new type, specifically designed to penetrate America's planned antimissile shield."

Pendergast nodded.

"What makes the missile special is a new aerodynamic form, combined with some special surface or coating, which together make it invisible to radar. It doesn't even leave a heat trace or turbulence wake on Doppler. But here's the rub: whatever it is the Chinese have done, it isn't working. Up to now, all their missiles have broken up on re-entry.

"That's where BAI comes in. This is right up their alley. We think the Chinese hired BAI to solve the problem. And we think they're solving it at the Florentine plant."

"How?"

"We don't know. The breakups seem to have had something to do with a resonance spike that occurs at re-entry. The shape of the missile is so constrained by having to remain invisible that it's almost unflyable. A similar problem occurred with the stealth bomber, but it was solved with some heavy computing power and wind-tunnel research. But here the missile is moving a hell of a lot faster, it's ballistic, and it's up against a much more sophisticated radar. The answer lies somewhere in the field of eigenvalue mathematics, Fourier transforms, that sort of thing. You know what I'm talking about?"

"At a basic level."

"The mathematics of vibrations, resonance, and dampening. It has to be perfectly aerodynamic while having a surface that's black to radar. This missile can't have any curves, hardness, or smoothness—those would cause reflection or turbulence you could see on the Doppler—and yet it has to be aerodynamic. If anyone can rise to the technical challenge, BAI can."

"Is this file for me?"

"Yes."

"Why?"

The agent looked at Pendergast for the first time, and his mask of expressionlessness fell away. What Pendergast saw was the face of a very, very tired man. "It's the same old story. The CIA is subject to partisan political pressure. Bullard has friends in Washington. I was told to deep-six the Bullard investigation. After all, he's raised millions for the reelection campaigns of a half dozen key senators and congressmen, as well as the president. Why, we're asked, is the CIA harassing a fine, upstanding citizen when there are so many foreign terrorists out there? You know the refrain."

Pendergast simply nodded.

"But screw it, this bastard is selling America down the river. He's a traitor, just like those good old American companies that sell dual-use technology to Iran and Syria. If Bullard gets away with this, the U.S. will have laid out a hundred billion dollars developing an antimissile system that will be obsolete on deployment.

And if that happens, it's the CIA that's going to get hammered. The administration will experience sudden and complete amnesia as to how they deliberately shut down our investigation. The Congress is going to demand an official inquiry on the so-called intelligence failure. We'll be everyone's whipping boy."

"Something we at the FBI know a little about."

"I spent eighteen months investigating Bullard, and I'll be goddamned if I'm going to let it go. I'm a patriotic American. I want you to nail Bullard. I don't want a nuclear missile to take out New York because some American businessman paid off a few congressmen."

Pendergast put the folder to one side. "Why me?"

"I've heard you're pretty good, even if you are FBI." The man allowed himself a cynical smile. "And I liked the way you dragged Bullard down to headquarters like a common criminal. That took guts. You really pissed some people off. Big time."

"Regrettable. But I fear it is not the first time."

"You better watch your ass."

"I shall."

"You won't find any smoking guns in the file; Bullard's covered his tracks well. You've got your work cut out."

He started the engine, flicked on the headlights, pulled through the turnaround, and headed back up to the traffic droning southward into lower Manhattan. He said nothing else until turning off the highway at 145th Street, the skyscrapers of Midtown like glowing crystals in the distance.

"You never heard of me, I never heard of you, and this conversation never took place. That file has been cleaned of intelligence markers, so even if it gets back to the CIA, no one will know where it came from."

"Won't they suspect you, anyway? It was your case."

"You worry about your ass, I'll worry about mine."

He left Pendergast a few blocks north of his house. As Pendergast was exiting the car, the man leaned toward him and spoke once again. "Agent Pendergast?"

Pendergast turned back.

"If you can't nail the bastard, kill him."

{ 32 }

The man calling himself Vasquez looked carefully around the little space where he would be spending the next several days of his life. A few minutes earlier he had tensed, preparing for an unexpected opportunity, when the door of the porte-cochère opened across the way. A quick check through the scope confirmed the target was leaving. However, another man had been with him. Vasquez had laid aside the rifle and made a note in his log: *22:31.04.* The two men walked to a car parked a few yards down the street, an unmarked law enforcement Chevy, obviously a government model.

As the car had pulled away, there'd been a brief flash of white in the doorway of the porte-cochère; Vasquez saw the retreating figure of a man in a tuxedo, shutting the door again. Butler, from the look of it. But who heard of a butler in this part of town?

Vasquez refused to allow himself any regret. Finishing a job so prematurely just never happened. Besides, it always paid to be overly cautious. Putting his notebook away, he went back to preparing his kill nest. The abandoned room of the old welfare hotel was a wreck.

There were used needles and condoms piled in a corner; a torn mattress on the floor with a dark stain in its middle, as if somebody had died on it. As his hooded light moved around the room, cockroaches fled in panic, their greasy brown backs flashing dully, countless legs rustling like leaves. But Vasquez was used to such things, and he was well pleased with his accommodations. He had, in fact, rarely seen a setup quite so ideal. He replaced the small piece of plywood from the boarded-up room's lone window and went back to his preparations.

Yes, this would do perfectly. The window faced north, looking out over the great dark bulk of the ruined mansion at 891 Riverside Drive. It was a crazy place for the target to live, but each to his own. Three stories down and across 137th Street was the porte-cochère, its semicircular driveway running under a brick and marble arch. He could just see the edge of the door the target used for ingress and egress: the one he had just come out of. So far he had used no other door—but then, Vasquez had been watching for only twelve hours.

Yes, this was a fine setup. In this part of Harlem, there were no inquisitive doormen hanging out in front of their buildings; no hidden video cameras; no old ladies who would call the police at the mere howl of an alley cat. Here, even gunshots didn't necessarily trigger a call to the police. What's more, Vasquez had found this abandoned building directly across from the target residence. It had a basement entrance hidden from the mansion, leading to an alley fronting 136th.

You couldn't ask for better.

The target, an FBI agent, seemed to be a man of regular habits. In the coming days, Vasquez would ascertain just how regular those habits were. As with hunting any animal, success lay in learning the creature's patterns of behavior. Vasquez intended to become an expert in this particular creature. He would learn by what doors he came and left, and when; he would ascertain who lived in the old mansion, who visited, what kind of security was in place. By understanding the movements, he would gain an insight into the man's psychology. Even people who varied their habits out of fear of assassination always varied them in a pattern. From what little he'd observed, he already realized he was dealing with an exceptionally cautious, intelligent target. But then, Vasquez always assumed at the beginning that the target was smarter, craftier, cleverer than he was. Vasquez had stalked and killed them all: federal agents, diplomats, mobsters, minor heads of state, even physicists. He'd been in the business twenty-two years in as many countries, and he had learned a trick or two. But it was wise to stay humble.

Without moving any of the original contents of the room, Vasquez began to unroll thick canvas tarps over the floor and partway up the walls, fixing them in place with gaffing tape. The room filled with the strong, pleasant smell of waterproof duck. Next he laid out his tools, mentally running through the checklist in his mind. They were all there, as he knew they would be, but he double-checked just to make sure. He picked up his Remington M21 bolt-action rifle, removed the box cartridge, made sure its small magazine was filled with the subsonic 7.62 by 51 military cartridges he preferred. The weapon was of an old design, but Vasquez was not interested in the latest frills or gimmicks: what mattered to him was simplicity, accuracy, and reliability. He rammed the magazine home, cranked a round into the chamber, examined the permanently fixed tactical telescopic sight. Satisfied, he put the weapon aside and carefully laid out packets of beef jerky and jugs of water sufficient for five days. Next, he set up his laptop computer, arranging a dozen freshly charged battery packs beside it. A pair of night-vision goggles was inspected and found to be in excellent order. Then, moving to a far corner, the man set up his washstand and toilet by the dim light of his torch. He would not be disturbed: the door had already been locked, screwed shut in the jambs with a battery-operated screwdriver, and light-sealed with the gaffing tape. A small bathroom window in the back provided fresh air.

Returning to the front of the room, he switched off the light and removed the piece of plywood from the shooting hole: a hole just large enough for the barrel and scope. He snapped open a bipod assembly and mounted it to the fore end of the stock. He very carefully positioned the rifle onto the porte-cochère, at head height. Then he reached for a handheld laser range finder, pointed it at the mansion's front door. It returned a distance of 30.66 meters. With a rifle that was accurate beyond five hundred yards, 30 meters was nothing. He would be shooting down through cool air with his target outside: the conditions he favored above all others. A few final adjustments and the weapon was ready.

His kill nest was complete.

Vasquez peered out again through the sight. The house was still and dark, the windows boarded up. This was not a normal home. Something illicit must be going on inside. But since it didn't make his target in any way erratic, Vasquez didn't really care. He had a job to do, limited in scope and restricted in time. He didn't care who it was who had hired him, or why. He cared about only one thing: the two million dollars that had appeared in his numbered account. That was all he needed to know.

He returned to his patient observation. Sometimes he liked to think of himself as a kind of naturalist, studying the habits of shy woodland creatures. He had the perfect blend of intelligence, discipline, and disposition for sitting in a blind in the jungle for weeks at a time, observing, taking notes, looking for patterns.

Only thing was, there was no money in that. And besides: nothing could compare with the thrill of the kill.

{ 33 }

It was almost midnight, D'Agosta saw from his watch, and Hayward was still at her desk. The rest of the Homicide Division was quiet as a tomb: just the night crew, working in their cubicles on the floor below. Hayward was alone. The only light, the only sound, came from the open door of her office. Funny, considering most New York City murders happened at night. *Like any other job,* D'Agosta thought to himself. *The average Joe doesn't want to log any more hours than necessary.*

He crept up to Hayward's door and listened. He could hear the tapping of her computer keyboard. She had to be the most ambitious cop he'd ever met. It was a little scary.

D'Agosta knocked.

"Come in."

The place was a disaster area: papers piled on every chair, the police-band radio squawking, a laser printer in a corner whining out some job. It was remarkably unlike the offices of most police captains, which were kept spotlessly clean and free of any real work.

She glanced up. "What brings you to brasstown so late?"

D'Agosta cleared his throat. This was going to be difficult. Pendergast—after dropping off the face of the earth for more than an hour—had just shown up in his hotel room thirty minutes before. Although he'd revealed precious few details of what happened, he had seemed almost *animated*, if such a thing was possible. And then he'd promptly sent D'Agosta off on an assignment—*this* assignment—because he'd known he had no chance at succeeding himself.

"It's Bullard again," he said.

Hayward sighed. "Move those papers and take a seat."

D'Agosta shifted a pile off one of the chairs and sat down. Hayward had unbuttoned her collar, taken off her hat, and let her hair down. It was surprisingly long, falling in big glossy waves below her shoulders. Despite the cluttered office, she looked cool somehow; fresh. She eyed him with a mixture of amusement and—what else? Affection? But no: that was his late-night imagination at work.

D'Agosta took out the folder and laid it on the desk. "Pendergast got this, I don't know how."

Hayward picked it up, glanced at it, dropped it like it was a piece of hot iron. "Jesus, Vinnie. This is classified!"

"No shit it's classified."

"No way am I going to read that. I never even saw it. Put it away."

"Let me just summarize what's in there—"

"God, no."

D'Agosta sat, wondering just how he was going to do this. Might as well get it over with.

"Pendergast wants you to put a tap on Bullard's phones."

Hayward stared at him for at least ten seconds. "Why doesn't he get it through the FBI?"

"He can't."

"Can't Pendergast ever do *any*thing by the book?"

"Bullard's too powerful. The FBI's a political creature, and not even Pendergast can change that. But you could get the U.S. Attorney's Office to issue a Title 3, no problem."

"I can't use a *classified* file to get Title 3 wiretap authority!" She was up from the desk, eyes flashing.

"No. But you could use the murder investigation as a hook."

"Vincent, are you *nuts*? There's no evidence against Bullard. No witness to put him at the scene of the crime. No motive, nothing to connect him with either the murders or the victims."

"The phone calls."

"Phone calls!" She paced behind the desk. "A lot of people make phone calls."

"His computer was stuffed with encrypted files. Hard encryption, virtually unbreakable."

"I encrypt e-mails to my mother. Vincent, that is *not evidence*. This is just the kind of thing that hits the *Times* front page, makes us look like we're blowing off people's constitutional rights. Besides, you know what a pain in the ass it is to get a wiretap authority. You've got to prove it's your last resort."

"You should read the file. It seems Bullard's been transferring military technology to the Chinese."

"I told you not to tell me what's in the file."

"He's got a company in Italy that's helping the Chinese develop a missile that can penetrate the U.S.'s planned missile shield."

"That's as far out of my jurisdiction as a pickpocket in Outer Mongolia."

"Bullard has big-time friends in Washington. He gives money to everyone's campaign. So neither the FBI nor the CIA wants to touch it."

She was pacing the room, flushed, her jet hair swaying across her shoulders.

"Look, Laura, we're both Americans. Bullard's a bad guy. He's selling our country down the river, and no one's doing a damn thing about it. All you need to do is come up with a good story for the judge. Okay, so maybe it's not strictly by the book."

"There's a reason for the book, Vincent."

"Yeah, but there also comes a time when you have to do what's *right*."

"What's right is to follow the rules."

"Not with something like this. New York City is still terrorist target numero uno. God knows who Bullard might sell his services to. Once this technology gets on the black market, we have no idea where it'll end up."

Hayward sighed. "Look. I'm a detective captain in New York City Homicide. The United States has hundreds of thousands of talented people—spooks, scientists, diplomats—employed to handle people like Bullard."

"Yeah. But right now, you're on the spot. The file

hints that something big is going down. Listen, Laura, nothing could be simpler than this wiretap. Bullard's in the middle of the Atlantic Ocean. We've got his satellite phone number, we've got a pen register of the numbers he's calling. It's all in the file."

"You can't tap a sat phone."

"I know. We'd get the taps on the land-based numbers of his cronies, monitor the conversations from their end."

"That won't help us if he calls a nonrecorded number."

"It's better than nothing."

Hayward took a few more turns around the room, then stopped in front of him. "This is not our problem. The answer's no."

D'Agosta tried to smile, found he couldn't. That was it, then. You didn't become the youngest female detective captain in New York City history by breaking the rules, being a maverick. He should have known the answer even before he asked the question.

He glanced up to find Hayward looking at him intently. "I don't like the expression on your face, Vincent."

He shrugged. "I gotta go."

"I know what you're thinking."

"Then I don't need to tell you."

Her face was coloring with anger. "You think I'm a careerist, don't you?"

"You said it, not me."

She stepped around the desk toward him. "You're a son of a bitch, you know that? I had to take a lot of shit as a T.A. cop, a lot of harassment from guys who thought I was working too hard. I'm not going to take that shit anymore. When a man's ambitious, it's called drive. When a woman's ambitious, it's careerism and she's a bitch."

Now D'Agosta felt himself flaring as well. Women were always broadening an argument into some kind of male-female thing. "That's just a smoke screen. Look, you can either do the right thing, or you can do the safe thing. And you're obviously on the side of safe. Fine. I won't stand in your way of becoming Commissioner Hayward." D'Agosta rose, picked up the bundle of papers he had put on the floor, put them back on the chair. Then he retrieved the classified folder from the desktop. When he turned, he found she was blocking the door.

He stood calmly, waiting for her to step aside. She didn't move.

He remained standing.

"I'm leaving now." He took a step forward but she still didn't move. She was so close to him he could feel her warmth, smell the fragrance of shampoo in her hair.

"That was a shitty thing to say." Her face remained flushed.

He tried to go around her, but she shifted and he almost ran up against her.

"Listen," she said. "I love this country as much as anyone. I also know I've done a lot of good work in this department, solved a lot of cases, put a lot of bad people behind bars. I'm effective *because* I play by the rules. So don't lay that bullshit on me."

D'Agosta said nothing. He stood where he was, mere inches from her, breathing hard, breathing in her anger, her perfume, the smell of her. He was conscious of her blue eyes, her ivory skin. He took a step toward her and their bodies touched. It was like a sudden electrical contact. They stood that way a moment, both breathing hard, their anger morphing into something else. He leaned forward and their lips met and he could feel her breasts pressing against him as they slowly kissed.

Her hand touched the back of his neck and she moved closer still, bringing their bodies into full contact, and then almost without knowing what he was doing he reached around with both arms, molded his hands to her form, and pulled her in hard against him. He could barely stand the rush of arousal that had engulfed him and he fought for breath as his lips slid lightly to her chin, kissing her, then down her neck, then over her shoulder. She shifted in his grasp, sighing; he could feel her hot breath move across his cheek as she took his earlobe between her teeth, first gently, then more sharply. She pulled him back toward her desk, leaned back, and he followed her down, keeping her hips locked against his. Now his hands fumbled with the buttons of her shirt, then the catch of her bra, and as he saw her breasts swing free he felt himself grow even harder. Her hands dropped from his shoulders, tracing lines down his torso, his stomach, then to the waistband of his pants, unbuckling his belt and loosening his zipper and slowly easing him free. Now the hand began to stroke him, slowly, and he gasped involuntarily as he reached for the hem of her skirt, slid his hand beneath it, and teased her panties free. She staggered a little as he entered her, thrusting her hips forward while arching her back, bringing him deep inside her. For a moment they remained like that, eyes locked. Hayward's lips parted; then her head sank backward, exposing her neck, and she let out a groan of desire. He wrapped his arms around her thighs and began sliding into her, again and again and again, gently, deliberately, the papers spilling to the floor...

...And then, in a sudden flood of pleasure, it was over. She held him, her dark hair wild, breathing hard, her limbs around his, contracting and relaxing in slowing spasms. They embraced each other for what seemed a very long time. And yet it was all too soon when she kissed him and gently pulled away. Only then did D'Agosta realize he still didn't understand what had just happened. He covered his confusion by turning from her, putting his clothes into some semblance of order. As he did so, he realized he couldn't even remember what had led to their sudden embrace. They had just come together like magnets. Nothing like this had ever happened to him before. He wasn't sure if he should feel elated, embarrassed, or nervous.

Behind him, he could hear her slow laugh. "Not bad," she said, her voice a little husky. "For a broken-down, washed-up loser, I mean. Next time, though, we should probably shut the door." She smiled at him from under a wild mop of black hair, a mottled flush fading below her neck, her breasts rising and falling heavily as she smoothed down her skirt. "You know what I like about you, Vincent?"

"No."

"You really care—about your work, about the case, and most of all, about justice. You *care*."

D'Agosta still felt out there, almost dizzy with what had happened. He ran his hand over his hair, adjusted his pants. He wasn't sure what she meant.

"I guess you earned that Title 3. With a little thought, I should be able to make something up."

He paused. "That wasn't why—"

She sat up, laid a finger on his lips. "Your *integrity* just earned you the Title 3. Not the—the other thing." Then she smiled again. "I'll tell you what. We kind of got things backwards here. Do what you have to do. Then you can take me out for a nice, long, romantic, candlelight dinner."

{ 34 }

The wire room of the lower Manhattan Federal Building was a nondescript space on the tower's fourteenth floor. To D'Agosta, it looked just like a typical office: fluorescent ceiling, neutral carpeting, countless identical cubicles forming a human ant farm. Depressing as shit.

He looked around guardedly, half hoping, half afraid he'd find Laura Hayward waiting for him. But there was only one of her detectives, Mandrell: the same guy who had called at lunchtime with news they'd obtained a Title 3 order from the U.S. Attorney's Office. The FBI, with its superior equipment, would execute the Title 3, in a joint operation with the NYPD. Coming through the NYPD had made it somehow politically acceptable.

"Sergeant," Mandrell said, shaking his hand. "Everything's set up. Is Agent, ah, Pendergast—"

"Here," said Pendergast, striding into the room. His beautifully cut black suit, pressed to perfection, shimmered under the artificial light. D'Agosta wondered just how many identical black suits the guy owned. Probably had rooms at the Dakota and the Riverside Drive mansion devoted to them.

"Agent Pendergast," D'Agosta said, "this is Detective Sergeant Mandrell of the Twenty-first Precinct."

"Delighted." Pendergast briefly shook the proffered hand. "Forgive me for not arriving earlier. I fear I took a wrong turn. This building is most confusing."

The Federal Building? Most confusing? Pendergast was a fed himself, he had to have an office in here somewhere. Didn't he? It occurred to D'Agosta that he'd never once seen, or been asked to visit, Pendergast's office.

"It's this way," Mandrell said, leading the way through a maze of cubicles.

"Excellent," Pendergast murmured to D'Agosta as they fell into step behind the detective. "I'll have to thank Captain Hayward personally. She really came through for us."

She came through, all right, D'Agosta thought with a private smile. The whole of the night before—Pendergast spirited away by the mysterious caller, his own totally unexpected encounter with Laura Hayward—seemed dreamlike, unreal. He had fought the temptation to call her all morning. He hoped she'd still want that long, candlelight dinner. He wondered if this would complicate their working relationship, decided it would, realized he didn't much care.

"Here we are," Mandrell said, stepping into one of the cubicles. It looked just like all the others: a desk with an overhanging credenza, a computer workstation with attached speakers, a few chairs. A young woman with short blonde hair sat at the workstation, typing.

"This is Agent Sanborne," Mandrell said. "She's monitoring the phone of Jimmy Chait, Bullard's right-hand boy here in the States. We have agents in adjoining cubicles logging the phones of another half dozen of Bullard's associates. Agent Sanborne, this is Sergeant D'Agosta of the Southampton P.D. and Special Agent Pendergast."

Sanborne nodded at them in turn, her eyes widening at the name of Pendergast.

"Anything?" Mandrell asked her.

"Nothing important," she replied. "There was some traffic a few minutes ago between Chait and another associate. Seems they're expecting a call from Bullard any time now."

Mandrell nodded, turned back to D'Agosta. "When was your last tap, Sergeant?"

"It's been a while."

"Then let me get you up to speed. Everything's done by computer these days, one workstation per phone number being monitored. The phone line goes right through this interface, and the conversation's recorded digitally. No more tapes. Agent Sanborne, who'll be transcribing the line sheets, can work the transport controls either by keyboard or foot pedal."

D'Agosta shook his head. It was a far cry from the low-tech setups he'd worked as a new jack cop in the mid-eighties.

"You mentioned Chinese?" Mandrell said. "Are we going to need a translator?"

"Unlikely," Pendergast replied.

"Well, we've got a man standing by, just in case."

The cubicle fell silent as Mandrell and Sanborne hovered over the screen.

"Vincent," Pendergast murmured, taking him aside.

"I've been wanting to tell you. We've made a very important discovery."

"What's that?"

"Beckmann."

D'Agosta looked at him sharply. *"Beckmann?"*

"His present whereabouts."

"No shit. When did you find out?"

"Late last night. After I called you to request this wiretap."

"Why didn't you tell me before?"

"I tried calling you as soon as I heard. There was no answer at your hotel. And your cell phone appeared to have been turned off."

"Oh. Yes, it was. Sorry about that." D'Agosta turned away, feeling a flush begin to spread over his face.

He was spared further questioning by a sudden beeping from the workstation.

"Call's coming in," said Agent Sanborne.

A small window appeared on her screen, filled with lines of data. "Chait's getting an incoming," she said, pointing at the window. "See?"

"Who's it from?" D'Agosta asked.

"The number's coming up now. I'll put it on vox."

"Jimmy?" came a high-pitched voice over the computer speaker. "Jimmy, you there?"

Sanborne began typing quickly, transcribing the call verbatim. "It's his home number," she said. "Probably his wife."

"Yeah," answered a deep voice with a thick New Jersey accent. "What you want?"

"When you coming home?"

"Something's come up." There was a faint roar in the background, like the rush of wind.

"No, Jimmy—not again today. We've got the Fingermans coming by this afternoon, remember? About the winter rental in Kissimmee?"

"Fuck that. You don't need me for that shit."

"Go ahead, take that tone with me. You're right, I *don't* need you for that *shit*. What I *need* is for you to stop by DePasquale's and pick up a few trays of sausage and peppers. I don't have a thing to serve."

"Then get your ass in the kitchen and cook something."

"Look, you—"

"I'll be home when I get home. Now get the fuck off, I'm expecting a call." And the line went dead.

There was a brief silence broken only by the click of keys as Agent Sanborne completed the transcription.

"Delightful couple," said D'Agosta. He motioned Pendergast aside. "How'd you find Beckmann, anyway?"

"With the help of an acquaintance of mine—an invalid, actually—who happens to be extremely good at tracking down troublesome nuggets of information."

"'Extremely good' sounds like an understatement. Nobody's been able to locate this guy. So where's this Beckmann at?"

But they were again interrupted by another beep from the computer. "We've got another one," said Sanborne.

"Incoming or outgoing?" asked Mandrell.

"Incoming. But the number must be blocked, I'm not getting any data on it."

There was a brief squeal over the speaker. "Yeah?" said Chait.

"Chait," a voice responded.

D'Agosta immediately recognized the gruff tone: it sent a thrill of hatred coursing through him.

Chait recognized it, too. "Yes, Mr. Bullard, sir," he said, his tone abruptly growing servile.

"Bullard will be using a satellite phone," D'Agosta said. "That's why you can't get a fix."

"Doesn't matter." Mandrell pointed to a string of numbers on the screen. "See that? It's the cell site of Chait's phone. It's the cellular node his phone signal's coming from, lets us determine his present location." He reached into the credenza, pulled out a thick manual, began leafing through it.

"Everything set?" Bullard asked.

"Yes, sir. The men have all been briefed."

"Remember what I said. I don't want any apologizing. Just do as I say. Walk it through, by the numbers."

"You got it, Mr. Bullard."

Mandrell looked up from the cell site manual. "Chait's in Hoboken, New Jersey."

"Everything's go," Bullard said. "The Chinese will be there on time."

"Location?" Chait asked.

"The primary, as discussed. The park."

Mandrell grasped D'Agosta by the arm. "Chait just changed cell sites," he said.

"What's that mean?"

"He's moving." Mandrell thumbed through the manual, looking up the new site. "Now he's in the middle of Union City."

"Mass transit wouldn't move that quickly," said Pendergast. "He must be in a car."

Bullard was speaking again. "Remember. They'll be expecting a progress report in exchange for the payment. You know what to give them, right?"

"Right."

Pendergast pulled out his own phone, dialing quickly. "Chait's on his way to a meeting. We've got to get a unit dispatched, triangulate on his location."

"I'll be expecting a report immediately after the meeting," said Bullard.

"I'll be back to you within ninety minutes."

"And Chait? No fuckups, you hear?"

"No, sir."

There was a click; a hiss of static; and the computer beeped once again to signal the connection had been broken.

"Cell site's changed again," Mandrell said, looking at the screen.

D'Agosta turned to Pendergast. "Within ninety minutes, he said? What the hell does that mean?"

Pendergast closed his phone, slipped it back into his pocket. "It means their meeting will take place before then. Come on, Vincent—we haven't a moment to lose."

{ 35 }

D'Agosta blew past the exit helixes of the George Washington Bridge and merged onto the express lanes, driving like hell. As the New Jersey Turnpike divided and the traffic began to thin a little, he seated the emergency bubble onto the dash, turned on its flasher, and began cranking the siren. Veering west onto I-80, he stomped hard on the pedal. The big engine of the pool sedan responded and they were soon rocketing along at a hundred miles an hour.

"Refreshing," murmured Pendergast.

The secure car-to-car frequency crackled into life. "This is 602. We've got a visual on the target. It's a TV van with a satellite dish, call letters WPMP, Hackensack, moving west on 80 near exit 65."

D'Agosta pushed his speed to one twenty.

Pendergast unhooked the mike. "We're just a few miles behind you. Hang back in another lane and keep out of sight. Over."

Everything had come together with remarkable speed. Pendergast had initiated a federal tail on Chait's cell signal, requisitioned a government vehicle, and put D'Agosta behind its wheel. The West Side Highway had been mercifully free of traffic, and it had taken them only ten minutes to clear Manhattan.

"Where do you think we're headed?" D'Agosta asked.

"Bullard mentioned a park. For now, that's all we know."

Out of the corner of his eye, D'Agosta noticed that, despite the speed, Pendergast had unbuckled his seat belt and was crouching forward. Now the agent was scratching his nails on the floor mat, rubbing his palms rapidly against it. D'Agosta had seen the man do strange things before, but this beat all. He wondered if he should ask, decided against it.

"Target leaving freeway at exit 60," the radio squawked. "Following."

D'Agosta slowed. Another minute, and he peeled off at the same exit.

"Target proceeding north on McLean."

"They're heading into Paterson," D'Agosta said. He'd never actually set foot in the city, though he'd passed it on the freeway countless times: a red-brick working town whose best days were probably about a hundred years gone. It seemed like a strange destination.

"Paterson," Pendergast repeated speculatively, wiping his dirty hands on his face and neck. "Birthplace of the American Industrial Revolution."

"Birthplace? Looks more like death's door to me."

"It's a city with a vigorous history, Vincent. Some of the historical neighborhoods are still quite beautiful. However, I'm banking on the fact that those are not where we're headed."

"Target leaving McLean," the voice on the radio said. "Heading left onto Broadway."

D'Agosta tore up McLean Highway, using the siren to punch his way through two red lights. To their right lay the Passaic River, brown and sullen in the autumn light. As he turned onto Broadway, shabby-looking and decrepit, he killed the siren and snapped off the flasher. They were close now: very close.

"Sergeant," Pendergast said abruptly, "head into this strip mall on our right, please. We need to make a quick stop."

D'Agosta glanced at him in surprise. "We don't have time."

"Trust me, we do."

D'Agosta shrugged. The operation was nominally FBI and Pendergast was in charge: Hayward had made sure of that. The lead car was FBI and he himself was Southampton P.D., which would offend nobody. Interstate police rivalries would be kept at a minimum. At the appropriate moment—when it was too late for a bunch of unbriefed town cops to screw things up—Pendergast would call in the locals.

The mall was a collection of dingy, glass-fronted stores set back from a parking lot heaved and cracked by time. It was half abandoned, and D'Agosta wondered just what the hell Pendergast was up to. Here he'd made good time, and now the agent was squandering it.

"There," Pendergast said. "At the far end."

D'Agosta sped up to the last storefront. A yellow Dumpster stood out front, pitted and scarred with age. Even before the car had stopped, Pendergast was out, running into the store. D'Agosta swore, punched the steering wheel. They were going to lose five minutes at least. He was used to Pendergast's inexplicable behavior, but this was too much.

"Target heading into East Side Park," came the cool voice from the lead car. "There's some kind of event going on. Looks like model rockets or something."

D'Agosta heard shouting and saw Pendergast trotting out of the shop, a bundle of clothes slung over one arm and a couple of pairs of shoes clutched in the other. Moments later a fat woman came bursting out.

"Help!" she bellowed. "Police! I hope you're proud of yourself, robbing the Salvation Army. Shithead!"

"Obliged, ma'am," Pendergast said, crumpling a hundred-dollar bill and tossing it over his shoulder as he jumped into the backseat. D'Agosta laid on the gas, leaving a streak of rubber and a cloud of smoke.

"I daresay that was no more than a two-minute detour," Pendergast said from the rear of the car. Looking into the mirror, D'Agosta saw he was peeling off his jacket and tie.

"Two minutes is a long time in this business."

"I'll have to send the Salvation Army people a little something to make up for my lack of manners."

"They're heading into East Side Park."

"Very good. Drive around the park, if you please, and enter from the south. I need a few more moments."

D'Agosta drove past the park—a wall of greenery to his left, rising above a concrete retaining wall—and made a left onto Derrom Avenue. Despite their proximity to seedy, sorry-looking Broadway, the houses here were remarkably large and well tended, relics of the days when Paterson had been a model city of industry.

Pendergast intoned from the back:

> *"Eternally asleep,*
> *his dreams walk about the city where he persists*
> *incognito."*

D'Agosta glanced again in the rearview mirror, almost jamming on the brakes in surprise when he saw a stranger staring back at him. But, of course, it was no stranger: it was Pendergast, transformed by some almost miraculous process of disguise.

"Have you ever read *Paterson* by William Carlos Williams?" the vagrant in the backseat asked.

"Never heard of it."

"Pity:

> *"Immortal he neither moves nor rouses and is seldom*
> *seen, though he breathes and the subtleties of his*
> *machinations*
> *drawing their substance from the noise of the pouring*
> *river*
> *animate a thousand automatons."*

D'Agosta shook his head and muttered to himself. He drove a few blocks, made another left, and entered the park beside a statue of Christopher Columbus.

East Side Park was an overgrown hillock of grass and the occasional shade tree, closely hemmed in on all four sides by houses. A lane wandered around its periphery, and D'Agosta eased the car onto it, passing a variety of pudding-stone outbuildings in various stages of disrepair. Concrete benches with green-painted wooden slats lined the roadway. Farther along, the lane veered in toward a height of land, which was crowned by a fountain surrounded by a black wrought-iron fence. Several cars were parked along the curb here, including their own lead vehicle, making the already narrow road almost impassable. Ahead, D'Agosta could see the TV van. It had pulled onto the grass between a brace of tennis courts and a baseball field. On the field itself, a small knot of kids was shooting off model rockets, supervised by half a dozen parents. A man with a television camera was standing by the van, filming the event.

"This is an exceptionally well planned meeting, Vincent," Pendergast said as they drove slowly past. "They're meeting in the middle of a park. No chance of being ambushed. And they're surrounded by noisy children and the roar of rockets, which will defeat any long-range electronic surveillance. That man with the camera is their lookout, with a perfect reason to be staring every which way through a telephoto lens. Bullard has clearly trained his men well. Ah, pull over a minute, please, Vincent: here come the Chinese."

In the rearview mirror, D'Agosta could make out a long black Mercedes, absurdly out of place, cruising slowly up the park drive behind them. It pulled onto the grass across the tennis courts from the van. Two big men with shaved heads and dark glasses got out, looking around carefully. Then a third, smaller man exited and began walking across the grass toward the van.

"What dreadful lack of subtlety," said Pendergast. "It appears these gentlemen have been watching too much television."

D'Agosta eased the car forward, coming to a stop

near the exit back onto Broadway. The hill fell away here and the trees were more numerous, blocking their car from view.

"Too bad I'm in uniform," he said.

"On the contrary: being in uniform, you will be the last one they suspect. I'm going to get as close as I can, see if I can learn more particulars about the meeting. You buy a donut and coffee over there"—he nodded to a dingy coffee shop across Broadway—"then wander into the park. Take a seat on one of the benches by the baseball diamond, where you'll have a clear line of fire should anything untoward occur. Let us hope, with these children around, that nothing of the sort occurs—but be ready for action regardless."

D'Agosta nodded.

Pendergast gave his eyes a vigorous rubbing. When his grubby hands fell away again, his eyes had lost their clear, silvery hue. Now they belonged to a tippler: uncertain, watery, red-rimmed.

D'Agosta watched Pendergast get out of the car and amble back up the rise. The agent was wearing a brown sport coat of dubious material, a faded stain between the shoulders; double-knit slacks a size too large; a pair of shabby Hush Puppies. His hair was several shades darker than usual—just how the hell had he managed that?—and his face was in need of a wash. He looked exactly like a man who was down but not quite out, clinging to a few shreds of respectability. And it wasn't just the clothes: his very gait had changed to a vague shuffle, his body language tentative, his eyes darting this way and that, as if prepared to ward off an unexpected blow.

D'Agosta stared another moment, marveling. Then

he exited the car, bought a coffee and a glazed donut in the coffee shop across the street, and headed back into the park. As he crested the little rise and approached the diamond, he could see the shorter Chinese man getting into the back of the television van. His large companions were hanging back about forty paces, arms crossed.

There was a *whooosh* as a model rocket went off to scattered cheers and clapping. All eyes turned skyward; there was a pop and the rocket came drifting back, floating beneath a red-and-white-striped miniature parachute.

D'Agosta eased himself onto a bench across the diamond from the van. He slipped the lid off his coffee, pretending to watch the rockets go off. This was strange: the would-be cameraman was now calling the kids together, apparently to film them. D'Agosta wondered if the cameraman was Chait, Bullard's main man in New York. He decided otherwise: Chait was no doubt inside the van with the Chinese honcho.

He turned his attention back to Pendergast. The agent was strolling along the walkway near the van. He paused, fished a racing form out of the trash, shook it clear of debris, then stopped to chat with the cameraman. It looked like he might be asking him for money. The man scowled and shook his head, motioning Pendergast to move on. Then the man turned back toward the children, gesturing for them to line up with their rockets.

D'Agosta felt a knot tighten in his stomach. Why the hell was the man organizing the kids like that, anyway? Something did not feel right at all.

Meanwhile, Pendergast had seated himself on the

bench next to the van, so close he could almost touch it, and was going through the racing form with a pencil stub, circling various horses and making notes.

Then—inexplicably—Pendergast stood up, went to the back door of the van, and knocked.

The cameraman came striding over immediately, gesticulating furiously, shoving Pendergast aside. D'Agosta resisted the impulse to reach for his gun. The back doors of the van opened; there was some loud talk; the doors slammed shut. The cameraman gestured angrily for Pendergast to move off, but instead, the agent shrugged and seated himself back down on the bench, returning to his study of the racing form, perusing it with languid ease, just as if he had all the money in the world to blow on the horses.

D'Agosta looked around. The two plainclothes FBI agents were strolling along the far side of the baseball diamond, talking. The Chinese goons didn't seem to have noticed them. Their attention was riveted on the van and what was going on inside. They seemed ready for something. *Too* ready. And there was the cameraman, still lining up the kids, as if he, too, was expecting something to happen at any moment.

D'Agosta felt an almost unbearable sense of apprehension. He asked himself why Bullard's men had gone to such trouble to place themselves in the midst of these kids. They had no inkling they were under surveillance. The tension was between them and their customers, the Chinese. He'd gathered as much from the wiretap, and now it was playing out here.

He started to calculate what would happen if the Chinese thugs pulled out weapons and opened fire on the van. The kids would be caught in cross fire. That's what it was all about: the kids were protection. Bullard's men were *expecting* a firefight: the cameraman was lining up the kids as a human shield.

D'Agosta dropped his coffee and donut and rose from the bench, hand on his piece. At the same moment, the back doors of the van flew open, and the little Chinese man got out as quickly and lightly as a bird. He began striding across the baseball diamond. He flicked his hand toward the two thugs—just the barest gesture—and broke into a run.

D'Agosta saw the two reach for their weapons.

Immediately, he dropped to one knee, steadied his grip on his handgun, and aimed. As soon as a weapon appeared—an Uzi, by the look of it—he squeezed off a round, and just missed.

Abruptly, all hell broke loose. There was the *pop! pop! pop!* of semiautomatic-weapons fire. Kids scattering, grown-ups yelling, grabbing their kids and running in terror or throwing themselves to the ground. An Uzi appeared in the cameraman's hand, too, but before he could fire, he was struck in the chest by a hail of gunfire and flew backward, slamming against the side of the van.

D'Agosta fired a second time at the goon he'd missed, stopping him with a well-placed round to the knee. The other turned toward the unexpected fire, swinging his Uzi and spraying automatic fire across the outfield; Pendergast, shielding two children with his own body, coolly dropped the man with a shot to the head. As the man went down, his Uzi swung wildly, still firing; small clouds of dirt erupted in the grass before Pendergast; then the agent fell sharply back, pushing the children out of harm's way as a spray of blood suddenly darkened his arm.

"Pendergast!" D'Agosta screamed.

The goon D'Agosta hit refused to stay down. Now the man had rolled over and was firing on the van, the rounds whanging its side and sending chips of paint flying. A burst of fire came from its front seat; the Chinese goon went down again; and the van pulled away with a squeal of tires.

"Stop them!" D'Agosta yelled at the two agents. They were already up and running, firing futilely, their shots ringing off the van's armored sides.

Now the head Chinese had reached the black Mercedes. As it roared to life, the two agents turned their fire toward it, blowing out the back tires as the car swerved into the lane. A round hit the gas tank, and the vehicle went up with a muffled thump, a ball of fire roiling skyward as the car left the lane and rolled gently into a grove of trees. The door flew open and a burning man got out, took a few halting steps, paused, and slowly toppled forward. In the distance, the television van was careening out of the park, vanishing into the warren of streets to the west.

The park was bedlam: kids and adults scattered across the ground, cowering and screaming. D'Agosta rushed to where Pendergast had fallen, relieved beyond measure when he saw the FBI agent was sitting up. The two Chinese were dead, and the cameraman, who'd practically been torn in half, was obviously on his way out, too. But no civilians had been so much as scratched. It seemed a miracle.

D'Agosta knelt in the grass. "Pendergast, you all right?"

Pendergast waved, face ashen, temporarily unable to speak.

One of the other FBI agents came running up. "Wounded? We got wounded?"

"Agent Pendergast. The cameraman's beyond help."

"Backup and medical are on the way." And, in fact, D'Agosta could now hear sirens converging on the park.

Pendergast helped one of the children he'd protected—a boy of about eight—to a standing position. His father rushed over and clasped the child in his arms. "You saved his life," he said. "You saved his life."

D'Agosta helped Pendergast up. Blood was soaking through one side of his dirty shirt.

"That fellow winged me," Pendergast said. "It's nothing, a flesh wound. I lost my wind, that's all."

Slowly, hesitantly, people began converging on the park from the surrounding houses, crowding around the burning hulk of the Mercedes and the nearby corpse. Newly arrived cops were shouting, covering the corners, setting up a cordon, yelling at the gathering crowd to keep back.

"Damn," said D'Agosta. "Those fuckers from BAI were expecting a firefight."

"Indeed they were. And no wonder."

"What do you mean?"

"I overheard just enough to learn Bullard's men were calling the deal off."

"Calling the deal *off*?"

"On the very eve of success, apparently. Now you can see the reason for the elaborate setup—the park, the children. They knew the Chinese would not be pleased. This was their attempt to avoid being shot to pieces."

D'Agosta glanced around at the carnage. "Hayward's gonna love this."

"She should. If we hadn't run that wiretap and been here to take down those shooters, I hate to think what might have happened."

D'Agosta shook his head and looked at the burning Mercedes, now being hosed down by a fire truck. "You know what? This case just keeps getting weirder and weirder."

{ 36 }

The Reverend Wayne P. Buck Jr. sat at the counter of the Last Gasp truck stop in Yuma, Arizona, stirring skim milk into his coffee. Before him lay the remains of his usual breakfast: white toast with a little marmalade, oatmeal without milk or sugar. Outside, beyond the flyspecked window, there was a grinding of gears: a large semi pulled off the apron, its steel tank flashing in the brilliant sun, heading west toward Barstow.

Reverend Buck—the title was honorary—took a sip of the coffee. Then, methodical in everything he did, he finished his breakfast, carefully cleaning the bowl with the edge of his spoon before setting it aside. He took another sip of coffee, replaced the cup gently in its saucer. And then at last he turned to his morning reading: the ten-inch stack of periodicals that lay tied in heavy twine on the far end of the counter.

As Buck cut the twine with a pocketknife, he was aware of a sense of anticipation. His morning reading was always a high point of the day: a trucker, whom he'd cured of fits at a camp revival several months before, always left a bundle of outdated newspapers for him outside the truck stop every morning. The papers varied from day to day, and Buck never knew what he'd find. Yesterday there'd been a copy of the *New Orleans Times-Picayune* in among the more common *Phoenix Sun* and *Los Angeles Times.* But his tingle of anticipation, he knew, extended beyond the selection of reading material.

Reverend Buck had been in the vicinity of Yuma almost a year now, ministering to the truckers, the waitresses and busboys, the migrant workers, the broken and wandering and uncertain souls that passed through on their way to some place and rarely lingering long. The work was its own reward, and he never complained. The reason there were so many sinners in the world, he knew, was that nobody had ever bothered to sit down and talk to them. Buck did just that: he talked. Read to people from the Good Book, let them know how to prepare for what was coming, and coming soon. He'd talk to the drivers, one at a time here at the counter; long-haul truckers just stopping in for a leak and a sandwich. He'd talk to groups of two or three regulars in the evenings, out back by the picnic tables. On Sunday mornings, fifteen, maybe twenty, at the old Elks lodge. When he could get a ride to the reservation, he'd preach there. Most people were receptive. Nobody had explained the nature of sin to them, the terrifying implacable promise of the End Days. When people were sick, he'd pray over them; when people were grieving, he'd listen to their problems, recite a parable or some words of Jesus. They paid him in pocket change; a few hot meals; a bed for the night. It was enough.

But he'd been here in Yuma a long spell now. There were other places, so many others, that needed to hear. Every day that went by meant there would be less time.

For truly I tell you, you will not have gone through all the towns of Israel before the Son of Man comes.

Buck was a firm believer in signs. Nothing that happened on this earth happened by accident. It was a sign that carried him from Broken Arrow, Oklahoma, to Borrego Springs, California, last year; another sign that had brought him from Borrego Springs here to Yuma a few months later. One of these days—maybe next week, maybe next month—there would be another sign. He might find it here in these stacks of newspapers. Or he might find it in the story of a passing trucker. But the sign would come, and he'd be gone, gone to some other remote spot with its full share of those in need of the balm of salvation.

Reverend Buck plucked the first newspaper from the pile: the previous Sunday's *Sacramento Bee.* He leafed rather quickly through the national and local pages—big cities like Sacramento could always be counted on for stories of murder, rape, corruption, vice, corporate greed. Buck had read enough such stories for a thousand cautionary sermons. He was more interested in the squibs and sidebars, the news bites taken off the wire feeds and recounted in odd corners of the paper for reader amusement. The tiny town where two brothers hadn't spoken to each other in forty years. The trailer park where every single child had left, a runaway. These were the stories that spoke to him; these were the signs that impelled him and his message.

The *Bee* completed, Buck turned to the next: *USA Today.* Laverne, the waitress, came over with coffeepot in hand. "Another cup, Reverend?"

"Just one more, thank you kindly." Buck practiced

moderation in all things. One cup of coffee was a blessing; two cups was an indulgence; three cups, a sin. He perused the paper, put it aside, and picked up a third: a day-old copy of the *New York Post.* Buck came across this tabloid only rarely, and he had nothing but scorn for it: the brazen mouthpiece of the world's most dissipated, sin-ridden city held no interest for him. He was about to put it aside when the headline caught his attention:

DESTRUCTION

Renowned Scientist Claims Recent Deaths Signal End of Days

by Bryce Harriman

More slowly, Buck turned the page and began to read.

October 25, 2004—A respected scientist yesterday predicted imminent destruction for New York City and possibly much of the world.

Dr. Friedrich Von Menck, Harvard scientist and Emmy Award-winning documentary filmmaker, says the recent deaths of Jeremy Grove and Nigel Cutforth are merely the "harbingers" of the coming catastrophe.

For fifteen years Dr. Von Menck has been studying mathematical patterns in the famous disasters of the past. And no matter how he cuts the data, one number shows up: the year 2004.

Von Menck's theory is based on a fundamental ratio known as the golden ratio—a ratio that is found throughout nature, as well as in such classical architecture as the

Parthenon and the paintings of Leonardo da Vinci. Von Menck is the first to apply it to history—with sinister implications.

Von Menck's research has revealed that many of the worst disasters that have befallen mankind fit the same ratio:

79 A.D.: Pompeii
426 A.D.: The sack of Rome
877 A.D.: Destruction of Beijing by the Mongols
1348 A.D.: The Black Death
1666 A.D.: The Great Fire of London
1906 A.D.: The San Francisco Earthquake

These and many more dates line up in ratios of uncanny precision.

And what do these natural disasters have in common? They have always struck an important world city, a city notable for its wealth, power, technology—and, Dr. Von Menck adds, neglect of the spiritual. Each of these disasters was preceded by small but specific signs. Von Menck sees the mysterious deaths of Grove and Cutforth as precisely the signs one would expect preceding the destruction of New York City by fire.

What kind of fire?

"Not any kind of normal fire," says Von Menck. "It will be something sudden and destructive. A fire from within."

As further evidence he cites passages from Revelation, the prophet Nostradamus, and more recent clairvoyants such as Edgar Cayce and Madame Blavatsky.

Dr. Von Menck left today for the Galápagos Islands, taking with him, he said, only his manuscripts and a few books.

Buck lowered the paper. The rest of the pile sat at his elbow, forgotten. He felt a strange sensation rise up his spine, spread down his arms and legs. If Von Menck was right, the man was a fool to believe he could take refuge on some faraway island. It put in mind some lines from Revelation, his favorite book of the Bible, which Buck frequently quoted to his flock: *And the kings of the earth, and the great men, and the rich men…hid themselves in the dens and in the rocks of the mountains…For the great day of His wrath is come; and who shall be able to stand?*

He raised his cup of coffee, but it no longer seemed to have any flavor, and he replaced it in its saucer. Buck had long believed he would see the End Days in his lifetime. And he had always believed in signs. Perhaps this sign was just larger than the others.

Perhaps it was very large, indeed.

Revelation, chapter 22: *Behold, I come quickly…*

Could this be what he'd been waiting for all these years? Did it not also say in Revelation that the wicked, the men with the mark of the beast on their foreheads, were taken first, in successive waves of slaughter? Just a few, here and there, would be taken. That's how it would start.

He read the article a second time. New York City. This was where it would begin. Of course, this was where it would begin. Two were taken. Just two. It was God's way of getting the word out to his chosen people, so they in turn could spread the message of repentance and atonement while there was still time. The wrath of God would never descend without warning. *Let he with ears hear…*

Behold, I come quickly... Surely I come quickly...

But New York City? Buck had never set foot beyond the Mississippi River, never been in a town much larger than Tucson. To him, the East Coast was Babylon, a foreign, dangerous, soulless region to be avoided at all costs, no place more so than New York. Was it meant to be? Was it, in fact, a sign? And more to the point: was *he* being called? Was this the great call from God he had been waiting for? And did he have the courage to follow it?

There was a chuff of air brakes outside the diner. Buck looked up in time to see the morning Greyhound cross-country express, traveling on I-10, stop outside. The sign above the driver's window read *New York City.*

Buck walked up just as the bus driver was about to close the door. "Excuse me!" he said.

The driver looked at him. "What is it, mister?"

"How much for a one-way ticket to New York?"

"Three hundred and twenty dollars. Cash."

Buck fished in his wallet and pulled out all the money he had in the world. He counted it while the bus driver tapped his finger on the wheel and frowned.

It amounted to precisely three hundred and twenty dollars.

As the bus pulled away from Yuma, Reverend Buck was sitting in the back, his only luggage the day-old copy of the *New York Post.*

{ 37 }

Vasquez eased away from the window, snugged the piece of wood back in place, turned on the hooded lantern, then stood and stretched. It was just past midnight. He rotated his head on his shoulders first one way, then another, working out the kinks. Then he took a long drink of water, wiping his mouth with the back of his hand. Despite a few surprises, the operation was going well. The target kept exceedingly irregular hours, coming and going at unpredictable times—except that every night, at one o'clock in the morning, he exited the house, crossed Riverside Drive at 137th Street, and took a stroll through Riverside Park. He always returned within twenty minutes. It seemed to be an evening constitutional; a turn around the block, so to speak, before going to bed.

Over the past forty-eight hours, Vasquez had come to realize he was dealing with a man of intelligence and ability, and yet a man who was also ineffably strange. As usual, Vasquez wasn't sure quite how he arrived at his conclusions, but he was rarely wrong about people and trusted his instincts. This man was something else. Even on the surface he was odd, with his black suit, marblelike complexion, and his quick, noiseless walk more like that of a cat than a man. Something about the way he moved spoke to Vasquez of utter self-confidence. Further, anyone who would go strolling in Riverside Park in the middle of the night had to be either crazy or packing heat, and he had no doubt the man possessed an excellent weapon and knew how to use it. Twice he had seen gang members who'd staked out the block quietly disappear when the target emerged. They knew a bad deal when they saw it.

Vasquez wrenched off a piece of teriyaki beef jerky and chewed it slowly, reviewing his notes. There seemed to be four inhabitants in the house: Pendergast, a butler, an elderly housekeeper he'd viewed only once, and a young woman who wore long, old-fashioned dresses. She wasn't his daughter or his squeeze—they were too formal with each other. Perhaps she was an assistant of some kind. The house had only one regular visitor: a balding, slightly overweight policeman with a Southampton P.D. patch on his arm. Using his computer and wireless modem, Vasquez had easily discovered the man was one Sergeant Vincent D'Agosta. He looked like a straight-ahead, no-bullshit type, solid and dependable, offering few surprises.

Then there had been a very strange old man with a wild head of white hair who had come by only once, late at night, scurrying along almost like a crab, clutching a book. Probably some kind of functionary, an Igor, a man of no importance.

The one o'clock walk was, of course, the time to do it. Hit him as he emerged from the semicircular drive.

Vasquez had gone over it again and again, figuring out the geometry of death. If the first round entered the man's head obliquely, the round would be deflected slightly by the inside curve of the skull and exit at an angle. The torque generated by the off-center hit would spin the target. As a result, the angle and pattern of the exit spray would suggest a shooter from a window somewhere down the street. The second round would strike him on the way down, spinning him further. The position of the body would help throw off the initial response, deflecting it down the block. In any case, he himself would be out the back and onto 136th Street practically before the body hit the ground, five minutes to the Broadway IRT train and gone. Nobody would notice him—a seedily dressed Puerto Rican runner heading home after a day of dubious employment.

Vasquez bit off another hunk of the dry meat. He wasn't sure just what it was that brought on a feeling of readiness, but he always knew when the time had come for the kill. It was now forty minutes to one, and it felt to him like that time had come. For two nights running, Pendergast had emerged at exactly 1 A.M. Vasquez felt certain he would do it again. This would be the night.

He took off his clothes and put on his getaway costume—warm-up suit open at the chest, heavy gold, puffy sneakers, thin mustache, cell phone—turning himself into just another cheap hustler from Spanish Harlem.

Vasquez extinguished the light, removed the small piece of wood from the corner of the boarded-up window, and got into position. Snugging his cheek against the composite stock—a stock that would never warp or swell in adverse weather—he carefully aligned the match grade barrel to the spot where the target's head would appear, right beyond the marble and brick wall that supported the porte-cochère. There the target always paused to speak to the butler, waiting to make sure the man shut and locked the door. It was a ten- or twenty-second pause: an eternity of opportunity for a shooter like Vasquez.

As he readied his equipment, Vasquez felt a faint twinge of uneasiness. Not for the first time, he wondered if the whole setup was just a little too easy. The one o'clock stroll, the little pause—everything seemed a little too perfect. Was he being set up? Did the target know he was there? Vasquez shook his head, smiling ruefully. He always had an attack of paranoia just before the kill. There was no way the subject could have detected his presence. What's more, the target had already exposed himself on a number of occasions. If he had known a shooter was tracking him, those deliberate exposures would take a level of sangfroid few human beings possessed. Vasquez had already had half a dozen chances to kill him cleanly. It was just that he'd never felt ready.

Now he did.

Slowly and carefully, he fitted his eye to the scope. The scope had a built-in compensator for bullet drop and had already been properly zeroed for windage. Everything was ready. He sighted through the crosshair grid. The central crosshairs were positioned just where the target would pause. It would be quick and clean, as always. The butler would witness it and call the police, but by then Vasquez would be gone. They would find his kill nest, of course, but it would do them no good. They already had his DNA, for all the good it did them. Vasquez would be back home by then, sipping lemonade on the beach.

He waited, gazing at the doorway through the scope. The minutes ticked off. Five minutes to one. Three to one. One o'clock.

The door opened and the target emerged, right on schedule. He took a few steps, turned, began speaking with the butler.

The rifle was already sighted in. Gently and evenly, Vasquez's finger began to apply increasing pressure to the trigger.

There was a sudden faint pop and flash of light from down the block, followed by a tinkle of glass. Vasquez hesitated, taking his eye from the sight; but it was just a streetlight failing as they always did in that neighborhood—or perhaps some young hoodlum-in-training with a BB gun.

But the moment had passed, and the man was now walking across the street, toward the park.

Vasquez leaned back from the rifle, feeling the tension drain away. He had missed his opportunity.

Should he catch him coming back? No, the man walked so swiftly back into the porte-cochère that he could not be sure of that perfect, off-center shot. No matter: it just wasn't in the cards. So much for his paranoia, for everything seeming a little too easy.

So he would be in his little nest for another twenty-four hours. But he wasn't complaining: two million dollars was just as acceptable for three days' work as it was for two.

{ 38 }

D'Agosta rode in the back of the Rolls in silence. Proctor was driving, and Pendergast sat beside him in the front passenger seat, chatting about the Boston Red Sox, which appeared to be the only topic of interest to Proctor, and which Pendergast in his mysterious way seemed to know all about. They were debating some statistical nuance of the 1916 pennant race that stupefied even D'Agosta, who considered himself a baseball fan.

"Where is it we're meeting this Beckmann again?" D'Agosta interrupted.

Pendergast glanced into the backseat. "He's in Yonkers."

"You think he'll talk to us? I mean, Cutforth and Bullard weren't exactly forthcoming."

"I imagine he'll be most eloquent."

Pendergast resumed his discussion, and D'Agosta turned his attention to the passing scenery, wondering if he'd completed all the necessary paperwork on yesterday's dust-up with the Chinese. This case was generating more paperwork than any he'd been involved with before. Or was it just all the new bullshit regulations that were keeping him hogtied? Pendergast never seemed to do any paperwork; D'Agosta wondered if the agent somehow still managed to keep above such mundane details, or if he simply worked all night filling out forms.

The Rolls had left Manhattan via the Willis Avenue Bridge and was now heading north through late Saturday morning traffic along the Major Deegan Expressway. Soon it left the Deegan for the Mosholu Parkway and made its way into the hard-core inner ring of suburbs that comprised the lower fringe of Westchester County. Pendergast had been his usual reticent self about where they were going. Dun-colored housing projects, aging industrial complexes, and strings of gas stations passed by in a blur. After a mile or two, they exited onto Yonkers Avenue. D'Agosta sat back with a sigh. Yonkers, the city with the ugliest name in America. What was Beckmann doing here? Maybe he had some nice place overlooking the Hudson: D'Agosta had heard talk of the city's waterfront revitalization.

But the waterfront was not their destination. Instead, the Rolls turned east, toward Nodine Hill. D'Agosta watched the passing road signs with little interest. Prescott Street. Elm Street. Except there didn't seem to be any elms here, only dying ginkgo trees that barely softened the dingy residential lines. As they drove on, the neighborhood grew increasingly seedy. Drunks and addicts now lounged on front stoops, watching the Rolls pass with scant interest. Every square inch of space was covered by illegible graffiti—even the tree trunks. The sky was the color of lead, and the day was becoming chilly. Here and there they passed vacant lots, reclaimed by weeds or sumac, patches of jungle in the middle of the city.

"Left here, please."

Proctor turned into a dead-end street and glided to a stop in front of the last building. D'Agosta stepped out, Proctor staying with the car.

Instead of entering the tenement, Pendergast headed for the end of the cul-de-sac: a twelve-foot cinder-block wall covered with still more graffiti. An iron door, studded with old rivets, streaked and scaly with rust, was set into the wall.

Pendergast tried the handle, then bent to examine the lock. He removed a pencil-thin flashlight from his pocket and peered into the keyhole, probing with a small metal tool.

"Going to pick it?" D'Agosta asked.

Pendergast straightened. "Naturally." He removed his sidearm and shot into the lock once, twice, the deafening reports rolling like thunder up the alleyway.

"Jesus, I thought you said you were going to pick it!"

"I did. With my pick of last resort." Pendergast holstered the .45. "It's the only way to unlock a solid block of rust. This door hasn't been opened in years." He raised his foot and gave the door a shove. It swung open with a groan of rusted metal.

D'Agosta peered through the doorway, astonished. Instead of a small weedy lot, the door opened on a vast overgrown meadow rising up a hill, covering at least ten acres, surrounded by decaying tenements. At the top stood a cluster of dead trees circling the ruins of what looked like a Greek temple: four Doric columns still standing, roof caved in, the whole structure shrouded in ivy. Directly before them was what once had been a small road. Now it was thick with weeds and poison sumac, rows of dead trees lining either side, their claw-like branches reaching into the gray sky.

D'Agosta shivered. "What's this, some kind of park?"

"After a fashion."

Pendergast began ascending the broken surface of the road, carefully stepping over chunks of frost-heaved asphalt, skirting four-foot weeds and dodging the poisonous sumac pistils. If he felt any lingering pain from the bullet graze of the day before, it did not show. On either side, beyond the dead trees, the weeds rose into a riot of overgrowth: ivy run rampant, brambles, and bushes. Everything was intensely green, growing with unnatural vigor and health.

After a few hundred feet, Pendergast paused, removed a piece of paper from his pocket, consulted it.

"This way."

He started down a path at right angles to the road. D'Agosta scrambled to follow, pushing through the chest-high growth, his uniform becoming covered with pollen dust. Pendergast moved slowly, peering left and right, once in a while consulting the diagram in his hand. He seemed to be counting. D'Agosta gradually became aware just what it was Pendergast was counting: almost invisible in the undergrowth were rows of low, gray slabs of granite set into the ground, each with a name and a pair of dates.

"Hell, we're in a cemetery!" said D'Agosta.

"A potter's field, to be exact, where the indigent, the friendless, and the insane were buried. Pine coffin, six-foot hole, granite tombstone, and a two-minute eulogy, all courtesy of the state of New York. It filled up close to ten years ago."

D'Agosta gave a whistle. "And Ranier Beckmann?"

Pendergast said nothing. He was moving through the ragweed, still counting. Suddenly he halted before a low granite stone, no different from any of the others. With a sweep of his foot, he knocked aside the weeds.

RANIER BECKMAN

1952-1995

A chill wind swept down from the hill, rippling the weeds like a field of grain. There was a distant rumble of thunder.

"Dead!" D'Agosta exclaimed.

"Exactly." Pendergast extracted his cell phone and dialed. "Sergeant Baskin? We have located the grave in question and are ready for the exhumation. I have all the forensics paperwork here. We shall await you."

D'Agosta laughed. "You've got quite a sense of theater, you know that, Pendergast?"

Pendergast shut the cell phone with a snap. "I didn't want to tell you until I was sure myself, and for that I needed to find the grave. There was a sad paucity of records on Mr. Beckmann. Those few that we managed to uncover were suspect. As you can see, they even misspelled his name on the tombstone."

"But you said Beckmann would be 'most eloquent.'"

"And so he will. While dead men tell no tales, their corpses often speak volumes. And I think Ranier Beckmann's corpse has quite a bit to tell us."

{ 39 }

Locke Bullard stood on the flying bridge of the Stormcloud. The air was crisp and sharp, the ocean flat-calm. It was a world reduced to its essentials. The ship throbbed beneath his feet; the cool breeze flowed past him as the ship plowed eastward at flank speed toward Europe.

Bullard lowered his cigar and stared forward at the point where the sky met the knife edge of ocean, his knuckles white on the rail. On this clear fall day, it really did look like the edge of the world, from which a ship could sail off into weightless oblivion. A part of him wished it would happen: that he could just drop off the world and be done with it.

He could do it now, in fact; he could wander to the back of the ship and slip off into the water. Only his steward would miss him and probably not for some time: he had spent most of the voyage locked in his cabin, having his meals delivered, seeing no one.

Bullard could feel himself trembling, every muscle tense, his whole body in the grip of powerful emotion, a terrible combination of rage, regret, horror, and astonishment. He could hardly believe what had happened, what had brought him to this point—here, in the middle of the Atlantic, heading eastward on such fateful business. Never in a million years of corporate scheming—with all his plotting, counterplotting, and preparation for every eventuality—could he have expected it would come to this. At least he'd been able to remove the wild card of that FBI agent, Pendergast: if Vasquez hadn't finished the job yet, he would soon.

And yet this was slight consolation.

He caught the glimpse of movement out of the corner of his eye. It was the slim figure of his steward, bobbing deferentially at the hatch. "Sir? The videoconference is in three minutes."

Bullard nodded, turned his eyes once more toward the horizon, hawked up a gobbet of phlegm, and rocketed it into the far blue. The cigar followed. Then he turned and descended.

The videoconference room was small, built just for him. The technician was there—why were they all weaselly men with goatees?—hunched over the keyboard. He rose when Bullard entered, bumping his head on a bulkhead in his haste. "Everything's set, Mr. Bullard. Just press—"

"Get out."

The man got out, leaving Bullard alone. He locked the door behind him, keyed in the passphrase, waited for the prompt, keyed in another. The screen flickered into life, split down the center into two images: the COO of Bullard Aerospace Industries in Italy, Martinetti; and Chait, his head man in the States.

"How'd it go yesterday?" Bullard asked.

The hesitation told Bullard there'd been a fuckup.

"The guests came with firecrackers. There was a party."

Bullard nodded. He'd half expected it.

"When they learned there was no cake, the party began. Williams had to leave suddenly. The guests all left with him."

So the Chinese had killed Williams and got their asses shot off in return.

"Another thing. The party got crashed."

Bullard felt a sudden constriction in his gut. Now, who the hell had done that? Pendergast? Christ, Vasquez was taking his precious time. Bullard had never met a man quite so dangerous. But if it was Pendergast, how had he learned about it? The files in the seized computer were strongly encrypted, no way they could have been cracked.

"Everybody else got home safely."

Bullard barely heard this. He was still thinking. Either their phones had been tapped or the feds had an informer in his top five. Probably the former. "There's a bird in the tree, maybe," Bullard said, speaking the prearranged code that indicated a phone tap.

This was greeted with silence. Hell, he almost didn't care anymore. Bullard turned to the image of his Italian COO. "You have the item ready and packed for traveling?"

"Yes, sir." The man spoke with difficulty. "May I ask why—?"

"No, god*damn* you to hell, you may not!" Bullard felt rage abruptly take him; it was like a seizure, beyond his control. He glanced over at the image of Chait. The man was listening, face expressionless.

"Sir—"

"Don't ask me *any* questions. I'll get the item when I arrive, and that'll be it. You'll never speak of it again, to me or anyone."

The man went pale and swallowed, his Adam's apple bobbing. "Mr. Bullard, after all the work we've done and the risks we've taken, I have the right to know why you are killing the project. I speak to you respectfully as your chief operating officer. I have only the good of the company at heart—"

Bullard felt the rage grow inside him like a heat, so intense it seemed to powder the very marrow of his bones. "You son of a bitch, what did I just tell you?"

Martinetti fell silent. Chait's eyes flickered this way and that, nervously. He was wondering if maybe his boss wasn't going crazy. It seemed a fair enough question.

"I *am* the company," Bullard went on. "I know what's for the good of the company and what isn't. You mention this again and *ti faccio fuori, bastardo.* I'll kill you, you bastard."

He knew no self-respecting Italian would stand for such an insult. He was right. "Sir, I hereby tender my resignation—"

"Resign, motherfucker, resign! And good riddance!" Bullard brought his fist down on the keyboard, again and again. On the fifth blow, the screen finally winked off.

Bullard sat for a long time in the darkened room. So the feds had been expecting them in Paterson. That meant they knew about the planned transfer of missile technology. Once, that would have been a disaster, but now it seemed almost irrelevant. At the last minute, the crime had been abandoned. The feds had jack and it would stay that way. BAI was clean. Not that Bullard gave a shit; he had bigger fish to fry at the moment.

Fact was, the feds knew nothing about what was *really* going on. He had gotten away just in time. Grove and Cutforth—Grove and Cutforth, and maybe Beckmann, too. They had to die; it was inevitable. But he was still alive and that's what counted.

Bullard realized he was hyperventilating. Christ, he needed air. He stumbled up from the console, unlocked the door, mounted the stairs. In a moment he was back on the flying bridge, staring eastward into blue nothingness.

If only he could just sail off the edge of the world.

{ 40 }

D'Agosta heard the faint squawking of a radio and looked up through the dense undergrowth. At first, nothing could be seen through the riot of vegetation. But within a few minutes, he began to catch distant flashes of silver, glimpses of blue. Finally a cop came into view—just a head and shoulders above the dense brush—forcing his way through the bracken. The cop spied him, turned. Behind him were two medics carrying a blue plastic remains locker. They were followed by two other men in jumpsuits, lugging a variety of heavy tools. A photographer came last.

The cop shouldered his way through the last of the brush—a local Yonkers sergeant, small and no-nonsense—and stopped before them.

"You Pendergast?"

"Yes. Pleased to meet you, Sergeant Baskin."

"Right. This the grave?"

"It is." Pendergast removed some papers from his jacket. The cop scrutinized them, initialed them, stripped off the copies, and handed the originals back. "Sorry, I need to see ID."

Pendergast and D'Agosta showed their badges.

"Fine." The policeman turned to the two workers in jumpsuits, who were busily unshouldering their equipment. "He's all yours, guys."

The diggers attacked the tombstone with vigor, crowbarring it up and rolling it aside. They cleared an area around the grave with brush hooks, then laid several big, dirty tarps across the clearing. Next they began cutting out the weedy turf with turf cutters, popping out squares and stacking them like bricks on one of the tarps.

D'Agosta turned to Pendergast. "So how did you find him?"

"I knew right away he had to be dead, and I assumed before his death he must have been either homeless or mentally ill: there could be no other reason why he'd prove so elusive in these days of the Internet. But learning more than that was a very difficult task, even for my associate, Mime, who as I mentioned has a rare talent for ferreting out obscure information. Ultimately, we learned Beckmann spent the last years of his life on the street, sometimes under assumed names, cycling through various flophouses and homeless shelters in and around Yonkers."

The turf was now stacked and the two workers began digging, their shovels biting alternately into the soil. The medics stood to one side, talking and smoking. There was another faint roll of thunder and light rain began to fall, pattering onto the thick vegetation around them.

"It appears our Mr. Beckmann had a promising start in life," Pendergast continued. "Father a dentist, mother a homemaker. He was apparently quite brilliant in college. But both parents died during his junior year. After graduation, Beckmann couldn't seem to find out what it was he wanted out of life. He knocked around Europe for a while, then came back to the U.S. and sold artifacts on the flea market circuit. He was a drinker who slid into alcoholism, but his problems were more mental than physical—a lost soul who just couldn't find his way. That tenement was his last place of residence." Pendergast pointed toward one of the decaying tenements ringing the graveyard.

Chuff, chuff, went the shovels. The diggers knew exactly what they were doing. Every movement was economical, almost machinelike in its precision. The brown hole deepened.

"How'd he die?"

"The death certificate listed metastatic lung cancer. Gone untreated. We shall soon find out the truth."

"You don't think it was lung cancer?"

Pendergast smiled dryly. "I am skeptical."

One of the shovels thunked on rotten wood. The men knelt and, picking up mason's trowels, began clearing dirt from the lid of a plain wooden coffin, finding its edges and trimming the sides of the pit. It seemed to D'Agosta the coffin couldn't have been buried more than three feet deep. So much for the free six-foot hole—typical government, screwing everyone, even the dead.

"Photo op," said the Yonkers sergeant.

The gravediggers climbed out, waiting while the photographer crouched at the edge and snapped a few shots from various angles. Then they climbed back in, uncoiled a set of nylon straps, slipped them under the coffin, and gathered them together on top.

"Okay. Lift."

The medics pitched in. Soon the four had hoisted the coffin out of the hole and set it on the free tarp. There was a powerful smell of earth.

"Open it," said the cop, a man of few words.

"Here?" D'Agosta asked.

"Those are the rules. Just to check and make sure."

"Make sure of what?"

"Age, sex, general condition...And most importantly, if there's a body in there at all."

"Right."

One of the workers turned to D'Agosta. "It happens. Last year we dug up a stiff over in Pelham, and you know what we found?"

"What?" D'Agosta was fairly sure he didn't want to know.

"*Two* stiffs—and a dead monkey! We said it must've been an organ-grinder who got mixed up with the Mafia." He barked with laughter and nudged his friend, who laughed in turn.

The workers now began to attack the lid of the coffin, tapping around it with chisels. The wood was so rotten it quickly broke loose. As the lid was set aside, a stench of rot, mold, and formaldehyde welled up. D'Agosta peered forward, morbid curiosity struggling with the queasiness he never seemed fully able to shake.

Gray light, softened by the misting rain, penetrated the coffin and illuminated the corpse.

It lay, hands folded on its chest, upon a bed of rotting fabric, stuffing coming up, with a huge stain of congealed liquid, dark as old coffee, covering the bottom. The body had collapsed from rot and had a deflated appearance, as if all the air had escaped along with life, leaving nothing but a skin lying over bones. Various bony protuberances stuck through the rotting black suit: knees, elbows, pelvis. The hands were brown and slimy, shedding their nails, the finger bones poking through the rotting ends. The eyes were sunken holes, the lips lopsided and drawn back in a kind of snarl. Beckmann had been a wet corpse, and the rain was making him wetter.

The cop bent down, scanning the body. "Male Caucasian, about fifty..." He opened a tape measure. "Six feet even, brown hair." He straightened up again. "Gross match seems okay."

Gross is right, D'Agosta thought as he looked at Pendergast. Despite the appalling decay, one thing was immediately clear: this corpse had not suffered the ghastly, violent fate that met Grove and Cutforth.

"Take him to the morgue," Pendergast murmured.

The cop looked at him.

"I want a complete autopsy," Pendergast said. "I want to know how this man *really* died."

{ 41 }

Bryce Harriman entered the office of Rupert Ritts, managing editor of the *Post*, to find the mean, rodentlike editor standing behind his enormous desk, a rare smile splitting his bladelike face.

"Bryce, my man! Take a seat!"

Ritts never talked quietly: his voice was high, and it cut right through a person. You might think he was deaf, except that his ferretlike ears seemed to pick up the faintest whisper from the farthest corner, especially when it concerned him. More than one editor had been fired for whispering Ritts's nickname from two hundred yards across a busy newsroom. It was an obvious nickname, just the substitution of one vowel for another, but it really got Ritts going. Harriman figured it was because he'd probably been called that as a child on the playground every day and never forgot it. Harriman disliked Ritts, as he disliked almost everything about the *New York Post*. It was embarrassing, physically embarrassing, to be working here.

He adjusted his tie as he tried to make himself comfortable in the hard wooden chair Ritts tortured his reporters with. The editor came around and seated himself on the edge of the desk, lighting up a Lucky Strike. He no doubt thought of himself as a tough guy of the old school: hard-drinking, tough-talking, cigarette-hanging-off-the-lip kind of guy. The fact that smoking on the job was now illegal seemed to make him enjoy it all the more. Harriman suspected he also kept a cheap bottle of whiskey and a shot glass in a desk drawer. Black polyester pants, scuffed brown shoes, blue socks, Flatbush accent. Ritts was everything that Harriman's family had trained him all his life, sent him to private school, given him an Ivy League education, never to be.

And here he was. Harriman's boss.

"This Menck story is fabulous, Harriman. Fucking fabulous."

"Thank you, sir."

"It was a real stroke of genius, Harriman, finding this guy the day before he left for the Virgin Islands."

"Galápagos."

"Whatever. I have to tell you, when I first read your piece, I had my doubts. It struck me as a lot of New Age bullshit. But it really hit a chord with our readers. Newsstand circ's up eight percent."

"That's great." Here at the *Post,* it was all about circulation. In the newsroom of the *Times*, where he used to work, "circulation" had been a dirty word.

"Great? It's fucking fabulous. That's what reporting is all about. Readers. I wish some of these other jokers around here would realize that."

The piercing voice was cutting a wide swath across the newsroom beyond. Harriman squirmed uncomfortably in the wooden seat.

"Just when the devil-killings story was flagging, you find this guy Menck. I have to hand it to you. Every other paper in town was sitting around with their thumbs up their asses, waiting for the next killing, but you—you went out and *made* the news."

"Thank you, sir."

Ritts sucked in a few quarts of smoke and dropped the cigarette on the floor of his office, grinding it in with his toe, where about twenty others lay, all nicely flattened. He exhaled with a noisy, emphysemic whistle. He lit another, looked up at Harriman, eyed him up and down.

Harriman shifted again in his chair. Was there something wrong with the way he was dressed? Of course not: it was one of those things he'd been schooled in from day one. He knew just when to break out the madras, when to put away the seersucker, knew the acceptable shade of cordovan for tasseled loafers. And anyway, Ritts was the last person who could criticize anyone else's taste in clothes.

"The *National Enquirer*'s picked up the story, *USA Today*, *Regis*, *Good Day New York*. I like the feel of this, Harriman. You've done well. In fact, well enough to make you a special correspondent at the crime desk."

Harriman was astonished. He hadn't expected this. He tried to control his facial muscles: he didn't want to be seen grinning like an idiot, especially to Ritts. He nodded his head. "Thank you very much, Mr. Ritts. I really appreciate it."

"Any reporter that pushes the circ up eight percent in a week is gonna get noticed. It comes with a ten-thousand-dollar raise, effective immediately."

"Thank you again."

The managing editor seemed to be observing Harriman with ill-concealed amusement, looking him up and down again, eyes lingering on his tie, his striped shirt, his shoes. "Listen, Harriman, as I said, your story touched a chord. Thanks to you, a bunch of New Agers and doomsday freaks have started congregating in the park in front of Cutforth's building."

Harriman nodded.

"It's nothing much. Yet. They're gathering spontaneously, lighting candles, chanting. Flying Nun kind of shit. What we need is follow-up. First, a story about these guys, a serious story, a respectful story. A story that'll let all the other freaks know there's a daily gathering they're missing out on. If we handle this right, we could build up quite a crowd up there. We could stimulate some TV coverage. Who knows, there might even be demonstrations. See what I'm getting at? Like I said: here at the *Post*, we don't sit around waiting for news to happen, we go out and *make* it happen."

"Yes, Mr. Ritts."

Ritts lit up again. "Can I give you some friendly advice? Just between you and me."

"Sure."

"Lose the repp ties and the penny loafers. You look like a goddamn *Times* reporter. This is the *Post.* This is where the excitement is. You sure as hell don't want to be back with those ass-puckered types over there, do you? Now, go on out and talk to every nut who's shaking a Bible. You've touched a nerve, now you've got to keep the pressure on, keep the story building. And bring in a couple of colorful personalities. Find the leader of this rabble."

"What if there isn't a leader?"

"Then *make* one. Set him up on a pedestal, pin a damn medal on him. I smell something big here. And you know what? In thirty years, I've never called a bad one."

"Yes, sir. Thank you, Mr. Ritts." Harriman tried to keep the contempt out of his voice. He would do what Ritts wanted, but he would do it in his own way.

Ritts sucked deep on his cigarette, tobacco hissing and spitting. Then he tossed the butt onto the floor and ground it out again with his foot. He coughed and smiled, displaying a rack of uneven teeth as yellowed as the stem of a corncob pipe.

"Go get 'em, Harriman!" he cackled.

{ 42 }

Vasquez worked off a piece of green chile beef jerky, chewed it meditatively, swallowed, and took a swig of bottled water. He went back to the cryptic crossword from the *Times* of London, pondered, made another entry, erased an earlier one, then set the puzzle aside.

He sighed. He always felt a little nostalgic at the close of an operation: knowing he would have to leave, that all his preparations and deliberations and the cozy little world he had created would quickly become ancient history, pawed over by police officers and photographers. At the same time, he looked forward to seeing sunlight again, breathing fresh air, and listening to the thunder of surf. Funny, though, how he never felt quite so free and alive outside as he did within a cramped kill nest, on the brink of a kill.

He checked his equipment yet again. He looked through the scope, made an infinitesimal correction with the windage adjuster, then raised his eye to examine the flash hider. Just a few minutes now. The box magazine held four rounds, with another in the chamber. All he'd need was two. Once again he shed his clothes and put on his disguise.

Five minutes to one. He glanced regretfully around his nest, at everything he would have to leave behind. How many times had he actually had the opportunity to finish a *Times* cryptic? He rested his eye against the scope and watched. The minutes ticked past.

Once again the door to the porte-cochère opened. Vasquez slowed his breathing, slowed his heart rate. Once again Pendergast's head and shoulders appeared in the reticle. This time Vasquez couldn't make out the butler, who must have been standing too far inside the door to be seen, but he was clearly there, because Pendergast was faced back toward the doorway, obviously talking to somebody. So much the better: an off-center shot to the back of the head would be just as hard to analyze later.

His breath suspended, timing his shots between heartbeats, Vasquez pressed his cheek against the pebbled stock and squeezed the trigger slowly. The weapon bucked in his hands; in a flash, he'd drawn the bolt, resighted, and fired again.

The first shot had been perfectly placed. It spun the target in exactly the right way, the next shot coming a split second later, entering just above the ear, the head exploding in all directions. Pendergast fell back into the shadows of the door frame and disappeared.

Vasquez now moved with a swiftness born of years of practice. Leaving the lights out, he threw the gun and laptop into a duffel, slung it over his shoulder, and snugged on the night-vision goggles that would help him to get out the back of the darkened building. He plugged the shooting hole, strode to the door, and with the battery-powered screwdriver backed out the four screws that held the door shut. Then he stripped off the gaffing tape sealing the jambs and quietly opened the door, stepping noiselessly into the hall.

A flash of light overloaded his goggles, blinding him; he tore them off, reaching down to pull out a sidearm, but a figure in the hallway moved too fast; he was slammed into the wall, still blinded, and the gun went skittering down the passage.

Vasquez swung wildly at his attacker, barely connecting, and received a tremendous blow to the ribs in return. He swung again, this time connecting solidly, dropping his assailant. It was the Southampton cop. In a fury, Vasquez yanked out his knife and leaped on him, aiming for the heart. A foot lashed out from one side; he felt it connect with his forearm, heard the snap, fell to the floor, and was immediately pinned.

The cop was on him. And there, beyond the brilliant glow of the lamp, *he* stood. Pendergast. The man he had just killed.

Vasquez stared, his mind instantly rearranging the facts.

It had been a setup. They must've known almost from the start what was going on. Pendergast had played his part perfectly. Vasquez had shot some dummy, some special-effects dummy. Mother of God.

He had failed. Failed.

Vasquez couldn't quite believe it.

Pendergast was staring at him closely, frowning. Suddenly his eyes widened, as if in understanding. "His mouth!" he said sharply.

D'Agosta shoved something wooden between his teeth, as he would for a dog or an epileptic. But it wouldn't do any good, Vasquez thought as the pain began to build in his broken arm. That wasn't where he carried his cyanide. The needle had been in the tip of his pinkie finger, shot off many years ago and now harnessed to another purpose. He pressed the prosthetic fingertip hard into his palm, felt the ampoule break, pressed the needle into his skin. The pain died away as numbness began stealing up his arm.

The day I fail is the day I die...

{ 43 }

The cab pulled up at the grand courtyard of the Helmsley Palace. D'Agosta hastened around the cab and opened the door for Hayward, who got out, looking around at the fanciful topiaries covered with lights, the Baroque facade of the Helmsley Palace rising around her.

"This is where we're having dinner?"

D'Agosta nodded. "Le Cirque 2000."

"Oh my God. When I said a nice dinner, I didn't mean this."

D'Agosta took her arm and led her to the door. "Why not? If we're going to start something, let's start it right."

Hayward knew that Le Cirque 2000 was possibly the most expensive restaurant in New York City. She had always felt uncomfortable when men spent a pile on her, as if money was somehow the way to her heart. But this time it felt different. It said something about Vinnie D'Agosta, about how he looked at their relationship, that boded well for the future.

Future? She wondered why that word had even entered her mind. This was a first date—sort of.

D'Agosta wasn't even divorced, had a wife and kid in Canada. True, he was interesting, and he was a damn good cop. *Take it easy and see where it goes—that's all.*

They entered the restaurant—jammed, even on a Sunday night—and were met by one of those maître d's who managed to convey an outward expression of groveling subservience while simultaneously projecting inner contempt. He regretted to inform them that, despite their reservation, the table wasn't ready; if they would care to make themselves comfortable in the bar, it shouldn't be more than thirty minutes, forty at the outside.

"Excuse me. Did you say forty minutes?" D'Agosta spoke in a quiet yet menacing way.

"There's a large party... I'll see what I can do."

"You'll *see* what you can do?" D'Agosta smiled and took a step closer. "Or you'll *do* it?"

"I'll do what I can, sir."

"I have no doubt that what you *can* do is get us a table in fifteen minutes, and that is what you *will* do."

"Of course. Naturally, sir." Now the maître d' was in full retreat. "And in the meantime," he went on, voice artificially high and bright, "I'll have a bottle of champagne sent to your table, compliments of the house."

D'Agosta took her arm and they went into the bar, which was decorated with a confusion of neon lights Hayward figured must somehow represent the "circus" theme of the restaurant. It was fun—if you didn't have to spend too long in there.

They sat down at a table, and a waiter soon appeared unbidden with menus, two glasses, and a chilled bottle of Veuve Clicquot.

She laughed. "That was pretty effective, the way you handled that maître d'."

"If I can't intimidate a waiter, what kind of a cop am I?"

"I think he was expecting a tip."

D'Agosta glanced at her quickly. "You do?"

"But you managed it all right and saved yourself some money."

D'Agosta grunted. "Next time I'll give him a fiver."

"That would be worse than nothing at all. The going rate is at least twenty."

"Jesus. Life is complicated at the top." He raised his glass. "Toast?"

She raised hers.

"To..." He hesitated. "To New York's finest."

She felt relieved he hadn't said what she expected. They clinked glasses. She sipped, looking at him while he studied the menu the waiter had left. It seemed he'd slimmed down a bit since she first ran into him at Cutforth's apartment. He'd mentioned something about working out every day, and it was pretty evident he wasn't kidding. Working out and shooting at the 27th Precinct range. She took in his hard, clean jawline, jet-black hair, soft brown eyes. He had a nice face, a really nice face. He seemed to be that rarest of finds in New York: a genuinely decent guy. With strong, old-fashioned values, solid, kind, steady—but no wimp, as proved by his surprise performance three nights before in her office...

She found herself blushing and tingling at the same time, and she covered it by raising her own menu. She glanced over the list of main courses and was horrified to see that the cheapest, the paupiette of black sea bass, was thirty-nine dollars. The cheapest appetizer was twenty-three dollars, for the braised pigs' feet and cheeks (no, thank you). Her eye looked in vain for anything under twenty dollars, finally coming to rest on the dessert menu, where the first item that caught her eye—a donut!—was ten dollars. Well, there was no help for it. She swallowed and began picking out her dishes, trying to avoid adding up the sums in her head.

Vincent was looking over the wine list, and she had to admit he hadn't lost any color, at least not yet. In fact, he seemed positively expansive.

"Red or white?" he asked.

"I think I'm going to have fish."

"White, then. The Cakebread Chardonnay." He shut the menu and smiled at her. "This is fun, don't you think?"

"I've never been in a restaurant like this in my life."

"Me neither, to tell you the truth."

By the time their table was ready, fifteen minutes later, the bottle of champagne was half gone and Hayward was feeling no pain. The maître d' seated them in the first dining room, a spacious chamber done in opulent Second Empire style with gilded moldings, high windows with silk brocade draperies, and crystal chandeliers, the effect curiously enhanced by suspended neon lighting and several floral arrangements as large as small elephants. The only drawback was the large party next to them, a table of loud people from one of the outer boroughs—Queens, by the accent. *Well, you can't bar people at the door because they have the wrong accent,* she thought.

D'Agosta ordered for them, and Hayward was once again impressed with his self-assurance, which she hadn't expected, especially in a place like this.

"Where'd you learn so much about haute cuisine?" she asked.

"Are you kidding?" D'Agosta grinned. "I recognized about half the words on the menu. I was just winging it."

"Well, you could have fooled me."

"Maybe it's all the time I'm spending with Pendergast. He's rubbing off on me."

She nudged him. "Isn't that Michael Douglas in the corner?"

He turned. "So it is." Turned back, unimpressed.

She nodded. "And look who's over there." A woman sat in a quiet corner by herself, eating a plate of french fries, dipping each one in a large dish of ketchup and pushing them into her mouth with evident satisfaction.

D'Agosta stared. "She kinda looks familiar. Who is she?"

"You been living under a rock? Madonna."

"Really? Must've dyed her hair or something."

"This would make a great scene in a novel. Maybe your next."

"There won't be a next."

"Why not? I loved those two books you wrote. You've got real talent."

He shook his head. "Talent—maybe. My problem is, I don't have the touch."

"What touch?"

He rubbed his fingers together. "The money touch."

"A lot of people never get one novel published.

You got two. And they were *good*. You can't give it up totally, Vinnie."

He shook his head. "Did I ever tell you this isn't my favorite subject?"

"I'll drop it if you want. For now. I actually wanted to ask you a question. I know we shouldn't be talking shop, but how in the world did Pendergast know that guy—what's his name, Vasquez—was gunning for him? Interpol's been chasing that killer for ten years, and he's a pro if ever there was one."

"I could hardly believe it myself. But when he explained, it made perfect sense. Bullard—who was no doubt behind it—felt threatened enough to set two goons on me after our first interview. Pendergast figured Bullard was desperate to leave the country and wouldn't let anybody stand in his way. He also figured Bullard would try again, this time against *him*. So he asked himself how a professional killer would do it. The answer was obvious: set yourself up in the vacant building across the street from his house. So right after we took Bullard downtown, Pendergast began watching the boarded-up windows of that building with a telescope. Soon enough, he noticed a fresh hole cut in the plywood. Bingo! That's when he let me in on it, told me what he was planning to do. Next, Pendergast established a routine so he could control when the man would strike."

"But how did he have the guts to walk in and out of his house, leaving himself exposed?"

"Whenever he stepped out of the building, he had Proctor train the telescope on the peephole. At one point, he had me shoot out a bulb on the street at a critical moment. That's when he tagged the man's weapon, knew the killer had missed his opportunity for the day. Figured he'd therefore act the next. So last night we had the dummy all ready for him. Proctor handled it perfectly, wheeled it out so just the upper part was visible."

"But why not just go in and take the guy out beforehand? Why run the risk?"

"No proof, for one thing. On top of that, the guy was barricaded in there—he might have slipped through our fingers. As you said, he was a real pro. And for sure he would have put up resistance. His vulnerable moment was while *he* was escaping. We just waited for him to run into our trap."

Hayward nodded. "That explains a lot."

"Too bad the guy took the suicide route."

Their first courses arrived, whisked to their table by no less than three waiters, with the sommelier hard on their heels to fill their wineglasses and another functionary to top off their water glasses.

"Now I've got a question for *you*," said D'Agosta. "How'd you make captain? So fast, I mean."

"There's no great mystery. I saw how things were going, so I went and got my M.S. from NYU in forensic psychology. A degree really helps these days—and, of course, it didn't hurt that I'm a woman."

"Affirmative action?"

"More like belated action. Once the lid of oppression was lifted off the force by Commissioner Rocker, naturally some of us rose to the surface. They looked around in a panic and realized there weren't any high-level women on the force—because they'd been discriminating against us forever—and began promoting. I was in the right place at the right time, with the right test scores and credentials."

"Ambition and talent had nothing to do with it?"

"I wouldn't say that." She smiled.

"Neither would I." Vincent sipped his wine. "Where'd you grow up?"

"Macon, Georgia. My dad was a welder, my mom a homemaker. I had an older brother, killed in Vietnam. Friendly fire. I was eight."

"I'm sorry."

Hayward shook her head. "My parents never recovered. Dad died a year later, Mom the year after that. Cancer, both of them, but I think it was more from grief. He was their pride and joy."

"That's really hard."

"That was a long time ago, and I had a wonderful grandmother in Islip who raised me. It helped me realize I was pretty much alone in this world and that nobody would kick ass for me. I'd have to do the kicking myself."

"You've done a good job of it."

"It's a game."

He paused. "You really shooting for commissioner?"

She smiled, saying nothing, then raised her glass. "Nice to have you back in the Big Apple where you belong, Vinnie."

"I'll drink to that. You don't know how I've missed this town."

"Best place in the world to be a cop."

"When I was a lieutenant, back during the museum murders, I never really appreciated it. I thought it would be great to get out of the city, live in the country, breathe fresh air for a change, listen to the birds chirping, watch the leaves turn color. I wanted to go fishing every Sunday. But you know what? Fishing is boring, the birds wake you up in the morning, and instead of Le Cirque, up in Radium Hot Springs you've got Betty Daye's Family-Style Restaurant."

"Where you can feed a family of four for what it costs here to buy a donut."

"Yeah, but who wants chicken-fried steak at four ninety-nine when you can have duck magret dusted with Espelette pimento for only forty-one bucks?"

Hayward laughed. "That's what I love about New York—nothing's normal. Everything's totally over the top. Here we are having dinner in the same room with Madonna and Michael Douglas."

"New York'll drive you crazy, but it's never boring."

She took a sip of wine and the waiter rushed over to refill her glass. "Is there really a town called Radium Hot Springs up there? It sounds like a joke."

"I've been there. I'm pretty sure it's real."

"What was it like?"

"I kid about it, but it wasn't a bad place. Small town, good values. Canadians are a friendly bunch. But it wasn't home. I always felt like an exile, you know what I mean? And it was too damn quiet. I thought I'd go crazy, I couldn't concentrate with all those chirping birds. Give me the roar of rock-solid Friday afternoon Midtown gridlock, stretching from river to river. Man, that's the voice of life itself."

Hayward laughed as their main courses arrived with a flurry of white-gloved waiters.

"I could definitely get used to this," said D'Agosta, leaning back and tucking into his duck magret, following it with a swig of Chardonnay.

Hayward placed a sea scallop *étuvée* in her mouth and savored it. She didn't believe she had ever tasted anything quite so good in her life. "You did well, Vinnie," she said with a smile. "You really did well."

{ 44 }

D'Agosta had never been in the place before, but everything about it was dismally familiar. At least the sharp tang of alcohol and formaldehyde and God only knew what other chemicals helped chase away a lingering hangover. He and Laura Hayward hadn't left the restaurant until 11:30 the night before. At the sommelier's suggestion, he'd splurged on a demi bottle of dessert wine—Château d'Yquem 1990, it had cost him a week's pay at least—and it had proved to be the most wonderful wine he'd ever tasted. The whole evening had proved wonderful, in fact.

What a tragedy that it had to be followed up by this.

The mingled smell of formalin, bodily fluids, and decomposition; the overly clean stainless-steel surfaces; the bank of refrigerating units; the sinister-looking diener lurking in the background; the attending pathologist—and of course the cadaver, star of the show, lying in the middle of the room on an old marble autopsy table, illuminated by its very own spotlight. It had been autopsied—disassembled was more like it—and a bunch of withered, sliced-and-diced organs lay arrayed around the corpse, each in its own plastic container: brain, heart, lungs, liver, kidneys, and a bunch of other dark lumps D'Agosta did not care to guess at.

Still, this wasn't as bad as some. Maybe it was because the parade of insects had come and gone and the corpse had decayed to the point where it was as much skeleton as flesh. Or perhaps it was because the smell of suppuration had almost been replaced by a smell of earth. Or maybe—D'Agosta hoped—maybe he was finally getting used to it. Or was he? He felt that familiar tightening in his throat. At least he'd been smart enough to skip breakfast.

He watched the doctor standing at the head of the corpse, round black glasses pulled down on his nose, thumbing through a clipboard. He was a laconic type, with salt-and-pepper hair and a slow, economical way of talking. He looked irritated. "Well, well," he said, flipping over papers. "Well, well."

Pendergast was restlessly circling the corpse. "The death certificate listed lung cancer as the cause of death," he said.

"I am aware of that," the doctor replied. "I was the attending physician *then*, and at your *request*, I have been hauled back here to be the attending pathologist *now*." The man's voice was brittle with grievance.

"I thank you."

The doctor nodded tersely, then went back to the clipboard. "I've performed a complete autopsy on the cadaver, and the lab results have come back. Now, what is it, exactly, that you would like to know?"

"First things first. I'm assuming you confirmed this is indeed the body of Ranier Beckmann?"

"Without question. I checked dental records."

"Excellent. Please proceed."

"I'll summarize my original records and diagnosis." The doctor flipped over some pages. "On March 4, 1995, the patient, Ranier Beckmann, was brought to the E.R. by ambulance. The symptoms indicated advanced stages of cancer. Tests confirmed an extensive-stage small-cell lung carcinoma with distant metastases. Essentially a hopeless case. The cancer had spread throughout the body, and general organ failure was imminent. Mr. Beckmann never left the hospital and died two weeks later."

"You're sure he died in the hospital?"

"Yes. I saw him every day on my rounds until he died."

"And your recollection, going back over a decade, is still clear?"

"Absolutely." The doctor stared at Pendergast over the tops of his glasses.

"Proceed."

"I conducted this autopsy in two stages. The first was to test my original determination of cause of death. There had been no autopsy. Standard procedure. The cause of death was evident, there was no family request, and no suspicion of foul play. The state obviously doesn't pay for an autopsy just for the hell of it."

Pendergast nodded.

"The second stage of my autopsy, as per your request, was to identify any unusual pathologies, conditions, wounds, toxins, or other irregularities associated with the body."

"And the results?"

"I confirmed Beckmann died of general organ failure associated with cancer."

Pendergast quickly fixed his silvery eyes again on the doctor. He said nothing: the skeptical look said it all.

The doctor returned the look steadily. Then he continued, voice calm. "The primary was a tumor in his left lung the size of a grapefruit. There were gross secondary metastatic tumors in the kidneys, liver, and brain. The only surprising thing about this man's death is that he hadn't showed up in the emergency room earlier. He must have been in tremendous pain, barely able to function."

"Go on," Pendergast said in a low voice.

"Aside from the cancer, the patient showed advanced cirrhosis of the liver, heart disease, and a suite of other chronic, but not yet acute, symptoms associated with alcoholism and poor nutrition."

"And?"

"That's all. No toxins or drugs present in the blood or tissues. No unusual wounds or pathologies, at least none detectable after embalming and almost ten years in the ground."

"No sign of heat?"

"Heat? What do you mean?"

"No indication that the body had experienced the perimortem application of heat?"

"Absolutely not. Heat would have caused a host of obvious cell changes. I've looked at forty, maybe fifty sections of tissue from this cadaver, and not one showed changes associated with heat. What an extraordinary question, Mr. Pendergast."

Pendergast spoke again, his voice still low. "Small-cell lung cancer is caused almost exclusively by smoking. Am I correct, Doctor?"

"You are correct."

"That he died of cancer is beyond a reasonable doubt, then, Doctor?" Pendergast allowed a skeptical tone to tinge his voice.

Exasperated, the pathologist reached down, grabbed two halves of a shriveled brown lump, and shoved them in Pendergast's face. "There it is, Mr. Pendergast. If you don't believe me, believe *this*. Take it. Feel the malignancy of this tumor. As sure as I'm standing here, *that's* what killed Beckmann."

It was a long, silent walk back to the car. Pendergast slipped behind the wheel—today he'd driven himself to Yonkers—and they exited the parking lot. As they left the gray huddle of downtown behind, Pendergast spoke at last.

"Beckmann spoke to us quite eloquently, wouldn't you say, Vincent?"

"Yeah. And he stank, too."

"What he said, however, was—I must confess—something of a surprise. I shall have to write the good doctor a letter of thanks." He swung the wheel sharply, and the Rolls turned onto Executive Boulevard, passing the on-ramp for the Saw Mill River Parkway.

D'Agosta looked over in surprise. "Aren't we heading back to New York City?"

Pendergast shook his head. "Jeremy Grove died exactly two weeks ago. Cutforth, one week ago. We came to Yonkers to get some answers. I'm not leaving until we have them."

{ 45 }

The bus inched through a long, white-tiled tunnel in stop-and-go traffic and emerged from an underpass, a long ramp amidst steel girders in semidarkness.

New York City, thought the Reverend Wayne P. Buck.

Beyond the web of steel, he could see limpid sunlight, sooty tenements, a brief glimpse of skyscrapers. The bus lurched back into darkness, the brakes chuffing as the line of traffic stopped again.

Buck felt an indescribable mix of emotions: excitement, fear, destiny, a sense of confronting the unknown. It was the same thing he had felt a couple of years ago, the day he'd been released from prison after serving nine years for murder two. It had been a long, slow slide for Buck: delinquency, failed jobs, booze, stealing cars, bank robbery—and then the fateful day when everything went wrong and he'd ended up shooting a convenience store clerk. Killing a poor, innocent man. As the bus crept forward again, his mind went back over the arrest, trial, sentence of twenty-five to life, the manacled walk into the bowels of the prison. A period of darkness, best forgotten.

And then, conversion. Born again in prison. Just as Jesus raised up the whore, Mary Magdalen, He raised up the alcoholic, the murderer, the man who had been cast away by all others, even his own family.

After his salvation, Buck began reading the Bible: again and again, cover-to-cover, Old Testament and New. He started preaching a little, a few words here, a helping hand there. He formed a study group. Gradually, he'd built up the respect and trust of the prisoners who had ears for the Good Word. He was soon spending most of his time assisting in the salvation of others. That, and playing chess. There wasn't much else to do: magazines were showcases of materialism, television was worse, and books other than the Bible seemed full of profanity, violence, and sex.

As parole grew near, Buck began to feel that his ministry in prison was preparation for something else; that God had a greater purpose for him which would be revealed in time. After he got out, he drifted from one small town to another, mostly along the border between California and Arizona, preaching the Word, letting God clothe and feed him. His reading began to expand: first Bunyan, then St. Augustine, then Dante in translation. And always, always, he waited for the call.

And now, when he least expected it, the call had come. God's purpose for him stood revealed. Who would have thought that his call would take him to New York City, the greatest concentration of spiritual bankruptcy and evil in all America? Vegas, L.A., and other such places were merely sideshows to New York. But that was the beauty of doing God's will. Just as God had sent St. Paul to Rome—into the black heart of paganism—so had He sent Wayne P. Buck to New York.

The bus stopped, lurched again, everyone's heads swaying in unison with the movements. They were now on some kind of concrete ramp, climbing a rising spiral between crisscrossed girders. It put Buck in mind of Dante's circles of hell. In a moment, the bus plunged back into darkness and the stench of diesel, the sound of air brakes hissing demonically. It seemed they were at the depot—but a depot such as Buck had never seen or imagined in all his born days.

The bus ground to a halt. The driver said something unintelligible over the public address system, and there was a great sigh of air as the door opened. Buck exited. The others all had to wait for their baggage, but he was a free man, without possessions or money, just as it had been six years ago when he walked out into the bright sunlight of Joliet.

Without knowing where he was going, he followed a crush of people down a series of escalators and through an immense terminal. Moments later he found himself outdoors, on the pavement of a great street. He stopped and looked around, feeling a rush of dread mingling with the spiritual vigor.

As I walked through the wilderness of this world... Jesus had spent forty days and nights in the desert tempted by the devil, and verily this was the desert of the twenty-first century: this wasteland of human souls.

He began walking, letting Jesus take him where He

would. Despite the crowded sidewalks, nobody seemed to notice him: the streams of humanity parted around him, then flowed together again behind him, like a river embracing a rock. He crossed a broad thoroughfare, walked down a canyonlike street thrown into deep shadow by buildings that rose on both sides. Within a few minutes, he arrived at another intersection, even wider than before, with roads coming in from all sides. Huge billboards and garish forty-foot neon marquees announced he was standing in Times Square. He looked skyward. It was a heady experience, surrounded by the mighty works of man, the modern-day glass and steel Towers of Babel. It was all too easy to see how one could be seduced by such a place; how quickly one could lose first one's conviction, then one's soul. He lowered his eyes again to the traffic, the noise, the great rush and press of humanity. The words of John Bunyan came to him again: *You dwell in the City of Destruction: I see it to be so; and, dying there, sooner or later, you will sink lower than the grave, into a place that burns with fire and brimstone: be content, good neighbors, and go along with me.*

Lost, all lost.

But perhaps not all: here and there, Buck knew, walked those who could still be saved, the righteous people with the grace of God in their souls. He did not yet know who they were, and it was likely even they didn't know. *Be content, good neighbors, and go along with me.* It was for them he had come to New York City: these were the ones he would pull back from the brink. The rest would be swept away in the blink of an eye.

For hours Buck walked. He could sense the siren-like

call of the city tugging at him: its urbane window displays, its unbelievable opulence, its stretch limousines. Buck's nostrils filled with the stench of rotting garbage one moment, and the next with the scent of expensive perfume from some lynx-eyed temptress in a tight dress. He was in the belly of the beast, for sure. God had entrusted him with a mission, God had given him his own forty days in the desert, and he would not fail.

He had spent his last nickel on the bus ticket and had not eaten at all during the ride. Somehow the hunger, the fasting, had sharpened his mind. But if he was to do God's will, he had to seek nourishment for his body.

His wanderings took him to a Salvation Army soup kitchen. He went in, waited in line, sat silently with the derelicts, and ate a bowl of macaroni and cheese with a couple slices of unbuttered Wonder bread and a cup of coffee. As he ate, he slipped the shabby paper out of his pocket and perused the soiled article yet again. It was God's message to him, and every time he read it he felt fortified, refreshed, determined. After his simple meal, he left and began walking again, a new spring in his step. He passed a newsstand and paused, his eye catching the headline of the *New York Post.*

THE END IS NIGH

Satanists, Pentacostals and Prophets of Doom Continue to Converge at Site of Devil Killing

He instinctively shoved his hand in his pocket before remembering he had no money. He paused. What to do? This headline was, without a doubt, another message from God. Nothing happened in this world without significance. Not even the slightest sparrow could fall from the tree...

He needed money. He needed a bed for the night. He needed a change of clothes. God clothed the lilies of the field; would He not clothe him? That had always been Buck's philosophy.

But sometimes God liked to see a little initiative.

Buck looked up. He was in front of a huge building, guarded by two massive stone lions—the New York Public Library, the legend said. A temple to Mammon, no doubt filled with pornography and immoral books. He hastened around the corner. There, beside a small but nicely manicured park, were a number of people with chessboards set up and ready for play. They weren't playing each other; they seemed to be waiting for passersby. He approached, curious.

"Play?" one of them asked.

Buck paused.

"Five dollars," the man said.

"For what?"

"Game of ten-second chess. Five dollars."

Buck almost walked on. It might be considered a form of gambling. But then he paused. Was this, too, a little help from God? Buck sensed these players were good; they had to be. But what did he have to lose?

He sat down. The man immediately moved his queen's pawn, and Buck countered, ten seconds for each move.

Ten minutes later Buck was sitting on a bench in the park behind the library, reading the *Post*. The article told of small gatherings of people in front of the building where the devil had taken the man named Cutforth. It even gave the address: 842 Fifth Avenue.

Fifth Avenue. The legendary Fifth Avenue. The Mephistophelean heart of New York City. It all fit together. He tore out the article and folded it up with the other, carefully slipping them into his shirt pocket.

He would not go there now; that could wait. Like David, he needed to gird his loins, prepare himself spiritually. He had not come to preach: he had come to do battle for the world.

He checked his pocket. Four dollars and fifty cents. Not nearly enough to find a bed for the night. He wondered just how God might help him multiply that money, as Jesus had multiplied the loaves and the fishes.

There were still a few hours before sunset. Jesus would help him, Buck knew. Jesus would surely help him.

{ 46 }

Beckmann's last known place of residence, as listed on the death certificate, was not far from the potter's field in which he was buried. Pendergast drove slowly past the decrepit building and parked before a package store a few doors down. Three old alcoholics sat on the front stoop, watching as they got out of the car.

"Nice neighborhood," said D'Agosta, looking around at the six-story brick tenements festooned with rusting fire escapes. Threadbare laundry hung from dozens of clotheslines strung between the buildings.

"Indeed."

D'Agosta nodded in the direction of the three rummies, who had gone back to passing around a bottle of Night Train. "Wonder if those three know anything."

Pendergast gestured for him to proceed.

"What? Me?"

"Of course. You are a man of the street, you speak their language."

"If you say so." D'Agosta glanced around again, then headed into the package store. He returned a few minutes later with a bottle in a brown paper bag.

"A gift for the natives, I see."

"I'm just taking a page from your book."

Pendergast raised his eyebrows.

"Remember our little journey underground during the subway massacre case? You brought a bottle along as currency."

"Ah, yes. Our tea party with Mephisto."

Bottle in hand, D'Agosta ambled up to the stoop, pausing before the men. "How are you boys today?"

Silence.

"I'm Sergeant D'Agosta, and this is my associate, Special Agent Pendergast. FBI."

Silence.

"We're not here to bust anyone's balls, gentlemen. I'm not even going to ask your names. We're just looking for any information on one Ranier Beckmann, who lived here several years back."

Three pairs of rheumy eyes continued staring at him. One of the men hawked up a gobbet of phlegm and deposited it gently between his badly scuffed shoes.

With a rustle, D'Agosta removed the bottle from the paper bag. He held it up. The light shone through it, illuminating pieces of fruit floating in an amber-colored liquid.

The oldest wino turned to the others. "Rock 'n' Rye. The cop has class."

"Beware of cops bearing gifts."

D'Agosta glanced at Pendergast, who was looking on from a few paces back, hands in his pockets. He turned back. "Look, guys, don't make a fool out of me in front of the feds, okay? Please."

The oldest man shifted. "Now that you've said the magic word, have a seat."

D'Agosta perched gingerly on the sticky steps. The man reached out a hand for the bottle, took a swig, spat out a piece of fruit, passed it on. "You too, friend," he said to Pendergast.

"I would prefer to stand, thank you."

There were some chuckles.

"My name's Jedediah," said the oldest drunk. "Call me Jed. You're looking for who again?"

"Ranier Beckmann," said Pendergast.

Two of the drunks shrugged, but after a moment, Jed nodded slowly. "Beckmann. Name rings a bell."

"He lived in room 4C. Died of cancer almost ten years ago."

Jed thought another moment, took a swig of the Rock 'n' Rye to lubricate the brain cells. "I remember now. He's the guy who used to play gin rummy with Willie. Willie's gone, too. Man, did they argue. Cancer, you say?" He shook his head.

"Did you know anything about his life? Marriage, former addresses, that sort of thing?"

"He was a college-educated fellow. Smart. Nobody ever came to visit him, didn't seem to have any kids or family. He might have been married, I suppose. For a while, I thought he had a girl named Kay."

"Kay?"

"Yeah. He'd say her name now and then, usually when he was mad at himself. Like when he lost at rummy. 'Kay Biskerow!' he'd say. As if he wouldn't have been in such a fix if she were there to look after him."

Pendergast nodded. "Any friends of his still here we could talk to?"

"Can't think of anybody. Beckmann mostly kept to himself. He was sort of depressed."

"I see."

D'Agosta shifted on the uncomfortable stoop. "When someone dies here, what usually happens to his stuff?"

"They clean out his room and throw it away. Except that John sometimes saves a few things."

"John?"

"Yeah. He saves dead people's shit. He's a little strange."

"Did John save any of Beckmann's possessions?" Pendergast asked.

"Maybe. His room's full of junk. Why don't you go on up there and ask? It's 6A. Top floor, head of the stairs."

Pendergast thanked the man, then led the way into the dim lobby and up the wooden staircase. The treads creaked alarmingly under their feet. As they reached the sixth floor, Pendergast laid a hand on D'Agosta's arm.

"I compliment you on your adroitness back there," he said. "Thinking to ask about his belongings was a clever move. Care to handle John, too?"

"Sure thing."

D'Agosta rapped on the door marked *6A*, but it was already ajar and creaked inward at his knock. It opened a little, then stopped, blocked by a mountain of cardboard boxes. The room was almost completely filled with vermin-gnawed cartons, stacks of books, all manner of memorabilia. D'Agosta stepped in, threading a narrow path between walls of assorted junk: old pictures, photo albums, a tricycle, a signed baseball bat.

In the far corner, beneath a grimy window, a space just big enough for a bed had been cleared. A white-haired man lay on the filthy bed, fully clothed. He looked at them but did not rise or move.

"John?" D'Agosta asked.

He gave a faint nod.

D'Agosta went over to the bed, showed his badge. The man's face was creased and sunken, and his eyes were yellow. "We just want a little bit of information, and then we'll be gone."

"Yes," the man said. His voice was quiet, slow, and sad.

"Jed, downstairs, said you might have saved some personal effects belonging to Ranier Beckmann, who lived here several years back."

There was a long pause. The yellowed eyes glanced over toward one of the piles. "In the corner. Second box from the bottom. *Beck* written on it."

D'Agosta laboriously made his way to the tottering stack and found the box in question: stained, moldy, and half flattened from the weight of the boxes on top.

"May I take a look?"

The man nodded.

D'Agosta shifted the boxes and retrieved Beckmann's. It was small; inside were a few books and an old cigar box wrapped in rubber bands. Pendergast came up and looked over his shoulder.

"James, *Letters from Florence*," he murmured, glancing at the spines of the books. "Berenson, *Italian Painters of the Renaissance.* Vasari, *Lives of the Painters.*

Cellini, *Autobiography.* I see our Mr. Beckmann was interested in Renaissance art history."

D'Agosta picked up the cigar box and began to remove the rubber bands, which were so old and rotten they snapped at his touch. He opened the lid. The box exuded a perfume of dust, old cigars, and paper. Inside, he could see a moth-eaten rabbit's foot, a gold cross, a picture of Padre Pio, an old postcard of Moosehead Lake in Maine, a greasy pack of cards, a toy Corgi car, some coins, a couple of matchbooks, and a few other mementos. "Looks like we found Beckmann's little chest of treasures," he said.

Pendergast nodded. He reached over and picked up the matchbook. "Trattoria del Carmine," he read aloud. His slender white fingers drifted over the coins and other mementos. Next he reached for the books, plucking the Vasari from the box and leafing through it. "Required reading for anyone wishing to understand the Renaissance," he said. "And look at this."

He handed the book to D'Agosta. Scrawled on the flyleaf was a dedication:

To Ranier, my favorite student,
Charles F. Ponsonby Jr.

D'Agosta took out a book himself. There was no inscription in this one, but as he rifled through it, a photograph dropped from between the pages. He picked it off the floor. It was a faded color snapshot of four youths, all male, arms draped around each other's necks, before what looked like a blurry marble fountain.

D'Agosta heard a sharp intake of breath from Pendergast. "May I?" the agent asked.

D'Agosta handed him the photograph. He stared at it intently, then handed it back.

"The one on the far right, I believe, is Beckmann. And do you recognize his friends?"

D'Agosta looked. Almost instantly he recognized the massive head and jutting brows of Locke Bullard. The others took a moment longer, but once recognized were unmistakable: Nigel Cutforth and Jeremy Grove.

He glanced over at Pendergast. The man's silvery eyes were positively glittering. "There it is, Vincent: the connection we've been looking for."

He turned to the man lying on the bed. D'Agosta had almost forgotten him, he had been so silent. "John, may we take these items?"

"It's what I've been saving them for."

"How so?" D'Agosta asked.

"That's what I do. I keep the things they treasured, in trust for their families."

"Who's *they*?"

"The ones that die."

"Do the families ever come?"

The question hung in the air. "Everybody has a family," John finally said.

It looked to D'Agosta like some of the boxes were so rotten and discolored they'd been sitting around for twenty years. It was a long time to wait for a family member to come calling.

"Did you know Beckmann well?"

The man shook his head. "He kept to himself."

"Did he ever have visitors?"

"No." The man sighed. His hair was brittle and his eyes were watering. It seemed to D'Agosta that he was dying, that he knew it, and that he welcomed it.

Pendergast picked up the small box of memorabilia and tucked it under his arm. "Is there anything we can do for you, John?" he asked quietly.

The man shook his head and turned to the wall.

They left the room without speaking. At the stoop, they passed the three drunks again.

"Find what you were looking for?" Jed asked.

"Yes," said D'Agosta. "Thanks."

The man touched his brow with his finger. D'Agosta turned. "What will happen to all the stuff in John's room when *he* dies?"

The drunk shrugged. "They'll toss it."

"That was a most valuable visit," Pendergast said as they got into the car. "We now know that Ranier Beckmann lived in Italy, probably in 1974, that he spoke Italian decently, perhaps fluently."

D'Agosta looked at him, astonished. "How did you figure that out?"

"It's what he said when he lost at rummy. 'Kay Biskerow.' It's not a name, it's an expression. *Che bischero!* It's Italian, a Florentine dialect expostulation meaning 'What a jerk!' Only someone who had lived in Florence would know it. The coins in that cigar box are all Italian lire, dated 1974 and before. The fountain behind the four friends, although I don't recognize it, is clearly Italianate."

D'Agosta shook his head. "You figured all that out just from that little box of things?"

"Sometimes the small things speak the loudest." And as the Rolls shot from the curb and accelerated down the street, Pendergast glanced over. "Would you slide my laptop out of the dash there, Vincent? Let us find out what light Professor Charles F. Ponsonby Jr. can shed on things."

{ 47 }

As Pendergast drove south, D'Agosta booted the laptop, accessed the Internet via a wireless cellular connection, and initiated a search on Charles F. Ponsonby Jr. Within a few minutes, he had more information than he knew what to do with, starting with the fact that Ponsonby was Lyman Professor of Art History at Princeton University.

"I thought the name was familiar," Pendergast said. "A specialist in the Italian Renaissance, I believe. Lucky for us he's still teaching—no doubt as professor emeritus by now. Bring up his curriculum vitae, if you will, Vincent."

As Pendergast merged onto the New Jersey Turnpike and smoothly accelerated into the afternoon traffic, D'Agosta read off the professor's appointments, awards, and publications. It was a lengthy process, made lengthier by the numerous abstracts Pendergast insisted on hearing recited verbatim.

At last, he was done. Pendergast thanked him, then slipped out his cell phone, dialed, spoke to directory information, redialed, spoke again briefly. "Ponsonby will see us," he said as he replaced the phone. "Reluctantly. We're very close, Vincent. The photograph proves that all four of them were together at least once. Now we need to know exactly where they met, and—even more important—just what happened during that fateful encounter to somehow bind them together for the rest of their lives."

Pendergast pushed the car still faster. D'Agosta shot a surreptitious glance in his direction. The man looked positively eager, like a hound on a scent.

Ninety minutes later the Rolls was cruising down Nassau Street, quaint shops on the left and the Princeton campus on the right, Gothic buildings rising from manicured lawns. Pendergast slid the Rolls into a parking space and fed the meter, nodding to a crowd of students who stopped to gawk. They crossed the street, passed through the great iron gates, and approached the enormous facade of Firestone Library, the largest open-stack library in the world.

A small man with a thatch of untidy white hair stood before the glass doors. He was exactly what D'Agosta imagined a Professor Ponsonby would look like: fussy, tweedy, and pedantic. The only thing missing was a briar pipe.

"Professor Ponsonby?" Pendergast asked.

"You're the FBI agent?" the man replied in a reedy voice, making a show of examining his watch.

Three minutes late, D'Agosta thought.

Pendergast shook his hand. "Indeed I am."

"You didn't say anything about bringing a *policeman*."

D'Agosta felt himself bristling at the way he pronounced the word.

"May I present my associate, Sergeant Vincent D'Agosta?"

The professor shook his hand with obvious reluctance. "I have to tell you, Agent Pendergast, that I don't much like being questioned by the FBI. I will not be bullied into giving out information on former students."

"Of course. Now, Professor, where may we chat?"

"We can talk right there on that bench. I would rather not bring an FBI agent and a policeman back to my office, if you don't mind."

"Of course."

The professor marched stiffly over to a bench beneath ancient sycamores and sat down, fussily cocking one knee over the other. Pendergast strolled over and took a seat beside him. There wasn't room for D'Agosta, so he stood to one side, arms folded.

Ponsonby removed a briar pipe from his pocket, knocked out the dottle, began packing it.

Now it's perfect, thought D'Agosta.

"You aren't the Charles Ponsonby who just won the Berenson Medal in Art History, are you?" asked Pendergast.

"I am." He removed a box of wooden matches from his pocket, extracted one, and lit the pipe, sucking in the flame with a low gurgle.

"Ah! Then you are the author of that new catalogue raisonné of Pontormo."

"Correct."

"A splendid book."

"Thank you."

"I shall never forget seeing *The Visitation* in the little church in Carmignano. The most perfect orange in all of art history. In your book—"

"May we get to the point, Mr. Pendergast?"

There was a silence. Ponsonby apparently had no interest in discussing academic subjects with gumshoes, no matter how cultivated. For once, Pendergast's usual charm offensive had failed.

"I believe you had a student named Ranier Beckmann," Pendergast went on.

"You mentioned that on the phone. I was his thesis adviser."

"I wonder if I could ask you a few questions."

"Why don't you ask him directly? I have no intention of becoming an FBI informant, thank you."

D'Agosta had run into this type before. Deeply suspicious of law enforcement, treating every question as a personal challenge. They refused to be flattered into compliance and fought you every step of the way, citing all kinds of spurious legalisms about the right to privacy, the Fifth Amendment, the usual bullshit.

"Oh, you didn't know?" Pendergast said, his voice smooth as honey. "Mr. Beckmann died. Tragically."

Silence. "No, I didn't know." More silence. "How?"

Now it was Pendergast's turn to be unforthcoming. Instead, he dropped another tantalizing nugget. "I've just come from the exhumation of his body... But perhaps this isn't an appropriate topic of conversation, seeing as how you two weren't close."

"Whoever told you that was misinformed. Ranier was one of my best students."

"Then how is it you didn't hear about his death?"

The professor shifted uneasily. "We lost touch after he graduated."

"I see. Then perhaps you won't be able to help us, after all." And Pendergast made a show of preparing to stand.

"He was a brilliant student, one of the best I've ever had. I was—I was very disappointed he didn't want to go on to graduate school. He wanted to go to Europe, do a grand tour on his own, a sort of wandering journey without any kind of academic structure. I did not approve." Ponsonby paused. "May I ask how he died and why the body was exhumed?"

"I'm sorry, but that information can be disclosed only to Mr. Beckmann's family and friends."

"I tell you, we were very close. I gave him a book at parting. I've only done that with half a dozen students in my forty years of teaching."

"And this was in 1976?"

"No, it was in 1974." The professor was very glad to offer the correction. Then a new thought seemed to strike him. He looked at Pendergast afresh. "It wasn't homicide . . . was it?"

"Really, Professor, unless you can get the permission of a family member to release this information—you *do* know someone in his family, I daresay?"

The professor's face fell. "No. No one."

Pendergast arched his eyebrows in surprise.

"He wasn't close to his family. I can't recall him ever mentioning them."

"Pity. And so you say that Beckmann left for Europe in 1974, right after graduation, and that was the last you heard of him?"

"No. I got a note from Scotland at the end of August of that year. He was preparing to leave some farming commune he'd joined and head to Italy. I felt it was just some stage he had to go through. To tell you the truth, these past dozen years I'd been half expecting to see his name turn up in one of the journals, or perhaps to hear of an art opening of his. I've often thought of him over the years. Really, Mr. Pendergast, I would appreciate hearing anything you might be able to tell me about him."

Pendergast paused. "It would be highly irregular..." He let his voice trail off.

D'Agosta had to smile. Flattery hadn't worked, so Pendergast had taken another tack. And now he had the professor begging him for information.

"Surely you can at least tell me how he died."

His pipe had gone out, and Pendergast waited while the professor drew out another match. As Ponsonby struck it, Pendergast spoke. "He died an alcoholic in a flophouse in Yonkers and was buried in the local potter's field."

The professor dropped the burning match, his face a mask of horror. "Good God. I had no idea."

"Very tragic."

The professor tried to cover up his shock by opening the matchbox again, but his shaking hands spilled them over the bench.

Pendergast helped pick them up. The professor poked them back one by one into the trembling box. He put his pipe away, unlit. D'Agosta was surprised to see the old man's eyes film over. "Such a *fine* student," he said, almost to himself.

Pendergast let the silence grow. Then he slipped Beckmann's copy of *Lives of the Painters* out from his suit coat and held it out to Ponsonby.

For a moment, the old man didn't appear to recognize it. Then he started violently. "Where did you get this?" he asked, grasping it quickly.

"It was with Mr. Beckmann's effects."

"This is the book I gave him." As he opened the flyleaf to the dedication page, the photograph slipped out. "What's this?" he asked as he picked it up.

Pendergast said nothing, asked no questions.

"There he is," Ponsonby said, pointing at the photo. "That's just how I remember him. This must have been taken in Florence in the fall."

"Florence?" said Pendergast. "It could have been taken anywhere in Italy."

"No, I recognize that fountain behind them. It's the one in Piazza Santo Spirito. Always a big hangout for students. And there, behind, you can just see the *portone* of the Palazzo Guadagni, which is a shabby student *pensione.* I say the fall because they're dressed that way, although I suppose it could have also been in spring."

Pendergast retrieved the picture, then asked offhandedly, "The other students in the photograph were also from Princeton?"

"I've never seen any of them before. He must have met them in Florence. Like I said, the Piazza Santo Spirito was a gathering place for foreign students. Still is." He closed the book. His face looked very tired and his voice cracked. "Ranier... Ranier had *such* promise."

"We are all born with promise, Professor." Pendergast stood up, then hesitated. "You may keep the book, if you wish."

But Ponsonby didn't seem to hear. His shoulders were bent, and he caressed the spine with a trembling hand.

As they drove back to New York in the gathering dusk, D'Agosta stirred restlessly in the front passenger seat. "Amazing how you extracted all that information from the professor without his even knowing it." And it *was* amazing, though also a little sad: despite the professor's arrogance and high-handedness, he'd seemed terribly moved by the death of a favorite student, even one not seen for three decades.

Pendergast nodded. "One rule, Vincent: the more unwilling the subject is to release information, the better the information is, once released. And Dr. Ponsonby's information was as good as gold." His eyes gleamed in the dark.

"It looks like they met up in Florence in the fall of '74."

"Exactly. Something happened to them there, something so extraordinary it resulted in at least two murders, thirty years later." He turned to D'Agosta. "Do you know the saying, Vincent, 'All roads lead to Rome'?"

"Shakespeare?"

"Very good. In this case, however, it appears all roads lead to Florence. And that is precisely where *our* road should lead."

"To Florence?"

"Precisely. No doubt Bullard himself is on his way there, if he's not there already."

"I'm glad there's not going to be any argument about my coming along," D'Agosta said.

"I wouldn't have it any other way, Vincent. Your police instincts are first-rate. Your marksmanship is astonishing. I know I can trust you in a tight spot. And the chances of ourselves ending up in just such a spot are rather good, I'm afraid. So if you wouldn't mind sliding out the laptop again, we'll book our tickets now. First class, if you don't mind, open return."

"Leaving when?"

"Tomorrow morning."

{ 48 }

D'Agosta let the cab drop him off at 136th Street and Riverside. After what happened on his first visit to Pendergast's crumbling old mansion, there was no way in hell he was going to trust public transportation. Still, caution prompted him to get off a block early. Somehow he felt Pendergast would prefer it that way.

He dragged the lone suitcase out of the backseat, handed fifteen dollars to the driver. "Keep the change," he said.

"Whatever." And the cabbie sped away. Seeing D'Agosta and his luggage outside the hotel, he'd clearly been hoping for an airport fare—and he hadn't been at all pleased to find out the actual destination was Harlem.

D'Agosta watched the cab take the next corner at speed and vanish from sight. Then he scanned Riverside Drive carefully, up and down, checking the windows, the stoops, the dark areas between the lampposts. Everything seemed quiet. Hefting the suitcase, he began trotting north.

It had taken about half an hour to prepare for the trip.

He hadn't bothered to call his wife—as it was, the next time he heard from her would probably be through a lawyer. Chief MacCready of the Southampton P.D. was delighted to hear he'd be taking an unscheduled trip as part of his modified duty with the FBI. The chief was in increasingly hot water over the slow progress of the case, and this gave him a bone to throw the local press: *SPD officer sent to Italy to follow hot lead.* Given a dawn departure, Pendergast had suggested they both spend the night in New York at his place on Riverside Drive. And now here he was, luggage in hand, just hours away from standing on his family's ancestral soil. It was both an exhilarating and a sobering thought.

The one thing he'd miss, he thought as he neared the end of the block, was his blossoming relationship with Laura Hayward. Though the frantic pace of the last few days had mostly kept them apart, D'Agosta realized he'd begun to feel, for the first time in almost twenty years, that constant, low-frequency tingle of courtship. When he'd called her from the hotel to say he was accompanying Pendergast to Italy in the morning, the line had gone silent for several seconds. Then she'd said simply, "Watch your ass, Vinnie." He hoped to hell this little jaunt wouldn't throw a monkey wrench into things.

Ahead, the Beaux Arts mansion at 891 Riverside rose up, the sharp ramparts of its widow's walk pricking the night sky. He crossed the street, then slipped through the iron gate and made his way down the carriageway to the porte-cochère. His knock was answered by Proctor, who wordlessly escorted him through echoing galleries and tapestried chambers to the library. It appeared to be lit only by a large fire that blazed on the hearth. Peering into the grand, book-lined room, he made out Pendergast near the far wall. The agent had his back to the door and was standing before a long table, writing something on a sheet of cream-colored paper. D'Agosta could hear the crackling of the fire, the scratch of the pen. Constance was nowhere to be seen, but he thought he made out—just at the threshold of hearing—the distant, mournful sound of a violin.

D'Agosta cleared his throat, knocked on the door frame.

Pendergast turned quickly at the sound. "Ah, Vincent. Come in." He slipped the sheet of paper into a small wooden box, inlaid with mother-of-pearl, that lay on the table. Then he closed the box carefully and pushed it to one side. It almost seemed to D'Agosta as if Pendergast was careful to shield its contents from view.

"Would you care for some refreshment?" he asked, stepping across the room. "Cognac, Calvados, Armagnac, Budweiser?" Though the voice was Pendergast's usual slow, buttery drawl, there was a strange brightness to his eyes D'Agosta had not seen before.

"No, thanks."

"Then I'll help myself, with your indulgence. Please have a seat." And moving to a sideboard, Pendergast poured two fingers of amber liquid into a large snifter.

D'Agosta watched him carefully. There was something unusual about his movements, a strange hesitancy, that—combined with Pendergast's expression—troubled D'Agosta in a way he could not quite describe.

"What's happened?" he asked instinctively.

Pendergast did not immediately respond. Instead, he

replaced the decanter, picked up the snifter, and took a seat in a leather sofa across from D'Agosta. He sipped meditatively, sipped again.

"Perhaps I *can* tell you," he said at last in a low voice, as if arriving at a decision. "In fact, if any other living person is to know, I suppose that person should be you."

"Know what?" D'Agosta asked.

"It arrived half an hour ago," Pendergast said. "It couldn't possibly have come at a worse time. Nevertheless, it can't be helped; we've come too far with this case to change direction now."

"*What* arrived?"

"That." And Pendergast nodded at a folded letter on the table lying between them. "Go ahead, pick it up; I've already taken the necessary precautions."

D'Agosta didn't know exactly what was meant by that, but he leaned over, picked up the letter, and unfolded it gingerly. The paper was a beautiful linen, apparently hand-pressed. At the top of the sheet was an embossed coat of arms: a lidless eye over two moons, with a crouching lion beneath. At first, D'Agosta thought the sheet was empty. But then he made out, in a beautiful, old-fashioned script, a small date in the middle of the page: *January 28.* It appeared to have been written with a goose quill.

D'Agosta put it down. "I don't understand."

"It's from my brother, Diogenes."

"Your brother?" D'Agosta said, surprised. "I thought he was dead."

"He is dead to me. At least, he has been until recently."

D'Agosta waited. He knew better than to say more.

Pendergast's sentences had grown hesitant, almost broken, as if he found the subject intolerably repellent.

Pendergast took another sip of Armagnac. "Vincent, a line of madness has run through my family for many generations now. Sometimes this madness has taken a benign or even beneficial form. More frequently, I fear, it has manifested itself through astonishing cruelty and evil. Unfortunately, this darkness has reached full flower with the current generation. You see, my brother, Diogenes, is at once the most insane—most evil—and yet the most brilliant member of our family ever to walk the earth. This was clear to me from a very early age. As such, it is a blessing we two are the last of our line."

Still, D'Agosta waited.

"As a young child, Diogenes was content with certain... experiments. He devised highly complex machines for the lure, capture, and torture of small animals. Mice, rabbits, opossums. These machines were brilliant in a horrible way. Pain factories, he proudly called them when they were ultimately discovered." Pendergast paused. "His interests soon grew more exotic. House pets began disappearing—first cats, then dogs—never to be found again. He spent days on end in the portrait gallery, staring at paintings of our ancestors... especially those who had met untimely ends. As he grew older—and as he realized he was being watched with increasing vigilance—he abandoned these pastimes and withdrew into himself. He poured forth his black dreams and his terrible creative energies into a series of locked journals. He kept these journals well hidden. Very well hidden, in fact: it took me two years of stealthy surveillance as an adolescent to discover them. I read only one page, but that was enough. I will never forget it, not as long as I live. The world was never quite the same for me after that. Needless to say, I immediately burned all the journals. He had hated me before, but this act earned his undying rage."

Pendergast took another sip, then pushed the snifter away, unfinished.

"The last time I saw Diogenes was the day he turned twenty-one. He had just come into his fortune. He said he was planning a terrible crime."

"A single crime?" D'Agosta repeated.

"He gave no hint of the details. All I can go on is his use of the word *terrible.* For something to be terrible to *him*..." Pendergast's voice trailed off, and then he resumed briskly. "Suffice to say, it will be anathema to rational contemplation. Only he, in his limitless madness, could comprehend its evil. How, when, where, against whom—I have no idea. He disappeared that very day, taking his fortune with him, and I have not seen or heard from him since—until now. This is his second notice to me. The first had the same date on it. I wasn't sure what it meant. It arrived exactly six months ago—and now this. The meaning is now obvious."

"Not to me."

"I am being put on notice. The crime will occur in ninety-one days. It is his challenge to me, his hated sibling. I suspect his plans are now complete. This note is equivalent to his flinging the gauntlet at my feet, daring me to try and stop him."

D'Agosta stared at the folded letter in horror. "What are you going to do?"

"The only thing I can do. I will wrap up this current

case of ours as quickly as possible. Only then can I deal with my brother."

"And if you find him? What then?"

"I *must* find him," Pendergast said with quiet ferocity. "And when I do—" He paused. "The situation will be addressed with appropriate finality."

The look on the agent's face was so terrible D'Agosta looked away.

For a long moment, the library was silent. Then, at last, Pendergast roused himself. One glance told D'Agosta the subject was closed.

Pendergast's voice changed back into its usual efficient, cool tone. "As liaison with the Southampton P.D., it seemed logical to suggest you as FBI liaison with the NYPD. This case began in the United States, and it may well end here. I've arranged for you, working with Captain Hayward, to be that liaison. It will require you to be in touch with her on a regular basis, via phone and e-mail."

D'Agosta gave a nod.

Pendergast was looking at him. "I trust you'll find that a satisfactory arrangement?"

"Fine with me." D'Agosta hoped he wasn't blushing. *Is there anything this guy doesn't know?*

"Very good." Pendergast rose. "And now I must pack for the trip and speak briefly with Constance. She'll be remaining behind, of course, to manage the collections and do any additional research we may require. Proctor will see that you're comfortable. Feel free to ring if you need anything."

He rose, offering his hand. "*Buona notte.* And pleasant dreams."

* * *

The room D'Agosta was shown to was on the third floor, facing the rear. It was exactly what he'd dreaded most: dimly lit and tall-ceilinged, with dark crushed-velvet wallpaper and heavy mahogany furniture. It smelled of old fabric and wood. The walls were covered with paintings in heavy gilt frames: landscapes, still lifes, and some studies in oil that were strangely disturbing if you looked at them too closely. The wooden shutters were closed tight against the casements, and no external noise filtered through the heavy stonework. Yet the room, like the rest of the house, was spotlessly clean; the fixtures were modern; and the huge Victorian bed, when he at last turned in, was exceptionally comfortable with fresh, clean sheets. The pillows had been aired and fluffed by some invisible housekeeper; the comforter, when he drew it up, was a luxuriously thick eiderdown. Everything about the room seemed guaranteed to provide an ideal night's sleep.

And yet sleep did not come quickly to D'Agosta. He lay in bed, eyes on the ceiling, thinking of Diogenes Pendergast, for a long, long time.

{ 49 }

Locke Bullard sat in the rear of the Mercedes as it cruised along the Viale Michelangelo above Florence, the great eighteenth-century villas of the wealthiest Florentines invisible behind enormous walls and massive iron gates. As the limousine passed the Piazzale, Bullard barely glanced out at the stupendous view: the Duomo, the Palazzo Vecchio, the Arno River. The car descended to the ancient gate of the Porta Romana.

"Cut through the old city," said Bullard.

The driver flashed his *permesso* at the policemen on duty at the gate, and the limo eased into the crooked streets, heading first north, then west, passing back through another gate in the ancient walls surrounding the city. The Renaissance palazzi turned into modest nineteenth-century apartment houses; these in turn gave way to anonymous blocks of apartments, built midcentury; and finally to hideous projects and high-rises of gray concrete. There were no highways, just a maze of jammed streets and decaying factories, punctuated here and there by tiny kitchen gardens or a few hundred square feet of vineyard.

In half an hour, the limousine was crawling through the shabby streets of Signa, one of the ugliest of the industrial suburbs, a gray expanse of buildings spread out in the floodplains of the Arno. Laundry hung on concrete balconies in the listless, dead air. The only reminder that this was Bella Tuscany was the distant green hills of Carmignano, the tallest topped by the barest outline of a castle.

Bullard saw nothing beyond the smoked windows, said nothing to the chauffeur. His craggy face was utterly blank, his deep-set eyes cold beneath the great jutting brows. The only sign of the great turmoil within were the slowly bulging muscles of his jaw, tensing and relaxing, again and again.

At last, the limo turned down an anonymous dead-end lane, arrived at a shabby chain-link fence with a gate and guardhouse. Beyond, the endless suburb stopped and a surprising new world began: a strange world of dark trees, vines, and a riot of ivy-covered mounds and shapes.

The limo was checked, then waved forward into the darkly fantastical landscape. From this closer vantage point, the green shapes could be descried as ruined buildings, so sunken in creepers as to look like natural cliffs. And yet these were not ancient ruins, like those so often seen in Italy. These heaps of fallen masonry were never visited by tourists. The ruins dated only back to the early decades of the twentieth century. As the limousine moved like a shark through the ruins, it passed old dormitories, treelined boulevards passing through rows of once-fine houses, past overgrown railroad sidings and wrecked laboratories—and, dominating it all, a brick smokestack that rose thirty stories into the blue Tuscan sky. The only clue as to what all this had once been was the faded remains of a sign painted on the stack, where *NOBEL S.G.E.M.* could still barely be discerned.

Security seemed deceptively slack. The chain-link fence along the outer perimeter was old and decrepit. A determined group of teenagers could have easily entered. And yet the ruined compound showed no sign of casual human trespass. There was no litter, no graffiti, no sign of campfires or broken wine bottles.

The limousine wound its way slowly along a maze of weed-choked roads, curving past a row of giant warehouses, now empty, windows like dead eyes, fields of wild strawberries growing around the cracked walls. The car continued through an archway in an old brick wall, past more ruins and heaps of brick and broken concrete, until it hit a second gate. This gate was far more modern than the first: attached to a sophisticated double perimeter of blastproof chain-link, topped with glittering coils of concertina, and surrounded by a wide motion-sensor field.

Again the limousine was inspected, this time much more thoroughly, before the gate opened electronically on well-oiled hinges.

And now a shocking contrast met the eye. Beyond one last ruined facade—drowning in vegetation—lay a manicured lawn, sweeping up to a gleaming building dressed in titanium and glass, an architectural masterpiece hidden among the ruins. It was framed by shrubbery that had been trimmed and shaped to perfection. An automatic sprinkler system cast an arc of water that glittered rainbows in the strong Florentine sunlight.

In front of the building stood three men. As the black car pulled up, one of them, clearly agitated but making a strong effort to suppress it, came over and opened the door.

"*Bentornato, Signor Bullard,*" he said.

Bullard got out, his enormous frame swelling as he stood up. Ignoring the proffered hands, he arched his back, stretched his arms. He seemed to be looking over the heads of the men as if they didn't exist. His massive, ugly, knotted face was an impenetrable mask.

"We should be pleased if you could lunch with us, sir, before—"

"Where is it?" Bullard cut him off.

There was a dismayed silence. "This way."

The small group turned, and Bullard followed them down the limestone walkway into the cool interior of the building. They passed down a corridor through two sets of automatic doors, each requiring a retinal scan from the leader of the group.

At one point, Bullard stopped and looked into a room leading off the corridor. The others paused expectantly. The room was a laboratory, full of equipment and whiteboards covered with formulas.

He stepped into the room, glanced at a nearby table covered with what appeared to be aircraft nose cones. Each was painted a different color, and a pin was stuck into each, bearing a label of notes and chemical formulas. In a sudden blind rage, Bullard raised his arm and swept the nose cones from the table. Then he turned back and, without a word, continued down the corridor.

They came to a third door, thicker and smaller than the others, made of stainless steel and brass.

There was a shout from behind. Everyone turned.

An elegantly dressed man was striding toward them, his face white with anger. "Stop," he said. "*Io domando una spiegazione, Signor Bullard, anche da Lei.* I demand an explanation, even from you." The man blocked their way, half the size of Bullard, almost noble in his outraged dignity.

There was a flash of movement, a grunt, and the man sank to the ground, punched in the gut. He clutched his midriff, groaning, and Bullard gave him a vicious kick with the toe of his shoe, so hard the snapping of the ribs was audible to all. The man gasped and rolled in agony.

Bullard turned to one of the men. "I fired this man. Martinetti was trespassing. I deeply regret that he resisted apprehension, assaulted a security officer, and had to be subdued by that officer."

He turned to one of the security officers escorting them. "Did you hear what I said?"

"Yes, sir," the man said in an American accent.

"Make it so."

"Yes, sir."

"Call a detail to remove this man and prefer charges against him for trespassing." Bullard stepped over the prostrate form and looked into the retinal scan himself. There was a click of disengaging metal, then the vault door swung open, exposing machined stainless steel and brass. Beyond lay a small vault. On one side were several hard drives, locked in transparent plastic cases and carefully stacked atop plastic filing cabinets. On the other was a small, rectangular box of polished walnut, surrounded by a cluster of sophisticated electronics:

climate-control sensors, humidity readouts, a seismograph, gas analyzer, barometers, and temperature gauges. Bullard strode over to the box, picked it up gently by the handle. It was so light that in Bullard's massive grip it seemed weightless. He turned.

"Let's go."

"Mr. Bullard, perhaps you might care to check the contents?"

Bullard turned to the man who'd spoken. "I'll check soon enough. If it isn't there, losing your jobs will be the least of your worries."

"Yes, sir."

The tension in the room was palpable. The men shifted uneasily, apparently reluctant to leave. Bullard brushed past them, started to duck through the vault door, turned back. "You coming?"

The men followed him out of the vault. The door hissed shut behind. Bullard stepped over Martinetti again and walked through the three sets of doors, the men in his wake, the only sound the clicking of heels on the polished corridors. In another few minutes, he was back at the curb, where the limousine sat idling. The men stood on the sidewalk uncertainly, looking at Bullard. There was no more mention of lunch.

Without a backward glance, Bullard got in the car, slammed the door. "To the villa," he said, placing the wooden box very carefully on his lap.

{ 50 }

D'Agosta stood at the windows of his suite in the Lungarno Hotel, looking out over the deep green of the Arno, the pale yellow palaces of Florence lining both banks, the Ponte Vecchio with its crooked little buildings perched out over the water. He felt strangely expectant, even a little light-headed. He wasn't sure if it was jet lag, the opulence of his surroundings, or the fact that he was in his country of origin for the first time in his life.

D'Agosta's father had left Naples as a boy with his parents, right after the war, to escape the terrible famine of '44. They settled on Carmine Street in New York City. His father, Vito, outraged by the rising power of the Mafia, had fought back by becoming a New York City cop, and a damn good one. His shield and awards still stood in a glass case on the mantel like holy relics: police combat cross, medal of honor. D'Agosta had grown up on Carmine Street, surrounded by Italian immigrants from Naples and Sicily, immersed in the language, the religion, the cycles of saints' days and celebrations. From childhood, Italy had for him taken on the air of a mythical place.

And now here he was.

He felt a lump rising in his throat. He had not expected it to be such an emotional experience. This was the land of his ancestors going back millennia. Italy was the birthplace of so much: art, architecture, sculpture, music, science, and astronomy. The great names of the past rolled through his mind: Augustus Caesar, Cicero, Ovid, Dante, Christopher Columbus, Leonardo da Vinci, Michelangelo, Galileo...The list stretched back more than two thousand years. D'Agosta felt certain no other nation on earth had produced such genius.

He opened the window and breathed in the air. It was something his wife never understood, his immense pride in his heritage. It was something that she had always thought a little silly. Well, no wonder. She was English. What had the English done but scribble a few plays and poems? Italy was the birthplace of Western civilization. The land of his ancestors. Someday he would take his son, Vinnie, here...

These delicious reveries were interrupted by a knock on the door. It was the valet with his luggage.

"Where would you like it, sir?" the valet said in English.

D'Agosta made a flourish with his hand and launched nonchalantly into Italian. *"Buon giorno guagliòne. Pe' piacère' lassàte ì valigè abbecìno o liett', grazie."*

The valet looked at him strangely, with what seemed to D'Agosta a fleeting look of disdain. "Excuse me?" he asked in English.

D'Agosta felt a brief swell of irritation. *"Ì valigè, aggia ritt', mettitelè' allà."* He pointed to the bed.

The valet placed the two bags by the bed. D'Agosta

fished in his pockets but could not find anything less than a five-euro note. He gave it to the valet.

"Grazie, signore, Lei è molto gentile. Se Lei ha bisogno di qualsiasi cosa, mi dica." And the valet left.

D'Agosta hadn't understood a word the man had said after "*Grazie, signore.*" It didn't sound at all like the language his grandmother spoke. He shook his head. It must be the Florentine accent throwing him off: he knew he hadn't forgotten *that* much. Italian was his first language, after all.

He looked around. This was like no hotel room he had ever stayed in before, the height of clean, understated taste and elegance. It was also huge: almost an apartment, really, with a bedroom, sitting room, marble bath, kitchen, and well-stocked bar, along with a wall of windows looking out over the Arno, the Ponte Vecchio, the Uffizi Gallery, the great cupola of the Duomo. The room must've cost a fortune, but D'Agosta had long ago given up worrying about how Pendergast spent his money, if indeed it was his money. The guy remained as mysterious as ever.

There came another soft knock on the door, and D'Agosta opened it. It was Pendergast. The detective, still dressed in his usual black—which somehow looked less out of place in Florence than it did in New York—glided in. He carried a sheaf of papers in one hand.

"Accommodations to your satisfaction, Vincent?"

"A bit cramped, lousy view of some old bridge, but I'll get used to it."

Pendergast settled on the sofa and handed D'Agosta the sheaf of papers. "You will find here a *permesso di soggiorno*, a firearm permit, an investigative authorization from the Questura, your *codice fiscale*, and a few other odds and ends to be signed—all through the count's good offices."

D'Agosta took the papers. "Fosco?"

Pendergast nodded. "Italian bureaucracy moves slowly, and the good count gave it a swift kick forward on our behalf."

"Is he here?" D'Agosta asked with little enthusiasm.

"No. He may come later." Pendergast rose and strolled to the window. "There is his family's palazzo, across the river, next to the Corsini Palace."

D'Agosta glanced out at a medieval building with a crenellated parapet. "Nice pile."

"Indeed. It's been in the family since the late thirteenth century."

Another knock came at the door.

"Trasite'," D'Agosta called, proud to be able to use his Italian in front of Pendergast.

The valet came in again, carrying a basket of fruit. "*Signori?*"

"Faciteme stù piacère' lassatele 'ngoppa' o' tavule."

The valet made no move toward the table, saying instead, "Where shall I put it?" in English. D'Agosta glanced at Pendergast and saw a twinkle of amusement in his eye.

"O' tavule," he answered more brusquely.

The man stood there with the fruit in his hand, looking from the table to the desk, finally placing it on the desk. D'Agosta felt a surge of irritation at his willful incomprehension—hadn't he given the man a big enough tip? Words he had so often heard from his father flowed unbidden off his lips. *"Allòra qual'è ò problema', sì surdo? Nun mi capisc'i? Ma che è parl' ò francèse'? Mannaggi' 'a miseria'.*"

The man backed out of the room in confusion. D'Agosta turned to Pendergast, to find the agent making a rare and unsuccessful attempt to suppress an effervescence of mirth.

"What's so funny?" D'Agosta said.

Pendergast managed to compose his features. "Vincent, I didn't know you had such a flair for languages."

"Italian was my first language."

"Italian? Do you speak Italian, too?"

"What do you mean, *too*? What the hell do you think I was speaking?"

"It sounded remarkably to me like Neapolitan, which is often called a dialect of Italian but is actually a separate language. A fascinating language, too, but, of course, incomprehensible to a Florentine."

D'Agosta froze. Neapolitan *dialect*? The thought had never occurred to him. Sure, there were families that spoke the Sicilian dialect where he grew up in New York, but he'd just assumed his own language was real Italian. Neapolitan? No way. He spoke *Italian*.

Pendergast, noticing the look on D'Agosta's face, continued. "When Italy was united in 1871, there were six hundred dialects. A debate began to rage as to what language the new country should speak. The Romans thought their dialect was the best, because, after all, they were *Rome*. The Perugians thought theirs was the purest, because that's where the oldest university in Europe was. The Florentines felt theirs was correct, because theirs was the language of Dante." He smiled again. "Dante won."

"I never knew that."

"But people continued to speak their dialects. Even when your parents emigrated, only a small portion of the citizenry spoke official Italian. It wasn't until the arrival of television that Italians began abandoning their dialects and speaking the same language. What you consider 'Italian' is actually the dialect of Naples, a rich but sadly dying language, with hints of Spanish and French."

D'Agosta was stunned.

"Who knows? Perhaps our researches will take us south, where you can shine. But for now, seeing as how it is getting on toward dinnertime, shall we head out for a bite to eat? I know a wonderful little *osteria* in Piazza Santo Spirito, where there is also a curious fountain I believe might be of interest to our investigation."

Five minutes later they were walking through the crooked medieval streets of Florence, which led them to a broad, spacious piazza, shaded by horse chestnut trees and shut in on three sides by lovely Renaissance buildings stuccoed in hues of ivory, yellow, and ocher. Dominating the end closest to the river was the plain facade of the Chiesa di Santo Spirito, severe in its simplicity. An old marble fountain splashed merrily in the center of the piazza. Students with backpacks clustered around it, smoking cigarettes and chatting.

Pendergast casually removed Beckmann's photograph from his pocket, held it up toward the fountain, and then slowly circled the piazza until the background matched. He stared for a long moment. Then he put the photo away.

"That's where the four of them stood, Vincent," he

said, pointing. "And there, behind, is the Palazzo Guadagni, now managed as a student *pensione.* We shall inquire there tomorrow to see if they remember any of our friends, although I do not hold out much hope. But let us dine. I find myself in the mood for linguini with white truffles."

"I could really do with a cheeseburger and fries."

Pendergast turned to him, a stricken look on his face. D'Agosta smiled back crookedly. "Just kidding."

They strolled across the piazza toward a small restaurant, the Osteria Santo Spirito. Tables had been set up outside, and people were eating and drinking wine, their lively conversation floating into the piazza.

Pendergast waited until they were shown to a table, then gestured for D'Agosta to sit. "I must say, Vincent, you are looking fitter these days."

"Been working out. And after that jaunt in Riverside Park, I've also been brushing up at the shooting range."

"Your firearm skills are the stuff of legend. That just might come in handy for the little adventure we'll be having tomorrow night."

"Adventure?" D'Agosta was tired, but jet lag only seemed to energize Pendergast.

"We are going to Signa to visit Bullard's secret laboratory. While you were unwinding in your hotel room this afternoon, I was speaking with various Florentine officials, trying to procure the files on Bullard and BAI's doings here. But even Fosco's influence got me nowhere. It seems Bullard is well connected with the right people—or at least knows where to spend his money. All I was able to procure was a long-outdated map of his plant site. In any case, it's clear we're not going to get anywhere through regular channels."

"I take it he doesn't know we're coming."

"Our visit will be in the manner of an insertion. We can get the gear we need tomorrow morning."

D'Agosta nodded slowly. "Could be exciting."

"Let us hope not *too* exciting. As I get older, Vincent, I have come to prefer a quiet evening at home to a bracing exchange of gunfire in the dark."

{ 51 }

Bryce Harriman walked north along Fifth Avenue, thread-ing his way through the crowds with practiced ease, his mind on the devil killings. Ritts was right: the Von Menck piece had really touched a nerve in the city. He'd been flooded with calls. Mostly from cranks, of course—this was the *Post*, after all—but still he couldn't recall a bigger reaction to a story. The whole business of the golden ratio and the way everything fitted so neatly with the historic dates, the aura of mathematics—for an ignorant person, it had all the ring of hard scientific fact. And, Harriman had to admit, it *was* a bit uncanny how the dates just happened to fall in line like that.

He passed the Metropolitan Club, glimpsing the marvels of old New York money within. That was *his* world in there, or rather, the world of his grandparents. Although he was approaching the age where he could start expecting the first of several prestigious club invitations (arranged by his father), he worried that his current position at the *Post* would be an impediment. He needed to get back to the *Times*, and fast.

This was the story that could do it.

Ritts loved him—at least as much as that reptile could love anyone. But a good story was like a fire. It needed to be fed. And this one was already guttering. He sensed Ritts's good favor could fade as quickly as it came, leaving him and his big new raise uncomfortably exposed. He needed a development, even if it was manufactured. That was what he hoped this return visit to Cutforth's building might provide. His earlier pieces had already swelled the ranks of the Bible-thumpers, devil worshipers, Goths, freaks, satanists, and New Agers who now gathered daily along the fringes of Central Park opposite the building. There had already been a couple of fistfights, some name-calling, a few visits by New York's finest to break things up. But it was all disorganized. All reactions needed a catalyst and this was no exception.

He was nearing 68th Street. He could already see the gatherings of freaks on the park side of Fifth Avenue, each in its own little clump. He sidled up to the milling groups, elbowing his way through the ring of rubberneckers. Nothing much had changed from the last time he was there, except the crowd had swelled. A satanist in black leather, clutching a Bud, was hurling curses at a New Ager in hemp robes. There was the smell of beer and pot, not unlike a rock concert. At the far end, a man in faded jeans and a Black Watch plaid short-sleeved shirt was speaking to a rather large crowd. Harriman couldn't hear what he was saying, but of all the acts going on in this circus, his seemed to be the biggest.

Harriman peeled out of the group of onlookers and inserted himself back in, much closer to the man. He was preaching, that much was clear; but he looked normal, and his voice, instead of cracking at the edge of hysteria, sounded calm, educated, and reasonable. Even as he spoke, the crowd around him was swelling. A lot of onlookers were attracted by what he was saying, and even some satanists and Goths were listening.

"This is an amazing city," the man was saying. "I've been here just twenty-four hours, but I can already safely say there's nothing else on earth like it. The tall buildings, the limousines, the beautiful people. It dazzles the eye, it surely does. This is my first time in New York City. And you know what strikes me most, more than the glitter and the glamour? It's the *hurry*. Look around you, friends. Look at the pedestrians. Look how fast they walk, talking into their phones or staring straight ahead. I've never seen a thing like it. Look at the people in the taxis and buses as they pass—even when they're not moving, they seem to be in a rush. And I know what they're all so busy with. I've been doing a lot of listening since I arrived. I've probably listened to a thousand conversations already, most of them one-sided, because people on this Manhattan Island seem to prefer talking into cell phones than talking to real people, face-to-face. What are they busy with? They're busy with *themselves*. With tomorrow's big meeting. With dinner reservations. With cheating on their spouses. With backstabbing a business associate. All sorts of plans and schemes and stratagems, and none of them any more foresighted than, say, next month's trip to Club Med. How many of all these busy folk are busy thinking thirty, forty years ahead—to their own mortality? How many of these folks are busy making their peace with God? Or thinking of the words of Jesus in Luke: *Verily I say unto you, This generation shall not pass away, till all be fulfilled*? Precious few, I'd guess. If any."

Harriman looked more closely at the preacher. He had sandy hair, neatly cut, a good-looking all-American face, well-developed arms, trim, neat, clean-shaven. No tattoos or piercings, no metal-studded leather codpiece. If he had a Bible, it wasn't in evidence. It was as if he was talking to a group of friends—people he respected.

"I've done something else since reaching New York," the man went on. "I've visited churches. *Lots* of churches. I never knew one city, no matter how big, could boast so many churches. But see, friends, here's the sad thing. No matter how many people were thronging the streets *outside*, I found every one of these churches empty. They're starving. They're perishing from neglect. Even St. Patrick's Cathedral—as beautiful a Christian place as I've ever seen in my born days—had only a sprinkling of worshipers. Tourists? Yes, indeed, by the hundreds. But of the devout? Less than the fingers on my two hands.

"And this, my friends, is the saddest thing of all. To think that—in a place of so much culture, so much learning and sophistication—there can be such a terrible spiritual emptiness. I feel it all around me like a desert, drying the very marrow of my bones. I didn't want to believe what I read in the papers, the awful stories that brought me here to this place almost against my will. But it's true, my brothers and sisters. Every last word of it. New York is a city devoted to Mammon, not God. Look at him," and he pointed to a well-dressed twenty-something passing by in a pinstripe suit, yakking into a phone. "When do you suppose was the last time he thought about *his* mortality? Or her?" He pointed to a woman with bags from Henri Bendel and Tiffany's, climbing out of a cab. "Or them?" His accusing finger aimed at a pair of college students, walking hand in hand down the street. "Or you?" His finger now swiveled across the crowd. "How long since *you* thought about your own mortality? It may be a week away, ten years, or fifty—but it's coming. As sure as my name is Wayne P. Buck, it's coming. Are you ready?"

Harriman shivered involuntarily. This guy was *good.*

"I don't care if you're an investment banker on Wall Street or a migrant worker in Amarillo, death has no prejudice. Big or small, rich or poor, death will come for us all. People in the Middle Ages knew that. Even our own forebears knew that. Look at old gravestones and what do you see? The image of winged death. And like as not the words *memento mori*: 'remember, you will die.' Do you think that young fellow ever stops to think about that? Amazing: all these centuries of progress, and yet we've lost sight of that one fundamental truth that was always, *always* the first thought of our ancestors. An old poet, Robert Herrick, put it like this:

"Our life is short, and our days run
As fast away as does the sun;
And, as a vapour or a drop of rain
Once lost, can ne'er be found again."

Harriman swallowed. His luck was holding. This guy Buck was a personal gift to him. The crowd was swelling rapidly, and people were shushing their neighbors so they could hear the man's quiet, persuasive voice. He didn't need a Bible—Christ, he probably had the whole thing in his head. And not only the Bible—he was quoting metaphysical poets as well.

He carefully reached over to his shirt pocket and pressed the record button on his microcassette recorder. He didn't want to miss a word. Pat Robertson with his Pan-Cake makeup couldn't hold a candle to this guy.

"That young man isn't stopping to think that every day he spends out of touch with God is a day that can never, ever be reclaimed. Those two young lovers aren't stopping to think of how their deeds will be held accountable in the afterlife. That woman loaded with shopping bags most likely never gave a thought to the *real* value of life. Most likely none of them even *believe* in an afterlife. They're like the Romans who stood blindly aside while our Lord was crucified. If they ever do stop to think about the afterlife, they probably just tell themselves that they'll die and be put in a coffin and buried, and that's it.

"Except, my brothers and sisters, that is *not* it. I've held a lot of jobs in my life, and one of them was a mortuary assistant. So I speak to you with confidence. When you die, that is *not* the end. It is just the beginning. *I've seen what happens to the dead with my own eyes.*"

Harriman noticed that the crowd, though growing all the time, had fallen utterly silent. Nobody seemed to move. Harriman realized he, too, was almost holding his breath, waiting to hear what the man would say next.

"Perhaps our important young man with the cell phone will be lucky enough to be buried in the middle of winter. That tends to slow things down a piece. But sooner or later—usually sooner—the dinner guests arrive. First come the blowflies, *Phormia regina*, to lay their eggs. In a fresh corpse, there's a population explosion of sorts. That kind of population growth—we're talking half a dozen generations here—adds up to tens of thousands of maggots, always moving, always hungry. The larvae themselves generate so much heat that those at the center must crawl out to the edges to cool before burrowing back in again to the task at hand. In time-lapse photography, it all becomes a boiling, churning storm. And, of course, the maggots are only the first arrivals. In time, the fragrance of decomposition brings a host of others. But I see no reason to trouble you with all the details.

"So much, my friends, for resting in peace.

"Perhaps, then, our young fellow with the cell phone might decide cremation is the way to go. This leaves no corpse behind to be violated, over slow years, by the beetles and the worms. Surely cremation is a quick, a dignified end to our human form. Aren't we told as much?

"Then let me be the one to tell you, my brothers and sisters, no death is dignified that befalls us outside the sight of God. I've witnessed more cremations that I can count. Do you have any idea how hard it is to burn a human body? How much heat is required? Or what happens when the body comes in contact with a six-hundred-degree flame? I will tell you, my friends, and forgive me if I do not spare you. You will learn there is a reason I do not spare you.

"First the hair, from head to toe, crisps in a blaze

of blue smoke. Then the body snaps to attention, just like a cadet in a parade review. And then the body tries to *sit up*. Doesn't matter that there's a casket lid in the way, it tries to sit up all the same. The temperature rises, maybe to eight hundred degrees. And it is now that the marrow boils and the bones themselves begin to burst, the backbone exploding just like a string of Black Cats.

"And still the temperature goes up. A thousand degrees, fifteen hundred, two thousand. The eruptions keep on, rattling the retort oven like gunshots—but again I will refrain from naming just what is exploding at this point. Leave me only say that this goes on for as long as three hours before the mortal remains are reduced to ash and fragments of bone.

"Why have I not spared you more of these details, my brothers and sisters? I will tell you why. Because Lucifer, the Prince of Darkness, who never sleeps in his tireless pursuit of corruption, will not spare you, either. And the fires of that crematorium burn far cooler, and far briefer, than the fires to which that important young man's soul is surely destined. Two thousand degrees or ten thousand, three hours or three centuries—these are nothing to Lucifer. These are but a warm spring wind passing for the briefest of moments. And when you try to sit up in that burning lake of brimstone—when you bump your head on the roof of hell and fall back into that unquenchable flame, burning so hot it surpasses all powers of my poor tongue to describe it—who will hear your prayers? Nobody. You already had a lifetime to pray, tragically squandered.

"And that is why I am here, my friends. Up in that beautiful building, towering so high over our puny heads, Lucifer showed his face to this great city and seized the soul of a man. A man named Cutforth. Revelation tells us that in the End Days, Lucifer will openly walk the earth. He has arrived. The death out on Long Island, the death right here: these are but the beginning. We have been given a sign, and we must act. And act now. It is not too late. The crypt or the crematorium urn, the maggot or the flame—you must all of you understand that it makes no difference. When your soul is laid bare before the judge of all, what will be your account? I ask you to look into yourself now, in silence; and in silence to judge yourself. And then, in a little while, we will pray together. Pray for forgiveness, and for the time still upon this earth, and in this doomed city, in which to find redemption."

Almost mechanically, without taking his eyes from Buck, Harriman slipped his cell phone out of his pocket and called the photo department, speaking very softly. It was Klein's shift, and he understood exactly what Harriman wanted. No caricature of a Bible-thumping preacher here. Just the opposite. Harriman would make the Reverend Buck look like a man the readers of the *Post* would respect: a man who seemed the most reasonable, thoughtful person alive.

And if you heard him speak, you might believe it yourself.

Harriman slipped the phone back into his pocket. This Reverend Buck might not know it yet, but soon—very soon—he was going to be page one news.

{ 52 }

The night was humid and fragrant. Crickets trilled in the close darkness. D'Agosta followed Pendergast along an abandoned railroad track between squalid-looking concrete apartments. It was midnight and the moon had just set, lowering a velvety cloak over the city.

The tracks ended, leaving only the railroad grade, which was crossed by a sagging chain-link fence running off into darkness on both sides. On the far side of the fence lay blackness, with just the faintest outline of large trees silhouetted against the night.

Following Pendergast, D'Agosta turned and walked along the fence for a few hundred yards until they reached a cluster of trees. In the center was a tiny clearing, carpeted with dead leaves and old chestnut burrs.

"We'll prep here," said Pendergast, setting down the bag he'd been carrying.

D'Agosta put down his own bag and took a few deep breaths. He was glad he'd begun working out after the chase through Riverside Park but wished he'd thought of it sooner. Pendergast didn't even seem winded.

Pendergast stripped off his suit, folding it up into

neat packets which he stowed in his bag. Underneath he was wearing black pants and shirt. D'Agosta stripped down to a similar costume.

"Here." Pendergast tossed D'Agosta a jar of face paint, taking another for himself, and began blackening his face with the tips of his fingers.

D'Agosta began to apply the paint as he examined the perimeter fence. It looked about as low-security as you could get: rusty and leaning, with numerous rends and tears. He took off his shoes and pulled on another pair Pendergast had supplied him with: black and tight-fitting, with smooth soles.

Pendergast slipped out his Les Baer and began applying blacking to the gun. D'Agosta winced; it was a hell of a thing to do to such a beautiful firearm.

"You need to do the same, Vincent. A single glint, no matter how small, would be all their spotters need."

D'Agosta reluctantly removed his weapon and began blacking it.

"Undoubtedly you are wondering if all this is really necessary."

"The thought had crossed my mind."

Pendergast tugged on a pair of black gloves. "The fence, as you've surely guessed, is deceptive. There are several rings of security. The first is purely psychological, which no doubt is one reason Bullard chose this site to begin with."

"Psychological?"

"The site was once Il Dinamitificio Nobel, one of Alfred Nobel's dynamite factories." Pendergast checked his watch. "One of the great ironies of history is that Nobel, who established the Nobel Peace Prize, made his fortune with what at the time was the cruelest invention in human history."

"Dynamite?"

"Exactly. Seventeen times more powerful than gunpowder. It revolutionized warfare. We're so used to mass killing, Vincent, that we've forgotten what war was like with only black powder, cannon, and bullets. A terrible thing, to be sure, but nothing like what it would become. Now a single bomb, instead of killing two or three, could kill hundreds. Shells and bombs could blow up entire buildings, bridges, and factories. With the invention of the airplane, bombs could level entire city blocks, burn cities to the ground, murder thousands. We tend to focus on the terror of nuclear weapons, but the fact is, dynamite and its derivatives have killed and maimed millions more than the atomic bomb ever did, or probably ever will." He slipped a clip into his weapon and quietly racked the slide.

"Right."

"Alfred Nobel had a patent on modern warfare. At the height of his success, he had hundreds of factories all over Europe making dynamite. These factories had to be built on large campuses like this one, because no matter how carefully they handled their materials, once in a while it went off, killing hundreds. He sited his factories in impoverished areas which would provide an endless source of desperate, expendable workers. This factory was one of his largest." He swept his hand toward the darkness beyond the fence.

"Nobel might have gone down in history as a thoroughly evil man had not a curious thing happened. In 1888 his brother died, and the newspapers of Europe mistakenly reported his brother's death as his own. 'The Merchant of Death Is Dead,' ran the headlines. Reading his own obituary shocked Nobel deeply, and made him realize how history would see him. His reaction was to establish the Nobel prizes—including the famed Peace Prize—as a way to redirect what would certainly have been the dreadful judgment of history on his life."

"Seems to have worked," muttered D'Agosta.

"Which brings me to the point. By the time this factory closed, hundreds of people had been killed in explosions. On top of that, many thousands had been devastated by some of the chemicals used in the manufacture of dynamite, chemicals that affected the brain. As a result, this is a cursed place. It is shunned by the locals. Except for the visits of a caretaker, the area saw no human beings until Bullard bought the property seven years ago."

"So Bullard's letting the rep of the place handle security for him," D'Agosta said. "Clever."

"It's a clever deterrent, at least for the locals. Nevertheless, there will be security, and probably quite sophisticated security at that. I can only speculate as to its nature—my inquiries, as you know, have not been fruitful. But I have a few tools that should aid us."

Pendergast removed a haversack from his bag and slung it over one shoulder. Reaching back into the bag, he removed several pieces of aluminum tubing and fitted them together, affixing a small disc to one end. He approached the fence, slowly moving the device back and forth. Reaching the fence, he bent down, sweeping the ground before him carefully. A small red light glowed faintly on the small disc.

Pendergast rose, stepped back. "As I suspected. There is a sixty-hertz alternating electromagnetic field, indicating electric current."

"You're saying that fence is electrified?" D'Agosta asked. "That old thing?"

"Not the fence itself. A pair of sensor wires are buried just inside to alert security if anyone passes over them."

"So how do we deactivate it?"

"We don't. Follow me."

Stowing their bags in the thicket, they crept along the fence until they reached a weak spot, where several large holes had been crudely patched with baling wire. Pendergast knelt and, with a few deft twists, unwired the largest. Then, carefully extending the detector through the hole, he scanned the ground inside the fence. Numbers glowed from a tiny LED screen on the disc.

He withdrew the device and, reaching for a stick, carefully scraped away the leaves and dirt, exposing a pair of wires. Then he repeated the process at another spot a few feet away, exposing more wires. Reaching into his haversack, he retrieved a pair of alligator clips mated to tiny electronic devices. He attached one of these clips to each end of the wire.

"What are you doing?"

"I'm using these clip-and-capacitor components to reduce our electromagnetic signature to that of a seventy-kilogram wild boar and its mate. They are common in this area, and no doubt Bullard's night security detail is plagued by boars roaming the fence line. Now, quickly."

They crawled through the hole, Pendergast swiftly wiring up the opening and removing the clips. Then, with another stick, he filled the holes and covered them with dead leaves. Finally, he pulled a small spritzer bottle and misted the disturbed ground. An acrid smell reached D'Agosta.

"Diluted boar urine. Follow me."

The two ran parallel to the fence for a few hundred yards, crouching low, until they reached a heavy thicket. As quietly as possible, they crawled deep inside.

"Now we wait for security to investigate. It will be a while. Regulate your breathing and stay calm. They'll be coming in with night vision and infrared, no doubt, so stay low and don't move. Since they're already assuming it's a boar, their search will not be long."

Silence fell. It was utterly black in the dense thicket. D'Agosta waited. To his left, Pendergast remained so motionless, so silent, that he seemed to disappear completely. The only noise was the faint rustle of wind, the occasional call of a night bird. Three minutes passed, then five.

D'Agosta felt an ant moving on his ankle. He reached down to flick it away.

"No," whispered Pendergast.

D'Agosta left the ant alone.

Soon he could feel it crawling over his shin, exploring with short, herky-jerky movements. It worked its way down to his shoe, where it began trying to dig into his sock. When he tried to think about something else, he realized his nose had begun to tickle. How long had they been still? Ten minutes? Jesus, remaining motionless like this was harder than running a marathon. D'Agosta could see absolutely nothing. A cramp had come up in his leg. He should have taken more care to seat himself comfortably. He longed to move. His nose was itching fiercely now, all the worse for his not being able to scratch it. More ants, emboldened by the investigations of their scout, began to crawl over his skin. The cramp in his leg grew worse, and he could feel his calf muscle twitching involuntarily.

Then came the faint sound of voices. D'Agosta held his breath. He could see the distant gleam of a light, almost obscured by leaves. More voices; a burst of static from a walkie-talkie; some desultory conversation in English. Then silence returned.

D'Agosta expected Pendergast to give the all-clear, but the FBI agent said nothing. Now all of his muscles were screaming with pain. One of his legs had gone to sleep, and the ants were all over him.

"All right." Pendergast rose and D'Agosta followed, hugely grateful, shaking out his legs, rubbing his nose, slapping away the ants.

Pendergast glanced at him. "Someday, Vincent, I will teach you a useful meditation technique, perfect for situations such as that."

"I could use it. Talk about agony."

"Now that we've bypassed the first layer of security, on to the second. Keep directly behind me and stay in my tracks as much as possible."

They moved through the woods, Pendergast still scanning with his device. The trees thinned and they emerged into an overgrown field. Beyond stood a row of ruined buildings, enormous brick warehouses with peaked roofs and vacant doors. Vines crawled up the sides, sprouting off in dark heads that nodded and swayed in the heavy air.

Pendergast consulted a small map, and they moved toward the first warehouse. Inside it smelled of mold and dry rot; their footsteps, even with the silent shoes, seemed to echo. They passed through a far door into a gigantic square surrounded by buildings. The cement of the square was riddled with cracks, through which thrust dark vegetation.

"What if they have dogs?" D'Agosta whispered.

"Loose dogs are a thing of the past. They're unpredictable, noisy, and often end up attacking the wrong person. Dogs are now only used for tracking. What we have to watch out for will be far more subtle."

They crossed the expanse of concrete. Nocturnal animals rustled in the foliage as they passed. At the far end of the courtyard was a grassy alley between two rows of ruined buildings, the heaps of masonry covered with ivy that, in the darkness, looked like spreading stains. Pendergast proceeded more cautiously now, using a small, hooded flashlight to illuminate their way. Halfway along the alley he paused, knelt, and examined the ground. Then he picked up a branch and gave a little poke to the grass ahead. He prodded harder, and the stick suddenly broke through into space.

"A pit," he said. "Notice that, with these ruins flanking either side, this alley is the only way to proceed."

"A booby trap?"

"Undoubtedly. But disguised to look like some part of the old factory, so that when the intruder falls in and is killed, nobody would be blamed."

"How did you spot it?"

"Lack of boar tracks." Pendergast carefully withdrew the stick and turned. "We shall have to make our way through one of these ruined laboratories. Take care: there may still be the odd bottle of nitroglycerin around, strategically placed to snag the unwary. We should consider this the next ring of security, Vincent; we must be both quiet and vigilant."

They entered a dark doorway and Pendergast flashed his hooded light around. The floor was covered with broken glass, rusty pieces of metal, broken tile, and bricks. Pendergast paused, then signaled to D'Agosta to back out.

Two minutes later they were in the concrete courtyard.

"What was wrong?" D'Agosta asked.

"Too much broken glass, too evenly spread, and the glass was too modern to be from the original factory. A noise trap, with sensors ready to pick up the telltale crunch of human feet. Motion sensors, too, I expect."

In the greenish glow of his lantern, Pendergast's face seemed troubled.

"What now?"

"Back to the pit."

They circled back around to the alleyway and Pendergast crept forward alone, prodding with a stick until he'd located the pit. Then he lay on his stomach, carefully parted the thick grass and vegetation, and shone his light into the dark hole. A moment later he withdrew, snapping off his light.

"Wait here."

And then he was gone, melting into the night.

D'Agosta waited. Pendergast hadn't told him to remain still and silent; he hadn't needed to. He crouched in the inky darkness, barely daring to breathe. Five minutes passed. Left alone, the tension began to take its toll. D'Agosta could feel his heart pounding in his chest.

Relax.

And then—as suddenly and silently as he had disappeared—Pendergast was back, a long plank in his hands. He laid it across the brushy opening, then turned to D'Agosta. "Beyond this, no talking unless absolutely necessary. Follow my lead."

D'Agosta nodded.

They crossed the wobbly plank, one after the other. On the far side, the brush was thicker, presenting a dark wall. Pendergast moved forward, probed with his sensor, sniffed. He briefly turned on the light, then turned it off again. They moved parallel to the brushy area, then veered into it on what appeared to be an animal trail.

The boars are saving our ass, D'Agosta thought.

They crept slowly through the thick brush. A brick wall loomed to their right: a blast wall, judging by its massiveness. In one place it had been knocked down by what D'Agosta guessed was an old explosion. They moved through this gap, still following the boar trail. D'Agosta could barely see Pendergast, and could hear even less: the man moved as silently as a leopard.

The trail petered out in a large meadow less overgrown than the others they had passed. Pendergast paused to reconnoiter, motioning for D'Agosta to stay back. At the far end lay the dark silhouette of more wrecked buildings and, beyond that, the faint glow of light.

Pendergast slipped a pack of cigarettes out of his pocket. Turning back toward D'Agosta, and very carefully shielding a cigarette with his hands, he lit up.

D'Agosta watched, astonished. Pendergast inhaled lazily, turned, and blew out a stream of smoke.

Not three feet in front of them, the drifting smoke revealed a brilliant beam of blue light: a laser. It was set just high enough to clear the back of a boar.

Pendergast got down on his stomach and began to slither forward through the tall grass, motioning D'Agosta to do likewise.

Slowly, painstakingly, they advanced across the field. Now and then Pendergast would take a drag on the concealed cigarette and blow a stream of smoke overhead, illuminating the laser beams that crisscrossed the field. Dark woods and ruins surrounded the verge of the meadow, and it was impossible to see where the beams were coming from. When the cigarette went out, he lit another.

In five minutes they were across. Pendergast ground out the stub of cigarette, rose, and moved at a crouch to an empty door frame, withdrawing his light and directing it inside. The beam briefly illuminated a long passageway, rooms fronted with metal bars facing each other across the corridor. To D'Agosta it looked almost like a prison. The ceilings had caved in, along with some of the walls, leaving a maze of broken masonry, beams, and tile.

Pendergast paused in the doorway to wave a handheld meter of some kind, then advanced cautiously. What was left of the edifice seemed about to collapse, and from time to time D'Agosta could hear the creaking and groaning of a beam or the rattle of falling plaster. As they moved through the vast crumbling space, the faint light ahead grew stronger, coming in through a row of shattered windows at the far end. Reaching the windows, they cautiously peered out.

An astonishing sight greeted D'Agosta's eyes. Beyond the ruined building was a double-chain-link fence, topped with concertina wire, enclosing a sweeping lawn swathed in light. A new building stood there behind trimmed shrubbery and flowers, a postmodern structure in glass, titanium, and white paneling, glowing like a crystal in the night. To the far right, D'Agosta could see a guardhouse and a gate in the fence.

They moved away from the window, and Pendergast sat against the wall. He seemed to be thinking. Several minutes passed before he roused himself and motioned D'Agosta to follow. Keeping low, they moved the length of the far wall and exited a side door. Thick brush and gooseberry bushes grew up to within about ten yards of the double fence, where the closely clipped lawn began.

They wormed their way into the brush and began crawling forward. Then D'Agosta felt Pendergast freeze. The sound of voices was rapidly approaching, along with the probing of a bright spotlight. D'Agosta flattened himself in the bushes, hoping to God his black outfit and face paint would keep him invisible. But the voices were getting close, too close; and they were loud; and the light was drawing ever nearer.

{ 53 }

D'Agosta lay motionless, hardly daring to breathe, while the beam of the spotlight lanced through the leaves and vines. The voices were even closer now, and he could make out what the men were saying. They were American. There were two of them, it seemed, and they were walking slowly along the inner perimeter of the fence. He felt a sudden, almost irresistible desire to look up. But then the brilliant beam landed square on his back, and he went still as death. The beam lingered, unmoving. The men had stopped. There was a scratching sound, the flaring of a match, followed by the faint smell of cigarette smoke.

"...real bastard," came one of the voices. "If it weren't for the money, I'd go back to Brooklyn."

"The way things are going, we might all be heading back," replied the other.

"The fucker's gone crazy."

A grunt of assent.

"They say he lives in a villa once owned by Machiavelli."

"Who?"

"Machiavelli."

"He's that new tight end for the Rams, right?"

"Forget it." The light abruptly swiveled away, leaving sudden darkness in its wake. It was a handheld torch, D'Agosta realized, carried by one of the men.

The cigarette arced through the darkness, landing near D'Agosta's left thigh, and the men continued on.

Several minutes passed. Then, abruptly, Pendergast was at his side.

"Vincent," he whispered, "the security here is considerably more sophisticated than I had hoped. This is a system designed not just to thwart corporate espionage, but to keep out the CIA itself. We can't hope to get inside with the tools at hand. We must retreat and plan another avenue of attack."

"Such as?"

"I have developed a sudden interest in Machiavelli."

"I hear you."

They crept back the way they had come, through the groaning, ruined building. The trip seemed longer than before. When they were halfway through, Pendergast paused. "Nasty odor," he murmured.

D'Agosta smelled it, too. The wind had shifted, and the scent of decay reached them from a far room. Pendergast opened a shutter on the flashlight, allowing a faint illumination. The greenish light disclosed what had once been a small laboratory, its roof caved in. Below, several heavy beams lay crisscrossed on the ground, and—protruding from them—a rotting, partly skeletonized head of a boar, its tusks broken off into stubs.

"Booby trap?" whispered D'Agosta.

Pendergast nodded. "Designed as an unstable, rotting building." He let the shaft of green light fall here and there, finally pausing on a doorsill. "There's the trigger. Step on that and you bring down the works."

D'Agosta shivered, thinking how he'd blithely crossed this very threshold not ten minutes before.

They passed carefully through the rest of the building, warning creaks of wood sounding occasionally over their heads. Beyond lay the broad field. It looked to D'Agosta like a lake of blackness. Pendergast lit another cigarette, then knelt and moved forward cautiously, blowing smoke before him once again, until the first laser beam became visible, pencil-thin and glowing dully. Pendergast nodded over his shoulder, and they returned to the laborious work of crawling through the field, keeping under the beams.

This time the process seemed interminable. When D'Agosta finally allowed himself a glance ahead, he was shocked to find they had only reached the middle of the field.

Just then there was a sudden commotion in the grass ahead of them. A family of hares burst into view, startled, leaping in several directions at once and bounding off into the blackness.

Pendergast paused, took in another lungful of smoke, and blew it at the spot where the rabbits had been. A crisscrossing of laser beams became visible.

"Nasty bit of luck," he said.

"Triggered the beam?"

"I'm afraid so."

"What do we do now?"

"We run."

Pendergast leaped up and flew like a bat across the field. D'Agosta rose and began to follow, doing his best to keep up with the agent.

Instead of heading back the way they had come, Pendergast was making for the woods to their left. As they approached the trees, D'Agosta heard distant shouts and the starting of car engines. A moment later, several pairs of headlights came sawing across the meadow, trailed by the much more brilliant beam of a mounted spotlight, as a pair of military-style jeeps came tearing around the ruined buildings.

Pendergast and D'Agosta crashed into the dense undergrowth of the woods, clawing through brambles and heavy brush. After a hundred yards, Pendergast took a sharp turn and continued at a right angle to their previous course, the haversack bouncing wildly on his shoulder. D'Agosta followed, heart hammering in his ears.

Pendergast took another sharp turn and they plunged on. Suddenly they emerged onto an old road filled with waist-high grass. They pushed through it, D'Agosta struggling to keep Pendergast in sight. Already he was growing winded, but fear and adrenaline spurred him on.

A powerful beam lanced down the length of the road and they dived to the ground. Once it swept past, Pendergast was up and running again, this time into another copse at the far end of the abandoned road. More beams flickered through the trees, farther away, and voices floated toward them over the sullen air.

Inside the copse, Pendergast stopped to pull out his map and scan it with the green flashlight while

D'Agosta caught up. Then they continued on, this time along a gentle rise. The woods grew thicker, and it seemed they had managed to put space between themselves and their pursuers. For the first time, D'Agosta allowed himself to hope they might escape, after all.

The trees thinned and D'Agosta saw a scattering of starlight. And then suddenly rising before them was an immensity of black—a wall, twenty feet high, all rotten bricks, dangling vegetation, and vines.

"This isn't on the map," said Pendergast. "Another blast wall—a late addition, it seems."

He glanced in either direction. Through the trees below, D'Agosta could see the flicker of flashlights. Pendergast turned and ran along the base of the wall. It curved along the top of a gentle ridge, its overgrown rim outlined against the night sky.

Ahead, where the wall descended, D'Agosta could see dancing lights through the vegetation.

"We climb," said Pendergast.

He turned, seized a root, pulled himself up. D'Agosta did likewise. He grabbed a stem, another, found a foothold. In his haste, one of the plants tore out of the wall, sending down a shower of rotting brick. D'Agosta dangled, recovered. He could see Pendergast already far above him, climbing like a cat. The lights below were coming up the hill, while another group to their right was also closing in.

"Faster!" Pendergast hissed.

D'Agosta seized a vine, another, slipping, scrambling, one leg scrabbling in space.

He now heard a cacophony of voices behind him. Pendergast was just reaching the top of the wall. There was a shot and the thud of the bullet on the wall to his right. One more hoist up, one more foothold.

Two more shots. Pendergast was reaching down, grabbing him by the arms, hauling him to the top. The lights had now reached the open area just before the wall, bobbing frantically, flashing up on the wall and hitting them.

"Down!"

D'Agosta was already throwing himself down on the crumbling, overgrown top of the massive wall. It was at least ten feet from side to side.

"Crawl."

Digging in his elbows and knees, he began to crawl across the top of the wall, keeping cover in the vegetation. There was a burst of automatic-weapons fire, the rounds snicking through the bush above, showering him with twigs and leaves.

They reached the other side—only to see more men there, arriving with dogs: silent dogs held on leashes. D'Agosta ducked back and rolled from the edge as more shots raked the bushes to one side of him.

"Jesus!" He lay on his back for a moment, staring at the unmoving stars.

The sudden baying of dogs reached his ears. The dogs had been released.

Now there were voices on either side, a babel of Italian and English. Powerful lights passed overhead, shone from below. D'Agosta could hear the rustle and scramble of climbing.

Pendergast was suddenly at his ear. "We stand up and run. Stay in the middle of the wall and run at a crouch."

"They'll shoot us."

"They're going to kill us, anyway."

D'Agosta stood, began to run—not exactly run, but push and crash through the heavy vegetation growing out of what must have once been a walkway at the top.

Lights raked the top of the wall, and a burst of gunfire sounded. And a voice: *"Non sparate!"*

"Keep running!" Pendergast cried.

But it was too late. There, in front of them on the wall, dark figures were mounting, blocking the way. Lights shone in their direction. D'Agosta and Pendergast dove to the rubble, flattening themselves.

"*Non sparate!*" someone shouted again. "Do not shoot!"

From behind, D'Agosta saw that a second group had surmounted the wall. They were surrounded. D'Agosta lay huddled in a pool of brilliant light, feeling exposed, naked.

"*Eccoli!* There they are!"

"Hold your fire!"

And then a voice—quiet and reasonable—said:

"You may both stand up now and surrender. Or we will kill you. Your choice."

{ 54 }

Locke Bullard stared across the table at the two men shackled to the wall. Two sons of bitches dressed in black special-ops outfits. They were Americans, that much was clear; probably CIA.

He turned to his security chief. "Wipe the paint off their faces. Let's see who they are."

The man pulled out a handkerchief and brusquely wiped off the paint.

Bullard could hardly believe his eyes. They were the two people he least expected: the police sergeant from Long Island and Pendergast, the FBI special agent. Immediately, he realized Vasquez had failed. Or more likely, run off with the money. Unbelievable. Yet even without Vasquez, it stunned Bullard to think these two had somehow followed him to Italy and managed to break through several layers of security at the lab. He kept underestimating them, again and again. He had to get out of that habit. These two were formidable. And that's exactly what he didn't need. He had something a lot more important to do than mess around with these two.

He turned to the security director. "What happened?"

"They penetrated outer security at the old railroad grade, made it as far as the second ring. They tripped the laser grid at the inner field."

"You found out what they're after? What they heard?"

"They heard nothing, sir. They got nothing."

"You sure they never made it past the second ring?"

"Absolutely, sir."

"Any comm devices on them?"

"No, sir. And none dropped. They came in deaf and dumb."

Bullard nodded, his shock slowly giving way to rage. These two had insulted him. They'd *damaged* him.

He cast his eye toward the fat one, who—as it happened—didn't look quite so fat anymore. "Hey, D'Agosta, you shed a few pounds? How's the hard-on problem?"

No answer. The fuck was looking at him with hatred. Good. Let him hate.

"And the not-so-special agent. If that's what you really are. Want to tell me what you're doing here?"

No response.

"Didn't get jack shit, did you?"

This was a waste of time. They hadn't penetrated the second, let alone the third, ring of security, which meant they couldn't have learned anything of value. Best thing now was to get rid of them. Sure, the feds would be all over the place tomorrow, but this was Italy, and he had friends in the Questura. He had five hundred acres in which to hide the bodies. They wouldn't find shit.

One hand was in his trouser pocket, rolling around some euros. The hand fell on his pocketknife. He removed it, opened the nail file, began idly cleaning his nails. Without looking up, he asked: "Wife still doing the RV salesman, D'Agosta?"

"You're a Johnny-one-note, you know that, Bullard? Makes me think you've had some problems along those lines yourself."

Bullard felt a surge of rage, which he quickly mastered. He was going to kill them, but first D'Agosta was going to pay a little. He continued with his nails.

"Your hit man fucked up," D'Agosta went on. "Too bad, him going the cyanide highway before he could implicate you. We'll still see you get stuck with a conspiracy rap, though. You'll do hard time. Hear me, Bullard? And once you're safely in the Big House, I'll personally make sure somebody makes you his number one bitch. Oh, you'll make some skinhead a nice punk, Bullard."

It was only through long practice that Bullard managed to keep his composure. So Vasquez hadn't run off with the money. He'd taken the job and failed. Somehow, he'd failed.

He reminded himself it hardly mattered now.

He examined his work, closed the nail file, opened the long blade. He kept it razor-sharp for occasions just like this one. Who knew: he might even get some information.

He turned to one of his assistants. "Put his right hand on the table."

While one guard grabbed D'Agosta's face in a meaty paw and slammed it back against the wall, the other unmanacled one hand, jerked it forward, and pinned it to the table. The cop struggled briefly.

Bullard eyed the class ring on the hand. Some shitty P.S. in Queens, probably. "Play the piano, D'Agosta?"

No answer.

He swiped the knife down across D'Agosta's right middle fingernail, splitting the tip of the finger.

D'Agosta jerked, gasped, pulling his finger free. Blood welled out from the wound: slowly at first, then faster. The man struggled wildly, but the guards regained a lock on him. Slowly, they forced the hand back into position against the table.

Bullard felt a flush of excitement.

"Son of a *bitch*!" D'Agosta groaned.

"You know what?" Bullard said. "I like this. I could do this all night."

D'Agosta struggled against the guards.

"You're CIA, aren't you?"

D'Agosta groaned again.

"Answer me."

"No, for chrissakes."

"You." He turned to Pendergast. "CIA? Answer me. Yes or no?"

"No. And you're making an even larger mistake than you made earlier."

"Sure I am." Why was he bothering? And what difference did it make? These were the bastards who had humiliated him in front of the whole city. He felt rage seize him again, and—more carefully now—he took the knife and sliced it hard across the table, taking the tip off D'Agosta's already damaged finger.

"Fuck!" D'Agosta screamed. "You *bastard*!"

Bullard stepped back, breathing hard. His palms were sweating; he wiped them on the sleeve of his jacket, took a fresh grip on the knife. Then he caught sight of the wall clock. It was already close to two. He couldn't let himself get caught up in a minor distraction. He had something more important to do before dawn. Something much, *much* more important.

He turned back to his security chief. "Kill them. Then get rid of the bodies. Dump their weapons with them. Do it over at the old shafts. I don't want any forensics left on the premises, especially not around the lab. You know what I mean: hair, blood, anything with DNA. Don't even let them spit."

"Yes, sir."

"You—," began Pendergast, but Bullard spun around and landed a massive uppercut in his stomach. Pendergast doubled over.

"Gag them. Gag them both."

The security men rammed balls of cloth into their mouths, then bound them tightly with duct tape.

"Blindfold them, too."

"Yes, Mr. Bullard."

Bullard looked at D'Agosta. "Remember how I promised to pay you back? Now your finger's as short as your dick."

D'Agosta struggled, making inarticulate sounds as the blindfold went on.

Bullard turned to his assistant, nodded at the table. "Clean up that mess. And then get the hell out of here."

{ 55 }

Gagged and blindfolded, hands cuffed behind his back, D'Agosta was herded along by one of the two security men. He could hear the chink of Pendergast's shackles beside him. They were moving through what seemed a long, damp underground passageway: the air stank of fungus, and he could feel the chill humidity soaking into his clothes. Or maybe it was his own sweat. His middle finger felt like it had been dipped in molten lead. It was pulsing in time to his heartbeat, the blood running freely down the small of his back.

There was something unreal about the whole situation. At any other time, the thought he'd just lost the end of a finger would be all-consuming. Yet right now only the pain itself registered. Everything had happened so quickly. Just hours before, he'd been relaxing in a luxurious suite. Just a few hours before, he'd been almost tearful at seeing his own native land at long last. And now here he was—a dirty cloth stuffed in his mouth, his eyes blindfolded, arms bound, being led to an execution-style death.

He couldn't really believe he was about to die. And

yet that was exactly what was going to happen unless either he or Pendergast could think of something. But they had been thoroughly searched. And Pendergast's most powerful weapon—his tongue—had been silenced. It seemed impossible, unthinkable. And yet the fact was he had only minutes left to live.

He tried to force the sense of unreality away; tried to forget the searing pain; struggled to think of some last-minute escape, some way to turn the tables on the two men that were so matter-of-factly leading them off to their deaths. But there was nothing in his training, nothing even in the detective books he'd read or written, to give him a clue.

They paused, and D'Agosta heard the groan of rusty metal being forced open. Then he was shoved forward, and the trilling of crickets and the humid night air hit his nostrils. They were outside.

He was prodded forward by what was undoubtedly the barrel of a gun. Now they were walking on what felt through the soft shoes like a grassy trail. He could hear the rustling of leaves above his head. Such small, insignificant sensations—and yet they had suddenly grown unbearably precious to him.

"Christ," said one of the men. "This dew is going to ruin my shoes. I just paid two hundred euros for them, handmade over in Panzano."

The other chuckled. "Good luck getting another pair. That old geezer makes like one pair a month."

"We always get the shit jobs." As if to underscore this, the man gave D'Agosta another shove. "They're soaked through already, goddamn it."

D'Agosta found his thoughts stealing toward Laura

Hayward. Would she shed a tear for him? It was strange, but the one thing he most wanted right now was to be able to tell her how he went out. He thought that would make it easier to bear, easier than just vanishing, than never knowing…

"A little shoe polish and they'll be like new."

"Once leather gets wet it's never the same."

"You and your fucking shoes."

"If you paid two hundred euros, you'd be pissed, too."

D'Agosta's sense of unreality grew. He tried to embrace the throbbing pain in his finger, because as long as he could feel that, he knew he was still alive. What he feared was when the pain ended…

Just a few more minutes now. He took a step forward, another, then stumbled against something in the grass.

A slap to the side of the head. "Watch your step, asshole."

The air had grown cooler, and there was a smell of earth and decaying leaves. He felt a terrible helplessness. The gag and blindfold robbed him of all ability to make eye contact with Pendergast, to signal, to do anything.

"The trail to the old quarry goes that way."

There was a rustling, then a grunt. "Jesus, it's overgrown in here."

"Yeah, and watch where you put your feet."

D'Agosta felt himself shoved forward once again. Now they were pushing through wet foliage.

"It's right up ahead. There's a lot of stones near the edge, don't trip." A guffaw. "It's a long way down."

More pushing through bushes and wet grass. Then D'Agosta felt himself brusquely halted.

"Another twenty feet," his man said.

Silence. D'Agosta caught a whiff of something wet and cold—the exhalation of stale air from a deep mine shaft.

"One at a time. We don't want to fuck this up. You go first. I'll wait here with this one. And hurry up, I'm getting bitten already."

D'Agosta heard Pendergast being pushed forward, heard the swish of wet footsteps through the undergrowth ahead. The first man had a tight hold on his cuffs, a gun barrel pushed hard into his ear. He should do something, he *had* to do something. But what? The slightest move and he was dead. He couldn't believe what was happening. His mind refused to accept it. He realized that, deep down, he'd been certain Pendergast would manage to do something miraculous, pull another rabbit out of his hat. But the time for that was past. What could Pendergast do: gagged, blindfolded, a gun to his head, standing at the edge of a precipice? The last small bit of hope drained away.

"That's far enough," came the voice from about thirty feet away, slightly muffled by the foliage. It was the second man, speaking to Pendergast. D'Agosta caught another whiff of cold air from the mine shaft. Insects whined in his ear. His finger throbbed.

It really was over.

He heard the sound of a round being racked into a pistol chamber.

"Make your peace with God, scumbag."

A pause. And then the sound of a gunshot, incredibly loud. Another pause—and then from far below, echoing up the shaft in a distorted way, the sound of a heavy object hitting water.

There was a longer silence, and then the man's voice came back, a little breathless. "Okay. Bring up the other one."

{ 56 }

Three A.M.

Locke Bullard stood in the enormous, vaulted *salone* of his villa, isolated on a hill south of Florence, his feelings betrayed only by the muscles working slowly above his massive jawline. He walked to the leaded windows that looked over the walled gardens, opened one with a shaking, knotted hand. The stars were obscured by clouds, the night sky perfectly black. A perfect night for this kind of business; as perfect as that other night had been, all those years ago. God, what he would give to undo that night...He shivered at the memory, or maybe it was just the cool breath of the wind sighing through the ancient trees in the *pineta* beyond the garden.

He stood at the window for some time, struggling to calm himself, to suppress a growing feeling of dread. Below, on the terrace, the indistinct white shapes of marble statues glowed faintly. Soon it would be over, he reminded himself. And he would be free. *Free.* But right now, he had to keep calm. He had to put his old, rational view of the world aside, if only for one night.

Tomorrow, he could tell himself it had all been a bad dream.

With a great effort he cleared his mind, tried to focus on something else, even briefly. Beyond the swaying tops of the umbrella pines, he could see the outlines of cypresses on the far hills, and then the distant cupola of the Duomo, next to Giotto's tower, brightly lit. Who was it that said only if you lived within sight of the Duomo were you a true Florentine? This was the same view Machiavelli had seen, exactly this: those hills, that famous dome, the distant tower. Perhaps Machiavelli had stood in this very spot five hundred years ago, working out the details of *The Prince*. Bullard had read the book when he was twenty. It was one of the reasons he'd jumped at the opportunity to own the villa Machiavelli was born and raised in.

Bullard wondered how Machiavelli would have reacted to this predicament. The great courtier would no doubt have felt the same things he did: dread and resignation. How do you make a choice when faced with a problem that has two solutions, both intolerable? He corrected himself: one was intolerable, the other unthinkable.

You accepted the intolerable.

He turned from the window and looked across the dim room at the clock on the mantelpiece. Ten minutes after three. He needed to make his final preparations.

He moved toward a table and lit a huge, ancient candle, whose glow illuminated an old piece of parchment: a certain page from a thirteenth-century grimoire. Then, taking up the ancient *arthame* knife that lay beside it, Bullard carefully began to score a circle in the terra-cotta floor of the room, working slowly, taking the utmost care to make sure the circle remained unbroken. When that was done, he took a piece of charcoal, specially prepared, and began to inscribe letters in Greek and Aramaic on the periphery of the circle, stopping now and then to consult the grimoire. He followed this by inscribing two pentagrams around it all. Next he inscribed a smaller circle—this one broken—beside the larger. He did not worry about being interrupted: he had dismissed all the security and the help. He wanted no chance of witnesses and—above all—no chance of interruption. When you were doing what he was about to do, *raising* what he hoped to raise, there could be no disruptions, no mistakes, nothing left out. The stakes were greater than his life—because, it seemed, the consequences would not end with his death.

He paused, preparations almost complete. It would not be long now. It would be over and then he could begin again. There would be, of course, minor loose ends to take care of: the disappearance of Pendergast and D'Agosta, for example; the Chinese and what had happened in Paterson. But it would be a relief to return to business as usual. Those problems, as tricky as they were, belonged to the real world, and he could handle them. They were small potatoes compared to *this*.

He went over the manuscript page again, then yet again, making sure he had missed nothing. Then, almost against his will, his gaze shifted to the old rectangular box sitting on the table. Now it was time for *that*.

He reached out, undid the brass latch. He caressed

the polished surface of the box and then—with a terrible reluctance—opened it. A faint scent of antique wood and horsehair wafted upward. He breathed it in: this ancient perfume, this priceless scent. With a trembling hand, he reached into the darkness of the box, stroked the smooth object inside. He did not dare take it out—handling it had always frightened him a little. It was not made for him at all. It was made for others. Others who, if he was successful, would never see it again...

A sudden rush of regret, anger, fear, and helplessness staggered him. He was almost overwhelmed by the sheer force of it. Incredible that a thought could virtually bring him to his knees. He gasped again, breathing hard; took a firm grip on the heavy table. What had to be done, had to be done.

He carefully closed the box, latched it, and placed it on the ground inside the smaller, broken circle. He wouldn't look at it again, wouldn't torture himself further. With a troubled heart, he glanced over at the clock. It responded by chiming out the quarter hour, the bell-like tones a strange counterpoint to the oppressive darkness of the room. Bullard swallowed, worked his jaw, and finally, with a supreme effort, spoke the words he had memorized so carefully.

It was the work of ninety seconds to complete the incantation.

At first, nothing happened. He strained, listening, but there was not a sound, not a sigh; nothing. Had he said it incorrectly? With the help gone, the place was as quiet as the tomb.

His eye drifted back to the manuscript page. Should

he recite it again? But no—the ceremony had to be performed precisely, without deviation. Repetition could have disastrous, unimaginable consequences.

As he waited, there in the faint light, he wondered if perhaps it wasn't true, after all: that it was all hollow superstition. But at this thought, such a desperate mixture of hope and uncertainty rose within him that he forced himself to push it aside. He was not wrong. There could be no other answer...

Then he felt, or thought he felt, a strange shifting of the air. A faint smell came to him, drifting across the *salone.* It was the acrid odor of sulfur.

A breeze shifted the curtains of the window. The room seemed to grow dimmer, as if a great darkness was encroaching from all directions. He felt himself go rigid with fear and anticipation. *It was happening.* The incantation was working, just as promised.

He waited, almost afraid to breathe. The smell got stronger, and now it almost seemed as if tendrils of smoke were drifting in the lazy air of the room, tendrils that licked about the windows and curled in the corners. He felt a strange sense of apprehension, of physical dread. Yes, it was a *physical* sensation, a harbinger of what was to come, and the air seemed to congeal with a rising warmth.

Bullard stood within the greater circle, his heart pounding, his eyes straining to see beyond the darkened doorway. A vague outline...a lumbering, slow-moving shape...

He'd done it! He'd succeeded! *He* was coming! *He was really coming...!*

{ 57 }

D'Agosta felt numb. The shot, the silence, and the final splash—this was really it.

"Come on," his minder said, giving him a push.

D'Agosta couldn't move; he couldn't believe what was happening.

"Move!" The man jabbed D'Agosta in the back of the head with his gun barrel.

He stumbled forward, mechanically trying to keep his footing among discarded pieces of stone. The moldy breath of the open shaft washed over him. Six steps, eight, a dozen.

"Stop."

Now he could feel the foul air tickling his nose, stirring his hair. Everything seemed abnormally clear, and time had slowed to a crawl. *Jesus, what a way to go out.*

The gun barrel pressed hard against his skull. D'Agosta squeezed his eyes tightly closed behind the blindfold, prayed for a quick end.

He took a shallow breath, another. Then came a deafening gunshot. He fell forward into space…

…Vaguely, as if at a great distance, he sensed a steel

arm shooting out from behind and hauling him back from the utter brink. The hand let go, and D'Agosta collapsed immediately onto the rock-strewn grass. A moment later he heard a body—not his—hitting the water far below.

"Vincent?"

It was Pendergast.

A snick and his blindfold was removed; another snick and Pendergast had cut off his gag. D'Agosta lay where he had fallen, stunned.

"Wake up, Vincent."

Slowly, D'Agosta came back. Pendergast was standing to one side, gun trained on his own minder, binding him to a tree. D'Agosta's man was nowhere to be seen.

D'Agosta stumbled woodenly to his feet. He felt a strange wetness on his face. Tears? Dew from the grass? It seemed a miracle. He swallowed, managed to croak, "How...?"

But Pendergast simply shook his head and glanced into the yawning mouth of the shaft. "I think his shoe troubles are over." Then he glanced at the remaining guard and flashed him a brief, chilling smile.

The man paled and mumbled something through his gag.

Pendergast turned to D'Agosta. "Show me your finger."

D'Agosta had forgotten all about it. Pendergast took his hand, examined it. "Done with a sharp knife. You're lucky: neither the bone nor the root of the nail was affected." He tore a strip of cloth from the hem of his black shirt and bandaged it. "It might be wise to get you to a hospital."

"The hell with that. We're going after Bullard."

Pendergast raised his eyebrows. "I'm delighted to hear that we are of the same opinion. Yes, now is a good opportunity. As for your finger—"

"Forget the finger."

"As you wish. Here's your service piece."

Pendergast handed him the Glock 9mm, then turned to his minder and aimed his own Les Baer at the man's temple. "You have one chance—only one—to tell us the best route out. I already know a great deal about the layout of this place, so any attempt to deceive will be detected and instantly answered with a bullet to the parietal lobe. Understand?"

The man couldn't talk fast enough.

An hour later, Pendergast and D'Agosta were driving south of Florence on the Via Volterrana, a dark, stone-walled road that curved along the hilltops south of the city. A faint scattering of lights winked from the surrounding hills.

"How did you do it?" D'Agosta asked. He could still hardly believe it. "I thought we were about to buy the farm."

They were still in their black stealth outfits, and only Pendergast's hands and face could be seen. In the dim light of the dashboard, his expression was hard and flat. "I have to admit a moment of discomfort back there myself. We were lucky they decided to separate, to kill us one at a time. That was their first mistake. The second was overconfidence and inattention. The third was my man keeping his gun pressed into me—which, of course, revealed exactly where the weapon was at all times. I always carry a few small tools in my shirt cuff, the hem of my trousers, other places. It's an old magicians' trick. I used these to pick the lock of my cuffs. Luckily, the Italian locks were rather crude. When we halted at the pit, I disarmed my opponent with a blow to the solar plexus, removed my blindfold and gag. I then shot the gun into the air while pushing a heavy rock into the quarry with my foot. Next I instructed my guard to order you brought forward—which he did as soon as he recovered his wind. I regret shooting your guard, but there would have been no way to manage both of them...I do not care for killing people in cold blood, but there was no help for it."

He fell silent.

D'Agosta felt his own anger grow. *He* had no sense of regret. His finger was throbbing painfully again, in time to the beat of his heart. *Bullard*. Pendergast had been correct: the man would pay dearly.

The car swung around a curve, and there, a half mile ahead, D'Agosta could see the outline of a villa silhouetted against the faint glow of the night sky, a crenellated tower on one end framed by cypress trees.

"Machiavelli's place of exile," murmured Pendergast.

The car dipped into a valley, cruising along an ancient wall. Pendergast slowed as they approached an iron gate, then turned off the road. They hid the car in an olive grove and approached the gate.

"I was expecting heavy security," Pendergast said after quickly examining the lock. "Instead, this gate's open." He peered through. "And the guardhouse appears to be unoccupied."

"Are you sure we're at the right villa?"

"Yes." He slowly eased the gate open, and they stepped into the darkness of the villa's great park. Two rows of cypresses lined a drive that led up a hill covered with more olive groves. Pendergast paused, dropping to his hands and knees to examine faint tread marks in the gravel of the drive. Then he stood, looked around, and nodded toward a dense forest of umbrella pines that lay to one side. "That way."

They moved through the pines, Pendergast stopping every now and then, apparently looking for guards or other signs of security. "Odd," he murmured to himself. "Very odd."

Soon they reached a thick hedge of laurel, immaculately clipped and impenetrable. They walked along the hedge to a locked gate, which Pendergast deftly picked. Beyond lay a formal Italian garden, low boxwood hedges laid in rectangular shapes, bordered by beds of lavender and marigolds. In the center stood a marble statue of a faun playing panpipes, water pouring from the pipes and splashing into a mossy pool below. Beyond rose the dark facade of the villa.

They paused to examine the huge structure. It was stuccoed in a pale yellow. A loggia ran across the fourth floor, just under the tiled roof: a row of columns topped by Roman arches. The only sign of life was a faint, flickering glow through the open leaded windows of what appeared to be a grand *salone* on the second floor.

Pendergast moved forward again and D'Agosta followed, the burbling fountain masking their footsteps. In another few minutes, they reached the outer wall of the villa itself. There was still no sign of any security.

"Strange," whispered Pendergast.

"Maybe Bullard isn't home."

They passed under one of the great windows of the *salone.* That was when the smell hit D'Agosta. It was just a fleeting whiff, yet it felt like a physical blow. Instantly his anger turned to disbelief, then to creeping dread.

"Sulfur."

"Indeed."

Fumbling half unconsciously for his cross, D'Agosta followed Pendergast around the side of the house to the great *portone* of the villa.

"It's open," Pendergast said, slipping inside.

After the briefest of hesitations, D'Agosta followed. They paused in the entryway, examining the great vaulted spaces of the *piano terra*, dark with ancient frescoes and trompe l'oeil.

The smell was stronger here. Sulfur, phosphorus—and burned grease.

Now Pendergast moved up the great sweep of stairs leading to the second floor and the *salone.* D'Agosta followed him down a vaulted hallway to a massive set of wooden doors, bolted and banded in iron. One was ajar, and a flickering light came from beyond.

Pendergast pushed it wide.

It took D'Agosta a moment to register. The light came, not from a burning candle or the great fireplace in the far wall, but from the middle of the room. There, in the center of a crude circle, something was in the last stages of burning, just a few licks of flame rising from charred lumps.

It was the outline of a human being.

With horror and disbelief, D'Agosta took in the smoldering, greasy outline; the ashy remnants of the skeleton, every fire-cracked bone in place, spread-eagled on the floor. There in its proper place was the belt buckle, there were the three metal buttons of a jacket. Where one of the pockets had been was now a fused lump of euros. The remains of a gold pen rested among the ashes of the upper ribs. The burned bones of one hand still sported a pair of familiar-looking rings.

But not all had burned. A single foot was perfectly preserved, burned only as far as the ankle. It looked absurdly like a movie prop, still encased in a beautifully polished handmade wing tip. And there at the other end was another piece of the body: just the side of the face, with one staring eye, a lock of hair, and a perfect pink ear, all intact, as if the fire that had consumed this person had suddenly ceased at a line drawn down the side of the head. The other half was mere skull, blackened, split and crumbled by heat.

Enough of the face remained to leave no doubt who this was. Locke Bullard.

D'Agosta found he'd been holding his breath. He let it out with a shudder, took in a lungful of what stank of sulfur and burned roast. As his faculties began to return, he noticed that the silk-draped walls and ceiling were covered with a greasy film. The large circle the body lay within appeared to have been incised into the floor, surrounded by mysterious symbols, the whole enclosed in a double pentagram. Nearby was a smaller circle—but this second circle was empty.

D'Agosta couldn't find the energy to turn away. He felt a snap and realized he'd been gripping his cross so hard he'd broken the chain. He looked down at the object in his hand, so familiar and reassuring. It seemed incredible that it could be true; that everything the sisters had told him so many years ago was, in fact, real: but at this moment, there wasn't the slightest doubt in his mind that this, *this*, was the work of the devil himself.

He glanced over at Pendergast and found he, too, was rooted to the spot, his face full of astonishment, shock—and disappointment. *This means the end of a theory*, D'Agosta thought to himself. *And the loss of a witness.* It was not just a shock. It was a terrible, perhaps even critical, blow to the investigation.

But even as D'Agosta stared, Pendergast took out his cell phone and started dialing.

D'Agosta could hardly believe his eyes. "Who are you calling?"

"I'm calling the carabinieri. Italian law enforcement. We are guests here, and it is important to play by the rules." He spoke briefly in Italian, snapped the phone shut, turned back to D'Agosta. "We have about twenty minutes until the police arrive. Let us make the most of it."

He began to make a quick tour of the crime scene, pausing at a small table on which several objects lay: an old piece of parchment, a strange-looking knife, a small pile of salt. D'Agosta simply watched, unable to bring himself to participate.

"My, my," said Pendergast. "Our friend Bullard had been consulting a grimoire shortly before his, ah, *demise*."

"What's a grimoire?"

"A book of the black arts. They contain instructions for raising demons, among other things."

D'Agosta swallowed. He wanted to get the hell out of here. This wasn't like Grove's death, or even Cutforth's—this had just happened. And this wasn't any normal killer. There was nothing Pendergast or any human law enforcement entity could do. *Hail Mary, full of grace...*

Pendergast was bending over the knife. "What do we have here? An *arthame*, by the looks of it."

D'Agosta wanted to tell Pendergast they had to get out, that forces a lot bigger than themselves were at work here, but he couldn't seem to form the words.

"Note that the circle enclosing Bullard has a little piece scratched out—do you see?—over there. It's been turned into a *broken* circle."

D'Agosta nodded mutely.

"On the other hand, the smaller circle beside it was never complete to begin with. I believe it was *constructed* as a broken circle." Pendergast walked toward it and bent down, examining the circle intently. He removed a pair of tweezers from his cuff and plucked something from the center of the circle.

"Right," D'Agosta managed to say, swallowing again.

"I'm very curious to know what was in this broken circle—an object evidently placed there as a gift to the, ah, devil."

"The devil." *The Lord is with thee...*

Pendergast examined the tip of his tweezers closely, turning it this way and that. Then his eyebrows shot up, a look of astonishment on his face.

D'Agosta stopped in midprayer. "What is it?"

"Horsehair."

And D'Agosta saw, or thought he saw, a flash of realization spread over the agent's pale features.

"What is it? What does it mean?"

Pendergast lowered the tweezers. "Everything."

{ 58 }

Harriman strolled past the Plaza Hotel and into Central Park, breathing in the crisp air with relish. It was a glorious fall evening, the golden light tinting the leaves above his head. Squirrels ran around gathering nuts; mothers pushed babies in strollers; groups of bicyclists and Rollerbladers glided past on South Park Drive.

His piece on Buck had run in the morning edition, and Ritts had loved it. The phones had been ringing all day, fax machines humming, reader e-mails flowing in. Once again, he'd touched a chord.

On this glorious evening, Bryce Harriman strolled northward, back to the site of his earlier triumph, in search of fresh glory. What was needed now was an interview with the good Reverend Buck himself—a *Post* exclusive. And if anyone could get that exclusive, he could.

As he came around the back of the Central Park Zoo and passed the old arsenal, he stopped in surprise. There was a tent here, an old canvas tent, pitched in the overgrown area just north of 65th Street along the Fifth Avenue side. As he walked up a small rise, more tents came into view. He crested the rise to find a veritable tent city spread before him, the smoke from dozens of fires rising into the autumn air.

Harriman paused, surprise changing to a glow of satisfaction. *He* had done this. He had kept the story alive, identified a leader, kept the people coming. And now *this*.

He moved into the outskirts of the camp. Some people, especially the numerous high school and college-aged kids, were wrapped only in newspapers; others had sleeping bags of various makes and colors; still others had makeshift tents made of sheets held up by sticks. A few had fancy tents from North Face and Antarctica Ltd.—trust fund brats from Scarsdale and Short Hills, probably.

Out of the corner of his eye, he saw a couple of cops along the Fifth Avenue wall, eyeing the situation. And to his left were more cops, just standing around, keeping a low profile. No wonder: there must be five hundred people camped in here.

He wandered into the encampment and down a makeshift alley between rows of tents. It was almost like a Depression-era shantytown, little narrow lanes built among the woodsy hollows and exposed rock faces: cooking fires, people sitting around on quilts and blankets drinking coffee. Here and there people were arriving with backpacks and setting up more tents. It had to extend at least to 70th Street: four square blocks of parkland. It was incredible. Had anything like this happened in New York before? Quickly, he got out his cell phone and ordered up a pool photographer.

Harriman then stopped to ask directions and within

minutes had located Buck's tent: a large army-surplus job near the camp's center. Just inside, he could make out Buck himself, seated at a card table and writing. He was a curiously dignified figure, and Harriman was reminded of old pictures he'd seen of Civil War generals. He hoped that damn photographer would hurry up.

As Harriman approached the entrance to the tent, a young man cut him off. "Can I help you?"

"I'm here to see Mr. Buck."

"A lot of people are here to see the reverend. He's busy, can't be disturbed."

"I'm Harriman from the *Post*."

"And I'm Todd from Levittown." The aide-de-camp stood firm, blocking the way, a kind of dreamy, supercilious smile on his face.

No asshole like a born-again asshole, Harriman thought. He glanced beyond the self-appointed guardian to Buck, working at his card table, ignoring them. What was that he saw, taped to the inside wall of the tent? A row of articles clipped from the *Post*. *His* articles. He felt emboldened.

"The reverend will want to see *me*." He pushed past the fellow, ducked into the tent, and strode over to Buck, hand extended. "Reverend Buck?"

The man rose. "And you are—?"

"Harriman from the *Post*."

"He just barged in, Reverend—," the aide-de-camp began.

But a slow smile was spreading across Buck's face. "Harriman. It's all right, Todd, I've been expecting this gentleman."

Deflated, Todd retreated to a corner of the tent,

while Buck shook the extended hand. Seen up close, he looked shorter than he did while preaching. He wore a simple checked short-sleeved shirt and a pair of chinos: no blow-dried helmet of hair or polyester suits for this preacher. His forearms were meaty and one sported a tattoo. His handshake was a crusher. Ex-prison, guessed Harriman.

"You've been waiting for me?" he asked.

Buck nodded. "I knew you'd come."

"You did?"

"It's all part of the plan. Won't you sit down?"

Harriman took a plastic seat at the card table and removed his microcassette recorder. "May I?"

"Be my guest."

Harriman turned it on, tested it, set it carefully on the table. "Perhaps we should begin with this plan of yours. Tell me about it."

Buck smiled indulgently. "I was referring to God's plan."

"Right. Okay. Which is?"

Buck spread his hands. "What you see all around you. I am nothing, just one flawed human trying my best to fulfill God's plan. You, Mr. Harriman, whether you know it or not, are a part of that plan, too. An important part, as it turns out. Your articles have swelled this crowd, brought people together—those with ears to hear and eyes to witness."

"Witness what?"

"The rapture."

"Excuse me?"

"God's promise to his followers in the End Days. When the faithful will be lifted into heaven while the wicked sink into filth and fire." Buck hesitated briefly. And in that hesitation, Harriman detected a flash—just a flash—of nervousness. Perhaps the man was a little scared at what he'd unleashed.

"What makes you think the End Days are here?"

"God sent me a sign. It was your article in the newspaper, the article on the deaths of Grove and Cutforth, that first brought me here all the way from Yuma, Arizona."

"And just who are all these people camped around you?"

"The saved, Mr. Harriman. Out there are the damned. Which are you?"

Harriman was taken aback by the suddenness of the question. Buck was eyeing him with an almost Rasputin-like intensity.

"Does it matter?" Harriman laughed weakly.

"Does it matter whether you spend eternity boiling in a lake of fire or lying sweetly in the lap of Jesus? Because the time has come to make a choice. These awful deaths have made that clear. No more sitting on the fence, wondering where the truth is. This question enters everyone's life at some point, and now that life-changing decision has suddenly, without warning, *come to you*. Remember Paul's Epistle to the Romans: *There is none righteous, no, not one... For all have sinned, and come short of the glory of God*. You must repent and be born again in the love of Jesus. You can wait no longer. So, Mr. Harriman: are you saved, or are you damned?"

Buck waited for a reply.

Harriman felt a cold sweat break out on the back of his neck. The guy was really waiting for an answer, and it was clear he wouldn't go on until he got one. What was he going to reply? Sure, he'd always considered himself a Christian, sort of—but not a Bible-thumping, proselytizing Christian.

"I'm still working it out," he finally said. How had he allowed Buck to set the agenda like this? Who was in charge of this interview, anyway?

"What's there to work out? The decision is simple. Remember what Jesus said to the wealthy man who desired eternal life: *Sell all that thou hast, and distribute unto the poor... For it is easier for a camel to go through a needle's eye, than for a rich man to enter into the kingdom of God.* Are you ready to give away your earthly goods, Mr. Harriman, and join me? Or will you walk away, like that rich man in the Gospel of Luke?"

Harriman thought about this. Had Jesus really said that? Something must have been lost in the translation.

Maybe another tack would break this impasse. "So when, Reverend, is all this going to happen?"

"If everybody knew when the Day of Judgment would dawn, we'd have a whole lot of converts the night before. It will come *when the world least expects it.*"

"But *you* expect it. And very soon."

"Yes. Because God has sent his faithful a sign, and that sign was the death that took place right across the street."

Harriman noted that the group of policemen in the distance had grown a little bigger. They were talking and taking notes. He realized abruptly this little Shangri-La wasn't going to last. If Christ didn't come soon, the police would. You couldn't have hundreds of people shitting in the bushes of Central Park forever.

And come to think of it, there *was* an odd smell wafting on the air…

"What will you do if the police move in to evict you?" he asked.

Buck paused, his face betraying another fleeting glimpse of uncertainty, but it was gone as quickly as it had appeared. The serene expression returned.

"God will be my guide, Mr. Harriman. God will be my guide."

{ 59 }

D'Agosta heard the sirens first, shattering the peace of the Tuscan countryside with their dissonant two-note ditty. Next came the headlights of two vehicles speeding around a nearby hill and sweeping up the drive. They ground to a halt before the villa with an audible spray of gravel. Police lights cartwheeled across the ceiling of the *salone*.

Pendergast rose from his crouch. The tweezers that had magically appeared from his clothing just as magically disappeared.

He glanced at D'Agosta. "Shall we retire to the chapel? We wouldn't want these good gentlemen to think we've been tampering with their crime site."

D'Agosta, still gripped with fear and dread, nodded dumbly. The chapel. That seemed like a good idea. A really good idea.

The chapel was in the traditional location at the far end of the *salone*, a tiny but exquisite Baroque room which could fit little more than a priest and half a dozen family members. There didn't seem to be any electric lights, so Pendergast lit a votive candle in a red glass holder, and they settled on the hard wooden benches to wait.

Almost immediately there was the sound of a door booming open; boots echoing in the downstairs hall; police radios blaring. D'Agosta was still holding his cross, his eyes on the small marble altar. The candle gave out a flickering reddish glow, and the air was redolent with frankincense and myrrh. He resisted the impulse to go down on his knees. He reminded himself he was a policeman, this was a crime scene, and the idea that the devil had come and claimed Bullard's soul was ridiculous.

And yet, in the perfumed darkness, it didn't feel the least bit ridiculous. His hand shook as it clutched the cross.

Now the carabinieri burst into the *salone.* D'Agosta heard a gasp; some muffled expostulations of shock; what sounded like a prayer being quickly intoned. Then came the familiar sounds of a crime scene being secured and floodlights being set up. A moment later the room beyond was bathed in almost unbearably bright light. A beam lanced into the chapel, striking the marble Christ behind the altar and setting it aglow.

A man appeared in the doorway, casting a long shadow. He was dressed, not in uniform, but in a tailored gray suit, a couple of gold leaves on his lapel signifying rank. He paused, staring. To D'Agosta, he seemed no more than an outline, framed in brilliant light, a short-barreled 9mm Beretta Parabellum in his hand.

"Rimanete seduti, mani in alto, per cortesìa," he said calmly.

"Remain seated, hands in view," translated Pendergast. "We're policemen—"

"Tacete!"

D'Agosta suddenly remembered they were dressed in black, their faces still half painted. God only knew what this police officer was thinking.

The man advanced, gun in hand, not exactly aimed at them but not quite aimed away, either. "Who are you?" he asked in lightly-accented English.

"Special Agent Pendergast, Federal Bureau of Investigation, United States of America." Pendergast's wallet was in his hand, and it fell open to reveal his shield on one side, his ID on the other.

"And you?"

"Sergeant Vincent D'Agosta, Southampton Police Department, FBI liaison. We're—"

"Basta." The man stepped forward. He reached for Pendergast's wallet, looked at the badge, the ID card. "Are you the one who called in the homicide?"

"Yes."

"What are you doing here?"

"We are investigating a series of murders in the United States, which that man"—Pendergast nodded out into the great room—"was connected to."

"Mafiosi?"

"No."

The man looked visibly relieved. "You know the identity of the deceased?"

"Locke Bullard."

The man handed back the wallet, gestured at their outfits. "Are these the newest uniforms among the FBI?"

"It's a long story, Colonnello."

"How did you get here?"

"You will find our car—if you haven't already—in the olive grove across the street. A black Fiat Stylo. I will, of course, prepare a formal report for you on all the particulars: who we are, why we're here. Some of it is already on file at the Questura."

"God, no. No reports. It is so inconvenient when facts get written down. At the proper time, we will talk about it over an espresso, like civilized human beings." The man moved out of the glaring backlight. For the first time, D'Agosta could see his features: prominent cheekbones, cleft chin, and deep-set eyes. He was about sixty, and he moved with a stiff military bearing, his graying hair brushed back, restless eyes taking in everything.

"I am Colonnello Orazio Esposito. Forgive me for not introducing myself earlier." He shook their hands. "Who is your liaison at the Questura?"

"Commissario Simoncini."

"I see. And what do you make of this..." He nodded again toward the great room. "This... *casino*?"

"It is the third in a series of murders, the first two of which took place in New York."

A cynical smile grew on Esposito's face. "I can see we're going to have quite a lot to talk about, Special Agent Pendergast. Listen. There is a nice little *caffè* in Borgo Ognissanti, just two doors down from the church and very near our headquarters. Shall we meet there at eight this morning? Unofficially, of course."

"It would be my pleasure."

"And now it would be better if you leave. We'll make

no note of your presence in the official report. To have the American FBI reporting a crime on Italian soil..." His smile broadened. "It just wouldn't do."

He briskly shook their hands and turned on his heel, crossing himself so rapidly as he passed the altar D'Agosta wasn't sure if he had done it at all.

{ 60 }

D'Agosta had seen a lot of police headquarters in his time, but the so-called barracks of the carabinieri in Florence beat them all. It wasn't a barracks at all, but rather a decaying Renaissance building—D'Agosta thought it was Renaissance, anyway—facing a narrow medieval street. It was huddled up beside the famous Ognissanti Church, its gray limestone facade streaked with dirt, every ledge and projection covered with needle-like spikes to ward off pigeons. Florence itself was nothing like what he'd imagined: even in the warm, mid-October light, the city seemed austere, its crooked streets always in shadow, the rough-cut stone facades of its buildings almost grim. The air smelled of diesel fumes, and the impossibly narrow sidewalks were clogged with slow-moving tourists dressed in floppy hats and khaki shorts, with packs on their backs and water bottles strapped to their waists, as if they were on an expedition into the Sahara rather than walking around perhaps the most civilized city in the world.

They had met the *colonnello* in the nearby café, as planned, and Pendergast had quickly brought him up to speed on their investigation—omitting, D'Agosta noticed, certain small but critical details. Now they were following him back to his office, single file, fighting a steady stream of Japanese tourists coming in the opposite direction.

The *colonnello* turned into the grand arched entryway of the barracks, over which hung a limp Italian flag—the first D'Agosta had seen since arriving in Italy. They passed through a colonnaded corridor and into a vast interior courtyard. Once elegant, the courtyard itself had been turned into a parking lot and was wall-to-wall with police vans and cars, packed together with such mathematical precision it seemed impossible to move one without moving them all. The windows looking down on the courtyard were all open, and from them issued a continuous clamor of ringing telephones, voices, and slamming doors, magnified and distorted by the confined space.

They turned into another vaulted corridor lined with stone pillars—the crumbling remains of religious frescoes still visible—past a battered statue of a saint; then up a massive flight of stone stairs and into a warren of modern cubicles constructed haphazardly out of what had once been a single pillared room.

"The *caserma,*" said Esposito as they walked, "was once the monastery connected to the Ognissanti Church. That large room is the secretarial pool, and beyond"—he waved his hand at a series of small but massive oaken doors giving onto tiny offices—"are the work spaces of the officers, built in the former cells of the monks."

They turned a corner and proceeded down yet

another vaulted corridor. "The refectory, where the monks used to eat, has an important fresco by Ghirlandaio that nobody ever sees."

"Indeed."

"Here in Italy, we make do with what we have."

Reaching the far end of the corridor, they went up another flight of stairs. From the landing, they passed through what D'Agosta realized must have once been a secret door in the wall; mounted a tiny circular staircase; passed through crowded rooms smelling of mold and overheated fax machines—and then suddenly arrived at a small, grimy door bearing nothing but a number. Here Esposito stopped with a smile. Then he pushed the door open and ushered them in.

D'Agosta stepped into a light-flooded room that ended in a wall of glassed-in columns and arches. Beyond lay a sweeping view southward, over the Arno River. Almost despite himself, he was drawn toward the view.

From above, finally, Florence looked like he had imagined it: a city of church domes and towers, red-tile roofs, gardens, and piazze, surrounded by steep green hills covered with fairy-tale castles. There was the Ponte Vecchio and the Pitti Palace; the Boboli Gardens; the dome of San Frediano in Cestello; and, beyond, the hill of Bellosguardo. It was a moment before he could shift his attention back to the room itself.

It was large and open, filled with rows of old mahogany desks. The floor, polished by five hundred years of feet, was inlaid in a striking array of colored marbles, and on the stuccoed walls hung giant paintings of old men in armor. There was a tense air in the room, and a number of men in suits at the desks were glancing nervously in their direction. The killing—and its bizarre particulars especially—were clearly on everyone's mind.

"Welcome to the Nucleo Investigativo, the elite unit of the carabinieri of which I am in charge. We investigate the major crimes." Esposito looked at D'Agosta sideways. "Is this your first visit to Italy, Sergeant D'Agosta?"

"It is."

"And how do you find it?"

"It's... not quite what I expected."

He could see a faint look of amusement in the man's eyes. Esposito's hand swept over the skyline. "Beautiful, no?"

"From up here."

"The Florentines..." He rolled his eyes. "They live in the past. They believe they created everything beautiful in the world—art, science, music, literature—and that is enough. Why do anything more? They've been resting on their laurels for four hundred years. Where I grew up we have a saying: *Nun cagnà 'a via vecchia p'a nova, ca saie chello che lasse, nun saie chello ca trouve.*"

"Don't live in the past—you will know what you've lost but not what you've found?" D'Agosta asked.

Esposito went still. Then he smiled. "Your family is originally from Naples?"

D'Agosta nodded.

"This is remarkable. And you actually speak Neapolitan?"

"I thought I grew up speaking Italian."

Esposito laughed. "This is not the first time I have heard of this happening. You are fortunate, Sergeant, to speak a beautiful and ancient language no longer taught in any school. Anyone can learn Italian, but only a real man can speak *napolitano.* I myself am from Naples. Impossible to work there, of course, but a marvelous place to live."

"Si suonne Napele viato a tte," D'Agosta said.

Esposito looked even more astonished. "'Blessed be you if you dream of Naples.' What a lovely saying. I've never heard it before."

"When I was a little boy, my grandmother used to whisper that in my ear every time she kissed me good night."

"And did you ever dream of Naples?"

"I sometimes dreamed of a city that I thought was Naples, but I'm sure it was all my imagination. I've never been there."

"Then don't go. Live in your dreams: they are always so much better." He turned to Pendergast. "And now—as you Americans say—to business."

He led them to a small sitting area in a far corner of the room, couches and chairs positioned around an old stone table. Esposito waved his hand. *"Caffè per noi, per favore."*

In moments, a woman appeared with a tray of tiny cups of espresso. Esposito took one, tossed it back, then drank a second just as quickly. He slipped out a pack of cigarettes, offered them around.

"Ah, you Americans never smoke." He took one himself, lit it, exhaled. "This morning, between seven and eight, I received sixteen telephone calls—one from the American Embassy in Rome, five from the American Consulate on the Lungarno, one from the U.S. State

Department, two from the *New York Times*, one from the *Washington Post*, one from the Chinese Embassy in Rome, and five from various unpleasant people in Mr. Bullard's company." He looked up, eyes twinkling. "Given that, and what you told me just now in the café, it's clear this Bullard was an important man."

"You didn't know him?" Pendergast asked.

"By reputation only." Inhale, exhale. "My colleagues at the *polizia* have a file on him already, which naturally they will not share with us."

"I could supply you with far more on Bullard, but it would do you no good. The information will only distract you, as it did me."

Esposito turned to the two carabinieri who were whispering together behind him. *"Basta' cù stì fessarie! Mettiteve à faticà! Maronna meja, chist' so propri' sciem'!"*

D'Agosta suppressed a laugh. "I understood that."

"I didn't," said Pendergast.

"He was just telling those men in, ah, Neapolitan, 'Cut the bullshit and get back to work.' "

"My men are foolish and superstitious. Half of them believe this to be the work of the devil. The other half think it the work of some secret society. As you know, Florentine nobility is rife with them." Inhale, exhale. "It appears to me, Mr. Pendergast, that we have a joker on our hands."

"On the contrary, our killer could not be more serious."

"But all this—*chest è 'nà scena rò diavulo*? Come, now. All this may scare my men half to death, but you?"

"I assure you there is a most purposeful design here."

"I see you already have a theory as to what happened to Mr. Bullard. Perhaps you will be kind enough to share it with me?" The *colonnello* leaned forward, elbows on his knees. "After all, I've already done you an enormous favor by not reporting your presence at the scene of the crime. Otherwise, you would be filling out paperwork from now until Christmas."

"I am grateful," said Pendergast. "But for now, there's little more I can tell you than what I mentioned last night. We're investigating two mysterious deaths that took place recently in New York State. Locke Bullard was a possible suspect. At the very least, he was involved in some extremely shady dealings. But as it happens, his own death patterns the first two."

"I see. And do you have any ideas? Conjectures?"

"It would be unwise for me to answer that question. And you wouldn't believe me if I did."

"*Va be'*. Well then, what now?" He leaned back, picked up yet another cup of espresso, and tossed it back like a Russian tosses back a shot of vodka.

"I would like you to do a search of all deaths in Italy over the past year in which the body was found burned or partially burned."

Esposito smiled. "*Another* favor..." He let his voice trail off into a cloud of smoke. "Here in Italy, we believe in the principle of reciprocation. I would like you to tell me, Mr. Pendergast, what you will be doing for *me*."

Pendergast leaned forward. "Colonnello, all I can say is, one way or another I *will* return the favor."

Esposito gazed at him for a moment, stubbed out his cigarette. "Well then. You're looking for a burned corpse in Italy." He laughed. "That would involve half the homicides in the South. The Mafia, Camorra, Cosa Nostra, the Sardinians—burning their victims after killing them is a time-honored tradition."

"We can safely eliminate homicides related to organized crime, family or business feuds, or any for which you've already caught the killer. We're looking for one that is isolated, perhaps an older person, probably rural."

D'Agosta stared at Pendergast. What was he driving at? There was an eager glint in his eyes. He was clearly hot on some trail and, as usual, wasn't sharing it with anyone.

"That will narrow things down tremendously," said Esposito. "I'll get someone on it right away. It might take a day or two—we are not nearly as computerized as your FBI."

"I am most grateful." Pendergast rose and shook Esposito's hand.

The policeman leaned forward and said, *"Quann' 'o diavulo t'accarezza, vo'll'ànema."*

As they exited into the sun, Pendergast turned to D'Agosta. "I find that I need to call on you again for a translation."

D'Agosta grinned. "It's an old Neapolitan proverb. *You need a strong heart to resist the devil's caresses.*"

"Appropriate." Pendergast inhaled. "What a fine day. Shall we go sightseeing?"

"What'd you have in mind?"

"I hear Cremona is lovely this time of year."

{ 61 }

D'Agosta stepped out of the Cremona train station into the warm sunlight of late morning. A wind had sprung up and was shaking the leaves of the plane trees in the broad piazza that lay before them. Beyond was the old part of the city, a cheerful medieval jumble of red-brick buildings rising from a maze of narrow streets. Pendergast chose one of these—the Corso Garibaldi—and began striding down it quickly, his black suit coat flapping behind him in the stiff wind.

With a sigh of resignation, D'Agosta hastened to keep up. He noticed the agent hadn't bothered to consult a map. Pendergast had spent most of the train ride talking about the history of the nearby marble quarries at Carrara, and the extraordinary coincidence that the source of the purest white marble in the world was located only a few dozen miles downriver from the birthplace of the Renaissance, giving the Florentine sculptors options other than black or green marble. He had deftly deflected D'Agosta's inquiries as to the reason why sightseeing had taken them here.

"Now what?" D'Agosta asked, sounding a little more irritated than he intended.

"Coffee." Pendergast swerved into a café and approached the zinc bar. D'Agosta felt his irritation swell.

"Due caffè, per favore," Pendergast said.

"Since when did coffee become your favorite drink? I thought you were a green-tea man."

"Usually, yes. But when in Rome—or Cremona, as the case may be..."

The coffees arrived, in the usual tiny espresso cups. Pendergast stirred his, tossed it down in the Italian manner. D'Agosta drank his more slowly, catching Pendergast's eye. There it was again: that look of eagerness.

"My dear Vincent, please don't think I'm being intentionally mysterious. In certain kinds of police work, there can be great danger in propounding theories. They take on a life of their own. They are like wearing colored spectacles, becoming the truth we see even when it is wrong. So I hesitate to bandy theories—especially with someone whose judgment I respect as much as yours—until I have proof in hand. That is why I have not asked for *your* theories, either."

"I don't have any theories."

"You will, before the day is up." He tossed a two-euro coin on the counter, and they went out. "Our first stop is the Palazzo Comunale, a fine example of medieval civic architecture, containing a notable marble chimneypiece by Pedoni."

"Heck, I've always wanted to see that chimneypiece."

Pendergast smiled.

A ten-minute walk brought them to the heart of the

city and a crooked piazza. On one side stood an enormous cathedral with a soaring tower. Pendergast gestured at it as they passed. "That is said to be the tallest medieval tower in Italy. Built in the thirteenth century, the height of a thirty-three-story skyscraper."

"Amazing."

"And here is the Palazzo Comunale." They entered a massive, unadorned medieval palace built of brick. A guard nodded at them as they passed the entrance, and D'Agosta wondered if it was Pendergast's air of utter self-confidence, or something else, that allowed them such easy entry. He followed Pendergast up a flight of stairs and down several stone corridors to a small, barren room. A glass case stood in its center, and an enormous Venetian glass chandelier hung from above, bristling with lightbulbs and giving the room the brilliance of a movie set. An armed guard stood nearby.

In the glass case were six violins.

"Ah!" said Pendergast. "Here we are: the Saletta dei Violini."

"Violins?"

"Not just any violins. What we are looking at is the history of the violin, in one case. Which is, in microcosm, a history of music."

"I see," said D'Agosta, letting a note of sarcasm creep into his voice. Pendergast would, eventually, get to the point.

"The first one, there, was made by Andrea Amati in 1566. You'll recall the violin Constance plays is also an Amati, though very much inferior to these. Those two beside it are by his sons; that one by his grandson. That next was built by Giuseppe Guarneri in 1689." Pendergast paused. "And that last one was made by Antonio Stradivari in 1715."

"As in Stradivarius?"

"The world's most celebrated violinmaker. He invented the modern violin and during his lifetime made eleven hundred, of which about six hundred survive. Although all his instruments remain among the greatest ever made, there was a period when he made a string of violins that had a most gloriously perfect tone—perhaps twenty or thirty. We call that his golden period."

"Okay."

"Stradivari was a man of many secrets. To this day, no one has ever solved the mystery of how he made such perfect violins. He kept his methods and formulas in his head, never wrote them down. He passed these priceless trade secrets on to his two sons, who took over his workshop, but when they died, all Stradivari's secrets died with them. Ever since, people have been trying to duplicate his violins. A number of scientists have tried to re-create his secret formulas. But to this day, Stradivari's secret has never been cracked."

"They must be worth a lot of dough."

"Not so long ago you could buy a good Strad for fifty or a hundred thousand dollars. But the market for violins has been ruined by the super-rich. Now a top Strad can fetch ten million or more."

"No shit."

"The best are priceless, especially those made during his golden period. In those instruments, he got the formula just right. Nobody really knows why. It's quite humbling, Vincent, to realize we can land a spaceship on Mars, we can build a machine to perform a trillion calculations a second, we can split the nucleus of the atom—but we still cannot make a better violin than could a man puttering around in a simple workshop three centuries ago."

"Well, he *was* Italian."

Pendergast laughed quietly. "One of the beautiful things about a Strad is that it has to be *played* in order to maintain its tone. It's alive. If you leave it in a case, it loses its tone and dies."

"What about these?"

"They are taken out and played at least once a week. Cremona is still the center of violinmaking, and there are many eager volunteers."

He clasped his hands behind his back, turned. "And now, for the *real* reason we came to Cremona. Stick close behind me, please, and don't get lost."

Pendergast led the way through a maze of back passages and narrow staircases to a side alley behind the palazzo. There they paused at least a minute while Pendergast made a careful inspection of the alley and surrounding buildings. Then, moving very quickly, he led D'Agosta through a winding series of ever more tortuous medieval streets, the ancient brick and stone buildings crowding in above. Some of the streets were so narrow they were dark despite the midday sun. Now and then, Pendergast would duck into a doorway or side alley and make another visual scan.

"What's up?" D'Agosta asked at one point.

"Just caution, Vincent; habitual caution."

They finally arrived at a street so narrow it could hardly admit a bicycle. It twisted into a dead end at what appeared to be a deserted shopfront, a plate-glass window rudely affixed to a medieval stone arch. The plate glass was cracked and taped and opaque with dirt. A metal grate had been fitted and locked over the front, where it seemed to have rusted in place.

Pendergast slid his hand through the grate and pulled a string. There was a small tinkle in the shop beyond.

"Would it compromise your investigation completely if you told me who we're visiting now?"

"This is the laboratory and workshop of *il dottor* Luigi Spezi, one of the world's foremost experts on Stradivari violins. He is a bit of a Renaissance man himself, being a scientist and engineer as well as a fine musician. His re-creations of the Stradivari violins are among the best in the world. But I warn you: he is known to be a little cranky."

Pendergast pulled again, and a voice rumbled from the back. *"Non lo voglio. Va' via!"*

Pendergast rang again, insistently.

A gray shape materialized behind the glass: an enormous, stooped man in a leather apron with long gray hair and a gray mustache. He waved both hands at Pendergast in a shooing motion. *"Che cazz'! Via, ho detto!"*

Pendergast took out a business card, wrote a single word on the back, and slipped it through the mail slot in the door. It fluttered to the floor. The man picked it up, read the back, and went very still for a moment. He looked up at Pendergast, looked down at the card—and then began the laborious process of unlocking the door and raising the grate. Within a minute, they had stooped beneath the arch and were standing in his shop.

D'Agosta looked around curiously. The walls of the shop were almost completely covered with the hanging bellies, backplates, and purflings of violins in various stages of carving. It had a pleasant smell of wood, sawdust, varnish, oil, and glue.

The man stared at Pendergast as if he were staring at a ghost. He was wearing a dirty leather apron, and he removed a pair of sawdust-covered glasses in order to peer at the agent more closely.

"So, Aloysius Pendergast, Ph.D.," he said in almost flawless English. "You have gotten my attention. What is it you want?"

"Is there a place where we can talk?"

They followed him through the confines of the narrow shop—perhaps eight feet wide—to a much larger space in the back. Spezi indicated for them to sit on a long bench. He himself perched against the corner of a worktable, folded his hands, and stared.

In the rear wall, D'Agosta could see a stainless-steel door, grossly out of place, with a single small window. On the far side of the window was a gleaming white laboratory, racks of computer equipment and CRTs bathed in unpleasant fluorescent light.

"Thank you for agreeing to see me, Dottor Spezi," Pendergast said. "I know you are a very busy man, and I can assure you we will not waste your time."

The man bowed his head, mollified slightly.

"This is my associate, Sergeant Vincent D'Agosta of the Southampton Police Department, New York."

"Very pleased." The man leaned forward and shook his hand. He had a surprisingly strong grip. Then he sat back again and waited.

"I propose an exchange of information," Pendergast said.

"As you wish."

"You tell me what you know of Stradivari's secret formulas. I will tell you what I know of the existence of the violin mentioned on my card. Naturally, I will keep your information secret. I will write nothing down and speak to no one about it, except to my associate, who is a man of complete discretion."

D'Agosta watched the man's deep pale eyes stare back at them. He appeared to be thinking about, perhaps even struggling with, the proposal. Finally he nodded curtly.

"Very well, then," said Pendergast. "I wonder if you could answer some questions about your work."

"Yes, but first: the violin. How in the world—?"

"First things first. Tell me, Dottore—since I am a man who knows nothing about violins—tell me what makes the sound of a Stradivarius so perfect?"

The man seemed to relax, evidently realizing he was not dealing with a spy or competitor. "This is no secret. I would characterize it as very lively. It is an *interesting* sound. On top of that, it has a combination of darkness and brilliance, a balance between high and low frequencies—a tone that is rich but as pure and sweet as honey. Of course, each Strad sounds different—some have a fatter tone, others are lean, even harsh; some are thin and quite disappointing. Some have been repaired and rebuilt so many times they can hardly be called original. Only six Strads, for example, retain their original necks. When you drop a violin, it's always the neck that breaks. But there are about ten or twenty that sound almost perfect."

"Why?"

At this, the man smiled. "That, of course, is the question." He rose, went to the steel door, unlocked it, and swung it open, revealing two hard-disk recording workstations and racks of digital samplers, compressors, and limiters. The walls and ceiling were covered with acoustic foam paneling.

They followed him in, and he shut and locked the door behind them. Then he switched on an amplifier, pulled up the faders on a nearby mixing console. A low hum began to sound from the reference speakers set high in the walls.

"The first really scientific test done on a Stradivarius was performed about fifty years ago. They hooked a sound generator to the bridge of a violin and had it vibrate the instrument. Then they measured how the violin vibrated in return. An absurd test, really, because it has nothing to do with the way a violin is played. But even such a crude test showed the Strad gave back an extraordinary response in the two-thousand-to-four-thousand-hertz range—which, not at all coincidentally, happens to be the range of sound that the human ear is most sensitive to. Later, high-speed computers allowed real-time processing of a Strad being played. Let me give you an example."

He turned to one of the digital samplers, used an attached keyboard to select an audio sample, sent the output to the mixer. The sweet sound of a violin filled the room.

"This is Jascha Heifetz playing the cadenza of Beethoven's violin concerto on the Messiah Stradivarius."

A complex series of dancing lines appeared on a

monitor sitting behind the mixer. Spezi pointed at them.

"That is a frequency analysis from thirty to thirty thousand hertz. Look at the richness of the low-frequency sounds! They give the violin its darkness, its sonority. And in the two thousand to four thousand range I mentioned, see how lively and robust it is. *This* is what fills the concert hall with sound."

D'Agosta wondered what any of this had to do with Bullard or the murders. He also wondered what Pendergast had written on the business card the man was still clutching in one fist. Whatever it was, it had clearly made this man remarkably cooperative.

"And these are the high frequencies. Look how they leap and flicker, like the flame of a candle. It's these transients that give the Strad that breathing, trembling tone, so delicate and fleeting."

Pendergast inclined his head. "So, Dottore—what's the secret?"

Spezi reached for the sampler and the music stopped. "There is no one secret. It was a whole catalog of secrets, some of which we've cracked, others we haven't. For example, we know exactly what kind of architecture Stradivari used. With computerized tomography, we can map a Strad perfectly in three dimensions. We know all there is to know about Stradivari's designs for the belly, backplate, purfling, f-holes—everything. We also know just what types of wood he used. We can make a perfect copy."

He turned to one of the computers, typed again, and the image of a beautiful violin appeared on its screen. "There it is. An absolutely perfect copy of the Harrison

Strad, down to the very nicks and scratches. It took me almost half a year, back in the early eighties, to complete." He glanced over at them with a mirthless smile. "It sounds *dreadful.* The real secret, you see, was in the *chemistry.* Specifically, the recipe for the solution Stradivari soaked his wood in, and the recipe for his varnish. This has been the thrust of my research ever since."

"And?"

The man hesitated. "I don't know why I am inclined to trust you, but I do. The wood Stradivari used was cut in the foothills of the Apennines and dumped green into the Po or Adige Rivers, floated downstream, and stored in brackish lagoons near Venice. This was purely for convenience, but it did something critical to the wood—it opened up its pores. Stradivari purchased the wood wet. He did not season it. Instead, he soaked it further in a solution of his own making—as far as I can deduce, a combination of borax, sea salt, fruit gum, quartz and other minerals, and ground, colored Venetian glass. He soaked it for months, perhaps years, while it absorbed these chemicals. What did they do to the wood? Amazing, complex, miraculous things! First, they preserved it. The borax made the wood tighter, harder, stiffer. The ground quartz and glass prevented the violin from being eaten by woodworms—but it also filled in the air spaces and gave it a brilliance and clarity of tone. The fruit gum caused subtle changes and acted as a fungicide. Of course, the real secret lies in the proportions—and those, Signor Pendergast, I will not tell you."

Pendergast nodded.

"Over the years, I've made hundreds of violins

from wood treated this way, experimenting with the ratios and the length of time in solution. The resulting instruments had a big, brilliant sound. But it was a *harsh* sound. Something was needed to *dampen* the vibrations, the overtones."

He paused. "Here is where the true genius of Stradivari comes in. He found that in his secret varnish."

He moused up the computer screen, clicked through a few menus. A new image appeared in black and white, a landscape of incredible ruggedness, looking to D'Agosta like some vast mountain range.

"Here is the varnish of a Stradivarius under a scanning electron microscope, 30,000x. As you can see, it is not the smooth, hard layer it seems to the naked eye. Instead, there are billions of microscopic cracks. When the violin is played, these cracks *absorb* and *dampen* the harsh vibrations and resonances, allowing only the purest, clearest tone to escape. That's the true secret to Stradivari's violins. The problem is, the varnish he used was an incredibly complex chemical solution, involving boiled insects and other organic and inorganic sources. It has defied all analysis—and we have so little of it to test. You can't strip the varnish off a Strad—removing even a little will ruin a violin. You'd need to destroy an entire instrument to get enough varnish to analyze it properly. Even then, you couldn't use one of his inferior violins. Those were experimental, and the varnish recipe changed many times. No—you'd have to destroy one from the golden period. Not only that, but you'd need to cut into the wood and analyze the chemistry of the solution he soaked them in as well as the interface between the varnish and the wood. For all these reasons, we have not been able to figure out exactly how he did it."

He leaned back. "Another problem. Even if you *had* all his secret recipes, you still might fail. Stradivari, knowing all that we don't, managed to make some mediocre violins. There were other factors to making a great violin, some apparently even beyond *his* control—such as the particular qualities of the piece of wood he used."

Pendergast nodded.

"And that, Mr. Pendergast, is all I can tell you." The man's face glittered with feverish intensity. "And now let us speak of *this*." He opened his hand and smoothed the crumpled business card. And for the first time, D'Agosta glimpsed what Pendergast had written on it.

It was the word *Stormcloud*.

{ 62 }

The man held out the card in a trembling hand.

Pendergast nodded in return. “Perhaps the best way to start would be for you to tell Sergeant D’Agosta what you know of its history.”

Spezi turned to D’Agosta, his face filling with regret. “The Stormcloud was Stradivari’s greatest violin. It was played by a string of virtuosi in an almost unbroken line from Monteverdi to Paganini and beyond. It was present at some of the greatest moments in the history of music. It was played by Franz Clement at the premiere of Beethoven’s violin concerto. It was played by Brahms himself at the premiere of his Second Violin Concerto, and by Paganini for the first Italian performance of all twenty-four of his caprices. And then, just before World War I—on the death of the virtuoso Luciano Toscanelli, may God curse him—it disappeared. Toscanelli went insane at the end of his days and, some say, destroyed it. Others say it was lost in the Great War.”

“It wasn’t.”

Spezi straightened abruptly. “You mean it still *exists*?”

"A few more questions if I may, Dottore. What do you know of the ownership of the Stormcloud?"

"That was one of its mysteries. It was always owned by the same family, apparently, who it was said purchased the instrument directly from Stradivari himself. It was passed down from father to son only in name, being on continuous loan to a string of virtuosi. That's normal, of course: most of the Strads today are owned by wealthy collectors who turn them over to virtuosi to play on long-term loan. Just so with the Stormcloud. When the virtuoso who was playing it died—or if he had the misfortune to give a bad concert—it was taken away by the family that owned it and given to another. There would have been intense competition for it. No doubt that is the reason the family remained anonymous—they didn't want to be harried and importuned by aspiring violinists. They made secrecy of their identity a strict condition of playing the violin."

"No virtuoso ever broke the silence?"

"Not as far as I know."

"And Toscanelli was the last virtuoso to play it."

"Yes, Toscanelli. The great and terrible Toscanelli. He died a syphilitic wreck in 1910, under strange and mysterious circumstances. The violin was not beside his body and was never found."

"Who *should* the violin have gone to after Toscanelli?"

"A good question. Perhaps the Russian child prodigy, young Count Ravetsky. Murdered in the revolution, though—a great loss. What a terrible century that was. And now, Mr. Pendergast—I am almost expiring from curiosity."

Pendergast reached into his pocket and slipped out a

glassine envelope, held it up to the light. "A fragment of horsehair from the bow of the Stormcloud."

The man reached out with trembling fingers. "May I?"

"I promised an exchange. It's yours."

The man opened it, removed the horsehair with a pair of tweezers, placed it on a microscope stage. A moment later the image appeared on a computer screen.

"It's definitely horsehair from a violin bow—you can see the grains of rosin, here, and the damage that playing has done to the microscopic scales on the shaft, there." He straightened. "Of course, any bow with the Stormcloud almost certainly isn't the original, and even if it was, the horsehair must have been replaced a thousand times. This is hardly proof."

"I'm well aware of that. It was only the first clue that led me on a string of deductions, the conclusion of which was that the Stormcloud still exists. It is here, Dottore, in Italy."

"If only it were so! Where did you get this hair?"

"From a crime scene in Tuscany."

"For God's sake, man: *who has it?*"

"I don't yet know for certain."

"How will you find out?"

"First, I need to learn the name of the family that originally owned it."

Spezi thought for a moment. "I'd start with Toscanelli's heirs—he was said to have had a dozen children from almost as many mistresses. God knows, one might still be alive somewhere—and now that I think of it, it seems to me there's a granddaughter or some such here in Italy. He was a notorious womanizer, drinker of absinthe, indiscreet in his later years. Perhaps he told one of his mistresses, who then might have passed it on to her issue."

"An excellent suggestion." Pendergast rose. "You have been most generous, Dottore. When I do learn more about the Stormcloud's whereabouts, I promise I shall share the facts with you. For now, I thank you for your time."

Pendergast led the way back out through the narrow streets with the same caution he'd shown in approaching Spezi's workshop. By the time they'd reached the café, however, he seemed to have satisfied himself on some point, and suggested they stop for another espresso. Standing at the bar, he turned to D'Agosta with a smile.

"And now, my dear Vincent—do you have a theory?"

D'Agosta nodded. "Most of one, anyway."

"Excellent! Don't tell me yet. Let us continue our investigations in silence just a little longer. The time will soon come when we need to share our conclusions."

"Fine by me."

D'Agosta sipped the bitter drink. He wondered if it was possible to get a cup of decent American coffee somewhere in Italy instead of this poisonous black stuff that stripped the inside of your throat and boiled in your stomach for hours afterward.

Pendergast tossed his off, then leaned against the bar. "Can you imagine, Vincent, what the Renaissance would have been like had Michelangelo's *David* been carved in green marble?"

{ 63 }

Captain of Detectives Laura Hayward sat in the orange plas-tic chair, coffee going cold in its Styrofoam cup. She was acutely aware of being both the youngest person, and the only female, in this room full of high-ranking police officers. The walls of the conference room were painted the usual pale puce. A picture of Rudolph Giuliani decorated one wall, framed together with a picture of the Twin Towers and, below, a list of police officers killed in the attacks. No picture of the current mayor, president of the U.S., or anyone else.

Hayward liked that.

Commissioner of Police Henry Rocker sat at the head of the table, his large hand permanently closed around a huge mug of black coffee, his permanently tired face gazing down the middle of the table. To his right sat Milton Grable, captain of patrol for the precinct in which Cutforth had been murdered and the tent city erected.

Hayward checked her watch. It was 9 A.M. sharp.

"Grable?" Rocker said, opening the meeting.

Grable cleared his throat, shuffled some papers. "As

you know, Commissioner, this tent city is becoming a problem. A big problem."

The only acknowledgment of this, it seemed to Hayward, was that the dark circles under Rocker's eyes grew darker.

"We got a couple hundred people living across the street from the most exclusive neighborhood in my precinct—the whole city, in fact—and they're trashing the park, pissing in the bushes, shitting everywhere—" His eyes darted to Hayward. "Sorry, ma'am."

"It's all right, Captain," Hayward said crisply. "I'm acquainted with both the term and the bodily function."

"Right."

"Proceed," the commissioner said dryly. Hayward thought she noticed a subtle flicker of amusement in Rocker's tired eyes.

"We're getting calls up the wazoo"—another glance at Hayward—"from important people. You know who I'm referring to, sir. They're demanding, they're *screaming*, for something to be done. And they're right. These people in the park have no permit."

Hayward shifted in her chair. Her job was on the Cutforth murder, not listening to some precinct captain talk about permits.

"It isn't a political protest, a question of freedom of speech," Grable went on. "It's a bunch of religious nuts, egged on by this so-called Reverend Buck. Who, by the way, did nine years in Joliet for murder two, shot some clerk over a pack of gum."

"Is that right?" Rocker murmured. "And why not murder one?"

"Plea-bargained it down. The point I'm making, Commissioner, is that we're not dealing with a simple fanatic here. Buck's a dangerous man. And the damn *Post* is beating the drum, doing all they can to keep things stirred up. It's getting worse by the day."

Hayward knew the facts already, and she half tuned Grable out, her mind turning to D'Agosta and Italy. She realized, with a twinge she didn't fully understand, that he was overdue for a phone update. Now, there was a real cop. And where did it get him? It was guys like Grable who got the promotions—desk jockeys.

"This isn't just a precinct situation. It's a problem for the whole city." Grable laid his hands on the table, palms-up. "I want a SWAT team to go in there and bring this man out before we have a riot on our hands."

When Rocker replied, his voice was gravelly and calm. "And that's just what we're here for, Captain: to figure out a way *not* to have a riot on our hands."

"Exactly, sir."

Rocker turned to a man sitting at his left. "Wentworth?"

Hayward had no idea who this was. She'd never seen him before, and there were no insignia on his suit to indicate rank. He didn't even look like a cop.

Wentworth turned, eyes half lidded, fingers tented, and took a long, slow breath before answering.

Psychologist, thought Hayward.

"As far as this, ah, *Buck* fellow is concerned," Wentworth drawled, "he's a common-enough personality type. Without an interview, of course, it's impossible to develop a firm diagnosis. But from what I've observed, he exhibits a marked psychopathology: possibly paranoid schizophrenic, potential for a Messianic complex. There's a good chance he suffers from a delusion of persecution. This is complicated by the fact that the man is prone to violence. I would definitely *not* recommend sending in a SWAT team." He paused thoughtfully. "The others are simply followers and will respond as Buck responds: with violence or with cooperation. They will follow his lead. The key here is getting Buck out of the picture. I would suggest that the movement will collapse of its own accord once Buck is removed."

"Right," said Grable. "But how do you get him out, if not with a SWAT team?"

"If you threaten a man like Buck, he'll lash out. Violence is the language of last resort for such a man. I would suggest sending an officer or two in there—unarmed, nonthreatening, preferably female and attractive—to take him out. A gentle and nonprovocative arrest. Do it quickly, surgically. Within a day, the tent city will be gone, his followers off to the next guru, or Grateful Dead concert, or whatever they were doing before they read those articles in the *Post*." Another long exhalation. "That is my considered advice."

Hayward couldn't help rolling her eyes. Buck, a schizophrenic? His speeches, as lovingly quoted in the *Post*, showed none of the disorganized thought processes you'd expect from schizophrenia.

Rocker, who was about to pass over her, caught her expression. "Hayward? Do you have something to contribute?"

"Thank you, sir. While I agree with some of Mr. Wentworth's analysis of the situation, I disagree with his recommendation, with all due respect."

She found Wentworth's watery eyes on her, clearly pitying her ignorance. Too late, she realized she had called him "Mr." instead of "Dr." A cardinal sin among academics, and his antagonism was palpable. Well, screw him.

"There's no such thing as a nonprovocative arrest," she went on. "Any attempt to go in there and take Buck away by force—even gently—won't work. If he's crazy, then he's crazy like a fox. He'll refuse to come. As soon as the cuffs appear, your two 'preferably female and attractive' cops will find themselves in a nasty situation."

"Commissioner," Grable interrupted, "this man is openly flouting the law. I'm getting a thousand calls a day from businesses and residents on Fifth Avenue—the Sherry Netherland, the Metropolitan Club, the Plaza. The phone lines are jammed. And you can bet that if they're calling me, they're calling the mayor." He paused, letting this sink in.

"I am acutely aware they have been calling the mayor," Rocker said, his voice low and unamused.

"Then you know, sir, that we don't have the luxury of time. We've got to do something. What other options are there besides arresting this man? Does Captain Hayward have a better idea? I'd like to hear it." He leaned back, breathing hard.

Hayward spoke coolly. "Captain Grable, these businesses and residents you mention should not be allowed to push the police into a hasty and ill-considered operation." *In other words,* she thought, *they can go fuck themselves.*

"Easy for you to say from your perch in the detective

bureau. These people are in my face every day. If you had solved the Cutforth homicide, we wouldn't have this problem, *Captain*."

Hayward nodded, keeping her face neutral. Score one to Grable.

Rocker turned to her. "Speaking of that, how is the investigation proceeding, Captain?"

"There's some new forensic evidence the boys in lab coats are going over. We're still checking the people on Cutforth's call list during his last seventy-two hours. And we're reviewing the security video cams from his apartment lobby, cross-checking them against residents and known visitors. And, of course, the FBI is following up some promising leads in Italy." This was thin, and Hayward knew it sounded that way. The fact was, they didn't have squat.

"So what's *your* plan for dealing with this guy Buck?" Grable, sensing he had the upper hand, faced her belligerently.

"I would advise an even less aggressive approach. Don't push it. Don't do anything to provoke things. Instead, send someone in there to talk to Buck. Lay it out for him. He's got hundreds of people there, ruining the park and disturbing the neighborhood. He is a responsible person at heart and will naturally want to do something about that; he'll surely want to send his followers home to shave, shit, and shower. That's how I'd put it. On top of that, I'd offer Buck a deal: if he sends his followers home, we give him a parade permit. Treat him like a rational human being. All carrot, no stick. Then, as soon as they've broken camp, fence the area under the guise of reseeding. And then give them a parade permit for eight o'clock Monday morning for the far corner of Flushing Meadows Park. That will be the last you see of them."

She saw another cynical glimmer in Rocker's eye. She wondered if it indicated agreement with, or amusement at, her suggestion. Rocker had a good rep among the rank and file, but he was notoriously hard to read.

"Treat him like a rational human being?" Grable repeated. "The man's a convicted murderer."

The psychologist chuckled. Hayward glanced at him, and he returned the look. His expression had become even more condescending. She wondered if he knew something she didn't. This was all beginning to look like a foregone conclusion.

"And if your plan doesn't work?" Commissioner Rocker asked her.

"Then I would defer to, ah, Mr. Wentworth."

"That's Doc—," began Wentworth, but he was interrupted by Grable.

"Commissioner, we don't have the time to try first one plan and then another. We need to get Buck out now. Either he comes nicely or in cuffs—his choice. We do it quick, at dawn. He'll be sweating in the back of a squad car even before his followers know he's missing."

Silence. Rocker was looking around the room. There were a couple of men who hadn't spoken. "Gentlemen?"

Nods, murmurs. Everyone, it seemed, agreed with the psychologist and Grable.

"Well," said Rocker, rising. "I have to go along with the consensus. After all, we don't have a psychologist on staff only to ignore his advice." He glanced at

Hayward. She couldn't quite read his expression, but she sensed something not unsympathetic in the look.

"We'll go in with a small group, as Wentworth suggests," Rocker continued. "Just two officers. Captain Grable, you'll be the first."

Grable looked at him in surprise.

"It's your precinct, as you took pains to point out. And you're the one advocating quick action."

Grable quickly mastered his surprise. "Of course, sir. Quite right."

"And also as Wentworth suggests, we'll send in a woman." Rocker nodded to Hayward. "That would be you."

The room fell silent. Hayward saw Grable and Wentworth exchanging glances.

But Rocker was still looking directly at her. *Keep things rational for me, Hayward*, the look seemed to say.

"Buck will appreciate two ranking officers. That should appeal to his sense of importance." Rocker turned. "Grable, you've got seniority and it's your operation. I leave it to you to organize the details and timing. This meeting is adjourned."

{ 64 }

The morning after the trip to Cremona was bright and crisp, and D'Agosta squinted against the noonday sun as he accompanied Pendergast back to Piazza Santo Spirito, across the river from their hotel.

"You checked in with Captain Hayward?" Pendergast asked as they walked.

"Just before going to bed."

"Anything of interest?"

"Not really. What few leads they'd been following up on Cutforth all turned into dead ends. The security video cams at his building told them nothing. It's the same with Grove, apparently. And now, all the top New York brass are preoccupied with this preacher who's taken up residence in Central Park."

This time, D'Agosta found the piazza not nearly as quiet as before: its tranquillity was spoiled by a large group of backpackers sitting on the steps of the fountain, smoking pot and passing around a bottle of Brunello wine, talking loudly in half a dozen languages. They were accompanied by at least ten loose dogs.

"Careful where you step, Vincent," murmured

Pendergast with a wry smile. "Florence: such a marvelous mixture of high and low." He raised his hand above the piles of dogshit and gestured at the magnificent building which occupied the southeast corner. "For example, the Palazzo Guadagni. One of the finest examples of a Renaissance palace in the entire city. It was constructed in the 1400s, but the Guadagni family goes back several more centuries."

D'Agosta examined the building. The first story was built in rough blocks of dun-colored limestone, while the upper floors were covered in yellow stucco. Most of the top floor was a loggia: a roofed portico supported by stone columns. The structure was restrained but elegant.

"There are various offices and apartments on the second floor, a language school on the third. And the top floor is a *pensione*, run by a Signora Donatelli. That, without doubt, is where Beckmann and the rest met back in 1974."

"Does this woman own the palazzo?"

"She does. The last descendant of the Guadagni."

"You really think she'll remember a couple of college students who visited three decades ago?"

"One can only try, Vincent."

They picked their way gingerly across the piazza and through an enormous pair of iron-studded wooden doors. A once-grand but now grimy vaulted passageway led to a stairway and a second-floor landing. Here, a shabby piece of cardboard had been hung on the cornice of a faded Baroque fresco. A hand-drawn arrow and the word *Reception* had been scrawled on the cardboard with a firm hand.

The reception room was incongruously small for such a giant palace: cluttered yet neat as a pin, bisected by a wooden transom, a battered set of wooden mail slots on one side and a rack of keys on the other. The room had only one occupant: a tiny old lady sitting behind an ancient desk. She was dressed with extraordinary elegance, her hair perfectly dyed and coiffed, red lipstick impeccably applied, with what looked like real diamonds draped around her neck and dangling from withered ears.

She rose and Pendergast bowed.

"Molto lieto di conoscerla, signora."

The woman responded crisply, *"Il piacere è mio."* Then she continued in accented English. "Obviously, you are not here to take a room."

"No," said Pendergast. He removed his ID, offered it to her.

"You are policemen."

"Yes."

"What is it that you want? My time is limited." The voice was sharp and intimidating.

"In the fall of 1974, I believe, several American students stayed here. Here is a picture of them." Pendergast took out Beckmann's photo.

She did not look at it. "Do you have the names?"

"Yes."

"Then come with me." And she turned and walked around the transom, through a back door, and into a much larger room. D'Agosta saw it was an old library of sorts, with bound books, manuscripts, and vellum documents filling shelves from floor to ceiling. It smelled of parchment and dry rot, old leather and wax.

The ceiling was coffered and had once been elaborately gilded. Now it was crumbling with age, the wood riddled with holes.

"The archives of the family," she said. "They go back eight centuries."

"You keep good records."

"I keep *excellent* records, thank you." She made a beeline to a low shelf at the far end of the room, selected a massive register, carried it to a center table. She opened the register, revealing page after page of accounts, payments, names, and dates, written in a fanatical, tiny hand.

"Names?"

"Bullard, Cutforth, Beckmann, and Grove."

She began flipping pages, scanning each with tremendous rapidity, each flip sending up a faint cloud of dust. Suddenly, she stopped.

"There. Grove." A bony finger, burdened with a huge diamond ring, pointed to the name. Then it slid down the rest of the page.

"Beckmann... Cutforth... Bullard. Yes, they were all here in October."

Pendergast peered at the register, but even he was clearly having trouble deciphering the minuscule hand.

"Did their visits overlap?"

"Yes." A pause. "According to this, one night only, that of October 31."

She closed the book with a snap. "Anything else, *signore*?"

"Yes, *signora*. Will you do me the courtesy of looking at this photograph?"

"Surely you don't expect me to remember some

slovenly American students from thirty years ago? I am ninety-two, sir. I have earned the privilege of forgetting."

"I beg your indulgence."

Sighing with impatience, she took the photograph, looked at it—and visibly started. She stared a long time, what little color there was in her face slowly disappearing. Then she handed the photograph back to Pendergast.

"As it happens," she said in a low tone, "I do remember. *That* one." She pointed to Beckmann. "Let me see. Something terrible happened. He and some other boys, probably those others in the photograph, went off somewhere together. They were gone all night. He came back and was terribly upset. I had to get a priest for him..."

She paused, her voice trailing off. Gone was the crisp confidence, the unshakable sense of self.

"It was the night before All Saints' Day. He came back from a night of carousing, and he was in a bad state. I took him to church."

"What church?"

"The one right here, Santo Spirito. I remember him panicked and begging to go to confession. It was long ago, yet it was such a strange occurrence it stuck in my mind. That, and the expression on the poor boy's face. He was begging for a priest as if his life depended on it."

"And?"

"He went to confession and right afterwards he packed up his belongings and left."

"And the other American students?"

"I don't recall. Every year they celebrate All Saints' Day, or rather the day before, which I believe you call Halloween. It's an excuse to drink."

"Do you know where they went that evening, or who they might have encountered?"

"I know nothing more than what I have told you."

The ring of a bell came from the front office. "I have guests to attend to," she said.

"One last question, *signora,* if you please," Pendergast said. "The priest who heard the confession—is he still alive?"

"That would have been Father Zenobi. Yes, Father Zenobi. He is now living with the monks of La Verna."

She turned, then paused and slowly glanced back. "But if you think you can persuade him to break the sacred seal of the confessional, sir, you are sadly mistaken."

{ 65 }

D'Agosta assumed that, upon leaving the palazzo, they would return directly to their hotel. But instead, Pendergast lingered in the piazza: strolling, hands in his pockets, eyes glancing first left, then right. After a few minutes, he turned to D'Agosta.

"Gelato? Some of the best in Florence, if I am not mistaken, can be found right here at Café Ricchi."

"I've given up on ice cream."

"I haven't. Indulge me."

They entered the café and approached the bar. Pendergast ordered his cone—tiramisu and *crème anglaise*—while D'Agosta asked for an espresso.

"I didn't know you had a sweet tooth," D'Agosta said as they leaned against the bar.

"I have something of a weakness for gelato. But our main reason for stopping here is to learn his intentions."

"*His* intentions? Whose intentions?"

"The man who's following us."

D'Agosta straightened up. "What?"

"No—don't look. He's nondescript, mid-thirties, wearing a blue shirt and dark pants. Quite professional."

Pendergast's cone arrived and he took a dainty bite. Then, suddenly, a change came over his face.

"He's just entered the *pensione*," he said. Abandoning his gelato, Pendergast dropped a few euros on the counter and strode out of the café, D'Agosta following.

"Are you afraid for the *signora*?"

"The *signora* is perfectly safe. It's the priest for whom I fear."

"The priest—?" Suddenly, D'Agosta understood. "Then we can stop this guy when he leaves the *pensione*."

"That would serve no purpose but to embroil us in endless legalities. Our best chance is the monastery itself. Come, Vincent: we haven't a moment to lose."

In twenty minutes, they were driving through the hills northeast of Florence, Pendergast at the wheel of their rented Fiat. Although D'Agosta had done more than his share of high-speed driving—and though Pendergast was clearly an expert—D'Agosta's heart was beating at an uncomfortable rate. The car was squealing around a series of hairpin curves, none of which had guardrails, at a terrifying clip. With each climbing turn, a rising sea of mountains swam into view before them: the great spine of the Apennines.

"I've been aware of surveillance for some time now," Pendergast said. "Since we found Bullard's body, and perhaps even before. At important moments—such as our trip to Cremona—I've managed to keep him at arm's length. I haven't yet confronted our shadower, hoping instead to learn who's behind him. I did not think he would take such a direct approach as he did just now in the piazza. It means we are getting close to the truth. It also means increased danger, for us and for those with crucial information—such as Father Zenobi."

The car squealed around another curve. D'Agosta braced himself against the lateral g-forces, sweat breaking out on his brow.

"I've seen you weasel information out of all kinds of people," he said when it was safe to draw breath again. "But if you can convince a priest to reveal a thirty-year-old confession, I'll swim all the way back to Southampton."

Another long, screeching turn, the car hanging practically over the edge of a chasm.

This time, D'Agosta almost had to pry his fingers from the dashboard. "Do you think we might slow down?"

"I don't think so." And Pendergast nodded over his shoulder.

The car made another semicontrolled skid around a corner, and as D'Agosta fell against the passenger window he got a terrifying glimpse back down the mountainside. About three switchbacks below he could see a motorcycle, black and chrome, its angular chassis exposed and gleaming. It was approaching fast.

"There's a motorcycle on our tail!" he said.

Pendergast nodded. "A Ducati Monster, S4R model, if I'm not mistaken. A four-valve twin, well over a hundred horsepower, light but very powerful."

D'Agosta glanced back again. The rider was dressed in red leather, wearing a helmet with a smoked visor.

"The man from the plaza?" he asked.

"Either him or somebody allied with him."

"He's after us?"

"No. He's after the priest."

"We sure as hell can't outrun him."

"We can slow him down. Get out your weapon."

"And do what?"

"I'll leave that to your discretion."

Now D'Agosta could hear the high-pitched whine of an engine in high gear, approaching from behind. They tore around another corner, scattering clouds of dust as the Fiat slewed, first right, then left. But already the motorcycle was biting into the same corner, leaning at an incredible angle, almost pegging the road. The rider straightened quickly and began closing the gap, preparing to pass.

"Hang on, Vincent."

The car swerved into the left lane just as the motorcycle came alongside, then swerved back with a shriek of rubber, cutting him off. D'Agosta looked back and saw the motorcyclist dropping back, preparing to make another run past them.

"He's coming on the right!" he shouted.

At the last minute, Pendergast jerked the car to the left again, correctly anticipating a feint; there was a screech of tires behind them as the motorcyclist dumped his rear brake and the bike rose in a reverse wheelie. The rider straightened, recovered. D'Agosta saw him reach into his jacket.

"He's got a gun!"

D'Agosta planted himself against the passenger door and waited, his own weapon at the ready. He doubted that a man on a motorcycle, going eighty miles an hour on a winding mountain road, could fire with any accuracy—but he wasn't going to take any chances.

With a burst of speed, the motorcycle closed again, the gun leveling, steadying. D'Agosta aimed his weapon.

"Wait until he fires," Pendergast murmured.

There was a bang and a blue puff, instantly whisked away; a simultaneous thump; and the back window went abruptly opaque, a web of cracks running away from a perfect 9mm hole. An instant later Pendergast braked with terrifying suddenness, throwing D'Agosta forward against the seat belt, then swerved and accelerated again.

D'Agosta unbuckled the seat belt, jumped into the backseat, kicked away the sagging rear window, steadied his gun, and fired. The cyclist swerved and dropped back behind a curve, kicking his way down through the gears.

"The bastard—!"

The car slid into the next corner, fishtailing on loose gravel and sliding perilously close to the cliff edge. D'Agosta knelt in the rear seat, hardly daring to breathe, aiming through the ruined window, ready to fire as soon as the motorcycle reappeared. As they ripped around another hillside, he saw the Ducati flash into view about a hundred yards back.

Pendergast downshifted, the engine screaming with the effort, the rpm needle redlining. The car went into another long, sickening turn.

As they accelerated out of the curve, the road emerged onto a shoulder of a mountain, heading straight through a long, dark forest of pine trees, tunneling into shade. A sign flashed past: *Chiusi della Verna 13km.* Keeping watch on their rear, D'Agosta could see a whirlwind of dancing pine needles thrown up by their passage.

...And there came the Ducati, swinging around the curve. D'Agosta aimed but it was an impossible shot, two hundred yards back from a moving car. He sat, awaiting his chance.

With a piercing whine, the motorcycle came surging forward, screaming into fifth, then sixth gear, approaching at ever-increasing speed. The man had put away his gun, and both his gloved hands were on the handlebars, his head lowered.

"He's going to try another run past us."

"No doubt." Pendergast stayed in the center of the road, accelerator floored.

But the car was no match for the Ducati. It came straight up behind them, accelerating all the way. *The thing must top out at a hundred and eighty*, D'Agosta thought. He knew it would try to turn and dart past them at the last moment, and there would be no way for Pendergast to guess if the rider would veer to the right or the left. He steadied his gun. He had vastly improved his shooting from many sessions at the 27th Precinct range, but with the vibration, the motion of the car, the motion of the bike—it was going to be tough. The bike was going at least twice their speed now, coming up on them fast...

D'Agosta squeezed off a shot, aiming low at the machine, and missed.

The car made a violent motion to the right as the bike came blasting past on the left—dual silencers flashing, rider leaning so far forward he seemed draped over the front fork—and was gone around the next curve.

"I lost that coin toss," Pendergast said dryly.

They were now approaching the curve themselves, their speed beyond any possibility of controlling the turn. Pendergast braked hard while simultaneously jamming on the gas pedal and twisting the wheel left. The car spun violently around, twice, perhaps three times—D'Agosta was too shaken to be sure—before coming to rest on the very edge of the cliff.

They paused just a moment, the acrid smell of burned brake pads wafting over the car.

"Fiat, for all its troubles, still knows how to make a decent vehicle," said Pendergast.

"Eurocar isn't going to like this," D'Agosta replied.

Pendergast jammed on the gas, and the car screeched back onto the road, accelerating into the next turn.

They tore through the fir forest once again before mounting another series of steep switchbacks, worse than the last. D'Agosta felt his stomach begin to rise uncomfortably. He allowed himself a single glance out over the edge. Far below—very, very far below—he could see the Casentino Valley, dotted with fields and villages. He looked quickly away.

Turn after turn they mounted, Pendergast driving in grim silence. D'Agosta reloaded and checked his gun: it beat looking out the window. Suddenly houses flashed past, and they whipped through the town of Chiusi della Verna, Pendergast leaning on the horn, pedestrians jumping into the doorway of a shop in terror as the car blasted by, clipping the side-view mirror from a parked van and sending it bouncing and rolling down the street. Just past town was another faded sign: *Santuario della Verna 6km.*

The road climbed steadily through a steep forest, one brutally sharp turn after another. And then suddenly they emerged from the trees into a meadow, and there—directly ahead but still a thousand feet above them—stood the monastery of La Verna: a great tangle of ancient stone, perched on a crag that seemed to hang over open space. It was windowless, so old and vast and scarred by time it looked a part of the cliff face itself. Despite everything, D'Agosta felt a chill go down his spine; he knew from Sunday school that this was perhaps the holiest Christian monastery in the world, built in 1224 by St. Francis himself.

The car blasted back into the forest and the monastery disappeared from view. "Have we got a chance?" D'Agosta asked.

"It depends on how quickly our man finds Father Zenobi. The monastery is a big place. If only they had a phone!"

The car careened around another turn. D'Agosta could hear a bell ringing, the faint sound of chanting floating toward him over the noise of the engine.

"I think the monks are at prayer," he said. He glanced at his watch. It would be the service of Sext: sixth hour of the Opus Dei.

"Yes. Most unfortunate." Pendergast pushed the car around the final bend, wheels slipping on ancient, mossy cobbles instead of asphalt.

The cobbled road—clearly never built to be driven upon—led up behind the monastery. There, at the stone archway leading through the outer wall of the monastery into a massive cloister, D'Agosta saw the Ducati lying on its tubular frame, fat rear wheel still spinning lazily.

Pendergast slewed to a stop and was out, gun drawn, even before the car was completely at rest. D'Agosta followed hard on his heels. They ran past the bike, across a stone bridge, and into the cloisters. A large chapel stood to the right, its doors wide, the vigorous sounds of plainchant rising and falling on the cool breeze. As they ran, the chanting seemed to hesitate, then die away in a ragged confusion.

They rushed into the church just in time to see the figure in red leather—his arm extended, rigid—fire point-blank into an old monk, who was kneeling, his hands raised in surprise or prayer. The report of the gun was shockingly loud in the confined space, reverberating even as the notes of the plainsong died away. D'Agosta shouted out in dismay, rage, and horror as the priest fell and the shooter raised his gun, execution style, taking careful aim for a second shot.

{ 66 }

In the predawn light, Hayward stood with Captain Grable on a rocky point just north of the Central Park Arsenal. From here, they commanded a good view of the tent city, still slumbering in the quiet morning air. They'd been briefed on the location of Wayne Buck's tent, and she could make it out clearly: a large green canvas job in the heart of the encampment.

Hayward's misgivings increased. This was no clean shot, in and out. The makeshift city had grown much larger than she realized: there had to be three hundred tents, maybe more, scattered through the foliage. And the landscape wouldn't help: deep green swales and leafy hollows, surrounded by grassy hummocks, their sides frequently exposing long swaths of dark gray rock. Through the thicket of tree branches, she could just make out—parked along Fifth—the cop car that would take Buck away. It was idling on the park side of the avenue, right opposite the entrance to Cutforth's building.

Fact was, this was just about the last place she wanted to be at the moment. By rights she should be pursuing the Cutforth murder. She shouldn't be out here—not anymore, not when there was an open homicide to be worked. It felt too much like the bad old days when she was a rouster for the transit police.

She glanced at Grable. She had talked to D'Agosta the night before, briefly, and now she wished he was here. There was a guy you could count on. As for Grable—

Grable adjusted his tie, squared his shoulders. "Let's circle around and come in from the west." He was sweating, his shirt plastered to his chest despite the cool morning.

Hayward nodded. "As I see it, the key here is *speed.* We don't want to be caught in there."

Grable swallowed, hiked up his belt. "Captain, unlike some in the force, I didn't waste my time in the classroom piling up degrees. I came up through the rank and file. I know what I'm doing."

There was a long moment while Grable looked down on the slumbering tent city. Hayward glanced at her watch. The light was coming up moment by moment, and the sun would rise within minutes. Why the hell was Grable waiting?

"We're running a little late, if you don't mind me saying so," she said.

"I don't operate on a timetable, Captain."

Hayward tried to suppress her misgivings. This was Grable's operation—Rocker had made that clear—and she was to follow his lead. Going in with a bad attitude wasn't going to do any good. And the plan might work. Hell, it *would* work if they could just get in and out fast enough, drag Buck to the waiting squad car before he'd even managed to wake up. *It could work*, she told herself, *as long as Grable moves fast. If you're going to arrest someone, you do it. You don't give them time to think about it first.* She glanced at Grable again, wondering why he was taking so long.

"Right," said Grable, noticing the glance. "Let's go."

They cut west through the low trees and brushy undergrowth, circling the flank of the tent city, sticking close to one side of a shallow defile. Soon they reached what looked like a herd path leading directly into the makeshift community. They were downwind now, and the odor of raw sewage and unwashed humanity hit Hayward hard.

Grable quickened his pace as they approached the fringes. A few people were already up, some cooking on little backpacking stoves, others wandering around.

Grable hesitated just inside the ragged outer ring of tents. Then he nodded brusquely to Hayward and they started forward again. Hayward nodded in a friendly way to those who were up and watching them pass. The ground flattened and the tents huddled closer together, forming narrow lanes and alleys. In a few minutes they had arrived at the center clearing around Buck's tent.

So far, so good, thought Hayward.

The front flap was tied on two side posts. Grable stopped before the entrance and called in a loud voice: "Buck? This is Captain Grable of the NYPD."

"Hey!" A tall, clean-cut fellow appeared out of nowhere. "What are you doing?"

"None of your business," said Grable brusquely.

Shit, thought Hayward. *Not like that.*

"There's no problem," she said. "We're just here to talk to the reverend."

"Yeah? What about?"

"Back off, pal," said Grable.

"What is it?" came a muffled voice from inside the tent. "Who's there?"

"Captain Grable, NYPD." Grable began untying the knotted drawstring that held the flap shut against one of the side poles. He had it almost undone when a hand reached from inside, closed over his, and removed it. The flap lifted and then Buck stood there, straight and stern. "This is my home," he said coldly and with dignity. "Do not violate it."

Cuff him, Hayward thought. *Cuff the son of a bitch and get the hell out.*

"We're New York City police officers, and this is public land. This isn't some private dwelling."

"Sir, I ask you once again to stand back from my home."

Hayward was astonished by the man's presence. She turned to see how Grable was going to handle it. She was shocked to see his face paling beneath the sheen of sweat.

"Wayne Buck, you are under arrest." Grable tried to unclip his handcuffs, but his hands were shaking slightly and it took longer than it should have.

Hayward couldn't believe it. Grable was out of his depth. That was the only answer. He'd ridden a desk so long he'd lost his street smarts—if he ever had them—and he'd forgotten how to deal with a fluid situation like this. That explained his hesitation back at the arsenal, his sweating, everything. He'd wanted the commissioner to send in a large party to deal with Buck, but when Rocker had given the job directly to him, he couldn't refuse. Now, with no SWAT team to back him up, confronted by the implacable Buck, he was losing his nerve.

Buck stared, making no move to cooperate, but not doing anything to resist, either.

The clean-cut man, who seemed to be Buck's bodyguard or aide-de-camp, turned, cupped his hands, and cried out in a tremendous voice, *"Arise! Arise! The cops are here to arrest the reverend!"*

There was a stirring, a sudden murmur of voices.

"Turn around and place your hands behind your back, sir," said Grable, but his voice was trembling.

Still Buck made no move.

"Arise!"

"Captain," said Hayward, her voice low, "he's resisting arrest. *Cuff him.*"

But Grable made no move.

In an instant, Hayward sized up the situation and realized their window of opportunity had already closed. Looking around, she recalled the time when—as a kid on a dare—she'd poked a stick into a hornet's nest. There was a moment, just a moment, of suspension...then a muffled hum just before the hornets came boiling out, madder than hell. That's what the tent city felt like. People were up but not yet out of their tents, a dull hum of activity that was about to explode.

"Defend the reverend! The police are here to arrest him! Arise!"

Now came the boiling. Suddenly, hundreds of people were up and out of their tents, pulling on shirts, moving toward them.

Hayward leaned in toward Grable. "Captain? We got trouble. Just be cool."

Grable's mouth sagged but no sound came out.

The crowd was pressing in, a wall of people quickly

forming at the front, others streaming in from every direction, ringing the tent, a babble of angry voices.

Shit. She turned to face the crowd. "Look, friends, we're not here to cause trouble."

"Liar!"

The cry went up. "*Blasphemers!*"

They pressed in. Buck said nothing, did nothing; he just stood there, the picture of dignity.

"Look," said Hayward, holding out her hands, keeping her voice calm, "there's just the two of us. Nothing to get excited about."

"Godless soldiers of Rome!"

"Keep your filthy hands off the reverend!"

This was even uglier than she thought. Grable was backing up instinctively, eyes roaming for an escape route that did not exist.

The crowd surged forward, growing angrier.

"Touch either one of us and it's assault," Hayward said, loudly but calmly.

This paused the front of the crowd; but with others behind pressing forward, it was only a matter of time before they were overwhelmed.

Grable dropped the handcuffs and went for his gun.

"Grable, *no*!" Hayward yelled.

Immediately, a roar went up. *"He's going to shoot! Murderer! Judas!"* The front wall surged forward.

Whang! went the gun into the air, the reaction to the sudden sound rippling through the crowd. And in that instant, Buck, standing only a few feet behind Grable, knocked the gun from his hand with one swift, sure motion.

Thank God, thought Hayward, keeping her hands in

sight and well away from her own piece. Something had to be done right away, or they were toast. She turned and spoke to Buck. "You better do something, Reverend. It's all in your hands."

Buck stepped forward, raising his hands. There was silence from the crowd, an instant stillness.

He let a moment pass, and then slowly lowered his arm and aimed a steady finger at Grable. "This man came here under the cloak of the Prince of Darkness to arrest me. But God has exposed his deceit."

Grable appeared speechless.

"These centurions, these soldiers of Rome, entered our encampment like skulking snakes, on the devil's own errand. And they have been defeated by their own shame and cowardice."

"Shame, cowards!"

Hayward took advantage of a lull to speak quietly to Buck. "We'd like to go now."

Another roar erupted from the crowd. *"Shame!"*

A stick flew out of the crowd, landing in the dust by their feet. She could see others being brandished above the crowd. People on the fringes had begun to hunt among the shrubbery for rocks.

Hayward leaned forward, speaking again in a low voice she hoped only Buck could hear. "Reverend Buck? What's going to happen to you and your followers if we get injured? Or taken hostage? How do you think the NYPD will react to that?" She smiled coldly. "It'll make Waco look like a Sunday barbecue."

There was a moment of silence. Then, not even acknowledging he'd heard, Buck raised his hands again and bowed his head. Once more a silence immediately fell.

"My people," he said. "My people. We are Christians. They may come with malice, but we must show them compassion and forgiveness." He turned to his aide-de-camp. "Open a way for the unclean ones, Todd. Let them go in peace."

Slowly, the sticks were lowered. A lane appeared amidst the shuffling throng. Hayward bent forward, face burning; picked up Grable's gun, tucked it into her belt. She turned away only to realize Grable wasn't following. He was still rooted in place.

"You coming, *Captain*?"

He started, looked around, then walked past without looking at her. After a moment, he broke into a trot. A great cheer rose up from the crowd. Hayward followed at a dignified walk, eyes straight ahead, struggling not to betray in any way—through expression, posture, voice—that she was enduring the worst humiliation of her entire career.

{ 67 }

A GUNSHOT, TERRIBLY LOUD, SOUNDED IN D'AGOSTA'S EAR. IT WAS Pendergast, firing over the heads of the crowd.

The assassin turned and saw them approaching. He glanced back down at the crumpled figure at his feet, looked quickly around him, then turned and fled. Monks in brown robes were clustered around their fallen brother, some praying, others crying out and gesticulating.

A number of monks were pointing to the back of the church. *"Da questa parte! È scappato di là!"*

Pendergast shot them a glance. "Vincent, after him!" He had his cell phone out and was already calling for a medevac helicopter.

A monk leaped up and grasped D'Agosta's arm. "I help you," he said in broken English. "Follow me."

They ran together through a door to the right of the altar; down a dark passageway and into an inner cloister; then across its courtyard and through a second stone passageway that abruptly terminated in the cliff face itself. Here they stopped. A lateral passage crossed their path, arches and pillars carved out of the living stone.

"He went this way." The monk turned and raced down the ancient, frescoed corridor. There was an iron door at its end, hanging ajar, and the monk threw it wide. Sunlight flooded the dark passage. D'Agosta followed the monk through the doorway and into open air. A dizzying stone staircase fell away below them, carved directly into the cliff face, no protection from a breathtaking drop save for a rotten iron railing.

D'Agosta leaned away from the cliff face, glanced over the railing. For a moment, vertigo overwhelmed him. Then he glimpsed the red-suited figure below, scrambling down the stone pathway.

"Eccolo!" The monk resumed the chase, robes flapping behind him. D'Agosta followed as quickly as he dared: the stairs were so polished by time, so damp with humidity, they felt as slippery as ice. The staircase was old and disused, so eroded in places they had to step over yawning blue space.

"You know where he's headed?" D'Agosta asked between gasps.

"To the forest below."

The stairway leveled off briefly, and they moved slowly over another gap. The iron railing had rotted away at this spot, and rough handholds were their only protection. A stiff, cold wind buffeted them.

A shot rang out from below. The monk slipped, clutched at a handhold, scrambled to regain his balance. D'Agosta pressed himself against the rock face. He was completely exposed, unable to help, unable even to move forward. With both hands clutching the rock he could not even unholster his gun.

Another shot rang out. D'Agosta felt a spray of rock

slash his face. Glancing down, he could make out the killer a hundred yards farther down the stairway, pointing his handgun directly at them.

There was no help for it: he couldn't just stand here, waiting to get shot. D'Agosta let go with one hand, desperately bracing himself against the cliff edge with his feet and his knees, and drew out his gun. Aiming as best he could, he fired once, twice.

Two close shots, missing by inches. The man gave a cry and ducked out of sight below. Meanwhile, the monk had recovered and moved on to a safer spot. D'Agosta felt himself slipping; he was going to have to drop his gun.

"A me!" said the monk.

D'Agosta tossed him the Glock, which the monk deftly caught. Then he pulled himself back into position and leaped over the gap. Just as he got to the far side, another shot rang out.

"Down!"

They crouched on the stone walkway, in the feeble cover of a small projecting rock. Another shot, another spray of rock.

Christ, thought D'Agosta, *we're pinned.* Unable to move forward, unable to go back. He would have to return fire again.

The monk handed him his gun.

D'Agosta slid out the magazine, checked it. Eight rounds left. He slapped it back in place.

"When I shoot, you go. *Capisci?*"

The monk nodded.

In one motion, D'Agosta rose, aimed, squeezed off a string of suppressing fire, just clipping the top of the rock behind which the shooter was crouching, keeping him down, unable to fire. The monk scrambled across the open section of trail, finding good cover at the far end where the pathway once again began to descend a crude staircase.

Magazine spent, D'Agosta ducked back behind the rocky projection. He slapped in his spare magazine, then ran across the open area until he reached the monk and the safety of the staircase, pausing to peer over a rocky wall. The shooter was nowhere to be seen.

Quickly, he rose and resumed the pursuit, the monk at his heels. Down and down they descended until, quite suddenly, they reached the bottom. There was a small vineyard here at the base of the cliff. Beyond rose a dense wall of forest.

"Which way?" D'Agosta asked.

The monk shrugged. "He is gone."

"No. We'll follow him into the forest."

D'Agosta took off again, half crouching, down the row of vines toward the trees. Within moments, they were inside the forest, the cathedral-like trunks surrounding them, silent and smelling of resin and cold, stretching ahead into darkness. D'Agosta scanned the ground, but there was no indication of footsteps in the thick bed of pine needles.

"Do you have any idea which way he went?" he asked.

"Not possible to know. Need dogs."

"Does the monastery have dogs?"

"No."

"We can call the police."

The monk shrugged again. "Takes time. For dogs, two, three days maybe."

D'Agosta looked back into the endless forest. "Shit."

Back at the chapel, the scene remained one of confusion. Pendergast was bending over the prostrate form of the monk, applying heart massage and artificial respiration. Several of the monks were kneeling in a half-circle, apparently led by the head of the order; others were standing well back, murmuring in low, shocked tones. As D'Agosta walked across the chapel, utterly winded, he could hear the distant beat of a chopper.

He knelt and took the old priest's frail hand. The man's eyes were closed, his face gray. In the background, the steady murmur of prayers continued, soothing in its measured cadence.

"I think he's suffered a heart attack," Pendergast said, pressing down on the man's chest. "The trauma of the gunshot wound. Still, with the medevac arriving, he might be saved."

Suddenly the monk coughed. A hand fluttered and his eyes opened, staring directly at Pendergast.

"Padre," said Pendergast, his voice low and calm, *"mi dica la confessione più terribile che lei ha mai sentito."*

The eyes, so wise and so close to death, seemed to understand all. *"Un ragazzo Americano che ha fatto un patto con il diavolo, ma l'ho salvato, l'ho sicuramente salvato."* He sighed, smiled, then closed his eyes and took one long, final, shuddering breath.

A moment later the paramedics burst in with a transport stretcher. There was an eruption of furious activity as they worked to stabilize the victim: one attached a cardiac monitor while another relayed the lack of vitals to the hospital and received orders in return. The stretcher was rushed back out the door, and within seconds the sound of the helicopter was receding again. And then it was over. The church seemed suddenly empty, the smell of incense drifting on the air, the steady sound of prayer adding a curious note of peace to a most shocking act of violence.

"He got away," D'Agosta gasped.

Pendergast laid a hand on his arm. "I'm sorry, Vincent."

"What did you say to the priest just now?"

Pendergast hesitated a moment. "I asked him to recall the most terrible confession he'd ever heard. He said it was from a boy—an American boy—who had made a pact with the devil."

D'Agosta felt revulsion constrict his stomach. So it was true, after all. It was really true.

"He added that he had certainly saved the boy's soul. In fact, he *knew* he'd saved his soul."

D'Agosta had to sit down. He hung his head a moment, still breathing hard, and then looked up at Pendergast. "Yeah. But what about the other three?"

{ 68 }

The Reverend Buck sat at the desk inside his tent, the beams of bright morning sun slanting through the door net and setting the canvas walls ablaze. Everybody in camp was still keyed up from the showdown with the police, still abuzz with energy. Buck could feel that same energy coursing through his being. The passion and belief of his followers had astonished, had heartened him. Clearly, the spirit of God was among them. With God, anything was possible.

The problem was, the police would not rest. They would act decisively, and act soon. His moment was about to arrive: the moment he had come so far, worked so hard, to fulfill.

But *what* moment? And how, exactly, would he fulfill it?

The question had been growing within him, gnawing at him, for days now. At first, it had been just a faint voice, a sense of disquiet. But now it never left him, despite his praying and fasting and penitence. God's path was unclear, His wishes mysterious.

Yet again he bowed his head in prayer, asking God to show him the way.

Outside, in the background, he could hear the excited hum of a hundred conversations. He paused to listen. Everybody was talking about the aborted attempt to arrest him. Strange that the police had sent in only two. They probably didn't want to make a show of aggression, have a Waco on their hands.

Waco. That little aside from the woman cop had sobered him up. It had been almost like a surgical thrust. She was something, that one. Couldn't be more than thirty-five, a real looker, self-assured as anything. The other was just another weak, vainglorious bully, like any number of the screws he'd dealt with in the Big House. But she—*she* had the confidence, the power, of the devil behind her.

Should he resist, put up a fight? He had tremendous power in his hands, hundreds of followers who believed in him heart and soul. He had the power of conviction and the Spirit, but they had the power of physical arms. They had the might of the state behind them. They had weapons, tear gas, water cannon. If he resisted, it would be a butchery.

What did God want him to do? He bowed, prayed again.

There was a knock on one of the wooden posts of the tent.

"Yes?"

"It's almost time for your morning sermon and the laying-on of hands."

"Thank you, Todd. I'll be out in a few minutes."

He needed an answer, if only for himself, before he

could face his people once again. They relied on him for spiritual guidance in this greatest crisis of all. He was so proud of them, of their bravery and conviction. "Soldiers of Rome," they'd shouted so aptly at the cops...

Soldiers of Rome—*that was it.*

Suddenly, like the cogs of some vast spiritual machine, a series of connections fell together like dominoes in his mind. *Pilate. Herod. Golgotha.* It had been there all the time, the answer he'd been searching for. He'd just needed the strength of faith to find it.

He knelt a moment longer. "Thank you, Father," he murmured. Then he rose, feeling suffused with light.

Now he knew exactly how he would face the armies of Rome.

He armed aside the tent flap and strode toward the preaching rock. He glanced around at the beauty of the morning, the beauty of God's earth. Life was so precious, such a fleeting gift. As he climbed the path that circled behind the rock, he reminded himself that the next world would be far better, far more beautiful. When the infidels came, a thousand strong, he knew exactly how he was going to deliver them unto defeat.

He raised his hands to a thunderous cheer.

{ 69 }

The cellar of the carabinieri barracks looked more like the dungeon it had once been than a basement, and as D'Agosta followed Colonnello Esposito and Pendergast through the winding tunnels of undressed stone, streaked with cobwebs and lime, he was half surprised to find no skeletons chained to the walls.

The *colonnello* paused at an iron door, opened it. "As you'll see, alas, we have yet to join the twenty-first century," he said as he gestured for them to enter.

D'Agosta stepped into a room wall-to-wall with filing cabinets and open shelves. Fascicles of documents sat on the shelves, tied up in twine. Some were so old and moldy they must have dated back centuries. An officer in a neat uniform of blue and white, with a smart red stripe down the outside of the slacks, stood and saluted crisply.

"Basta," said the *colonnello* in a tired voice, then gestured at some old wooden chairs arranged around a long table. "Please sit."

As they seated themselves, the *colonnello* spoke to the younger officer, who in turn produced a dozen folders and laid them on the table. "Here are the summaries of the homicides that fell within your requirements: unsolved murders over the last year in which the victim was found burned. I have been through them myself and found nothing of the slightest interest. I am much more concerned about what happened up at La Verna this morning."

Pendergast took the first folder, opened it, slid out the case summary. "I regret that more than I can say."

"I regret it even more. Things were tranquil here until you arrived—and then..." He opened his hands and smiled wanly.

"We are almost there, Colonnello."

"Then let us pray you get there, wherever 'there' may be, as soon as possible."

Pendergast began reading through the case summaries, passing each to D'Agosta as he completed it. The only sound was the gentle whisper of forced air, carried into the basement by shiny aluminum ducts that snaked along the vaulted ceilings in a futile attempt to bring fresh air into these depths. D'Agosta looked at each case and its associated photograph, struggling to comprehend the Italian, able to get the gist but no more. Occasionally he jotted down a note—more to have something to report to Hayward on their next call than for his own recollection.

In less than an hour, they'd gone through them all.

Pendergast turned to D'Agosta. "Anything?"

"Nothing stood out."

"Let us take a second pass."

The *colonnello* glanced at his watch, lit a cigarette.

"There's no need for you to stay," said Pendergast.

Esposito waved his hand. "I am quite content to be buried down here, out of reach, my cell phone dead. It is not so pleasant upstairs, with the Procuratore della Repubblica calling every half hour—thanks again, I fear, to you." He looked around. "All that's lacking is an espresso machine." He turned to the officer. *"Caffè per tutti."*

"Sissignore."

D'Agosta heaved a sigh and began leafing again through the barely comprehensible files. This time he paused at a black-and-white photo of a man lying in what looked like an abandoned building. The corpse lay curled in a cracked cement corner, very badly burned. It was a typical police photo, sordid, vile.

But there was something else. Something wrong.

Pendergast instantly detected his interest. "Yes?"

D'Agosta slid the photo over. Pendergast scrutinized it for a few seconds. Then his eyebrows shot up. "Yes, I do see."

"What is it?" asked the *colonnello*, reluctantly leaning forward.

"This man. You see the small pool of blood there, underneath him? He was burned *and then* shot."

"And so?"

"Usually victims are shot, then burned, to conceal evidence. Have you ever heard of burning a man first and then shooting him?"

"Frequently. To extract information."

"Not over half the body. Torture burning is localized."

Esposito peered at the photo. "That means nothing. A maniac, perhaps."

"May we see the complete file?"

The *colonnello* shrugged, rose, shuffled to a distant cabinet, then returned with a fat bundle of documents. He put it on the table, cut the twine with his pocketknife.

Pendergast looked through the documents, pulled one out, began to summarize in English: "Carlo Vanni, aged sixty-nine, retired farmer, body found in a ruined *casa colonica* in the mountains near Abetone. There was no physical evidence recovered at the site, no fingerprints, fibers, shell casings, prints, tracks." He glanced up. "This does not look like the work of a maniac to me."

A slow smile gathered on the *colonnello*'s face. "Even among the carabinieri, incompetence has been known to occur. Just because no evidence was recovered does not mean there *was* no evidence to recover."

Pendergast flipped the page. "A single shot to the heart. And what's this? Some droplets of molten aluminum recovered by the *medico legale*, burned deep into the man's flesh."

He flipped another page.

"Now, this is even more intriguing. Several years before his murder, Vanni was accused of molesting children in the local community. He got off on a technicality. The police theorized that the murder was simple vengeance, and it appears they did not try very hard to find the killer."

The *colonnello* stubbed out his cigarette. "*Allora*. A revenge killing, someone from the community. The killer wanted to make this pedophile suffer for what he had done. Hence the burning, then the shot to the heart. It explains everything."

"It would seem so."

A long silence.

"And yet," said Pendergast, almost to himself, "it's too perfect. If you wanted to kill someone, Colonnello, but it made no difference who it was, who would you choose? A man exactly like this: guilty of a heinous crime but never punished for it. A man with no family, no important connections, no job. The police aren't going to exert themselves to find the killer, and the townspeople will do all they can to hinder the investigation."

"That is too clever, Agent Pendergast. Never in my life have I dealt with a criminal who would be capable of such sophisticated planning. And why kill someone at random? It is like something out of Dostoevsky."

"We are not dealing with an ordinary criminal, and our killer had a very specific reason to kill." Pendergast laid the file down and gazed at D'Agosta. "Vincent?"

"Worth pursuing."

"May I have a copy of the report of the *medico legale?*" Pendergast asked.

The *colonnello* murmured to the officer, who had just returned with the coffee. The man took the folder to a photocopy machine, returning with the copy a moment later.

The *colonnello* handed it to Pendergast, then lit a cigarette, his face creased with irritation. "I hope you are not going to ask me for an exhumation order."

"I'm afraid we are."

Esposito sighed, smoke dribbling out of his nostrils. "*Mio Dio.* This is all I need. You realize how long this will take? At least a year."

"Unacceptable."

The *colonnello* nodded. "That's Italy." A thin smile worked itself into his face. "Of course..."

"Of course what?"

"You could always go the unofficial route."

"You mean, grave robbing?"

"We prefer to call it *il controllo preliminare.* If you find something, *then* you do the paperwork."

Pendergast rose. "Thank you, Colonnello."

"For what? I said nothing." And he made a mock bow. "Besides, the place is out of my jurisdiction. A satisfactory arrangement for all concerned—save perhaps Carlo Vanni."

As they were leaving, the *colonnello* called after them. "Do not forget to pack *panini* and a good bottle of Chianti. The night, I fear, will be long and chilly."

{ 70 }

The church where Carlo Vanni was interred lay in the foothills of the Apennines above the town of Pistoia, at the end of a winding road that seemed to climb forever through darkness. Their replacement Fiat wound back and forth, the headlights stabbing into darkness at each turn.

"We should be prepared for company," said Pendergast.

"You think they know we're here?"

"I know it. A car's trailing us. I glimpsed it a couple of times three or four switchbacks down the mountain. He'll have to park below the church, and I don't intend to be surprised. Are you familiar with the move-and-cover approach to an objective?"

"Sure."

"You'll cover me while I move, then I'll signal you to follow, like this." And he gave a low hooting sound indistinguishable from an owl's.

D'Agosta grinned. "Your talents always manage to surprise me. Rules of engagement?"

"We're dealing with a potential killer, but we can't shoot first. Wait for the first shot, then shoot to kill."

"Meanwhile, you're down."

"I can take care of myself. Here we are." Pendergast slowed, making the final turn. "Check weapons."

D'Agosta removed his Glock, ejected the magazine, made sure it was at its maximum fifteen-round capacity, slammed it home, and racked the slide. Pendergast drove past the church and parked in a turnout near the end of the road and exited the vehicle.

The smell of crushed mint rose around them. It was a chill, moonless night. There was a scattering of bright stars above the dark line of cypresses. The church itself stood below, faintly silhouetted against the distant glow of Pistoia. Crickets trilled in the darkness. It was a perfect place for a tomb robbing, thought D'Agosta—quiet and isolated.

Pendergast touched his shoulder and nodded toward a dark copse of trees about a hundred yards downhill. D'Agosta crouched in the shadows of the car, gun drawn, as Pendergast darted silently down toward the copse, disappearing into the darkness.

A minute later, D'Agosta heard a low hoot.

He rose, moved quickly toward the trees, and joined Pendergast. Beyond stood the church: small and very ancient, built of stone blocks with a square tower. The front entrance—a Gothic arch over a wooden door—was closed.

Pendergast touched D'Agosta's arm again, nodded this time toward the entrance. D'Agosta retreated into the shadows, waiting.

Pendergast shot across the courtyard in front of the church. D'Agosta could just make out his silhouette, black against black, before the door. There was the sound of a locked door being tried. This was followed by the faint scraping of iron against iron as Pendergast picked the lock, and then a dull creak as the door opened. Pendergast slipped quickly inside. Within moments, another hoot of an owl. Taking a deep breath, D'Agosta ran across the open piazza and past the door. Pendergast immediately closed it behind him and, inserting a narrow device into the keyhole, relocked it.

D'Agosta turned, crossed himself. The interior of the church was cool and smelled of wax and stone. A few candles guttered before a painted wooden statue of the Virgin, throwing a dim orange light across the small nave.

"You take the left side, I'll take the right," said Pendergast.

They moved down opposite walls of the ancient church, guns drawn. It was empty save for the statue of the Virgin, a confessional with a drawn curtain, and a rough altar with a crucifix.

Pendergast crept up to the confessional, took hold of the curtain, jerked it aside.

Empty.

D'Agosta watched him put his gun away and glide to a small, rusted iron door set into a far corner. He bent over the lock and—with another rattle and scrape—opened it to reveal a descending stone staircase. Pendergast switched on his flashlight and probed into the murk.

"This isn't the first tomb I've disturbed," murmured Pendergast as D'Agosta drew up beside him, "but it promises to be one of the most interesting."

"Why was Vanni buried down here, and not in a cemetery outside?"

They passed through the doorway, and Pendergast gently closed and locked the door behind them. "Because of the steep hill, the church has no outside *camposanto.* All the dead are buried down in the crypts, cut into the hillside underneath the church."

They descended the staircase to find themselves in a low, vaulted space. D'Agosta's nostrils filled with the smell of mold. To the left, the flashlight revealed some medieval sarcophagi, several with the bodies of the deceased carved in marble on the lids, as if asleep. One was shown in a suit of armor; another was dressed as a bishop.

D'Agosta followed Pendergast to the right. This passageway led past more old tombs, decorated with sculptures and relief, ending in another iron door. In a moment, Pendergast had it open.

The flashlight disclosed a much cruder tunnel beyond, fashioned out of the rock itself. Shelves were cut into the rude walls, each with its own pile of bones, a skull, and bits of rag. Some of the skeletons had rings on their bony fingers, or bits of jewelry and necklaces scattered among the rib cages. There was the faint rustling of mice, and a few furry bullets shot across the dirt floor, heading for cover. Farther on were rows of newer tombs, narrow edge out, as in a mausoleum. Each niche was covered with a marble plaque.

As they walked, the dates on the plaques grew more recent. Some had photographs of the deceased affixed to the front, unsmiling nineteenth- and early-twentieth-century faces marked by hardship and disappointment. A scattering of vacant crypts with blank marble plaques appeared. Others had a name and birthdate but no date of decease. Pendergast swept his flashlight from left to right and back again as they progressed. Ahead, D'Agosta could make out the terminal wall of the crypt. And there, isolated at the end, in the bottom row, was the tomb they were looking for:

CARLO VANNI
1948-2003

Pendergast reached into his suit coat and removed a thin cloth, which he quickly spread on the stone floor in front of the crypt. Next, he produced a narrow crowbar and a long metal blade with a curved end. He shimmed the blade behind the marble plaque, moved it slowly along all four edges, then stuck the crowbar into the newly created joint and gave a sharp tug. The plaque popped loose with a faint cloud of dust. Pendergast caught it deftly and laid it on the cloth.

The dark hole exhaled a nasty, burned smell.

Pendergast shone his flashlight into the niche. "Give me a hand, please."

D'Agosta knelt beside him. He avoided looking in the hole; it didn't seem decent somehow.

"You grab the left foot, I'll grab the right, and we'll slide him out. It's our good fortune that Vanni's niche is at floor level."

Now D'Agosta forced himself to look. In the dimness, all he could see were the soles of two shoes, each with a hole in it.

"Ready?"

D'Agosta nodded. He reached in, grabbed the shoe.

"On second thought, grasp it above the ankle. We wouldn't want the foot coming off at the anklebone."

"Right." D'Agosta moved his hand up, around the pant leg. It felt like grabbing a knotty bone, except there was a crackle of something else under there, like parchment, that almost turned his stomach. The smell was appalling.

"At the count of three, pull slowly and easily. One, two, three..."

D'Agosta pulled, and after a moment of sticky resistance, the body came free and began sliding out, surprisingly light.

"Keep going."

D'Agosta backed up, pulling as he went, until the corpse was entirely out of the niche. A nest of earwigs was exposed, the panicked insects racing off in all directions. D'Agosta jumped back, slapping at several that had dashed up his leg.

Carlo Vanni lay before them, arms crossed, hands folded around a crucifix, eyes wide open but black and wrinkled. The lips had drawn back from the teeth, which were no more than rotten stumps. The man's white hair had been slicked down with some formidable substance, because not a strand was out of place. The suit had holes in it from insect activity but was otherwise intact, if a bit dusty. The only obvious sign of burning was on the hands themselves, which were black and twisted, the fingernails curled up in little scrolls.

"Hold the light, please, Vincent."

Pendergast bent over the body, placed a knife at the corpse's throat, and in one motion slit the clothes from neck to navel. He pulled them aside. Paper wadding, used to bulk up the suit, filled the sunken abdomen. Pendergast pulled this away to reveal a blackened torso, skin peeling away in dusty burned sheets. Burned ribs sprang from the rib cage, charred ends exposed.

D'Agosta made an effort to keep the light steady.

Pendergast removed a piece of paper from his pocket and laid it beside the body. D'Agosta saw it was the copy of the M.E.'s report, a photocopy of an X-ray showing the location of the drops of metal. Next, he fitted a jeweler's loupe to his eye, bending close to the body as he adjusted the objective. With the knife in one hand and a pair of surgical tweezers in the other, he began to poke into the abdomen. Faint crackling sounds rose up.

"Ah!" He held up a frozen droplet of metal, suspended between the tweezers, then dropped it into a test tube and reapplied himself to the corpse.

From the darkness behind them came a sound.

D'Agosta straightened immediately, turning the light back down the crypt. "You hear that?"

"A rat. The light, if you please?"

D'Agosta returned the light to Vanni, heart pounding. There was a lot to be said for waiting for the paperwork to come through. A year? Make that two.

There was another sound and D'Agosta swept the light back. A rat the size of a small cat crouched and blinked, showing its teeth with a little hiss.

"Shoo!" D'Agosta kicked some dirt at it and it slunk away.

"The light?"

D'Agosta swung the light back. "Nasty buggers."

"Here's another." Pendergast put a long dribble

of frozen metal into the test tube. "Interesting. This metal penetrated more than six inches of flesh. These droplets weren't merely splattered on the corpse: they entered the body at high velocity. The result, I would guess, of a small explosion."

Pendergast extracted a third and fourth droplet, stoppered the tube, removed the loupe. Everything disappeared back into his suit. "I think we're done here," he said, glancing up at D'Agosta. "Let's return Mr. Vanni to his resting place."

D'Agosta bent and, once again taking hold of the corpse, helped shove him back into the niche.

Pendergast whisked the bits and pieces of the body that had broken off onto the M.E.'s report and tipped them into the niche. He then removed a small tube of construction cement, dabbed it around the edges of the marble plaque, and fitted it back in place, tapping here and there to seal it.

He stepped back, looked at his handiwork. "Excellent."

They exited the crypt and climbed into the church. The door was still closed and locked. Pendergast unlocked it, and D'Agosta covered him while he flitted across the courtyard. A moment later he heard Pendergast's voice. "It's all right."

D'Agosta stepped out into the warm night, immeasurably relieved to be free of the tomb. He brushed at his arms and legs, feeling the smell, the mold, still clinging to his clothes. Ahead, Pendergast was pointing toward the darkness of the hill. A pair of taillights could be seen winding down the mountainside a half mile below them.

"That's our man." His light came on, revealing

unfamiliar shoe tracks clearly outlined in the short, dew-laden grass.

"What was he doing?"

"It seems they no longer want to kill us. Rather, they are merely anxious to keep track of how much we know. Now, why do you think that is, Vincent?"

{ 71 }

Hayward never liked the sensation of déjà vu, and she was feeling it especially strongly this afternoon, sitting in the same room, with the same people, listening to the same arguments she'd heard twenty-four hours earlier. Only now it was ass-covering time. It reminded her of musical chairs: as soon as the music stopped in this room, some poor schmuck would no doubt be left standing, ass exposed and ready to be kicked.

Grable seemed to be trying hard to make sure that exposed ass was hers.

He was in the middle of a long-winded account of the botched arrest attempt, an account that somehow transformed his own craven and erratic behavior into restraint and heroism. The story went on and on, the climax coming when he was obliged to fire into the air to warn the savage crowd. As a result they'd been able to depart in good order, upholding the dignity of the New York City Police Department, even if they had failed in their objective of arresting Buck. Throughout the account, there was the faint implication that he had done all the work, taken all the risks, while Hayward had been a reluctant participant at best. He even managed to give the impression of refraining from criticism, as if she'd been a dead weight on the whole operation.

If he was as good in the field as he is at ass-covering, Hayward thought grimly, *we wouldn't be here right now.* She considered responding, but decided she didn't want to play that particular game. If she pointed out that Grable had run like a cur with its tail tucked between its legs, that he had fired in panic and lost his gun—well, it might set the record straight, but it would do her no good. Her mind wandered, tuning out the parade of half-truths.

One bright note was that Pendergast and D'Agosta seemed to be making progress in Italy. And Pendergast was out of her hair, no doubt making some Italian police officer's life miserable. On the other hand, she missed D'Agosta. Missed him even more than she'd thought she would.

It was Wentworth's turn next, and she made an effort to concentrate. He expounded at length on the psychology of crowds, trotting out quotations on megalomania from file cards specially prepared for the occasion. It was a huge smokescreen of words and theories, piled one on top of another, signifying nothing. This was followed by some neighborhood honcho, talking about how upset the mayor was, how everybody was up in arms, how all the important people of the city were beside themselves that nothing was being done.

No one, it seemed, had any ideas on how to get Buck out of Central Park.

Rocker heard them all out with the same tired expression on his face, an expression which betrayed nothing of his inner thoughts. Finally, the tired eyes came to rest on her.

"Captain Hayward?"

"I have nothing to add." She said it perhaps a little more curtly than she intended.

Rocker's eyebrows raised just slightly. "So you agree with the gentlemen here?"

"I didn't say that. I said I had nothing to add."

"Did you find out anything more on Buck's record? An outstanding warrant, perhaps?"

"Yes," said Hayward, having spent part of the morning on the phone. "But it isn't much. He's wanted in Broken Arrow, Oklahoma, for violating parole."

"Violating parole!" Grable laughed. "What a joke. The laws he's broken here include assaulting a police officer, resisting arrest, attempted kidnapping—I mean, we got enough here to put him away for years."

Hayward said nothing. Fact is, the parole violation was the only charge that would stick. As far as the others went, there were dozens of witnesses who would testify truthfully that Grable had drawn and fired his gun with no real provocation, that Buck had not, in fact, resisted arrest, that the crowd had parted like the damn Red Sea to let them go, and that Grable had run, leaving his gun in the dust.

Rocker nodded. "What now?"

Silence.

Rocker was still looking at Hayward. "Captain?"

"I'd suggest just what I suggested in the first meeting."

"Even after your, ah, unpleasant experience this morning?"

"Nothing happened this morning to change my mind."

That produced a long, leaden silence. Grable was shaking his head, as if to say, *Some people never learn.*

"I see. You suggested going in alone, is that right?"

"Right. I go in there and ask for Buck's cooperation in sending his people home for a shower and change of clothes. We'll promise him a parade permit in return. Treat him with respect. Deliver a fair, honest warning."

There was a snort of derision from Grable.

Rocker turned. "Captain Grable, you have something to say?"

"I was *there*, Commissioner. Buck is crazy. He's a dangerous ex-murderer. And his followers are like Jonestown, real fanatics. She goes in there alone, without a large force to protect her, they'll take her hostage. Or worse."

"Commissioner, I respectfully disagree with Captain Grable. It's been almost a week now, and Buck and his followers have been reasonably well behaved and orderly. I believe it's worth a try."

Wentworth had joined in the head-shaking.

"Dr. Wentworth?" Rocker said.

"I would give Captain Hayward's plan a very low probability of success. Captain Hayward is not a psychologist, and her prognostications of human behavior are simply lay opinion, not based on scientific study of human psychology."

Hayward looked at the commissioner. "I'm not one to toot my own horn, sir, but the fact is, I do have an M.S. in forensic psychology from NYU. Since I believe Dr. Wentworth is an assistant professor at the College of Staten Island—CUNY, it's understandable that we never met academically."

In the uncomfortable silence, it seemed to Hayward that Rocker might even be suppressing a little smile of his own.

"I stand by my earlier comment," Wentworth said acidly.

Rocker ignored him, still speaking to Hayward. "And that's it?"

"That's it."

"You better have a SWAT team standing by to extract Captain Hayward, along with paramedics, for when the inevitable occurs," said Grable.

Rocker looked down at his hands, his brow creased. Then he raised his head again. "Sunday is the day after tomorrow. I'd already decided on using the relative calm to go in with overwhelming force and arrest this man. But I hate to take a step like that until all avenues have been tried. I'm inclined to let Captain Hayward have a shot at it. If she can get Buck out of there without tear gas and water cannon, I'm all for it." He turned to Hayward. "You do your thing at noon. If it doesn't work, we move in, as scheduled."

"Thank you, sir."

A beat. "Hayward, are you *sure* this plan of yours is going to work?"

"No, sir."

Rocker smiled. "That's all I wanted to hear—a little goddamned humility for a change." His eyes raked the rest of them, then returned to Hayward. "Go to it, Captain."

{ 72 }

D'Agosta looked out at the vague outlines of the island looming off the ferry's port bow, rising steep and blue from the sea, shimmering slightly in the midmorning light. Capraia: outermost of the Tuscan islands, a mountaintop lost in the wide ocean. It looked unreal, almost fairylike. The Toremar car ferry chiseled its way forward, squat steel bows stubbornly parting the turquoise water as it plowed toward its destination.

Pendergast stood beside D'Agosta, sea breeze ruffling his blond hair, his finely cut features like alabaster in the glare of the sun. "A most interesting island, Vincent," he was saying. "Once a prison for the most dangerous and intelligent criminals in Italy—Mafia capos and serial escapees. The prison closed in the mid-sixties, and now most of the island is a national park."

"Strange place to live."

"It is actually the most charming of all the Tuscan islands. There is a small port and a tiny village on a bluff, connected by the island's only road, which is all of half a mile in length. There's been no ugly development, thanks to the fact that the island doesn't have any beaches."

"What's the woman's name again?"

"Her name is Viola Maskelene. Lady Viola Maskelene. I couldn't find out much about her on short notice—she's a private person. It seems she spends her summers on the island, leaving at the end of October. Travels the rest of the year, or so I've been informed."

"You sure she's home?"

"No. But I prefer to take the chance of surprising our quarry."

"Quarry?"

"In an investigative sense. We're dealing with a sophisticated and well-traveled Englishwoman. As the only great-grandchild of Toscanelli's greatest love, she is in the best position to know the family secrets."

"She might be a tough nut to crack."

"Quite possibly. Hence the surprise approach."

"How old is she?"

"I assume middle-aged, if my calculations are correct."

D'Agosta glanced at him. "So what's the family story?"

"It was one of those torrid nineteenth-century affairs one reads about. The stuff of opera. Viola Maskelene's great-grandmother, a famous Victorian beauty, married the Duke of Cumberland, thirty years her senior and as cold and correct a man as you could find. Toscanelli seduced her only a few months after her marriage, and they carried on a legendary affair. An illegitimate daughter came of the union, and the poor duchess died in childbirth. That child was Lady Maskelene's grandmother."

"What did the duke have to say about all that?"

"He may have been cold, but he also seems to have

been a rather decent sort. After his wife's death, he took steps to legally adopt the child. The greater titles and estates were entailed away, but the daughter inherited a lesser title and some land in Cornwall."

The ferry throbbed beneath their feet, and the island seemed to gain weight and substance as they approached. As they stood silently, Pendergast drew the test tube out of his pocket. He held it up, the melted droplets taken from Vanni's corpse the night before glittering in the sun. "We haven't spoken yet about these."

"Yeah. But I've been thinking about them."

"So have I. Perhaps, Vincent, the time has come at last for each of us to turn over a card."

"You first."

Pendergast smiled faintly and held up a finger. "Never. As the officer in charge, I reserve the right to call your hand."

"Pulling rank on me?"

"Precisely."

"Well, I'd say those drops came from some device which malfunctioned, spraying molten metal into Vanni and burning him terribly."

Pendergast nodded. "What kind of device?"

"Some device meant to torch Vanni. Same device that killed the others. But in Vanni's case, it didn't seem to work, so he had to be shot afterwards."

"Bravo."

"Your theory?"

"I reached the same conclusions. Vanni was an early victim—perhaps a test subject—of a highly specialized killing device. It appears we are dealing with a flesh-and-blood assassin, after all."

Now the ferry was slipping past surf-scoured volcanic cliffs and into a small harbor. A row of crumbling houses, stuccoed yellow and red, crowded the quay, hillsides rising steeply behind them. The ferry maneuvered into port, and a single car and a scattering of passengers got off. Almost before D'Agosta's feet were on firm ground, it was backing out again and heading to its next stop, the island of Elba.

"We have four hours before the ferry returns on its homeward swing." Pendergast pulled out a little piece of paper, scrutinized it. "Lady Viola Maskelene, Via Saracino, 19. Let's hope we find *la signorina* at home."

He set off down the quay toward a bus stop, D'Agosta at his side. Within moments, an old orange bus wheezed into view, struggled to turn around in the lone narrow street, then opened its doors. They boarded; the doors creaked shut; and the bus began groaning and wheezing its way back up the frighteningly steep slope that seemed to rise straight out of the foaming sea.

In five minutes, they were in the village at the far end of the road. The doors creaked open again and they descended. An ancient peach-colored church sat on one side, a tobacconist on the other. Cobbled lanes ran off at odd angles, too narrow to admit a car. A giant, ruined castle, completely overgrown with prickly pears, dominated the headland before them. Behind the village mounted a series of empty, scrub-covered mountains.

"Charming," said Pendergast. He pointed at a street sign, carved on an old marble plaque and cemented into the wall of a building, reading *Via Saracino.* "This way, Sergeant."

They walked down a lane between small whitewashed houses, the numbers mounting slowly. Soon the town ended and the lane turned to dirt, bounded by stone walls enclosing garden plots of small lemon trees and microscopic vineyards. The air carried the scent of citrus. The lane made a sharp curve, and there—at the edge of the cliff, all by itself—stood a neat stone house shaded by bougainvillea, overlooking the blue immensity of the Mediterranean.

Pendergast slipped down the path, entered the patio, and knocked on the door.

Silence.

"C'è nessuno?" he called.

The wind sighed through the rosemary bushes, carrying the fragrance of the sea with it.

D'Agosta looked around. "There's someone over there," he said. "A man, digging." He nodded toward a small, terraced vineyard a hundred yards away, where a figure was turning earth with a spade. The man was wearing a battered straw hat, old canvas pants, and a rough shirt unbuttoned partway down the front. Seeing them, the person straightened up.

"Correction: a woman digging." Pendergast set off down the path with a vigorous step. Reaching the vineyard, they stepped gingerly through clods of freshly turned earth. The woman watched them approach, leaning on her shovel.

Pendergast paused to offer the woman his hand, giving his usual little half-bow. In response, she removed her straw hat, shook out a mass of dark glossy hair, and took the hand.

D'Agosta froze. *This is no middle-aged woman.*

She was stunningly beautiful, tall, athletic, and

slender, with spirited hazel eyes, high cheekbones, skin tanned and freckled from the sun, nose still flaring from the effort of digging.

After a moment, he realized Pendergast, after having bowed, had straightened again but seemed rooted to the spot, still holding her hand, saying nothing but looking into her eyes. The woman appeared to be doing the same. There was a moment of utter stillness. D'Agosta wondered if they had known each other before—it almost seemed as if they recognized each other.

"I am Aloysius Pendergast," Pendergast said after a long moment.

"I'm Viola Maskelene," she replied in a rich, warm English accent.

As they released each other's hand, D'Agosta realized Pendergast had uncharacteristically forgotten to introduce him. "And I'm Sergeant Vincent D'Agosta, Southampton Police."

The woman turned to him, as if noticing him for the first time. But the smile she gave him was full of warmth. "Welcome to Capraia, Sergeant."

Another awkward silence. D'Agosta glanced at Pendergast. He had a most uncharacteristic look of surprise on his face, as if somebody had just dropped a scoop of ice cream down his back. What was going on?

"Well," said Lady Maskelene with another smile, "I assume you're here to see me, Mr. Pendergast?"

"Yes," he said hastily. "Yes, we are. It concerns—"

She held up her finger. "A hot vineyard is no place to have a civilized conversation. Let's go back to my house and enjoy something cool on the *terrazza*, shall we?"

"Yes, of course."

She smiled again: a dazzling, dimpled smile. "Follow me." She set off across the field, her big boots clomping through the clods of earth. The *terrazza* was shaded by a pergola draped with wisteria, and bordered by blooming rosemary and miniature lemon trees. It was like being perched on the edge of the known world, the cliffs dropping away to an infinity of blue, stretching to the horizon and merging imperceptibly with the sky. The expanse was broken by a single, tiny black reef, about a mile offshore, which only served to increase the sense of distance, of infinity.

Lady Maskelene seated them around an old tiled table, in battered wooden chairs, and then disappeared into the house. A minute later she returned with a wine bottle without a label, filled with a pale amber liquid; some glasses; a bottle of olive oil; and a battered clay platter heaped with thick pieces of rough-cut bread. She set down the glasses and, moving around the table, filled them with white wine. As she passed D'Agosta his glass, he caught her faint scent, a perfume of grapevines, earth, and the sea.

Pendergast took a sip. "Is it yours, Lady Maskelene?"

"Yes. The olive oil is mine also. There's something marvelously satisfying about working your own piece of ground."

"Complimenti." Pendergast took another sip, dipped a piece of the rough bread in a dish of olive oil. "Excellent."

"Thank you."

"Allow me to tell you why we've come, Lady Maskelene."

"No," she said in a low voice, looking not at him, but far out to sea, her hazel eyes almost blue in the intense light, a strange smile on her lips. "Don't spoil this... particular moment just yet."

D'Agosta wondered just what particular moment she might be talking about. The faint sound of surf and the cries of seagulls drifted from the edge of the cliff.

"What an enchanting villa you have here, Lady Maskelene."

She laughed. "A villa it is not—just a simple seaside bungalow. That's why I love it. Here I have my books, my music, my vines, my olive trees—and the sea. What more could you ask for?"

"You mentioned music. Do you play an instrument?"

A hesitation. "The violin."

Now we're getting somewhere, thought D'Agosta. As usual, Pendergast was sliding into the subject sideways.

"You are here year-round?"

"Oh, no. I'd get bored. I'm not *that* much of a recluse."

"Where do you spend the rest of your time?"

"I lead a rather decadent life. Fall in Rome, December in Luxor, at the Winter Palace."

"Egypt? That's a curious place to spend the winter."

"I'm directing a small dig in the Valley of the Nobles."

"You're an archaeologist, then?"

"An Egyptologist and philologist. There's a difference, you know—we study a great deal more than dirt, pots, and bones. We've been excavating the tomb of a Nineteenth Dynasty scribe, full of fascinating hieratic inscriptions. Of course, the tomb was looted in antiquity, but fortunately all the looters wanted were the gold and gems. They left the scrolls and inscriptions intact. We found the scribe himself in his sarcophagus, holding a bundle of mysterious scrolls full of magical formulas which we have yet to unroll and translate. They're exceedingly delicate."

"Fascinating."

"And then, come spring, I go to Cornwall, the family place."

"Spring, in England?"

She laughed. "I love mud. And freezing rain. And sprawling on a fur rug in front of a roaring fire reading a good book. How about you, Mr. Pendergast? What do *you* love?"

The question seemed to take Pendergast by surprise, and he covered his confusion with a sip of wine. "I love this wine of yours. Fresh, simple, unpretentious."

"It's made from malvasia vines brought to the island almost four thousand years ago by Minoan traders. For me, the flavor somehow evokes history itself, the Minoans crossing the wine-dark sea in trireme ships, bound for distant islands..." She laughed, sweeping her black hair from her face. "I'm an incurable romantic. When I was a child, I wanted to grow up to be Odysseus." She looked at Pendergast. "And you? When you were a child, what did you want to be?"

"A great white hunter."

She laughed. "What a curious ambition! And did you become one?"

"In a way. But on a hunt in Tanzania...I discovered quite suddenly that I had lost the taste for it."

More silence. D'Agosta gave up trying to make sense of what tack Pendergast was taking. He sipped the wine with renewed interest. It was very pleasant, if a bit dry. And the bread was fabulous, thick and chewy, the olive oil so fresh it was spicy. He dipped a piece of bread, stuffed it in his mouth, followed with another. He hadn't eaten breakfast and had been a bit too severe with his diet. He glanced surreptitiously at his watch. If Pendergast didn't hurry things up, they'd miss the ferry.

Then, to D'Agosta's surprise, the woman brought the subject up herself.

"Speaking of history, there's quite a lot of that in my own family. You know of my great-grandfather, Luciano Toscanelli?"

"I do."

"He did two things in life exceptionally well: playing the violin and seducing women. He was the Mick Jagger of his age. His groupies were countesses, baronesses, princesses. Sometimes he would have two or three women in a day, and not always at different times." She laughed lightly.

Pendergast cleared his throat, took a piece of bread.

"He had one great love, however, and that was my great-grandmother. The Duchess of Cumberland. He gave her an illegitimate daughter, my grandmother." She paused, looked at Pendergast curiously. "This *is* why you came, isn't it?"

It took Pendergast a moment to reply. "Yes, it is."

She sighed. "My great-grandfather ended up like so many in the days before penicillin: with a bad dose of venereal disease."

"Lady Maskelene," said Pendergast hastily, "please don't think I have come to pry into your family's private affairs. I really only have one question that needs answering."

"I know what that question is. But first, I want you to know the history of my family."

"There is no need—"

Maskelene blushed, her hand touching the buttons of her shirt. "I want you to know it up front, that's all. Then we won't have to speak of it again."

D'Agosta listened with surprise. *I want you to know it up front.* Up front of what? Pendergast seemed equally nonplussed. In any case, when he had no answer for this, she began again.

"So my great-grandfather got syphilis. It eventually progressed to the tertiary stage, where the spirochetes attack the brain. His playing changed. It grew bizarre. He gave a concert in Florence where he was pelted by the audience. The family who owned the violin demanded it back. He wouldn't give it up. He fled to escape them and their agents, traveling from city to city, driven by a rising insanity and aided by countless women. The family's agents and private detectives pursued him doggedly—but quietly, because keeping the family name secret was of the utmost importance. My great-grandfather stayed one step ahead. He played in his hotel rooms at night: insane, shocking, even terrifying renderings of Bach, Beethoven, Brahms, executed—so the story goes—with enormous technical virtuosity but cold, strange, all wrong. Those who heard him say it was as if the devil himself had taken up the violin."

She paused.

"Go on," said Pendergast gently.

"The family who owned the Stormcloud was very powerful. They were related by blood to some of the royal families of Europe. Even so, they couldn't catch my great-grandfather. They pursued him from one end of Europe to the other. The chase finally ended in the small village of Siusi in the South Tyrol. There, under the peaks of the Dolomites, they cornered him. He was betrayed by a woman, naturally. He escaped out the back of a small *albergo* and fled into the high mountains with nothing but the violin and the clothes on his back. He ascended the great Sciliar. Do you know it?"

"No," said Pendergast.

"It's a high Alpine plateau wedged between the peaks of the Dolomites, cut by ravines and sheer cliffs. They say it's where the witches once held their black masses. In the summer, a few hardy shepherds graze their flocks there. But this was fall and the Sciliar was deserted. That night it snowed heavily. The next day they found his body, frozen to death, in one of the deserted shepherd's huts. The Stormcloud was gone. There were no tracks in the snow around the hut, no clues. They concluded that on the way up the Sciliar, in the grip of madness, he had flung the violin into the Falls of the Sciliar."

"Is this what you believe?"

"Reluctantly, yes."

Pendergast leaned forward. His normally calm, almost honeyed southern tones had taken on an unusual intensity. "Lady Maskelene, I am here to tell you that the Stormcloud exists."

Her eyes gazed at him steadily. "I've heard that before."

"I will prove it to you."

She continued looking at him with a grave, steady

face. Finally she gave a wan smile and shook her head sadly. "I'll believe it when I see it."

"I *will* get it back. And I will place it in your hands myself."

D'Agosta listened with surprise. He might be wrong, but he was pretty sure Pendergast's aim in coming here wasn't to inform this woman of the violin's existence. Fact was, he felt surprised Pendergast even mentioned it.

She shook her head more vigorously. "There are hundreds of Stormcloud fakes and copies out there. They were churned out by the gross in the late nineteenth century, sold for nine pounds apiece."

"When I bring you the violin, Lady Maskelene—"

"Enough of this 'Lady Maskelene' business. Every time you say that, I think my mother must have stepped into the room. Call me Viola."

"Certainly. Viola."

"That sounds better. And I'll call you Aloysius."

"Of course."

"What an unusual funny name, though. Did your mother read a lot of Russian novels?"

"Unusual names are a tradition in my family."

Viola laughed. "Just as musical names were in mine. Now tell me about the Stormcloud. Where in the world did you find it? If you did really find it, that is."

"I'll tell you the whole story when I bring it to you. You'll play it—and then you'll know."

"It is too much to hope for. Still, I should love to hear it before I die."

"It would also clear your family name."

Maskelene laughed, waved her hand. "What rot. I

hate being called Lady Maskelene, if you want to know the truth. Titles, family honor—that's nineteenth-century rubbish."

"Honor is never out of date."

She looked at Pendergast curiously. "You're a rather old-fashioned sort, aren't you?"

"I don't pay much attention to current fashions, if that's what you mean."

She looked his black suit up and down with an amused smile. "No, I suppose you don't. I rather like that."

Again Pendergast looked nonplussed.

"Well"—she stood up, her brown eyes catching the light off the water, a smile dimpling her face—"whether you find the violin or not, come back anyway and tell me about it. Will you?"

"Nothing would please me more."

"Good. That's settled."

Pendergast looked at her gravely. "Which brings me to the point of my visit."

"The big question. Ah." She smiled. "Go ahead."

"What is the name of that powerful family that once owned the Stormcloud?"

"I can do better than give you a mere answer." She reached into her pocket, removed an envelope, and laid it before Pendergast. In a lovely copperplate hand was written, *Dr. Aloysius X. L. Pendergast.*

Pendergast looked at it, his face draining of color. "Where did you get this?"

"Yesterday, the current Count Fosco—for that was the family that once owned the violin—paid me a surprise visit. Surprise is hardly the word—I was bowled over. He said you'd be coming, that you were friends, and that he wanted me to give you this."

Pendergast reached down and slowly picked up the envelope. D'Agosta watched as he slid his finger under the flap, tore it open, and pulled out a card, on which was written in the same generous, flowing hand:

Isidor Ottavio Baldassare Fosco,
Count of the Holy Roman Empire,
Knight Grand Cross of the Order of the Quincunx,
Perpetual Arch-Master of the Rosicrucian Masons of Mesopotamia,
Fellow of the Royal Geographical Society, etc., etc.,
desires the pleasure of your company
at his family seat,
Castel Fosco,
Sunday, November 4

Castel Fosco
Greve in Chianti
Firenze

Pendergast looked sharply at D'Agosta and then back at Lady Maskelene. "This man is no friend. He's extremely dangerous."

"What? That fat, charming old count?" She laughed, but the laughter died when she saw the expression on his face.

"He's the one who has the violin."

She stared. "It would be his, anyway—wouldn't it? I mean, if it were found."

"He brutally murdered at least four people to get it."

"Oh, my God—"

"Don't say anything to anyone about this. You'll be safe here, on Capraia. He would have killed you already if he thought it was necessary."

She stared back. "You're frightening me."

"Yes, and I'm sorry, but sometimes it's good to be afraid. It will be over in two or three days. Please be careful, Viola. Just stay here and do nothing until I return with the violin."

For a moment, she did not reply. Then she stirred. "You must go. You'll miss the ferry."

Pendergast took her hand. They stood quite still, looking at each other, saying nothing. Then Pendergast turned and quickly walked through the gate and down the trail.

D'Agosta leaned against the fantail of the ferry, watching the island dissolve on the horizon in much the same way it had appeared: with a sense of expectancy, of a fresh beginning. Pendergast stood beside him. Since they had left the small house on the bluff, the agent hadn't said a word. He stared back over the churning wake, apparently lost in thought.

"Fosco knew that you knew," said D'Agosta. "That's what saved her."

"Yes."

"This whole thing. It was just an elaborate plot to get the violin, wasn't it?"

Pendergast nodded.

"I knew from the beginning that fat bastard had something to do with it."

Pendergast didn't respond. His gaze was far away.

"Are you all right?" D'Agosta finally risked asking.

Pendergast started, looked over. "Quite all right, thanks."

The island had finally disappeared. As if on cue, the low outline of the Tuscan mainland began to materialize on the eastern horizon.

"What now?"

"I accept Fosco's invitation. It's one thing to know, quite another to have proof. If we want to get Fosco, we have to get whatever machine he used to commit these murders."

"So why did Fosco give you an invitation?"

"He wants to kill me."

"Great. And you plan on accepting?"

Pendergast turned away and gazed back out to sea, his eyes almost white in the brilliant light. "Fosco knows I'll accept, because it's the only chance to gather the evidence we need to put him behind bars. If we don't do it now, he will be back to haunt us next month, perhaps, or a year from now, or ten years..." He paused. "And what's more, he'll always be a danger to Viola—Lady Maskelene—for what she knows."

"I get it."

But Pendergast was still looking out to sea. When he spoke again, his voice was very low. "It ends tomorrow, in the Castel Fosco."

{ 73 }

Bryce Harriman sat at the old table, taking notes in the harsh light of a Coleman lantern, the Reverend Buck across from him. It was almost midnight, but he wasn't the least bit sleepy. The day before, he had filed a crackerjack story, about the failed attempt to arrest Buck. He had pieced it together from a half dozen witnesses, and it was juicy: the swaggering police captain coming in to arrest Buck, how he'd panicked and run, leaving it to the other captain—a woman—to straighten things out. Great copy. In the long run, it might turn out to be more than just great copy: he'd begun putting out feelers at the *Times*, and they seemed receptive to a job interview. This new article would be gravy. And thanks to Buck, he was now the only journalist allowed in the tent city. With this second piece appearing hot on the heels of the first, he was going to score a double whammy. And he would be there tomorrow, too, just in case there was a showdown with New York's finest.

Judging from the mood in the camp, it was going to be a mess. Since the botched arrest, the whole place had been on edge, restless, belligerent, like a powder keg ready to go. Even at midnight, more than a day after the would-be raid, everyone was still awake, the prayers and camp meetings sounding shrilly through the darkness. A lot of the kids he'd noticed on his first visit to the tent city were gone—a night or two of sleeping on the hard ground, without an Internet connection or cable TV, had sent them scurrying home to their comfy suburbs. What remained was the hard-core element, the real zealots. And there was no shortage of those: there had to be at least three hundred tents here.

Buck himself was different. Gone was the flicker of uncertainty, the faint aura of surprise and wonder that he had possessed before. Now he seemed almost transcendentally calm and assured. When he looked at Harriman, it was as if he was looking right through him to another world.

"Well, Mr. Harriman," he was saying, "have you gotten what you came for? It's almost midnight, and I usually deliver a message to the people before retiring."

"Just one other question. What do you think's going to happen? The NYPD aren't just going to walk away, you realize."

He had half expected the question to shake Buck up a bit, but instead, the man seemed to settle even deeper into something like serenity. "What will happen will happen."

"It may not be pretty. Are you ready?"

"No, it won't be pretty, and yes, I am ready."

"You say that almost as if you know what's going to happen."

Buck smiled knowingly but said nothing.

"Aren't you concerned?" Harriman asked more insistently.

Again that enigmatic smile. *Damn, you can't quote a smile.* "We're talking tear gas maybe, cops swinging billy clubs. No more fun and games."

"I put my trust in God, Mr. Harriman. Who do you trust?"

Time to wrap this up. "Thank you, Reverend, you've been very helpful." Harriman rose.

"And thank you, Mr. Harriman. Won't you stay a few minutes to hear my message to the people? As you say, something is about to happen. And as a result, my sermon this evening will be somewhat different."

The reporter hesitated. He had to be up at five, ready to go. He was pretty sure the cops were going to do their thing tomorrow, and it might begin early. "What's it on?"

"Hell."

"In that case, I'll stay."

Buck rose and signaled one of his men, who came over, helped him don a simple vestment, and then accompanied him out of the tent. Harriman followed in their wake, pulling his recorder out of one pocket, trying to ignore the heavy reek of the encampment. They were headed, he knew, to a huge glacial erratic that reared out of the earth to the west of the tent city and which was now universally called the "preaching rock."

The bustle of the camp died away as Buck went out of sight behind the massive boulder, climbed the grassy hummock to the rear, then reappeared on its lofty crag. He raised his hands slowly. Watching from below, Harriman found hundreds of people drifting in out of the darkness to surround him.

"My friends," he began. "Good evening. Once again

I thank you for joining me on this spiritual quest. It's been my custom, in these evening talks, to speak to you of this quest: to explain why we are here and what it is we must do. But tonight my subject will be different.

"Brothers and sisters, you will soon face a trial. A great trial. We won a mighty victory here yesterday, thanks be to God. But the agents of darkness are not easily turned back. Therefore, you must be strong. Be strong, and accept *the will of God*."

Harriman, listening with recorder raised, was surprised by Buck's tone and manner. His voice was quiet, but it rang with an iron conviction he'd never heard before, even in the very first sermon delivered outside Cutforth's building. There was a strange look in Buck's bright eyes: a look of anticipation mingled with an almost stoic resignation.

"I have spoken to you many times about what we have come here to achieve. Now, on the eve of your trial to end all trials, I must take a moment to remind you of what we are up against and who your enemy is. Remember my words even when I am no longer among you."

The eve of your *trial. Who* your *enemy is. No longer among* you. Since his last meeting in Buck's tent, Harriman had begun reading the Bible—just a little, here and there—and the words of Jesus came back to him now: *Whither I go, thou canst not follow me now; but thou shalt follow me afterwards.*

"Why, my friends and my brothers, were our medieval ancestors—unsophisticated and unlettered in other ways—so much more God-fearing than people today? But I speak the answer even as I ask the question.

Because they had the *fear* of God. They knew what rewards awaited the chosen few in heaven. And they also knew what awaited the sinful, the wicked, the lazy and unbelieving.

"The fault lies not just with the people. Today's clergy are even more at fault. They sugarcoat the word of God, make light of his warnings, tell their flocks that hell is merely a metaphor or an antique concept with no actual reality. God's love is expansive and forgiving, they tell us. They lull their flocks into a false sense of entitlement. As if a baptism here, a few good deeds there, a communion or two, is a ticket to heaven. My friends, this is a tragic mistake."

Buck paused to glance around at the hushed multitude.

"God's love is a tough love. In this city, as in all great cities, people die every day. They die by the hundreds. At what point do you suppose all those poor souls begin to realize the *real* fate that lies in store for them? At what point do the scales fall from their eyes and they learn their entire life has been a lie—that they've spent it running from the light ever deeper into the darkness—and that they now have nothing but unimaginable torment to look forward to? There is no way to know for sure. But I believe at least some people *have* a glimpse of it in their last moments. I believe that, for these people, there is a creeping sense that something is terribly wrong: something far, far worse than the act of dying itself. In those last moments, as the soul begins to separate from the body, the fabric of everyday reality is ripped asunder. And suddenly they can see into the void beyond. Then comes a terrible oppression; overwhelming fear; rising heat. They cannot scream, they cannot flee. This is no panic attack that will pass; this is merely the foretaste of what is to come. This is a step onto the first tread of the long stairway down into hell.

"And what is hell itself like? Our ancestors were told it was a burning lake of fire, of sulfur and brimstone, in which one was eternally submerged. A terrible furnace whose flames bring no light, but merely darkness made visible. And in a simpler time, such a depiction was enough."

He stopped again to look around, fixing first one, then another, with his eyes.

"Mind you, I do believe this is hell for some. But it is not the only hell. There are countless hells, my brothers and sisters. There is a hell for *each* of us. Lucifer may be no match for our God. Yet he was a very mighty angel indeed, and as such, has powers far beyond our poor comprehension.

"You must remember something, and remember it always: Lucifer, the devil, was cast out of heaven because of his overmastering envy and evil. In his implacable jealousy, his unquenchable thirst for revenge, he now uses us as his pawns. Just as the rejected child hates a favored rival, he hates us for what we are: beloved children of God. And which of us can hope to comprehend the depths of his bottomless rage? Each human he corrupts, each soul he takes, is for him a victory: a fist shaken up at God.

"He knows our individual weaknesses, our petty desires; he knows what triggers our vanity or our greed or our lust or our cruelty. We have no secrets from him.

He has handcrafted temptations for each one of us; he has strewn our path with a thousand ways to veer into darkness. And once he has successfully lured a soul into his kingdom—once he has won, yet again—do you think Satan will be content to leave that soul in a *generic* hell? Think again, my friends: think again. He who knows all our weaknesses also knows all our fears. Even those we may not know ourselves. And to complete his victory, to make his victim's suffering *supreme*, he will fashion each individual hell to be the most unendurable for its particular inhabitant. And worst of all, it will be a hell that lasts forever. And ever. *And ever.* For some, that may well mean a burning lake of fire. For others, it may mean an eternity nailed up in a black coffin, motionless, lightless, speechless, as insanity doubles and redoubles over long eons. For others, it might mean, say, eternal suffocation. Imagine that for a moment, my friends. Imagine that you've held your breath for two minutes, maybe three. Imagine the desperate need for oxygen, the exquisite torture. And yet in hell, there is no release of breath, no drawing in of good sweet air. Nor is there the blankness of oblivion. There is simply that moment of maximal agony, prolonged forever."

Maximal agony, prolonged forever. Despite himself, Harriman shivered in the warm night.

"Other hells might be more subtle. Imagine the man who always feared going crazy, doing so over decades or even slow centuries. And then beginning the process over. And over. Or imagine the doting mother, forced to watch—again and again and again—how after her own passing her children slide into poverty and neglect, drug addiction, depression, maltreatment, and death."

Here he stopped, and stepped up to the very edge of the rock.

"Take a moment to think of the very worst hell you could imagine for yourself. And then realize that Satan, who knows you even better than you know yourself, could fashion one far worse. And he will. *He already has.* In anticipation. Because he has only one salve for his bitter pain: the despair, the desperate pleadings, the cries and sufferings of his victims."

Buck paused again. He took a deep breath, then another. Then, in an even lower voice, he went on.

"I've said there was a hell for each of us. That hell is there, waiting for each one of you. Satan has made your hell so very easy to find, with a wide and comfortable road leading straight to it. It is far, far easier for us to go with the flow, to stroll unthinking down that broad pleasant avenue, far easier than to search for the rough, hidden turnoff that leads to heaven. We must fight against the lure of the easy road. It is a fight, my friends; a fight to the death. Because that is the only way—*the only way*—we are going to discover that difficult trail to heaven. I ask you to remember this in the trials we are about to face."

And then he turned and stepped down out of sight.

{ 74 }

When D'Agosta entered Pendergast's hotel suite, he found the agent at breakfast. The table was set with assorted fruits, breakfast rolls, and the inescapable and inevitable tiny espresso. Pendergast was nibbling daintily at poached eggs and reading what looked like a set of faxed documents. For a brief moment, D'Agosta thought of the earlier meal they'd shared, back in Southampton, when this case was still brand-new. It seemed a distant memory indeed.

"Ah, Vincent," Pendergast said. "Come in. Would you care to order something?"

"No, thanks." Although it was a beautiful morning and sunlight gilded the rooms, D'Agosta felt as if a threatening cloud was hanging over them both. "I'm surprised you've got an appetite."

"It's important I take some refreshment now. I'm not sure how long it will be until my next meal. But that shouldn't stop you: come, have a croissant. These Alsatian plum preserves from Fauchon are delightful." He put the faxes aside and picked up *La Nazione*.

"What's that you were reading?"

"Some faxes from Constance. I'll need all the, ah, ammunition I can gather for what's to come. She has proven most helpful."

D'Agosta stepped forward. "I'm coming with you," he said grimly. "I want to get that straight here and now so there won't be any questions later."

Pendergast lowered the paper. "I assumed you'd make such a demand. Let me remind you the invitation was for me alone."

"I doubt that fat-assed count would have any objections."

"You're probably right."

"I've come all this way. I've been shot at more than once, lost the end of a finger, almost been pushed off a cliff, almost been *driven* off a cliff."

"Right again."

"So don't expect me to spend the evening relaxing by the pool with a few cold ones while you're in Fosco's lair."

Pendergast smiled faintly. "I have one more errand to run before leaving Florence. Let's discuss it then."

And he raised the paper once again.

Two hours later, their car stopped on a narrow street in Florence, outside a vast, austere building of rough stone.

"The Palazzo Maffei," Pendergast said from behind the wheel. "If you wouldn't mind waiting here a moment? I won't be long." He got out of the car, approached a brass plaque of door buzzers set into the facade, scanned the names, and pressed one. A moment later, a muffled voice rasped over the intercom. Pendergast answered. Then the great door buzzed open and he vanished inside.

D'Agosta watched, curious. He'd picked up enough Italian to know that what Pendergast said into the intercom hadn't sounded right. It sounded more like Latin, to tell the truth.

Getting out of the car, he crossed the narrow street and examined the buzzers. The one Pendergast pressed was labeled simply *Corso Maffei*. This told D'Agosta nothing, and he returned to their rental car.

Within ten minutes, Pendergast emerged from the building and got back into the driver's seat.

"What was that all about?" D'Agosta asked.

"Insurance," Pendergast replied. Then he turned to look intently at D'Agosta. "The chances of success in this venture are not much better than fifty-fifty. I have to do this. You do not. I would personally prefer it if you didn't come."

"No way. We're in this together."

"I see you are determined. But let me just remind you, Vincent, that you have a son and what appear to be excellent prospects for advancement, promotion, and a happy life ahead of you."

"I *said*, we're in this together."

Pendergast smiled and laid a hand on his arm—a strangely affectionate gesture from a man who hardly ever showed affection. "I knew this would be your answer, Vincent, and I am glad. I have come to rely on your common sense, your steadiness, and your shooting ability, among other excellent qualities."

D'Agosta felt himself unaccountably embarrassed and he grunted a reply.

"We should reach the castle by midafternoon. I'll brief you on the way."

The road running south from Florence into Chianti wound through some of the prettiest country D'Agosta had ever seen: hills striped with vineyards turning yellow in fall colors, and pale gray-green olive groves; fairy-tale castles and gorgeous Renaissance villas sprinkled on hills and ridges. Beyond loomed a range of forested mountains, dotted here or there with a grim monastery or an ancient bell tower.

The road loosely followed the ridges above the Greve River. As they passed over the Passo dei Pecorai, the town of Greve came into view far below, lying in a low valley along the river. As they came around another bend in the road, Pendergast pointed a finger at his side window. "Castel Fosco," he said.

It stood on a lonely spar of rock far up in the Chiantigian hills. From this distance, it looked to D'Agosta like a single massive tower, crenellated and time-worn, rising above the forest. The road turned, dipped, and the castle disappeared. A moment later Pendergast turned off the main road, and after a confusing series of turns onto ever-smaller lanes, they arrived at a mossy wall with an iron gate. The marble plaque beside it read *Castel Fosco.* The open gate was rotten and rusted, and it seemed to have settled crookedly into the very ground itself. An ancient dirt road ran up from the gate through some vineyards, climbing a steep hillside and disappearing over the brow of the hill.

As they wound their way up the hillside, Pendergast nodded toward the terraced vineyards and groves that lined the road. "A rich estate, apparently, and one of the largest in Chianti."

D'Agosta said nothing. Every yard they drove farther into the count's domain seemed to increase the sense of oppression that hung over him.

The road topped the ridge and the castle came into view again, much closer now: a monstrous stone keep perched on a crag far up the mountainside. Built into one side of the keep was a later, yet still ancient, addition: a graceful Renaissance villa with a pale yellow stuccoed exterior and red-tile roofs. Its rows of stately windows stood in strong contrast to the grim, almost brutal lines of the central keep.

The entire structure was surrounded by a double set of walls. The outermost was almost completely in ruins, consisting mostly of gaps of tumbled stone, broken towers, and crumbling battlements. The inner curtain was in much better repair and acted as a kind of retaining wall to the castle itself, its enormous ramparts providing fields of level ground around the exterior. Beyond the castle, the slopes of the mountain rose yet another thousand feet into a wild, forested amphitheater, jagged outcrops forming a serrated semicircular edge against the lowering sky.

"Over five thousand acres," said Pendergast. "I understand it dates back more than a millennium."

But D'Agosta did not reply. The sight of the castle had chilled him more than he cared to admit. The sense of oppression grew stronger. It seemed insane, walking into the lion's den like this. But he'd learned to trust Pendergast implicitly. The man never did anything without a reason. He'd outfoxed the sniper. He'd saved them from death at the hands of Bullard's men. He'd saved their lives many times before, on earlier cases. Pendergast's plan—whatever it was—would work.

Of course it would work.

{ 75 }

The car came around a final turn and passed the ruined outer gate. The castle rose above them in its stern and immense majesty. They proceeded down an avenue of cypress trees with massive ribbed trunks and stopped at a parking area just outside the inner curtain. D'Agosta peered at this wall through the passenger window with deep misgiving. It towered twenty feet over his head, its great sloping buttresses streaked with lime, dripping moss and maidenhair ferns. There was no gate in this inner wall, just a spiked and banded pair of wooden doors at the top of a broad stone staircase.

As they got out of the car, there was a humming sound, followed by a deep scraping noise, and the doors opened at an invisible cue.

They mounted the stairs, passed through a hulking doorway, and stepped into what seemed like another world. The smooth lawn of the inner ward ran for a hundred yards to the skirt of the castle itself. To one side of the lawn lay a large, circular reflecting pool surrounded by an ancient marble balustrade, ornamented at its center by a statue of Neptune astride a sea monster. To the right stood a small chapel with a tiled dome. Beyond was another marble balustrade overlooking a small garden that stepped down the hillside, ending abruptly at the fortified inner wall.

There was another scraping noise, and the ground trembled; D'Agosta turned to see the great wooden doors rumbling closed behind them.

"Never mind," murmured Pendergast. "Preparations have been made."

D'Agosta hoped to hell he knew what he was talking about. "Where's Fosco?" he asked.

"We'll no doubt see him soon enough."

They crossed the lawn and approached the main entrance of the massive keep. It opened with a creak of iron. And there stood Fosco, dressed in an elegant dove-gray suit, longish hair brushed back, his smooth white face creased with a smile. As always, he was wearing kid gloves.

"My dear Pendergast, welcome to my humble abode. And Sergeant D'Agosta, as well? Nice of you to join our little party."

He held out his hand. Pendergast ignored it.

The count let the hand drop, his smile unaffected. "A pity. I had hoped we could conduct our business with courtesy, like gentlemen."

"Is there a gentleman here? I should like to meet him."

Fosco clucked disapprovingly. "Is this a way to treat a man in his own home?"

"Is it any way to treat a man, burning him to death in his own home?"

A look of distaste crossed Fosco's face. "So anxious

to get to the business at hand, are we? But there will be time, there will be time. Do come in."

The count stood aside, and they walked through a long archway into the castle's great hall. It was quite unlike what D'Agosta had expected. A graceful loggia ran along three sides, with columns and Roman arches.

"Note the Della Robbia *tondi*," said Fosco, gesturing toward some painted terra-cotta decorations set into the walls above the arches. "But you must be tired after the drive down. I will take you to your quarters, where you can refresh yourselves."

"Our rooms?" Pendergast asked. "Are we spending the night?"

"Naturally."

"I'm afraid that won't be necessary, or even possible."

"But I must insist." The count turned and seized an iron ring on the open castle door, drawing it shut with a boom. With a dramatic flourish, he removed a giant key from his pocket and locked it. Then he opened a small wooden box mounted on the nearby wall. Inside, D'Agosta saw a high-tech keypad, wildly out of place amidst the ancient masonry. The count punched a long sequence of numbers into the keypad. In response, there was a clank, and a massive iron bar shot down from above, sliding into a heavy iron bracket and barring the door.

"Now we are safe from unauthorized invasion," said Fosco. "Or, for that matter, unauthorized departure."

Pendergast made no answer. The count turned and, moving in his peculiar light-footed way, led them through the hall and into a long, cold stone gallery. Portraits, almost black with age, lined both walls, along with mounted sets of rusted armor, spears, lances, pikes, maces, and other medieval weaponry.

"The armor is of no value, eighteenth-century reproductions. The portraits are of my ancestors, of course. Age has obscured them, fortunately—the counts of Fosco are not a pretty race. We have owned the estate since the twelfth century, when my distinguished ancestor Giovan de Ardaz wrested it from a Longobardic knight. The family bestowed the title 'cavaliere' on itself and took as its coat of arms a dragon rampant, bar sinister. During the time of the grand dukes, we were made counts of the Holy Roman Empire by the electress palatine herself. We have always led a quiet existence here, tending our vines and olive groves, neither meddling in politics nor aspiring to office. We Florentines have a saying: *The nail that sticks out gets hammered back in.* The House of Fosco did not stick out, and as a result, we never felt the blow of the hammer during many, many shifts of political fortune."

"And yet you, Count, have managed to stick yourself out quite a bit these past few months," Pendergast replied.

"Alas, and much against my will. It was only to recover what was rightfully ours to begin with. But we shall talk more of this at dinner."

They passed out of the gallery and through a beautiful drawing room with leaded-glass windows and tapestried walls. Fosco gestured toward some large landscape paintings. "Hobbema and van Ruisdael."

The drawing room was followed by a long series of graciously appointed, light-filled chambers, until quite suddenly the character of the rooms changed abruptly.

"We are now entering the original, Longobardic part of the castle," Fosco said. "Dating back to the ninth century."

Here the rooms were small and almost windowless, the only light admitted by arrow ports and tiny, square openings high on the walls. The walls were calcined, the rooms bare.

"I have no use for these dreary old rooms," said the count as they passed through. "They are always damp and cold. There are, however, several levels of cellars, tunnels, and subbasements below, most useful for making wine, *balsamico*, and *prosciutto di cinghiale*. We hunt our own boar here on the estate, you know, and it is justly famous. The lowest of those tunnels were cut into the rock by the Etruscans, three thousand years ago."

They came to a heavy iron door, set into an even heavier stone wall. Deeper within the castle, D'Agosta could see that the stonework was beaded with moisture.

"The keep," Fosco said as he unlocked the door with another key.

Immediately inside was a wide, windowless circular staircase that corkscrewed its way up from the depths and curved out of sight above their heads. Fosco removed a battery-powered torch from a wall sconce, turned it on, and led the way up the stairs. After five or six revolutions, they stopped at a small landing containing a single door. Opening it with yet another key, Fosco ushered them into what looked like a small apartment, retrofitted into the old castle keep, its tiny windows overlooking the valley of the Greve and the rolling hills marching toward Florence, far below. A fire burned in a stone fireplace at one end, and Persian rugs covered the terra-cotta floor. There was a comfortable sitting area in front of the fire; a table to one side well furnished with wines and liquors; a wall of well-stocked bookshelves.

"*Eccoci quà!* I trust you will find your chambers comfortable. There are two small bedrooms on either side. The view is refreshing, don't you think? I am concerned that you brought no luggage. I will have Pinketts furnish you with anything you might need—razors, bathrobes, slippers, sleeping shirts."

"I very much doubt we will be staying the night."

"And I very much doubt you will be leaving." The count smiled. "We eat late, in the Continental fashion. At nine."

He bowed, backed out of the door, shutting it with a hollow boom. With sinking heart, D'Agosta heard a key rasp in the lock, and then the footsteps of the count disappearing quickly down the stairway.

{ 76 }

The staging area for the move on Buck's encampment was a maintenance parking lot behind the arsenal, well out of sight of the tent city. Commissioner Rocker had called up no fewer than three NYPD riot control divisions, along with a SWAT team, two hostage negotiators, officers on horseback, two mobile command units, and plenty of rank and file with helmets and bulletproof vests to manage the arrests. Then there were the fire trucks, ambulances, and prisoner transport vans, all standing by at a discreet distance on 67th Street.

Hayward stood at the northern fringe of the staging area, giving her radio and weapon a final check. The crowd of uniformed officers milling around with batons and riot shields was enormous, not to mention various operations specialists with wires dangling from their ears and even a few confidential informants dressed as tent city residents. She understood the reason for the overkill: if you went in, you went in with overwhelming force, and nine times out of ten the opposition caved. The worst thing you could do was let them think they might have a chance if they made a stand.

And yet these people thought they had God behind them. These weren't striking bus drivers or municipal workers with spouses and kids, two cars in the driveway. These were true believers. They were unpredictable. Her approach made more sense.

Didn't it?

Rocker appeared out of the crowd, strode over, and laid a hand on Hayward's shoulder. "Ready?"

She nodded.

He gave her a fatherly pat. "Radio if you run into heavy weather. We'll move in early." He glanced at the array of men and equipment behind them. "I hope to hell none of this is necessary."

"So do I."

She could see Wentworth at one of the mobile command units, wire dangling from his ear, talking, gesturing this way and that. He was playing cop, having the time of his life. He glanced in her direction and she turned away. It would be humiliating if she failed. Not only that, it would seriously damage her career. Wentworth had already predicted failure, and it was only through Rocker's support that her mission had been approved at all. Not for the first time since the last meeting, she wondered why she'd stuck her neck out. This was not the way to advance a career. How many times had she seen that those who went with the flow rode the tide to success? D'Agosta's attitude must be rubbing off on her.

"Ready?"

She nodded.

Rocker released her shoulder. "Then have at it, Captain."

She took one more look back at the safety of the

staging area. Then she set off along a walkway that curved north around the arsenal, taking her badge from her pocket and clipping it to her jacket as she did so.

In a few minutes, the straggling outer tents of the encampment came into view. She slowed, getting a feel for the crowd. It was noon, and people were moving around everywhere. There was the smell of frying bacon in the air. As she neared the first line of tents, people stopped to stare. She nodded in a friendly way, receiving hostile looks in response. The crowd seemed a lot more tense than on Friday—and no wonder. They weren't stupid. They knew they weren't going to get away with threatening police officers. They were waiting for the second shoe to drop. She just had to make sure they realized she wasn't that shoe.

She entered one of the crooked lanes, feeling all eyes on her, hearing whispered comments. The words *Satan* and *unclean* reached her ears. She kept a friendly smile on her face, an easiness in her walk. She remembered her professor in Social Dynamics saying a crowd was like a dog: if you showed fear, it would bite; if you ran, it would chase.

The path was familiar, and in less than a minute, she found herself approaching Buck's tent. He was sitting at a table out front, reading a book, totally absorbed. The same officious man who had accosted her and Grable two days before—Buck had called him Todd—suddenly appeared in front of her. Already a crowd was forming. Nothing ugly: just curious, silent, and hostile.

"You again," the man said.

"Me again," Hayward replied. "Here to chat with the reverend."

"They're back!" the man cried to the others, stepping forward to block her way.

"Not 'they.' Just me."

The murmur of the crowd rose like an electric buzz. The air was suddenly tense. Hayward glanced back, surprised at how large the crowd was growing. *Focus on Buck.* But he remained reading at the desk, ignoring her. From here, she could make out the title: *Foxe's Book of Martyrs, Reader's Digest Edition.*

Todd advanced to the point where he was almost—but not quite—touching her with his body.

"The reverend can't be disturbed."

Hayward felt a twinge of something uncomfortably like doubt. Was this plan of hers really going to work? Or was Wentworth right, after all?

She spoke loudly enough for Buck to hear. "I'm just here to talk. I've got no arrest warrant. I just want to talk to the reverend, one human being to another."

"Prevaricator!" someone shouted from the crowd.

She had to get past this aide-de-camp blocking her way. She took a step forward, brushing him.

"That's assault, Officer," Todd said.

"If the reverend doesn't want to talk to me, let me hear him say it himself. Let the reverend make his own decisions."

"The reverend asked not to be disturbed." They were still touching, and it gave Hayward the creeps, but she sensed a back-down in the making.

She wasn't wrong. Todd took a step back, still blocking her way.

"Roman!" came a cry from the crowd.

What is it with this Roman shit? "All I ask is five

minutes of your time, Reverend," she called, leaning around Todd. "Five minutes."

At last, Buck laid down the book with great deliberation, rose from the table, and finally raised his head to look at her. The instant her eyes met his, she felt a chill. On Friday he'd seemed a little unsure of what he'd wrought; perhaps amenable to persuasion. But today there was a coolness, a calmness, a sense of utter self-confidence she had not seen before. The only emotion she sensed in him was a passing flicker, perhaps, of disappointment. She swallowed.

"Excuse me." She tried to step past the guardian.

Buck nodded to the man, who took a step to the side. Then Buck looked back at her, but the look was such she was unsure whether he was seeing her, or seeing through her.

"Reverend, I've been sent by the NYPD to ask you and your followers a favor." *Keep it chatty, informal, nonintimidating.* That's what she had learned in negotiations training. *Let them think they're making the decisions.*

But Buck showed no sign of having heard.

The crowd had fallen ominously silent. She didn't turn, but she sensed it had grown enormous by now—no doubt much of the encampment.

"Look, Reverend, we've got a problem. Your followers are ruining the park, trampling the bushes, killing the grass. On top of that, they've been using the surroundings as a public latrine. The neighbors are complaining. It's a health hazard, especially for you all."

She paused, wondering if any of this was sinking in. "Reverend, can you help us out here?"

She waited. Buck said nothing.

"I need your help."

She heard restless murmuring in the crowd behind her. People were flowing in around the back side of Buck's tent, filling her field of vision. She was truly surrounded now.

"I've got a deal to offer you. I think it's a fair deal. A straight deal."

Ask what it is, asshole. It was crucial to get him talking, asking questions, *anything.* But he said nothing. He continued looking at her, looking *past* her. Christ, she had somehow misjudged him—or something had changed since their last visit. This was not the same man.

For the first time, the real possibility of failure loomed before her.

"You want to hear it?"

No response.

She forged gamely ahead. "First, the health hazard. We don't want you or your followers to get sick. We'd like you to give your people a day off. That's all—a day off. Let them go home, shower, have a hot meal. In return, we'll give you a parade permit that'll allow you to gather lawfully with the city's blessing. Not like this, wrecking the park, annoying residents, earning the disrespect of the whole city. Look, I've heard you talk. I know you're a fair guy, a straight shooter. I'm giving you a chance to go legit, earn some respect—and still get your message out."

She stopped. *Don't say too much. Let him come round.*

All around them, an air of expectancy had grown. Everyone was waiting for the reverend to speak. It all depended on Buck.

At last, he moved. He blinked, raised his hand

slowly, almost robotically. The tension increased with the silence. It was so silent, in fact, Hayward could hear birds chirping in the trees around them.

The hand came around and pointed at her.

"Centurion," he said in a voice so low it was barely more than a whisper.

It was like the release of pressure from a cooker. *"Centurion!"* came the sudden cry of the crowd. "*Soldier of Rome!*" The throng jostled and shoved as it began to close in.

For the first time, Hayward felt a stab of real fear. Failure was becoming a foregone conclusion, but there was more than her career at stake now. This crowd was dangerously aroused.

"Reverend, if your answer is no—"

But Buck had turned away, and now, to her overwhelming dismay, he was entering his tent, lifting the flap, disappearing inside. More people streamed in where he'd stood, filling the gap.

He'd left her to the mercy of the crowd.

She turned to face them. *Now it was time to get the hell out.* "All right, folks, I know when to take no for an answer—"

"Silence, Judas!"

Hayward saw sticks once again, swaying above the heads. It amazed her how ugly a crowd could get, so quickly. She had failed, failed miserably. Her career was ruined, no question. The real question was whether she could get out in one piece.

"I'm leaving," she said loudly and firmly. "I'm leaving, and I expect to be allowed to leave peacefully. I am an officer of the law."

She moved toward the wall of people, but this time no path opened. She kept walking, expecting, hoping for, them to fall back. But they didn't. Several hands reached out and shoved her back—hard.

"I came in peace!" she said loudly, trying to keep the tremor out of her voice. "And I'm leaving in peace!" She took another step toward the wall of people, coming face-to-face with Todd. He was brandishing something in one hand. A rock.

"Don't do anything stupid," she said.

He raised his hand as if to throw. She immediately took a step toward him, looking into his eyes, just as one would do with a dangerous dog. It was always the crazies who got to the front of a hot crowd. The followers stayed back, hoping for a good lick once the adversary was down and helpless. But these front ones, they were the killers.

Todd took a step back. "Judas bitch," he said, waving the rock threateningly.

Reaching down inside and searching for calm, Hayward quickly reviewed her options. If she pulled her piece, that would be the end. Sure, by firing into the air she might drive them back for a moment, but they would be on her in a flash and she'd be forced to shoot into the crowd. And then she'd be dead meat. She could call Rocker, but it would be ten minutes at least before he could mobilize and move in. Blood would be up, and he'd meet immediate resistance. By the time they reached her... God, she didn't have ten minutes, she didn't even have five.

The only one who could control this crowd was Buck, and he was in his tent.

She backed up, turning in a slow circle. The crowd was so thick she couldn't even see his tent anymore. And she was being pushed away from it, as if the crowd wanted to keep the unpleasantness of what was to come away from him. Taunts and chanting rose from all sides.

She searched her mind desperately for something useful from her training. Crowd psychology was something that interested her, especially after the Wisher Riots a few years back. Problem was, an angry crowd did not behave like a normal human being. A crowd did not respond to the cues of body language. A crowd did not listen to anything except itself. You could not reason with a crowd. A crowd would enthusiastically commit an act of violence no single member would normally condone.

"Centurion!" Todd had taken another step forward, emboldened, the crowd consolidating behind him. Hysterically angry. They weren't going to hurt her—they were going to kill her.

"Buck!" she shouted, turning, but it was hopeless, he couldn't hear over the taunts of the crowd.

She faced them again. "You call yourselves Christians?" she screamed. "Look at you!"

Wrong move. It just pushed their anger up a notch. But it was all she had left.

"Ever heard of turning the other cheek? Loving thy neighbor—"

"Blasphemer!" Todd shook his rock, the crowd flowing with him.

She was really frightened now. She took a step back, felt herself shoved from behind. Her voice cracked. "In the Bible, it says—"

"She's blaspheming the Bible!"

"You hear her?"

"Shut her up!"

A dead end. Hayward knew she was out of time. She had to figure out something before the stones came raining down. Once the first was thrown, it wouldn't stop until it was over.

The problem was, she'd exhausted all her options. There was nothing left to do.

Nothing.

{ 77 }

At five minutes to nine, D'Agosta turned from the window to see Pendergast rising calmly from the sofa, where he had been lying motionless for the past half hour. Earlier, the agent had established he could open the door with his lock-picking tools, but he seemed uninterested in exploring, so he'd relocked it and they had waited.

"Good nap?" He wondered how Pendergast could sleep at a time like this. He felt so keyed up it seemed he'd never be able to sleep again.

"I wasn't napping, Vincent—I was thinking."

"Yeah. So was I. Like how are we going to get out of this place?"

"Surely you don't think I have brought us in here without a well-conceived plan of departure? And if my plan does not work, I am a great believer in improvisation."

"Improvisation? I don't like the sound of that."

"These old castles are full of holes. One way or another we'll escape with the evidence we need and return with reinforcements. Reinforcements that will only be convinced by the evidence. Coming here, Vincent, *was* our only option—aside from giving up."

"That's not an option in my book."

"Nor in mine."

There was a knock at the door. It opened and Pinketts stood there, in full livery. D'Agosta's hand drifted toward his service piece.

Pinketts gave a slight bow and said, in his plummy English, "Dinner is served."

They followed him back down the staircase and through a series of rooms and passageways to the dining *salotto.* It was a cheerful space, painted yellow, with a high vaulted ceiling. The table had been laid with silver and plate, an arrangement of fresh roses in the middle. There were three places set.

Fosco was standing at the far end of the room, where a small fire burned in the grate of an enormous stone fireplace, surmounted with a carved coat of arms. He turned quickly, a little white mouse scampering over his fat hand and running up his sleeve.

"Welcome." He put the mouse away in a small wire pagoda. "Mr. Pendergast, you will sit here, on my right; Mr. D'Agosta on my left, if you please."

D'Agosta seated himself, edging his chair away from Fosco. The count had always given him the creeps; now he could hardly stand to be in the same room. The man was a fiend.

"A little *prosecco*? It is my own."

Both men shook their heads. Fosco shrugged. Pinketts filled his glass with the wine, and the count raised it.

"To the Stormcloud," he said. "Pity you can't toast. Have some water, at least."

"Sergeant D'Agosta and I are abstaining tonight," replied Pendergast.

"I have prepared a marvelous repast." He drained the glass and, on cue, Pinketts brought out a platter heaped with what looked to D'Agosta like cold cuts.

"Affettati misti toscani," said Fosco. "Prosciutto from boar taken on the estate, shot by myself, in fact. Won't you try some? *Finocchiona* and *soprassata*, also from the estate."

"No, thank you."

"Mr. D'Agosta?"

D'Agosta didn't answer.

"Pity we don't have a dwarf handy to taste the food. I so dislike eating alone."

Pendergast leaned forward. "Shall we leave the dinner aside, Fosco, and settle the business at hand? Sergeant D'Agosta and I cannot stay the night."

"But I insist."

"Your insistence means nothing. We will go when we choose."

"You will not be leaving—tonight, or any other night, for that matter. I suggest you eat. It will be your last meal. Don't worry, it isn't poisoned. I have a much cleverer fate in mind for you both."

This was greeted by silence.

Pinketts came and poured a glass of red wine. The count swirled it in his glass, tasted it, nodded. Then he looked at Pendergast. "When did you realize it was me?"

Pendergast's reply, when it came, was slow. "I found a fragment of horsehair at the site of Bullard's murder. I knew it came from a violin bow. At that point, I recalled the name of Bullard's boat: the *Stormcloud*. It all came together: I realized then that this case was merely a sordid attempt at theft through murder and intimidation. My thoughts naturally turned to you—although I'd long been sure the business went beyond Bullard."

"Clever. I didn't expect you to put it together so quickly—hence the unseemly rush to kill the old priest. I regret that more than I can say. It was unnecessary, stupid. I had a momentary panic."

"'Unnecessary'?" snapped D'Agosta. "'Stupid'? We're talking about murdering another human being here."

"Spare me the moral absolutism." Fosco sipped his wine, folded a piece of prosciutto onto his fork, ate it, recovered his good humor. He glanced back at Pendergast. "As for me, I knew you were going to be a problem within five minutes of encountering you. Who'd have expected a man like you would go into law enforcement?"

When he didn't receive an answer, he raised his glass in another toast. "From the very first time I met you, I knew that I would have to kill you. And here we are."

He took a sip, set down the glass. "I had hoped that idiot Bullard would pull it off. But, of course, he failed."

"You put him up to that, naturally."

"Let us just say that, in his frightened condition, he was susceptible to suggestion. And so now it is left to me. But first, don't you think you should congratulate me on a beautifully executed plan? I extracted the violin from Bullard. And as you know well, Mr. Pendergast, there are no witnesses or physical evidence to connect me to the murders."

"You have the violin. Bullard once had it. That can be established beyond the shadow of a doubt."

"It belongs to the Fosco family by legal right. I still have the bill of sale, signed by Antonio Stradivari himself, and the chain of ownership is beyond question. A suitable period will pass following Bullard's death; then the violin will surface in Rome. I've planned it down to the last detail. I will make my claim, pay a small reward to the lucky shopkeeper, and it will come to me free and clear. Bullard told no one why he needed to remove the violin from his laboratory, not even the people at his company. How could he?" Fosco issued a dry chuckle. "So you see, there is nothing, Mr. Pendergast, no evidence at all against me. But then, I have always been a most fortunate man in such matters." He bit off a piece of bread. "For example, there is an extraordinary coincidence at the very heart of this affair. Do you know what it is?"

"I can guess."

"On October 31, 1974, in the early afternoon, while on my way out of the Biblioteca Nazionale, I ran into a group of callow American students. You know the type—they throng Florence all year long. It was the afternoon of All Hallows' Eve—Halloween to them, of course—and they'd been drinking to excess. I was young and callow myself, and I found them so astonishingly vulgar that they amused me. We fell in for the moment. At some point, one of the students—Jeremy Grove to be precise—went on a tear about religion, about God being rubbish for the weak mind, that sort of thing. The sheer arrogance of it annoyed me. I said that I couldn't speak on the existence of God, but I did know one thing: that the devil existed."

Fosco laughed silently, his capacious front shaking.

"They all roundly denied the existence of the devil.

I said I had friends who dabbled in the occult, who had collected old manuscripts and that sort of thing, and that, in fact, I had an old parchment which contained formulas on how to raise Lucifer himself. We could settle the question that very night. The night was perfect, in fact, being Halloween. Would they like to try it? Oh, yes, they said. What a marvelous idea!"

Another internal disturbance shook Fosco's person.

"So you put on a show for them."

"Exactly. I invited them to a midnight séance in my castle, and then rushed back myself to set it all up. It was a great deal of fun. Pinketts helped—and, by the way, he isn't English at all, but a manservant named Pinchetti who happens to be both a clever linguist and a lover of intrigue. We had only six hours, but we did it up rather well. I've always been a tinkerer, a builder of machines and gadgets, and incidentally a designer of *fuochi d'artificio*—fireworks. There are all sorts of secret passageways, trapdoors, and hidden panels in the cellars here, and we took full advantage of them. That was a night to remember! You should have seen their faces as we recited the incantations, asked the Prince of Darkness to bring them great wealth, offered their souls in return, pricked their fingers and signed contracts in blood—especially when Pinketts activated the theatrics." He leaned back, pealing with laughter.

"You terrified them. You scared Beckmann so much it ruined his life."

"It was all in good fun. If it shook up their pathetic little certainties, so much the better. They went their way and I went mine. And here comes the coincidence so marvelous I feel it must be predestination: thirty years later, I discovered to my horror that one of these philistines had *acquired* the Stormcloud."

"How did you learn?" Pendergast asked.

"I had been on the track of the Stormcloud almost my entire adult life, Mr. Pendergast. I made it my life's goal to return that violin to my family. You've been to see Lady Maskelene, so you know its history. I knew perfectly well Toscanelli had not thrown it into the Falls of the Sciliar. How could he? As crazy as he was, he knew better than anyone what that violin represented. But if he didn't destroy it, then what had happened? The answer is not so mysterious. He froze to death in a shepherd's hut up on the Sciliar, and then it snowed. There were no footprints in the snow. Obviously, someone had found him dead with the violin *before* it snowed and had stolen the violin. And who was this someone? Just as obviously, the man who owned the hut."

Pinketts whisked away his plate, then returned bearing another of *tortelloni* with butter and salvia. Fosco tucked into it with relish.

"Remember how I told you I loved detective work? I have a rare talent for it. I traced the Stormcloud from the shepherd, to his nephew, to a band of Gypsies, to a shop in Spain, to an orphanage in Malta—this way and that it traveled. I shudder to think of the times it was left in the sun; packed in a case with a few threads of straw and thrown into the back of a truck; left unattended in some school auditorium. *Mio Dio!* Yet it survived. It ended up in France, where it was sold in a lot of junk instruments to a lycée. Some clumsy oaf in the orchestra dropped it, chipped one of the scrolls, and it was taken to a violin shop in Angoulême for repair. The man who owned the shop recognized it, substituted it, and sent back another instrument in its place." Fosco clucked disapprovingly. "What a moment that must have been for him! He knew he could never acquire legal title to it, so he smuggled it to America and quietly put it up for sale. It took a long time to find a buyer. Who wanted a Stradivarius if you couldn't play it as a Strad? If you could never establish title to it? If it might be taken from you at any moment? But he finally did find a buyer—in Locke Bullard. Two million dollars—that was all! I found out three months after the deal had closed."

A dark furor passed over Fosco's face, rapidly clearing as Pinketts carried in the next course, a *bistecca fiorentina*, sizzling from the fire. Fosco carved off a piece of almost raw meat, placed it in his mouth, chewed.

"I was perfectly willing to buy it from Bullard, even paying a handsome price, despite the fact it was mine to begin with. But I never got to the point of making an offer. You see, Bullard was going to destroy the violin."

"To crack Stradivari's secret formulas once and for all."

"Exactly. And do you know why?"

"I know Bullard was not in the business of making violins, nor did he have any interest in music."

"True. But do you know the business his company, BAI, *was* into? With the Chinese?"

Pendergast did not reply.

"Missiles, my dear Pendergast. He was working on *ballistic missiles.* That's why he needed the violin!"

"Bullshit!" D'Agosta interjected. "There can't possibly

be a connection between a three-hundred-year-old violin and a ballistic missile."

Fosco ignored this. He was still looking at Pendergast. "I sense you know rather more than you let on, my good sir. In any case, I penetrated their laboratory with a mole in my employ. Poor fellow ended up with his head crushed. But before that happened, he did tell me just what Bullard planned to do with the violin."

He leaned forward, eyes flashing with indignation. "The Chinese, you see, had developed a ballistic missile that could theoretically penetrate the United States' planned antimissile shield. But they had a problem with their missiles breaking up on re-entry. To make the missile invisible to radar, you know, one can't have any curved or shiny surfaces. Look at the strange angular shapes of your stealth fighters and bombers. But this wasn't a bomber flying at six hundred miles an hour: this was a ballistic missile re-entering the atmosphere at ten times that speed. Their test missiles broke up under uncontrollable resonance vibrations during atmospheric re-entry."

Pendergast nodded almost imperceptibly.

"Bullard's scientists realized the solution to this problem lay in the *Stradivari formula for the varnish.* Can you imagine? You see, the key to the Stradivari varnish is that, after a few years of playing, it develops billions of microscopic cracks and flaws, too small to be seen. These are phenomenally effective in dampening and warming the sound of a Stradivari. This is also why the violin must be played regularly—otherwise, the cracks and flaws start knitting back up. Bullard was designing a high-performance coating for those Chinese missiles that would do the same thing—a coating that would have billions of microscopic flaws to dampen the vibrational resonance of re-entry. But he had to figure out *precisely* what the physics was, why those cracks and flaws did what they did. He had to know how they were distributed three-dimensionally in the varnish; how they made contact with the wood; how wide, long, and deep they were; how they connected to each other."

Fosco stopped talking long enough to eat some more steak and sip his wine.

"To do that, Bullard needed to cut up a golden period Strad. Any would do, but none were for sale—especially to him. And then along came the black-market Stormcloud. *Ecco fatto!*"

D'Agosta stared in mingled repulsion and disbelief as the count wiped his red and greasy lips on an oversize napkin. It seemed outrageous, impossible.

"Now you see, Pendergast, why I needed to go to such lengths. It was worth a billion to Bullard on the Chinese deal alone. With more money to come as he resold the technology to a host of other eager buyers. I *had* to get the violin quickly, before he destroyed it. He had already brought it to his Italian laboratory, where it was guarded under truly impenetrable security. And that's when it came to me. I'd use the only leverage I had: our first and only encounter, thirty years ago. I'd *frighten* Bullard into giving up the violin!"

"Through murdering the others who had been at the staged devil raising."

"Yes. I would kill Grove, Beckmann, and Cutforth, making it look in each case like the devil had finally come for their souls. Beckmann seemed to have disappeared, so that left only Grove and Cutforth. Only two. Whatever I did, it had to be utterly convincing. Bullard was an ignorant, blustering man with few religious impulses. I needed a way to kill them that was so unique and dreadful that the police would be baffled, that would generate all kinds of talk about the devil—and most important, that would convince Bullard. It had to be heat, naturally. And that was how I came to invent my little device. But that is another story."

He paused for another sip of wine.

"I prepared the scene of Grove's death with great care. I began by calling and alarming him with a story of a terrible visitation I'd had; how I feared Lucifer was coming for us because of the ceremony years before, how we had to do something. He was skeptical at first, so I had Pinketts set up a few bits of stage business in his house. Strange sounds, smells, and the like. Remarkable how a few props can undermine the conviction of even the most arrogant man. He grew frightened. I suggested some kind of atonement for his sins; hence, the peculiar dinner party. I loaned him my beloved cross. The poor fool gave me the keys to his house, the codes to the alarm system—everything I needed.

"His death worked like a charm. Almost immediately Bullard was on the phone to me. I was careful to ensure all my calls were made from an untraceable phone card. I continued playing the role of terrified count. I told him of strange things that had happened to me, sulfurous smells, disembodied sounds, uncomfortable tingling sensations—all the things, of course, that would happen to him later. I pretended to be convinced the devil was coming for all of us: after all, we had offered our souls in the compact we made thirty years before. The devil had completed his side of the bargain; now it was time for us to fulfill ours.

"After sending Bullard off to stew about this, it was time to deal with Cutforth. I had Pinketts here purchase the apartment next to his, posing as an English baronet, to assist with the various, ah, *arrangements.* Like Grove, Cutforth scoffed at the idea at first. He'd been convinced my little show back in 1974 was a fraud. But as details of Grove's death emerged, he grew increasingly nervous. I didn't want him *too* nervous—just nervous enough to call Bullard and alarm him further. Which, of course, he did."

He issued a dry laugh.

"After Cutforth's death, your vulgar tabloids did a fabulous job beating the drum, whipping people into a frenzy. It was perfect. And Bullard fell apart. He was out of his mind. Then the *colpo di grazia*: I called Bullard and said that I had managed to cancel my contract with Lucifer!"

Fosco patted his hands together with delight. Watching, D'Agosta felt his stomach turn.

"He was desperate to know how. I told him I'd located an ancient manuscript explaining the devil would sometimes accept a gift in return for a human soul. But it had to be a truly unique gift, something of enormous rarity, something whose loss would debase the human spirit. I told him I'd sacrificed my Vermeer in just such a way.

"Poor Bullard was beside himself. He had no Vermeer, he said; nothing of value except boats, cars, houses, and companies. He begged me to advise him what he should buy, what he should give the devil. I told him it had to be something utterly unique and precious, an object that would impoverish the world by its loss. I said I couldn't advise him—naturally he couldn't know I was aware of the Stormcloud—and I said I doubted he owned anything the devil would want, that I had been hugely fortunate to have a Vermeer, that the devil surely would not have accepted my Caravaggio!"

At this witticism, Fosco burst into laughter.

"I told Bullard that, whatever it was, the devil had to have it immediately. The thirty-year anniversary of our original pact was nearing. Grove and Cutforth were already dead. There was not enough time for him to acquire something of the requisite rarity. I reminded him the devil would be able to see into his heart, that there would be no cheating the old gentleman, and that whatever he offered had better fit the bill or his soul would burn forever.

"That's when he finally broke down and told me he had a violin of great rarity, a Stradivarius called the Stormcloud—would that do? I told him I couldn't speak for the devil, but that I hoped for his sake it would. I congratulated him on being so fortunate."

Fosco paused to place another piece of dripping meat into his mouth. "I, of course, returned to Italy far earlier than I let on to you. I was here even before Bullard arrived. I dug an old grimoire out of the library here, gave it to him, told him to follow the ritual and place the violin inside a broken circle. Within his own, unbroken circle, he would be protected. But he must send away all his help, turn off the alarm system, and so forth—the devil didn't like interruptions. The poor man did as I asked. In place of the devil, I sent in Pinketts, who is devil enough, I can tell you. With theatrical effects and the appropriate garb. He took the violin and retreated, while I used my little machine to dispense with Bullard."

"Why the machine and the theatrics?" Pendergast asked quietly. "Why not put a bullet in him? The need to terrify your victim had passed."

"That was for *your* benefit, my dear fellow! It was a way to stir up the police, keep you in Italy a while longer. Where you would be easier to dispose of."

"Whether we will be easy to dispose of remains to be seen."

Fosco chuckled with great good humor. "You evidently think you have something to bargain with, otherwise you wouldn't have accepted my invitation."

"That is correct."

"Whatever you think you have, it won't be good enough. You are already as good as dead. I know you better than you realize. I know you because you are like me. You are *very* like me."

"You could not be more wrong, Count. I am not a murderer."

D'Agosta was surprised to see a faint blush of color in Pendergast's face.

"No, but you *could* be. You have it in you. I can see it."

"You see nothing."

Fosco had finished his steak and now he rose. "You think me an evil man. You call this whole affair sordid. But consider what I've done. I've saved the world's greatest violin from destruction. I've prevented the Chinese from penetrating the planned U.S. antimissile shield, removing a threat to millions of your fellow citizens. And at what cost? The lives of a pederast, a traitor, a producer of popular music who was filling the world with his filth, and a godless soul who destroyed everyone he touched."

"You haven't included our lives in this calculation."

Fosco nodded. "Yes. You and the unfortunate priest. Regrettable indeed. But if the truth be known, I'd waste a hundred lives for that instrument. There are five billion people. There is only one Stormcloud."

"It isn't worth even one human life," D'Agosta heard himself say.

Fosco turned, his eyebrows raised in surprise. "No?"

He turned and clapped his hands. Pinketts appeared at the door.

"Get me the violin."

The man disappeared and returned a moment later with an old wooden case, shaped like a small dark coffin, covered with the patina of ages. Pinketts placed it on a table next to the wall and withdrew to a far corner.

Fosco rose and strolled over to the case. He took out the bow, tightened it, ran a rosin up and down a few times, and then—slowly, lovingly—withdrew the violin. To D'Agosta, it didn't look at all extraordinary: just a violin, older than most. Hard to believe it had led them on this long journey, cost so many lives.

Fosco placed it under his chin, stood tall and straight. A moment of silence passed while he sighed, half closing his eyes. And then the bow began moving slowly over the strings, the notes flowing clearly. It was one of the few classical tunes D'Agosta recognized, one that his grandfather used to sing to him as a child: Bach's *Jesu, Joy of Man's Desiring*. The melody was simple, the measured notes rising, one after another, in a dignified cadence, filling the air with beautiful sound.

The room seemed to change. It became suffused with a kind of transcendent brightness. The tremulous purity of the sound took D'Agosta's breath away. The melody filled him like a presence, sweet and clean, speaking in a language beyond words. A language of pure beauty.

And then the melody was over. It was like being yanked from a dream. D'Agosta realized that, for a moment, he'd lost track of everything: Fosco, the killings, their perilous situation. Now it all came back with redoubled vengeance, all the worse for having been temporarily forgotten.

There was a silence while Fosco lowered the violin. Then he spoke in a whisper, his voice trembling. "You see now? This is not just a violin. It is *alive*. Do you understand, Mr. D'Agosta, why the sound of the Stradivarius is so beautiful? Because it is mortal. Because it is like the beating heart of a bird in flight. It reminds us that all beautiful things must die. The profound beauty of music lies somehow in its very transience and fragility. It breathes for a shining moment—and then it expires. That was the genius of Stradivari: he captured that moment in wood and varnish. He *immortalized* mortality."

He looked back at Pendergast, eyes still haunted. "Yes, the music always dies. But *this*"—he held up the violin—"will never die. It will outlive us all a hundred times over. Tell me now, Mr. Pendergast, that I have done wrong to save this violin. Please, say that I have committed a crime."

Pendergast said nothing.

"I'll say it," said D'Agosta. "You're a cold-blooded murderer."

"Ah, yes," Fosco murmured. "One can always count on a philistine to lay down absolute morality." He carefully wiped down the violin with a soft cloth and put it away. "Beautiful as it is, it isn't at its best. It needs more playing. I've been exercising it every day, fifteen minutes at first, now up to half an hour. It's healing already. In another six months, it will be back to its perfect self. I will loan it to Renata Lichtenstein. Do you know her? The first woman to win the Tchaikovsky Competition, a girl of only eighteen but already a transcendental genius. Yes, Renata will play it and go on to glory and renown. And then, when she can no longer play, my heir will loan it to someone else, and his heir to someone else, and so it will go down the centuries."

"Do you have an heir?" Pendergast asked.

D'Agosta was surprised by the question. But Fosco was not; he seemed to welcome it.

"Not a direct heir, no. But I shall not wait long to furnish myself with a son. I have just met the most charming woman. The only drawback is that she is English, but at least she can boast an Italian great-grandfather." His smile broadened.

As D'Agosta watched, Pendergast grew pale. "You are grotesquely deluded if you think *she* will marry you."

"I know, I know. Count Fosco is fat, revoltingly fat. But do not underestimate the power of a charming tongue to capture a woman's heart. Lady Maskelene and I had a marvelous afternoon on the island. We are both of the noble classes. We *understand* each other." He dusted his waistcoat. "I might even go on a diet."

This was greeted by a short silence. Then Pendergast spoke again. "You've showed us the violin. May we now see this little device that you spoke of? The device that killed at least four men?"

"With greatest pleasure. I'm very proud of it. Not only will I show it to you, I'll give you a demonstration."

D'Agosta felt a chill. *Demonstration?*

Fosco nodded to Pinketts, who took the violin and left the room. Within moments he returned with a large aluminum suitcase. Fosco unlatched the case and raised the lid, exposing half a dozen pieces of metal nestled in gray foam rubber. He began removing them, screwing them together. Then he turned and nodded to D'Agosta.

"Will you please stand over there, Sergeant?" he asked quietly.

{ 78 }

"Buck!" Hayward screamed again, fighting against an almost overwhelming panic. "Don't let them do this!" But it was hopeless; the roar of the crowd drowned out her voice, and Buck was in his tent, flaps closed, out of sight behind a wall of people.

The crowd was closing in now, the noose tightening fast. The ringleader—Buck's aide-de-camp, bolstered by increasingly frenzied followers—raised the hand with the rock. Watching him, Hayward saw his eyes widen, his nostrils flare. She'd seen that look before: it was the look of someone about to strike.

"Don't!" she shouted. "This isn't what you're about! It's against everything you stand for!"

"Shut up, centurion!" Todd cried.

She stumbled, righted herself. Even at this moment of extreme danger, she realized she could not show fear. She kept her eyes on Todd—he was the greatest threat, the match for the powder keg—and let her gun hand hover near her piece. As a last resort—a very last resort—she'd have to use it. Of course, once she did, that would be the end. But she wasn't going to go down like a cat under a pack of dogs.

Something about all this isn't right. Something was going on; something was being played out here that she didn't understand.

The cries of the crowd, their strange epithets, made no sense. *Centurion. Soldier of Rome.* What was this talk? Something Buck was subtly encouraging in recent sermons? And speaking of Buck, why had he seemed disappointed when she arrived—and then just walked away? Why the glassy, expectant look in his eyes? Something had happened to him, between this visit and the last.

What was it?

"Blasphemer!" Todd screamed. He took another step closer.

In response, the crowd tightened around Hayward. She had barely enough room to turn around now. She could feel rancid breath on the back of her neck; feel her heart beating like mad. Her hand strayed closer to the butt of her gun.

There was a pattern here, if only she could see it. There *had* to be.

She fought to stay rational. Her only way out of this was Buck himself. There was no other.

Quickly, she went back over her knowledge of deviant psychology, over Buck's possible motivations. What had Wentworth said? *Possibly paranoid schizophrenic, potential for a Messianic complex.* Deep down, she was still convinced Buck was no schizophrenic.

But a Messianic complex . . . ?

The need to be the Messiah. Perhaps—just perhaps—Wentworth was more right on that point than he knew.

Then, in an instant of revelation, it came to her. All of Buck's new hopes, new desires, were suddenly laid bare. This talk about Romans—they weren't talking about Roman Catholics. They were talking about real Romans. Pagan Romans. Centurions. *The soldiers who came to arrest Jesus.*

She suddenly understood the script Buck was following. *That* was why he ignored her, walked back into the tent. *She didn't fit into his vision of what had to happen.*

She faced the crowd, addressed them in her loudest voice. "A band of soldiers are coming to arrest Buck!"

This had a galvanic effect on the crowd. The yelling faltered a little, front to back, like the ripple of a stone on a pond.

"Did you hear!"

"The soldiers are coming!"

"They're coming!" Hayward yelled encouragingly.

The crowd took up the cry as she hoped they would, acting as a megaphone to Buck. *"The soldiers are coming! The centurions are coming!"*

There was a movement in the crowd, a kind of general sigh. As one group moved back, Hayward saw that Buck had reappeared at the door of his tent. The crowd seethed with expectation. Todd raised his rock once again, then hesitated.

It was the opening she needed. Momentary, but just enough to call Rocker. She slipped out her radio and bent forward, shielding herself from the crowd.

"Commissioner!" she called out.

For a moment, static. Then Rocker's voice crackled over the tiny speaker.

"What the hell's going on, Captain? It sounds like a

riot. We're mobilizing, we're going in *now* and getting your ass *out*—"

"No!" Hayward said sharply. "It'll be a bloodbath!"

"She's using her radio!" Todd screamed. "Betrayer!"

"Sir, *listen to me.* Send in thirty-three men. Thirty-three *exactly.* And those undercover cops you've been using for on-site intel, the ones dressed like Buck's followers? Send in one of them. *Just one.*"

"Captain, I have no idea what you're—"

"Shut up, please, and *listen.* Buck has to act out the passion of Christ. That's how he sees himself. He's New York's sacrificial lamb. There's no other explanation for his behavior. So we've got to play along, let him act it out. The undercover cop, he's the shill, he's Judas, he's got to embrace Buck. Do you hear, sir? *He's got to embrace Buck.* And then the cops move in and make the cuff. You do that, Commissioner, *and there'll be no riot.* Buck will go peacefully. Otherwise—"

"But thirty men? That's not enough—"

"*Thirty-three.* The number in a Roman band."

"Get her radio!" Hayward was jostled. She spun away, shielding her radio.

"Are you telling me Buck thinks—"

"Just do it, sir. *Now!*"

Hayward felt herself shoved hard from behind. She lost her grip on the radio, and it went flying into the crowd.

"Agent of darkness!"

Hayward had no idea if Rocker had understood. More to the point, she didn't know how the crowd would act. Buck might have his script, but would this frenzied mob follow it, too?

She looked toward Buck, who was now wading into the crowd. "Make way for the soldiers of Rome!" she yelled. "Make way!" She pointed southwest, the direction she knew the police would come from.

It was amazing: people were turning, looking. Buck himself was looking. He was standing, calm and tall, waiting for the drama to begin.

"Here they come!" others were yelling. "*Here they come!"*

There was a surge of confusion, a scuffling as the rest of the group began to arm themselves with rocks and sticks. Suddenly Buck held up his arms, tried to say something. The sound of the crowd fell.

"He's about to speak!" people called out. *"Silence, everyone!"*

Buck intoned in a deep, penetrating voice, "Make way for the centurions!"

This took everyone by surprise. Some took tighter grips on their makeshift weapons; others looked over their shoulders, in the direction of the approaching police. Still others looked at Buck, uncertain they had heard him correctly.

"This is as it should be!" Buck cried. "It is time to fulfill that which the prophets have spoken. Make way, my brothers and sisters, make way!"

The cry was taken up, at first raggedly, then with growing conviction. *"Make way!"*

"Do not fight them!" Buck cried. "Drop your weapons! Make way for the centurions!"

"Make way for the centurions!"

Buck spread his hands, and the crowd began to part hesitatingly before him.

As she watched, Hayward felt a flush spread through her limbs. It was working. The attention of the crowd had shifted from her. Only Todd, the aide-de-camp, seemed not to accept the change. He was still staring from her to Buck and back again, as if too caught up in the frenzy of the moment to shift direction.

"*Traitor!*" he barked at her.

And now, right on cue, a phalanx of cops came running through the distant trees toward them. Rocker *had* understood, after all: he'd come through. They waded into the outer fringes of the crowd, shoving and pushing with their riot shields. But already, with Buck's exhortations, the people were falling back.

"Let them pass!" Buck was crying, arms spread.

Now the cops were barreling down the open lane, trampling tents, shoving aside stragglers. As they broke into the open area before Buck's tent, there was a moment of panic and struggle. Todd raised his rock, fury twisting his features. "You did this, you *bitch*—!"

And the rock came flying, striking a glancing blow to Hayward's temple. She staggered back, fell to her knees, feeling the hot trickle of blood.

Suddenly Buck was there, his strong arms around her, raising her up and staying the crowd with his hand. "Put up thy swords! They have come to arrest me, and I will go with them peacefully! This is the will of God!"

Dazed, Hayward looked at Buck. He dabbed at her wound with a snowy handkerchief. "Suffer ye thus far," he murmured. His face was radiant, suffused with light.

Of course, she thought. *Even this is part of the script.*

There was more confusion. Someone embraced Buck—the shill at last—she heard Buck saying, "Judas, betrayest thou me with a kiss?"—and then the cops were all around, and he was pulled away from her. The cut on her head was bleeding freely, and she felt woozy.

"Captain Hayward?" she heard somebody call out. "Captain Hayward's been hurt!"

"Officer down! We need a medic!"

"Captain Hayward, you all right? Did he assault you?"

"I'm all right," she said, shaking away the wooziness as cops crowded around her, everyone trying to help. "It's nothing, just a scratch. It wasn't Buck."

"She's bleeding!"

"Forget it, it's nothing. Let me go." They released her reluctantly.

"Who was it? Who assaulted you?"

Todd was staring, humanity shocked back into him, horrified at what he'd done.

Hayward looked away. Another arrest right now could be disastrous. "Don't know. Came out of nowhere. It doesn't matter."

"Let's get you to an ambulance."

"I'll walk by myself," she said, brushing off yet another proffered arm. She felt embarrassed. It *was* nothing: scalp wounds always bled a great deal. She looked around, blinking her eyes. An immense silence seemed to have settled on the crowd. The police had the cuffs on Buck and had formed a semicircle around him, already moving him out. The crowd looked on, stunned, while Buck exhorted them to remain calm, be peaceful, hurt no one.

"Forgive them," he said.

All the momentum was gone. Buck had ordered them to stand down, and they had obeyed.

It was over.

{ 79 }

Immediately, D'Agosta pulled out his service piece and drew down on the count. "No fucking way," he said.

The count stared at the gun, sighing condescendingly. "Put away that gun, you fool. Pinketts?"

The manservant, who had left the room, now returned, carrying a large pumpkin in both arms. He set it down on the hearth before the fireplace.

"It is true, Sergeant D'Agosta, you would have been a much more effective demonstration. But it would have caused such a *mess*." Fosco went back to assembling the device.

D'Agosta moved slowly backward, slipping his gun back into his holster as he did so. Somehow, the act of drawing his weapon brought fresh resolve. He and Pendergast were both armed. At the first indication of trouble, he would have no hesitation about taking out both the count and Pinketts. Except for some kitchen help, there didn't seem to be any other servants around—but he knew that, with the count, appearances were deceptive.

"There we go." Fosco hefted the assembled machine,

which looked something like a large rifle, made primarily of stainless steel, with a bulbous dish at one end and a barrel sporting half a dozen buttons and dials at the other. "As I said, I knew I had to kill Grove and Cutforth in such a way that the police would be utterly baffled. It had to be done with heat, of course. But how? Burning, arson, boiling—much too common. It had to be mysterious, unexplainable. That was when I recalled the phenomenon known as spontaneous human combustion. You know the first documented case of it was here in Italy?"

Pendergast nodded. "The countess Cornelia."

"Countess Cornelia Zangari de' Bandi di Cesena. Most dramatic. How, I wondered, could a similarly devilish effect be duplicated? Then I thought of *microwaves.*"

"Microwaves?" D'Agosta repeated.

The count smiled patronizingly at him. "Yes, Sergeant. Just like your own microwave oven. They seemed perfect for my needs. Microwaves heat from the inside out. They can be focused, just like light, to—say—burn a body while leaving the rest of the environment intact. Microwaves heat water far more selectively than dry materials, fats, or oils, so they would burn a wet body before heating the rugs or furnishings. And they have an ionizing and heating effect on metals with a certain number of valence electrons."

Fosco ran a hand over his device, then laid it on the table next to him. "As you know, Mr. Pendergast, I'm a tinkerer. I love a challenge. It's quite simple to build a microwave transmitter that would deliver the necessary wattage. The problem was the power supply. But I. G.

Farben, a German company which my family was connected with during the War, makes a marvelous combination of capacitor and battery capable of delivering the requisite charge."

D'Agosta glanced at the microwave device. It looked almost silly, like a cheap prop to an old science fiction movie.

"It would never work as a weapon of war: the top theoretical range is less than twenty feet, and it takes time to do its work. But it suited my purposes perfectly. I had quite a time working out the kinks. Many pumpkins were sacrificed, Sergeant D'Agosta. At last, I tested it on that old pedophile in Pistoia—the one whose tomb you examined. There was a bit of a meltdown—the human body takes a lot more heating than a pumpkin. I rebuilt the device with improvements and used it more successfully on the terrorized Grove. It wasn't quite enough to set the man on fire, but it did the job. Then I arranged the scene to my satisfaction, packed up, and left, locking everything and turning the alarm back on. With Cutforth it was even simpler. As I said, my man Pinketts had rented the apartment next door and was undertaking 'renovations.' He made a marvelous elderly English gentleman, poor man, all bent over and muffled up against the chill."

"That explains why they couldn't identify a suspect from the security video cams," D'Agosta said.

"Pinketts used to be in the theater, which frequently comes in handy for my purposes. In any case, the weapon works beautifully through walls made of drywall and wooden studs. Microwaves, my dear Pendergast, have the marvelous property of penetrating drywall like light through glass, as long as there is no moisture or metal. There could of course be no metal nails in the wall between the two apartments, because metal absorbs microwaves and would heat up and cause a fire. So Pinketts opened our side of the wall, removed the nails, and replaced them with wooden dowels. When it was all over, he put our side of the wall back up. The whole operation was disguised as part of the remodeling job. Pinketts himself did the honors on Cutforth while I was at the opera with you. What better alibi than to contrive to spend the evening of the murder with the detective himself!" Fosco heaved in silent mirth.

"And the smell of sulfur?"

"Sulfur burned with phosphorus in a censer, injected through the wall at cracks around the molding."

"How did you burn the images into the wall?"

"The hoofprint in Grove's house was done directly, focusing the microwave. The image in Cutforth's apartment had to be done indirectly—Pinketts couldn't get into the apartment—by focusing the device against a mask. That was a little trickier, but it worked. Burned the image right through the wall. Brilliant, don't you think?"

"You're sick," said D'Agosta.

"I am a tinkerer. I like nothing more than solving tricky little problems." He grinned horribly and picked up the device. "Now please stand back. I need to adjust the range of the beam. It wouldn't do to scorch us as well as the pumpkin."

Fosco raised the ungainly thing, slid its leather strap over his shoulder, aimed it at the pumpkin, adjusted some knobs. Then he pressed a rudimentary kind of trigger. D'Agosta stared in horrified fascination. There was a humming noise in the capacitor—that was all.

"Right now the device is working up from its lowest setting. If that pumpkin were our victim, he would begin to experience a most awful crawling sensation in his guts and over his skin about now."

The pumpkin remained unaffected. Fosco turned a knob, and the humming went up a notch.

"Now our victim is screaming. The crawling sensation has gotten unbearable. I imagine it's like a stomach full of wasps, stinging endlessly. His skin, too, would start to dry and blister. The rising heat within his muscles would soon cause the neurons to begin firing, jerking his limbs spasmodically, causing him to fall down and go into convulsions. His internal temperature is soaring. Within a few more seconds he'll be thrashing on the ground, biting off or swallowing his tongue."

Another tick of the dial. Now a small blister appeared on the skin of the pumpkin. It seemed to soften, sag a bit. A soft pop, and the pumpkin split open from top to bottom, issuing a spurt of steam.

"Now our victim is unconscious, seconds from death."

There was a muffled boiling sound inside the pumpkin, and the fissure widened. With a sudden wet noise, a jet of orange slime forced itself from the split, oozing over the floor in steaming rivulets.

"No comment necessary. By now, our victim is dead. The interesting part, however, is yet to come."

Blisters began swelling all over the surface of the pumpkin, some popping with little puffs of steam, others breaking and weeping orange fluid.

Another tick of the dial.

The pumpkin split afresh, with a second rush of boiling pulp and seeds squeezing out in a hot viscous paste. The pumpkin sagged further and darkened, the stem blackening and smoking; more fluid and seeds oozed from the cracks along with jets of steam. And then suddenly, with a sharp popping sound, the seeds began to explode. The pumpkin seemed to harden, the room filling with the smell of burned pumpkin flesh; then, with a sudden *paff!*, it burst into flame.

"*Ecco!* The deed is done. Our victim is on fire. And yet, if you were to place your hand on the stone next to the pumpkin, you would find it barely warm to the touch."

Fosco lowered the device. The pumpkin continued to smolder, a flame licking the stem, sizzling and crackling as it burned, a foul black smoke rising slowly.

"Pinketts?"

The servant, without missing a beat, picked up a bottle of *acqua minerale* from the dinner table and poured it over the pumpkin. Then he gave the bubbling remains a deft kick into the fire, heaped on a few more sticks, and retired again to the corner.

"Marvelous, don't you think? And yet it's much more dramatic with a human body, I can assure you."

"You're one sick fuck, you know that?" said D'Agosta.

"This man of yours, Pendergast, is beginning to annoy me."

"Clearly a man of many virtues," Pendergast replied. "But I think this has gone on long enough. It is time for us to get to the remaining business at hand."

"Quite, quite."

"I have come here to offer you a deal."

"Naturally." Fosco's lip curled cynically.

Pendergast glanced at the count a moment, his looks unreadable, letting the silence build. "You will write out and sign a confession of all that you have told us tonight, and you will give me that diabolical machine as proof. I will escort you to the carabinieri, who will arrest you. You will be tried for the murders of Locke Bullard and Carlo Vanni, and as an accomplice in the murder of the priest. Italy has no death penalty, and you will probably be released in twenty-five years, at the age of eighty, to live the remainder of your days in peace and quiet—if you manage to survive prison. This is your side of the bargain."

Fosco listened, an incredulous smile developing on his face. "Is that all? And what will you give me in exchange?"

"Your life."

"I wasn't aware my life was in your hands, Mr. Pendergast. It seems to me it's the other way around."

D'Agosta saw a movement out of the corner of his eye. Pinketts had withdrawn a 9mm Beretta and had it trained on them. D'Agosta's hand moved toward his own weapon, unstrapped the keeper.

Pendergast stopped him with a shake of his head. Then he removed an envelope from his pocket. "A letter identical to this one has been placed with Prince Corso Maffei, to be opened in twenty-four hours if I have not returned to reclaim it."

At the name of Maffei, Fosco paled.

"You are a member of the secret society known as

the Comitatus Decimus, the Company of Ten. As a member of this society, which dates back to the Middle Ages, you inherited and were entrusted with certain documents, formulas, and manuscripts. You abused that trust, in particular on October 31, 1974, when you went through a mock ceremony using those same instruments to frighten a group of American students. Then you compounded it with these killings."

The paleness had given way to mottled fury. "Pendergast, this is absurd."

"You know better than I it is not. You belong to this secret society by virtue of your title. You had no choice in the matter: you were born into it. You didn't take it seriously as a young man; you thought it a joke. Only years later did you realize the severity of that mistake."

"This is all bluster, a poor attempt to save your own skin."

"It's your skin you should be concerned about. You know what awaits those who break the society's seal of silence. Remember what happened to the marchese Meucci? The ten men who head the Comitatus have enormous money, power, and reach. They will find you, Fosco—you know that."

Fosco said nothing, simply staring back at Pendergast.

"As I said, I will give you your life back by retrieving that letter—but only after I have received your signed confession and escorted you to the carabinieri headquarters. The violin you may keep. It is yours, after all. A fair deal, when you consider it."

Fosco tore open the letter with a fat hand and began to read. After a moment, he paused and looked up. "This is infamy!"

Pendergast merely watched as Fosco returned his attention to the document, hands visibly shaking.

D'Agosta observed this interchange with growing comprehension. Now he understood the purpose of Pendergast's stop that morning, a stop he had referred to as "insurance." He had been depositing the copy of his letter with this Prince Maffei. How Pendergast had put all this together, and exactly what it meant, D'Agosta didn't know. No doubt he would learn in time. But his overwhelming feeling was one of relief. Once again, Pendergast had saved their asses.

The count lowered the document abruptly. His face had gone white.

"How did you know this? Someone must have already broken the seal of the Comitatus! Someone else must pay, not me!"

"I learned it from you, and nobody else. That is all you need to know."

Fosco appeared to be struggling to master himself. He placed the letter on the table, faced Pendergast. "Very well. I had expected a strong opening move, but this one does you credit. Twenty-four hours, you say? Pinketts will escort you back to your rooms while I consider my riposte."

"No fucking way," said D'Agosta. "We're leaving. You can telephone our hotel when you're ready to hand over the confession." He glanced at Pinketts, who had his gun trained on them, the muzzle moving back and forth. D'Agosta figured the chances were pretty good that—if he timed it right—he could put a bullet in Pinketts before the man could react.

"You will go to your quarters and await my answer," the count said imperiously.

When nobody moved, he gave an almost imperceptible nod to Pinketts.

All it took was a faint movement in the man's hand, and D'Agosta had dropped, rolled, and fired in one smooth, endlessly practiced move. Without even a cry, Pinketts staggered back against the wall, Beretta still in hand, firing once above their heads. D'Agosta rose to his knee and fired two more shots. Pinketts jerked, the gun skidded across the floor, coming to rest in a corner. Pendergast had his own gun out and was now aiming at the count.

Slowly, Fosco raised his hands.

Suddenly, men appeared in the doorways leading out of the dining room: rough-looking men in peasant dress, guns in hand, faces set. They came in orderly, deliberately, without haste, sure of themselves. In a moment, more than half a dozen had entered, guns aimed at Pendergast and D'Agosta.

There was a long silence, interrupted only by a long, gargling rattle from Pinketts that wheezed off into silence.

Fosco's hands were still raised. "We seem to be at a standoff," he said. "How very theatrical. You kill me, my men kill you." Though the words sounded light, they held a harsh, chill undertone.

"Let us walk out of here," said D'Agosta. "And nobody'll get killed."

"You've already killed Pinketts," Fosco replied crisply. "Here you are, the man who dared lecture me on the sanctity of human life. Pinketts, who was my best and most loyal servant."

D'Agosta took a step toward the count.

"Agent Pendergast!" Fosco said, turning and raising his voice. "A moment's reflection will show you this is a game you cannot win. At the count of three, I will order D'Agosta killed. I will die too, at your hand. *You*, on the other hand, will live to ponder how you brought death to your partner. You know me well enough to know it's not a bluff. You *will* lay down the gun—because you have the *letter*."

He paused. "One."

"It's a bluff!" D'Agosta shouted. "Don't fall for it!"

"Two."

Pendergast laid down his weapon.

The count paused again, hands still in the air. "Now, Mr. D'Agosta, you haven't put down *your* gun. Do I need to say that last number, or can you understand the situation has gone against you? Even with your remarkable marksmanship, you will not succeed in dropping more than one or two of my men before you are sent back to your Maker."

D'Agosta slowly lowered his gun. He still had a second strapped to his leg, and he knew Pendergast had one, too. The game was not over by a long shot. And they still had the letter.

Fosco looked from one to the other, eyes glittering. "Very well. My men will escort you to your rooms while I consider your offer."

{ 80 }

Dawn was finally breaking through the tiny windows of the keep when Pendergast emerged from his room. D'Agosta, sitting by the fire, grunted an acknowledgment. He had spent the night tossing restlessly, unable to sleep, but Pendergast seemed to have had no difficulty.

"Excellent fire, Vincent," he said, smoothing the front of his suit and taking a seat nearby. "I find these fall mornings a bit chilly."

D'Agosta gave the fire a savage poke. "Nice sleep?"

"The bed was an abomination. Otherwise, passable, thank you."

D'Agosta heaved on another log. He hated all this waiting, this not knowing, and was unable to completely suppress his irritation at Pendergast's going directly to his room the night before without a satisfactory explanation.

"How did you know about that secret society business, anyway?" he asked a little gruffly. "I've seen you pull a rabbit out of a hat before, but this one took the cake."

"What a delightful mixed metaphor. I had a suspicion

that Fosco was involved in some way or another, even before I found the horsehair from the Stormcloud at the site of Bullard's killing."

"When did you first suspect him?"

"You recall the associate I mentioned, Mime? I had him perform Internet background checks on the recent activities of all who were at Grove's last party. His research eventually picked up the fact that, six months ago, Fosco quietly purchased a rare seventeenth-century Florentine cross from an antique dealer on the Via Maggio."

"The one he gave Grove?"

"Exactly. And recall the count himself was careful to point out to me that, had Grove lived only one more day, he would have been forty million dollars richer."

"Yeah. Anytime someone volunteers an alibi, something's fishy."

"The count's Achilles' heel is his volubility."

"That *and* his big mouth."

"I began to search for weaknesses in the count. He was clearly a dangerous man, and I felt we needed every advantage we could get—just in case. You may recall the comment of the *colonnello*'s, back at his barracks, about secret societies. He said the Florentine nobility was 'rife with them.' I began to wonder if Fosco belonged to such a secret society, and if so, whether it might be used against him in some way. The Florentine nobility are among the oldest in Europe—their lineages go back to the 1200s. Most of their ancient titles are associated with various arcane orders and guilds, some going as far back as the Crusades. Most have secret documents, rites, and so forth. The Knights

Templars, the Black Gonfaloniers, the Cavaliers of the Rose—there are many others."

D'Agosta nodded silently.

"Some of these societies take themselves extremely seriously, even if their original function has long passed and all that remains are empty observances and ceremonies. The count, coming from one of the most ancient families, surely belonged by hereditary right to a number of them. I e-mailed Constance, who managed to unearth several possibilities. I followed up with some of my own contacts here in Italy."

"When?"

"The night before last."

"And here I thought you were fast asleep in your hotel suite."

"Sleep is an unfortunate biological requirement that both wastes time and leaves one vulnerable. At any rate, I uncovered hints of the existence of the Comitatus Decimus, the Company of Ten. It was a group of assassins formed during the most contentious years of the thirteenth century, long before the Medici came to power. One of the founders of the order was a French baron named Hugo d'Aquilanges, who brought to Florence some peculiar manuscripts full of the dark arts. Using these manuscripts, the group conjured up the devil—or so they believed—to aid in their midnight assassinations. They swore blood secrecy to each other, and any violation was punishable by immediate death. The cavaliere Mantun de Ardaz da Fosco was another of the founders; he passed membership with the title to his son and so forth, down to our Fosco. Their line, apparently, was also the keeper of the library of the Comitatus. It was these ancient documents Fosco used in conjuring up the devil for Bullard and the rest on All Hallows' Eve. Whether he planned to use those documents from the beginning, I can't be sure. But he would have learned Beckmann could read Italian and that Grove, even as a student, was knowledgeable about old manuscripts. Fosco couldn't pass off any old manuscript—it had to be the real thing. I believe that he simply could not resist the fun. Of course, he didn't realize at the time what it meant—or what penalties his breach of secrecy would incur. You see, members aren't inducted into the order until they reach the age of thirty."

"But you still haven't explained how you knew Fosco belonged."

"The research indicated that when the hereditary member is inducted into the society, he is marked with a black spot—a tattoo, really—using a bottle of ashes from the corpse of Mantun de Ardaz, who was drawn, quartered, and burned in the Piazza della Signoria for heresy. This black spot is placed directly over the heart."

"And when did you get a glimpse of *that*?"

"When I interviewed him at the Sherry Netherland. He wore an open-necked white shirt. Of course, at the time I didn't understand its significance—it merely looked like a large mole."

"But you remembered it."

"A photographic memory can be quite useful."

Abruptly, Pendergast motioned for D'Agosta to be silent. For about a minute they waited, motionless. Then D'Agosta heard footsteps, a soft knock.

"Come in," Pendergast said.

The door opened and Fosco slipped through, followed by half a dozen men with guns. He bowed. "Good morning to you both. I trust you passed a decent night?"

D'Agosta did not reply.

"And how was your night, Count?" Pendergast asked.

"I always sleep like a baby, thank you."

"Funny how most murderers do."

Fosco turned to D'Agosta. "You, on the other hand, look a little peaked, Sergeant. I hope you haven't caught cold."

"You make me sick."

"There's no accounting for taste," Fosco said with a smile. Then he glanced back at Pendergast. "As promised, I've considered your offer. And I have brought you my riposte."

He reached inside his jacket and withdrew a smooth white envelope. He held it out to Pendergast, eyes twinkling.

D'Agosta was startled to see Pendergast go pale as he took the envelope.

"That's right. The very letter you left with Prince Maffei. Unopened and unread. I believe the word here is *check*, Mr. Pendergast. Your move."

"How did—?" D'Agosta began. Then he fell silent.

Fosco waved his hand. "Mr. Pendergast didn't count on my brilliance. I told Prince Maffei that my castle had been burglarized and that I was concerned for the safety of the Comitatus's most secret manuscript—which, as the librarian of the Comitatus, I of course had in my possession. I asked him if he would hold it himself for safekeeping until the burglars had been caught. Naturally he took me to his most secure repository, where I felt sure he would have placed your letter. I didn't know, of course, what you had said to him about the letter, so I felt it was better not even to mention it. The old fool opened his vault to put in the manuscript, and there, amidst all his moldy old papers, was a fresh, crisp envelope! I knew it had to be yours. A quick sleight of hand and the letter was mine. When you fail to return, the prince Maffei will open his vault and find nothing, and no doubt begin to worry about the toll old age is taking on his feeble mind." Fosco laughed silently, his capacious front shaking, holding out the envelope.

There was a silence as Pendergast stared at the envelope. Then he took it, opened it, glanced at the sheet inside, and let it fall to the ground.

"I said *check,* but perhaps I should have said *checkmate*, Mr. Pendergast." He turned to the men standing in the doorway. They were dressed in rough woolen and leather clothing, each pointing a firearm. Another man, in a stained suede jacket, stood behind them. He had a small, sharp face and was watching them with intelligent eyes.

D'Agosta's hand crept toward his gun. Pendergast noticed, made a brief suppressing motion.

"That's right, D'Agosta. Your superior knows it is futile—only in the movies can two men overpower seven. Of course, I am quite willing to see you both die right here and now. But then," he added teasingly, "don't lose hope—there's always the chance you might escape!" He chuckled and turned. "Fabbri, disarm these gentlemen."

The man in the leather jacket stepped forward, held out his hand. After a moment, Pendergast removed his backup weapon and handed it to him. With a huge sense of foreboding, D'Agosta reluctantly gave the man his own as well.

"Now search them," said the count.

"You first, Mr. Pendergast," Fabbri said in a heavily accented voice. "Remove your jacket and your shirt. Then stand over there with your arms up."

Pendergast did as ordered, handing each article of clothing to Fabbri. When Pendergast removed his shirt, D'Agosta noticed for the first time that the agent wore a chain around his neck, with a small pendant attached: a strange design of a lidless eye hovering over the image of a phoenix, rising from the ashes of a fire.

One of the peasants shoved Pendergast toward the wall. Fabbri began patting him down expertly. He quickly found a stiletto.

"There will be lock-picking tools as well," said the count.

Fabbri searched Pendergast's collar and cuffs, finally removing a small tool kit held there with Velcro. Other things appeared: a syringe and needle, some small test tubes.

"You've got quite an arsenal tucked away in that suit of yours," Fosco said. "Fabbri, set it all on the table over here, if you please."

Removing a stitching knife, Fabbri proceeded to cut open the linings of Pendergast's suit, searching them thoroughly. Out came other items—tweezers, some small folded packets of chemicals—which the man placed on the table.

"His mouth. Check his mouth."

The man opened Pendergast's mouth, checked his teeth, looked under his tongue.

D'Agosta recoiled in horror at this indignity. With the discovery of each additional tool, he'd felt his hopes dim further. But Pendergast had a lot of tricks up his sleeve. He'd get them out of this somehow.

Fabbri directed Pendergast to step to one side and bend his head forward so he could search his hair. Pendergast complied, his arms still raised, positioning himself so he was facing away from the half-circle of men and the count, who was examining the items on the table with murmurs of interest. Now Fabbri's back was turned to D'Agosta, while Pendergast was facing him. And D'Agosta was amazed at what he saw.

He saw Pendergast, moving his hands ever so slightly, extract a tiny piece of metal from between the ring and little fingers of his left hand. Somehow he had managed to palm this at the beginning of the search.

"All right," Fabbri said. "Lower your arms and step over here."

Pendergast did as directed. With a motion so fleeting D'Agosta wasn't even sure he'd seen it, Pendergast tucked the piece of metal beneath Fabbri's own jacket collar—using the man himself as a hiding place.

Next, Fabbri examined Pendergast's shoes, cutting off the heels with a knife and stabbing through the sole in several places. This produced a second lock-picking set. He frowned and returned once again to Pendergast's suit.

At last, the search was completed, leaving Pendergast's clothes in tatters.

"Now the other one," said Fosco.

They repeated the same process with D'Agosta, stripping him and unstitching everything, subjecting him to the same humiliating search.

"I would leave you both bare," said the count, "but the dungeons of this castle are *so* damp. I would hate to see you catch cold." He nodded toward their clothes. "Get dressed."

They did so.

Fabbri spun them around and manacled their hands behind their backs. *"Andiamoci."*

The count turned and stepped out of the apartment. Fabbri followed, then Pendergast and D'Agosta. The half dozen thugs brought up the rear.

Down the circular staircase they went, out of the keep and back into the ancient rooms of the castle. The count led the way back to the dining *salotto*, then through the kitchen and into a large, drafty pantry. An arched opening was set into the far wall, with a staircase descending out of sight. The group descended this into a deep, vaulted tunnel, its walls weeping moisture and encrusted with calcite crystals. Silently they walked past storerooms and empty galleries of stone.

"Ecco," said the count, stopping before a low doorway. Fabbri stopped in turn, and Pendergast, his eyes on the ground, clumsily stumbled into him from behind. Fabbri cursed and pushed him away, sending the agent sprawling to the stone floor.

"Get in," said the count.

Pendergast rose to his feet and ducked into the tiny room beyond the doorway. D'Agosta followed. The iron door slammed, the metal key turned, and they were in darkness.

The count's face appeared at the small grating set into the door.

"You'll be secure here," he said, "while I attend to a few final details. And then I will be back. You see, I have prepared something special, something *fitting*, for you both. For Pendergast, a literary end—something out of Poe, actually. And for D'Agosta, murderer of my Pinchetti, I will use my microwave device one more time before destroying it, and with it the last evidence of my involvement in this affair."

The face vanished. A moment later, the faint illumination of the corridor was extinguished.

D'Agosta sat in the dark, listening to the echo of retreating footsteps. In a moment, all was silent save for the faint dripping of water and the flutter of what D'Agosta thought must be bats.

He shifted, pulled his torn clothes more tightly around him. Pendergast's voice came to him through the darkness, so low as to be almost inaudible.

"I don't see any reason to delay our departure. Do you?"

"Was that a lockpick I saw you hiding under Fabbri's collar?" D'Agosta whispered.

"Of course. Most obliging of him to carry it for me. Naturally, I stumbled into him just now in order to reclaim it. And now I have little doubt that Fabbri or one of the others is outside, guarding us. Bang on the door, Vincent, and see if you can't get a response from him."

D'Agosta banged and shouted: "Hey! Let us out! *Let us out!*"

The echoes slowly died away in the corridor beyond.

Pendergast touched D'Agosta's arm and whispered again. "Keep making noise while I pick the lock."

D'Agosta shouted, yelled, and swore. A minute later, Pendergast touched his arm once again.

"Done. Now listen. The man waiting in the dark no doubt has an electric torch, which he'll turn on at the slightest indication of funny business. I'm going to find him and take care of him. You keep making noise as a diversion, and to cover any sounds of my crawling through the dark."

"Okay."

D'Agosta once again took up the cry, stomping around and demanding to be let out. It was pitch-black, and he could see nothing of what Pendergast was doing. He yelled and yelled. Suddenly there was a loud thump outside, followed by a thud. Then a beam of light stabbed through the low opening.

"Excellent work, Vincent."

D'Agosta ducked back out beneath the low doorway. There, about twenty feet away, was Fabbri, facedown on the stone floor, arms flung wide.

"Are you sure there's a way out of this pile?" D'Agosta asked.

"You heard the squeaking of bats. Right?"

"Right."

"There must be a way out."

"Yeah, for a bat."

"Where bats fly, so shall we. But first we must get our hands on the machine. It's our only real evidence against the count."

{ 81 }

They made their way back through the dark stonework of the storage cellars and furtively climbed the ancient stairway to the pantry. Pendergast checked the room carefully, then motioned D'Agosta forward. Slowly, they moved from the pantry to the kitchen: a huge room with parallel tables of oiled pine and marble, and a massive fireplace replete with grills and racks. Cast-iron cookware hung on great hooks and chains from the ceiling. No sounds issued from the dining *salotto* beyond. All appeared deserted.

"When Pinketts retrieved the weapon," whispered Pendergast, "he came through this kitchen, and was gone no more than a minute. It has to be close."

"Why would it still be in the same place?"

"Remember what Fosco said. He's planning to use it once more—on you. Other than the dining area, there are only two ways out of this room. The pantry we just came through, and *that*." He pointed to a door leading into what looked like an old meat locker.

At that moment, footsteps sounded from beyond

the dining room. They flattened themselves behind the door of the kitchen. Voices spoke in Italian, too indistinct to make out, but approaching.

"Let's keep looking," Pendergast said after a moment. "Any moment now the alarm might be raised."

He ducked into the meat locker: a cool stone room hung with prosciutti and salami, shelves groaning under the weight of massive wheels of aging cheeses. Pendergast shone Fabbri's torch around the crowded space. There was a gleam of aluminum on one of the upper shelves.

"There!" D'Agosta grabbed the case.

"Too bulky," Pendergast said. "Get rid of the case and let's assemble the weapon."

They opened the case, and—with a little difficulty—Pendergast screwed together the various parts. He handed it to D'Agosta, who slung it over his shoulder by its attached leather strap. Then they hurried back into the kitchen. More voices, this time from the dining room itself. Then the hiss of a radio. A voice rasped out, loud, full of panic.

"Sono scappati!"

A flurry of activity, followed by retreating footsteps.

"They've got radios," Pendergast murmured. He paused only another moment. Then he dashed back through the kitchen and across the dining room, D'Agosta following, weapon bouncing on his shoulder. They ran out into the central gallery, past the age-darkened portraits and luxurious tapestries.

Dim voices could be heard ahead.

"This way," Pendergast said, nodding toward a small open door. They ran through it to find themselves in an old armory. Rusted swords, armor, and chain mail hung from the walls. Without a word, Pendergast took down a sword, examined it, put it back, took down another.

The voices grew louder. And then a group of men passed by the doorway, running at top speed toward the dining room and the kitchen.

Pendergast peered out, and then motioned to D'Agosta.

They continued down the gallery, then veered away through a maze of elegant chambers, arriving at last in the small, damp, windowless rooms surrounding the old keep. D'Agosta heard no footsteps but their own. It seemed they were temporarily in luck: nobody expected they'd head for the heart of the castle instead of making toward the outer walls.

No sooner had this thought occurred to him than he heard a voice ahead, talking furiously. He looked around. There was no place to hide in this series of bare stone rooms.

Pendergast swiftly got behind the door, D'Agosta crouching at his back. A man appeared in the doorway, jogging, radio in hand. Pendergast raised his sword with one swift motion; the man grunted, then sprawled forward onto the floor, run through, blood running out over the paving stones.

In an instant, Pendergast had retrieved the man's handgun, a 9mm Beretta. He handed the sword to D'Agosta and gestured for him to follow.

Ahead yawned the entrance to a circular staircase,

leading down into darkness. They began flying down the steps, two at a time. Then Pendergast raised his hand.

Footsteps rang faintly from below. Someone was running up toward them.

"How many thugs does the fat fuck employ?" D'Agosta muttered.

"As many as he wants, I imagine. Stay still. We have the advantage of surprise and altitude." And Pendergast aimed the gun carefully down the curve of the stairs. Moments later, a man in peasant dress appeared. Pendergast fired without hesitation, then knelt beside the crumpled form, retrieved his weapon, and tossed it to D'Agosta.

A second man was shouting up from below. *"Carlo! Cosa c'è?"*

Pendergast darted down the stairs, tattered suit flapping behind him, and—leaping toward the second man—sent him sprawling backward with a kick to the head. He landed lightly, paused to pluck the man's gun from his hand, and thrust it into the waistband of his trousers.

They ran down the dank corridor leading away from the staircase. Behind them, D'Agosta could hear shouts and cries. Pendergast switched off the flashlight to make them less of a target, and they continued forward in almost complete darkness.

Ahead, the tunnel divided. Pendergast stopped, examined the ground, the ceiling.

"Note the guano? The bats fly out this way."

They took the left-hand tunnel. Now a faint light appeared in the distance behind them. A shot rang out, whining off stone. D'Agosta stopped to return fire. Their pursuers hung back.

"What about the microwave weapon?" he asked.

"Useless in this situation. Takes too long to operate, doesn't have the range. Besides, we don't have the time now to figure out how to use it."

The tunnel branched again. D'Agosta smelled fresh air ahead, then caught a faint glow of light. They ran around another corner, then another—and suddenly came up against a thick grate of iron bars, bright light streaming in between them. D'Agosta could see that the grate opened onto the cliff below the castle. Beyond, he could make out the steep flanks of the mountain, to the left plunging into a deep ravine and to the right rising to pinnacles and crags.

"Shit."

"I expected something like this," said Pendergast. He swiftly examined the bars. "Ancient, but sound."

"What now?"

"We make a stand. I'm counting on that shooting ability of yours, Vincent."

Pendergast flattened himself against the last angle of the tunnel, and D'Agosta did the same. The men were coming up faster now—judging by the footsteps, there were at least half a dozen of them. D'Agosta turned, aimed, squeezed off a shot. In the dimness, he saw one of the figures fall. The rest scattered, flattening themselves against the rough rock walls. There was an answering blast of a shotgun. This was followed by the fast stutter of an automatic weapon: two short bursts, the bullets caroming off the ceiling in showers of sparks and stone.

"*Shit!*" D'Agosta said, shrinking back involuntarily.

"Keep holding them, Vincent, while I see what I can do about these bars."

D'Agosta crouched low, ducked briefly around the corner, fired. The automatic weapon returned fire, the bullets once again ricocheting off the ceiling, thudding into the ground in a scattered pattern not far from D'Agosta.

They're deliberately aiming for the ricochet.

He yanked his magazine out of the grip, examined it. It was a ten-shot magazine: six bullets were visible, plus the one in the chamber.

"Here's the spare clip," Pendergast said, tossing it to him. "Conserve your fire."

D'Agosta glanced at it: full. He had seventeen shots.

Another short burst of automatic-weapons fire came zinging off the ceiling, thudding into the ground directly before his feet.

Angle of incidence equals angle of refraction, D'Agosta vaguely remembered from his pool-shooting days. He fired at the place where he'd seen the rounds ricochet off, fired a second time, each time aiming for a smooth patch of stone, carefully angling for the ricochet.

He heard a cry. *Score one to mathematics.*

Now a fusillade of shots came ricocheting in. D'Agosta rolled back just in time, half a dozen rounds slapping the ground where he had been.

"How's it going?" he called over his shoulder.

"More time, Vincent. Buy me time."

More bullets came in off the ceiling, with a spray of broken stone.

Time. D'Agosta had no choice but to return fire

again. He crawled up to the angle, peered around. A man had ducked out from the shadows and was running up to a closer position. D'Agosta fired once and winged the man, who retreated with a cry.

Now Pendergast was firing his own gun in measured shots. Glancing back, D'Agosta could see him shooting into the masonry holding the grate in place.

More shots came in, landing about him in irregular spots. D'Agosta squeezed off another round.

Pendergast had emptied his magazine. "Vincent!" he called.

"What?"

"Toss me your gun."

"But—"

"The gun."

Pendergast caught it, took careful aim, and fired point-blank into the masonry at each point where the bars were cemented. The cement was old and soft, and the shots were taking effect, but still D'Agosta winced, unable to prevent himself from counting the wasted bullets. *One, two, three, four, click.* Pendergast popped out the spent magazine, tossed it aside. D'Agosta handed him the spare. The fire from around the corner had intensified. They had only moments before they were overrun.

Seven more shots rang out. Then Pendergast paused, crouched.

"Kick together. On three."

They gave the grate a violent kick, but it remained immobile.

Pendergast fired two more shots, then tucked the gun into his waistband.

"Kick again. From the ground."

They lay on their backs, cocked their legs, struck the grate together.

It moved.

Again, then yet again—and now it came free, clanging down the cliff face with a shower of rocks and pebbles.

They stood and approached the edge. The rough rock went straight down at least fifty feet before beginning to level out.

"Shit," D'Agosta murmured.

"No choice. Toss the device. Look for brush, the gentlest landing place possible. Then climb down."

D'Agosta leaned out, tossed the microwave weapon down into a thick patch of bushes. Then, swallowing his terror, he turned and eased himself over the edge. Sliding down slowly, holding fast to the mortar of the grate with his hands, he found a purchase for his feet. Then another descent, another purchase. In a moment, his face was below the edge of the chamber, clinging to the cliff face.

And then Pendergast was suddenly beside him. "Go sideways as you descend. It's easier to see footholds, and you'll make a more difficult target."

The rock was shelving limestone, dreadfully sheer but offering abundant hand- and footholds. While it probably would have provided little challenge to a professional rock climber, D'Agosta was terrified nonetheless. His feet kept slipping, and his leather-soled shoes were almost useless.

Down he went, gingerly, one hand after the other, trying not to scrape his hurt finger against the sharp rocks. Pendergast was far below already, descending swiftly.

Shots echoed from the opening above, followed by a tremendous fusillade, followed by silence. Then a rush of voices: *Eccoli! Di là!*

D'Agosta glanced up to see a few heads craning out over the gulf. A hand with a gun appeared, aiming right at him. He was a sitting duck. Christ, it was over.

Pendergast's gun cracked from far below: his final round. The shooter was hit square in the forehead; he staggered, fell, then came hurtling silently past, headed for the rocks below. D'Agosta looked away, resumed his descent as quickly as he dared.

From the opening above came more commotion. D'Agosta saw another figure appear cautiously, this time with the automatic weapon in hand. D'Agosta recognized the stubby form of an Uzi.

He flattened himself against the rock. Pendergast had vanished out of sight below. Where the hell was he?

He heard the Uzi go off in short bursts, rounds humming past his ear. He tried fishing out with his leg, searching for another foothold, but realized he was protected only by a thin shelf of rock overhead; if he moved again, he would be exposed.

Another burst confirmed the fact: he was pinned.

"Pendergast!"

No answer.

More shots came, stinging his face with splinters of stone. He shifted one foot, probed.

Another burst, and he felt one of the rounds nick his

shoe. He pulled his leg back. He was hyperventilating now, gasping for breath as he clung to the tiny purchase. He had never felt so terrified in his life.

More shots, the stone fragmenting.

They were shooting *through* the thin shelf above him. Even if he didn't move, they'd get him. He felt blood running down his cheek from where the stone chips had cut him.

Then he heard a single shot, this time from below; a scream from overhead; and then another man hurtled past, Uzi flying.

Pendergast. He must have reached the bottom and retrieved the dead man's weapon.

D'Agosta began to climb down in a panic, slipping, recovering, slipping again. There was another shot from below, then another—Pendergast covering him, keeping the opening above clear of men.

The rock began to level out a little and he half climbed, half slid the last twenty feet. Then he was on his feet at the top of a scree slope, soaked in perspiration, heart hammering, his legs like jelly. Pendergast was here, crouched behind a rock, firing up again at the opening.

"Get the device and let's go," he said.

D'Agosta rose, scrambled down to the thicket of bushes, and retrieved the weapon. One of its bulbs was slightly dinged, and the device looked a little smudged and scratched, but otherwise it seemed undamaged. He slung it over his shoulder and raced for the cover of the trees. Pendergast joined him a moment later.

"Down. To the Greve road."

They took off downhill, leaping and running

through chestnut trees, the sound of shots behind and above growing fainter and fainter.

And then, suddenly, Pendergast stopped again.

In the ensuing silence, D'Agosta heard a sound rising from below. The measured baying of dogs.

A lot of dogs.

{ 82 }

Pendergast listened for a moment, then he turned to D'Agosta. "The count's boar-hunting dogs. With their handlers. Coming up from below."

"Oh, my God..."

"They're trained to fan out into an impenetrable line, trap their prey, and surround it. We've no choice. We've got to go up and over the top of the mountain. That's our only chance to escape."

They turned and began scrambling up through the steep woods, moving at an angle to the slope, away from the castle. It was a tough, nasty ascent: the chestnut forest was full of brush and brambles, the ground wet and the leaves slippery. D'Agosta could hear the baying of the dogs below, dozens and dozens it seemed, overlapping into a cacophony of noise. The sounds echoed clear across the valley, from one end to the other. They seemed to be getting closer.

They climbed through an especially steep section of forest and broke out onto a gentler slope, planted in vines, leaves yellow in the fall air. They ran uphill between the rows, stumbling and panting through the wet clods, sticky earth clinging to their shoes.

There was no question: the dogs were gaining.

At the far end of the vineyard, Pendergast paused a second to reconnoiter. They were in a couloir between two mountain ridges. Above, the ridges narrowed as they approached the summit, about half a mile away. The castle lay below them on its own projecting shelf of rock, grim and dark.

"Come on, Vincent," Pendergast said. "There's not a moment to lose."

The vineyard gave way to another steep slope, thickly covered with chestnut trees. They thrashed their way upward, briars tearing at their already tattered clothes. The broken wall of some ancient ruin came into view overhead, an old *casa colonica* sunken in vines. They climbed past the ruin and its outbuildings and entered an overgrown clearing. Again Pendergast paused to examine the hillside above them.

D'Agosta felt his heart was going to explode. The microwave device was a dead weight across his shoulder. Staring down the ridgeline, gasping for breath, he caught a brief glimpse of several of the dogs below, running, baying. Their line was tightening. He could now make out the distant whistling and shouting of the handlers.

Pendergast was staring intently upslope, where the couloir narrowed toward the summit. "I see a glint of steel."

"Men?"

Pendergast nodded. "Have you ever hunted boar?"

"No."

"That's precisely how we're being hunted. Like boar. Up there, where that draw narrows, will be the hunters. Perhaps a dozen, maybe more, arranged in blinds. Their field of fire will completely cover the upper part of the ridge." He nodded, almost as if in approval. "It's a standard hunt. The dogs flush out the boar and drive them up a narrowing valley toward a ridgeline, where they are forced to break cover and are taken down by the hunters."

"So what do we do?"

"We don't behave like boar. Instead of running *away* from the dogs, we head sideways."

He turned and ran along the slope, at right angles to the fall line, following the rise and fall of the topography. The baying of the dogs was closer, their sounds echoing back among the rises of land, making it appear as if the animals were approaching from all sides.

The steep flank of the mountain lay perhaps a quarter mile in front of them. If they could get over that, D'Agosta thought as they stumbled forward, they could outflank the dogs and head downhill again. But the forest grew ever steeper and denser, slowing them down. And then, quite suddenly, they reached the lip of a small but very steep ravine, a stream at its bottom plunging down over sharp boulders. On the other side, perhaps twenty feet away, was a cliff of wet, moss-covered rock.

It was impassable.

Pendergast turned back. The dogs seemed very close now. D'Agosta could even hear the crackling of twigs, the breaking of brush, the curses of the handlers.

"We can't cross this ravine," Pendergast said. "That

leaves only one choice. We must go up, try to creep through the line of hunters."

Pendergast pulled out the handgun he'd taken from the fallen man, checked the magazine. "Three rounds left," he said. "Let's go."

They resumed their climb. It seemed incredible to D'Agosta that he could go any farther, but adrenaline—and the dreadful baying of the boar hounds—kept him moving.

After a few minutes, the forest thinned and it grew brighter. They crouched, then crept forward slowly. Above, the forest gave way completely to meadows and brushy draws. D'Agosta caught his breath in dismay. The draws were full of impenetrable brush; the meadows were open and bare, dotted with isolated copses of trees. The land rose another quarter of a mile, hemmed between the two ridges of rock, finally topping over a barren summit. It was like a shooting gallery.

Pendergast examined the summit for at least a minute, despite the rapidly approaching dogs. Then he shook his head.

"It's no good, Vincent. It's suicide to go farther. There will be too many men up there, and they've no doubt been hunting boar in this valley all their lives. We'll never break through."

"Are you sure? Sure the men are up there, I mean?"

Pendergast nodded, looking back up the ridge. "I can see at least half a dozen from here. It's impossible to say how many others are hidden behind the rock blinds." He paused, as if considering. Then he spoke rapidly, almost to himself. "The ring is already closed on either side and above. And we can't go down: we'll never penetrate the line of dogs."

"Are you positive?"

"Not even a two-hundred-pound male boar, moving through heavy brush at thirty miles an hour, can get past those dogs. As soon as the boar hits the line, the dogs converge, and..."

He stopped. Then he looked at D'Agosta, eyes glittering.

"Vincent, that's it. There is a way out. *Listen to me.* I will head directly downhill. When I hit the line of dogs, their cry will bring the others, and they'll bunch. Meanwhile, you move a couple of hundred yards laterally, that way, quick as you can. Then go slowly downhill. *Slowly.* When you hear the cornering cry of the dogs—it's an unmistakable sound—you'll know I've hit the line and they're baying at me. The line will break as the dogs converge, and *that's* when you can pass. Then, and *only* then. Is that clear? *Listen for the cornering cry.* When you break through, head straight to the Greve road."

"And you?"

Pendergast held up the gun.

"With three shots? You'll never do it."

"There's no other way."

"But where will I meet up with you? The Greve road?"

Pendergast shook his head. "Don't wait for me. Get the *colonnello* and return in full force as soon as possible. *In full force.* You understand? Take the machine—you'll need it to convince him."

"But..." D'Agosta stopped. And then—only then—

did the full consequences of Pendergast's intentions reveal themselves to him.

"The hell with that," he said. "We go together."

The baying grew closer.

"Only one of us can get through. There's no other way. Now, *go!*"

"I won't. No way... I'm *not* leaving you to the dogs..."

"*Damn* you, Vincent, you *must!*" And without another word, Pendergast turned his back and took off downhill.

"No!" D'Agosta shouted. *"Noooo—!"*

But it was too late.

He felt paralyzed, rooted to the spot in disbelief. Pendergast's thin black figure was leaping like a cat down the hill, gun upraised—and then it vanished into the trees.

There was nothing to do but follow the plan. Almost robotically, D'Agosta began scrambling along the hill, moving laterally, until he had gone about three hundred yards. He turned, prepared to descend.

Then he stopped. Ahead, in a thickly wooded copse beneath a spur of rock, stood a lone figure. From any other vantage point, he would have been invisible below the outcropping of rock. He stood very still, looking at D'Agosta.

Jesus, D'Agosta thought. *This is it.*

He reached for the microwave device, thought better of it. The man wasn't armed; or, if he was, his weapon was out of sight. This situation was better handled with bare hands. He gathered himself to leap forward.

But then he hesitated. Though the man was dressed

in peasant garb, he seemed different from the rest of Fosco's men. He was very tall and slender, perhaps four inches taller than Pendergast, and he wore a closely trimmed beard. There was something strange about his eyes. They were different colors: the left was hazel, the right an intense blue.

Maybe he's a local, D'Agosta thought. *Or a poacher, or something. Great fucking time to be out for a stroll.*

Suddenly, he became aware of the dogs again. They were still baying: a regular, measured sound, as before.

No more time to waste. The man had turned calmly away from him, uninterested. D'Agosta began descending slowly, waiting for the change in the dogs' cry. He glanced back once and saw the stranger, still motionless, looking intently downslope.

D'Agosta turned back and continued slowly and carefully down through the forest. *Forget him.* The important thing now was Pendergast. He would escape. He had to, he *had* to...

And then, suddenly, off to his right and below, he heard a single dog barking hysterically, its voice sounding a much higher, more urgent note than before. He paused, listening. Another took up the cry, then a third. In a moment, the whole line had taken it up. D'Agosta could hear them converging on a single spot with a babel of high-pitched barking. Then came the report of a gun, the shriek of a dog. The frenzy increased in pitch. It was a terrifying sound, interrupted by a second shot, then a third. These were followed in turn by the lower boom-*boom* of an old, heavy-caliber carbine. D'Agosta could see nothing through the dense brush, but he could hear what was happening all too clearly.

This was his chance. Hugging the machine close to him, D'Agosta ran downhill as hard and fast as he could, leaping, ripping through brambles, stumbling, recovering, running on and on. He broke through a small clearing, and there—far off to his right now—he caught one last glimpse of Pendergast: a lone figure in black, surrounded by a boiling pack of dogs, a dozen or more men converging from two sides and below, each with heavy rifles trained on him. The din was incredible, the frenzied ring of dogs closing in, the bolder ones dashing forward, attempting to tear out chunks of flesh.

D'Agosta kept running, running—and then he was past the line, the dogs' terrible ravening cry now behind and above him. He kept on going, the nightmarish shrieking of the dogs, the cursing and shouting of the handlers, ringing ever more faintly in his ears. The hunt was over, the quarry cornered—only it wasn't a boar, it was a human being. Pendergast. And he wasn't going to escape: not this time, he wasn't.

{ 83 }

Buck sat on the cot in his cell at the Manhattan Detention Center, listening and waiting. It was a modern, sterile facility, all white walls and fluorescent lighting, the lights recessed behind caged glass. Despite the fact that it was past midnight, he could hear a lot of noise from the other prisoners, who were banging on the bars, yelling, arguing, demanding lawyers. Some were shouting in unintelligible languages that sounded harsh, almost barbarous.

He'd been processed, fingerprinted, photographed, showered, given a change of clothes. He'd been fed, given a copy of the *Times*, been offered a phone to call a lawyer—and told absolutely nothing. It seemed he'd been in the cell forever. Every hour that passed turned the screw another notch. When would it begin? Is this what Christ felt, waiting to be brought before Pontius Pilate? He would have preferred almost anything—beating, torture, abuse—to this interminable wait. And this environment was sterile, suffocating. What was worse, he'd been given a cell to himself. His treatment was almost cruel in its courtesy. He wondered how much longer he could stand these people coming and going with his food: these people who never answered his questions, never looked him in the eye, never said a word.

He knelt to pray. When would *it* happen? When would the walls shake, the voices sound on high, the ground open to swallow the unclean? When would the screams of the damned fill the air, the kings and princes run to hide among the rocks, the four horsemen of the Apocalypse appear in the sky? He didn't even have a window to look out of, no way to see anything.

The suspense was literally killing him.

Yet another guard appeared: a large black man in a blue uniform, carrying a tray.

"What's this?" Buck asked, looking up.

No answer. The man opened the sliding tray in the bars, set it down, slid it in, shut the slot, turned, and walked away.

"What's happening out there?" Buck cried. "What's—?"

But the orderly had disappeared.

Buck rose and sat down again on the bunk. He looked at the food: a bagel with cream cheese and jelly; a chicken breast sitting in some congealed gravy; some grayish green beans and carrots; a dollop of hardening mashed potatoes. The sheer banality of it made him sick.

Now, above the usual prison sounds, he heard something else: voices, a clang, a sudden burst of shouting from the other prisoners. Buck stood up.

Was it starting? Was it starting at last?

Four police officers appeared down the hall, heavily armed, billy clubs swinging from their hips, swaggering in formation. For him: they were coming *for him.* He felt a tingle of anticipation. Something would happen now. It might be very hard. It would no doubt test him to the utmost. But whatever it was, he would accept it. It was part of God's great plan.

They halted outside his cell. He stared back at them, waiting. One stepped forward and read from a card clipped to a green folder.

"Wayne Paul Buck?"

He nodded, stiffening.

"You're to come with us."

"I'm ready," he said, defiantly but with quiet dignity.

The man unlocked the cell. The others stood back, guns at the ready.

"Step out, please. Turn around and place your hands behind your back."

He did as he was told. It was going to be bad, very bad: he could feel it. The cold steel of the cuffs went around his wrists, and there was a click: a portent of things to come.

"This way, sir."

Sir. The mocking was beginning.

They marched him silently down the hall to an elevator, rose a few floors, then down another sterile corridor to a gray metal door. They knocked.

"Come in," said a feminine voice.

The door opened, and Buck found himself in a small office with a metal desk, a single window looking out over the nightscape of lower Manhattan. Sitting at the desk was *that* one, the female cop who had led the centurions in to arrest him.

He stood proudly before her, unbowed. She was his Pontius Pilate.

She accepted the folder from the lead cop. "Have you had access to a lawyer?" she asked.

"I don't need a lawyer. God is my advocate." He noticed, for the first time, how pretty she was—and how young. She had a discreet bandage above her ear, where she had been hit with the rock. He had saved her from death.

The devil has many faces.

"As you wish." She rose, pulled her jacket off a hook, slid into it, then nodded to the policemen. "Is the marshal ready?"

"Yes, Captain."

"Let's go, then."

"Where?" Buck asked.

Her only answer was to lead the way down the hall. They took another elevator down and out through a maze of corridors into the yard, where an unmarked police car sat, idling, gleaming beneath a dozen sodium lamps. A uniformed cop was behind the wheel. A small, heavyset man in gray polyester stood beside the passenger door, hands clasped before him.

"You can uncuff him," Hayward said to the cops. "Put him in the back, please."

They uncuffed him, opened the door, eased him in. Meanwhile, Hayward was talking to the man in the suit, giving him the green folder and a clipboard. He signed the clipboard, handed it back to her, got in beside the driver, and slammed the door.

Now Hayward leaned in at the rear window. "You're

probably wondering what's going to happen to you, Mr. Buck."

Buck felt a rush of emotion. This was it: he was being led away, taken to meet his end, his supreme moment. He was ready.

"This gentleman is a U.S. marshal, who is going to escort you by plane back to Broken Arrow, Oklahoma, where you are wanted for parole violation."

Buck sat there, stunned. This couldn't be. More mockery. It was a trick, a ruse.

"Did you hear me?"

Buck did not acknowledge. It *had* to be a trick.

"The D.A. decided not to file any charges against you here in New York—too much trouble. And to tell you the truth, you didn't really do anything all that wrong, outside of exercising your right of free speech in a rather misguided way. We were lucky, avoided a riot, managed to disperse the crowd peacefully once you left. Everyone went home and the area's now fenced. Soon the Parks Department will be giving it a thorough cleaning and reseeding, which it needed anyway. So, you see, no real harm was done, and we felt it better to let the whole incident die a quiet death and be forgotten."

Buck listened, hardly able to believe his ears.

"And what about me?" he finally managed to say.

"Like I said, we're shipping you back to Oklahoma, where there's a parole officer really anxious to talk to you. We don't want you. They had a prior and wanted you back. Nice ending all around."

She smiled, laid her hand on the side of the car. "Mr. Buck? Are you all right?"

He didn't answer. He *wasn't* all right. He felt sick. This wasn't what was supposed to happen. It was a trick, a vicious trick.

She leaned in just a little farther. "Mr. Buck? If you don't mind, there's something personal I'd like to say to you."

He stared at her.

"First of all, there's only one Jesus and you aren't Him. Another thing: I'm a Christian, and I try to be a good one, although I may not always succeed. You had no right to stand there when I was at the mercy of that crowd, point your finger at me, and pass judgment. You should take a good look at that passage in the Gospel of Matthew: *Judge not, that ye be not judged... Thou hypocrite, first cast out the beam out of thine own eye; and then shalt thou see clearly to cast out the mote out of thy brother's eye.*"

She paused. "I always liked the King James Version the best. Now, listen. You worry about *yourself* from now on, being a good citizen, keeping out of trouble, and obeying the law."

"But... You don't realize... It's going to happen. I warn you, it's coming." Buck could barely articulate the words.

"If there's a Second Coming in the works, you sure as heck won't get advance notice—that much I *do* know."

With that, she smiled, patted the side of the car, and said, "Farewell, Mr. Buck. Keep your nose clean."

{ 84 }

In the elegantly appointed dining room within the main massing of the Castello Fosco, the count waited, quite patiently, for his dinner. The walls of the fifteenth-century villa were extremely thick, and there was no sound at all save the faint mechanical whirring of Bucephalus from a white T-stand nearby, applying his artificial beak to an artificial nut. The stately windows of the room looked out over a spectacular landscape: the hills of Chianti, the deep valley of the Greve. But Fosco was content to sit in his heavy oak chair at one end of the long table, reviewing—with delicious tranquillity—the events of the day.

His reverie was broken by the shuffle of feet in the passageway. A moment later his cook, Assunta, appeared, bearing a large serving tray. Placing it at the far end of the table, she presented the dishes to him one by one; a simple *maltagliati ai porcini*; oxtail, served *alla vaccinara*; *fegatini* grilled over the fire; a *contorno* of fennel braised in olive oil. It was the simple, homely fare his cook excelled at and Fosco preferred while in the country. And if Assunta's presentation lacked the polish and subtlety of Pinketts—that, alas, could not be helped.

He thanked her, pouring himself a glass of the estate's exceptional Chianti Classico as she left the room. And then he applied himself to his dinner with relish. Although he felt famished, he ate slowly, savoring every bite, every mouthful of wine.

At last, meal complete, he rang a small silver bell that lay near his right hand. Assunta reappeared.

"Grazie," he said, dabbing the corners of his mouth with a huge linen napkin.

Assunta curtsied a little awkwardly.

The count rose. "Once you have cleared away, you may take a few days off."

The cook glanced at him inquiringly without raising her head.

"*Per favore, signora*. It has been months since you visited your son in Pontremoli."

The curtsy deepened. *"Mille grazie."*

"Prego. Buona sera." And the count turned lightly on his heel and left the dining room.

Once the cook had departed, the castle would be empty of servants. His men had done their work and departed. Even the groundskeepers had been given a few days' absence. Only Giuseppe, the ancient dogmaster, remained on the estate: as it happened, he could not be spared.

It was not that Fosco distrusted his retainers: they all had ancient ties to his family, some going back as far as eight hundred years, and their loyalty was without question. It was simply that he wanted to finish this business undisturbed.

He moved slowly and purposefully through the huge rooms of the castle: the *salone*; the hall of portraits; the hall of armor. His stroll took him back through time: first, through the older, thirteenth-century additions, then into still older chambers, built half a millennium earlier. Here there was no electricity, no modern conveniences such as plumbing or central heating. The warren of small, windowless rooms grew dark and oppressive, and Fosco stopped to pull a torch from a wall sconce and light it. Turning to an ancient worktable nearby, he picked up something else and tucked it into his waistcoat. Then he took a side passage and continued on and down: down into a subterranean warren of tunnels cut into the living rock.

Many of the extensive basements of the Castello Fosco were taken up with the production of the estate. A great many rooms were devoted to winemaking: filled with bottling machinery and fermentation vats, or with countless small barrels of French oak. Others were given over to the aging of boar hams: deep, cool spaces from whose ceilings hung countless hams, still covered in coarse fur. Still others were used for storing olive oil or making *balsamico*. But here—far beneath the bulk of the castle's stronghold—there were no such large and well-ventilated spaces. Narrow vaults dug deeply into the beetling cliff face of limestone, and stairs corkscrewed down toward old wells and chambers unused for half a millennium.

It was one of these staircases that Fosco now descended. The air was chill, the walls slick with damp. The count slowed further: the hand-cut steps were slippery, and if he fell there would be nobody to hear his cries.

At last, the staircase ended in a labyrinth of narrow vaults, lined in ancient brick. Niches were cut into the walls, and each contained a skeleton: some long-deceased family member or—more likely, given the sheer number—fallen allies from wars fought a millennium ago. The air was bad here, and Fosco's torch guttered as he threaded his complex path.

As he penetrated deeper into the maze, the ancient walls grew more uneven. He passed several places where they had fallen away from the rock, leaving heaps of scattered bricks. Skeletons lay in thick profusion, as if dumped and abandoned where they lay, the bones chewed and scattered by rats.

The vault finally ended in a cul-de-sac. The darkness here was so thick, so complete, that Fosco's torch barely penetrated. He took another step forward, waved the torch in a cautious arc into the last recess ahead of him.

The guttering flame revealed the figure of Agent Pendergast, head lolled forward onto his chest. His face was scratched and bleeding in a dozen places. His normally immaculate black suit was shredded and dirty, the jacket lying in a heap at his feet. His hand-tailored English shoes were covered in thick Tuscan mud. He appeared unconscious and would have sunk to the ground before Fosco if not for the heavy chain bound tightly across his chest. This was fixed to an iron staple set into the limestone wall, and was padlocked to a second iron staple on Pendergast's far side. His wrists hung limply at his sides, secured by additional lengths of chain fixed to the rear wall of the niche.

Fosco's first sweep of the torch had been a careful one. He had learned, even now, not to underestimate his opponent. But Pendergast was clearly immobilized, helpless. Emboldened, the count brought the torch forward again.

As the light of the torch crossed his face, Pendergast stirred. His eyes fluttered open.

Instantly, Fosco stepped back. "Agent Pendergast?" he crooned. "Aloysius? Are we awake?"

Pendergast did not answer, but his eyes remained open. He moved his limbs weakly, flexed his manacled hands.

"Please forgive me, but I'm afraid the restraints are necessary. As you shall soon understand."

When there was no response, the count continued. "You no doubt feel weak, barely able to stir. And you may be experiencing a certain degree of amnesia. Phenobarbital does have that effect at times: it seemed the easiest way to return you to the castle without undue exertions. So allow me to refresh your memory. You and the good sergeant D'Agosta grew tired of my hospitality and desired to leave. I, naturally, took objection. There was a nasty struggle, I'm afraid, in which my beloved Pinketts perished. You had deposited some paperwork I was obliged to reclaim. Then came your escape attempt. Sergeant D'Agosta made good his escape, I fear. But the important thing is that *you're* back, my dear Agent Pendergast: back safely again in the bosom of Castel Fosco! And I insist you remain here, as my guest. No, really—I'll hear no objection."

Fosco placed the torch carefully into an iron wall mounting. "I beg your pardon for the scant accommodation. Still, these chambers are not without their natural charm. You'll notice the white webwork that gleams from the cavern walls? It's nitre, my dear Pendergast—you of all people should appreciate the literary allusion. And thus understand what is to follow."

And to underscore this, the count slipped his hand into his waistcoat and slowly withdrew a trowel.

Staring at it, Pendergast's dull, drug-heavy eyes gleamed briefly.

"Aha!" the count cried, pleased. "It is *not* lost on you! Let us then proceed with all haste." And turning to one side, he swept away a heap of tumbled bones, revealing a large quantity of freshly slaked mortar.

Using the trowel, he laid a thick line of mortar along the front lip of the recess. Then he moved to one of the piles of collapsed brick and, two at a time, brought the bricks back to the niche, laying them carefully in a line atop the mortar. Within a few minutes, the first course of bricks was in place and Fosco was troweling another layer of mortar along its top.

"How wonderful these bricks are!" he said as he worked. "They are many centuries old, made from the very clay of the hillside. See how massive: none of your trifling English bricks for Fosco! I've called for a great deal of lime in the mortar—nearly two parts lime to each part sand—but then I want your final habitation to be as strong as possible. I want it to last through the ages, my dear Pendergast. I want it to last until the final trump is sounded!"

Pendergast said nothing. But his drug-clouded eyes had cleared. They watched Fosco work with an almost feline stoicism—if, Fosco reflected, stoicism was the correct word. Finishing the second course of bricks, he paused to return the gaze.

"I've been preparing this for some time," he said. "Quite some time, in fact. You see, ever since our first meeting—at the memorial service for Jeremy Grove, when we had our little disagreement over the Ghirlandaio panel—I realized you were the most formidable opponent I had ever faced."

He paused, waiting. But still Pendergast said nothing, did not move except to blink his eyelids. And so Fosco returned to his work and—with the energy of a sudden surge of anger—laid the third, fourth, and fifth course of bricks.

When he laid the last brick of the sixth course in place, he paused once more. The brief anger had passed and he was again himself. The wall reached now to Pendergast's waist. Throwing back the tails of his coat, Fosco perched daintily on the old pile of bricks to rest. His gaze fell almost kindly on the prisoner.

"You'll note I'm laying the bricks in Flemish bond, alternating the headers with the stretchers," he said. "Beautiful, is it not? I could have been a mason, perhaps, had I so chosen. Of course, building such a wall is time-consuming. Consider it my final gift. My *parting* gift. You see, once the last brick is in place, it will not take long—perhaps a day, perhaps two, depending on how much air seeps through these ancient walls. I am no sadist. Your death will not be unduly prolonged—though I imagine slow suffocation in the dark might not be quite as merciful as one would hope. It cannot be helped."

He sat for a moment, catching his breath. Then he went on, his voice now almost meditative.

"Do not think, Signor Pendergast, I take this

responsibility lightly. I realize that by entombing you here, I rob the world of a great intellect. It will be a duller place without you. However, it will also be safer, for me and those like me: men and women who would prefer to pursue their destinies unfettered by laws devised by their inferiors."

He glanced into the recess. With the wall half complete, the niche lay in deepest shadow. Only the gaunt lines of Pendergast's bloodied face reflected in the torchlight.

The count looked at him quizzically. "Still nothing? Very well: let us continue." And he pulled himself to his feet.

The next three tiers were laid in silence. Finally, as Fosco put the last brick of the ninth course in position and smoothed fresh mortar across its top, Pendergast spoke. The wall had reached the level of his pale eyes, and his voice echoed hollowly inside the new-made vault.

"You must not do this," he said. His voice had none of its usual creamy, almost lazy precision.

This, Fosco knew, was a side effect of the phenobarbital. "But my dear Pendergast, it is done!" He troweled off the mortar and returned to the brick pile.

The tenth course was half laid before Pendergast spoke once more. "There is something I must do. Something unfinished, of great importance to the world. A member of my family is in a position to do great harm. I must be allowed to stop him."

Fosco halted, listening.

"Let me complete that task. Then I will return to you. You... you may then dispose of me as you see fit. I give you my word as a gentleman."

Fosco laughed. "Do you take me for a fool? I am to believe you shall return, willingly, like Regulus to Carthage, to meet your end? Bah! Even if you do keep your word, when should I expect you? Twenty or thirty years from now, when you have grown old and tired of life?"

No answer came from the darkness of the niche.

"But this task you mention. It intrigues me. A family member, you say? Give me more details."

"Free me first."

"That is impossible. But come—I see we are simply bandying words. And I weary of this task." And more quickly now, Fosco finished the tenth course and started on the eleventh and last.

It was when only a single stone remained to be fitted and mortared into the wall that Pendergast spoke again. "Fosco"—the voice was faint, sepulchral, as if emerging from the deepest recesses of a tomb—"I ask you, as a gentleman and a human being. Do not place that brick."

"Yes. It does seem a shame." And Fosco hefted the final brick in his hand. "But I'm afraid the time has come for us to part. I thank you for the pleasure of your company these last few days. I say to you, not *arrivederla*, but *addio*." And he forced the last stone into place.

As he smoothed away the last bit of excess mortar, Fosco heard—or thought he heard—a sound from the tomb within. A low moan, or exhalation of breath. Or was it just the wind, crying through the ancient catacombs? He pressed his head to the freshly laid wall and listened intently.

But there was nothing further.

Fosco stepped back, kicked a pile of scattered bones

into position before the wall, then grabbed the torch and made his way hastily through the rat's nest of tunnels to the ancient stairwell. Reaching it, he began to climb—a dozen steps, two dozen, three—heading for the surface and the warm evening sunlight, leaving the restless netherworld of shadows far behind.

{ 85 }

D'Agosta sat silently in the backseat of the car as it moved up the winding mountain road. The countryside was as beautiful as it had been two days before: the hills clad in autumn raiment, shining rust and gold under the early morning sun. D'Agosta barely noticed. He was staring up at the cruel-looking keep of Castel Fosco, just now rising into view above its spar of gray rock. Merely seeing the castle again brought a chill not even the convoy of police cars could allay.

He shifted the weight of the canvas bag from one leg to the other. Inside was Fosco's diabolical weapon. The chill evaporated before the furious, carefully controlled anger that burned within him. D'Agosta tried to channel that anger: he'd need it for the encounter to come. The maddening, excruciating twelve-hour delay was finally over. The paperwork, the warrant, had finally come through; the bureaucracy had been satisfied. Now he was back here, on the enemy's home ground. He had to stay calm, stay in control. He knew he had only one shot to save Pendergast—if indeed Pendergast was still alive—and he wasn't going to blow it by losing his cool.

Colonnello Esposito, sitting beside him, took a last deep drag on his cigarette, then ground it out in an ashtray. He'd been quiet during the drive, moving only occasionally to light a new cigarette. Now he, too, glanced out the window.

"A most formidable residence," he said.

D'Agosta nodded.

Esposito pulled out a fresh cigarette, reconsidered, replaced it, and turned to D'Agosta. "This Fosco you describe seems a shrewd character. It will be necessary to catch him red-handed, secure the evidence ourselves. We will therefore go in fast."

"Yes. Good."

Esposito ran a hand over his brushed-back gray hair. "He is also clearly one who leaves nothing to chance. I worry that Pendergast may be..." His voice trailed off.

"If we hadn't waited twelve hours—"

The *colonnello* shook his head. "One cannot change the way things are." He fell silent while the cars passed the castle's ruined outer gate and made their way along the avenue of cypress trees. Then he stirred again. "One request, Sergeant."

"What?"

"Let me do the talking, if you please. I will make sure the conversation is in English. Fosco speaks English well?"

"Perfectly."

D'Agosta was more exhausted than he ever remembered being. Every limb ached, and his skin was scratched and torn in countless places. Only his iron resolve to rescue Pendergast, his fear about what his friend might be undergoing at the hands of the count, kept him going. *Maybe he's still alive,* he thought. *Back in the same cell. Of course he is. He must be.*

D'Agosta prayed briefly, fervently, that this would prove the case. The alternative was too dreadful to contemplate.

The cars pulled into the graveled parking area just outside the inner wall. Here, in the deep shadow of the stone buttresses, it was chilly. D'Agosta opened the car door and stepped out briskly despite his aches and pains.

"The Fiat," he said. "Our rented car. It's gone."

"What model?" Esposito asked.

"A Stylo, black. License IGP 223."

Esposito turned to one of his men and barked an order.

The castle seemed deserted, almost preternaturally quiet. The *colonnello* nodded to his men, then led the way quickly up the stone steps to the banded doors.

This time, the doors to the inner ward did not open by themselves. In fact, it took five minutes—and increasingly agitated raps by the *colonnello*—before they groaned slowly open. There, on the far side, stood Fosco. His gaze traveled over the knot of policemen, coming to rest at last on D'Agosta. He smiled.

"Why, my heavens! It's Sergeant D'Agosta. How are you finding Italy?"

D'Agosta did not reply. Just the sight of the grotesque count brought on a rush of loathing. *Keep it cool,* he reminded himself.

Fosco was puffing just a bit but otherwise seemed his jovial, unflappable self. "Please excuse my delay in responding. I wasn't expecting any company today."

Then he turned toward the *colonnello*. "But we haven't yet been introduced. I am Fosco."

"I am Colonnello Orazio Esposito of the Nucleo Investigativo," Esposito said brusquely. "We have a warrant to search these premises. I would ask you to step aside, sir."

"A warrant!" Surprise bloomed on the count's face. "What's it about?"

Esposito ignored him, walking past, barking orders to his men. He turned to the count. "My men will need access to all parts of the castle."

"Of course!" The count hastened across the lawn of the inner ward, past the purling fountain, and into the fastness of the dark and brooding keep, putting on a remarkable front of surprise and alarm, mingled with subservient cooperation.

D'Agosta maintained a stony silence, keeping his canvas bag well away from Fosco. He noticed that, this time, none of the massive doors scraped closed behind them.

The count led the way down the central gallery and into a room D'Agosta hadn't seen before: a large and elegant library, its walls covered with ancient volumes, leather spines stamped and gilded. A fire crackled merrily on the hearth.

"Please, gentlemen," Fosco said, ushering them in. "Have a seat. Can I offer you sherry? A cigar?"

"I'm afraid there is no time for pleasantries," Esposito said. He reached into his pocket, withdrew a sheet of paper bearing official stamps, laid it on the table. "Here is the warrant. We will search the basements and cellars first, then work our way up."

The count had taken a cigar from a carved wooden box. "Of course I shall cooperate, but I'd like to know what it's about."

"Sergeant D'Agosta has leveled very grave charges against you."

"Against *me*?" the count said. He glanced at D'Agosta. "Whatever are you talking about?"

"Kidnapping, attempted murder—and the accusation that you are still holding Pendergast."

The surprise on Fosco's face deepened. "But this—this is outrageous!" He lowered the cigar, looking from D'Agosta to Esposito and back again. "Sergeant, is this true? Do you make such accusations?"

"Let's go," said D'Agosta impatiently. Although he kept his tone level, he seethed inwardly at the masterful acting. The count truly looked like a man struggling with shock and disbelief.

"Well. If that is the case, who am I to protest?" Fosco examined the cigar, snipped off the end with a tiny silver clipper, lit it. "But you may put away that warrant, Officer. I give you and your men free run of the castle. Every door is open to you. Search where you will. Please allow me to assist you in any way I can."

Esposito turned briskly to some of the carabinieri, speaking in Italian. The men saluted, fanned out, disappeared.

Esposito turned back to D'Agosta. "Sergeant, perhaps you could take us to the room where you were incarcerated for the night. Count, you will accompany us."

"I would insist upon it. The Foscos are an ancient and noble family, and we value our honor above all else.

These charges must be addressed, and settled, immediately." He glanced back at D'Agosta with just a trace of indignation.

D'Agosta led the way down the gallery, through the drawing room, and into the long procession of elegant chambers. The count followed, walking in his peculiar light-footed way, pointing out various works of art and sights of interest for the *colonnello*, who ignored him. The remaining two carabinieri brought up the rear.

Then came a point where D'Agosta lost his way. He looked around, stepped forward, stopped again. There had been a door in this stuccoed wall—hadn't there?

"Sergeant?" Esposito said.

"Perhaps I could be of assistance?" Fosco volunteered.

D'Agosta glanced through one doorway, backtracked, looked through another. It had been less than twenty-four hours; he couldn't have forgotten. Could he? He advanced, touched the stucco, but it was old, crumbling, anything but fresh.

"The sergeant said the apartment where he was held prisoner was in the tower itself," the *colonnello* told Fosco.

The count cast a puzzled gaze on the *colonnello*, turned to D'Agosta. "There is only one apartment in the tower, but it is not this way."

"Take us to it."

The count led them quickly through a series of passages and low, dark stone rooms, barren of furnishings.

"This is the oldest part of the castle," Fosco said. "Dating back to the ninth century. It's rather cold and depressing. There are no modern amenities like electricity or plumbing. I never come here myself."

Within a minute, they had reached the heavy iron door of the keep. Fosco opened it with difficulty, the lock rusty. The door creaked open, Fosco brushing away cobwebs. He led the way up the staircase beyond, the echo of feet filling the stony spaces. Reaching the landing, D'Agosta paused before the door of their apartment. It was ajar.

"Is this it?" Esposito asked.

D'Agosta nodded.

Esposito beckoned to his men, who came forward, opened the door, and stepped inside. Esposito followed, D'Agosta on his heels.

The snug apartment where he'd spent the night before last was gone. The rugs, bookshelves, and furniture were nowhere to be seen. Lights, plumbing fixtures—everything that had been retrofitted into the space was now gone. Instead, he gazed into a chill, dark vault filled with decaying lumber, broken stone carvings, moldering stacks of heavy draperies. A massive iron chandelier, twisted and rusting, lay on the floor. Everything was coated in a thick mantle of dust. It looked like a storage area for the cast-off detritus of past centuries.

"Sergeant—are you sure this is the room?"

D'Agosta's astonishment gave way to puzzlement, then anger. "Yes, but it wasn't like this. It wasn't like this at all. There were bedrooms, a bathroom—"

The room fell silent.

So that's the game, D'Agosta thought. "The count has used the twelve hours it took to get the warrant to fix things. To disguise everything."

Esposito ran his finger over the dust on an old, wormy table, rubbed it between thumb and finger, then looked at D'Agosta rather intently. He turned to the count. "Are there any other apartments in the tower?"

"As you can see, this occupies the entire upper floor."

Esposito looked back at D'Agosta. "All right. What next?"

"We went down to dinner." D'Agosta was careful to keep his voice calm. "In the main dining room. Fosco said we'd never leave the castle alive. There was an exchange of gunfire. I killed his manservant."

The count's eyebrows shot up again. "Pinketts?"

Within five minutes, they were stepping into the cheery dining *salotto.* But it was as D'Agosta had begun to fear: there were no bloodstains, no sign of any struggle. The remains of a single breakfast lay on the table.

"You'll excuse me, I hope," Fosco said, gesturing toward the half-eaten meal. "You caught me breakfasting. As I said, I was not expecting visitors. And I gave the staff a few days off."

Esposito was strolling around the room, hands clasped behind his back, examining the walls, searching for chips or holes that would indicate bullet marks. He asked, "Sergeant, how many rounds were exchanged?"

D'Agosta thought a moment. "Four. Three went into Pinketts. The other should be somewhere on the wall above the fireplace. If it hasn't been plastered over."

But of course there was no mark: none at all.

Esposito turned toward the count. "This Pinketts, may we meet him?"

"He's back in England for a few weeks. Left the day

before yesterday—a death in the family, I understand. I would be glad to give you his address and telephone number in Dorset."

Esposito nodded. "Later."

Another silence fell over the room.

He's not English! D'Agosta almost shouted. *And his name's not Pinketts!* But he knew there was no point in arguing about it now. Fosco had clearly prepared things all too well. And he would not allow himself to rise to the bait—not in front of the *colonnello.*

Find Pendergast. That's the most important thing.

Two of the carabinieri returned, speaking rapidly in Italian to the *colonnello.* Esposito turned to D'Agosta. "My men found no sign of the car in the garages or anywhere else on the grounds."

"He's obviously disposed of it."

Esposito nodded thoughtfully. "What was the rental company?"

"Eurocar."

Esposito turned back to his men, spoke in Italian. The men nodded and left.

"After Fosco returned from Florence, we were locked in an old storeroom," D'Agosta said, struggling against a growing sense of panic. "In the cellars. I can lead you there. The stairway's just off the pantry."

"Please." And Esposito gestured for him to proceed.

D'Agosta led the group out of the dining room, through the large and empty kitchen, and into the pantry beyond. The staircase leading down to the storage cellars was now covered by a massive armoire, copper pots and cookware hanging from its ancient brass hooks.

Bingo! D'Agosta thought.

"The stairway's behind there," he said. "He's covered it up with that armoire."

Esposito nodded to his two men, who moved it with great difficulty. D'Agosta felt himself go cold. The stairway was gone. In its place was bare wall, ancient and dusty as the rest of the room.

"Feel it!" he said, unable now to keep the frustration and mounting horror from his voice. "He's bricked it in! The mortar's got to be still wet!"

The *colonnello* stepped forward, removed a penknife from his pocket, and stabbed its point into the mortar. Small, dried pieces crumbled away in a train of dust. He dug it in farther, probing. Then he turned and, without a word, handed the knife to D'Agosta.

D'Agosta knelt, felt along the bottom. The wall looked old, dusty—there were even what appeared to be cobwebs exposed by the moving of the armoire. He stepped back, looked around the room. No mistake: this was the right place.

"The count has covered it up. Disguised it somehow. *There was a door here.*"

Another, longer, silence fell. Esposito's eyes met D'Agosta's, then looked away.

Seeing the speculative look, D'Agosta felt a renewed sense of steely determination settle over him. "Let's join your men. Search the whole goddamned place."

An hour later, D'Agosta found himself back in the central gallery. They had explored more passages, salons, rooms, vaults, basements, and tunnels than he'd ever imagined one castle could hold. The castle was so large, so sprawling, it was impossible to know whether or not they had covered all its drafty spaces and dank stairwells. All his muscles quivered with weariness. The canvas bag with the microwave weapon hung like a dead weight by his side.

As the search progressed, Esposito had grown increasingly quiet. Throughout it all, Fosco had stayed by their side, solicitous, patient, unlocking every door, even suggesting new routes of inquiry from time to time.

Now, the count cleared his throat. "Could I suggest we return to my library? We can talk more comfortably there."

As they seated themselves around the fire, one of the carabinieri came in and whispered in Esposito's ear. The *colonnello* nodded, then dismissed the man with a gesture, his expression unreadable. Fosco once again offered him a cigar, and this time Esposito accepted. D'Agosta watched all this with a sense of growing disbelief. He felt rage taking over now, almost beyond his ability to control, combined with a sense of horror and grief. It was unreal, a nightmare.

Esposito spoke at last, his voice neutral. "My men looked into the Stylo. It was returned to Eurocar at 13:00 yesterday. The chit was signed by A. X. L. Pendergast, paid for with an American Express card belonging to Pendergast. A Special Agent A. X. L. Pendergast had a reservation on a flight to Palermo at 14:30 from Firenze Peretola. We're still trying to find out whether he was, in fact, on that flight. The airlines these days are so difficult..."

"*Of course* it will appear he was on the flight! Can't you see what Fosco's game is?"

"Sergeant—"

"It's all *bullshit!*" D'Agosta said, rising from his chair. "Orchestrated by Fosco! Just like he walled up the passageway, disguised the apartment. Just like he's planned *every fucking thing!*"

"Sergeant, please," Esposito said quietly. "Control yourself."

"You said yourself we were dealing with a determined man!"

"Sergeant." The voice was firmer.

D'Agosta stood, almost out of his mind with rage, frustration, and grief. Fosco had Pendergast's credit card. What did it mean? And now the bastard was slipping through his fingers. Pendergast was gone, vanished. He made an almost superhuman struggle at control—if he lost it, he would never have another chance. He had to find a chink in the count's armor. "He's not in the castle, then. They've taken him into the woods, up on the mountain. We've got to search the area."

Esposito puffed thoughtfully on the cigar, waiting for D'Agosta to finish. Then he spoke. "Sergeant D'Agosta. In your story, you claim the count killed four people to get back a violin—"

"*At least* four people. We're just wasting time here! We have to—"

Esposito raised a hand for silence. "Excuse me. You claim the count killed these men with that device you're carrying."

"Yes." D'Agosta tried to control his breathing.

"Why don't you show it to the count?"

D'Agosta pulled the microwave device from the bag.

"My goodness," Fosco said, staring with great interest. "What is that?"

"The sergeant tells us it is a microwave weapon," Esposito said. "Designed by you, and used by you, to burn to death Mr. Locke Bullard, a peasant from Abetone, and two other people back in the United States."

Fosco looked first at the *colonnello*, then at D'Agosta, astonishment and then—pity?—on his face. "The sergeant says this?"

"Correct."

"A machine, you say? That zaps people, turns them into smoking piles of ash? That I built?" He spread his hands, astonishment on his face. "I should like to see a demonstration."

"Sergeant, perhaps you'd care to demonstrate the device for us and the count?"

D'Agosta looked down at the weapon, turned it over in his hands. Fosco's skeptical tone went unrefuted by the *colonnello*, and no wonder: the device looked almost cartoonish, a Flash Gordon confection.

"I don't know how to use it," D'Agosta said.

"Try," said Esposito, an edge of sarcasm in his voice.

It occurred to D'Agosta that if he could get it working, it might be his only chance to turn the tide. It was his last chance.

He pointed it toward the fireplace hearth, where—as if placed as a deliberate challenge—sat a fresh pumpkin. He tried to clear his mind, tried to remember precisely what Fosco had done before. He turned a knob, pulled the trigger.

Nothing happened.

He spun more dials, pressed a button, aimed, pulled the trigger.

Still nothing.

For all he knew, it had been damaged during the escape, when he tossed it into the bushes. He fiddled with the dials, pulling the trigger again and again, hoping for the low hum he'd heard during the demonstration. But the machine remained silent, cold.

"I think we've seen enough," said Esposito quietly.

Slowly, very slowly, D'Agosta replaced it in the canvas bag. He could hardly bring himself to look at the *colonnello.* The man was staring at him, his face a mask of skepticism. No, not just skepticism: pure disbelief, anger—and pity.

From over Esposito's shoulder, Fosco also stared. Then—very slowly and deliberately—Fosco reached into his collar, drew out a chain with a medallion at the end, and draped it carefully over his shirtfront, patting it familiarly with a plump hand.

With a sudden, burning shock of recognition, D'Agosta recognized the medallion: the lidless eye over a phoenix rising from the ashes. Pendergast's own chain. Fosco's private message was all too terribly clear.

"You bastard—!" And D'Agosta lunged for the count.

In a moment, the carabinieri leaped on D'Agosta and pulled him back, restraining him against a far wall of the library. The *colonnello* quickly placed himself between D'Agosta and Fosco.

"The son of a bitch! That's Pendergast's chain! There's your proof! *He killed Pendergast and took it!*"

"Are you all right?" Esposito asked the count, ignoring D'Agosta.

"Quite all right, thank you," Fosco said, sitting back and smoothing his capacious front. "I was startled, that is all. To settle the question once and for all, so there can be *no doubt*—" He turned the disc over, and there, on the reverse of the medallion, evidently worn by time, was an intricate engraving of the count's own crest.

Esposito looked at the crest, then turned to stare at D'Agosta, dark eyes glittering. D'Agosta, clamped in the arms of six men, could barely move. He tried to regain control of himself, his voice. The way the count had said *So there can be no doubt,* with that peculiar emphasis on the words *no doubt*... It was a message aimed directly at D'Agosta. It was a message that told him he was too late. Those twelve hours maneuvering for the warrant had proved fatal. The desperate hope D'Agosta had been fighting to hold on to—that the count might have kept Pendergast alive, a prisoner—guttered and died. Pendergast was dead. *So there can be no doubt*...

Esposito extended his hand to Fosco. *"Abbiamo finito qui, Conte. Chiedo scusa per il disturbo, e la ringrazio per la sua pazienza con questa faccenda piuttosto spiacevole."*

The count inclined his head graciously. *"Niente disturbo, Colonnello. Prego."* He glanced in D'Agosta's direction. *"Mi dispiace per lui."*

Esposito and Fosco shook hands. "We'll be going now," Esposito said. "There is no need to show us out." And with this he bowed deeply to Fosco and left the room, ignoring D'Agosta.

The carabinieri holding D'Agosta released him. D'Agosta picked up the canvas bag and headed for the door. A red mist hung before his eyes. In the doorway, he stopped to look back at Fosco. "You're a dead man," he said, barely managing to speak. "You—"

But the words died in his throat as Fosco swiveled to stare at him in turn, his large features and wet lips spreading into a horrible grin. It was like nothing D'Agosta had ever seen before—malevolent, triumphant, a grotesque leer of exultation. If the count had spoken the words out loud, the message couldn't have been clearer. *He had murdered Pendergast.*

And then the smile was gone, hidden behind a cloud of cigar smoke.

Colonnello Esposito said nothing during the walk back along the gallery, across the manicured lawn, through the gate of the inner ward. He remained silent as the cars made their way down the narrow road, past the cypress trees and olive groves. It was not until they were on the main road back to Florence that he turned to D'Agosta.

"I misjudged you, sir," he said in a low, chill voice. "I welcomed you here, gave you credentials, cooperated with you in every way. In return, you disgraced yourself and humiliated me and my men. I will be lucky if the count doesn't bring a *denuncia* against me for this invasion of his home and insult to his person."

He leaned a little closer. "You may consider all your official privileges revoked from this moment on. The paperwork to have you declared persona non grata in Italy will take a little time—but if I were you, *signore,* I would leave this country by the next available flight."

Then he sat back, stared stonily out the window, and spoke no more.

{ 86 }

It was approaching midnight when Count Fosco finished his evening constitutional and, puffing slightly, returned to the main dining *salotto* of the castle. Whether in town or country, it was his habit, before turning in, to take a short stroll for his health's sake. And the long galleries and corridors of Castel Fosco offered an almost endless variety of perambulations.

He took a seat in a chair facing the vast stone fireplace, warming his hands before the merry blaze, dispelling the damp embrace of the castle. He'd take a glass of port and sit here awhile before retiring: sit here, and contemplate the end of a successful day.

The end, in fact, of a successful undertaking.

His men had been paid off and had all melted away, back into the huts and tenant farmhouses of his estate. The small detachment of police had gone, along with Sergeant D'Agosta and his fire and bluster. The man would soon be on a flight back to New York. The servants would not return until the next morning. The castle seemed almost watchful in its silence.

Fosco rose, poured himself a glass of port from a

bottle on an ancient sideboard, then returned to his comfortable chair. For the past few days, the walls of the castle had rung with noise and excitement. Now, by comparison, they seemed preternaturally quiet.

He sipped the port, found it excellent.

It was a great pity, not having Pinketts, or rather Pinchetti, here to anticipate his every need. It was a great pity, to think of him at rest in an unmarked tomb within the family vault. The man would be difficult, even impossible, to replace. Truth to tell, sitting here by himself, in this vast empty edifice, Fosco found himself feeling just the least bit lonely.

But then, he reminded himself, he was *not* alone. He had Pendergast for company—or, at least, his corpse.

Fosco had faced many adversaries in the past, but none had shown the brilliance or tenacity of Pendergast. In fact, had it not been for Fosco's home soil advantages—his moles in the police and elsewhere, the maturity of his long-laid plans, the scope of his contingency arrangements—the story might well have ended differently. Even so, he'd felt just the least bit anxious. And so Fosco had made sure this evening's constitutional took him back down—very deep down indeed—to Pendergast's current domicile. Just to make sure. As expected, he'd found the newly mortared but carefully disguised wall as he left it. He'd rapped on it, listened, called softly, but, of course, there was no answering response. Almost thirty-six hours had passed. No doubt the good agent was already dead.

He sipped the port, sank back in the chair, basking in the reflections of a successful outcome. There was, of course, one loose end: Sergeant D'Agosta. Fosco reflected on the fury, the impotent murderous rage, on the policeman's face as he'd been led off the grounds. Fosco knew this rage would soon fade. And in its place would come first resignation, then uncertainty, and then—ultimately—fear. Because by now D'Agosta surely must know the kind of man he was dealing with. He, Fosco, would not forget. He would snip off that loose end, finish the business, make D'Agosta repay the debt he incurred for shooting Pinchetti, and in so doing retrieve his clever little invention.

But there was no hurry. No hurry at all.

As he sipped his port, Fosco realized there was, in fact, a second loose end. Viola, Lady Maskelene. He thought of her, tending her bit of vineyard, strong limbs made tawny by the Mediterranean sun. Her bearing, her movements, had a mix of good breeding, catlike athleticism, and sexuality he found deliciously intoxicating. Her conversation sparkled like no other woman's he had met. She was bursting with vitality. She would bring warmth to any place she visited—even Castel Fosco...

A faint sound, like the scurry of dead leaves on stone, came from the darkness beyond the room.

Fosco paused in mid-sip.

Slowly, he put the glass down, stood, and walked to the main entrance to the *salotto.* Beyond lay the long gallery, lit only by the moon and the occasional wall sconce. Long ranks of suited armor lined the walls, glowing faintly in the pallid light.

Nothing.

Fosco turned thoughtfully. The old castle was full of rats; it was high time he had the head gardener in again to deal with them.

He began walking back toward the fire, feeling a chill that could not entirely be explained by the cool air.

Then he stopped again. There was one thing, he knew, that would put him in fine high spirits.

Taking a tack away from the fire, he made for the small doorway that led into his private workshop. He crossed the dark room, threading his way through a maze of lab tables and freestanding equipment, until he reached the wooden paneling of the rear wall. He knelt, ran one fat hand along the polished wainscoting, found a tiny detent. He pressed it. One of the wooden panels above his head popped ajar with a faint snick. Rising, the count pulled the panel wide, exposing a large safe retrofitted into the stonework of the wall. He punched a code into the safe's keypad, and its door sprung open. Carefully, reverently, the count reached inside and pulled out the small, coffin-shaped wooden case that held the Stormcloud Stradivarius.

He carried the case into the dining *salotto* and placed it on the table against the wall, well away from the heat of the fire, leaving it closed, so it would slowly accustom itself to the change in temperature. Then he returned to his seat. Compared to the chill of the lab, it was deliciously warm before the fire. He took another sip of port, thinking about what he would play. A Bach chaconne? A flashy Paganini? No: something simple, something clean, refreshing...Vivaldi. "La Primavera," from *Le Quattro Stagioni*.

After a few minutes, he rose again, walked over to the violin, undid the brass fastening, and lifted the lid. He did not play it, not yet: it would need at least another ten minutes to adjust to the ambient temperature and humidity. He merely gazed dotingly on its wondrous and mysterious finish, its sensual lines. Staring at the violin, Fosco felt a joy, a sense of completion, flood through him.

He returned to his comfortable chair, loosened his cravat, undid his waistcoat. The Stormcloud was back where it belonged: in the family seat. *He* had snatched it from the jaws of oblivion. It had been worth the expense, the extravagant planning, the danger, the lives. It was worth any cost, any struggle. As Fosco stared at it, glowing crimson in the warm reflected firelight, it seemed to him that the instrument was not of this world. Rather, it was the voice—the song—of the better world to come.

It was now very warm in the room. He rose, took up a poker, pushed the logs back a little, turned his chair from the fire. "La Primavera." The sweet, lively melody coursed through his mind as if he was already playing it. Five more minutes. He removed his cravat and unbuttoned the top button of his shirt.

A log cracked loudly in the fireplace, startling him; he sat bolt upright, the port sloshing out of his glass and spilling onto his open waistcoat.

He sat back slowly, wondering at the sense of unease. Nerves: the affair had taken more of a toll on him than he'd thought. His stomach gave a small lurch, and he set down the glass of port. Perhaps he should have taken something stronger as a *digestivo*: a drop of Calvados, a grappa, or, even better, one of the excellent herbal digestives produced by the monks at Monte Senario.

A most unpleasant sensation of poor digestion now infused his stomach. He rose, lumbered over to the sideboard—how uncharacteristically heavy he felt on his feet!—and took out a small bottle of Amaro Borghini, filled a small glass with the reddish-brown liquid, and returned to the chair. His stomach was protesting vociferously, and he took a swallow, then a second, of the bitter liqueur. And as he did, he heard another sound, like a footfall, at the door.

He half rose, but felt weak and sank back. Naturally, there was nobody there. There couldn't be. The servants had all been given a few days off. It was his imagination playing tricks with him. It was the strain of the last few days. He was getting on in years for business such as this.

His innards were almost boiling with indigestion and he drained the glass, shifting in his chair, trying to get comfortable. The heat in the room had grown oppressive, but, blast it, there was no one to douse the fire. He fetched a deep, shuddering sigh. He would calm himself, then take out the Stormcloud and restore his previous mood with a leaping rendition of "La Primavera."

Only calmness did not come. He felt a strange oppression creep stealthily over him—a pressure that seemed to build slowly, layer on layer, from within. This was not indigestion; he was getting ill. He mopped his brow with a handkerchief, aware that his heart was beating uncomfortably fast. He had caught a chill in the crypts, no doubt, hefting those heavy bricks, brought out by his unwise second visit to those clammy, nitred depths. He would take a holiday; leave tomorrow, in fact. The isle of Capraia, he told himself, would be a perfect spot…

He extended a trembling hand toward the glass of

amaro, but the liqueur suddenly tasted wrong, like hot pitch and vinegar in his mouth—hot, even, in his hand. Burning hot. He rose with a cry, the glass falling away and dashing to pieces against the floor. Fosco whirled, stumbled, righted himself.

Porca miseria, what was happening?

He gasped, felt his eyes smart, felt his mouth go dry, his heart accelerate. For a moment, he wondered if he was having a fit of some kind, or perhaps a heart attack. He'd heard heart attacks often began with a feeling just like this: a feeling that something, *something,* was terribly wrong. But there was no localized pain to his chest or arm. Instead, the terrible oppression within grew, and still grew, until it enveloped him. His very guts seemed to writhe. He looked around frantically, but there was nothing—not the bottle of port, not the violin, not the furniture or the rich tapestries—nothing to give any aid or explanation.

His insides felt as if they were crawling, boiling. He felt his mouth twitching, his eyes blinking uncontrollably, grimacing, his fingers jerking. The heat was like being suffocated with a burning blanket. His skin felt as if it was covered with a blanket of bees. Now fear and heat rose within him as one: an unendurable, irresistible heat that had nothing to do with the fire on the hearth—

Suddenly he knew. He *knew.*

"D'Agosta—!" he choked, but his throat closed up and no more words came out.

He whirled toward the closed door of the *salotto,* staggered forward, fell over the side table with a crash, rose to his knees. His muscles were jerking spasmodically, but with an enormous effort of will, he began to crawl forward.

"Bastardo—!" It came out like a choked cry. As he did so, his limbs began to take on a life of their own, twitching and jerking with a horrible violence, but he had only a few more feet to go; he gave one superhuman lurch, seized the door handle. It was burning hot, and he felt his skin popping and sizzling, yet he clung tenaciously, heaved, turned—*locked*.

With a suppressed shriek he sank, collapsing at the door, writhing. The heat grew, and grew, like lava spreading itself through his veins. A terrible piercing whine, like the buzz of a monstrous gnat, filled his head. What was that he smelled burning? All of a sudden the count went rigid. His jaws clamped together involuntarily, grinding with such force his teeth chipped and split. Now, unbidden, his many sins and excesses paraded before him in a terrible blur. As the heat continued to grow—intolerable yet still increasing, an inferno of agony he could never have imagined possible—Fosco felt his vision grow dim and strange. His eyes jerked around the room, coming to rest on the fire, while reality itself began to distort, fall away, and he began to see things *beyond*...

...Oh, dear Jesus, what is that dark shape rising in the fire...?

And now, summoning every last ounce of willpower he possessed—despite the teeth grinding into meal and the blood that filled his mouth and the swelling tongue that refused to move—Fosco began to slur, in something between a gargle and a groan, the words of the Lord's Prayer.

Pater noster...

He felt his skin blister, his oiled hair curl and smoke. He clawed his hands across the stone floor in agony, tearing away the nails in his efforts to get out the words:

...Qui es in coelis...

Over the shrieking buzz in his ears, Fosco could hear—as if rising from the deepest depths of the earth—the rich and terrible laughter, not of Sergeant D'Agosta, not of any earthly being...

...Sanctificetur...

He tried, with the last of a supreme effort of will, to continue the prayer, but the subcutaneous fat was boiling beneath the skin of his lips:

...Sanctiferrrrrrrr...

And then came the point where no sound, not even a scream, was possible to utter.

{ 87 }

Bryce Harriman ducked into the stale, smoke-fouled office of his editor, Rupert Ritts. He had been waiting for this moment a long, long time, and he was determined to enjoy it, drag it out as long as possible. It would be a story he'd tell his kids and grandkids, put in his memoirs. One of the moments he'd savor the rest of his life.

"Harriman!" Ritts came around from behind his desk—his idea of a show of respect—and seated himself on one corner. "Take a seat."

Harriman sat. Why not? Let Ritts talk a bit first.

"That was quite a piece you wrote on Hayward and that man, Buck. I'm almost sorry that cracker preacher got his ass sent back to Oklahoma. I hope he decides to move back to the Big Apple once his parole is up." He laughed and picked a piece of paper from his desk. "Here's something I bet you'll be interested to hear: newsstand circ for the week ending today." He waved the paper in Harriman's face. "Nineteen percent above this same time last year, six percent above last week, sixty percent sell-through."

Ritts grinned, as if the newsstand circulation and

sell-through figures of the *New York Post* were the be-all and end-all of Harriman's existence. Harriman kicked back in the chair, listening, a practiced smile on his face.

"And look at this. Advertising revenues up three and a half."

Another pause so that Harriman might absorb and glorify in the stupendous news.

Ritts lit a cigarette. He snapped the lighter shut, exhaled. "Harriman, don't ever say I don't give credit where credit is due. This was your story from beginning to end. You did it. Sure, I helped with some ideas here and there, gave you the benefit of my experience, nudged you in the right direction once or twice—but this was your story."

Ritts paused, as if waiting. For what? Effusive, genuflecting thanks? Harriman leaned back and listened, still smiling.

"Anyway, as I was saying, *you* did this. You've been noticed, and I mean *noticed*, by the powers on high."

Who was that? Harriman wondered. The big cheese himself? That would be a joke. The guy probably couldn't even get into his father's club.

Now Ritts dropped his bomb. "Next week, I want you to be my guest at the annual News Corporation dinner at Tavern on the Green. This wasn't just my idea—although I heartily approved. It was"—and now his eyes flashed upward as if a heavenly host had issued the invitation—"*his* idea. He wants to meet you, shake your hand."

Meet me, shake my hand. This was beautiful. God, this was beautiful. He couldn't wait to tell his friends about this.

"It's black tie—you got one of those? If not, I rent mine at a place opposite Bloomingdale's. Discount Tux, best deal in the city."

Harriman could hardly believe his ears. What a bozo. Not even *ashamed* to admit he rented his tuxes. "I have one or two, thanks," he said coolly.

Ritts looked at him a little strangely. "You all right? You do know about the annual dinner, right? I mean, I've been in this business thirty years and let me tell you, this is *something special.* It's Thursday evening, drinks at six in the Crystal Room, dinner at seven. You and a guest. Bring your squeeze, if you have one."

Harriman sat forward. "I'm afraid that won't be possible."

"Come alone, then. No problem."

"You don't understand. I can't come at all. I'm otherwise engaged."

"What?"

"I'm *busy.*"

There was a shocked silence. And then Ritts was off his perch. "You're *busy*? Aren't you listening? I'm talking about dinner with *the man himself*! I'm talking about the *News Corp. annual fucking dinner*!"

Harriman rose and dusted his sleeve, on which Ritts's ashes had fallen as he'd waved his cigarette around in excitement.

"I've accepted an appointment as a reporter at a newspaper called the *New York Times.* Perhaps you know of it." Harriman slipped an envelope out of his pocket. "My letter of resignation." He laid it on the desk, right on the shiny place where Ritts usually perched his ass.

There it was. Said and done. He'd drawn it out about as long as he could. There was no point in wasting any more time: he had a new office to fix up, a lot to do. After all, Bill Smithback would be returning from his extended honeymoon on Monday to find the surprise of his life: Bryce Harriman, associate reporter, fellow colleague, occupying the office next door.

Now, *that* would be something.

God, life was good.

He turned and walked to the door, turning just once to get a final look at Ritts, standing there, mouth open, for once with nothing to say.

"See you around, old chap," Harriman said.

{ 88 }

The big jet hit the tarmac with a jolt; tipped back into the air at an angle; then settled once more onto the ground, thrust reversers screaming.

As the plane decelerated, a lazy voice came over the P.A. system. "This is your captain speaking. We've landed at Kennedy Airport, and as soon as we get clearance, we'll taxi to the gate. Meanwhile, y'all please keep your seats. Sorry about that bit of turbulence back there. Welcome to New York City."

Faint applause arose here and there from a sea of ashen faces, then died quickly away.

"Bit of turbulence," muttered the man in the aisle seat. "Is that what he calls it? Shit on a *stick*. You couldn't pay me enough to get back in a plane after this."

He turned to his seatmate, nudged him with his elbow. "Glad to be back on the ground, pal?"

The nudge brought D'Agosta back to the present. He turned slowly away from the window, through which he'd been staring without really seeing, and glanced at the man. "What's that?"

The man snorted in disbelief. "Come on, stop playing it cool. Me, my own life passed before my eyes at least twice the last half hour."

"Sorry." And D'Agosta turned back to the window. "Wasn't really paying attention."

D'Agosta walked woodenly through Terminal 8 on his way out of customs, suitcase in one hand. All around him, people were talking excitedly, hugging, laughing. He passed by them all, barely noticing, eyes straight ahead.

"Vinnie!" came a voice. "Hey, Vinnie. Over here!"

D'Agosta turned to see Hayward, waving, walking toward him through the crowds. Laura Hayward, beautiful in a dark suit, her black hair shining, her eyes as deep and blue as the water off Capraia. She was smiling, but the smile did not reach quite as far as those perfect eyes.

"Vinnie," she said, embracing him. "Oh, Vinnie."

Automatically, his arms went around her. He could feel the welcoming tightness of her clasp; the warmth of her breath on his neck; the crush of her breasts against him. It was like a galvanic shock. Had it really been only ten days since they last embraced? A shudder passed through him: he felt strange, like a swimmer struggling upward from a very great depth.

"Vinnie," she murmured. "What can I say?"

"Don't say anything. Not now. Later, maybe."

Slowly, she released him.

"My God. What happened to your finger?"

"Locke Bullard happened."

They began to move through the baggage area. A silence grew between them, just long enough to become awkward.

"How's it been here?" he asked at last, lamely.

"Not much has happened since you called last night. We've still got ten detectives working the Cutforth murder. Technically. And from what I hear, that Southampton chief of police is catching holy hell for lack of progress on Grove."

D'Agosta gritted his teeth, started to speak, but Hayward put a finger to his lips.

"I know. I know. But that's the nature of the job sometimes. Now that Buck's out of the picture and the *Post* has moved on to other things, Cutforth's finally off the front page. Eventually it'll become just another unsolved murder. Along with Grove's, of course."

D'Agosta nodded.

"Amazing that it was Fosco. I'm floored."

D'Agosta shook his head.

"It's a hell of a thing, knowing who the perp is but being able to do nothing."

There was the ring of a claxon; an amber alarm flashed overhead; and a carousel nearby began to move.

"I *was* able to do something," he said in a low voice.

Hayward looked at him sharply.

"I'll explain in the car."

Ten minutes later they were on the Van Wyck Expressway, halfway back to Manhattan, Hayward at the wheel. D'Agosta sat beside her, idly looking out the window.

"So it was all about a violin," Hayward said. "The whole damn thing. A lousy violin."

"Not just any violin."

"I don't care. It wasn't worth all those deaths. And it *especially* wasn't worth—" But here she stopped, as if hesitant to break some unspoken code between them. "Where is it now?"

"I sent it by special courier to a woman on the island of Capraia. Comes from a line of violinists. She'll restore it to the Fosco family at a time of her choosing, when the new heir is settled in. Somehow, I think that's what Pendergast would have wanted."

It was the first time Pendergast's name had passed between them.

"I know you couldn't explain on the phone," she went on. "But what happened, exactly? After you took the Italian police to Fosco's castle yesterday morning, I mean."

D'Agosta did not reply.

"Come on, Vinnie. It'll be better if you talk about it."

D'Agosta sighed. "I spent the rest of the day combing the Chianti countryside. Talking to farmers. Talking to villagers. Anyone who might have seen anything, heard anything. Checking my hotel for messages. Of course, there was nothing. But I had to be sure, you see—absolutely sure..."

Hayward waited. After a moment, he went on.

"The thing is, deep down, I was already sure. We'd searched the castle. And then there was that look Fosco gave me, that awful look. If you'd seen it..." He shook his head. "Close to midnight, I drifted back to the castle. Went in the same way we'd come out. I took the time to figure out how the microwave device worked. And then I... used it. One last time."

"You brought Fosco to justice. Avenged your partner. I'd have done the same thing."

"Would you?" D'Agosta asked quietly.

Hayward nodded.

D'Agosta shifted restlessly. "There's not much more to tell. I spent this morning back in Florence, checking hospitals, morgues, police reports. More to keep busy than for anything else. And then I boarded the plane."

"What did you do with that weapon?"

"Disassembled it, smashed the pieces, and deposited them in half a dozen garbage cans around Florence."

She nodded. "And what are your plans now?"

D'Agosta shrugged. He hadn't given this any thought. "I don't know. Go back to Southampton, I guess. Face the music."

A small smile crept over her face. "Didn't you hear what I said? It's the chief who's facing the music. He got back from vacation and was so eager to hog the limelight that now it's all coming back to roost. Braskie's running against him in the next election, odds-on favorite to win."

"Even worse for me."

She changed lanes. "There's something else you should know. They've suspended the NYPD hiring freeze. That means you can work the city again. Get your old job back."

D'Agosta shook his head. "No way. I've been away too long. I'm old goods."

"It hasn't been *that* long. They're rehiring by

seniority. And with your experience in Southampton, and as FBI liaison..." She paused to negotiate the ramp onto the Long Island Expressway. "Of course, it couldn't be in my division. But they've got openings in several of the downtown precincts."

D'Agosta sat a moment, letting this penetrate. Then he looked at her sharply. "Wait a minute. My old job back, openings downtown. You didn't have anything to do with this, did you? Have a talk with Rocker, or something like that?"

"Me? You know the kind of cop I am. By the book. Miss Straight Arrow." But her smile seemed to deepen briefly.

Up ahead, the maw of the Queens-Midtown Tunnel loomed, gridworks of tile illuminated by fluorescent tubes. Hayward merged smoothly into the E-ZPass toll lane.

From the passenger seat, D'Agosta watched her: the beautiful lines of her face, the curve of her nose, the little furrow of concentration as she negotiated the evening traffic. It was wonderful just to see her again, to be here by her side. And yet he could not escape the sense of desolation that enveloped him. It was like a hollowness he carried around, a vacuum that could not be filled.

"You're right," he said as they entered the tunnel. "It doesn't matter if that violin's the most precious ever made. It wasn't worth Pendergast dying. Nothing was worth that."

Hayward kept her eyes on the road. "You don't know he's dead."

D'Agosta didn't answer. He'd told himself this

already: once, twice, a thousand times. When everything had been stacked against them—when there seemed no way they could possibly survive—Pendergast had always saved them. At times, it had seemed almost miraculous. And yet, this time, Pendergast had not reappeared. This time, it felt different.

Then there was that other feeling, the one that made him almost physically ill. It was the image of Pendergast, there in the clearing, surrounded by dogs. Everyone—the hunters, the handlers, the beaters—closing in. *Only one of us can get through. There's no other way.*

D'Agosta felt his throat close up. "You're right. I have no proof. Except maybe *this*." He reached into his pocket, drew out Pendergast's platinum chain and pendant: a lidless eye over a phoenix, rising from fiery ash, now pitted and partly melted. The chain he'd retrieved from Fosco's burning, smoking corpse. He stared at it a moment. He balled the hand into a fist, pressed a knuckle against his teeth. He felt a ridiculous impulse to burst into tears.

The worst of it was, D'Agosta knew he was the one who should have been left on that hill. He wished, more than anything else, that he had been left on that hill.

"Anyway, he would have contacted me by now. Or you. Or *some*body." He paused. "I don't know how I'm going to tell Constance."

"Who?"

"Constance Greene. His ward."

They drove through the rest of the tunnel in silence, finally emerging into the Manhattan night. Then he felt Hayward take his hand.

"Let me off anywhere," he said, sick at heart. "Penn Station's fine. I'll take the LIRR out to Southampton."

"Why?" she replied. "There's nothing for you out there. Your future's here, in New York City."

D'Agosta remained silent as the car cruised west: past Park, past Madison, past Fifth.

"You have a place to stay in town?" she asked.

D'Agosta shook his head.

"I—," Hayward began. Then she, too, fell silent.

D'Agosta roused himself, glanced at her. "What?" It was hard to tell, but in the reflected light of the streetlamps, he thought she was blushing.

"I was just thinking. If you're coming back to the NYPD, working here in the city...well, why not stay with me? For a while," she added hastily. "You know. See how it works out."

For a moment, D'Agosta didn't answer. He just looked back out at the lights passing over the windshield.

Then he realized, quite abruptly, he had to let go. Let go, at least for the moment. The past was over and done. Tomorrow was an unknown, still to come. He had no control over either. All he could control, all he could live, was the here and now. Knowing this didn't make things any better, really—but it did make them easier to bear.

"Look, Vinnie," Hayward said in a low voice. "It doesn't matter what you say. I just can't believe that Pendergast is dead. My gut tells me he's still alive. The guy's as close to indestructible as a body can be. He's cheated death a thousand times. He'll do it again somehow. I *know* he will."

D'Agosta smiled faintly.

Ahead, a traffic light turned red. She eased to a stop, then turned to look at him.

"So, you coming back with me, or what? It's not polite to make a lady ask twice."

He turned to her, squeezed her hand.

"I think I'd like that," he said, his smile broadening. "I think I'd like that very much."

{ Epilogue }

A chill November sun illuminated, but did not warm, the bleak stone ramparts of Castel Fosco. The garden was deserted; the marble fountain purled and splashed for no one. Beyond the castle walls, dead leaves swirled over the gravel of the parking area, obscuring the tracks of the many vehicles that had come and gone earlier in the day. Now all was quiet. The narrow road leading down the mountainside was empty. A single raven sat on the battlements above, gazing silently over the valley of the Greve.

The coroner's van had removed Fosco's body around mid-morning. The police lingered a little longer, snapping photos, taking statements, looking for evidence but finding nothing of value. Assunta, who had discovered the corpse, had been borne away, ashen and distraught, by her son. The few remaining servants had also gone off, taking advantage of the unexpected vacation. There seemed little reason to stay. Fosco's nearest relation, a distant cousin, was vacationing on the Costa Smeralda of Sardinia and would not arrive for several days at least. Besides, none were eager to linger in a place to which death had made such a gruesome visitation. And so the castle was left to brood in shadows and silence.

Nowhere was the silence more profound than in the ancient passageways that riddled the rock far beneath the basements of the castle. Here there was not even the rustle of the wind to disturb the dusty tombs and stone sarcophagi of the forgotten dead.

The deepest of these passages, carved by Etruscans into the living rock more than three thousand years before, twisted down into black depths and came to an end in a horizontal tunnel. At the far end of this tunnel stood a brick wall with a small scatter of bones lying before it. Though the tunnel was dark, even with the aid of a torch it would have been almost impossible to tell the wall had been built only forty-odd hours before, sealing up an ancient tomb, the bones of its former occupant, an unknown Longobardic knight, swept out and left lying in the dirt.

The ancient tomb that lay behind the brick wall was just large enough to contain a man. Inside that tomb there was no sound. Darkness reigned so profoundly that even the very passage of time seemed suspended.

And then a muffled sound broke the stillness: a faint footfall.

This was followed by a rattle, as if a bag of tools had been set down on the ground. Silence descended briefly once again. And then came an unmistakable sound: the scrape of iron against mortar, the sharp rap of a hammer against a cold chisel.

The rapping went on in a low, measured cadence, methodical, like the ticking of a clock. Minutes passed, and the sound stopped. Another silence, and then there were the faint sounds of scraping, the abrasion of brick against mortar; a few more sharp raps—and suddenly a faint light appeared in the tomb, a glowing crack that outlined the rectangular shape of a brick in the upper portion of the wall. With a soft, slow grating, the brick was withdrawn, millimeter by millimeter. Then it was gone, and a soft yellow light shone through the newly opened hole, penetrating the darkness of the tomb.

A moment later, two eyes appeared in the glowing rectangle, gazing in with curiosity, perhaps even anxiety.

Two eyes: one hazel, one blue.

An Aside to the Reader

Some readers will note we have done something quite unusual in *Brimstone.* Perhaps certain English professors will shake their heads and wonder that such a vile offense could have been committed against great literature.

We are speaking of how we've brazenly lifted the character of Count Isidor Ottavio Baldassare Fosco from the pages of *The Woman in White*, the great novel by the Victorian author Wilkie Collins, and inserted him bodily into *Brimstone.*

For those not familiar with Collins, he invented the modern detective novel with the publication of his work *The Moonstone. The Woman in White*, published a few years earlier in 1860, was in our opinion his greatest novel and one of the most popular books of the Victorian Age. Today it is well-nigh forgotten.

We apologize for purloining the character of Count Fosco. Yet it is the highest tribute we can pay to one of our favorite writers, who has certainly influenced our own fiction. We owe an enormous debt to Wilkie Collins, as do all writers of detective fiction (whether they know it or not). If, perchance, this prompts some of our more adventurous readers to pick up *The Woman in*

White, we will be very pleased. And to those critics who protest the pilfering of Fosco as a trangression against literature, we respond:

Braveggia, urla! T'affretta
a palesarmi il fondo dell'alma ria!

Acknowledgments

Lincoln Child would like to thank Bruce Swanson, Mark Mendel, Pat Allocco, Chris and Susan Yango, Jerry and Terry Hyland, Anthony Cifelli, M.D., Norman San Agustin, M.D., and Lee Suckno, M.D., for their friendship and assistance. Ongoing thanks to Special Agent Douglas Margini for his advice on New York, New Jersey, and federal law enforcement matters. Thanks to Jill Nowak for an insightful reading of the text. Bob Przybylski was very useful in nailing down some of the firearms details. Thanks also to Monsignor Bob Diacheck for reading and commenting on the manuscript. Thanks to my family, nuclear and extended, for putting up with an eccentric writer. Special thanks to my wife, Luchie, and my daughter, Veronica, for their love and support.

Douglas Preston is greatly indebted to Alessandro Lazzi, who kindly invited me to observe a wild boar hunt on his estate in the Tuscan Apennines. I thank Mario Spezi for providing much useful information on the workings of the Italian carabinieri and criminal investigation in general. I would like to express my appreciation to Mario Alfiero for his help with Neapolitan dialect. Some of the settings in the novel would not have been possible without the kind help of many people: in particular, the Cappellini family, owners of the Castello di Verrazzano in Greve; the Matta family, proprietors of Castello Vicchiomaggio; the monks of La Verna and Sacro Speco, Subiaco. I would also like to thank Niccolò Capponi for his help and our Italian translator, Andrea Carlo Cappi, for his advice and support. I thank Andrea Pinketts for the lending of his illustrious name. And last but not least, once again I thank my family, who can never be thanked enough: Isaac, Aletheia, Selene, and Christine.

And, as always, we want to thank in particular those people who make the Preston-Child novels possible: Jaime Levine, Jamie Raab, Eric Simonoff, Eadie Klemm, and Matthew Snyder.

In closing, we would like to distance ourselves from any misinterpretation of scripture by Wayne P. Buck, or any misapplication of the golden ratio by Professor Von Menck. All persons, police departments, corporations, institutions, governmental agencies, and locations both American and Italian mentioned in this novel are either fictitious or used fictitiously.

Dear Friend and Reader,

About a dozen times a year we send a short, entertaining note to a select group of our readers. It brings you information available nowhere else. We call it *The Pendergast File*. Each missive includes a surprise or shock: an outlandish bit of Pendergast history, a marvelous giveaway, a contest, hidden clues to buried treasure, upcoming book signings, snide and nasty comments about reviewers we dislike, and other amusing tidbits.

In short, The Pendergast File is not your ordinary "newsletter."

If you would like to sign up for The Pendergast File, please go to our website, www.PrestonChild.com, and click on the signup button. You can opt out at any time.

With warm regards,
Doug & Linc

P.S. We will never, ever, under any circumstances, share your e-mail address or information.

About the Authors

The thrillers of Douglas Preston and Lincoln Child "stand head and shoulders above their rivals" (*Publishers Weekly*). Preston and Child's *Relic* and *The Cabinet of Curiosities* were chosen by readers in a National Public Radio poll as being among the one hundred greatest thrillers ever written, and *Relic* was made into a number-one box office hit movie. Coauthors of the famed Pendergast series, Preston and Child are also the authors of *Fever Dream*, *Cold Vengeance*, and *Gideon's Sword*. Preston's acclaimed nonfiction book, *The Monster of Florence*, is being made into a movie starring George Clooney. His interests include horses, scuba diving, skiing, mountain climbing, and exploring the Maine coast in an old lobster boat. Lincoln Child is a former book editor who has published four novels of his own, including the huge bestseller *Deep Storm*. He is passionate about motorcycles, sports cars, exotic parrots, and nineteenth-century English literature.

Readers can sign up for The Pendergast File, a monthly "strangely entertaining note" from the authors, at their website, www.PrestonChild.com. The authors welcome visitors to their alarmingly active Facebook page, where they post regularly.

In a new assignment from his mysterious employer, Gideon Crew must steal a priceless artifact—and unearth an ancient Greek treasure that may change human history…

Please turn this page for a sneak preview of

The Lost Island

{ 1 }

The conference room at Effective Engineering Solutions emptied. Everyone left, leaving Gideon Crew alone with Eli Glinn and Manuel Garza in the spare room, high above the streets of Manhattan.

With his withered hand, Glinn motioned Gideon to a chair at the conference table. "Gideon, please, sit down."

Gideon took a seat. He sensed already that this meeting—which had begun with a celebration of his successful completion of the latest project for EES—was morphing into something else.

"You've had quite an ordeal," Glinn said. "Not just the physical manhunt, but the, ah, emotional toll as well. Are you sure you want to jump right into something new?"

"I'm sure," Gideon replied.

Glinn looked at him carefully—a long, searching look. Then he nodded. "Excellent. Glad to hear you'll be continuing with us as our..." he paused, searched for a word, "...our special deputy. We'll engage you a suite at a hotel around the corner, so you'll have a place to stay while we find you an apartment. I know how you hate to be away from your beloved Santa Fe, but it's a very interesting time to be in New York. Right now, for example, there's a special exhibition at the Morgan Library—the Book of Kells, on loan from the Irish government. You've heard of the Book of Kells, of course?"

"Vaguely."

"It's the finest illuminated manuscript in existence, considered to be Ireland's greatest national treasure."

Gideon said nothing.

Glinn glanced at his watch. "Then you'll come have a look at it with me? I'm a great fancier of illuminated manuscripts. They'll be turning a new page of the book every day. Very exciting."

Gideon hesitated. "Illuminated manuscripts are not exactly an interest of mine."

"Ah, but I was so hoping you'd accompany me to the exhibition," said Glinn. "You'll love the Book of Kells. It's only been out of Ireland once before, and it's only here for a week. A shame to miss it. If we leave now, we'll just catch the last hour of today's showing."

"Maybe we could go Monday."

"And miss the page displayed today—forever? No, we must go now."

Gideon started to laugh, amused at Glinn's earnestness. The man's interests were so arcane. "Honestly, I couldn't care less about the damn Book of Kells."

"Ah, but you will."

Hearing the edge in Glinn's voice, Gideon paused. "Why?"

"Because your new assignment will be to steal it."

{ 2 }

Gideon followed Eli Glinn into the East Room of the Morgan Library. Despite its being packed with visitors, entering the magnificent space was nevertheless an overwhelming experience. Gideon hadn't been in the Morgan for years—he always found its treasures too tempting—and immediately became entranced all over again with the vaulted and painted ceilings, the two-story tiers of rich books, the massive marble fireplace, the opulent tapestries, furniture, and thick burgundy rug. Glinn, operating the joystick of his electric wheelchair with one clawlike hand, moved into the room aggressively, cutting the line and taking advantage of the fact that people tended to yield to the handicapped. Soon they had moved to the front of the line, where a large glass cube contained the Book of Kells.

"What a room," murmured Gideon, looking around, his eyes instinctively picking out the many visible details of high security, starting with the hyperalert guards, the single entrance, the camera lenses winking in the ceiling moldings, the motion-sensor detectors and infrared laser placements. Not only that, but—in entering the room—he had observed the side edge of a massive steel pocket door, ready to seal the space off at a moment's notice.

Glinn followed his eye toward the ceiling. "Magnificent, isn't it?" he said. "Those murals are by the artist H. Siddons Mowbray, and the spandrels feature the twelve signs of the zodiac. J.P. Morgan belonged to an exclusive dining club that admitted only twelve members, each of whom was given a Zodiac code name. They say the arrangement of the signs and other strange symbols painted in the ceiling relate to key events in his personal life."

Gideon's eye fell to the grand fireplace adorning one end of the hall. Even in its intricately carved recesses he could make out the faint presence of security devices, some of which he had never seen before and had no idea what they did.

"That tapestry over the fireplace," Glinn continued, "is sixteenth-century Netherlandish. It depicts one of the seven deadly sins: avarice." He issued a low chuckle. "Interesting choice for Mr. J. Pierpont Morgan, don't you think?"

Gideon turned his attention to the glass cube that contained the Book of Kells. It was clearly bulletproof, and not the standard blue kind, either, but white glass—he guessed a P6B standard—which rendered it not only bulletproof but blastproof, hammerproof, and axeproof as well. He stared intently into the case, ignoring the fabulous and irreplaceable treasure it contained, his eyes instead picking out and categorizing the many layers of security within—motion sensors, atmospheric pressure sensors, infrared heat detectors, and even what looked like an atmospheric composition sensor.

Clearly any disturbance would trigger the instant shutting of that steel door—sealing the room and trapping the thief inside.

And that was just the security he could see.

"Breathtaking, isn't it?" murmured Glinn.

"It's scaring the shit out of me."

"What?" Glinn looked startled.

"Excuse me. You mean the book..." He looked at it for the first time. "Interesting."

"That's one way of putting it. Its origins are shrouded in mystery. Some say it was created by St. Columba himself around 590 A.D. Others believe it was created by unknown monks two hundred years later, to celebrate Columba's bicentennial. It was begun at Iona and then carried to the Abbey of Kells, where the illumination was added. And there it was kept, deeply hidden, as the abbey was raided and looted again and again by pagan Viking marauders. But they never found that book."

Gideon looked at the manuscript more closely. Despite himself, he was drawn in, enthralled by the fantastically complex abstract designs on the page, almost fractal in their depth.

"The page on display today is folio 34r," Glinn told him. "The famous Chi Rho monogram."

"Chi Rho? What's that?"

"Chi and Rho are the first two letters of the word *Christ* in Greek. The actual narrative of Jesus's life starts at Matthew 1:18, and that page was often decorated in early illuminated gospels. The first word of the narrative is *Christ.* In the Book of Kells, those first two letters, Chi Rho, consume the entire page."

The crowds began to back up behind them and Gideon felt someone's elbow giving him a faint nudge.

Glinn's whispery voice continued. "Look at the labyrinth of knotted decoration! You can see all kinds of strange things hidden in there—animals, insects, birds, angels, tiny heads, crosses, flowers. Not to mention Celtic knots of stupendous complexity, a mathematician's dream...And then the colors! The golds and greens and yellows and purples! This is the greatest page from the greatest illuminated manuscript in existence. No wonder the book is considered Ireland's greatest national treasure. Just *look* at it."

This was the first time Gideon could remember hearing anything approaching enthusiasm in Glinn's voice. He leaned closer, so close his breath fogged the glass.

"Excuse me, but there are people waiting," came an impatient voice from behind him.

As a little test, Gideon reached out and put his hand on the glass.

Instantly a low beeping sounded and a guard called out: "Hands off the glass, please! You, sir—hands off!"

This stimulated the impatient crowd. "Come on, friend, give someone else a chance!" came another voice. Others murmured their agreement.

With a long sigh of regret, Glinn's withered finger touched the joystick and the wheelchair moved aside with a hum, Gideon following. A few moments later they were back out on Madison Avenue, the traffic streaming past, cabs blaring. Gideon blinked in the bright light.

"Let me get this straight. You want me to *steal* that book?"

He felt Glinn's hand touch his arm reassuringly. "No, not the entire book. Just that one little folio page we were looking at, number 34r."

"Why?"

A silence. "Have you ever known me to answer a question like that?" Glinn asked pleasantly, as their limousine came gliding up to take them back to little West 12th Street.

{ 3 }

Three days later, Gideon Crew, fresh from a swim in the rooftop pool of the ultrahip Gansevoort Hotel, stood stark naked in his suite high above the meatpacking district of New York, staring down at a king-size bed overspread with diagrams and schematics—which mapped out, in minute detail, the security system of the East Room of the Morgan Library.

The loan of the Book of Kells by the Irish government to the Morgan Library had taken eight years to arrange. It had been fraught with difficulty. The main reason was that in the year 2000, one of the book's folios had been sent to Canberra, Australia, for exhibition. Several pages were damaged by rubbing and a loss of pigment—the vibration of the plane's engines were blamed—and the Irish government was now loath to risk another loan.

James Waterman, the billionaire Irish-American founder of the Waterman Group, had made it a personal mission to bring the book to the United States. A man known for his charisma and charm, he managed to persuade the Irish prime minister, and finally the government, to release it—under stringent conditions. One of those conditions was a total overhaul of the security system of the East Room of the Morgan Library, which Waterman paid for himself.

Waterman had initially tried to put the manuscript on display at the Smithsonian. Museum security, however, had proven unwilling to provide the necessary high-tech face-lift, and the effort had fallen through. Secretly, Gideon was pleased to hear this. Although he had dreadful memories of Washington, D.C. as a child—after all, that was where his father had been killed—in later years he had gone back occasionally to visit and found the town to be a somewhat boring, even sleepy, collection of handsome monuments and timeless documents. But just weeks before, he'd been summoned to Washington to receive a medal for his recent accomplishments at Fort Detrick. And to his dismay—perhaps because of 9/11, perhaps simply as a result of red tape and the inevitable bureaucratic accretion—what had once been a pleasant and relaxed Capitol was now more like an armed camp. The Metropolitan Police; Capitol Police; Park Police; State Department Police; U.S. Mint Police; Secret Service Police, "Special" Police (*achtung!*)—in fact something like two dozen different police forces, he'd learned—now choked the city with their presence: all armed, and all with the power to pull over and arrest any luckless driver or visitor. (This according to one of Gideon's cab drivers, himself formerly on the Job.) Looking around at all the redundant cops, with their overlapping fiefdoms, Gideon could practically smell his tax dollars burning away.

The final straw came when he later received a robot traffic ticket in the mail: some pole-mounted camera-radar had observed him driving up New York Avenue at a few miles over the 35 mph speed limit, and—snagging an image of his license plate—had mailed him a ticket for $125. No, there seemed no viable way to protest the ticket short of traveling back to Washington to defend himself. And, of course, the actual event was so vague in his memory there was no way to reconstruct it: had there been a 35 MPH sign posted anywhere nearby? Had he truly been speeding? Where the hell, exactly, was New York Avenue? Many days had passed—how was an honest citizen to recall? In Gideon's opinion it was, pure and simple, an officially sanctioned scam to extract an outrageous fine—and if he didn't pay the $125 in short order, it would double to $250. So Gideon had done two things: first, paid the fine; and second, vowed not to return to D.C. for a long, long time. What had once, in his opinion, been a beautiful and abiding symbol of the country's greatness had degenerated into a city-state obsessed with balancing its grossly swollen budget (those two dozen police departments) by dinging hapless citizens and tourists instead of protecting them. George Orwell would have been proud.

Or maybe, fresh from his trout stream, Gideon was just feeling the pain of reentry into urban existence. But either way, there wasn't a chance in hell he was going back to the Smithsonian.

Now—as his thoughts returned to the present and he circled the bed—Gideon began wondering how Glinn had managed to get hold of the complete engineering, wiring, and electrical diagrams of that security system. Here was every circuit, every sensor, every spec, spelled out in minute detail. Lot of good it was going to do him. He had never in his life seen a security system like this—he had never even *imagined* a security system like this. There were the usual multiple layers, redundant and hardened systems, backup power supplies, and everything a burglar might expect. But that was just the beginning.

The East Room itself was now, essentially, a vault. It had originally been constructed of double-laid walls of Vermont limestone block almost three feet thick. The single entry into the room came equipped with a divided steel pocket door that would drop down from the ceiling and rise up from the floor the instant an alarm was triggered, sealing the room. There were no windows anywhere, light being incompatible with the preservation of books. The vaulted ceiling was of poured reinforced concrete, incredibly thick. The floor was a massive slab of reinforced concrete, covered with marble. To all this original reinforcement had been retrofitted, at the Irish government's request, an outer layer of steel plating and sensors.

At night, the room was completely sealed up. Inside, it was secured by crisscrossing laser beams, motion detectors, and infrared sensors of several wavelengths, including one that would pick up even the smallest hint of body heat. Quite literally, not even a mouse (and probably not even a cockroach) could move inside the room without being detected. There were cameras running day and night, the monitors manned by highly trained, hand-picked security guards of the highest caliber.

During the day, when the exhibition was open to the public, people had to leave behind all their bags and cameras and pass through a metal detector. There were guards inside and outside the hall, and more cameras than a Las Vegas casino. The cube in which the book sat contained an atmosphere of pure argon. Inside the cube were sensors that would immediately go off if they detected a whiff of any other atmospheric gas, even in levels as low as one part per million. If the book was disturbed, the steel doors would seal the room so quickly that not even an Olympic runner could carry it from the case to the exit before it shut.

For days, Gideon had looked for weaknesses in the system. All systems had vulnerabilities, and almost always those vulnerabilities were related either to human fallibility, programming glitches, or to a system too complex to be completely understood. But the designers of this system had taken those limitations into account. While this system was indeed complex, it was modular, in the sense that each component was fairly simple and independent of the others. The programs were simple, and some layers of security were entirely mechanical, with no computerized controls at all. The redundancy was such that multiple systems could fail or be compromised without affecting the ultimate security of the book.

There was, of course, a way to turn the system on and off, because the pages of the book were turned on a daily basis. But even this had been exceedingly well planned. To shut down the system required three people, each with a simple, independent code that they had memorized. There were no physical keys or written codes or anything that could be stolen. And these three people were untouchable. They were John Waterman himself, the president of the Morgan Library, and the deputy mayor of New York City. While one might be corruptible or susceptible to social engineering, two would be extremely difficult and three impossible.

And what would happen if one of them died? In that case there was a stand-in, a fourth person—who happened to be the prime minister of Ireland himself.

What about fire? Surely in the case of an emergency, Gideon reasoned, the book would have to be quickly moved. But the specs dealt with that possibility in an unusual way. The book would not be moved in case of a fire. It would be fully protected in situ. The glass cube was designed to be a first line of defense, able to withstand a serious fire on its own; the second line was a fireproof box that rose from inside the cube to enclose the book, protecting it from even the most prolonged fire. And the East Room had redundant, state-of-the-art firefighting components in place that would stifle any fire well before it got going. There were similar systems protecting the book against earthquake, flood, and terrorist attack. Just about the only thing it wasn't protected from was a direct nuclear strike.

With a long sigh, Gideon strolled over to his closet and flipped through his clothes. It was time to get dressed for dinner. He had taken, as a loose cover, the persona of a young, hip dot-com millionaire, a persona he had used before with success. He took out a black St. Croix mock turtleneck, a pair of worn Levi's, and some Bass Weejuns—he had to mix it up a *little*, after all—and pulled them all on.

He hadn't eaten anything all day. This was usual. Gideon preferred one elegant and extraordinary dining experience to three cheap squares. Eating for him was more ritual than sustenance.

He checked his watch again. It was still too early to dine, but he felt restless after three days cooped up in this room, staring at diagrams. He had yet to find a hole, a chink, even the slightest hairline crack in this security system. Since he'd started stealing from art museums and historical societies when he was a teenager, he had come to believe that there was no such thing as a perfect security system. Every system was vulnerable, either technologically or through social engineering.

That had always been his certitude. Until now.

Christ, he needed a break. He went into the bathroom, combed his wet hair, then slapped on some Truefitt and Hill aftershave balm to cover up the lingering smell of chlorine from the pool. He left his suite, hanging the DO NOT DISTURB sign on the doorknob on his way out.

It was a hot August evening out in the meatpacking district. The beautiful people were out in the Hamptons, and instead the cobbled streets were packed with young, hip-looking tourists—the meatpacking district had become one of the chicest neighborhoods in Manhattan in recent years.

He walked around the block to the Spice Market, sat down at the bar, and ordered a dark and stormy. As he sipped the drink, he indulged in one of his favorite activities, observing the people around him and imagining every detail of their lives, from what they did for a living to what their dogs looked like. But try as he might, he couldn't get into the groove. For the first time in his life, he had run into a security system designed by truly intelligent people—people even smarter than him. The damned Book of Kells was going to be harder to steal than the *Mona Lisa*.

As he pondered this, his mood, already foul, deepened. The people around him—well heeled and sophisticated, talking, laughing, drinking, and eating—began to irritate him. He began to imagine they weren't people, but chattering monkeys engaged in complex grooming rituals, and that eased his annoyance.

His drink was empty. Long ago he had learned it was a bad idea for him to order a second one—not that he had a drinking problem, of course—but after two he seemed to pass a line that led to a third, and even a fourth, and that would inevitably lead him to seek out one of those sleek, blond, chattering monkeys...

He ordered a second drink.

As he sipped it, feeling marginally better about the state of the world as the alcohol kicked in, a little idea came to him. If it was truly impossible to steal the Book of Kells—and deep down he knew it was—he would simply have to get someone else to take it out of the room for him...with the full cooperation of those three people. This would require a level of social engineering far more sophisticated than any he had ever attempted before.

And a way to do just that began to materialize in his very crooked, half-soused mind.

His third drink arrived, and he cast his eye about the elegant bar. There was a woman at the far end, not necessarily the most beautiful woman in the room—she was slightly plump and wore glasses—but what he personally found most attractive in a woman was that she possessed a mordant, intelligent gleam in her eye. She was looking around, and it seemed to Gideon that she found this scene as amusing as he did.

He picked up his almost finished drink and walked over. He glanced at the stool. "May I?"

She looked him up and down. "I think so. Are you in the computer business?"

He laughed and put on his most self-deprecating look. "No, but I am WYSIWYG. Why do you ask?"

"The Steve Jobs uniform—black mock turtleneck and jeans."

"I don't like thinking about what I'm going to wear in the morning."

She turned to the bartender. "Two Beefeater martinis, straight up, two olives, dirty."

"You're buying me a drink?"

"Any objection?"

He leaned forward. "Not at all, but how did you know what I was drinking?"

"I've been watching you since you came in."

"Really? Why me?"

"You look like a lost boy."

Gideon found himself flushing. This woman was perhaps a little too keen in her observations and he felt unmasked. "Aren't we all a bit lost?"

She smiled and said, "I think we're going to get along."

The drinks arrived and they clinked glasses.

"To being lost," said Gideon.